CLEANSING HUNT

BOOK TWO

of

THE EARTHSOUL PROPHECIES

Greg Park

BLADESTAR
PUBLISHING

CLEANSING HUNT

A Bladestar Book
Published by Bladestar Publishing
Orem, Utah

www.BladestarPublishing.com

ISBN: 0-9787931-9-6
Library of Congress Control Number: 2006935185

Maps and sketches by Matthew Furner Broderick
Jacket art by Melissa Douglas
Jacket design by Michael Spencer

Printed in the United States of America

For Tilly
atanami en koires

ACKNOWLEDGMENTS

To all those who have helped with this project, I offer my heartfelt thanks. To my wife for the countless hours she spent reading and editing the manuscript and for listening to me talk through my ideas. To my children — my two biggest fans — for begging Dad to read each new part as it was written. To Amber Park, Craig Child, Joani Elliott, Idell Oliver, Aerwyn Whitlock, Brian Saxton, and Jeff Shurtliff for providing feedback. To Matthew Broderick, Emily Hawkins, and Melissa Spencer for artwork. To my enthusiastic students at Timpanogos High School — too many to name — for pestering me each and every day for a "book update." And lastly, I offer my heartfelt thanks to God for giving me the skills, imagination, and patience to make all of this possible.

CONTENTS

Seven Gifts of *Ta'shaen*

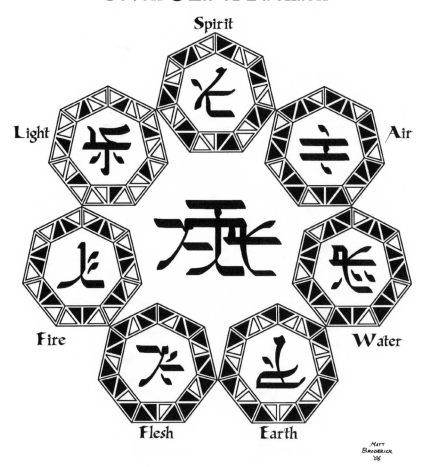

Spirit

Light

Air

Fire

Water

Flesh

Earth

MATT
BRODERICK
'06

THE NINE LANDS

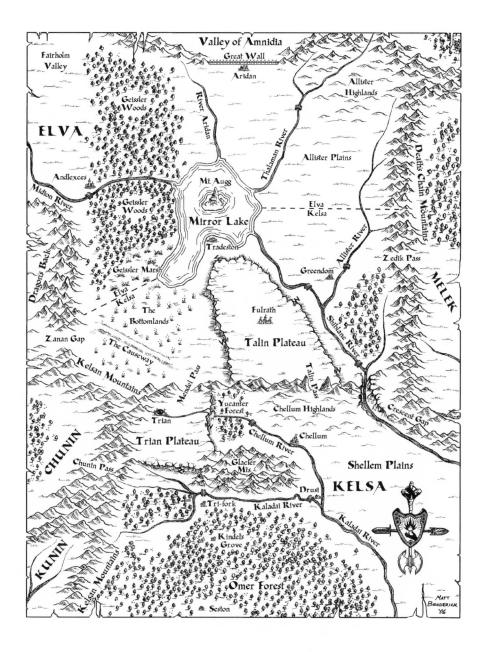

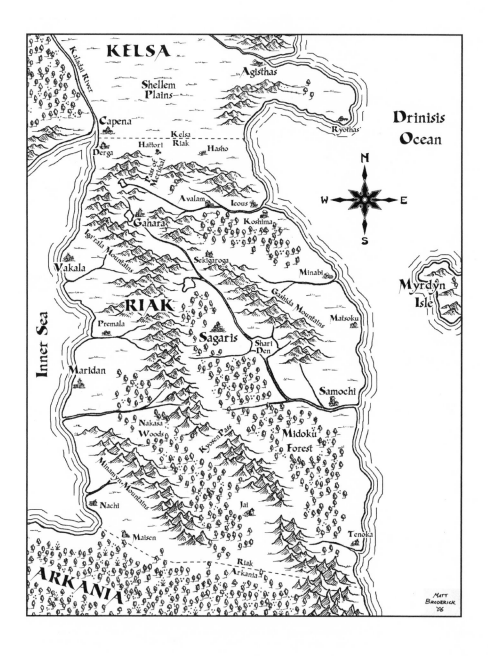

The City of Trian
and its Major Routes

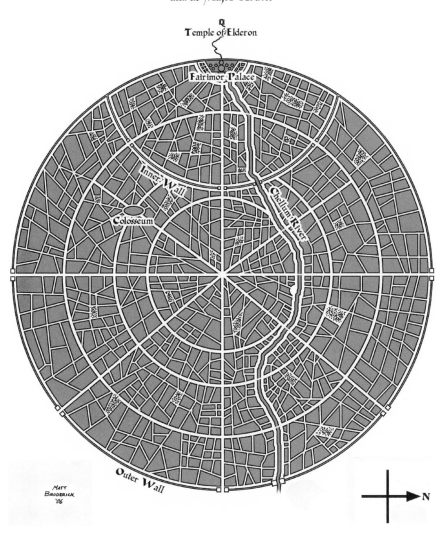

And it will come to pass that the blood of Fairimor shall be corrupted, and the Sons of the Birthright shall turn against the Light of Creation, forsaking their heritage and leaving the city of their birth. And you will see my hand in all their works, for they will be servants unto the dark, servants unto me as I pour out my wrath upon all the nations of the world. And then shall ye know that I am the god of this world. Then shall ye know what it is to fear.

~Taken from an epistle written by
Throy Shadan to the Kings of Elva
and Kelsa in A.S. 1387

PROLOGUE

Glimmers of the Future

Night has fallen, but the sky over Trian flickers red — flashes of color that paint the low-hanging clouds the color of blood. Most of the outer city is in flames.

From where he stands in the relative darkness at the eastern rim of the Overlook, Jase Fairimor watches the fires in horror. A few pockets of resistance still remain amid the blazes consuming whole quadrants, dark pools that appear calm despite the tremendous chaos around them. The look is deceiving, Jase knows. For those are the areas where the fighting is at its worst. That is where hordes of Darklings are smothering the last few groups still trying to hold ground against them.

Lightning rains down on the inner wall, deadly spears of corrupted Earthpower that kill and scatter Trian's troops like ants. Jase sees a section of the inner wall collapse and watches a mass of armored Darklings pour through the gap. Those defenders closest to the breach rush to engage the vile creatures but are quickly swallowed by a sea of bristling fur and black-lacquered armor. A few moments later the first Shadowhounds appear in the streets and on the rooftops several blocks deeper in the city.

Jase frowns. It won't be long now.

In the courtyard below the Overlook, a squad of armored men stands facing the deserted streets leading in from the city. With swords and spears in hand and helmets and breastplates gleaming, they stand with the quiet dignity of men who will soon meet their Creator and know it. They are the last line of defense for Fairimor Palace and the Dome, the last of an army that has been swallowed by a swarm of evil far larger than anyone could have imagined.

Jase gazes down on the men with sadness. They will die with honor, he knows. But die they will. And then it will be up to him.

Trian is lost, but he will not let the Darkling armies have the prize they so ravenously desire. He will not let them take the palace or the Temple of Elderon.

Gripping the Talisman of Elsa tightly, he prepares to seize enough of the Power to collapse the cliffs behind the city and bury the Temple of Elderon, the palace, the Dome, and the Overlook beneath a mountain of rubble. It is the least he can do after failing to heal the Earthsoul.

He sighs resignedly. Because of him, Kelsa is getting a firsthand look at Con'Jithar. Because of him, Hell has come to earth. And it is only beginning. When the Earthsoul fails completely, the world will become a place of death and savagery worse than anything happening in the outer city. Maeon will reign supreme, and his last act of mockery toward the Creator will be to place his throne in the palace created for the Fairimor family by the hand of Elderon Himself.

Jase sets his jaw firmly. *Only I won't let that happen,* he vows. He just hopes it will atone, in small part at least, for his failure.

He thinks about that failure and wonders how it came to pass. It hadn't happened all at once, but he still should have seen it coming. He'd certainly had enough warnings.

He shakes his head sadly. A slight misuse of Ta'shaen here, a little indiscretion there, and slowly but surely he'd moved down the path to Agla'Con until he'd lost both his birthright as a descendant of Elsa and his Seven Gifts of Power.

Now he is forced to steal Ta'shaen the way those he despises above all living flesh do. He is like them now, and he hates himself for it. *But I will never be one of you,* he thinks. *I've failed the Light of Creation, but I will never serve Maeon.*

He glances down to find the inner wall breached completely and a mass of Darklings and other shadowspawn flowing through the streets toward the palace like a river of pitch.

The heavy tramp of booted feet sounds on the paving stones as they near the Overlook, and the soldiers waiting to engage them lower their spears in anticipation. A few moments pass, and Darklings come into the lamplight at the far end of the courtyard. There they stop, a wall of armor and steel that may as well stretch into Con'Jithar for all the chance the men have of stopping it.

Darkling eyes glow with a feral light as they study the trophy they have come to claim for their master. A moment later their beastly howls rend the air, and they charge forward, a wave of bristly fur and spikes, razor sharp teeth and claws. The last of the human defenders meet the rush, and cries of pain reach Jase's ears as they are quickly overwhelmed and killed.

Shadowhounds run with the Darklings, hulks of liquid night that defy the very laws of nature as they move up the sheer face of the Overlook. He watches them spill over the rim and move to encircle him, and he takes hold of the Power.

They feel the corruption coursing through him and stop their advance, momentarily confused that he is an Agla'Con. They watch warily but make no move to attack as he continues to draw in as much of Ta'shaen as he can stand. It flows into him in a river of fire so vast it chars his bones and scorches his soul.

He does nothing with it, however. He simply continues to draw in more and more — an ocean of raw energy sufficient to shatter the moon. His vision blurs, and a roaring fills his ears. The Shadowhounds shrink back in fear as the very air around him begins to crackle with heat. Throughout the city the fighting ceases, and all heads, both human and shadowspawn, turn toward the glow coming from the Overlook.

With his Awareness thus extended, he can see the surprise and fear in every face. This is nothing, he tells them proudly, and the truth of the statement makes him want to throw his head back and laugh.

For when he finally reaches his breaking point, the entire world is going to feel it.

Jase jerked upright in a tangle of blankets and cast about in alarm. His skin was hot with sweat, and the veins in his head and neck throbbed violently with each beat of his heart. When his vision cleared, he found that his room was dark save for the soft, grey-white glow of dawn filtering through the window. Only the muffled warble of a morning bird on the balcony disturbed the silence.

He sighed in relief at finding everything intact and lay back against the pillows to cool down. He'd been so certain that he'd embraced the Power while asleep that he'd expected to wake and find the room on fire. He closed his eyes and found Ta'shaen still tingling along his Awareness, a shimmering ocean of Earthpower waiting to be embraced. And there, just audible at the far reaches of his mind was... a voice.

It was the same ambient whisper that had spoken to him last night when it had guided him to the top of the Dome. Only this time it wasn't guiding; it was warning. Warning of both the present and the future.

His eyes snapped open in shock.

The future.

The dream of Trian's fall hadn't been a dream at all. It had been a vision. A prophecy. He knew it as surely as he knew he lived. Ta'shaen had spoken to him of the future!

The thought turned his blood to ice. The future he had seen had come about because he had failed to heal the Earthsoul. No. It was worse than that. He had become one of the enemy. Con'Jithar had come to Trian early because he'd lost his birthright.

He pressed his palms to his eyes and willed the images of the ruined city away. *Never*, he vowed. *I will never become an Agla'Con. I will die first.* The white hot image of how the vision had ended flashed through his mind and he shuddered. If he were to draw as much of the Power as the vision hinted he was capable of, he truly could challenge Maeon.

But at what price?

The vision hadn't lied when it suggested he could shatter the moon. That much Earthpower could lay waste to an entire continent. In a confrontation with Maeon, that much of *Ta'shaen* could ruin the world.

But the vision had warned of something equally horrible. By becoming an Agla'Con, he had made himself unworthy to take up a Talisman of Elsa and heal the Earthsoul; he had ruined the world before the battle at Trian had even begun. He hadn't destroyed the world directly, but his failure had been just as complete. That failure had ensured Maeon's victory, allowing him to reign supreme in the world of death and misery left behind.

Even knowing that he had stood against Maeon until the very end did little to ease the pain of knowing he had been responsible for the death of every living creature on earth. By failing to live up to his birthright, it was as if he had killed them all himself.

He rose and moved to the balcony. Pulling open the doors, he stepped out into the morning air and let it cool his skin while he searched for a bright spot among all the gloom and doom of the warning. There really wasn't much to take heart from, and he rubbed his eyes wearily. *At least I saved the temple from desecration*, he thought, then frowned to himself. *Yeah, by destroying it.* He shook his head and turned his attention outward.

Trian spread below in a patchwork of streets and buildings washed of color by the all-encompassing grey of early morning. A few people moved in the streets, early-risers eager to start the day and a handful of soldiers finishing their nightly patrols.

He watched them for a time and wondered how many of them had died defending Trian in his vision. Gideon had told him that visions of the future weren't always set in stone. The future was the end result of actions taken in the present. *Actions can be changed*, he had said, *and so can the future.*

Jase nodded. It wouldn't happen as he'd seen.

The Elvan Prophet Elrien opened his eyes to the grey of early morning and pursed his lips grimly. The last vestiges of the vision of Trian's destruction still flickered through his mind, and he entertained them with a great deal of trepidation. For the Earthsoul to send such a grave warning to the Fairimor lad meant the potential for the vision to come to pass was startlingly real. Jase had already slipped into the realm of Agla'Con on several occasions. What was to keep it from happening for good? If the Sons of the Birthright turned to the Shadow, Con'Jithar would swallow the world without a fight.

He rose from his bed and moved to the window to gaze at the Allister Plains spreading before him in a sea of greens and yellows. They were a stark contrast to the desolation on the northern side of the Great Wall, and he hoped to keep them that way. He knew the Shadan'Ko would never breach the wall, but he did worry that Jase Fairimor might be more dangerous than the Twisted Ones and all of Maeon's other servants combined. The vision had certainly hinted as much.

He took a deep breath to calm himself. He would have to trust that Gideon Dymas would keep the boy on the right path. If anyone understood the dangers of crossing into the realm of the Agla'Con, it was Gideon. He had lost his birthright because of just such a transgression a long time ago.

Yes, Gideon would know what to do. With the Earthsoul failing so quickly, however, he wondered if there would be time enough to see things through to the end.

CHAPTER 1

A Call for War

Clutching the Blood Orb of Elsa tightly in his fist, Jase Fairimor watched the sun rising in the east and pressed his lips into a frown. He'd stood here since waking from the dream of Trian's destruction, too troubled by what he'd seen to return to bed. The fate of Trian — the fate of the world — was in his hands, and he was starting to wonder if he would be up to the challenge. He'd been so confident last night when he'd followed the whisperings of the Talisman to the top of the Dome and thrown back the night. He had known that what he'd done had been the fulfillment of prophecy. He'd felt good about accepting his birthright.

But then the vision had come. A vision of the future, to be sure, and one that had him wanting to hide under a mountain. *Too late for that,* he thought. *Every person in the Nine Lands probably saw what I did. And every one of them will wonder what it means.*

He sighed. At least it would give his enemies cause to wonder. He just hoped it made them fear him... at least as much as he feared himself.

Turning back into the room, he moved to the porcelain tub the servants had filled the night before. He momentarily considered taking a cold bath but worked up enough courage to clear his mind and open himself to *Ta'shaen.* Then, with more control than he'd shown in weeks, he channeled a tendril of Fire into the water until it was nice and hot. *Figures,* he thought darkly. *I only foul up when there are people around to see it.* The incident on top of the Dome aside, of course. He'd embraced the Power properly then, too... and alerted every Power-sensitive being within five hundred miles.

Shaking his head in disgust at the workings of fate, he slipped into the tub until only his head was above the water. Closing his eyes, he tried to relax. The High Tribunal would be gathering in a few short hours, and the decisions made there would change the future as well. Hopefully it would be for the good.

It was two full hours later before he was finally ready to leave his room — it had taken that long for him to come to terms with the warnings in the vision. He was still haunted by the images of Trian's destruction, haunted even more by the fact that it had been his fault. As terrifying as it was, though, it steeled his resolve to learn to use the Power wisely and appropriately.

He glanced at himself in the mirror and frowned. He hoped the horror of what he'd seen didn't still show in his eyes when he reached the dining hall. He didn't want to have to explain what he'd seen to the others. He knew there would be no getting out of explaining how he'd lit the top of the Dome bright as noonday.

The bulge of the Talisman of Elsa beneath his shirt caught his eye and he reached up to touch it, vowing to let the ancient blood help him through all of this. It was, after all, the cause of most of it. *It knows who the enemy is,* Gideon had said. *It is alive with the spirit of Elsa.*

If that's true, he thought, *then Elsa has an interesting concept of irony.*

For if there was only one thing to be gleaned from the vision, it was that he *could be* the enemy. And with Aethon watching for a chance to pull him over into the realm of the Agla'Con, he wasn't sure if the Talisman had done the right thing in announcing him to the world. The proverbial gauntlet had been thrown; Aethon and the others were sure to respond.

He pushed the thoughts away and fastened his attention on his image in the mirror. The clothes he'd chosen to wear were similar to those he'd worn in Chellum — clothes equal to his rank as a Prince of Trian. It still made him nervous to think of himself that way, but the impression others had of him was critical. He hoped the dark blue uniform with tiny bars of silver stitched into the hems of the sleeves and lapel would do the trick. He didn't know if he liked the delicate silver chains linking the three rows of buttons across his chest or the bright red stripe running down the outseam of both legs, but it was the best he could find. Especially considering that the chains, silver stitching, and stripes paled in comparison to the Blue Flame of Kelsa sewn over his heart — the hundreds of tiny gems glittered every time he moved. Talia would like it, though. So would his mother... if she could see it.

"Keep her safe, Daris," he whispered at the mirror, then turned away.

Two warders stationed outside his door fell in step behind him and followed silently as he made his way through the Fairimor home. He didn't need to see the look on their faces to know that they were wondering if they were even necessary now that they knew what he was capable of. *Of course you're necessary*, he told them silently, *because most of the time I'm as clumsy as a one-legged blind man.*

When he reached the dining hall, he found everyone except his aunt, uncle, and Gideon already gathered at the table.

Thorac wore his brass-colored chainmail over a green and grey uniform bearing the insignia of Ambassador General of Chunin. His beard had been trimmed, and his long reddish hair hung in a single thick braid down his back. He didn't have his axe, but a short sword was belted around his waist.

Elliott and Seth each wore the dark grey of House Chellum, and the capes fastened around their necks had the Fighting Panther of Chellum embroidered in gold on the back. As usual, both wore their swords. Endil and Andil each wore a uniform similar to his, and it was obvious from the look in Andil's eyes that he was nervous about being given a voice on the council.

General Eries and his Elvan Master of Spies sat near Talia, and the three were talking quietly. Talia, he noted appreciatively, was absolutely stunning. The blue and green dress she'd chosen matched her eyes. Her long, tri-colored hair hung loosely about her shoulders. It made taking his eyes off her more difficult than usual.

Seth looked up as he came in and chuckled. "We were starting to wonder if you were going to show up," he said. "The tribunal starts in less than an hour."

"I had trouble finding something to wear," he lied. "Nothing seems to fit me anymore."

"Well, get something to eat," the captain ordered. "It's going to be a long day."

"Especially since it has already been a long night," General Eries said, a knowing look in his eyes. "Or should I say a very bright one?"

Jase cringed. "Sorry about that," he told them, then cringed again when he saw Elliott gaping in surprise.

"That was you?" the Chellum Prince asked, his eyes wide with wonder. "I thought it was Gideon."

"So did I," Seth said, reaching up to pull at his mustache. "But it does make more sense now that I know it was you."

"What are you talking about?" Jase asked, not entirely sure he wanted an answer. He took a seat across the table from General Eries and helped himself to the breads and fruits Allisen had prepared.

"Prophecy," Croneam answered, looking at Seth and nodding. When Seth motioned for him to continue, Croneam turned his gaze back on Jase. "The *Dy'illium* makes mention of such an occurrence in the Book of Gariel. I don't have it memorized, but it goes something like this: *Watch ye, therefore, for a night of blood, when the house of Fairimor shall be defiled by the Shadow. For behold, Elsa's sons shall prove victorious, and the Dome of the Birthright shall be crowned with Fire."*

Teig Ole'ar leaned forward. "There is a similar prophecy in the *Eved'terium*, but I won't try to quote it for fear of doing it injustice."

"Yes," Croneam said. *"For behold, the house of Fairimor shall be crowned with Fire; yea, Fire and Light shall throw back the night, even to the lifting of the Veil of Darkness cloaking the lands of thine inheritance.* I read them both last night while you were up on the Dome fulfilling them."

"Prophecy," Jase grumbled. "I'm becoming very irritated by the fact that my life isn't my own anymore."

"Sure it is," Croneam countered. "You still have a choice in everything you do. Tell me, what led you to the top of the Dome? A vision? A whispering?"

"Both," Jase answered, shifting his shoulders uncomfortably.

"So why did you follow them?" Croneam asked.

"I don't know," Jase told him. "Curiosity perhaps."

"Is that all?"

Jase hesitated. "I suppose I wanted to believe it might be real."

"But you weren't forced to go?"

"No," he answered. "I chose to."

Croneam leaned forward, a twinkle of understanding in his hazel eyes. "What do you think would have happened if you had ignored the vision and the whispering?"

"The prophecy wouldn't have been fulfilled, I guess."

"Wrong," Croneam said firmly. "It simply wouldn't have been fulfilled last night. The scriptures don't say exactly when or by whom the prophecy will be fulfilled, only that it *will* be fulfilled. If you had chosen to ignore the whispering, the Earthsoul would have whispered to you some other time. If you were to continue to ignore Her call, She would simply select someone else who would listen."

"I hate to cast doubt on your theological optimism," Elliott interjected, "but what if time runs out before these prophecies can be fulfilled? I mean, what if the dark prophecies — and I know there are some — what if the dark side wins out before the prophecies of light come to fruition? What if the Earthsoul dies before Jase can heal Her?"

Croneam shrugged. "We'll have to have faith that won't happen."

"Faith," Elliott grumbled, "isn't much good against a sword-wielding Darkling. It wasn't faith that stopped the killing last night, but this." He shook his sword in his fist. "In a fight like that, I'll take cold hard steel over something

I can't see, anytime. Faith didn't keep a dozen women from getting their throats cut by those vermin. Faith didn't stop the awful from happening."

Croneam leaned forward and looked Elliott in the eyes. "The *awful*, as you so aptly named it, was also prophesied," he said softly. "If not, then the night of blood spoken of in the *Dy'illium* is yet to be fulfilled. Not a very comforting thought, all things considered."

Frowning, Elliott fell silent.

Croneam studied him for a moment then continued. "Some things happen for a reason," he said softly. "Some things simply happen. You can't explain them. You can't even come to terms with some of them. All you can do is pick up the pieces and move on. To do nothing mocks the agency given you by the Creator. To do nothing is to give Maeon the victory without a fight. You know bloody well his minions are exercising their agency — doing all in their power to bring the dark prophecies to pass. And what's more, they believe in those prophecies. They have faith in them. Rely only on your sword if you wish, young Prince. I'm going to look to a higher power for help."

An awkward silence fell over the group and stretched to uncomfortable lengths. It wasn't until Talia and Teig began to talk quietly to one another that the others in the group followed suit, trading small talk designed to cover their nervousness. And they were nervous, Jase knew. He could see it in their eyes and hear it in their voices. Everyone except Seth, Elison, and Croneam, he amended. Those three looked ready for war.

He picked at his food and stayed silent, preoccupied with the images of the vision. He knew he needed to tell Gideon what he'd seen, but the Dymas still hadn't arrived. A glance at the large grandfather clock showed only a half hour remained before the start of the tribunal. If Gideon didn't join them soon, any sharing of the vision would have to wait until this afternoon.

As the minutes wore on, the chatting gradually ceased until only the loud ticking of the clock remained. Finally, Elison rose from the table. "Time to go," he said. "Most of the lesser tribunal members have undoubtedly gathered already. They will be eager to see what we have to say."

"And not so eager to accept it," Seth muttered.

During the minutes prior to a meeting, the Dome usually thundered with a din of voices so loud it made communicating with the person next to you difficult. Today, however, was different. The Dome was subdued, almost hushed. The five tiers of seats were filled, but those occupying them kept their voices low as they talked, occasionally casting frightened glances in the direction of the Overlook and frowning worriedly. It was easy to see why they were concerned.

The shattered remains of the doors had been removed, and the framework within the *chorazin* had been rebuilt enough for canvas to be hung over the opening. Six *Bero'thai* stood guard in front.

Jase let his gaze sweep across the rest of the Dome and pursed his lips grimly. The carpets had been removed from the area of battle. So had the tables and other furniture that had been damaged. To him, the emptiness of those areas was as bad as if they'd still been covered with blood. Everyone knew what had taken place; removing what had been ruined only served to show how far into the Dome the Darklings had come.

He frowned. By now, the rumors about the battle had likely tripled the true awfulness of it all. From the way most of the delegates were looking around the Dome, it may as well have still been littered with bodies.

He and the others reached the tribunal area and moved to their seats along the outside of the curving table where they could face the lesser judges and the five tiers of seats rising behind them. Thorac moved to a cluster of tables to the left of the tiers and was joined by the ambassadors of Elva and Zeka. The *Bero'thai*, arrows notched in their bows, fanned out around the main table and took up positions where they could watch the proceedings.

Jase found his nameplate and took his seat, not at all pleased to be sitting near the center of the table. He'd hoped for a seat near either end where he could stay mostly out of the collective line of sight. Here, he may as well have a sign painted on his forehead. Or a target.

To his right, three empty seats displayed nameplates for Gideon, Randle, and Cassia. The half-moon shape of the table made it possible to see the faces of each delegate, and he followed them around the bend. Endil occupied the seat next to Cassia and was followed by Elliott and Talia. The next four seats were empty, but smooth orbs of polished blue crystal the size of an apple sat next to each nameplate. Communicator Stones. *Ta'shaen*-activated talismans linked to sister stones in one of the other large cities. He could see the names Agisthas and Marik on the first two, but the following two weren't visible.

Stalix Geshiann and the other three Chief Judges finished out the last four seats, and Jase studied them intently. Judge Zeesrom met his gaze and nodded a greeting. Jase returned the nod before looking to his left.

Croneam Eries and Elison Brey occupied the two closest seats. They were followed by Seth, Andil, and Elders Nesthius and Zanandrei. The last three seats were empty, but Communicator Stones sat next to the nameplates. He could just make out the name on the nearest: General Crompton of Capena.

He faced forward once more and sat back in his chair, letting his eyes travel across the five tiers rising before him. A hundred and forty-four seats made up the twelve lesser councils, but he doubted more than a handful would know who he was if not for the nameplate. Their curiosity was evident as they studied him and the other newly appointed members of the council. He did his best to regard them coldly, letting his eyes sweep across them with feigned indifference. It was the only way he could keep his knees from knocking together.

The flat-eyed stares of the twelve lesser judges sitting at the other table were harder to ignore. They resented his being where he was and were doing little to hide their contempt. He met their gazes squarely and even managed a mocking smile. He was pleased to see them scowl.

Next to him, Croneam chuckled. "Good boy," he said softly. "Let those pig-headed fools know you don't think much of them."

Jase cast a sideways glance at the old general. "What else can I do?" he whispered. "I feel like a bug about to have body parts removed by a group of malicious children."

Croneam chuckled again but said nothing.

A moment later Elison rose and whistled sharply. "Delegates of Trian," he said, "please rise and welcome Randle Fairimor, High King of Kelsa and Keeper of the Blue Flame."

Everyone rose and all eyes turned toward the door of the inner palace where Randle and Cassia were entering the Dome. Gideon walked at their heels, and behind him came a dozen Elvan *Bero'thai*. Randle wore a dark blue uniform trimmed in gold and carried a short scepter in the crook of his arm, a polished staff of Silverwood with a large blue crystal cut into the shape of a flame set in its end. The crystal flame caught the sunlight streaming through the windows and shimmered like a real flame near the King's elbow. Cassia held his other hand and looked stunning in her blue velvet dress.

Gideon's face was a mask of seriousness as he followed in the King and Queen's wake. His eyes glittered almost as brightly as Randle's scepter. He wore a grey shirt and pants and a dark grey cloak similar to the one he'd worn when he'd first arrived in Kindel's Grove. The blue flame medallion centered his chest.

Jase followed Gideon with his eyes as he drew near, and the big Dymas met his gaze. A faint smile touched Gideon's lips and, with a flit of his eyes, he indicated the source of his amusement. Jase looked up to see all hundred plus members of the lesser councils staring at the Dymas dumbfoundedly. Many looked worried — the older members anyway — since they understood the full import of Gideon's return. Even the lesser judges did little to conceal their surprise.

Randle took his seat, and those at the table followed. There was a collective swishing of clothes and a ripple of murmurs as the twelve lesser councils settled in above them. Once everything quieted, Randle stood to address them.

"Dymas, if you'd please," he said, gesturing to the stones. Jase felt Gideon draw on *Ta'shaen* and the seven Communicator Stones flared blue, filling the empty seats with the glowing, semi-transparent images of the Kings and Governors of the other ruling cities. Although he'd never seen the stones work, he'd heard enough from his mother to know that the link made it possible for them to function as if they were truly sitting at the table.

"Honorable members of the lesser tribunals," Randle continued, "we of the Kelsan High Tribunal welcome you to this emergency session. It is under the most dire of circumstances that we gather this day. Our nation is threatened once more by enemies of old, and it is our duty as leaders to confront it."

He paused and let his eyes travel the length of the tiers. "Already lives have been lost in this war, as evidenced by the vacancies in your midst." He gestured with his scepter, and the crystal flame flashed blue. "It grieves me, and it angers me, but it also steels my resolve. Those who took part in this assault have been destroyed. Those who orchestrated it will be hunted down and destroyed as well."

Jase watched as the majority of tribunal members nodded their agreement, their faces grimly determined. The lesser judges, however, kept their faces smooth. Glancing down both sides of the crescent-shaped table, he saw a variety of emotions on the faces of the High Tribunal. Most notable was Elder Nesthius. The aging High Priest's eyes were bright with excitement as he watched Randle speak.

It surprised him that a man of the church, especially the High Priest, would show so much eagerness for war, but then he thought of Gideon. The Dymas was both a Prophet and a warrior and had served Elderon in both capacities for three centuries.

As if drawn by his stare, Elder Nesthius turned to regard him. The High Priest's gaze locked on his, and for a brief moment Jase was powerless to look away. It gave him the feeling that Nesthius was taking his measure. When Randle starting speaking again, the spell was broken and Jase hurriedly looked away. Elder Nesthius may be over ninety, but he had the intensity of a forest fire.

"The attack last night was savage and powerful," Randle said, "but it was nothing more than a single gust of wind from an approaching storm. A storm so vast and potentially destructive that we will need every weapon at our disposal to combat it. It is for this purpose that we have gathered. It is for this purpose that I wish to invoke Military Law and Power and turn matters over to the Core Tribunal so they may counter this growing threat."

A ripple of mutters swept through the lesser tribunals, and heads pulled together in conversation. Randle drew all eyes back to him as he continued. "To explain the seriousness of the danger we face, I call upon the Guardian of Kelsa's Flame, Gideon Dymas."

Gideon rose to face the shocked silence. "I know many of you thought me dead," he said. "I know some of you are disappointed that I am not." There was a ripple of uncomfortable laughter before Gideon continued. "But the truth is, I was captured and imprisoned, and I spent the last twenty years in a Shadan Cult dungeon. A month ago members of the rightful government of Melek learned of my imprisonment and freed me. And for that, the nation of Kelsa owes them a great debt. For not only did they free me, but they freed the truth behind the resurgence of the Shadan Cult, the rise of the Con'Kumen, and the reasons behind these recent acts of aggression. They freed the truth of the danger we face."

He paused and looked around, and Jase realized the Dymas had everyone's attention. If he didn't know better, he would say half of them were holding their breath. "Throy Shadan has been refleshed once again and is preparing to pick up where he left off at the Battle of Greendom. His armies are twice what they were twenty years ago."

At the far end of the table, Chief Judge Zeesrom raised his hand in question. "Yes, councilor?" Gideon asked.

"But for Shadan to be refleshed means the mission to heal the Earthsoul failed. Is that correct?"

Good, Jase thought, *Zeesrom is with us.* He knew what Talia had told the man. Apparently, the Chief Judge had decided she was speaking the truth.

"Yes," Gideon answered, turning back to face the lesser tribunals. "And though it grieves me to say it, the Earthsoul is still dying." A mumbling of voices filled the Dome as those in the assembly turned to each other to express their shock and disbelief. Most people knew of the prophecies concerning the Earthsoul, and Jase thought most people believed them to some extent. But many of those seated before him looked skeptical as they studied Gideon intently.

"The mission to the Soul Chamber was discovered by Shadan, and we were attacked. The Talisman was rendered useless. Areth Fairimor and his warders were killed. Benak Fairimor and I were taken to Melek and imprisoned. The only good news is that I was able to deal such a blow with *Ta'shaen* that Shadan was sent back into Con'Jithar and has only now been able to return to the world of the living." His eyes were icy cold as he surveyed his audience.

"But his minions have not been idle the past twenty years. They have spawned an army far greater than anything Kelsa has faced before. If I were to elaborate, you would think Con'Jithar itself was coming for us."

A wave of murmurs swept the crowd once more, but Jase could see that doubt was starting to fade. It was being replaced, he realized, with fear.

Randle stood. "What to do about Shadan's return and the state of the Earthsoul are matters for the Core Council," he said, and the chatter died at the sound of his voice. "War is imminent." He glanced at the canvas-covered doors to the Overlook. "War is already upon us," he amended. "Shadan's armies, led by his cult, are massing for an invasion of our nation. There is evidence Riak is involved as well." He turned to Gideon who continued.

"I have seen this army," the Dymas said. "It is made up largely of Meleki soldiers blinded by the lies of the Shadan Cult, but there are enough Darklings and other shadowspawn to decimate the city of Trian without cultist help." He leaned forward for emphasis. "Even worse, this army is led by a numerous host of Agla'Con and K'rrosha. They are gathered east of Zedik Pass and could begin marching at any time."

A deep hush fell over the Dome, and Jase looked up to see fear in nearly every face.

Randle's words cut through the silence. "You know what we face. I ask you to give us the power to combat it. And so it is with heavy heart that I, Randle Fairimor, call for a vote to invoke Military Law and Power."

Gideon spoke first. "I vote yes."

"As do I," said Cassia, rising to stand beside her husband.

Croneam rose, followed closely by Elison, Seth, and Andil. "Yes," they said and remained standing.

Jase rose. "Yes," he said and felt all eyes turn to regard him.

"Yes," said Elliott, and Talia was only a heartbeat behind him.

The glowing images of the Kings of Marik, Tetrica, and Agisthas rose to cast their supporting votes as well. All along the main table, the High Tribunal was coming to its feet — Elders Nesthius and Zanandrei, the younger helping his elder rise; Chief Judge Zeesrom; and the bluish images of the Governors of Tradeston, Fulrath, and Capena; General Crompton — all of them voting in favor, their faces set, their eyes narrowed with determination.

Judgment Seat Geshiann and the other two Chief Judges remained sitting. Across from them, the twelve lesser judges did likewise.

Jase felt a rush of anger wash through him. They were three votes short of what was necessary to invoke wartime authority, and it was obvious the fifteen judges knew it. Their faces were smug, their eyes challenging.

He cast a sideways glance at Randle. The King's face was a mask of anger as he glared at the lesser judges, but there was a hint of something else in his face as well — worry perhaps, or maybe sadness. Without the freedom Military Law and Power would give the Core Council, they would have to fight with the lesser councils each and every time they needed to do something to fight the war with Shadan. It made him want to take hold of them with the Power and shake some sense into them.

He looked to Gideon, fully expecting to see anger in the big man's eyes, and blinked in surprise when he found him smiling. He followed Gideon's gaze and discovered why.

All along the five tiers, people were standing in a symbolic gesture of approval, their faces hard as they gazed down at the judge who headed their council. Within a matter of moments, every person in all of the five tiers was standing.

Jase turned his attention to the lesser judges and smiled when he saw that they were unaware of the multitude of eyes fastened on them from behind. He caught the attention of one of the judges and pointed to the tiers. The man glanced over his shoulder and stiffened in surprise, then nudged the judge next to him. One by one the rest of the lesser judges looked behind them. Each time their surprise was evident by the way they stiffened.

He watched them for a moment longer, then turned to regard Judgment Seat Geshiann and the other two Chief Judges. Their anger was obvious, but only a fool would ignore what had just happened. To do so would mean the end of a career.

Judge Geshiann stood. "Yes," he hissed, and the rest of the judges followed his lead.

Randle nodded and lifted the blue-flame scepter from the table. "It is done," he said. "Military Law and Power is hereby invoked and the governing of Kelsa transferred to the twelve members of the Core Council until such time as our enemies are vanquished and peace is restored. For the honor of God, the Flame of Kelsa, and the liberty of the people, it shall be so."

"Amen," Elder Nesthius said, and a ripple of 'amens' swept through the crowd.

"All delegates are asked to return to their duties and proceed as normal until further notice," Randle told them. "The governing of Trian is still in your hands. The war is in the hands of the Core. We will keep you informed of our decisions and let you know what you can do to assist in the war effort. Thank you for coming, and God bless."

Jase watched as the delegates from the lesser councils began filing out and marveled at how smoothly things had gone. After the difficulties he'd witnessed at the Chellum Council, he'd anticipated more resistance. It made him wonder if last night's attack had influenced the outcome.

He glanced at the ruined doors of the Overlook and nodded in satisfaction. Of course it had, he decided. The Con'Kumen's brazen assault had influenced a vote for the very thing which would make destroying them more feasible. The irony of it all was exquisite.

CHAPTER 2

Word from the South

Gideon watched the last of the delegates pass out of the Dome, then waited for the two warders to close the doors behind them before turning back to the thirty-six members of the Kelsan High Tribunal. The twelve lesser judges were clearly unhappy with what had taken place. So were Judge Geshiann and the two who'd sided with him. Only Judge Zeesrom seemed unperturbed by the outcome. *A good man,* he decided. *And one deserving of a reward.*

He glanced up at the empty tiers and smiled. The sight of so many people rising to show their support of the vote had been marvelous to behold, but he wasn't overly surprised by their reaction. If there was one thing he had learned over the past three centuries, it was that nothing raised the flag of unity among the normally quarrelsome politicians faster than the spilling of Kelsan blood, especially when some of it was theirs. The grim-faced determination with which they'd stared down the judges gave him hope for winning the war.

He turned his attention to the blue, semi-transparent images of the Communicator Stones and inhaled deeply. It didn't take a tremendous amount of Earthpower to make them work, but so many over such a long distance would be draining if he had to maintain the link for very long. And without Dymas at the other ends to ward the links, the enemy might be able to listen in on the conversation.

As if sensing his thoughts, Randle rose to address the council. "Members of the High Tribunal," he said, "I am grateful the vote was unanimous. It would pain me to think we had division among us." His voice held a hint of sarcasm, and he looked pointedly at the judges before continuing. "Now that Military Law and Power is official, I am going to dismiss all but the members of the Wartime Council and those few members who are vital to our success against this growing evil." He turned to the glowing images of the three Governors. "We will be in touch by means other than the Communicator Stones until such time as Dymas can be found to secure your end of the link. Thank you for your support." He nodded, and Gideon let the three stones wink out.

Randle turned to the lesser judges. "I'm sure Judgment Seat Geshiann will keep you informed as to the proceedings of the Core Council," he said dryly. "If we need your assistance for anything, we'll let you know." His voice was curt and dismissive, and Gideon was pleased with the effect it had on the judges. Scowling, they retrieved their papers and began making their way out of the room. Chief Judges Arivata and Gerdon moved to join them.

Judge Zeesrom, however, stopped at Gideon's shoulder and leaned close. "Beware of those fourteen," he whispered. "They are not pleased with how things have gone."

"And you?" Gideon asked, arching an eyebrow.

Zeesrom placed a hand on his shoulder and squeezed gently. "I am glad you are back," he said softly. "My knowledge and influence as a Chief Judge are at your disposal. If that fails, you shall have my sword."

"Thank you," Gideon said and watched Judge Zeesrom move off. It was obvious he was in no hurry to catch up to his colleagues. Not surprising since he had acted in opposition to them all. He shook his head in admiration at the man's courage. As soon as this meeting was over, he would speak with Randle about offering Zeesrom protection. He turned to find the King watching him.

"We'll look out for Zeesrom," Randle whispered, then glanced down the table. "Elder Zanandrei," he called, but Elder Nesthius raised a hand to stop him.

"With your permission," the aging High Priest said, his papery voice tired. "I would like him to stay. I need him to help me get around. And besides," he said, his face pinching into a smile, "I might not be around long enough to see this war through to its end anyway. Since Elder Zanandrei will be my replacement, let this be his training."

"As you wish," Randle said, then turned to the tables where the ambassadors were waiting. "Everyone else is invited to stay as well." He gestured them toward the table. "Please join us." He turned to Elison. "Move chairs around to the other side of the table so we aren't spread out so far. It's fine when facing the lesser tribunals, but it makes my neck hurt to keep looking back and forth."

Judge Geshiann moved up to Randle. "If the church is to have additional representatives," he said with a sour look toward Elder Zanandrei, "then I would like one of my Chief Judges to be allowed to stay as well."

Randle waved his hand irritably. "Fine," he said curtly, then turned to one of the warders. "Go fetch Judge Zeesrom and invite him to return." The warder left at a trot, and Judge Geshiann returned to his seat with a smug smile on his face. Gideon watched him for a moment, then dismissed him from his thoughts. The man was as childish as the rest of his family.

When the chairs were in place and everyone had settled in, Randle nodded in satisfaction. "Gideon Dymas will take things from here," he said.

Gideon looked around at those who remained. The four Communicator Stones still in use had been placed directly across from him, and the glowing images of General Crompton and Kings Marik, Agisthas, and Tetrica watched him and the others without speaking. Even knowing how the stones worked, they were a marvel to behold.

He let his eyes travel the table. Seth, Elison, and Croneam sat to the left of the stones, and Elders Nesthius and Zanandrei and Judges Zeesrom and Geshiann sat to the right. He, the Fairimors, and the Chellums had remained where they were. Thorac and the ambassadors from Elva and Zeka had moved to the seats next to Jase.

Seeing that everyone was present, he opened himself more fully to the Power and created a ward against eavesdropping. A thick invisible shield of Spirit and Air settled around the table like a bubble.

"Before I discuss the issues at hand," he said, "I need to explain a few things about the stones for the benefit of those who've never seen them used. I have warded our end against those who might seek to hear what we discuss, but I can do nothing about the other ends of the four links. It's highly unlikely our enemies are aware of the links yet, but continued use of *Ta'shaen* to communicate over such a distance will eventually be discovered. I will give you what information I can today. After that, you'll have to rely on written communications until you have someone who can ward your end as well."

The four blue images nodded, so he continued. "I want a full call to arms issued in each of your cities," he told them. "Lord Marik, Lord Tetrica, I want you to send every soldier not directly responsible for peace-keeping in your cities to Capena. General Crompton, I want you to solidify the front lines between Kelsa and Riak. You know better than I do what is needed, so I leave our southern border in your hands. King Agisthas," he said, turning to regard the portly image, "send half your troops to Fulrath and the other half to Crescent Gap. Defending Fulrath does little good if the enemy sneaks in from the south."

"Yes, Dymas," the King said.

"The enemy we face," he continued, "is more than sword-bearing soldiers. There will be shadowspawn and Agla'Con. There will also be K'rrosha. We will need Power-wielders trained for battle if we are to stand against those. Some have answered the call sent by Lord Fairimor to come forward and be trained, but they are not nearly enough. And what is worse, we have none but myself to train them." He let his eyes move along the table. "I refuse to believe I am the last of my kind. The Dymas are out there, gentlemen. Find them. Do whatever is necessary. Go door to door if you have to. Tell them Gideon Dymas has need of their services once more. Post notices in every village and neighborhood detailing the nature of the threat we face. Tell them of the Agla'Con. You can even tell them Shadan has returned, I don't care. But find them."

He leaned forward and placed his hands on the table. "As you do these things be wary. Be ready for an attack at any time, in any place. The Agla'Con have created a talisman that acts much the same as the Veilgates of the Old World. They can pass through this gate and appear anywhere they choose as if stepping from thin air. Nowhere is safe. No place is secure. Twice now they have used it — once to send Darkling troops into Chellum Palace, and then a second time to send a small army into the heart of the Chellum army as it marched to Fulrath. If they choose to, they could open this gate and drop Shadowhounds in our laps."

He saw the fear in their eyes as they contemplated his words.

It was Elder Zanandrei who broke the silence. "How many Agla'Con are we talking about?" he asked.

Croneam answered for him. "According to my Master of Spies, the Meleki army alone has five hundred or more."

"Five hundred!" King Agisthas gasped. "What's to keep them from simply stepping through this gate of theirs and conquering any of our cities on their own?"

"Several things," Gideon said patiently. "First: Shadan, arrogant fool that he is, wants credit to go to his cult. Second: even being so numerous, the Agla'Con couldn't maintain their hold on what they captured. Using the Power is draining. They need the Meleki and Darkling armies to occupy the places they conquer. And third: the Agla'Con are needed to control and direct the shadowspawn they have created. Without the Agla'Con to keep them in check, the shadowspawn would turn on each other and the rest of the Meleki host."

"I see," Agisthas said, sounding only partially relieved. "I don't suppose there is a way to eliminate the Agla'Con?"

"By myself?" Gideon scoffed. "We'd need at least a third their number in Dymas to even challenge them. I'd prefer half. Two to one odds aren't insur-mountable."

"If the Dymas are trained for battle," Croneam added. "Even with the Gifted who may come forward to help, it's unlikely any of them will have been trained for battle."

Gideon nodded. "Which is why it's so critical that we find Dymas. I can't train them all myself." He turned and glanced briefly at Jase. "I barely have time to train those I do know about. Not only do we need Dymas with skill and power, but we need Dymas who have the nerve to train the Gifted quickly. We don't have time for reservations about their safety. Keeping them from hurting themselves will do little good if they aren't ready when Shadan's forces show up to kill them."

He took a calming breath. "There is one more reason the Agla'Con can't simply attack us on their own," he said, getting back to Agisthas' question. "Probably the biggest reason. While it is true that they hate us terribly, they don't like each other very much either. They spend as much time plotting against one another as they do plotting against us. They are as likely to start fighting amongst themselves as to attack Kelsa if they think they can gain something by it."

"And thankfully so," Seth added, "or it would be over for us already."

"With five hundred Agla'Con, I'm not so sure it isn't," Judge Geshiann said.

"It's definitely not a war we can win," Gideon told them. He saw General Crompton stiffen, but he continued before the general could speak. "Not without first healing the Earthsoul and sending Shadan and the other Refleshed from the world of the living. Healing the Earthsoul will also lessen Maeon's power. He is the real enemy in this war. It is to him that Shadan and the Agla'Con look for leadership and power. Heal the Earthsoul, and we can better fight what's left."

"So, in essence, we are back where we were twenty years ago," Judge Zeesrom said.

Gideon looked around the table. "I'd say we are in worse shape than that."

"Do we have a Talisman of Elsa?" Croneam asked.

"No," Gideon answered. "And that is the heart of our problem."

Jase listened intently as Gideon spoke to the Core, even though it was information he already knew. The sense of urgency in the Dymas' voice cast new light on the situation and caused Jase to wonder if there was more the aged warrior-prophet wasn't telling. If nothing else, it made him realize that Gideon would rather be out fighting the evil directly instead of acting as a diplomatic advisor to Randle.

Not me, he thought. For him this time of diplomacy, boring as it may be, was valuable. It was giving him time to think things over. And the fact that no one was trying to kill him at the moment was an added bonus. Yes, he felt a sense of urgency about the upcoming conflict, but for an entirely different reason. Where

Gideon seemed anxious to attack, he was nervous to even think about embracing the Power. He needed to gain control of his abilities with *Ta'shaen* before his fears came true and he killed any number of his friends and associates. He fingered the bulge of the Talisman beneath his shirt and wondered again at Gideon's words concerning it.

It can protect the world from you.

It can protect you from yourself.

It knows who the enemy is.

From the three statements came two unsettling prospects. First: he was as dangerous as the enemy. Second: he was his own worst enemy. If both were true, it meant a third prospect might be true as well: if he didn't learn some control soon, the Talisman might consider him an enemy as dangerous as those he was fighting against. The thought tied his stomach in knots.

He was wrenched from his musings by Croneam's question. "Do we have a Talisman of Elsa?"

"No," Gideon answered. "And that is the heart of our problem."

"What do we do?" the image of General Crompton asked.

"With the council's permission," Gideon replied, motioning for Elison.

The captain withdrew five more Communicator Stones from a leather bag and placed them in front of empty chairs.

Gideon waited until Elison returned to his seat before continuing. "I would like to contact the Kings of Zeka, Chunin, and Elva. As was the case twenty years ago, we need their help in fighting this war. Shadan and his armies threaten them as well. I realize that ambassadors are here from all three nations, but for this first meeting I think it wise to involve the Kings directly. After today, Thorac Shurr of Chunin, Emish Kaitan of Elva, and Benin Jizo of Zeka will speak for their countries." He turned to the three and bowed appreciatively. "Thank you, once again, for answering the call."

Thorac dipped his head in a bow. "It is our privilege to be here," the little man answered. Beside him the Elvan and Zekan ambassadors uttered their agreement.

Jase felt Gideon draw on more of the Power and watched the Communicator Stones flare to life, filling the empty chairs with images of blue light.

"Can you all hear me?" Gideon asked. When they nodded, he turned back to the rest of the council. "Let me introduce Tohan Nanda, King of Chunin's Southern Kingdom," he said, indicating a young-looking man with a close-cropped beard. "And this is Luas Olwen of the Middle Kingdom, and Prad Moirai of the Northern." The stone-faced Kings inclined their heads politely.

"Orais Reiekel, King of Elva," Gideon continued, and the slender image inclined his head politely.

"It is a pleasure to see you once again, Dymas," the Elvan King said.

Gideon acknowledged the greeting with a nod and gestured to the last image. "Salamus Pryderi of Zeka."

"It's an honor to, as it were, meet you," Pryderi said, glancing around the room. "I must say this is an odd experience. We are several hundred leagues from one another, yet I can see you all as if we truly sat at the same table."

"It makes planning a war much easier," Gideon commented, obviously amused with the young King's amazement. "You've read the reports sent to you by Randle Fairimor detailing the nature of the danger we face?" he asked, and the five Kings nodded.

"I realize you each face difficulties of your own," he said, gesturing to King Reiekel, "such as the Shadan'Ko attacking the Wall of Aridan." He looked at Tohan Nanda. "Or the Kunin massing along your southern border. But my heart tells me these and many other things like them are but small pieces of a larger danger." He paused and looked at each member, flesh and glowing image alike. "The Earthsoul is dying, and Maeon's power grows. The Shadan Cult, Kunin, Riak, the Shadan'Ko, the Con'Kumen, and every other group massing to fight against us are part of this war. All are being stirred to anger by the Dark One."

He made a fist. "We can, and must, fight all these smaller battles — preserving our freedom is essential if we are to address the larger fight — but winning these smaller battles is pointless if we fail to accomplish the true task." There was a touch of desperation in his voice as he added, "We need to heal the Earthsoul. We must find a Talisman of Elsa."

"What does this Talisman look like?" Lord Nanda asked.

Jase looked up as Gideon turned to him. "My young friend here has the Blood Orb that Areth took on the failed mission twenty years ago. It was rendered useless to its true purpose by shadowspawn when we were attacked, but it remains a powerful weapon nonetheless. Show them, Jase."

He did as Gideon asked and held it up so the red-gold orb glimmered as it spun in the gripping talons.

"It is an orb of purest gold," Gideon told them. "Perfectly round and heavier than gold should be. It cannot be melted down or damaged in any way. This one was located in the temple here in Trian. It was in the inner sanctum in a small three-legged stand of silver, placed there by the hand of Fairimor himself after the temple was completed."

He shook his head. "The Temple of Elderon in Andlexces had one as well, but Siamon Fairimor carried it into battle against Shadan in A.S. 1407. Some believe it was the reason Shadan was defeated, but I consider Siamon's actions to be the biggest blunder in Kelsan history. That Talisman was also rendered useless to its true purpose. It was lost a few years later." He pursed his lips. "I've been to other Old World temples — in Chunin and Elva — but those Talismans were missing as well, probably carried off by someone else who didn't understand their importance. Most of the temples we know about are those built after the destruction of the Old World, such as the temple in Chellum, and none of them contain a Blood Orb. They were built to worship Elderon. The Old World temples were built to facilitate the Rejuvenation by keeping the Talismans safe."

"Are we sure these Old World temples still exist?" King Agisthas asked.

"Yes," Croneam Eries said. "The scriptures speak of them several times." He glanced at Gideon. "May I?" At Gideon's nod he continued. "When Maeon killed Elsa, her blood mingled with the dust of the earth and sprang forth in diverse places as Talismans of great power. Wherever those Talismans were found, a temple was built; both to keep the place sacred and to hold the Blood Orb until it was needed. But remember, that happened more than six thousand years ago. The destruction of the Old World changed everything. Of the hundreds of temples built in honor of Elsa's blood mingling with the earth, only those Gideon mentioned are known to us today."

"But," Gideon added, "with so many temples having been built, it's possible that we can find one containing a viable Talisman."

"Where do we look?" Judge Zeesrom asked.

"Everywhere," Gideon answered. "But more specifically we must discover and search any ruins known to have been from the Old World. I know it's a long shot, but if we are to find a lost Temple of Elderon, it will be in those places."

"May I see the Blood Orb?" Salamus Pryderi asked, and his glowing image leaned forward.

Jase handed the Talisman to Gideon, and it was passed down the table to Talia who held it before Pryderi's semi-transparent face. "I have seen its like," he said, and Jase felt his heart skip a beat.

Gideon's face was bright with excitement. "Where?"

Pryderi looked up. "Two months ago some ruins were discovered by one of our logging companies harvesting trees in the Callisar Mountains forty miles southwest of Thesston. I ordered the logging put on hold until our archeologists could determine what they had found. I journeyed there myself last week when they finally managed to open a door to a chamber on the upper floor of the largest structure. It contains an altar of crystal." He glanced back at the Talisman. "And inside the altar is an orb of gold about that size."

"Word from the south," Gideon said, and the tone of reverence in his voice was so profound that Jase looked at him in surprise. So did everyone else. The

Dymas ignored them all. His eyes, glittering with conviction, remained fastened on Pryderi. "Who else knows of this?" he asked.

"In addition to the loggers... a handful of archeologists, a few warders assigned to guard the place, and a handful of politicians who drew up the legislation to have it protected."

"A worthwhile cause," Gideon told him. "Because it seems you've found a lost Temple of Elderon."

CHAPTER 3

Dire Warnings

"... a lost Temple of Elderon."

The words hung in the air like the sounding of a trumpet, and it was all Gideon could do to contain his excitement. Every eye turned to regard him silently, and he could see what everyone was thinking. They wanted to know how he was so sure the golden orb in the temple was a Blood Orb without seeing it. How, even if it was a Talisman of Elsa, could he know it would still be viable? He decided to put their concerns to rest and tell them the truth.

He glanced at Elder Nesthius. "When I first arrived in Trian, I went to the Temple of Elderon in search of answers. While I knelt in prayer, the voice of the Earthsoul came to me and told me to be patient. She told me that word would come from the south." He looked to Pryderi. "What your people discovered *is* a Talisman of Elsa," he declared. "*Ta'shaen* is confirming it as we speak."

"Shall I have it removed from the ruins then?" Pryderi asked. "I could have it in Trian inside of two weeks."

"No," Gideon answered sharply — more sharply than he'd intended — and he raised an apologetic hand. "No," he said again, moderating his tone. "It can only be removed from the temple by a firstborn son of the blood of Elsa or else it becomes defiled and cannot be used to heal the Earthsoul."

"It's part of the birthright," Elder Nesthius added. "It must be taken up by a Fairimor for the ancient blood to be awakened properly. If other hands remove it from the temple, the link between the old blood and the new is broken. The temple may look run down, but it is still a holy place."

"But even removed by someone other than one of Elsa's sons," Gideon cautioned, "the Blood Orb remains a weapon of tremendous power. When her blood mingled with the dust of the earth, it created a powerful link to *Ta'shaen*. Anyone with ability in the Power, Dymas or Agla'Con, can use it to draw upon a reservoir of Earthpower far greater than anything they could wield on their own."

"What do you mean?" Judge Geshiann asked.

Gideon gestured for the Talisman to be returned. When it reached him, he held it for a moment, letting it dangle for all to see. "When this Talisman was defiled so that it could no longer be used to heal the Earthsoul, I used its reservoir of Earthpower to strengthen the Veil, and then to battle Shadan when he felt what I was doing and left the Battle of Greendom to confront me. There is no way I could have stood against him otherwise. I am not strong enough to contend with an Agla'Con as powerful as Shadan. He was the strongest to ever walk the earth, and his power has only slightly decreased since his death."

He was quiet a moment before continuing. "After I destroyed Shadan, I used the remainder of the reservoir to finish strengthening the Veil against Shadan's immediate return. That is why it took him twenty years to be refleshed."

The memory of the battle inside Mount Tabor made him tremble, but it was the truths he was forced to withhold that turned his words to bile. "This particular Blood Orb's reservoir has been used, but it remains a weapon of great power. The one your loggers discovered, Lord Pryderi, is a thousand times more powerful." He handed the Talisman back to Jase. "If it were to fall into the wrong hands..." He trailed off meaningfully before turning back to gaze at the image of the Zekan King.

"Select fifty of your best and most trusted warders," he told Pryderi, "and have them guard the temple grounds and the Blood Orb at all costs. A viable Talisman in the hands of the enemy could bring the Veil down as readily as I was able to strengthen it. If that happens, we will be facing Maeon as well as Shadan."

"I'll put half my army there," Pryderi replied, but Gideon waved him off.

"Too large a group will draw unnecessary attention and create the kind of curiosity we want to avoid, even among the warders. Simply choose your best fifty and tell them they are to protect the discovery until experts can be brought in to study the artifacts. They don't need to know what they guard, only that it's sacred."

"That's near enough the truth," Pryderi said. "I'll have them out there before nightfall. How long before one of the sons of Elsa can come and retrieve it? Now that I know what it is, the sooner it's removed from my custody the better I'll feel."

"We will leave tomorrow," he assured the King. "We'll need nine days to reach Tetrica, and two more to sail to Thesston — " He cut off when he saw Seth shaking his head.

"If you'll allow me to pick the horses," the Chellum captain said, "I can shave two days off the time to Tetrica."

Gideon nodded and turned back to Pryderi. "Give us nine days then," he said and let his gaze sweep across the group. "I still want a full search to be made for any other lost temples, and I want to be contacted the moment anything is found. I hate to plan for the worst, but if anything should happen to Pryderi's discovery, I want others found to replace it."

They assured him that a thorough search would be made, and he told them how communications would proceed until such time as he felt it safe to use the stones again. "The less they are used," he said, "the less likely it is that our plans will be discovered."

"Is discovery really such a threat?" Elder Zanandrei asked. "I mean, are the Agla'Con really so adept at eavesdropping?"

Gideon turned to regard the church leader with a frown. "They are," he answered firmly. "But what is worse — " he cut off, his words stifled by a warning tickle of *Ta'shaen*.

He had intended to tell them about Zeniff — to speak of how the man, a member of Kelsa's own governing council, had betrayed the first mission to heal the Earthsoul — but a surge of Earthpower stayed his tongue. It was something he had experienced before, and he knew better than to ignore such a powerful warning.

Suddenly it occurred to him that the warning may have come because Zeniff was sitting at the table with them and would lash out if discovered. He glanced around the table in horrified silence. *How could I have been so careless?* he wondered. *Why did I not consider that the traitor might be among the Core members instead of just among the lesser councils?*

He suddenly wished that Lord Pryderi hadn't mentioned the finding of the Elsa Talisman in front of these people. If Zeniff was indeed among this group, he may very well decide to try to fetch the Talisman for himself.

Alarmed, he let his eyes move down the table. Who among all these could have sold their souls to Maeon? Not Randle or Cassia, he decided. And not Seth or Elder Nesthius either. The younger generation could be ruled out as well — Endil, Jase, and the others had been in diapers when the mission was betrayed. Talia had yet to be born.

Stalix Geshiann and Bresdin Zeesrom had been lesser judges at the time of the first mission and hadn't been privy to the information. Neither had Elder

Zanandrei. That left generals Eries and Crompton, Elison Brey, and Kings Marik, Agisthas, and Tetrica from the Kelsan representatives, and the ambassadors and Kings of Elva, Chunin, and Zeka.

Orais Reiekel he dismissed immediately; the Elvan people were not capable of such treason. Lord Pryderi was new to the council, as was Lord Nanda. He refused to believe that Elison or Croneam could have turned to the dark; Thorac was just as unlikely. He studied those who remained. It simply didn't seem possible that any of them could be guilty of such horrific treason. Unfortunately, he would be suspicious of them all until Zeniff was discovered.

He realized that everyone was watching him, waiting for him to continue.

"But what is worse..." Seth prompted, helping him remember what he'd been about to say.

"But what is worse," he continued, hoping they couldn't sense the fear that was washing through him, "is that some Agla'Con have the ability to pry into another person's mind." *Not that it matters,* he thought darkly, *since Zeniff probably already knows everything.* He let his eyes move along the faces at the table. *Who could it be?*

"Certainly you would feel such a thing," King Reiekel said. "Thought Intrusion is, as I understand it, forbidden."

"If I were in close proximity to the crime when it occurred, I would feel it," Gideon told them. "It doesn't require a tremendous amount of *Ta'shaen* to accomplish, just a willingness to become the target of a Cleansing Hunt."

"What of the Dainin?" Elison asked. "Have they pledged their support as well?"

"The Dainin," Gideon said, "do things according to their own time, and after their own designs. They haven't made official contact with Lord Fairimor, but I doubt they are sitting idly by while Shadan rallies his forces."

Croneam leaned forward to glance down the table at Randle. "I received an official notice from the Dainin stating that they have invoked a Cleansing Hunt and that they will inform us if the one they hunt is taken on our soil."

"Good," Gideon replied. "I knew we could count on the *Nar'shein Yahl.*" He turned back to the image of the Elvan King. "Returning to your question, Lord Reiekel, I think a better question to ask is: Do we have enough Gifted among us to warn of any abuses with the Power? The Agla'Con will think twice about seizing *Ta'shaen* if there is a risk they might be discovered." He turned to Lord Pryderi. "You don't happen to have any Dymas you could send along with the warders, do you?"

Maybe Zeniff will hesitate to take the Talisman if he fears he will have to fight for it, he thought darkly. He held his breath as he waited for Pryderi's answer.

The Zekan King nodded. "I know of two I can send," he replied. "Assuming I can find them. And assuming they will be willing to help."

"Do your best," Gideon told him, then turned to glance at Elison who had risen. He followed the captain's gaze to find three warders approaching the council area. A robed figure walked among them, his hood pulled down low around his face to hide his identity.

"Ah," Gideon said, motioning them forward. He opened a hole in the protective shield he'd created against eavesdropping and allowed the hooded figure inside. Closing the hole behind him, he pulled a chair close to his with a tendril of Air and gestured for the figure to sit. "I was hoping you would be able to join us," he said warmly. "And I thank you for coming so quickly."

Dark hands spider-webbed with purple reached up to pull back the hood, and it dropped away to reveal the chiseled face and white mane of a Meleki. All along the table the members of the war-time council gasped, their eyes filled with disbelief as they stared at a man so many of them considered to be the enemy. All except for the images of Lord Agisthas and General Crompton. Those two, Gideon noted, looked angry. Downright hostile in fact.

"It is an honor to be here," the Meleki replied. "A tremendous honor indeed."

Ignoring Crompton's scowl, Gideon let his eyes sweep the table. "Ladies and gentlemen of the council," he said, "let me introduce Hulanekaefil Nid, High King of Melek."

Jase blinked in surprise as Gideon introduced the Meleki King, and all along the table there were several audible gasps. Most of the members of the tribunal recovered quickly, but the image of General Crompton leaned forward to stare accusingly at Gideon. "What is the meaning of this... this outrage?" he growled. "We are at war with the Eastland and you bring their King to sit in council with us?"

Gideon made a placating gesture. "Be at ease, General," he soothed. "We are at war with the Shadan Cult and those who serve Maeon. They are the enemy, not the Meleki people. High King Nid has been fighting them for the past two decades as well."

"Then why bring him here?" Judge Geshiann asked. "Let him stay in his own land where he belongs. If it weren't for the fanatical nature of the Meleki people, there wouldn't be a Shadan Cult."

General Crompton nodded his agreement, and beside him King Agisthas did likewise. The rest of those seated at the table kept their faces smooth, but Jase sensed that many of them shared the Chief Judge's sentiment. It was difficult for him to control his anger.

Beside him, Gideon opened his mouth to rebuke them, but Seth beat him to it.

"And what of the fanatical nature of the Con'Kumen?" he snarled. "Have you forgotten them so quickly? Those we have captured and killed have been Kelsan, you know. And their leaders wore the robes of Shadan Cult priests." He leaned forward and his eyes narrowed dangerously. "This isn't a war between nations; it's a battle between those who serve the Creator and those sworn to Maeon."

"And how do we know this Meleki isn't sworn to the dark?" General Crompton countered. "How do we know this isn't some ploy to gain advantage in the upcoming war?"

"Precisely," Judge Geshiann added. "Deception is part of the Meleki lifestyle. It's highly unlikely that — "

Gideon had heard enough. "Silence!" he shouted, rising to his feet and leaning across the table toward Judge Geshiann. "This man is here by my invitation. He is as loyal to our cause as Lord Fairimor and as trustworthy as Lord Reiekel." He glared at Geshiann hatefully. "Much more trustworthy than you, Judge Geshiann. Or you, General Crompton. Either of you slander him or his people again, and the High Tribunal will have need to fill a vacancy."

Jase cringed. Threatening a member of the council was almost as serious as threatening a member of the royal family. Regardless of his title as the Guardian of the Blue Flame, Gideon may have overstepped his bounds. It was obvious from the outrage in the Chief Judge's eyes that he thought so.

"How dare you threaten me!" he growled, rising to face Gideon.

From the corner of his eye Jase saw all the warders tense, and he glanced at Elison to see how he would react. He looked surprisingly calm. Beside him, Seth actually looked amused. Jase turned back as Judge Geshiann raged on.

"You think because you have sat with this council for three centuries that you can play the rest of us as pawns in some twisted game? Sorry to disappoint you, Dymas, but I will not be moved. And I will not accept this... this..." he glanced scornfully at High King Nid, "this *Darkling* as anything but an enemy to Kel — "

He cut off, his eyes bulging, and Jase could feel the tendrils of Air Gideon had seized him with.

"I warned you," Gideon said menacingly. "Now it's time to die."

"Gideon," Randle said sharply, "release him."

The Dymas glanced at Randle, his eyes and face hard, and for a moment Jase thought he might crush Geshiann's neck anyway. Finally, he conceded.

Gasping for air, the Chief Judge reached up to rub his throat.

Gideon's eyes bored into him. "I defer to Lord Fairimor's wishes this time," he said softly, his tone chilling. "But if you offend again, I will kill you."

He sat down, and Jase let his eyes move along the table. Everyone looked stunned by what had just occurred. Even Elison. Only Seth and Croneam Eries seemed unperturbed by Gideon's uncharacteristic show of anger.

"And what of me?" General Crompton asked. "Are you going to reach across the leagues between Trian and Capena to silence me? Because I will not be silent on this matter. I have spent my entire life fighting Melek and Riak, and now you expect me to cast aside all animosity and trust one of them with the security of our nation?"

"Yes," Gideon answered. "That is exactly what I'm asking."

"And if I refuse?" Crompton asked, his voice hard.

Croneam leaned forward so he could look over at Crompton's glowing image. "Then I will have you stripped of your command and thrown in prison for insubordination," he said sharply. "Good heavens, man, what's gotten into you?"

Crompton shrugged. "I'm just not sure having a Meleki sit with this council is the wisest course of action."

"Well, I am," Croneam said fiercely. "And you will hold your peace. That's an order."

"Yes, sir," Crompton said, his tone neutral. He turned his gaze on Gideon. "And my apologies, Dymas. It's in my job description to be paranoid."

Jase held his breath as Gideon studied Crompton for several moments. "Apology accepted," Gideon said at last. "And I'm grateful for your concern about our nation. But you must trust me. As the Chief Judge said, I have sat with this council for three centuries; I'm not going to compromise its security now." He glanced pointedly at Judge Geshiann. "Others I'm not so sure about."

High King Nid, who had watched the entire exchange without so much as a frown or raised eyebrow, reached over and put his hand on Gideon's arm. "Perhaps if you show them," he said, his voice calm, "their fears concerning me can be put to rest."

"Show us what?" Elder Zanandrei asked.

"Why we should be thanking this man instead of scorning him," Gideon replied. He motioned for the warder holding a copper urn, and the man set it in the center of the table. Jase felt a tickle of Earthpower, and flames sprang up in the urn.

"Look into the fire," he told them.

The corridor was wide, the ceiling high and lost in shadow. Numerous side passages intersected the corridor, some stretching into blackness, others glimmering with flickers of red.

Gideon glanced toward those glimmers and frowned. There were Agla'Con everywhere in the fortress. Hundreds of them. And yet it was the dark passages that troubled him most — those areas held nightmares he couldn't begin to imagine. If he hadn't seen some of them firsthand, he wouldn't have believed.

The K'rrosha holding the chain fastened to the collar around his neck noticed the errant glance and gave the chain a sharp tug.

"Eyes forward," it rasped. "Nothing in there need concern you."

"Everything concerns me," Gideon told it darkly.

The K'rrosha laughed, a chilling sound devoid of all humanity. "It must be frustrating," it hissed tauntingly, "to kill someone only to have him come back as a Deathman." It glanced over at him, its eyes flaring. "This body may be the flesh of another, but my memory is my own. I haven't forgotten the Battle of Capena. Nor will I forget how you murdered my brothers even as they tried to flee." He rattled the chain for emphasis. "I'm going to enjoy watching you die."

Gideon held his tongue. Instead, he looked to the end of the corridor where seven Shadan Cult priests were waiting in the antechamber fronting the great hall of Shadan's fortress. Their hoods were pulled close about their faces, but he could tell from their hands that they were all Meleki. One of them gestured to the K'rrosha as they approached.

"We'll take him from here," the Meleki said. "You are dismissed."

The K'rrosha hesitated. "I was told to take him directly to Shadan," it rasped, but the Meleki shook his head.

"Plans change," he growled, then held out his hand for the chain.

Reluctantly, the K'rrosha handed it over. The priest gave a sharp tug and started back the way Gideon and the K'rrosha had come. "This way," he said roughly. "We must make ready for your death."

When the K'rrosha started to follow, one of the priests barred his way. "You are no longer needed, Deathman," he said. "Return to your post."

The K'rrosha's eyes flared, but he dipped his head in acquiescence. "As you command, Agla'Con."

As the priests led him down the corridor, Gideon studied them quietly. In spite of the earlier bravado, he sensed that they were nervous. Then again, the entire fortress had been tiptoeing around in anxious trepidation since Shadan's return yesterday.

The Agla'Con holding the chain noticed his stare and turned to regard him silently for a moment. When they passed beneath a lamp burning in a wall bracket, the hooded head tilted back far enough for lamplight to shine on the man's face.

Gideon's eyes went wide, and he looked over his shoulder at the others.

High King Nid chuckled softly. "They are with me," he whispered, then lowered his face into darkness. "And they know their duty."

Up ahead, two Agla'Con emerged from a side passage and moved toward them. They moved to the side to let him and the others pass, but Gideon could see the curiosity in their eyes. To date, only K'rrosha had been allowed to hold his leash. Lord Nid noticed the looks as well and rattled the chain.

"It must be terrible to be bound against using the Power," he taunted, his voice filled with scorn. "But I must say, you look good collared like a dog."

"If not for this collar," Gideon growled back, putting an edge in his voice, "I'd cut your filthy hearts out."

"Silence, cur," King Nid replied, giving the leash a tug, "or I'll remove your tongue. Shadan said nothing about leaving you intact." When the Agla'Con were out of earshot, Lord Nid leaned close. "We need to get out of here before their curiosity turns to suspicion."

They reached a large rotunda and moved toward the main entrance of the fortress. There were nearly a dozen Agla'Con in the room, and the exit was guarded by a pair of K'rrosha holding Power-wrought scepters.

"This might be a problem," Gideon muttered, and beside him Lord Nid grunted. Without hesitating, they approached the exit.

The talismans in the ends of the K'rrosha's scepters flared to life as they were lowered to bar the way. "Halt," one of them hissed, "and state your intention."

"My intention," High King Nid said, reaching up to pull back his hood, "is to set this man free."

The entire room fell quiet, and all eyes turned to regard Lord Nid in disbelief — disbelief that quickly turned to shouts of alarm as many recognized him for who he was. Taking advantage of the initial surprise, Lord Nid opened himself to the Power and, with a quick flick of his hand, cleaved the K'rrosha guards in two with a narrow blade of Fire. Then he turned toward Gideon and deftly sliced the collar from his neck.

The six men who'd come with Nid threw off their robes to reveal an assortment of weapons, and daggers were drawn and hurled into the crowd. Cries of pain filled the room as black-robed figures began crumpling to the floor. Four of the men drew swords and took up positions at the sides of the other two. Obviously Dymas, those two were sending columns of Fire streaking into the side passages.

Freed from the collar's restraining power, Gideon sent tendrils of killing heat lancing through several Agla'Con who were preparing to strike back. With smoldering holes in their chests, they dropped among the lifeless bodies littering the floor.

There was a flash of black as Shadowhounds bounded in from a side corridor and raced toward him. He channeled a stream of blue fire to intercept them, but the hounds slipped past — only Hulanekaefil's quick action saved them from being torn to shreds.

The outcast King struck the stone beneath the hounds, exploding everything upward in a gout of superheated grit. The hounds vanished behind the blinding spray.

"Strike the ceiling," Lord Nid shouted. "Collapse it on their heads."

Gideon lashed out, pummeling the stone above with several stabs of lightning. The high-domed ceiling fell in a great smoking rumble, and the entire room trembled with the impact. Gideon sent several more stabs horizontally down the main corridor and saw a number of bodies somersault into death, their corpses outlined in silvery white. There were many more that remained on their feet, though, protected from the killing strike by shields of Air and Spirit. He could feel the corruption in the Power they wielded; he could feel how many were rushing to join the battle.

"Let's get out of here," he shouted. Turning to the fortress' main gate, he exploded it outward with a massive fist of Air. He had only taken a few steps when the air behind him flashed into a killing heat. Pulling a shield of Spirit around him, he turned to search for his companions. Lord Nid was a few paces away, crouched beneath a shield of his own, and a few paces beyond that, smooth disruptions in the flames showed where two more shields held the fires at bay. Everyone else, Agla'Con and Meleki warder alike, had been incinerated.

Lord Nid motioned toward the door and began making his way forward, pulling the protective shield along with him. Behind him, the other two shields merged into one, and the Meleki Dymas retaliated. One maintained the shield while the other channeled a barrage of lightning that threatened to collapse this part of the fortress.

Gideon turned to help them, but Lord Nid's shout brought him up short.

"They know their duty," the Meleki King shouted. "Don't let them die for nothing. Quickly now. They will cover our escape."

Pursing his lips into a tight frown, Gideon followed Lord Nid's lead, and together they fled out into the darkness and down the narrow road splitting a sea of midnight-colored sands.

When the Viewing faded, Gideon looked around the room, and his face pinched into the same frown he'd worn in the Viewing. "Now maybe you realize that our allies will come to us from all lands. As Captain Lydon stated earlier, this isn't a war between nations so much as it is a war against the servants of Maeon. Lord Nid and many of his people started fighting this war long before the Con'Kumen showed up in Trian." He glanced around the room, his face still a mask of stone. "I owe him my life. Many at this table owe him an apology."

The awkward silence that followed was finally broken by General Crompton. The shimmering blue image dipped his head in a bow. "Lord Nid," he began, clearing his throat. "I beg forgiveness for my earlier words against you. I see now that you are indeed a friend of this tribunal. And if you don't mind my saying, what you did for Gideon Dymas is the most courageous act I have ever witnessed. It may also be the craziest."

There was a nervous chuckle from some of the others before Crompton continued. "You have my admiration and respect," he said sincerely. "If ever you find yourself in Capena, I would be honored to have you join me in my home. But if such an opportunity should never arise, then let it suffice to say that I would be honored to ride out with you to battle. I would fight at your side any time."

Several members of the tribunal muttered in agreement, but Judge Geshiann remained silent. Croneam Eries glared at him for a moment before turning his attention back to Lord Nid. "I share General Crompton's sentiment," he said, "and I thank you for what you have done for Kelsa."

Talia Chellum leaned forward so she could look into Lord Nid's face. "The Dymas who covered your escape," she said, her voice sympathetic, "they were your warders?"

High King Nid's face remained smooth, but his words were filled with sadness as he answered. "They were my sons."

This time the silence that fell over the table was suffocating as those present wrestled with the enormity of the Meleki King's sacrifice. It was a sacrifice far larger than any they had ever been required to make, and when Gideon looked into their faces he saw sympathy mingled with what could only be described as a morbid sense of awe. Talia, he noted, had tears forming in her eyes.

"I'm sorry," she said, breaking the silence. "And I share your grief. They were obviously exceptional men."

Lord Nid nodded. "They were. They knew going in that we might not be coming out alive. I forbade them from coming with me, of course..." he hesitated, a fond smile creeping across his face, "but they disobeyed me. It is the only time in their lives that I can remember them doing such a thing." He shook himself free of the memory and returned his gaze to Talia.

"And I appreciate your sympathy, Lady...." He left off, waiting.

"Chellum," she replied. "Talia Chellum."

After a long silence, Randle cleared his throat. "To return to the point of discussion before Lord Nid arrived," he said, "Lord Pryderi is going to guard the Talisman until it can be retrieved by the Fairimors. The rest of us will prepare to meet the armies of Shadan and Riak and continue the hunt for the traitorous Con'Kumen. If we are lucky, the Fairimors will rejuvenate the Earthsoul before Shadan launches his attack and we will only have to contend with a living enemy."

He looked at those around him and smiled. "It won't be easy, but my heart tells me we can win this. For those of you who are distant, we will keep in touch through other means until it is safe to use the Communicator Stones. Until that time, farewell. For the honor of God, and liberty of all our peoples, let it be so."

"Let it be so," they echoed, and Gideon released the Power, severing the last of the communication links. When the shimmering images faded, he turned to those who remained.

"You all know your duties," he told them. "I suggest you attend to them." Rising, he let the shield against eavesdropping vanish and started for the inner palace.

Elder Nesthius called to him, and he waited as the aging High Priest worked his way around the end of the table. As he neared, Nesthius motioned for Elder Zanandrei to hold back so he could approach alone. "I'm pleased at your safe return," the High Priest said. "I was starting to wonder if I would live long enough to see it happen."

"You knew I would come back?" Gideon asked, surprised.

Nesthius nodded. "I hear the voice of the Earthsoul from time to time as well," he said, then looked around to make sure no one was listening. "I had a vision last night," he whispered, his voice concerned. "In it, your young apprentice had become corrupted and was unable to rejuvenate the Earthsoul. He didn't give himself over to Maeon, but it didn't matter. In the end, he himself destroyed most of Kelsa."

Gideon frowned. "A prophecy?" he asked, a cold pit settling in his stomach.

"A warning," Nesthius said. "A very serious warning."

"Thank you for telling me," he said, taking the old man's hand and clasping it warmly. "I'll keep my eyes on him."

He released the High Priest's hand and started down the carpeted aisle splitting the Dome's interior. His eyes settled on Jase's back and he frowned. *Don't turn to the Agla'Con,* he admonished silently. *Don't make me have to kill you.*

Back in the inner palace, Jase and the others went to their rooms to change into less formal clothes before gathering once more in the Fairimor home. At Gideon's invitation, Croneam Eries and Teig Ole'ar joined them, and Allisen made sure that they were fed. The aging General and his Elvan Master of Spies would be leaving for Fulrath within the hour, and Cassia had made a fuss about not letting them leave on an empty stomach. Lord Nid was with them, and the three were talking quietly as they ate.

Jase waved a greeting to them, then moved to where Elliott sprawled on one of the sofas in the library half of the room. The Prince's eyes were narrow with thought as he fingered the hilt of his sword, and his lips were pressed into a frown. Jase took a seat opposite his friend and watched him without speaking.

A moment later Endil joined them, and Jase saw from his frown that he was worried about what the next few days would bring. Endil didn't leave the palace often, so the prospect of leaving the country in search of a Talisman of Elsa was more than a little unsettling for the young Prince. Jase knew how he felt — this would be the third time in as many weeks he'd had to leave a place he called home.

Endil noticed him watching, and smiled self-consciously. "It's not easy, is it?" he asked. "Having all this responsibility."

"No. It's not," Jase answered, then glanced at the others. "Fortunately, we don't have to bear the burden alone."

Endil's brow furrowed, and Jase could tell he was considering what he would say next. "I envy you," he said at last. "For your abilities, I mean. It must be nice to be able to defend yourself and those around you with the Power."

Jase stared at him.

"I mean it, Jase," Endil continued. "Part of the burden I feel is from the burden I place upon others because of my lack of training in the Power and the more traditional forms of combat you learned from Seth and Daris. I've been too busy with the bureaucratic side of things to learn much of that."

Jase was quiet a moment, considering. "I want you to have my dartbow," he said. "I haven't used it since becoming a Dymas, and it really should have gone to you anyway since it belonged to Grandfather."

Endil looked stunned. "Are you sure? I know how much it means to you."

Jase smiled at him. "It's yours. As soon as we finish here, I'll go get it out of my room."

Gideon and General Eries joined them at the sofas, and Elliott breathed out dramatically as they neared. "Well, the tribunal went more smoothly than anticipated."

Taking a chair to Croneam's left, Elison nodded his agreement. "Yes, it did. But I have to admit, when Geshiann and the other two Chief Judges didn't cast their vote, I thought we were done for. I could see in their eyes what they were thinking. Even the four who answer to Judge Zeesrom had their hackles up."

Talia, who had slipped into the room without Jase seeing, pulled her hair back into a pony tail and began tying it with a ribbon. "Judge Zeesrom took an awful risk by voting for Military Law and Power," she said, moving to sit by Gideon. "It's very likely the other judges will seek to ruin his career now."

"Perhaps," Elison replied. "But after the show of support from the members of the lesser councils, I don't think they will dare. The twelve lesser judges still have to answer to those who elected them. You can bet the members of their councils won't forget how their elected representatives sat in defiance of the High Tribunal. If anything, Zeesrom probably achieved some kind of hero status by being the only judge to voluntarily side with the council."

"I hope you're right," Talia told him. "I like Judge Zeesrom. I'd hate for anything bad to happen to him."

"I'm more worried how the lesser judges are going to react to Gideon's threatening to kill the Chief Judge," Randle said darkly. "That was very foolish of you, Gideon. Very foolish indeed."

Jase cringed and turned to watch how Gideon would react. Surprisingly, the Dymas laughed. "I suppose it was," he said, "but at least those pompous fools know I mean business. Besides, it felt good. House Geshiann has been a thorn in my side for two and half centuries."

"Would you have really killed him?" Endil asked.

"No," Gideon replied, "but he doesn't know that, does he?"

"And I think we ought to leave it that way," Elison added, then looked meaningfully at Gideon. "And I think it's safe to say he isn't the Agla'Con we suspect to be among us. He certainly would have retaliated otherwise."

"Perhaps," Gideon answered. "It's hard to tell how an Agla'Con will react. Yes, they have an instinct for survival, but they would cut their own throat if Shadan told them to." He blew out his cheeks resignedly. "Since we don't know what orders this Agla'Con has received or who those orders may have come from, we are going to have to suspect everyone outside of this room. Someone on the tribunal is an Agla'Con, that much I know. The Earthsoul manifested the truth of it to me while we sat in council."

"Then this Agla'Con knows where the Blood Orb is and what we are planning to do to retrieve it," Randle said, his face dark with anger.

"They know an approximate location," Gideon countered. "There is no reason to believe they can find it before we get there. The forests around Thesston are thick and the terrain mountainous. If we hurry, I have every reason to believe we will get there first."

"I hope so," Randle muttered, "or we will be in trouble."

"You have no idea," Lord Nid said. "A Blood Orb in the hands of an Agla'Con with the right knowledge could win the war for Shadan in a single stroke. An Agla'Con with the right knowledge and skill could bring down the Veil and usher Con'Jithar into the world of the living."

There was a heavy silence as all in the room considered the Meleki King's words.

Finally, Elliott spoke. "So what now?" he asked. "Who goes to Zeka to retrieve the Talisman with Jase?"

Jase turned to study Gideon's face while the Dymas considered Elliott's question. He looked amused. "Who do you think should go with him?" Gideon asked.

Elliott sat up. "You, obviously," he said, then looked at Seth. "And Seth, of course." He adjusted his sword as if considering, then added, "And I should probably ride along as well." He kept his face smooth, but the eagerness in his eyes was unmistakable.

Gideon's amusement increased. "You? Why you?"

Elliott's face hardened. "Because I want to," he said, and there was a sudden edge to his voice.

"I don't think that's wise," Seth said, but Gideon held up a hand to silence him.

"You can come," he told Elliott. "So long as you stay out of trouble."

Elliott looked insulted. "When have I ever caused trouble?"

"I'm going too," Talia said, and Seth shook his head.

"Absolutely out of the question!" he growled, shooting her a look that could have caused a Shadowhound to faint. Talia's eyes narrowed angrily, but Seth continued before she could speak. "What do you think this is, a bloody vacation? I will not — "

"Seth," Gideon said firmly, and the captain broke off, scowling. "She is needed. It is the will of the Earthsoul."

Seth's face was livid, but he shrugged. "If you say so," he hissed.

"If we are going by coach," Thorac said, "I think I'd like to go as well." When everyone looked at the Chunin in surprise, he shrugged. "I might as well. I don't have anything better to do. Sitting around in the palace is boring, and Endil certainly isn't much of a chess player."

Endil stiffened momentarily, then laughed. "I suppose I'm not."

"What of my son?" Randle asked. "Will you need him to go as well?"

"Yes." Gideon replied. "Should anything happen to Jase, Endil will have to remove the Talisman from the temple."

Randle nodded, and Jase could see the worry already present in his eyes. Cassia's face paled visibly, and tears formed at the corners of her eyes. It made him wonder how Brysia would react if she were to find out about all of this. He decided it was best she didn't know.

"We will leave at first light," Gideon told them. "Bring what you need to make the journey bearable, but remember we need to make haste."

Elison rose. "Seth and I will select the horses and ready the coaches," he told them. "How many warders do you want to accompany you?"

"None," Gideon replied. "They will only slow us down."

"I'll select a dozen," Seth answered as if he hadn't heard, "from among the *Bero'thai*. And we'll find the best horses to carry them." He turned away before Gideon could reply.

Croneam chuckled and elbowed Teig. "He kind of reminds me of Governor Prenum," he said, then rose to face Gideon. "I'm leaving," he said. "I'll have Fulrath ready to march to Zedik Pass within the month."

"Thank you," Gideon said, moving to shake Croneam's hand. "Journey safely, my friend. With any luck, we'll have the Earthsoul healed by the time you're ready to march. Without Shadan and the other Refleshed to lead the cultist army, this war will be much easier."

"Dymas," Lord Nid said, moving to stand beside Croneam, "I wish to accompany General Eries to Fulrath. When his men march to Zedik Pass, I will go with them. My knowledge of the enemy and my skills as a Dymas will be theirs."

Gideon smiled approvingly. "I thought you might want to reenter the fight," he said with a smile. "And you have my blessing." He took the Meleki King's hand. "Kelsa owes you a great debt, my friend. I want you to stay alive long enough for us to repay it."

"I'll do my best," Lord Nid said, then moved to the table to collect his things.

"God's speed, Dymas," Croneam said, starting for the door, "and good luck."

Jase smiled as he watched Croneam go. *God's speed,* he repeated silently. *That's what we need right now.* He took a breath and let it slowly out. Three weeks round trip to retrieve the Elsa Talisman and another two to journey to the Soul Chamber to heal the Earthsoul. Five short weeks before life could get back to normal.

CHAPTER 4

Forbidden Indulgence

Zeniff finished reading the note from Ren Troas, owner of the inn called *The Proud Flame*, then looked up at Ren's daughter. She stood before him unblinking, her face smooth as she awaited his reply. If she was nervous to be in the presence of an Agla'Con, she didn't show it. Ren, on the other hand, would have been sweating buckets. It was probably the reason the cowardly innkeeper always sent the girl to deliver these messages.

He glanced at the note again and frowned. *Your brother arrived from the Mae'rillium estates in Seston and wishes to see you. Come to The Proud Flame to meet him.* Ren was an idiot when it came to writing messages, but he knew what the innkeeper meant, so it wasn't all bad. In the past, some of Ren's notes had been so confusing he'd had to send for the man to have him report in person.

He reached up to scratch his cheek. *Who do I know in Seston?*

There were scores of *Mae'rillium* in his service but none as far south as Seston. Unless one of them had moved without notifying him; a possibility to be sure, but not likely. No. If anything, it was a trick by one of his rivals. After the amount of Earthpower used by the Fairimor lad last night, any Agla'Con within fifty miles of Trian was likely to come to investigate. It was possible one of them was trying to see if he still lived so they could move in and stake a claim.

He looked again at the girl. Whoever it was that wanted to see him would have to wait. "Tell your father that I will see this messenger from Seston tomorrow. I have too much to do today to be bothered by something this trivial."

"As you wish, Agla'Con," the girl said, dropping a quick bow and turning away.

When she was gone, Zeniff turned and gazed out the window, letting his thoughts return to the Kelsan High Tribunal. The swiftness with which Randle had obtained a vote for Military Law and Power was maddening. And it was partly his fault. He'd underestimated the members of the lesser councils. In light of last night's attack, he had been certain they would shy away from taking action against the Con'Kumen. He had believed their fear would overshadow their determination to fight back. He'd been wrong.

He hated being wrong.

And yet, there was good to be found in all of this. True, the vote had been gained, but it was a small battle lost, not the entire war. If anything, the discovery of the Talisman of Elsa had opened a new front against Kelsa. It was a front he intended to attack, exploit, and conquer — all without leaving the comfort of the palace. He didn't have to. Gideon and the Fairimor boys would do all the legwork. All he had to do was wait for them to return from Zeka with the Blood Orb in hand, and then he would take it from them.

He smiled at the thought. Gideon would be gone for weeks. More than enough time to reorganize the Con'Kumen and prepare for the taking of Fairimor Palace. When the Dymas returned, he would kill him, take the Blood Orb, and use the incredible reservoir of Earthpower it accessed to destroy all those who might dare stand against him.

He nodded to himself. Yes. Learning of the Zekan ruins had been most advantageous. It had certainly been easier than twenty years ago when he'd had to spy for every scrap of information. The ease of learning the truth this time almost took the sting out of the failed reprisal. In fact, without a vote for Military Law and Power, he might never have learned of the Talisman of Elsa at all. If he didn't know better, he'd say Maeon had taken a hand in things.

Let Gideon and the Fairimors go traipsing across two nations and back; he'd be ready for them when they returned. And once he relieved them of the Blood Orb, he might even decide that Aethon had outlived his usefulness. With the power of the Elsa Talisman at his disposal, he could kill The First and his two idiot brothers and take control of the entire Hand of the Dark.

He smiled again. Yes. That was what he would do. He would take the Talisman of Elsa and use it to become Maeon's right hand man. Then, when the Earthsoul failed, he would be exalted above all other Agla'Con.

"Good luck, Gideon," he said. "I'll be waiting for my prize."

Chuckling, he removed his formal judge's robes and put on a nondescript-looking shirt and pants. After he sent one of his Agla'Con to kill Croneam Eries, he planned on visiting a few of his chapter houses to begin making preparations for his conquest of Trian. He wanted everything ready when Gideon and his group delivered the Talisman right into his hands.

Muriell Troas returned to *The Proud Flame* to find her father sitting at the table with three men. The three were travel-worn and dirty and wore nondescript clothes and cloaks, but she knew instantly what they were. She didn't need to see the black robes of an Agla'Con to know that these were men of power. Dark power. Their eyes glimmered with a feral light, eager and hungry. In contrast, Ren looked like a chicken on the chopping block.

Keeping her face smooth, she approached the table. "Welcome, Agla'Con," she said politely, then turned to her father. "I delivered the message to Zeniff," she told him, but when his face turned pale, she realized she had said something she shouldn't have.

One of the Agla'Con, the pale-haired Zekan, glanced suspiciously at Ren. "What message?" he asked darkly.

"Just that a messenger from a *Mae'rillium* in Seston arrived with a message. I do not know what the message is. The messenger was stubborn and wouldn't tell me."

"He is still here?" another of the three asked. He was Riaki, Muriell realized, and as deadly looking as a lion despite only having one arm.

"He is asleep upstairs," Ren replied.

"Then we will deal with him shortly," the Riaki said, and the Zekan nodded.

The third Agla'Con, Kelsan-born by the look of him, turned to regard Muriell with eyes filled with suspicion. "Are you sworn to Zeniff?" he asked.

Muriell shook her head. "No. My allegiance is to Jendus Zanandrei. He's Second High Priest in the — "

"We know who he is," the Zekan snarled, then softened his voice when the Kelsan shot him a warning look. "Please go and fetch him for us. Your father will write the note."

Muriell waited while Ren scribbled out the message, then she moved to the counter where she folded it and sealed it with a dabble of hot wax. She retrieved her veil from her room and was on her way out the back door when the Zekan Agla'Con stopped her.

"Tell him nothing of who we are," he warned. "If you do, your father will need to find a different set of legs to deliver his messages."

"Yes, Agla'Con," she replied and slipped out the door.

After leaving the Dome, Elder Zanandrei helped Elder Nesthius return to his study, then made his way through the halls of the outer palace to his own room. He mulled things over as he walked, still amazed by the ease with which Gideon

Dymas and Randle Fairimor had manipulated the council. The overwhelming support the lesser councils had shown for Military Law and Power hadn't been overly surprising — their anger at the Con'Kumen reprisal was still too fresh for them to think clearly. But the manner in which Gideon had so easily learned the location of a Talisman of Elsa was mind-boggling. One might almost think the Earthsoul Herself had gotten involved.

No matter. He knew what was necessary to thwart their efforts. It would only take a moment to write a note to his contacts in Melek. A few days at most and Aethon Fairimor would know what had transpired.

He knew Zeniff wouldn't send word to Aethon. The bloody Agla'Con had his own agenda when it came to fighting this war as evidenced by the failed reprisal. No. If anything was to come of the information he'd learned during today's discussion, he would have to initiate it.

He had to be careful, though. If Zeniff found out his loyalty was to Aethon, the Agla'Con would squash him like a bug. His eyes narrowed in anger at the thought. He hated Zeniff with a passion — had, on more than one occasion, considered killing him. But the man was so highly favored of Shadan that he had taken no action against him. Yet.

Besides, he had more important things to do, such as taking control of the Church of Elderon. And then he, Elder Jendus Zanandrei, would become High Priest of the Church of Elderon. From there, he could turn things over to Maeon.

He reached his study and paused as a young woman rose from the sofa in the adjacent antechamber. Her head was covered, and her face was veiled for confession. When she spoke, however, he recognized her voice and knew she wasn't here to repent of her sins.

"Elder Zanandrei," she said, checking to see that they were alone. "I have a message from one of your Brethren." She handed him a note and turned to go, but he caught her arm.

"Are you sure you don't want to stay?" he asked.

"We don't have time for that today," she said coyly. "The message is most urgent."

"Too bad," he said, letting her go. "You are looking particularly sinful today."

She gave him a look that always warmed his blood, then turned and moved away down the corridor. He watched her a moment, regretting her haste, then broke the seal on the note. It was in Ren's terrible hand, two hastily scrawled lines that read: *Three lost sheep have requested spiritual guidance. Come to* The Proud Flame *to save their souls.*

He crumpled the note and stuffed it in his pocket. *Three lost sheep, huh?* he thought. Ren was an idiot when it came to writing messages. If not for the grace and skill of his daughter, the owner of *The Proud Flame* would have been discovered by Elison Brey a long time ago.

He gazed down the corridor in the direction Muriell had gone and sighed resignedly. He supposed he may as well go see what this was all about. If it didn't take too long he might be able to spend some time with the sinful young lady after all.

When Jendus Zanandrei stopped inside the doors of *The Proud Flame* and took a look around, he saw right away that things had changed in the Con'Kumen chain of command. Ren sat at a table with three other men, and the innkeeper's face was as white as the towel he was using to mop the sweat from his forehead.

When the three men sitting with Ren looked up and he got a good look at their faces, he suddenly understood Ren's nervousness. All three were Agla'Con generals in Shadan's armies and had sworn allegiance to Aethon. He had met them the day he'd sworn his own oath to Aethon. If his memory served him correctly, their names were Borilius Constas, Falius Tierim, and Gwuler Hom.

He was surprised to find them here, and though he didn't share Ren's fear, he knew it would be best to be cooperative and cautious. He joined them at the table and took a seat next to the sweating Ren.

"To what do I owe the honor?" he asked, pleased with how calm he'd kept his voice. As the soon-to-be High Priest of the Church of Elderon, his place among the Hand of the Dark was just as prestigious as theirs, Zeniff's, or even Aethon's for that matter. If Maeon placed any emphasis on irony it might be more prestigious. Still, Agla'Con were unpredictable, so he kept his tone neutral. His rank of *Mae'chodan* would mean nothing if they killed him.

"Elder Zanandrei," Falius said, his smile never touching his eyes, "we understand things in the Dome have been rather chaotic of late. Care to fill us in?"

Borilius nodded. "Yes. What has Brother Zeniff been up to?"

Zeniff. He should have known they would start with him. For many of the Agla'Con, the man was a thorn that could neither be lived with nor removed. Then again, Aethon had made changes to the Hand of the Dark before. Perhaps he'd decided Zeniff's meddling had finally overshadowed his usefulness. *Perhaps,* he thought with a glimmer of hope, *these three have come to kill him.*

"Gideon Dymas and members of the military have been raiding our chapter houses," he began, "so Zeniff retaliated by attacking the Dome with a dozen K'rresh and however many Darklings they carried in."

"You didn't see it?" Falius asked.

"Are you kidding?" he scoffed. "After I informed Aethon of Zeniff's plan, I stayed as far away from the Dome last night as I could. You know how unpredictable shadowspawn are."

"What happened?" Gwuler Hom urged.

"Jase Fairimor, the King's nephew — apparently he is a Dymas of considerable strength — killed the Agla'Con, K'rresh, and half the Darklings."

The three Agla'Con looked at each other, and he could tell this was something they hadn't anticipated. "What of Gideon Dymas?" Falius asked.

"He didn't arrive until after the battle was over. Zeniff had arranged a diversion for him, hoping for more casualties. Obviously, he didn't anticipate the Fairimor lad's abilities."

"We felt him," Gwuler said. "The boy is strong."

"It is why we have come to Trian," Borilius added. "Aethon sent us to kill Gideon and capture the boy. Apparently, he is interested in his potential."

Jendus pursed his lips thoughtfully. So Aethon wanted to make Jase Fairimor into an Agla'Con did he? Not a bad idea if it could be done. He wondered if Zeniff had considered it as well. Not that he would be able to do much about it. Or these three either, for that matter. He knew a good soul when he saw one, and Jase Fairimor had a good soul.

"Then you'd better hurry," he told them. "They leave for Thesston tomorrow morning." Again the three men looked at each other before speaking, their displeasure evident in their faces.

"Why?" It was Borilius who voiced the question.

He met the Zekan's gaze without flinching. "The Kelsan High Tribunal met this morning," he said, deciding it best to tell them all he knew. "Elder Nesthius asked if I might stay since I am to be his replacement. I was allowed to stay and learned some very interesting things. Things that could very well save our cause from ruin." He paused and looked at Ren for a moment. He'd forgotten the innkeeper was there. It was very obvious from the nervous twitching of his left eye that he wished he weren't. He looked on the verge of throwing up.

Jendus looked questioningly at the three Agla'Con.

"It's fine if he hears," Borilius said. "Perhaps it will make him understand the full extent of his stupidity for sending word to Zeniff."

"But I didn't know," Ren moaned, and Borilius gestured with his finger. Ren's eyes bulged, and he choked for breath.

"Continue," Borilius said as if nothing out of the ordinary had happened.

"Gideon Dymas used Communicator Stones to contact all the major cities of Kelsa, as well as the Kings of Zeka, Chunin, and Elva. They are united against us I'm afraid. They know of the army in Melek and have a pretty good idea of how many of your kind are leading it. They even know of the artificial T'rii Gate."

"We know all this," Falius hissed bitterly. "Tell us something new."

"Salamus Pryderi has discovered what he thinks is a Talisman of Elsa," he told them and watched surprise flash across each of their faces. "That's why Gideon Dymas and the Fairimor lad are leaving tomorrow. They're going to Thesston to retrieve the Blood Orb."

He could tell by the smiles creeping over their faces that they were pleased. He hoped it meant they would let him live. Bracing himself, he waited.

"Tell no one else of this," Falius said after a moment. "We report to Aethon directly. We will let him know what you have learned. You are dismissed."

Nodding, Jendus rose and brought his fist to his chest. "It will be as you say, Agla'Con."

After Elder Zanandrei left, Falius turned to his two companions. "We will have to act quickly," he told them. "Zeniff knows of the Elsa Talisman as well and may try to take it for himself." He ground his teeth in frustration. Being stripped of their command of shadowspawn and other creatures of the dark was going to make competing with Zeniff difficult.

Borilius shook his head. "I know how Zeniff thinks," he said. "He isn't going to work for anything he doesn't think he has to. Think about it. Where will Gideon go once he retrieves the Talisman?"

"To the Soul Chamber," Gwuler answered, but Falius realized what Borilius was hinting at and nodded his understanding.

"By way of Trian," he said. "Zeniff is counting on Gideon to come back to Trian before he goes north. Zeniff, lazy fool that he is, will simply wait here for the Talisman to come to him."

"Yes," Borilius said. "It is how the man thinks."

"So the only people we need to beat to Thesston are Gideon and his companions."

They were quiet a moment as they contemplated this new information. To Falius, it was a godsend. Well, a demon-send anyway; he'd quit believing in Elderon a long time ago. Delivering the Talisman to Aethon would put them back in his good graces and earn back their places as leaders in Shadan's army. If they managed to kill Gideon and capture the boy Fairimor in the process, their places at Maeon's side would be assured.

"But getting to Thesston quickly poses a problem," Falius continued. "Gideon and his crew have tremendous resources available to make their journey a speedy one." He frowned darkly. "I for one don't relish the thought of riding a horse all that distance. Coming to Trian in such a manner was painful, not to mention degrading. We are Agla'Con; we should not be forced to travel like commoners."

Borilius and Gwuler exchanged glances. "What are you suggesting?" the Zekan asked. "That we defy Aethon's punishment and try to enlist the aid of shadowspawn — K'rresh perhaps — to travel to Thesston?"

"With what we stand to gain I think he would overlook the violation of his orders."

"Not Aethon," Borilius said emphatically, and Gwuler nodded his agreement. "He is too proud. He would accept the Blood Orb and still have our heads removed for disobedience." He paused and his face twisted distastefully. "I do not relish the idea of traveling like a commoner either, but I'm afraid we have no choice. Perhaps we can use a coach to make it a little more bearable, but..." he leaned forward and his face hardened, "I would be willing to crawl to Thesston if it meant regaining Aethon's favor."

"There is another way," Gwuler told them, and Falius could tell by the Riaki's manner that whatever he was about to tell them held as much danger as promise. "I have contacts in Riak that not even Aethon knows about. These contacts have... resources."

"No shadowspawn," Borilius said firmly, but Gwuler was shaking his head.

"They aren't shadowspawn," Gwuler replied. "But using them may invoke a wrath I fear almost as much as Aethon's if I am discovered."

"And these resources are...?"

"A secret," Gwuler said firmly, and the look he gave Borilius was deadly.

The Zekan shrugged innocently. "I would never dream of using my talent on you," he said. "Not with — "

Falius cut him off. "You are sure you can reach these contacts?" he asked. If Gwuler felt it necessary to keep things a secret, he supposed he could humor him. As long as it meant he wouldn't have to ride a horse again. And as long as it put them ahead of Gideon and the others.

"I will send my bladehawk at once," Gwuler replied. "It may take a few days for these resources to arrive, but once they do, I can have us in Thesston in a few hours. Finding the lost temple will take even less time."

"Do what you need to," he said, then turned to Ren. The innkeeper's face was turning purple as he continued to struggle for breath, and his eyes had rolled back in their sockets. They knew his loyalty was to Zeniff, and because of that, they couldn't risk leaving him alive. His daughter, however... she seemed like the intelligent type. They would make her an offer she couldn't refuse and then take over this branch of Zeniff's network by setting her up in her father's place.

Borilius had read her mind enough to know she was in love with Zanandrei, so her loyalties were already leaning toward their cause. She would make a fine replacement for Ren.

He gestured to Borilius, and the bones in Ren's neck cracked as he slumped forward onto the table.

Falius turned to Gwuler. "Go fetch the girl," he said. "And congratulate her on her new inheritance. *The Proud Flame* is now hers."

Borilius chuckled. "And she is ours."

It was late afternoon before Droe Strembler woke and prepared to go down to the common room of *The Proud Flame*. He would have slept longer if Ren's daughter hadn't awakened him to say someone was waiting to see him. It was the first decent rest he'd had in over a week, and he rolled out of bed grudgingly. If not for the fact that the person waiting for him might be Zeniff, he'd have told her to go away. That and the realization that he was starving.

The last food he'd eaten was last night after he'd identified himself to Ren and told him of the message for Zeniff. He'd probably told Ren more than he should have, but the innkeeper had been so eager to help — fixing him an excellent dinner, having a hot bath drawn up, and providing him with new clothes — that he hadn't been able to stop himself. He suspected being alone in the saddle for six days had contributed to the loosening of his tongue as well, but he wasn't going to admit he'd been lonely.

Standing in front of the mirror, he snugged the sling on his injured arm, then stretched his tired back, enjoying the smooth feel of the new shirt. Being a member of the Brotherhood sure had its advantages. Being on the errand of a *Mae'rillium* made it that much better. Smiling, he left his room.

He cleared the stairs and was several steps into the common room before he noticed that something was markedly different. The common room should have been bustling this time of day, but all was quiet. The place was deserted.

Ren's daughter — he thought her name was Muriell — came in from the kitchen and motioned him to a corner table. "I'll bring you something to eat in a moment," she said pleasantly.

"Where is this person who wanted to see me?" he asked.

She gestured to the stairs. "He'll be along shortly," she said and slipped back into the kitchen.

He eased himself behind the table, keeping his back to the wall out of habit, and waited for his food to be brought. A few minutes passed, and the kitchen door swung inward. It wasn't Muriell.

Three men — a Kelsan, a Zekan, and a Riaki with only one arm — crossed the room toward him. Grim-faced and haggard-looking, they let their eyes sweep the room as if to ensure they were alone, then stopped in front of his table.

"Good evening, *Brother*," the Kelsan said, flashing a Con'Kumen hand signal.

"Evening," Droe replied, keeping his hand on the table. He didn't need to return the signal. They obviously knew he was one of them. Though which one was Zeniff, he couldn't say.

"Mind if we join you?" the Zekan asked, taking a chair without waiting for a reply. The other two joined him, positioning themselves as if to block his escape. He suddenly regretted his paranoid habit of keeping a wall at his back. He felt cornered. "Ren told us you have a message for Zeniff," the Zekan continued. "This message is from a *Mae'rillium* in Seston."

Droe looked at each one of them in turn and slowly nodded. "I do," he said. "Which one of you is Zeniff?"

"There has been a change in plans," the Kelsan said, his smile far from friendly. "You will give your message to us instead."

"Sorry, fellas," he said. "I have my instructions." Who did these three think they were? Interfering in the affairs of a *Mae'rillium* was no small thing. Even if it wasn't, he wouldn't tell these men anything without first making sure he could profit by it. Maybe not even then. He didn't like their arrogance. "Perhaps you should mind your own business."

"You don't know who we are," the Riaki said. It wasn't a question.

"I know you are in the Brotherhood," he said, "and that is well and fine. But you have no right to interfere here. The *Mae'rillium's* command was that I give my message only to Zeniff. He put me under oath to do so." He leaned forward and glared at them. "You know what that means, don't you?"

By their expressions they did. Oath-breaking in the Con'Kumen was the highest form of treason and was punishable by death — a very welcome death by the time the executioners got around to killing you.

The Zekan placed his hands on the table, and a gleam of red colored one fist. "You know what this is, I assume?"

Droe stared at the talisman, the first traces of fear creeping into his heart.

"Even in the Brotherhood," the Zekan continued, "a *Mae'rillium* is nothing more than a flea compared to an Agla'Con. Tell us what we want to know and we will let you live."

The other two men displayed talismans as well, but Droe glanced at them disdainfully. He didn't like being threatened, and he didn't like people sticking their noses into his business. He'd been in the Brotherhood long enough to know that they couldn't use their powers without alerting Zeniff or anyone else who might be able to wield *Ta'shaen*. They were bluffing.

But if they were intent on violence, Agla'Con weren't known for their skill with conventional weapons; his military training should be enough to fight them off. He shifted his weight slightly, ready to use the dagger tucked behind his belt.

"I'll tell you what," he said defiantly. "After I deliver my message to Zeniff, I'll come back here and you can pay me for what I know." He reached down and rattled his coin purse. "The *Mae'rillium* in Seston was generous enough with his gold." He let his hand slide from the purse to his dagger.

The Riaki Agla'Con leaned forward. "Fool," he hissed. "We come to Trian on the errand of Aethon Fairimor. His wishes supercede all else. Tell us what we need to know or you will die!"

More threats. No action. These Agla'Con were powerless and they knew it. He smiled at them. It felt good to stare them down, pompous, arrogant fools that they were, and he locked eyes with the Zekan. "I've given you my answer," he said. "Now if you'll excuse me."

He moved to get up, but the Riaki shoved the table violently forward. The edge caught Droe across his midsection, and he felt his already injured ribs crack under the pressure as the three men pinned him against the wall.

The pain was terrible, and he gasped for breath, struggling to push the table away. With only one good arm, they were too strong for him. He was reaching for the dagger at his side when the Zekan leaned forward.

"Bad idea," he said, and the talisman in his hand flared red.

The inside of Droe's head exploded into pain and his vision blurred. He tried to scream, but the Agla'Con's power had him. His body refused to respond. His fingers, spasmodically clutching at the dagger, quickly numbed. He lost feeling everywhere but inside his head.

Something dark entered his thoughts; he could see it in his mind's eye, a serpentine coil of blackness slipping through his mind, invasive and searching. It pressed against a place near the back of his mind, and there was a flash of color as the events of the past week became visible in his head, a barrage of sounds and images he was powerless to control. He knew what was happening, and the realization made him want to retch. The Agla'Con was stealing his thoughts.

The *Mae'rillium* and the Waypost cell came into view for a moment, then slid past as his memory continued to move backward toward the events in Scloa. With a jarring flash, the Waypost cell jumped into focus once more as the Agla'Con recognized the moment.

"*You will travel to Trian,*" the cowled head said softly, "*to the inn known as* The Proud Flame. *The innkeeper will assist you in reaching the Agla'Con known as Zeniff who resides in Fairimor Palace. He will not know me, but you will tell him that Daris Stodd, warder to the Sister Queen of Kelsa, is here in Seston with his charge. Tell him that Daris is disrupting the Con'Kumen effort here in the south and ask him to send word as to what he would like me to do about it."*

The cowled head dipped closer, and a bag of gold was offered. For an instant the man's face was visible in the moonlight, and Droe blinked in surprise. He was young, much younger than most Mae'rillium he'd encountered, but made of iron and steel. The killing light in his eyes could have belonged to a Shadowhound.

The images inside his head faded slightly, and the faces of the three Agla'Con appeared behind the blurred haze. The Zekan, he saw, was smiling.

A searing white-hot pain lanced through his thoughts like a heated blade, and he shrieked as everything vanished into black.

As Droe Strembler slumped forward, Falius turned to glare at Borilius in anger. The Zekan had released the Power and was tucking his talisman away in his vest. He had a very satisfied grin on his face.

Falius suspected Borilius' pleasure came as much from killing the man as from the morbid joy he seemed to take from entering another's thoughts. Regardless of whatever value the information might have, however, this reckless use of a forbidden talent was inexcusable. With Zeniff and Gideon Dymas a short two blocks away, it was stupid as well.

"We could have killed him without using the Power," he scolded. "Invading another's thoughts is bad enough by itself. Using thought to kill someone is bound to attract the attention of our enemies sooner or later. I can feel the residue of what you did, and even to me, one long sworn to the shadow, it feels corrupt. Are you deliberately trying to draw the attention of the *Nar'shein Yahl?* Do you want them to invoke a cleansing hunt for you?" He gave the Zekan his best scowl. This was the third time inside of a week that Borilius had done this.

"Relax," Borilius replied. "I didn't use enough of the Power for it to be felt outside of this room. And what's more, I learned something of extreme value. It seems the Sister Queen of Kelsa is in a place called Seston."

Falius narrowed his eyes at him. "I know this place," he said, "but as to how valuable it is..." he trailed off, waiting for Borilius to explain.

"Brysia Fairimor is Jase Fairimor's mother," Borilius said. "Since we must go to Zeka anyway, why not stop in this Seston long enough to drop in on the Sister Queen?"

A grin stole over Gwuler's face. "We can use the mother to capture the son. He will certainly come to rescue her. If we bait him well enough, we can lure him right to a T'rii Gate and hand him, his mother, and the Elsa Talisman over to Aethon. And since Gideon will undoubtedly choose to pursue the Talisman instead of the Sister Queen, we won't have to face him and the boy at the same time. If we plan this right, we can separate them long enough to kill Gideon. With him out of the way, leading the boy to a Veilgate will be easy."

"But which gate?" Borilius asked. "I know of only two and neither is anywhere near Thesston."

"There is one in Arkania," Falius told them. He didn't like giving away his secrets any more than Gwuler did, but in light of what they stood to gain, keeping such knowledge to himself was foolhardy. He shrugged off the suspicious looks they gave him. "I was assisting Aethon when he discovered it. It is near the mouth of Illiarensei, but isolated in heavy jungle. The nearest village is several miles away. It would be a good place to wait in ambush for the boy."

"Are we strong enough to open it ourselves?" Gwuler asked.

"With a Talisman of Elsa to draw on, I think we can handle it." Falius replied. "But if not, simply trying to open the gate will be enough to alert Aethon, assuming he's in the Meleki camp. He linked each of the gates we discovered to the artificial one he created."

Borilius' eyes narrowed. "Why haven't you told us this before?" he asked darkly.

Falius was unfazed by the anger in the Zekan's voice. "Because I didn't think it necessary," he replied flatly. "What I did with Aethon before I was assigned to lead the army with you two is really none of your business."

"We all have secrets," Gwuler said, directing his words to Borilius. "What matters is that we have an opportunity to redeem ourselves in Aethon's eyes."

"Yes," Falius said, "and when we pull this off, our place in the Hand of the Dark will be exalted."

CHAPTER 5

Tough Questions

Colonel Calis Hurd paused in the garden of his estate and stared silently at his manor home, unsure if he really wanted to enter. In the week since Shavis Dakshar had left Tey Eries and her two Shizu guardians behind, it had started to feel less like his home and more like a prison. Even worse, it was starting to feel like a trap. It was an extremely uncomfortable position to be in, and he simply didn't know what to do.

His first thought had been to run — to leave Fulrath and his stagnating military career and try to find a new life in some remote corner of Kelsa. What stopped him was the knowledge that if Shavis didn't come looking for him, his brethren in the Con'Kumen would. They were very possessive of those who'd sworn allegiance. Once joined, the only way your membership was canceled was if you died. And you prayed it wasn't at their hands.

No. Running wasn't an option. But neither was sitting on his hands waiting for Shavis to find information that could tie him to the Con'Kumen. If Shavis learned the truth about the Deathstrike, it would mean a violent and painful death at the hands of a Shizu. It would certainly be as bad as dying at the hands of the Brotherhood.

He blew out his cheeks wearily. If only he could turn this situation with the Shizu to his advantage. If he could somehow kill Tohquin and Raimen, he could dispose of the girl, then set a trap for Shavis and kill him when he returned. He could be rid of the whole unpleasant mess. Except killing a Shizu was something he had no idea how to do, especially the girl's two guardians. He never saw more than one of them at a time — how they managed that disturbed him to no end

— but he knew they were there, *always* within striking distance. It made marching in with twenty of his brethren to take the child by force all but impossible. One of the two was bound to survive and report to Shavis. And since it was obvious how the Shizu felt about betrayal, attempting to kill them would be signing his own death warrant.

He had even considered trying to deliver the girl to her grandfather — an act that would have him hailed as a hero — but he couldn't come up with an explanation plausible enough to be believed. Besides, the little brat was clever for her age and far too free with her tongue. One word to Croneam about what had really happened and...

He shuddered. Death was all around him, and he couldn't see a way out.

"You look as if you are plotting something," a voice said from behind him, and he jumped. Whirling, he found Raimen standing within the protective shadows near the manor wall fingering his sword. His eyes, visible through the slit in his *koro* mask, were bright with mirth.

Calis ground his teeth. How they managed to sneak up on him with such ease was starting to wear on his nerves. "What I plot, I plot," he told the Shizu coldly. "It need not concern you."

"Everything concerns me," Raimen replied, sounding amused.

Amused! He felt like drawing his sword. *Bloody Shizu with their bloody sneaking abilities,* he thought angrily. *It has to be the Power. They must have some Gift of Ta'shaen. There is no other explanation for how they do what they do.*

As if reading his thoughts, Raimen bowed slightly, took one step backward, and... vanished.

"Bloody Shizu!" he muttered, turning back to his home and stomping away. From somewhere in the shadows behind him came the soft sound of chuckling.

He slammed the door behind him, flung his cloak on the table, then moved down the hall to his study. What he found there disturbed him more than Raimen's vanishing act.

Tohquin sat cross-legged on an imported rug facing Tey, and there was a deck of colorful cards spread between them. The child giggled as she collected a match, and Tohquin praised her for being so smart. With sword strapped across his back and a pouch of bladestars hanging at his waist, it was a sight more unsettling than if he'd been killing the girl. His *koro* mask lay on the floor beside him, and he was smiling. *Smiling!*

Shizu are assassins, he wanted to shout. *The ultimate dealers of death. Their very name instills fear into all who hear it. They don't play card games with children!*

The two looked up as he entered, but if Tohquin was embarrassed to be caught playing a child's game, there was no sign of it. If anything, he looked as amused as Raimen had. *It must show in my face,* Calis thought. *I've got to quit letting things surprise me.*

"What do you want?" Tey asked, scowling at him.

"This is my study," he told her firmly, then modified his tone when he saw Tohquin's eyes narrow dangerously. "I have work to do. So if you two could move to another room, I would appreciate it." Humbling himself to the child rankled horribly, but there was no way around it. The Shizu scared him to death.

Three days ago he had forgotten himself and shouted at Tey, and Tohquin had knocked the wind out of him with a punch that had probably cracked a rib. *I will figure a way out of this,* he told her silently. *Then, you little brat, I'll do more than shout at you.*

When Tohquin looked to the child for approval, Calis frowned. Both Shizu had been doing that more of late — deferring to her wishes — and the little beast was making life miserable. She must have been in a good mood tonight, though, because she shrugged. "Okay, but we're taking the rug with us. It's softer than the dumb wood floors in the other rooms."

"Fine," Calis said as meekly as he could. *Con'Jithar, that child is a brat!* He watched Tohquin help gather up the game and shook his head in bewilderment at the contrast between the colorful cards and the black-lacquered sword hilt strapped across the Shizu's back. The smile Tohquin flashed Tey as he handed her the cards was definitely at odds with his Shizu attire. It was difficult for Calis to squash the uneasy feeling he got from watching the assassin interacting so peacefully with the child.

"Remember," Tey said, backing off the rug as Tohquin rolled it. "I'm winning."

"You always do," Tohquin said, the fondness in his voice unmistakable. Hefting the rug, he followed her from the room.

Calis scowled at the empty doorway. *Fondness from a Shizu!* he thought, shaking his head. He never should have involved himself with the Riaki people. They were all crazy.

Pouring himself a glass of brandy from the liquor cabinet, he moved to his chair. There had to be a way to get out of this mess, some way to use it to his advantage.

He sat in nervous silence as the evening shadows lengthened across the room and night drew near. When the bell rang for the merchants in the outer city to begin shutting down for the night, his agitation had reached the point where he felt like shouting. Because no matter how hard he thought about things, no matter which avenues he considered, he simply couldn't figure out how he was going to save his neck.

Raimen Adirhah of Clan Gahara watched as Colonel Hurd left for the fortress and wondered at the urgency of the message clutched tightly in the man's fist. He suspected it had to do with last night's glow of light over the Kelsan heartland, but in a military city, it could be anything. And yet he suspected the light. The sheer magnitude and brilliance of it had been awe-inspiring, and he wondered once again what could have caused it. He wasn't particularly religious, but he recognized the fulfilling of prophecy when he saw it. He just wished he knew what prophecy it was and how it would affect the Riaki nation.

When Hurd was gone, Raimen loosed his hold on *Ta'shaen* and slipped back into Hurd's manor to check on Tey. He found her sitting at the table eating a bowl of wheat mush sweetened with honey. Her hair was a mass of tangles from the night's sleep, and her tiny bare feet dangled below the hem of the blue nightgown Tohquin had acquired from a merchant's shop in the outer city.

"Tohquin tells me you beat him in cards last night," he said, pulling open the curtains to let in the morning light. He pulled off his *koro* and ran his fingers through his jet black hair.

"I sure did," Tey said, a dabble of mush running down her chin. "He doesn't remember the colors as good as I do."

Raimen looked at Tohquin standing near the stove and smiled. "That's because he is going soft in the head."

"I wonder," Tohquin said, "if we're both going soft in the heart."

Raimen laughed. "Only for Tey Eries, Princess of Clan Gahara," he said, taking a chair opposite her at the table.

"Am I really a princess?" Tey asked, her eyes going wide with excitement.

"All little girls are."

"My daddy said that too," she told him.

"He was a smart man," Raimen said, looking away.

"He's dead," she said.

The words stung his ears and he looked at Tohquin to find his face pinched with bitterness. Neither of them knew how to respond.

Tey continued eating, unaware of the awkward silence. After a time she spoke. "Do you have a little girl at your house? Are you daddies?"

"Tohquin is," Raimen said, looking into Tey's eyes. A piercing blue, they sparkled with life. It made knowing what happened to her family all the more painful. "His little princess is about your age too, I believe."

"Yes," Tohquin said. "And she beats me in cards just like you do."

"Do you miss her?"

Tohquin nodded. "Very much."

"Then how come you don't go home and see her?" she asked, tilting her head and propping it with an elbow on the table.

"Because I have to stay here and keep you safe," he said, and Raimen could tell the smile was forced. "Besides, Gahara is a long way from here."

"Oh," Tey said and returned to her mush.

Raimen and Tohquin regarded each other quietly, and Raimen wondered what his friend was thinking. If it was even close to the thoughts he was having, his days as a Deathsquad member were numbered. Doing one's duty to country, it seemed, was easier if you didn't have to think about your targets as people. Learning of the Eries family had changed things for both of them. Perhaps it was time for Tohquin to go home to his family. *Perhaps it is time for me to start looking for a wife.*

Another question by Tey brought him out of his thoughts. "How long do we have to stay here?"

"Only until Shavis returns," he answered.

"How long will that be?" she asked, wiping her mouth with the back of her hand.

"Not long," Tohquin assured her.

"Good. Because I hate it here."

"So do I, little one," Raimen said. "So do I." He looked at Tohquin who nodded in agreement.

It was quiet a moment, and Tey's face was crunched up in thought. Suddenly she hopped off the chair and asked, "What are we going to do today?"

Tohquin smiled. "Go get dressed and then I'll teach you how to play *kiisho*. I'm sure Hurd has a chess board we can use."

"Is it hard?" Tey asked.

"It won't be for you," Tohquin said, ruffling her already messy hair.

She skipped off to the room they'd established as hers, and they could hear her talking to herself as she picked through the clothes Tohquin had acquired for her. They looked at one another and grinned sheepishly.

"Soft in the head and the heart," Tohquin murmured.

Raimen fixed his gaze on his friend's face. "Hurd is up to something."

"Good," Tohquin replied. "I hope he gives me a reason to kill him." He frowned. "I've seen how he looks at the little one. He would kill her if he could. The man has no honor."

"I, too, would like to kill him," Raimen replied. "But it is not for us to do." He paused as Tey stuck her head from the room.

"Do you like this one?" she asked, holding up a light green shirt with yellow flowers embroidered across the front.

"It's lovely," Raimen said.

Tey smiled and ducked back into the room, and Raimen turned to face Tohquin. "We must wait for Shavis," he continued. "If Hurd turns out to be in this Hand of the Dark..." he let his words trail off.

"I hope he is," Tohquin said. "Anyone who gives himself over to Maeon deserves to die."

Raimen glanced out the window to the battlements of the fortress proper visible through the trees. "It makes me wonder," he said softly. "If someone as high in rank as Hurd is doing Maeon's will in Kelsa, how many others are there like him?" He turned back and met his friend's gaze. "How many of our own Highseats might be Maeon's servants as well?"

Tohquin's face was a mask of stone as he considered.

It was a question neither of them wanted to answer.

と

A flicker of fire appeared in the dark squares of the windows, a gentle dance of color that quickly grew to a blazing inferno. Glass cracked beneath the heat and columns of smoke billowed outward, writhing masses of greyish-orange stretching skyward. From the shadow of the nearby barn, Shavis Dakshar of Clan Gahara watched as his men slipped away from the burning home and moved toward him. Their dark silhouettes were sharply outlined by the brilliant conflagration behind them.

Standing beside him, pale-faced Sallen Zeph, with his overly-large ears and beady eyes, fidgeted anxiously. His eyes, glowing yellow with excitement in the flickering shadows, only enhanced how much he looked like an overgrown rat. "The Great Lord of the Dark will be pleased with our deeds here this night," he breathed heavily, ringing his hands. "We will be well rewarded."

Shavis frowned at the rat-faced man. "What did you say?" he asked softly.

Sallen licked his lips, his eyes never leaving the flames consuming General Eries' home. "I said the Great Lord Maeon will be pleased with our work here tonight."

"Have you been in his service long?" Shavis asked.

"Three years," Sallen replied proudly. "I swore my oath in Capena along with many of your Shizu friends from the Samochi and Vakala clans. The Brotherhood was pleased to have more of your kind in the order. Four who took the oath with me are in the squad who is to hit the secondary target. They were pleased that you had been assigned to the Deathstrike as well. Gahara's reputation is well-known among the Con'Kumen."

"I see," Shavis said, turning to look at the whirling vortex of flame that had once been General Eries' home. Too late to stop it now, he thought grimly. But perhaps

there is time to stop the other.

His men stopped before him, their eyes shining in the slits of their masks.

"No one was home," Raimen told him. "Perhaps the Samochi squad will find him at the secondary target."

"It is just as well he wasn't here," Shavis told them, turning to look at their guide. "Sallen was telling me how pleased Maeon will be with our service here tonight. Isn't that right, Sallen?"

Five Shizu heads turned to regard Sallen as he huffed himself up grandly. "Yes. The Great Lord will — "

Sallen's head rolling backward off his shoulders and the thud of his body collapsing at their feet was punctuated by the hiss-click of Shavis' sword returning to its scabbard.

He turned his gaze on his men. "Clan Gahara has been misled," he told them. "This man was an agent of Maeon and a member of the so-called Con'Kumen."

"So the rumors are true," Raimen said.

"Yes," Shavis said, grinding his teeth. "And from what Sallen told me, it seems this strike was ordered by the Con'Kumen and not by Highseat Dromensai." He glanced scornfully at the headless corpse. "I am not Maeon's pawn," he hissed, "and neither is Clan Gahara."

He turned away from the flames of the failed Deathstrike, glad in his heart that General Eries had not been home. "Come," he said. "Clan Samochi is involved in this treachery. We must move quickly if we are to stop the second strike."

Shavis let the memory trance fade and opened his eyes to stare into the small cookfire on the ground before him. He inhaled deeply, letting the warm night air of the Shellum Plains fill his lungs, and did his best to ignore the weariness that was starting to find its way into his body. *Jiu* meditation may be relaxing and restorative, but he was definitely starting to grow tired. Traveling four hundred miles in seven days could do that to a man. Especially on foot.

He wished the Myrscraw that had delivered him and his men to Greendom hadn't been sent away by the Samochi fools — the huge birds could have covered the distance between Fulrath and Gahara in a single night. He took another deep breath and sighed. At least the return trip to Fulrath would be fast and easy. *Assuming I can secure another Myrscraw.*

No one outside of Riak, and very few within, knew of the massive sea birds. They were reserved for long-range Deathstrikes, and only the most elite Deathsquads could use them. The birds were the most closely guarded secret of the Shizu, since the ability to appear anywhere in the Nine Lands virtually at will had a way of striking fear into people and added to the Shizu mystique.

The thought raised a question that made him frown. Why had the Samochi squad sent the birds away? This wasn't a suicide mission. It was a simple strike on an aging general. There was no way Shizu secrecy could have been compromised. Why had Samochi seen fit to change procedure? What had they known that he didn't? Something dark, he decided and pushed the thought away for later.

He massaged his feet for a minute, then adjusted the ties on his leg wraps and checked the soft-soled boots for damage. It was too bad that stealing horses was forbidden by the Shizu code; there had been plenty of good animals on Talin Plateau. Not that they would have gotten to Gahara any faster — he and his men could cover the same distance on foot that most horses could — it was simply a matter of comfort over the long haul.

He glanced out at the night. A league to the west, the watch lights of Capena sparkled brightly, but the interior of the city was dark, its inhabitants asleep. To the north and east, the Shellem Plains stretched into blackness broken only occasionally by dots of light marking a homestead or ranch. Ten leagues to the south, the Iga'rala Mountains rose from the darkness near the Kelsan-Riaki border, a jagged outline of snow-capped peaks against the backdrop of stars. He and his men would reach them before morning and be well into Gahara Prefecture before noontime tomorrow. By sunset they should be within sight of Gahara City.

Thoughts of his beloved home made him smile. Located in a broad valley between two mountain ranges, Gahara was second only to Sagaris in size, but second to none for beauty. With its buildings and roads nestled among the great Kairus trees, many of them thousands of years old, it was a splendid balance of civilization and nature. Gahara Castle, like so many other notable structures in the city, was constructed entirely of wood. Several buildings were centuries old but were in as fine a condition as the day they were built.

Not once had any of the dozens of civil wars that had devastated so many other cities during Riak's history ever touched Gahara. Riaki Highseats vying for power had always gone for the Imperial Seat in Sagaris as a way of claiming control of Riak. Only then did they turn their attention outward, usually without strength enough to push their authority much farther than Vakala or Samochi. And because the Highseats of Gahara had always been content to let the clans of the other prefectures tear each other apart so long as they stayed out of the Iga'rala Mountains, Gahara remained unscathed.

A hundred years ago, an usurping clan seized control of Sagaris and then tried to take Gahara as well, but it proved to be their undoing. Clan Gahara beat them so decisively that all outlying clans urged Gahara to claim the Imperial Seat in Sagaris. Halian Padershi had been appointed Emperor and had ruled for two decades. It was a record of longevity for the position, and all of Riak had prospered.

But sadly, Emperor Padershi let a misunderstanding between himself and the Highseat of Gahara stir up his anger to the point that he sent an army to take Gahara. The army had been destroyed and Padershi removed from power.

Shavis shook his head in disgust. If the clans of Riak had spent less time fighting each other and more time fighting Kelsa, the lands of their First Fathers would already be theirs. Kelsa would be a subjugated nation, and peace would have been established. So much unnecessary bloodshed would have been avoided.

He studied the outline of the Iga'rala Mountains and snorted in disappointment. He had been certain that the current Emperor's announcement of a treaty with Melek and the subsequent plan to invade Kelsa would be the campaign to end all wars between the three nations. Peace would finally come, and Riak would rise as the greatest nation in the world.

His discovery that the Con'Kumen were behind the Deathstrike on General Eries, however, made him question the purity of the Emperor's motives.

If this war had nothing to do with restoring the Riaki people to the land of their First Fathers but was, instead, the means the Con'Kumen and the fanatics of the Shadan Cult had devised to seize power, he wanted no part of it. He would not let Riak, and more importantly Gahara, be tools in the hands of Maeon. *I will discover who the Riaki members of the Con'Kumen are,* he vowed. *And then I will destroy them.*

Rising, he kicked dirt on the cookfire and called to his men. "Come," he said and watched as they materialized out of the dark. He still hadn't spoken to them about the light that had filled the northwestern sky a few short hours ago, and he could see in their eyes that they were concerned by what it might mean. Especially Railen since he claimed to have felt it as well as seen it. But, since he had no answers, he left the speculating to them.

He looked them over for a moment, then turned and began to run. Without a word, they fell into stride beside him.

Setting a pace that would kill a horse, he focused on his breathing and let his hatred of Maeon and those who served him fuel his strength.

Perched on a mountainside in the heart of Cresdraline Forest, Aethon Fairimor's castle retreat resembled any of the other Meleki estates scattered about the country. It was well-constructed, well-furnished, and surrounded by some of the finest woodlands the country had to offer. And like those other estates, it was well guarded... just not by anything natural.

Standing at the balcony railing high in the central tower, he could see the Shadowhounds patrolling the forested area outside the castle wall in his mind's eye. With his Awareness thus extended, he felt the presence of the approaching Satyr long before the creature materialized from the shadows near the castle's main gate. The two K'rrosha standing guard moved to block its way with their scepters, and the Satyr crouched aggressively, scythe-like blades flashing beneath its flaring cloak.

Aethon pursed his lips in irritation. For the creature to have reacted in such a way meant it wasn't one of his; most likely it had come to deliver a message. That it had come to the main gate instead of sneaking into the castle told Aethon it had been sent by someone who knew how angry it made him when the bloody things showed up in his room unannounced. He'd destroyed six or seven before word finally trickled back through the Agla'Con network that he didn't like those kinds of surprises. Satyrs were difficult shadowspawn to replace, and taming them enough so they wouldn't turn on you took longer than the act of creating them.

That last thought made him chuckle. But reconditioning those already tamed by someone else was very easy if you knew what part of their brain to tweak. Changing the orders for the two Satyrs Zeniff had sent into the Dome last night had taken less than a minute once he'd pinpointed their location in Kradan Colgra's chapter house. It had been stretching his Awareness over such a distance that had taken every bit of skill and strength he had. His head still hurt from the effort.

Imagining how badly Zeniff must have reacted to the interference, however, made it all worth it. The man was a meddlesome nuisance, to say the least, and last night's attack in Fairimor Dome showed that he was starting to take matters concerning the war into his own hands. If not for the fact that Maeon, and Shadan as well for that matter, viewed the Kelsan judge as such an integral part of the plan to destroy Trian, Aethon would have killed him a long time ago. For now he would have to be content that his use of one of Zeniff's Satyrs to deliver a message would have the man pulling his beard out by the roots as he tried to figure out who had done it.

Down in the courtyard, the K'rrosha moved aside to let the Satyr pass, and the shadowy creature moved down the stone walkway toward the castle. Aethon drew in his Awareness until it covered nothing more than the room behind him. Focusing on the doorway, he took hold of the Power in case the Satyr proved to be more than a simple messenger and waited for it to arrive.

It entered without knocking and stopped just inside the door. Like all Power-sensitive creatures, it could feel that he held *Ta'shaen* and knew its survival depended upon its behavior. The distance between it and the balcony was just a hair longer than what it could cover with one of its lunges.

"I's have a message for The First," it mewed softly. "Shadan is displeased with Melek's lack of progress, and he is angered by the light of prophecy that lit the night above Kelsa. He demands an explanation for both." It took a step forward, and Aethon wove a fine, blade-like band of Spirit, positioning it midway between him and the Satyr. If it lunged for him, it would be cut in half.

"You's will report to the Pit immediately," it told him. "The Destroyer of Amnidia awaits." With that, it took a step backward and disappeared through the shadowed doorway.

Using his Awareness, Aethon followed its exit from the castle.

When it was gone, he turned back to the window to gaze out across the forest. *So, Shadan is concerned by the light of prophecy is he? Well, he should be.* The crowning of Fairimor Dome with Fire was the prophesied start of the Third Cleansing. All those Gifted who had witnessed it would surely respond to its call. *But,* he added, *if I can turn Jase, a legion of Gifted won't be enough to stop us.*

The boy had the potential to become the most powerful Agla'Con to ever live, and he had already shown he was capable of crossing over into the realm of the Agla'Con. The right nudge at the right time, and Jase's crossing over would be irrevocable. It was obvious that Zeniff thought so too; the man had had ample opportunity to kill the young Fairimor but hadn't.

He shook his head in awe at the boy's strength, glad in his heart that his own attempts to eliminate him had failed. It made him wonder if Maeon had taken a hand in preserving the boy. Nothing would please the Dark One more than to add another Fairimor to his list of servants.

Reaching up to rub his chin, he traced the rugged outline of the Death's Chain with his eyes. In a week or two, he decided, he would see what kind of a nudge he could give the boy to convince him to join Maeon's cause. If Jase refused, he would die.

Moving to his wardrobe, he donned the uniform that marked him as Maeon's first among the living. If he had to face Shadan again, he wanted the Dreadlord to have a visual reminder of how important he was to this war.

When he was ready, he took a deep breath and opened a hole in the Veil. With a quick thrust of his Awareness, he checked to make sure he wasn't walking into a trap, then stepped through to his study in Shadan's Keep. This was not going to be pleasant.

CHAPTER 6

Proper Uses

As Aethon Fairimor strode down the corridor leading to Shadan's throne room, the look in his eyes sent every Agla'Con in his path scurrying hastily aside. None of them so much as made eye contact with him. *And that is just the way I want it*, he thought, pinching his face into a deeper frown. *They need to know I am still in control*. Despite his long, confident strides and determined face, however, the bravado was false. Inside, he was terrified. A cold pit of fear had settled in his stomach, and no matter what he did, he couldn't force it away.

Facing Shadan had never been a pleasant experience to begin with. Since being deprived of the privilege of killing Gideon, the refleshed Dreadlord had become intolerable. Sixteen lower-ranking Agla'Con had died in the past ten days alone — killed by Shadan in a moment of rage after delivering messages about the progress of the war that Shadan hadn't found pleasing. Most of those who'd been killed had died simply because they'd made mention of Gideon. The Dome of Fairimor Palace being crowned with Fire had likely increased the Dreadlord's irritability tenfold.

Aethon inhaled deeply and held it a moment before letting it go. He hoped his position as first among the living still counted for something in Shadan's eyes. It certainly did in Maeon's. Likely, it was the only thing that had kept Shadan from lashing out at him as he had the other sixteen. Shadan may be the driving force behind the cultist armies, but it was the Fairimor Three who were fighting the real war of trying to bring down the Veil. Shadan was a fool, but he certainly couldn't be stupid enough to ruin a chance to bring a speedy death to the Earthsoul. Maeon needed the Fairimors alive; their blood was too precious to be spilt.

He turned a corner and two Agla'Con had to leap out of his way to keep from getting trampled. Aethon barely noticed, too preoccupied with his thoughts. If he could somehow get his hands on a Talisman of Elsa, he could use its reservoir of Earthpower to rend the Veil so irreparably that Maeon's tides of darkness could flow into this world unchecked. The Dark One wouldn't have to wait the weeks, or even months, it might take for the Earthsoul to fail completely; he could join the fight immediately.

He pursed his lips determinedly. *If I can get my hands on a Talisman of Elsa, I can usher Con'Jithar into this miserable world once and for all. And then,* he thought with satisfaction, *we will see who sits higher in Maeon's eyes... me or Shadan.*

The thought made him smile. Seventy years ago, when he and his brothers had first sworn their allegiance to the Great Lord of the Dark, he had received a promise that he, Aethon Fairimor, first among his brethren in life, would be first among the legions of darkness when Maeon took control of the Earthsoul. Shadan had his part to play in all of this, certainly, but it was Maeon who really ran things. It was Maeon who had provided the power necessary to reflesh Shadan in the first — scratch that — the second place. And it was the Fairimor Three who opened the rent from this side of the Veil and allowed him to come through.

He frowned with disgust. Shadan had been a pompous, self-absorbed fool when he'd been alive; being dead for eight hundred years had only made it worse. That he was so important to Maeon's plans was frustrating. If not for him and his stupid cult, this war would be much easier to run.

He reached the doors of the throne room and paused as two K'rrosha pushed them open for him. Without sparing a glance for either, he moved inside. The copper urns still burned, but the frenzied crowd of worshipers was noticeably — and thankfully — absent. Aethon's boots echoed loudly off the high-domed ceiling as he walked.

Shadan sat in his throne at the top of the dais, gazing into a red crystal set in the end of a black iron scepter. He looked up, and his eyes flared brightly, turning the grey flesh of his face the color of blood. Aethon stopped at the foot of the dais and went to one knee just long enough to show some semblance of respect before rising once more. When Shadan frowned Aethon smiled inwardly. *Respect for how high you sit in Maeon's eyes,* he thought, *not reverence for you.* He waited quietly, refusing to flinch under Shadan's fiery gaze.

"Your failures continue to mount," Shadan hissed.

Aethon let his face harden into a frown. "My failures?" he asked, his voice harsh. "My failures?" he repeated, lacing his voice with scorn. His anger had the best of him, but anger was better than fear so he pressed on. He didn't shout, but there was enough heat in his words to cause Shadan to flinch. It was the slightest of movements, but it was enough to give Aethon courage.

"Was it *my* failure when I effectively cut off trade between Elva and Kelsa by poisoning Mirror Lake with shadowspawn the size and like of which have never before been known to our kind? Was it *my* failure when Croneam Eries escaped assassination because *you* preferred to use Shizu instead of a Satyr so Kelsa would look to Riak instead of Melek and your presence here would stay hidden? How about when I learned to rend the Veil? Or when I constructed an artificial T'rii Gate so the rending would be easier to accomplish? Was it *my* failure when I created links between our gate and the *chorazin* Veilgates of the Old World that lie scattered across the world? Was it *my* failure when those three idiots you put in charge of the Meleki camp followed your instructions to attack the Chellum army in Talin Pass and found a bloody booby trap that obliterated all those they sent through?"

He stopped and glared at Shadan with every bit of anger he possessed, deliberately holding the dead man's gaze without blinking. He could have gone on, of course. There were a dozen more examples of just how much he'd done for this war while Shadan, arrogant fool that he was, had done so very little.

The dead warlord's eyes flashed into a killing rage, and Aethon wondered if he'd gone too far with his anger. Shadan leaned forward and casually waved a finger. It was a small, seemingly insignificant movement, but Aethon found himself struggling for breath as wave after wave of excruciating pain flooded through him. His knees gave out, and he collapsed into a thrashing heap at the foot of the dais, writhing in agony and trying not to scream.

He fully expected to see whole sections of his flesh being peeled away and acid being poured over the wounds, but amazingly, his skin remained intact. The pain was nothing more than a trick of the Power. It was a small consolation in light of the agony, however, and he clenched his teeth to keep from howling as he waited for Shadan's anger to run its course.

When the torture finally ended, he pushed himself to his feet and waited to be addressed. He'd been right in his assumption that Shadan couldn't kill him, and though it had been a painful theory to test, he was encouraged by the possibilities it presented. He lowered his head to hide the smile which threatened to creep across his face. Shadan must have taken it as an act of obeisance because he spoke.

"Know your place, Fairimor," he hissed, his raspy voice filled with scorn. "I am in charge of this war until Maeon comes. Challenge me again and we will both find out how serious he is about you staying alive."

He sat back in his throne, his eyes flaring brightly. "For now your duties remain the same. But I want Croneam Eries killed and our plans for taking control of the Fulrath High Command accelerated. You will then make ready for the merging of our army with Riak's and finish linking the Veilgates of the Old World with the one in the Meleki camp. And I want you to discover who lit the skies of Kelsa last night. I want that person destroyed."

His staff suddenly flared red, and Aethon found it difficult to breathe as an invisible fist closed around his throat. "But most of all," Shadan added, "I want you to find Gideon Dymas and kill him. As long as he lives, you are a failure."

The words stung as much as the choking grip, but Aethon nodded. "Yes, Deathlord," he said when Shadan released him, putting enough humility in his voice to avoid another confrontation. "It shall be as you say."

た

From the window of his study in Fulrath's main fortress, Calis Hurd gazed out at the city and smiled. It was a city with one less general to worry about with Croneam away in Trian. *The old fool,* he thought. He should have sent Joneam. The younger Eries would have had more of an impact with the Kelsan High Tribunal than his father. Trian's politicians were sure to react to his reinstatement with the same hesitation and doubt that still plagued much of the tribunal here. If it hadn't been for Governor Prenum's intervention, Croneam's appeal would likely have been rejected. True, the council was militarily minded, but even they recognized when an old horse needed to be put out to pasture.

That last thought turned sour as soon as it came, and he reached up to rub the socket of his missing eye wearily. Only Croneam wasn't an old horse. He was a dragon. A dragon back in control of the most awesome military force in all of Kelsa. He had left Fulrath, though, and right now that was all that mattered. As much as he hated to admit it, the old wardog made him nervous. Some might see Croneam as a weathered old has-been, but Calis didn't. He knew what Croneam was capable of, and frankly, the old man scared him to death.

The Brethren were wary of him also, else they wouldn't have gone to so much trouble to try to have him eliminated. He rubbed his chin thoughtfully. Somehow they had known Croneam would renounce his retirement and desire to lead Fulrath once again, and their respect of his abilities had prompted them to act. If only Aethon Fairimor had contacted him sooner. He could have arranged the Deathstrike properly, and he wouldn't be in this bloody mess!

Croneam showing up in Fulrath the very day Sallen had left was the very rottenest of luck. If he'd have known Croneam was coming, he wouldn't have had to rely on the blabbering fool to guide the Shizu to Croneam's home. At least Sallen had been killed before he could say anything truly incriminating. There was no doubt in his mind that Shavis would have already killed him if he had learned the truth.

From what he'd seen of Shavis' skill as a Shizu, he suspected a strike inside the fortress itself would have presented no problem whatsoever. The bloody Shizu were even more deadly than he'd thought. For them to so suddenly have a conscience was frustrating to no end.

He shook his head angrily. Too bad he'd been unable to contact his Brethren in Samochi quick enough to postpone the strike. If he could have done that, Croneam wouldn't know he was a target and Shavis wouldn't be hunting the Con'Kumen.

He could do nothing about Shavis; he just hoped the Shizu didn't find what he was looking for or the world wouldn't be large enough to hide him from the man's wrath. Croneam, on the other hand, *could* be dealt with — especially since he had gone to Trian and wouldn't be back for at least a week. *A week*, he thought with a smile, *that I can use to start changing my luck.*

He moved back to his desk and took a seat, glancing only briefly at the stack of papers he'd been assigned to review. A colonel, and here he was doing the garbage work of any dimwit lieutenant. Colonel Phanon had gotten off easy with his transfer to Capena. Then again, Phanon hadn't been in on the Brotherhood's plan to eliminate Croneam, and eventually Joneam as well. *And add Governor Prenum to the list*, he thought darkly. *The meddling hag.*

He backhanded the stack of papers off his desk and slammed his fist down hard. If not for her support, the military council may have voted the other way. *Curse this bloody, rotten luck.* Closing his good eye, he took a steadying breath. At least he had the pleasure of knowing Tress Eries' death had caused Croneam a great deal of anguish. *And*, he thought with satisfaction, *I have his granddaughter. Sort of.*

Rising, he moved to the small liquor cabinet in the corner and poured himself a drink of brandy, then stepped to the window where he could watch Fulrath begin preparing for night. The streets of the outer city were empty of merchants, and all along the battlements of both the inner and outer walls armed men had assumed their posts. He could see the roof of his home visible among the trees outside the fortress proper and hissed in frustration.

"Bloody Shizu!"

He dreaded going home — the prospect of facing Raimen and Tohquin again was simply too much to deal with right now. For a moment he contemplated sleeping here in his study.

He frowned. But it was his house, for hell's sake! He wouldn't be driven out by the likes of *them*. He glared at the rooftop of his home and gripped the glass in his hand so tightly it made his knuckles hurt. *Bloody assassins and their bloody fatherly affection.* He took the rest of the brandy in one swallow, barely flinching as it burned his throat.

A week with Croneam gone might be the break he needed to find a solution to his problems. There were hundreds of Con'Kumen in Fulrath, and though he didn't know them all by sight, he had their names. They wouldn't know him, but his giving them the secret sign should quell any doubts they might have long enough for him to establish how high he stood in the Brotherhood. Holding the rank of *Mae'chodan* had its advantages.

Once they knew how high he stood in Maeon's eyes, he shouldn't have any problem enlisting their help. Assuming, of course, that they didn't already have orders from someone of higher standing in the Brotherhood. If they did, they wouldn't hesitate to turn on him in order to protect their own interests. It was risky, but no more so than waiting for King Fairimor's extermination order on the Con'Kumen to be carried out.

It didn't take long to realize the benefits of acting far outweighed the risks of doing nothing. First thing tomorrow morning he would contact some of his Brethren. A week was more than enough time to arrange for the murder of Joneam and Lenea.

The thought made him smile. *Let Croneam come home to another funeral. While he is grieving, he will be that much easier to kill.*

He turned from the window to find a Satyr standing in the middle of the room. His breath caught in his throat, and he froze in horror, his blood quickly turning to ice.

The black-cloaked shadowspawn stood motionless, its slitted green eyes shining as it studied him with a look of feral hunger. One of the rarest of all shadowspawn, Satyrs were used mainly as messengers for the highest-ranking Agla'Con, but there was enough talk of them being used for murder that he steadied himself and waited to die.

Hoping for a show of meekness, he lowered his gaze and waited to see what would happen. There wasn't much else he *could* do. If the Satyr was here to kill him, it would happen. He swallowed, trying to ignore the blood pounding in his temples, and prayed for a miracle. Satyrs were very messy assassins.

"The Brethren are displeased," the Satyr hissed. "*The* Brethren."

"Aethon?" Calis asked, and the Satyr's robes flared outward as if caught in a sudden wind. Steel blades flashed brightly in two sets of clawed limbs.

"You will address him as *The First*," the creature snarled. Calis nodded wordlessly, and the Satyr's robes settled into place once more.

"The First is displeased with your lack of results," the Satyr mewed. "Croneam Eries still lives. Your promise to kill him and place members of the Con'Kumen in places of authority here in Fulrath goes unfulfilled."

"But I — "

The Satyr moved so swiftly Calis could only blink before it had him. Two clawed hands seized the front of his uniform while two more pressed scythe-like blades against his throat. "Living or dying?" the Satyr purred, tilting its head as if listening to some far away voice. After a moment it pressed its face close, and the chill of winter flowed across Calis' skin as it spoke. "Two weeks from the time Croneam Eries returns to Fulrath... that is how much time you have to make good on your promise." It released its grip on his uniform, but its blades stayed at his throat. Calis' knees wavered, and he barely steadied himself in time to keep from getting his throat cut.

The Satyr seemed hesitant to pull the blades away, and Calis was certain the creature was disappointed at not being allowed to kill him. "Fulfill your oath, *Mae'chodan*," it mewed, then backed away into a shadowed corner of the room. A moment later it vanished as if it had never been.

Calis sagged to his knees and tried desperately not to vomit. *What have I gotten myself into?*

た

Raimen Adirhah, nine-year veteran of elite Deathsquad Alpha of Leif Iga and its current bladestar champion, chuckled softly as he gazed down at Tey Eries sitting on the rug at his feet. Giggling softly to herself, the little girl was teasing a grey and white striped kitten with a piece of string, causing it to bound about clumsily. It finally caught the string in its mouth and flopped over on its back, flailing with its tiny claws. Tey pulled at its tail, and it leapt up and scampered away, bringing a squeal of delight from the little girl.

Raimen glanced at Tohquin and found him grinning. The kitten was another one of his gifts. He had sensed her boredom and had gone out into the city proper looking for something to keep her entertained. They knew she liked cats; she had been playing with one the night her parents died.

He reached up and rubbed at his eyes. He found himself thinking about her parents more and more of late, of how they and the grandmother hadn't deserved to die. It was the first time since becoming Shizu that he found himself questioning his choice of career. It was the first time he'd ever thought of the targets of a Deathstrike as actual people. People with lives, loves, and feelings. And while it was true that the targets of Deathstrikes were usually criminals or enemies of clan or country, he knew that sometimes they weren't. Tey's grandmother hadn't been part of the strike, but he had witnessed firsthand how she had been killed.

He clenched his fist in anger. If only he'd gotten there a step sooner, he could have saved her. The thought made him want to swallow one of his bladestars.

From a military standpoint, trying to kill General Eries had been wise because of how prominently he factored into the upcoming war. The problem was, the strike hadn't been ordered by the military — it had come from the Con'Kumen.

His squad being used as a pawn by the Hand of the Dark, coupled with his growing conscience about those who had been ruthlessly killed by the Samochi squad, had him questioning the honor of his position as a Shizu. It also made him wonder about the purity of the Emperor's motives at ordering such strikes. Not all of Riak's clans were as honorable as Gahara. It was entirely possible the Shizu were so greatly feared because Deathsquads were perceived as indiscriminate butchers rather than efficient military strike teams.

Who was he kidding? Of course the world saw them as butchers. The willingness of clans like Samochi to kill everyone who happened to be in the presence of the target had made it that way. And Samochi wasn't alone. There were many who killed when it wasn't necessary. He was glad Gahara wasn't one of them.

But, he realized bitterly, even those who were legitimate targets were still people. People who would be loved and missed by those who knew them. It was a thought he could no longer push away, and the bitterness inside him continued to grow. Guilt had him by the throat and was slowly choking away his life.

With that guilt, however, came a desire to somehow right the wrongs he may have done over the past nine years. He also wanted to change the popular notion of the Shizu — to restore them to the days when they were feared but grudgingly respected.

"It will be dark soon," Tohquin said, bringing him out of his thoughts. "I think I'll go wait outside for Hurd."

"You enjoy scaring him too, don't you?"

Tohquin grinned. "Very much," he said, embracing *Ta'shaen* and bending the light around him so that he seemed to disappear.

"How does he do that?" Tey asked, looking up from the kitten.

Raimen leaned forward and glanced around mysteriously. "Magic."

"Joselyn Rai is magic," Tey said, returning to her teasing of the kitten. "One time my brother broke his arm, and she used magic to make it better."

"Is that so?"

"Uh-huh. And one time when I was really sick, she made me better too."

"Magic is a nice thing to have around," Raimen said. "So long as it's used properly."

So long as it's used properly, he thought grimly, reaching up to run his fingers through his hair. *Words that can be applied to Riaki Deathsquads as well as to the Power.*

He glanced down at Tey. Perhaps it was time for Leif Iga to reevaluate how and to whom they deployed their Shizu. Perhaps, he thought with a smile, the Shizu could hunt the Con'Kumen as a way of making at least a partial restitution for the mistakes of the past. He certainly hoped so. For if he had learned only one thing during this time, it was that the family of Tey Eries — and countless others before them — deserved justice.

CHAPTER 7

Limitations

The sharp crack of wooden swords was followed by a *whump* of flesh being struck, and the last of the eight Highwaymen fell with a groan. Whirling away from the stricken man, Daris spun to a stop, his practice sword held out behind him, his free hand extended before him in a Shizu pose.

He relaxed his concentration and let time and motion return to normal around him. Glancing at the fallen men, he raised his sword hilt to his forehead in salute, then turned to find Greig and Tomlin staring at him in open-mouthed wonder. A short distance away, seated on a bench in the shade of a covered walkway, Brysia studied him with tight-lipped contemplation. Next to her, Maira wore a look of morbid awe.

Daris did his best to ignore the two women and moved instead toward Greig and Tomlin. Both Brysia and Maira had been acting differently toward him the last week — a direct result, he knew, of his perceived emotional withdrawal from Maira. He knew he had hurt her feelings, especially after the nice evening they'd had together, but he wasn't about to address the issue with either woman. Gideon's message had destroyed any chance of a relationship with Maira. At least until the war with Shadan was over. Maybe not even then.

As for Brysia's sudden desire to see him retire... he hoped the whipping he'd given the Highwaymen proved that he wasn't as old and decrepit as she'd been hinting. There were only two ways for him to retire now. One was to turn her back over to Benak if he ever returned — an event he didn't think likely — the other was to die. Now that the prophecies were starting to be fulfilled, option two was becoming more and more likely with each passing day.

That last thought made him glance involuntarily toward the north. He still hadn't spoken to Brysia about the light that had filled the northern sky last night because he feared she would sense he knew more than he was telling. He had no idea what prophecy had been fulfilled, but he suspected she might. And if she even remotely suspected that Gideon or Jase might be involved, there would be no stopping her return to Trian. He couldn't allow that to happen, not without word from Lord Fairimor that it was okay to do so. Trian was simply too dangerous a place.

He pushed the thought away as he reached Greig and Tomlin.

"That was amazing," Tomlin said at last. He handed Daris a rag so he could wipe his face but stopped when he noticed it wasn't needed. Daris had bested the eight men so quickly, he hadn't even broken a sweat. Tomlin tossed the rag away.

Greig chuckled. "I've seen better," he said teasingly. "They are only Highwaymen, after all. Saddles and crossbows are their forte, not swords."

Before Daris could respond, Brant Callison moved up to them. "Those are pretty big words coming from an *apprentice*," he told Greig. "Perhaps you would like to try to duplicate your mentor's feat."

Greig looked around at the faces of the Highwaymen gathering to listen and his jaw set determinedly. "I'd love to," he answered, unbuckling his sword and handing it to Tomlin. He took a practice sword from one of the men Daris had beaten and turned to those still waiting for a chance to practice. "Select your best nine," he told Brant, then moved into the open.

Daris cringed inwardly. *Nine?* He knew Greig was cocky, but this was ridiculous. The boy was going to get slaughtered. The grins on the faces of the assembling Highwaymen showed they thought so as well. They looked eager to make the young warder eat his words.

Brant pointed to eight men, motioning them toward the barrel of practice swords, then unbuckled his own sword and moved to join them. Daris wasn't surprised; Brant was as good as any of them. Plus, he liked to lead by example.

Greig blinked when he saw that Brant would be one of the nine, but he quickly smoothed his features and put on an air of calm indifference.

Daris smiled. This was going to be interesting.

As the nine men approached, Greig went into a defensive stance, bringing one foot forward and holding his sword low and slightly to the right. His eyes darted from face to face as the Highwaymen entered the circle, and Daris could tell the young warder was sizing up the competition.

Brant motioned with his sword, and four of the nine men circled around in a flanking maneuver, coming in toward Greig's back.

There's their first mistake, Daris thought. Greig had deliberately left that avenue open — he was baiting them. And Brant had fallen for it. *Or has he?* Daris amended when he saw Brant motion again. Four more men moved around to come in from the other side.

Keeping his eyes fastened on Brant, Greig used his peripheral vision to keep track of the others. If he looked to either side now, the opposite group would attack.

Good boy, Daris thought. *Don't let them bait you.*

The Highwaymen stopped, and a heavy silence fell over the area as everyone held their collective breath. And then something happened that Daris, and more obviously Greig from the look of him, didn't expect — Brant raised his sword and strode directly at the young warder.

Greig held his stance until it became evident that Brant meant to attack, then launched himself at the Waypost captain in an attempt to get a quick kill. Brant deflected the blow, then deftly stepped aside as the rest of the Highwaymen rushed in.

Spinning away from Brant, Greig engaged the Highwaymen to his right and put two of them out of action with strikes to the head and neck. He locked swords with the third, then shoved the man away and ducked beneath a swipe from the fourth. He struck the man on the wrist, knocking his sword away, then scored a kill with a thrust to his chest.

He snatched the fallen sword up with his free hand, scored a kill against the man he'd shoved, then whirled, both swords humming, into the midst of the other four Highwaymen. Two went down almost immediately. A third took a blow to the knee, staggered, and was finished with a swipe across the back. The fourth knocked the sword from Greig's left hand but was removed from the fight by the other. He dropped with a groan, and Greig whirled away again... right into the tip of Brant's outstretched sword. It took the young warder in the midsection, dropping him with an astonished blast of exhaled air.

Brant lowered his sword, then leaned forward and offered his hand to Greig, helping him to his feet.

Daris stepped up to them. "That was a fine bit of fighting," he told Greig. "Right up to the part where you got killed." He met Brant's gaze briefly before turning his attention back to Greig. "It's not enough to know what one is capable of," he said, taking on a lecturing tone, "you must also know your limits."

Sitting in the shade of the Waypost's covered walkway, Brysia gave a little laugh. "That's more than a little ironic coming from you," she chided. "You've been ignoring said limits since we arrived in Seston. Particularly when you consider what happened in Scloa."

"What happened in Scloa was well within my range of abilities," Daris told her flatly, trying to keep his irritation out of his voice. They'd already been over this a dozen times; why did she feel it necessary to bring it up again? Especially in front of so many people?

"The injury to your shoulder says differently," she countered. "The days of you going against a dozen or more men on your own are over, Daris. Why can't you see that?"

"I can see it," he said mildly. He wasn't about to let himself be drawn into an argument with her in front of Brant and the others, not with the knowledge he had of her verbal skills. He'd never once won an argument with her — none worth mentioning anyway — and he didn't think a victory could be won here either. He wasn't lying when he said it was important to know one's limits.

He made his way toward her. "Which is why I am working to train assistants. With their help I don't have to exceed my limits." He shot a quick glance at Greig. "Assuming I can keep their enthusiasm in check, of course."

When he reached Brysia, he gently took her hand in his. "I promised Benak I would look after you," he said, knowing even as he spoke that the words would sting Maira's heart. It couldn't be helped; both women needed to know where his duty lay. Maira, as lovely and enticing as she was, could have no place in his life until his promise to Benak had been fulfilled.

"*En 'liott kel, en jyosai, sa bies en semairei,*" he told her in the Old Tongue, then whispered for Maira's benefit, "My sword is yours, my lady, as is my life."

Brysia sighed resignedly. "So you keep telling me," she said and released his hand. Motioning to Maira, she rose and moved away down the boardwalk. Hend, Matail, and Robil took up positions around her.

Daris rejoined Greig and Tomlin where they were engaged in banter with Brant.

"What was that all about?" Tomlin asked.

"Nothing I couldn't handle," Daris answered, making it clear by his tone that he wanted the matter dropped. He was sure Brysia had spoken to the two young warders about her feelings concerning his eventual retirement, but he didn't want to discuss it with either of them.

He turned to Brant. "Choose eleven of your best men," he said. "And then join them in the practice circle. I'll be along shortly."

Brant's expression was one of disbelief, but he nodded and moved to do as instructed. "Oh, and Brant," Daris called, "I want them in full armor."

Brant's disbelief turned to all-out shock, and he shook his head as if he were wondering if all warders were crazy.

Daris turned back to find Greig and Tomlin looking equally shocked.

"Have you lost your mind?" Greig asked. "If the Highwaymen don't crack your skull, Mistress Wyndor will."

"Only if she finds out," Daris replied darkly, hoping to make the hint obvious. He glanced around guardedly. "When the last man falls, I want you two to come at me as well. Hold nothing back. If you do, you will regret it."

Tomlin glanced at Greig. "Why do I get the feeling we are going to regret it anyway?"

Chuckling, Daris moved to the barrel of practice swords and removed two that suited him, then strode into the practice circle to await Brant and his men. It took them several minutes to don their armor, so he used the time to clear his mind and relax his muscles.

He took a deep breath. Five years had passed since he'd last gone against a dozen men. Ten since he'd faced men with any real skill. And despite Greig's wisecrack about these Highwaymen, Daris knew they were skilled. Add the armor they now wore, and this would be as tough a challenge as he'd faced since he'd saved Xia and been raised to warder.

Back then, however, he'd been a lot like Greig: young, cocky, and eager to prove to others just how good he was. Today, he simply wanted to prove to himself that he wasn't the feeble has-been that Brysia kept hinting at. He knew his limits. Today he planned on exceeding them. At least as far as fighting the Highwaymen was concerned. There was no telling what might happen once Greig and Tomlin entered the fray.

As Brant and his men approached, Daris took a sword in each hand and turned to face them. He knew the captain had instructed his men on how they should attack, and he didn't want to let them carry out their plan. When they were all inside the circle, he whirled each sword once and began death's dance.

Standing in the shade next to the Waypost command center, Brysia watched Daris square off against the Highwaymen and closed her eyes in defeat. She'd suspected he might do something like this. For a week now he'd been acting like something was bothering him — a quiet irritation that had nothing to do with her playing matchmaker between him and Maira. This was something else entirely, and she wished she knew what it was.

Beside her, Maira chewed her lip nervously. "What is he doing?" she asked, then gasped as Daris launched himself at the Highwaymen.

Brysia pursed her lips distastefully. "Acting like a fool."

But, she added silently, he was still the deadliest fool she knew. *What is bothering you, Daris? What aren't you telling me?* If she didn't know any better, she would say it had something to do with last night's fulfilling of prophecy. But she doubted that he knew what prophecy had been fulfilled. She wasn't entirely sure herself, though she suspected it may have been the crowning of Fairimor Dome with Fire. She'd read the passage a long time ago and wasn't completely sure what it had to do with the upcoming war. If Daris did know of the prophecy, however, it might explain today's behavior.

She pushed the thought away and watched in amazement as Daris scored kills on seven of the Highwaymen almost immediately and forced the other five to retreat to the edge of the circle. There they clustered together for a moment before launching an attack of their own.

Daris tossed one of his swords away and stood his ground, meeting the counterattack in a series of whirls and spins that put Brant and one other soldier out of action and forced the other three to give ground.

The sharp *whack whack whack* of the combatants' swords echoed across a compound that had been stunned to silence by the sheer ferocity of Daris' attack. Even the normally boisterous Greig was at a loss for words. Standing at the circle's edge, he and Tomlin watched their mentor's movements in awe. The boys were good, but they were getting a firsthand look at how experience was as important as skill.

Beside her, Maira was breathing heavily — whether from excitement or fear, Brysia couldn't say — and her eyes were wide. Her hands were clenched tightly in front of her. So tightly, in fact, her knuckles had turned white. It made Brysia wonder if seeing this side of Daris' character would cause Maira to reconsider her feelings toward him. Yes, he was gentle and caring towards those whom he loved; but he was as fierce as a Shadowhound and as deadly as a Riaki Deathsquad toward his enemies. *And,* she added darkly, *when he knows something I don't, he's as unpredictable as a Kelsan politician.*

Another highwayman dropped with a groan, and the remaining two fell back, the look in their eyes one of disbelief mingled with fear. It was only a matter of time now. Daris was just too good for them. *And much better than I've been giving him credit for.*

But then she saw Greig and Tomlin take up practice swords and ready themselves at the edge of the circle and rolled her eyes in disgust. *But he's still just as foolish.*

As the last highwayman fell beneath Daris' sword, his two warders-in-training attacked, bringing their wooden swords to bear with a grace the other twelve men had lacked. Daris met them in the center of the circle, and the clacking of swords became so rapid it seemed to blend together into one continuous sound. Daris kept Greig and Tomlin in front of him, circling away so they couldn't pin him between them.

A short time later Tomlin tripped over a fallen practice sword, momentarily losing his concentration, and Daris caught him across the side of the head with a swipe that dropped him like a rock. Spinning away from his fallen apprentice, Daris caught Greig's sword with his and they locked hilts, standing face to face and grinning at one another like madmen.

"You're next," Daris said, shoving Greig away and launching himself at the young man with a ferocity that made Brysia cringe.

The macabre dance continued for several tense minutes as both men pressed relentlessly for a weakness, and Brysia was amazed at Daris' stamina. He really hadn't lost anything due to age, she decided. If anything, he looked even more deadly than when she'd first taken him on as a warder. As the duel continued, though, Daris started to give ground. Greig was young and quick, and the look in his eyes showed how much he wanted to prove himself in front of the Highwaymen.

The sharp cracking of their swords rose to a fevered pitch, then cut off with a loud, simultaneous *thump* of wood on flesh. Greig staggered away in a mumbling of curses, clutching the side of his neck and shaking his head to clear his vision; Daris reached down to rub his ribs. Both would have been killing blows, Brysia knew, but as far as scoring was concerned, Daris was the victor. A *dead victor,* she added wryly.

She turned to Maira. "I've seen enough of this foolishness for one day," she said. "Let's go."

Turning to follow Brysia, Maira shook her head in bewilderment at what she had witnessed, as impressed as she was mortified by Daris' ability with a sword. In the ten years that he and Brysia had been coming to Seston, she had never seen him fight until today. Sure, she'd heard stories from Jase about Daris' ability as a swordsman. She simply hadn't given them much thought, having always discounted them as the tales of an overexcited young man. Now that she had seen what Daris was capable of, she realized that Jase was a lousy storyteller. Either that or he had deliberately toned down the stories to avoid upsetting her.

"Is that what it was like at Drusi Bridge?" she asked, turning to study Brysia.

Brysia regarded her quietly for a moment, her Elvan eyes sparkling. "Minus the blood and death," she said. "Does it bother you to know that Daris has killed to keep me safe?"

"It used to," she replied. "But I've been able to see the man inside the warder. His love for and loyalty to you is really quite a beautiful thing. I admit I am jealous."

Brysia reached over and took her hand, giving it a squeeze. "He loves you too, you know. He hasn't said it aloud, but I can see it in his eyes. Give him some time and he will come around."

Maira smiled. "I hope so."

Brysia looked like she would say more but pursed her lips tightly when she spied Iveera Silliam and several of her friends rounding the corner in front of them. The Seston Gossipers, as Daris had come to call them, spotted them as well and let their conversation die. With noses turned upward, they studied her and Brysia with airs of disdain as they approached, moving side by side so as to take the whole of the boardwalk. She and Brysia would either have to step aside into the street or push right through their midst. Judging from the determined frown on Brysia's face, Maira realized it was going to be the latter.

Good. I've had it with Iveera's holier-than-thou attitude. Her husband may be the Mayor, but it didn't give her the right to treat people so poorly. And the rumors she'd been spreading about Brysia were downright awful. Maira braced herself. If the chance presented itself, she might put a shoulder or an elbow into the hag.

The decision was taken from her when Hend, noticing the looks passing between the two groups, moved up out of the street and plowed right through the midst of the women, scattering them the way he might a gaggle of geese. Iveera, Maira was pleased to note, was so startled, she stepped from the boardwalk and into a puddle of mud.

"Beggin' your pardon," Hend said with no trace of sincerity in his voice. "I guess the sun was in my eyes, so's I didn't see you there." He grinned at Brysia, then turned and started away down the boardwalk as if nothing had happened. Behind them, Matail and Robil laughed openly. They cut off when Brysia shot them both a dark look.

When they were well away from Iveera and her friends, Brysia called to Hend. "I appreciate you looking out for us," she told him. "But Maira and I are more than a match for those women."

"Precisely why I intervened," Hend said evenly. "We can't be having you sendin' them to visit the Healer, now can we, *Mistress Wyndor?*" The emphasis he placed on her alias was obvious.

Brysia gave a little laugh, shaking her head in defeat. "You are right, of course," she told him, then turned to smile at Maira. "Apparently, Daris isn't the only one who can act like a fool."

Maira nodded. *But,* she thought sadly, *he is the only one who won't acknowledge it.* And she didn't mean his desire for swordplay either. He was simply too duty-bound to Brysia to acknowledge what lay in his heart.

Glancing over her shoulder at the Waypost, she frowned. *Don't make me wait too long, Daris. I need you in my life.*

Daris accepted the mug of ale from Brant and leaned back in his chair. After three hours of sword practice with the Highwaymen, it was a much-needed break. Especially, considering that his shoulder ached to beat hell. Obviously the wound he'd received in Scloa wasn't fully healed. He listened to the noise and commotion still taking place out in the compound for a moment, then focused his attention on Brant. He found the young captain watching him.

"I must say," Brant began, "that you are the most talented swordsman I have ever seen. I think even that young smart-mouth Greig has a newfound respect for your abilities."

Daris shrugged. "Well, there's nothing like a good thrashing to awaken one's sense of humility." He smiled with admiration. "But, I'll tell you what, Greig is the most talented swordsman that *I've* ever seen. He's twice as good as I was at that age, and better than I am now. If he would rely more on intuition and less on the strict adherence to the forms, he would be nigh on unbeatable."

They fell silent then, each left to his own thoughts while they sipped their drinks, and Daris found himself thinking about Jase. The boy could have been a Blademaster as well if he'd stuck with his training. As it was, he was better with a sword than any of the Highwaymen that had taken part in today's practice. Considering all that might be happening in the boy's life right now, the ability to defend himself was likely proving invaluable. Even for a fully trained Dymas, the time often came when ability with the Power wasn't enough to stay alive. It was the reason Gideon had become a Blademaster in spite of all he could do with *Ta'shaen.*

And Jase, untrained as he was, would need all the help he could get. *Keep him safe, Gideon,* Daris urged silently. *Or you will be answering to both me and Brysia.*

The sound of booted feet at the doorway pulled him from his thoughts and he looked up as Captain Yelan Falistan entered with two of his men. Daris glanced at the clock. They were back from patrol early. Three hours early, in fact.

"Look who we found," Captain Falistan said as three men, shackled hand and foot and chained to one another, shuffled in behind him.

Daris' eyes narrowed with contempt. The men were some of the Con'Kumen prisoners who'd escaped from the Waypost a week earlier. They scowled at him but said nothing.

"Where did you find them?" Brant asked, the excitement in his face obvious.

"In Kerns," Falistan answered, then added for Daris' benefit, "It's a little town about fifteen miles to the east. They've been hiding out in the loft of a barn owned by the man who turned them in. He became suspicious when his hens suddenly stopped laying eggs, but it wasn't until his cow stopped giving as much milk that he realized someone was stealing from him. He was waiting for us this morning out on the highway and asked us to investigate." He glanced at the three men and frowned. "Lucky for him he didn't try to confront them himself since they'd rearmed themselves. One of them had Herriman's sword."

Daris frowned. Herriman was one of the Highwaymen killed the night the men had escaped. "Did they give you any trouble?" he asked. If they had inflicted any more casualties on the ranks of the Highwaymen, he would have them executed right here and now.

"No," Captain Falistan replied. "Thanks to the old man, we took them by surprise."

Daris rose and moved to stand in front of the men. They looked worn and tired, and in spite of the defiant looks they were giving him, they looked afraid. *Good,* he thought. *I want them to be terrified.* "We have some things to discuss," he told them. "How well you cooperate will determine whether or not I let you live."

"Con'Jithar take you," one of the men snarled, then gasped for air as Daris punched him so hard he felt the man's ribs crack.

"Rule number one," Daris said as if nothing had happened, "is that you will not speak to me unless I ask you a direct question. Rule number two is that you will address me as Captain Stodd." He glanced at the one whom he had punched. "And rule number three," he said, lacing his voice with all the scorn he could muster, "is that the Con'Kumen are vermin scum in need of eradication. The only thing keeping me from sending you to meet your dark lord right now is my curiosity as to how you escaped."

He turned to Brant. "Toss them in separate cells and station a dozen of your best men outside each. No one is to enter the cells without me to accompany them."

He turned a hard stare back on the men. "I'm looking forward to our chat," he told them. "Try not to disappoint me."

Brant waited until Captain Falistan led the Con'Kumen from the room before he spoke. "What are you going to do with them?" he asked, more than a little alarmed by Daris' hostility toward the men. "I know you have full juris-diction here, but torture is not the Kelsan military's way. I will not allow it."

Daris chuckled. "Torture? Who said anything about torture? I'm just trying to scare a little common sense into those scum. I'm hoping their imaginations running wild tonight with what I *could* do to them will convince them to be honest with me."

"You're not going to hurt them, then?"

"Of course not," Daris answered, sounding slightly offended. "At least not until I have their heads removed for the crimes they've committed."

"That I can live with," Brant told him. "So what *are* you going to do?"

Daris smiled. "I'm going back to *The Rose of the Forest* to clean up and have a nice dinner. Then I'm going to try to avoid having my skin removed by Mistress Wyndor, since I'm sure that young smart-mouth, as you like to call him, will manage to let it slip that I fought again after she left."

"The nice dinner I envy you for," Brant told him, "but you have my sympathies regarding the other. Mistress Wyndor is, ah, how shall I put it? A formidable woman."

"You have no idea," Daris chuckled. "You really have no idea."

Sipping at her tea, Brysia waited while Eimei cleared away the dinner plates, silently impressed with the joy and pride the girl took in her work. Glavin Roe, the owner of *The Rose*, had hired a real gem when he'd hired this girl. Hopefully the stingy innkeeper was paying her what she was worth. Probably, or Eimei would have gone elsewhere. She was a masterful cook, and was as beautiful as she was talented. That beauty wasn't lost on Greig and Tomlin who were watching her with un-warderly preoccupation.

"Was everything to your satisfaction?" Eimei asked.

"It was excellent," Brysia told her, and Daris and Maira nodded their agreement. Greig and Tomlin, she noted with a frown, were so spellbound by the girl that they could only nod. When they noticed Daris frowning at them, however, they shook themselves free of her spell, and their faces returned to the serious, detached masks that all warders were famous for.

Eimei appeared not to notice, but Brysia saw a slight smile tugging at the corners of the girl's mouth and knew she hadn't been fooled. "I'll bring out dessert in a moment," Eimei told them as she started for the kitchen. "Carrot cake with a creamy frosting. It's one of my specialties."

"It sounds wonderful," Brysia told her.

When Eimei was gone from the room, Daris leaned forward to glare at his two young apprentices. "That kind of preoccupation with the opposite sex is a sure path to getting your throats cut," he told them. "Or weren't you listening when I told you about Jimsalon Fairimor?"

"We were listening," Tomlin said, sounding truly abashed. Beside him Greig nodded.

"Who is Jimsalon Fairimor?" Maira asked.

Brysia turned to look at her. "He was High King of Kelsa from A.S. 1346 to 1384," she said. "And like our young warders here, he was known to appreciate a pretty face. A little too much, in fact. It ruined his marriage and almost brought about the ruin of Kelsa."

The shock in Maira's eyes was obvious. "What did he do?"

"The question," Daris said darkly, "is what didn't he do?"

Brysia took a sip of her tea before continuing. "Shortly after his wife left him — taking their son Siamon and moving to Andlexces — Jimsalon was befriended by a young politician named Throy Shadan... who also had an *appreciation* for the opposite sex. He surrounded himself and King Fairimor with dozens of beautiful women — I suppose a better word for them would be concubines — and Fairimor Palace became nothing short of a brothel."

She pursed her lips, truly disgusted by this unpleasant piece of her family's history and unable to continue.

"In short," Daris continued for her, "the warders became so distracted by all the beautiful women that it cost them their lives. Apparently, Shadan had been planning all along to seize control of Trian, and his entourage of scantily clad women was part of the plan. One night a celebration was held, where the most beautiful of the women danced for those stationed in the palace. During that dance, the rest of those loyal to Shadan killed Jimsalon and his warders and took control of the palace."

"Are you saying Eimei is dangerous?" Greig asked jokingly.

Brysia scowled at him, irritated by his inability or unwillingness to take things seriously. The boy may be a fantastic swordsman, but his lack of seriousness concerning matters such as this told her he would never be able to replace Daris. She glanced at Daris and wondered if he was thinking the same thing. His face was hard, and the set of his jaw showed that he was irritated with Greig as well.

"Only as dangerous as your preoccupation with her good looks makes her," Daris replied evenly. "Remember that you are a warder, Greig. Your only preoccupation should be with the safety of Mistress Wyndor. Everything else is secondary. Allowing yourself to dwell on those other things is to put your charge, as well as yourself, at risk. I'm sure Jimsalon didn't see his concubines as a threat. I'm sure that many of them had no knowledge of Shadan's plan to usurp the throne and were as shocked as everyone else when the killing started."

He leaned forward and there was a fire burning in his eyes that surprised even Brysia. She had seen it only a few times before and knew that the discussion of Jimsalon Fairimor had opened an old wound. It took her only a moment to realize that part of what he was telling his two young warders was directed at her and Maira as well.

"The point is this," he said fiercely, "distractions get warders killed. An enemy never attacks us at our strongest point; they look for a weakness. And if that weakness comes in the form of a pretty face or a well-shaped bottom, then you know bloody well the enemy will try to exploit it. And then the object of your preoccupation is at risk as well. The enemy won't hesitate to kill her to get to you. It's the reason — " he cut off as Eimei came into the room bearing a tray of desserts.

Daris leaned back in his chair and waited while Eimei served everyone, but his eyes never left the faces of Greig and Tomlin.

Brysia watched them as well. To their credit, both young men were watching Eimei with the detached professionalism expected of them. It seemed neither of the two had taken the chastisement lightly. Judging from the hurt in Maira's eyes, neither had she. It made Brysia want to reach across the table and slap Daris across the face. The only thing that stayed her hand was the knowledge that he was right.

When Eimei was gone, Daris continued. "It's the reason that warders don't get married," he told them, glancing briefly at Maira. "Being a husband interferes with our ability to perform our duty."

Maira's face remained smooth, but Brysia could tell it came because of considerable effort. Her hands were knotted in her lap, and she was trembling. She looked on the verge of tears. What Daris said next only made it worse.

"That's not to say that we don't experience these desires," he told Greig and Tomlin, then turned to gaze at Maira. "Or that we don't know what it is like to love a woman and want to be with her. It simply means that we will be unable to act on those desires until our duty is fulfilled."

He turned back to Greig and Tomlin. "And we will fulfill our duty," he told them. "Because we must."

A long silence ensued, and Brysia studied Daris intently. This wasn't just another hint for her to cease playing matchmaker between him and Maira. Nor was it simply another refusal to retire. Daris was troubled by something far larger than either of those two things — something which had him upset enough that he felt it necessary to erect a wall between himself and all those whom he cared about. She decided to find out what it was.

"Daris," she said softly, "what's troubling you? And I don't mean the obvious." She glanced meaningfully at Maira.

Daris raised his hands in defeat. "Jase was right when he said there is no hiding things from you," he said, a slight smile creeping over his face. It vanished just as quickly. "I received a message from Lord Fairimor," he said, then hesitated as if he might not continue. "He informed me that Throy Shadan has been refleshed. Death's Third March is already underway."

Brysia's reaction to the news of Shadan's return wasn't what Daris expected. There was no fear or alarm in her eyes. No concern. She didn't even seem surprised. All she did was raise an eyebrow at him. Impressive, since everyone else in the room was gaping openly.

"And how long have you known this?" she asked, a hint of irritation in her voice.

He shrugged. "About a week."

"I see," she said, her voice edged with anger. "And you didn't inform me until now because..." she trailed off, waiting for him to speak.

"Because Lord Fairimor told me not to," he answered. "He didn't want you to worry."

"When is he going to stop treating me like his baby sister?" Brysia groaned. Then her face hardened once more, and Daris flinched when she pointed a finger at him. "No more secrets," she said hotly. "From now on you will inform me the moment you learn anything new."

He bowed his head deferentially. "Yes, *en jyosai*," he said, grateful for the loophole she had given him. *Anything new*, she had said. That meant unless she asked, he didn't have to tell her about Gideon and Jase. Even then he still might lie to her.

He didn't like the deception, of course, but Gideon and Jase had a job to do; they couldn't afford Brysia becoming the kind of distraction that might get them both killed. As distasteful as this dishonesty was to him, it, too, was part of his duty. And, as he had done all his life, he would do his duty.

CHAPTER 8

Rock and Stone

With the afternoon sun hidden behind the cliffs overhead, the road through Mendel Pass was deep with shade. It was so deep, in fact, it reminded Hulanekaefil Nid of the canyon pass leading into the Pit. But only slightly. Here the road was cared for and the way smooth, and their destination was a beautiful, grassy lowland, not the godforsaken sands of K'zzaum. He shuddered involuntarily at the memory of his descent into the Pit to rescue Gideon and their subsequent retreat ahead of an entire legion of K'rrosha Shadowlancers. How he and Gideon had managed to evade so many was as much a mystery as it was a miracle.

He exhaled slowly. And for the country of Melek, it had been a costly miracle. With both his sons dead, the two-hundred-year reign of the Nid family might be nearing its end. Unless his grandsons were still alive somewhere in Melek, he was the last of his bloodline. When he was gone, the monarchy would most likely be transferred to the Shim family. And that was assuming he and those loyal to him could wrest it from the iron clutches of the Shadan Cult. *Bloody parasites, and their bloody religion,* he added darkly.

Riding beside him, Croneam Eries spoke, bringing him out of his thoughts. "So what did you think of the Fairimor lad?" he asked.

"His strength is impressive," Hul answered. "But his lack of control is frightening. I was still outside of Trian when the battle inside the Dome was fought, and I could feel him wielding the Power. He very nearly crossed into the realm of the Agla'Con. I know you and Gideon believe him to be a figure of prophecy, but I am starting to worry that Jase might fulfill some for the dark side as well."

"It's a possibility, to be sure," Croneam conceded. "We'll just have to pray it doesn't happen."

"I hear he had a close encounter with a Satyr," Hul said after a moment. "One that should have ended with his death but didn't. That means the Satyr was delivering a message. Any idea who may have taken an interest in the boy?" He could tell by Croneam's expression that this was something he hadn't considered.

Croneam shook his head. "No. Do you?"

Hul shrugged. "I suspect Aethon Fairimor, though, in truth, it could be any high-ranking Agla'Con."

"Does Gideon know about this?" Croneam asked.

"I don't know. I had hoped to talk to him about it, but we ran out of time. Knowing Gideon as I do, though, I'm sure he is aware of it. I just don't know how he will handle it. There isn't much he can do anyway. That only a message was sent is a good thing. I have no doubts the boy would be dead if the Satyr had been sent to kill him."

"That's true enough," Croneam agreed. "Satyrs are formidable. Only a fool deliberately steps in front of them."

Hul gave a hearty laugh. "You are no fool, Croneam Eries," he said, then grinned at the surprised look on the general's face. "I heard about your encounter with the Satyr as well. And well done. I thought only a Dymas could defeat one of those bloody creatures."

Croneam shrugged. "I got lucky."

Smiling, Hul fell silent. He and Croneam had never met before this morning, but already he liked the man. He'd known *of* him for four decades, of course. The name Croneam Eries was a legend in the land of Melek. Those loyal to the kingdom admired and respected him; those in the Shadan Cult feared and hated him. His final stand against Shadan's armies during the Battle of Greendom was mythical, earning him a kind of hero status among the Meleki people that was usually reserved for one who was Meleki-born. The only other man not Meleki with Croneam's reputation was Gideon Dymas. He suddenly wondered if either man knew how the vast majority of Melek viewed them.

Not likely, he decided. Both men were too busy doing their jobs to focus on their egos. And it was a good thing too. It was the pride of Throy Shadan that started all of this in the first place.

They rode on in silence, and a short while later they reached the wooden pole marking the summit. After a brief pause to rest the horses and stretch their own tired muscles, they began their descent. They'd gone less than a mile when they heard a rumbling above them.

"Rock slide!" one of the warders shouted, pointing to a stream of boulders cascading toward them. "Ride for your lives!"

"Hold your positions," Hul shouted as he embraced the Power and spread a thick shield of Air above them. "And stay together. Keep the horses close."

The warders did as they were told, watching in wide-eyed terror as the river of stone rumbled toward them. Croneam, on the other hand, watched calmly, his face confident as he deftly kept his tawny-colored mare under control.

Hul ignored them all as he opened his Awareness and focused his attention on the largest of the boulders bouncing toward them. He would need to destroy them lest they punch through his shield. The rest, as long as they didn't hit all at once, he should be able to hold off. Maybe.

He closed his eyes and let the steep slope above him come into luminescent focus in his mind's eye. When the largest boulders were a dozen yards out, he struck.

Croneam watched the rocks rumbling toward him and held his breath. He had full confidence in High King Nid's abilities to protect them, but it was a frightening sight nonetheless. And he didn't think it was a natural occurrence either. A whisper in his mind told him this had been caused by an Agla'Con. He was glad Hul had decided to come with them. Evading the slide on horseback would have required a miracle. As it was, things were about to get ticklish.

The rumbling quickly turned deafening and Croneam readied himself for whatever Lord Nid was about to do. He didn't have to wait long.

The largest of the tumbling boulders blew apart in a spray of dust and everything disappeared behind the thick layer of grit that settled against the shield Lord Nid had woven above them. Craters of dust appeared and disappeared on the surface of the shield as smaller boulders pelted the protective layer and bounced away, causing the air around the eleven men to reverberate with each massive thump.

Two of the horses reared in fright, throwing the warders clear, then bolted from beneath the protection of the shield. Both were struck instantly, and Croneam was glad the thundering of the stones drowned out the sounds of their dying. The area beyond Lord Nid's shield disappeared beneath a crushing layer of death, and a cloud of dust washed over everything, obscuring Croneam's vision and causing him to cover his mouth and nose in order to breathe.

As the shield above them continued to shake and tremble, Lord Nid's face grew tight with the effort of holding it up, and Croneam's fear that the Meleki wouldn't have strength enough to outlast the slide came true a moment later when a massive boulder struck the southern edge of the shield, punching its way through. It struck the ground and took a sideways bounce, clipping one of the horses in the rump and knocking it into a second. Both animals went down, and the warders were tossed clear. One landed in the rubble outside the shielded area and disappeared from view.

Croneam pursed his lips sadly, not needing to see the man's crushed and tattered form to know that he was already dead. If this lasted much longer, they would all be sharing the fallen warder's fate.

Holding his horse steady, he listened as the rumbling began to subside, eventually dying to nothing more than intermittent thumps against the shield. Lord Nid stood motionless, his eyes closed, his copper-colored face pinched in concentration. The fine lines of purple spider-webbing his skin had grown more pronounced — a sign, Croneam decided, of the Meleki King's anger.

When all had faded into silence, Lord Nid tilted the shield to the side and dumped a layer of rubble that would have filled three or four wagons. Letting the shield drop, he moved to the warders who'd been thrown and healed them of their injuries. Then he healed the horses. When he turned to regard the warder buried beneath the pile of boulders, a look of sadness washed over his face. With a gentle wave of his hand, he removed the pile of stones with the Power, then wrapped the man in his cloak to hide the injuries. The limp form floated over to lay across an empty saddle. When Lord Nid sagged tiredly, Croneam knew he had released the Power.

He dismounted and moved to stand beside him. "You did well, Dymas," he told the Meleki King. "The rest of us owe you our lives."

Lord Nid frowned. "But it wasn't enough," he said quietly. "And that has been the story of my life. I give my all only to learn I couldn't give enough."

Croneam put a hand on his shoulder and looked him in the eye. "We all have our limits," he told him. "But when we give our all, we *are* giving enough."

Lord Nid nodded, but he didn't seem convinced. Turning, he pointed to the cliff face where the rock slide had originated. "I probed the area with my Awareness," he said, "and discovered that this was not a natural occurrence. It was the work of an Agla'Con. I felt the signature corruption left behind by the wielder. A very clever wielder since the majority of the work was done earlier today, making it so that only a small amount of the Power was needed to trigger it." He clenched his teeth angrily. "The enemy knew we would be coming."

"Then why not simply attack us with the Power instead of trying to make it look like an accident?" Teig Ole'ar asked, moving his horse near.

"Because *that* I would have felt," Lord Nid replied firmly. "And I would have sent the fool who attacked us to join Maeon in Con'Jithar."

Croneam studied the cliff face for a moment before speaking. "Then it seems our enemy knows their limits as well. But more importantly," he added, turning to study Lord Nid, "it means whoever did this knew you would be coming with us. They were trying to kill you."

Surprisingly, the Meleki King chuckled. "That, too, is the story of my life."

Teig Ole'ar stepped from the boardwalk of the Mendel Pass Waypost barracks and made his way toward the line of horses tethered along the outside of the corral. Croneam was already there, checking the straps on his saddle. Beyond him the eastern horizon was nothing more than a faint strip of early morning grey above the bulk of Talin Plateau. Apparently, the aging general was eager to make up the time they'd lost due to yesterday's event in the pass. The loss of two horses had forced some of the warders to ride double, and that had slowed them down. Today they would ride hard.

The riding he didn't mind. It was the idea of going back through the Tunnel that tied his insides into knots. All that stone above him, the feeling of a lack of air — it made him want to give up his job as Master of Spies and go hide in Elva. Riding through the Tunnel the first time was the most nerve-wracking thing he'd ever done.

Moving to the line of horses, he greeted Croneam, then began checking over his own saddle as well. He didn't expect to find anything wrong with it, he just needed to do something to keep his mind off the inevitable return to the Tunnel. Unfortunately, nothing helped, and by the time the rest of the warders arrived and Croneam started away down the road, Teig felt like he was going to throw up. *I walked into the heart of darkness,* he told himself. *I saw Maeon reach through the Veil. I witnessed the Night of Blood in the Dome. I'll be fine.*

Besides, he added, *I've already ridden through the bloody thing once. What's another thirty-six miles through an eight-hundred-year-old tunnel?*

None of the rationales he could devise, however, did anything to calm his nerves.

So it was with a great deal of trepidation that he followed Croneam and the others from the main highway leading to Tradeston and angled across the grasslands toward a point several leagues north of the West Talin Rampway. It was a secluded area, partially hidden by clusters of paperbarks and dense stands of willows. The face of the plateau looming above was nearly vertical, a towering mass of grey-brown stone that gave no indication of the secret passage leading through it.

Shaking his head resignedly, he rode in self-imposed silence.

They reached the edge of the sheltering paperbarks shortly after midday and Croneam gestured with his hand. "The Kelsan Government owns all the land surrounding this area," he told Lord Nid. "The Fulrath High Command has stewardship over it. Several thousand acres that are off-limits to civilians. We tell them it is used for training horses and such, but really it is to keep this area secure. The Highwaymen from the two nearest Wayposts patrol it, but even they don't know what it is they are really protecting."

Croneam turned his horse down a narrow pathway through the willows, and Teig heard the *thump thump* of several deer bounding away. From the corner of his eye he saw several flashes of brown.

"Not that it would matter if someone did come here," the general added once they reached the hollow fronting the cliff face. "The Dymas who constructed the Tunnel warded it against discovery. There are only a handful of people with the knowledge to open it. And only if they have one of these." He held up the medallion he'd pulled from his pocket, a silver disk with the Fighting Lion of Fulrath raised in its center. The other side was centered with a large rectangular crystal of some sort.

Croneam dismounted and moved to the cliff face to trace a series of fine crags with his fingertips. The general moved a half dozen paces to his right, then stopped to feel around the underside of a slight outcropping. Nodding, he raised the medallion and pressed the crystal against the stone.

There was a click as the medallion attached itself to the stone and a soft stony hiss as a small section of the cliff slid aside to reveal a wheel similar to the one Teig had seen at the Fulrath end of the Tunnel. Croneam turned the wheel, and two massive slabs of stone that only moments before had been indistinguishable from the cliff face swung inward to reveal a passage that stretched away into blackness.

One of the warders moved inside to turn the wheel that activated the first stretch of glowstones, and Teig and the others followed. When they were all inside, Croneam removed the medallion and hastened inside as the doors began to swing slowly shut.

Teig watched longingly as the outside world shrank to a narrow slit and vanished with a grating boom. The sound reverberated behind him, long and hollow, and a chill raced up his spine. Taking a deep breath, he turned to face what he now knew to be his greatest fear.

"It's very quiet in here," Lord Nid said softly.

"No more so than a tomb," Teig commented dryly, aware that his shoulders were already hunching beneath the weight of the earth above his head. "Come on," he said, urging his horse forward. "The sooner we get going, the sooner we can get out of this hellhole."

Croneam laughed. "Lead the way, Master of Spies, and I shall tell of the wonders I discovered in the natural caverns through which this tunnel passes. Marvelous sights they were, and visible without the use of torch or glowstone. Did you know that there is a lichen that grows in the deep that makes its own light? Pretty amazing stuff, I assure you. Saved my life after I was attacked by wolfrats and the bloody things ran off with my glowstones. I would have likely fallen into one of the many bottomless holes if not for the lichen."

Teig pressed his eyes shut and did his best to ignore Croneam's words. It was difficult, but the laughing of the warders helped some. So did the *clop clop* of the horses' hooves echoing around them. He never would have guessed that General Croneam Eries, hero of the Battle of Greendom, would have such a wicked and torturous sense of humor.

Croneam took hold of the wheel that controlled the mile-long stretch of glowstones behind them but hesitated when he noticed a soft glow in the distance ahead. He checked the number on the wheel and found that they were still four miles short of the chamber beneath Fulrath's main fortress. Standing beside him, Tren, the warder who'd been about to activate the mile-long stretch ahead of them, saw it too.

"Someone else is in the Tunnel," Tren said. "Two, maybe three, sections ahead."

"I see it," Croneam said, then turned to Lord Nid. "Can you use your Awareness to get a look at who it is?" he asked.

"Already there," the Meleki King said, his eyes closed, his brow furrowed in concentration. After a moment, he spoke. "Unless you have a twin brother who's managed to cheat aging, I'd say it is your son."

Croneam gave a sigh of relief. "Good. After everything else that has gone wrong lately, I feared the enemy had discovered our secret."

"Don't be too happy," Lord Nid continued. "They are inspecting an area of damage along one side of the Tunnel."

"Another earthquake," Croneam muttered, and behind him Teig groaned.

"Don't worry, Master of Spies," Lord Nid told him, his eyes still closed. "The damage is minor. Nothing that would lead to the collapse of the hundreds of feet of earth above your head."

Teig shivered noticeably, and Croneam snorted a laugh, amused that the Meleki King had finally decided to join in the teasing. "Light the way," he told Tren. "Let's go see what my son is looking at."

"Don't just stand there," Joneam shouted. "Shoot the bloody thing!"

Crossbow strings twanged loudly as Generals Taggert Enue and Thad Chathem fired, and the wolfrat gave a hissing snarl of pain as the bolts took it in the side. Claws scratching loudly on the stone of the Tunnel floor, the wounded creature turned and bolted away down the passage.

Joneam growled a curse as he watched the creature getting away, then blinked in surprise when he spotted a group of men on horseback coming toward them. His surprise spiked sharply when, fifty or so yards short of the men, the wolfrat burst into flaming chunks of flesh that quickly flared to ash.

He turned to General Gefion. "It seems my father has a Dymas with him."

"Good," Gefion replied. "Maybe he can use the Power to seal this hole."

"I'm more concerned with the hole in the fortress," Joneam told him. "Wolfrats are only a minor nuisance compared to some of the other creatures that live in the deep. Not to mention the fact that the caverns running through the plateau now represent a pretty substantial threat to security."

"Do you really think anything besides a wolfrat could find their way around in that godforsaken maze?" General Gefion asked.

"I'm certainly not willing to risk it," Joneam insisted. "The sooner we close off the damaged areas the better."

"I'm not going to argue with that," Gefion said, then raised a crossbow and shot a wolfrat that was poking its head into the Tunnel. The bolt took the creature in the head and it dropped without a sound. "That's how you're supposed to shoot them," he told Taggert. "How did you get to be a general with such horrible aim?"

Taggert huffed himself indignantly, and Joneam turned away before their routine banter could resume. He moved instead toward his father and the other men coming up the Tunnel. Footsteps behind him caught his attention and he turned to find Elam Gaufin coming as well.

"I don't think I can make it through another one of their gab sessions," Elam told him. "I had to listen to Taggert all the way from Chellum." He glanced over his shoulder, his eyes narrowing with irritation. "The man never shuts up."

Joneam withheld comment. He'd known Taggert since the Battle of Greendom; and if Elam thought the general was talkative now, he should have seen him back then. The man could have talked a Darkling to death.

"Well met, General Eries," Croneam said when he reached them. "Well met, Captain Gaufin."

"Welcome back, Father," Joneam said. "I see you have a new friend."

Croneam nodded. "Let me introduce Lord Hulanekaefil Nid, High King of Melek."

To cover his astonishment, Joneam gave a slight bow. "Lord Nid," he said politely. "Welcome to Fulrath."

"Thank you, General," the Meleki replied. "It is a pleasure."

"Thank you for killing the wolfrat," Joneam told him. "You're a Dymas, I presume?"

"A very skilled one," Croneam said before Lord Nid could speak. "And one who has done things to change the course of the war." He gestured toward General Gefion and the others. "But come, we will talk of that later. Right now I want to know what happened."

Teig Ole'ar peered into the hole opened by the earthquake and tried unsuccessfully to suppress a shudder. General Gefion tossed a torch inside, but the dismal flame did little more than emphasize just how endless the narrow cavern beyond seemed to be. Greenish-yellow eyes stared at him from the black beyond the reach of the flame. *Wolfrats,* he decided. *Or worse.* Perhaps traveling through the Tunnel wasn't so bad after all. It was certainly safer than the maze of darkness that lay beyond the reach of General Gefion's torch.

Croneam clapped him on the shoulder, and Teig nearly bit his tongue in half to stifle a yelp. He turned to find the general gazing into the hole as well.

"Except for the wolfrats and a few other creatures like them," he said conversationally, "most of what lies in there is beautiful."

"I'll take your word for it," Teig told him, "since I don't plan on ever going into such a place." Croneam, he decided, was either the bravest man alive or else he was crazy.

Joneam stepped up to his father. "There is a similar break in section one of the Tunnel and a smaller break in the floor of a storeroom in the fortress' lower chamber. It's not much more than a crack, but it leads to a massive underground cavern that branches off in seven or eight directions."

"You went down it?" Teig asked, unable to hide his astonishment. Apparently, Joneam was as crazy as his father.

"Only as far as the cavern," Joneam told him. "I don't have a death wish." He glanced pointedly at his father. "Unlike some others who have gone into the labyrinth that is down there."

"The question I have," General Gefion said, cutting off whatever response Croneam had for Joneam, "is what to do about these holes." He turned to Lord Nid. "Can you..." he waved his hand at the rent, "...fix it with the Power?"

The Meleki King shook his head. "Not without alerting every Power-sensitive person or thing within five miles of the city. The amount of *Ta'shaen* required to fuse stone, and the time it would take to do it, would allow any

Agla'Con in the area to pinpoint this exact location. Your secret tunnel would be discovered."

"The wolfrat you destroyed," Elam Gaufin began, pointing down the Tunnel, "could not that also have been felt by an Agla'Con?"

"No," Lord Nid replied. "The strike was quick, and the amount of *Ta'shaen* needed was minimal. An Agla'Con would have had to be right here in the Tunnel to feel it."

Croneam laughed. "He wouldn't have destroyed it at all, but he thought it was a Shadowhound."

Lord Nid shrugged. "It was an honest mistake," he said. "The blasted thing was as big as a Shadowhound, and I've had far too many encounters with shadowspawn lately to just stand there and watch it bear down on me." He returned his attention to General Gefion. "The safest bet for the Tunnel," he continued, "will be to seal it off with regular stones and mortar."

"I agree," Croneam said. "I'll send a group of warders back down to see to it. In the meantime," he added, turning to Tren, "I want you and Avin to stay here and make sure no more wolfrats come into the Tunnel." He took a bundle of food from one of the saddlebags and tossed it to him. "Those who come to seal the Tunnel will relieve you." He gestured to two more of the warders. "Mindar and Percin will guard the break in section one."

"Excellent," Teig told them. "Now, can we get moving? I'm starting to feel like I can't breathe."

Croneam chuckled. "Lead the way, Master of Spies. Just keep a sharp eye out for any more wolfrats."

Teig tried to scowl at the aging general, but it was ruined by a shiver of disgust. Croneam burst out laughing, and Teig knew the general's teasing would make for a long two miles to the fortress.

ㅊ

After two days in a saddle, the cushioned, high-backed chairs of his study seemed softer than usual, and Croneam sighed wearily as he settled in. Taking a seat across the rug from him, Lord Nid sighed as well. The purple maturation lines crisscrossing his copper face had paled considerably since this morning, showing his fatigue. In light of all he'd done with the Power to save them in Mendel Pass, Croneam wasn't surprised. As soon as they were finished discussing a few items with Joneam, he would make sure the Meleki King was given a good meal and a quiet, well-furnished room.

There was a light rap on the door, and Joneam entered with a pitcher of ale and three mugs. Closing the door behind him, he moved to a small table and poured them each a drink. He served Lord Nid, then handed a mug to Croneam and took a seat.

"General Gefion has gone down to oversee the repairs to the Tunnel and the storeroom," he told them. "Taggert and Elam decided to return to their men." He took a sip of his ale. "You know, I like those two," he said. "Especially Elam. Seth Lydon chooses his men well."

"And what of our Elvan Master of Spies?" Croneam asked.

An amused smile broke over Joneam's face. "He went for a walk out in the Free Zone. Said he needed to be out in the open for a while. All that *rock and stone*, as he put it, has him on the verge of a nervous breakdown. You'd never know by looking at him that he waltzed into the center of Shadan's army, got a look at Maeon, and jumped through a hole in the Veil."

Lord Nid choked on his ale. "He did what?"

Joneam looked at him. "You didn't know? What did you three talk about for two days?"

"Everything but that, obviously," Lord Nid replied.

"Teig isn't much of a conversationalist," Croneam told his son, then changed the subject. "Have you learned anything about Tey?"

Joneam frowned. "Nothing." His demeanor sobered further, and Croneam thought he saw a hint of resignation in his son's eyes. That and a deep sadness. "And with as long as she has been gone," he added, "I'm starting to doubt we ever will."

"We'll find her," Croneam assured him. "Deep in my heart I know it." He steeled himself for his next question. "What of Cam and Hena?" he asked.

"They're doing better," Joneam said. "They've started talking more, and the nightmares aren't as frequent. Grief is starting to turn to anger — for Hena at least. Cam still has moments when he is inconsolable. He seems unwilling to accept that his parents aren't coming back."

Noticing the confused look on Lord Nid's face, Croneam took a moment to explain. "The night of the Dragon Festival," he began, doing his best to ignore the cold fist of grief starting to close around his heart, "two Riaki Deathsquads came for me in Greendom." He stopped, his throat tightening with pain and rage. Neither he nor Joneam had spoken of the incident very much. Thinking about it now was like shoving a knife through his already wounded heart. *Focus on your rage*, he told himself. *Your grief will only cripple you.*

"I was here in Fulrath," he continued, his voice full of bitterness. "The Shizu killed my wife and my son and daughter-in-law. They spared two of my grandchildren, Cam and Hena, but took Tey, the youngest, when they left. The kidnapping isn't unusual — the Riaki often take hostages to use as barter — but we have received no word from Riak. No demands. No offer to trade Tey for anything. Nothing."

"Equally troubling," Joneam added, "is the fact that one of the squads — the one that took Tey — killed the second squad. All six of their bodies were found at my brother's house. I know enough about the Shizu code to tell you that is highly unusual. Forbidden, in fact."

"The dead squad bore the mark of Samochi," Croneam said. "Obviously, they have a rival willing to break the code to get what they want. As painful as the loss of my family is, it shows me once again that Riak is politically unstable. It is an instability I plan to exploit. I'm going to give our neighbors to the south a war they will never forget."

Lord Nid was quiet for a moment before speaking. "I will keep Tey in my prayers," he said softly, "and I will go to Cam and Hena at once. I can't remove the memory of what happened to their parents, but I can lessen the pain of that memory and give them comfort through *Ta'shaen*. I can speed up their emotional healing."

"I would appreciate that," Croneam told him. "When we finish here, Joneam will take you to the children. They are staying with his wife and children at his estate. You can stay there until it is time to march to Zedik Pass. Joneam has an extra room that will certainly be quieter than any here in the fortress."

Lord Nid dipped his head in gratitude. "After everything I have been through lately, that will be a most welcome respite."

"Well, I also think it would be wise to keep your presence here a secret." Croneam told him. "The way some on the High Tribunal acted toward you was but a shadow of the hard feelings that might exist among the men who fight Meleki Shadan Cultists on a regular basis. I certainly don't want some over-zealous soldier putting an arrow in your back."

He turned back to Joneam. "We will need to address the bureaucracy and the Merchants' Guild as soon as possible," he said, "and begin plans for an evacuation of all non-military personnel. Greendom will also need to be evacuated, as well as all outlying farms and villages. I don't know how much time we have before Shadan's armies will begin marching through the pass, but I suspect it won't be long."

Perched atop a jagged peak overlooking Zedik Pass, Zeniff's K'rresh fidgeted anxiously, and he reached down to pat its neck. "Easy my pet," he soothed.

"We'll fly soon enough."

Sitting straight once more, he gazed at the vast expanse of campfires spreading out from the eastern mouth of the pass and smiled smugly. This was a moment he wanted to enjoy. He'd come to the Meleki camp to see if he could discover who had tampered with the Satyr he'd used during the attack in the Dome. Instead he had learned about Aethon's artificial T'rii Gate. He'd also gotten close enough to the gate while Aethon was using it to learn how the rending was done. It was valuable knowledge, to be sure, and something he would very much like to duplicate. He simply wasn't strong enough on his own to do it.

With something like Aethon's gate to assist him, however, it might be possible to rend the Veil without help from other Agla'Con, and he would be free to carry out his plans for the conquest of Trian.

He glanced down at the much smaller cluster of campfires at the mouth of the narrows, midway through Zedik Pass, then turned his attention back to the main camp. It angered him that Aethon had managed to keep such a marvelous creation hidden from him. Even worse was how his spies in the Meleki camp had failed to mention it in any of their reports. *It must be new,* he thought. *Otherwise I would have known of it.* The only other possibility was that his spies had been killed or turned against him by Aethon — something that was very plausible considering how the bloody, self-righteous fool liked to meddle in other people's affairs.

Well, he thought, reaching up to scratch his cheek, *I can do a fair bit of meddling myself.* One or two more trips into Aethon's camp to study the gate and he should be able to create a gate of his own. True, he wasn't as strong as Aethon or Gideon, or even as strong as that fool Shalan Ras had been, but he was a fast learner and as skilled as Gideon himself when it came to most things.

He smiled. Unlocking the secret of Aethon's gate should return him to an equal standing with the traitorous Fairimor. *And then I will see what I can do about reorganizing the Agla'Con hierarchy.*

Satisfied that the night had been productive after all, he urged his K'rresh into the air and started back toward Trian. Gideon and the others would be leaving for Thesston this morning — may have left already if he knew anything about the aging Dymas — so life in the palace should return to normal for a while. At least as far as he was concerned. Not being able to seize the Power for the past week had grated on his nerves as badly as the loss of so many of his chapter houses.

But that is about to change, he thought with a smile. *With Gideon and Jase away, Elison Brey and that bloody Breiter Lyacon will be easy prey.* A few days to follow their movements, and he would be ready for them when they raided the next chapter house. Only this time they would find more than a handful of unsuspecting Con'Kumen worshipers. This time they would walk into the jaws of hell.

He threw his head back and laughed. With Death's Third March poised and ready at Zedik Pass and the Con'Kumen organized in Trian, Kelsa was about to be crushed from within as well as from without. "The end is near," he told the night sky. "And I will be victorious."

Yes, he thought. *And then Trian will be mine.*

CHAPTER 9

Feelings that Linger

Dawn was still an hour away when Jase climbed into the coach bound for Thesston and took a seat next to Talia. He smiled at her, then turned to gaze out the window. For reasons he couldn't explain, leaving Fairimor Palace was proving more difficult than he'd imagined it would be. His acceptance of his birthright had a lot to do with it, especially now that he had issued a challenge to Shadan, Aethon, and any number of others who might take exception to his crowning the Dome with Fire. It didn't seem right to leave so soon after drawing the kind of attention that might provoke an attack. Without him or Gideon around to combat any shadowspawn, he feared Elison and Breiter might have to face more than they could handle.

Then again, he amended, *it was me and Gideon that drew the shadowspawn here in the first place.* Leaving was probably the best thing they could do. He hoped so; he didn't want to think he might be abandoning his friends to their doom. He hoped they would be careful in their efforts to eradicate the Con'Kumen.

Elison shut the coach door and peered through the window. His moonlit profile held a smile as he spoke. "You stay out of trouble."

"That's funny," Jase said. "I was about to say the same thing to you."

Elison's smile deepened, and he thumped the door to signal the driver. "Be careful," he said and vanished as the coach lurched forward.

"You too," Jase whispered into the dark, unable to suppress the sadness washing through him.

Across from him, Thorac grunted. "Don't worry about him," the Chunin said. "Elison has more sand in his craw than a black-crested fighting rooster."

"Don't those fight to the death?" Elliott asked.

"Ah, yes. I suppose they do," Thorac answered. "Sorry, Jase. Bad comparison."

"I knew what you meant," he said, shooting Elliott a dark look.

"Ignore my idiot brother," Talia whispered into his ear, and her warm breath sent a pleasant shiver through him.

He turned to smile at her, and there was enough light from the glowposts lining the streets for him to see the smile she flashed in return. She leaned against him and lay her head on his shoulder. Normally, the confining interior of a coach made him feel like he was suffocating, but the soft warmth of Talia's body and the sweet scent of her hair chased the feeling away. Maybe this wouldn't be such a bad way to travel after all.

Fifteen leagues and several hours later, Jase changed his mind about the coach. It was hot and stuffy, and if he had to listen to one more of Thorac's or Elliott's stories, he was going to puke. To make matters worse, Talia had switched to the other coach shortly after sunup. She'd said it was so she could practice using her Gift under Gideon's direction, but he suspected it was to get away from her brother. He shook his head. *Whatever possessed them to ride in the same coach in the first place?*

He'd wanted to move to the other coach as well, but Endil hadn't wanted to trade, and Gideon wouldn't allow two Fairimors to be in the same coach in case they were attacked. *We must protect the last of the Fairimor bloodline,* he had said. *One of you has to make it to Thesston and back.*

So here he was, stuck in a dark box on wheels with two talkative fools who couldn't get enough of the sound of their own voices. He'd tried reading the book Gideon had given him — a collection of historical battles between Dymas and Agla'Con and the prophecies those battles had fulfilled — but reading while the countryside of Trian Plateau flowed past his window made him feel sick to his stomach. His only options at that point had been to sleep or look out the window. Unfortunately, the view of Trian Plateau was lackluster at best, nothing more than fields and grassland interspersed occasionally by a village or ranch.

Leaning back in the cushioned seat, he closed his eyes and forced himself to relax. Thorac and Elliott continued to prattle on about the many *manly* adventures they'd had, but he ignored them as best he could. He focused instead on the pounding of the horses' hooves and the rumble of the wheels on the highway and let the sounds drown out Elliott and Thorac.

It seemed only minutes before the coach creaked to a halt and he sat up, casting about groggily. He rubbed the sleep from his eyes and peered out the window. The warders still formed ranks around them, but Jase could see a cluster of buildings beyond and a group of Highwaymen moving about. They had reached the Southern Rim Waypost.

The coach door opened, and Seth motioned them out. "We're swapping some of the horses for fresh ones," he told them. "Feel free to stretch your legs while we wait."

Jase was happy to oblige and eased himself out of the coach to stretch his aching muscles. A short distance away Talia and Endil were doing the same. Talia saw him and smiled warmly. He was about to smile in return when Elliott made a snide remark. Jase scowled at him, then turned away to enjoy the fresh air and the view. Mostly it was to keep himself from punching the Chellum Prince in the mouth.

To the west the sun was dropping behind the Kelsan Mountains, and the low angle painted the underside of the clouds in hues of purple and orange. A line of darker clouds was building above the jagged horizon to the southwest, a wall of black that spoke of heavy rains. Thorac noticed them as well.

"That makes me even more thankful to be riding in a coach," the Chunin commented. "The only thing worse than riding one of those demons you call a horse, is doing so while you're wet."

"I would ride in the worst of storms *naked* if it meant I didn't have to listen to any more of your stories," Jase told him, then walked away before Thorac or Elliott could respond. When he looked back, he found them looking at one another as if they had no idea what he was talking about. Jase rolled his eyes in disgust.

"...an hour to reach the bottom of the rampway," he heard Seth tell Gideon as he drew near. "But with fresh horses we can be in Tri-fork by nightfall. The horses will have the night to rest."

"Good," Gideon said. "Have two warders ride ahead to Tri-fork and obtain lodgings for us at one of the inns. One of the nicer inns, since Randle is paying."

"Yes, Dymas," Seth answered, then moved away.

"There you are," Gideon said when he spotted Jase. "How is the trip so far?"

"I'd tell you," Jase replied, "but I'd have to use a lot of profanity to describe it completely, and we have a lady present."

Talia smiled. "If you're talking about my brother, any words you used couldn't be worse than those I chose."

"I'll say," Endil said, adjusting the dartbow belted around his waist as he moved to join Elliott and Thorac at the other coach.

"I guess that means you'll be riding with us the rest of the way," Talia said, flashing a smile that quickened Jase's pulse.

Before he could return the smile, Gideon destroyed all hope of a pleasant ride. "Excellent," the big Dymas said, clapping him on the shoulder. "It will give us time to work on your abilities with *Ta'shaen*."

"Great," Jase said with mock enthusiasm. "I can't wait."

By the time they reached the outskirts of Tri-fork, however, Jase would have done anything to be back in the other coach, his friends' manly-adventure chatter or no. Listening to Elliott and Thorac babble was nothing compared to the torture Gideon had put him through by having him hone his Awareness of *Ta'shaen* and the unseen spiritual world it opened to his mind's eye. The practice was grueling and left him with a raging headache. Still, he had mastered it to the point that he picked up on the residue of evil left behind by the Shadowhound attack on Breiter's decoy at Tri-fork Bridge.

"Excellent," Gideon said. "As old as that disturbance is, your sensing it is remarkable."

"It's like a stain," Jase said, his eyes still closed. In the shimmering blue outline that was the spiritual fabric of the world, the area where the Shadowhounds had attacked was clouded — a murky film of black against an otherwise luminescent landscape.

He opened his eyes to find Gideon looking at him. "Some acts of evil are so great," the Dymas said, "that the stain, as you called it, lingers. For weeks, months, or even years. Sometimes it can linger indefinitely. There are places where the very fabric of life itself has turned dark. Places like the Pit, Shadan's throne room, and other chambers dedicated to the worship of Maeon." He paused briefly. "Or, as is the case with the Valley of Amnidia, an entire region."

"Where the Soul Chamber is," Jase said. "Wonderful."

"Getting there will be difficult, certainly," Gideon answered, "but I've done it before. As long as we are careful not to use the Power, we should be able to slip through the area unnoticed. *Ta'shaen* draws the Shadan'Ko the same way it draws other shadowspawn."

Jase nodded but said nothing, choosing instead to gaze out the window at the lights of Tri-fork glimmering in the distance ahead.

They reached the village a short time later, and the driver turned down a wide side street. A few people were still moving about outside, but most of the village's residents had retired for the evening. The coaches creaked to a stop in front of *Tri-fork Inn*.

"Get something to eat and get to bed," Gideon told them as they exited the coach. "We will be leaving first thing in the morning."

Jase wasn't going to argue. He was tired and hungry, and he had a headache from being cooped up all day. He took Talia by the arm and escorted her inside.

The common room of the inn was mostly empty — not surprising considering the late hour — but it was brightly lit for those few patrons not yet willing to retire for the evening. In one corner a group of rough-looking men played cards, while near the door, a man and woman were finishing a meal. A few other men and women were scattered about, sipping at drinks as they talked quietly to one another. They looked up as he and Talia entered but quickly began studying the inside of their glasses when Gideon came in with Elliott and Thorac.

Jase couldn't tell if it was the sight of the big Dymas in his forbidding robes that caused the people to look away or the weapons displayed by Elliott and Thorac. Whatever the case, it was obvious the people didn't like what they saw. Some of the frowns being directed into those drinks looked downright hostile.

Wait until they get a look at the warders guarding this place, he thought, moving farther into the room. *That will change their attitudes.*

The sound of booted feet on the stairs at the far end of the room caught his attention, and he looked up to see Seth and another man coming down from the rooms above. Judging by the apron around the man's waist, Jase surmised he was the inn's owner. Seth spotted them and moved to speak with Gideon. The innkeeper stayed a few steps behind and wrung his hands nervously as he eyed the twin swords nestled on Seth's hips.

"This place will do," Seth told them. "Eight rooms in a single hallway, and stairs leading out the back of the building should we need to leave quickly. If you'd like, I can have the coaches wait near the stairs until morning."

Gideon glanced around the room. "That will be fine," he said, keeping his voice low. "Do the warders have a schedule for keeping watch?"

"Yes."

The innkeeper stepped forward timidly. "But Master Zephan," he said to Seth, "I can assure you there will be no trouble. Masil and Dramblin there," he said, indicating two of the men playing cards, "work for me. They are quite capable of keeping the peace."

Seth eyed the two men for a second, then turned his gaze on the innkeeper. "I'm sure they are, Master Heathser, if by trouble you mean drunken misconduct or a card game gone sour. They may even be able to handle a cutpurse or two. But..." he leaned forward and his voice dropped to a whisper, "those who would do us harm are none of those. Masil and Dramblin would be dead before they knew what it was they faced."

The innkeeper blinked and swallowed. "I'll take your word for it."

"Good," Seth said. "I lost a friend in Tri-fork a few weeks ago. A messy affair out on the bridge...." He hesitated to let the words sink in, then added, "Trust me when I say your men are way out of their league."

Master Heathser's face paled. "Ah, yes, I heard about that," he said with a shudder. "And I'm, ah, sorry about your friend."

Seth turned back to Gideon. "Food has already been taken to the rooms. I know it will be a sacrifice for some, but I think we can do without a bath." He looked pointedly at Talia. She muttered something unintelligible, and Seth smiled at her. With a gesture toward the stairs he bowed with mock sincerity. "I'm sure my lady will survive," he told her, and the glare she threw at him only made his smile broaden.

"Master Heathser," Gideon said, "thank you for your hospitality. If there is anything else we need, we'll let you know."

The dismissal was obvious, and the innkeeper beat a hasty retreat for the kitchens.

"Master Zephan?" Jase asked, arching an eyebrow.

"I've found it wise not to use my real name when traveling," Seth told him darkly. "A principle you of all people should understand."

"I wasn't questioning the principle," Jase countered, careful to keep his voice down. "But Zephan in the Old Tongue means 'lost one'."

"Wrong," Seth countered. "It means 'one who hides.' Appropriate considering our circumstances."

Thorac yawned as he moved past. "The night is slipping away," he said. "The rest of you can stand here in the doorway if you want, but I need food and sleep."

"Endil," Seth said, "go with him. You two are sharing a room. Elliott will share with Gideon. And Jase, before he gets his hopes up, will be in my room. Talia needs her privacy." The Chellum captain grinned at him. "It is the last room on the left. Your bunk is the top. That way I can kick you in the back if you snore."

Jase's smile was withering.

Gideon chuckled. "I'll set a perimeter warding," he told Seth. "Nothing fancy, but your warders will know if any shadowspawn come near."

"That will be fine," Seth replied as he started for the door. "I'll have the coaches moved around back."

Gideon motioned toward the stairs. "Go get some sleep, Jase. Morning will be here sooner than you think."

By the time the third nightmare woke him, Jase was thinking morning couldn't arrive soon enough. His back hurt from the lumps in the mattress, and the bed was a few inches too short for him to fully stretch out. Plus it squeaked when he moved, and he was afraid he was keeping Seth awake as well.

But the nightmares were the main cause of his insomnia, horrifying images that once again had him wielding *Ta'shaen* like an Agla'Con. It was enough to sour his stomach and wet the sheets with his sweat.

He rolled onto his other side, trying to keep the squeaks to a minimum, and closed his eyes once more. Careful not to embrace the Power itself, he reached out with his Awareness and let the soothing tingle of Earthpower caress his mind. For once, he did it right. He fell asleep a few minutes later.

He stands in a blackened, desolate wasteland. All around him the skeletal shapes of trees stab skyward, misshapen daggers with bark scarred and pitted as if burned by acid. The sky is a murky, swirling mass of clouds. Smoke the color of blood rises from fissures in the ground. To the north a mountain rages in fury, spewing columns of black smoke as glowing rivers of red magma snake down its slopes. Fires dance through a ruined forest at the mountain's base where fingers of molten rock ignite trees in their passing. Lightning stabs earthward as the rising smoke fuels a growing storm. Flashes of white light the area around him.

He's been here before. Three times already, in fact, and he knows now what to expect.

He doesn't have to wait long before they appear. Hundreds at first, and then thousands, the Shadan'Ko slip from the broken landscape around him, drawn, he knows, by the Talisman pulsating at his chest.

They are repulsive creatures, more animal now than human, twisted by the evil stain left behind by Throy Shadan and his Agla'Con during the Battle of Amnidia. Their eyes glow with a feral light, and they growl deeply in their throats, a horrifying mewing that sounds like a rabid lion.

The first three times he'd come to this place, he had lashed out at them with the Power, burning them and the surrounding trees to ash. Each time, he had awakened with a gasp to find himself in an inn in Tri-fork. He knows this is a dream. This very moment his body lies in a bunk above Seth Lydon. He is aware of it even now, so many hundred leagues to the south. He can feel the uncomfortable lumps and the not-quite-long-enough length of the bed.

But none of that matters. Only the Shadan'Ko matter.

He knows the dream is trying to tell him something. He knows that he failed the first three times he came here. Gripping the Talisman, he draws in an ocean of Ta'shaen and prepares to strike them down again if necessary. He watches them advance, but this time he withholds his strike.

When they are within a dozen feet of him, a strange thing happens: the Shadan'Ko begin to kneel, prostrating themselves before him in a display of reverence. Those few who gaze up at him do so with eyes filled with what can only be described as hope —

eyes that show a faint trace of humanity in an otherwise savage face.

"Make us whole," *they whisper, and the Power flares within him.*

Jase sat up with a start, jarring the bed so roughly that Seth stirred below him.

"What's wrong?" the captain asked.

"The Shadan'Ko," he answered, still somewhat dazed. "They... they came to me for help."

Seth grunted. "Those miserable creatures are beyond help," he muttered. "Go back to sleep."

Jase lay back down and fingered the Talisman on his chest. *Beyond help,* he agreed silently. But now he wasn't so sure.

Breakfast the following morning was a meal even Andil would have had a hard time complaining about, a feast of sausages and eggs and sweetbreads as good as anything Allisen could have fixed. It was a man's meal if ever he saw one. And plenty of it.

Master Heathser knew what he was about when it came to feeding a dozen warders and those they guarded. Jase figured Tri-fork's location midway between two Wayposts had taught the innkeeper a thing or two about cooking for large groups of men. He'd heard Captain Nian complain about military food, so it was likely the Highwaymen made up a large percentage of Heathser's customers.

"Isn't there any fruit?" Talia asked as she eyed the sausages with disgust.

"My lady," Heathser said, sounding offended. "The food I prepare is according to season. And it is spring. Any fruit I had was gone months ago." He set another tray of sweetbreads before the warders at an adjacent table, then returned to the kitchen.

"This isn't Chellum Palace," Seth told her. "Heathser can't afford to pay the prices fruit merchants charge to ship things this far north." He leaned forward and his eyes were hard. "You would do well to remember that we are no longer in Chellum or Trian. Questions such as the one you just asked tend to arouse the wrong kind of curiosity. Even the dumbest of thieves would get the idea you might be *accustomed* to fruit out of season. That you can afford it is the next logical conclusion. Let's not draw any more attention to ourselves than necessary."

Talia looked pointedly at the Elvan warders seated around the room before turning back to Seth. "My mistake," she said flippantly. "I'm sure we blend right in."

Jase had to work hard to suppress a smile, but Seth was not amused.

"Give a thief reason to believe the payoff outweighs the risk of robbing and even a group our size can be attacked. With as many enemies as we seem to already have, I'd appreciate it if you didn't add robbers to the list."

Talia was silent as she glared back at Seth, and her eyes glittered emerald fire. Jase braced himself for an explosion, but it never came. After a moment, Talia's anger faded. "As usual, you are right," she said softly. "And I'm sorry."

Seth shrugged and went back to his food.

For the rest of the meal, conversation was at a minimum. The other patrons, what few there were with so many warders filling the place, kept their eyes fastened on their own tables as if ignoring the armed men might make them disappear. Talia picked at her food but ate little, and Seth watched her without comment. When the last of the warders finished and rose to leave, Seth rose with them.

"We'll leave as soon as you finish," he told them. "If you want to pick what coach you ride in, I'd get out there before Elliott and Thorac." Jase followed Seth's gaze to where the Prince and the Chunin were gabbing around mouthfuls of food.

Bloody...! They're at it already. "I'm finished," he said and stood.

Talia rose with him, and they went out to stake their claim on a coach.

"Warder," Talia called to one of the men as they neared.

"Yes, my lady?"

"Will you fetch me that leather case there on the coach? The blue lacquered one with the funny shape."

"Of course," he answered and turned from the horse he was hitching to retrieve it for her.

"I could have gotten it for you," Jase whispered.

"I know you could have," she said. "But Elliott is the one who *borrowed* it from Fairimor Palace, and he'll be furious when he finds it's missing. Let him be mad at me, not you."

"What's in it?"

She smiled. "You'll see."

She didn't open it until they were safely inside the coach, and Jase found himself staring at an extremely fine-crafted guitar. It was cherry-colored with ivory pegs and looked like it would sound incredible. Talia set the case on the floor next to her feet and held the guitar on her lap without playing.

"Once we're moving," she said, patting the glossy instrument. "Maybe it will help the time pass a little more pleasantly."

"I'm sure it will," he said. "As long as you don't want me to sing with you. My mother says I sound like a tone deaf cat with a hangover."

"Oh, come now, you can't be that bad," she said.

"Trust me," Jase told her emphatically. "At Church Day services I've been asked by those sitting near me to hum the words instead of sing them."

"How rude," she said, but he could tell she was trying not to smile.

The door opened, and Talia tightened her grip on the guitar, flinching as if she were considering trying to hide it somewhere. She relaxed when she saw it was Gideon.

He climbed in and sat across from them. His eyes fell on the guitar. "Well," he said, his face brightening. "I had considered riding in the other coach today so I could speak with Endil, but it looks as if the entertainment is in here."

Talia smiled. "You don't mind, then?"

"It will be a pleasure," he told her.

A moment later the door opened again and Seth stuck his head in. "Everything is ready, Dymas," he said. "I am going to ride ahead with a couple of the warders to make sure the way is clear."

"That will be fine," Gideon told him. "But we don't need to go as far as we had originally planned. We will be staying in Kindel's Grove this evening."

"It will cost us valuable time," Seth warned. "I thought we had decided on Jenin. Stopping before then negates what we have done to this point. I thought the goal was to reach Thesston as quickly as possible."

"It is," Gideon said, "but we *must* stop in Kindel's Grove. I can't explain why. But the feeling is one I can't ignore. When the Earthsoul whispers, I obey."

Seth was quiet a moment, his eyes narrow as he weighed Gideon's words. "It will be as you say, Dymas," he answered, and for once there was no bitterness in his words. Jase realized that whatever had just passed between the two men was something that had happened many times before. Seth, it seemed, was wise enough to trust Gideon's premonitions in spite of how it affected the job he had undertaken to do.

"Be wary," Gideon continued. "I'm sensing other stirrings in *Ta'shaen* that hint of trouble to come."

"Any idea what kind of trouble?" Seth asked.

Gideon shook his head. "No. But something is... wrong. I can't pinpoint what exactly — it may be nothing — but it feels like something big is about to happen."

"Of course it is," Seth said. "We haven't been attacked in over two days. We're long overdue."

"I'm serious," Gideon said darkly.

"So am I," Seth answered, then turned to Talia. "I know it isn't much," he said, handing her a small bundle wrapped in cloth, "but it's all I could find in a town this small." He closed the door before she could say anything. He called for the driver to move out, and the coach lurched into motion.

Jase watched curiously as Talia loosed a knot to reveal an apple, a banana, and a half dozen strawberries. She gasped in surprise and smiled, but tears formed at the corners of her eyes for the warder who, in spite of harsh lectures, had found her the breakfast she wanted.

Jase smiled. Many times while growing up, he had experienced similar acts of kindness from the grizzled warrior. Each time he had been as surprised and delighted as Talia was now. He suspected that Seth's hard-nosed approach to life made these little moments that much more meaningful. The man may look hard as stone on the outside, might even act as if he had no heart, but actions like this destroyed the facade. Underneath his rough exterior, Seth Lydon had the heart of an angel.

Talia offered him a strawberry, but he refused; Seth's gift was for her. He tried not to watch too openly as she ate, but it was hard. She was so incredibly beautiful that even something as commonplace as eating was a sight to behold. The way the little muscles of her jaw worked...

He forced himself to look out the window, once again embarrassed by his thoughts. The world was dying, every Agla'Con in the world was looking to kill him, and he sat here wondering what it would be like to kiss that part of her neck just below her jaw. He really was an idiot.

When she finished eating, she positioned the guitar on her lap and began to play.

Jase watched her fingers move along the strings and marveled once again at her talent for music. He didn't recognize the tune she was playing, but it didn't matter. It was beautiful. Almost as beautiful as the woman playing it, he thought, sneaking a look at her face. Her eyes were closed and her head bobbed slightly as she followed the rhythm in her mind.

When Gideon began to sing, he and Talia stared at him in wonder. The Dymas' voice was strong and deep, a perfect match for the music.

> *From the mountains, plains, and isles of the sea,*
> *come ye people of the earth and rejoice in what will be.*
> *The bridegroom from the heartland and the maiden from the east*
> *are joined by power unending, behold the marriage feast.*
> *And in this holy union, salvation's seed is sown.*
> *Soon comes the child Fairimor, the one who'll lead us home.*
> *Raise your voices up t'ward heaven, in songs of praise and joy,*
> *for the ancient blood will rise again, awakened by a boy.*

When the song ended, Talia and Gideon sat looking at each other.

"I didn't know there were words to that music," Talia said after a moment.

"I didn't think anyone knew the music," Gideon said. "It is titled *The Marriage Feast* and refers to the joining of Temifair and Imor. It is an old song, a very old song, in fact. Written more than a thousand years ago, if my memory serves me. Where did you learn it?"

"The libraries at Jyoai College have many collections of music," she answered. "This was one I learned to play there."

"Jyoai, you say?" Gideon said, pursing his lips thoughtfully. "I guess I shouldn't be surprised. They have many things other libraries don't, with particular attention given to the arts." He smiled. "What else do you have stored in that lovely head of yours?"

Talia smiled at the compliment and closed her eyes as she considered. "There is this one," she said and began playing. It was a softer piece than the first, with a sad almost mournful sound to it. "It was untitled as well, but I learned it anyway. I know it sounds sad, but there is something very beautiful about it."

When Gideon didn't respond, Jase looked up to find the Dymas' eyes glistening and his face pinched tight with pain. Talia saw it too and stopped playing.

"I'm sorry," she said hurriedly, "I didn't mean..."

"Don't stop," Gideon said softly. "It's all right. I just haven't heard that one for quite some time. It surprised me, that's all."

"Do you know the words?" Talia asked.

"There are no words," Gideon replied, motioning for Talia to continue. "No words could ever do justice to the pain I felt when I composed that song."

"You composed it?" Talia gasped, her fingers tripping over the strings. She recovered quickly, but amazement still painted her face.

"I wasn't always a Dymas," he told them as if that explained everything. When they continued to stare at him, he went on. "Music was one of many things I loved to do." He shrugged. "One of many things I had to give up in order to do what was needed of me. There wasn't time to do both."

"There is time now," Talia said, handing him the guitar.

Gideon hesitated, so she pressed it forward even more firmly. "Please, Dymas," she said. "It will be good for you to play again."

Gideon nodded and rested the instrument on his lap. His large fingers dwarfed the strings, but he played as deftly and delicately as Talia had. It was the same sad tune, but the knowledge that Gideon had composed it, made it sound that much more heart-wrenching. It made Jase wonder what had happened to inspire such a sad tune, but he knew better than to ask. Anything that could have wounded Gideon's heart so horribly was probably best left unknown.

He leaned back in his seat and listened in awe until Gideon finished.

"That was wonderful," Talia said, clapping her hands in approval. "I feel honored to have heard it played by the creator."

"And I'm honored that you liked it enough to learn it," Gideon replied as he returned the guitar to her. "And a little surprised. I thought I had destroyed every last copy of that music."

"Why would you want to do that?" Talia gasped, truly horrified.

Gideon made a placating gesture with his hand. "You've made me glad that I didn't. But please, let's hear something with a little more joy in it, shall we? Do you know *The Tale of Glendair?*"

Talia played a few notes. "Is this it?"

"Perfect," Gideon said, then turned to Jase. "Come on, Jase. Let's hear you sing too."

Talia smiled her encouragement, and Jase shrugged. "Okay, but I warned you."

Reaching the Omer Forest Waypost came as a disappointment to Talia, but she climbed out of the coach to stretch her legs anyway. She, Jase, and Gideon had been having such a marvelous time singing — well she and Gideon had sung; Jase had... well... perhaps his mother's assessment of his abilities had been accurate after all. She smiled at him as he climbed out of the coach, and he looked around self-consciously. A few of the warders had shouted comments about his singing as they'd rode near the coach, and none had been very nice. They were eyeing him now as he stretched his legs, and several were still muttering insults.

Jase's face flushed red, but Talia couldn't tell if it was from anger or embarrassment. Impulsively she stepped over and kissed him on the cheek. "I think you have a lovely voice," she whispered and watched his face turn a deeper shade of red. The warders, she noted with some satisfaction, stopped their muttering.

"Oh no," Jase said, and Talia followed his gaze to see Elliott striding toward them.

Fortunately he didn't seem angry. "Gideon thanked me for letting him borrow the guitar," he said, then cast a wondering glance to where the Dymas stood speaking with the Waypost commander. "I didn't know he knew how to play."

"Neither did we," Talia told him, "but he is very good. You should listen to him sometime."

"I'd like to. Do you still have it in your coach?"

"I'll get it for you," she said and moved to retrieve it. She snugged it back in its case and fastened the catches before handing it to him. "I'm glad you thought to sneak it out of the Dome," she told him. "It has a lovely sound."

Elliott cast an embarrassed look at Jase. "I didn't steal it," he said. "Your aunt said I could borrow it." Shrugging his shoulders uncomfortably, he moved away.

When he was gone, Talia looked at Jase. "It seems Gideon took the blame for my borrowing the guitar from Elliott," she said. "That's twice today someone has done something unexpectedly nice for me."

Jase reached up and touched the spot on his cheek where she'd kissed him. "You deserve it for all the nice things you do for others."

She smiled warmly at him. "When I kissed you," she admitted, "it was only partly to silence the warders. It was mostly because I wanted to." She leaned in close and whispered, "Perhaps when there aren't so many eyes around, I'll give you a real kiss."

The earlier color in his cheeks was nothing compared to the flush of red that came next, and she grinned at him before turning to walk away, leaving him standing in shocked silence. She glanced back only once to see him staring after her. She knew she had been extremely forward with him, not just recently, but ever since they were kids. She simply couldn't help herself. He was gorgeous, and she loved him with all of her heart. It was a very nice feeling knowing that he felt the same. A very nice feeling indeed.

CHAPTER 10

Return to Kindel's Grove

Riding on top of the coach, Jase watched the leafy canopy streaming overhead and breathed in deeply. He loved traveling Forest Road, and not just because of the cool, leafy smell of the air or the vast stretches of deep shade, but because the road itself was in such great shape. He loved the stretch of road so much, in fact, that he'd talked Gideon into letting him ride up on top with the driver so he could fully enjoy it. The Dymas had refused at first, but Jase had argued that it was necessary to show the driver where to turn off to his home. Nevermind that Seth could ride there in his sleep; he'd wanted — needed — to ride up in the open air. Spending time beneath such a beautiful canopy while cooped up in the tiny confines of a coach was a crime against nature.

Besides, he'd needed some time away from Talia. The girl had really rattled his insides when she'd kissed him at the Waypost. And her promise of a *real* kiss had jumbled his wits so badly he could barely think. He could imagine what a real kiss from her might be like, and that was the problem — it made it hard to imagine anything else *but* kissing her.

And he didn't want to imagine. He wanted to kiss.

So here he sat, trying to keep his mind off her but unable to do so. The driver was about as much of a conversationalist as a glowstone and hadn't said more than six words in the last ten miles. *At least the air is nice,* he thought. *It sort of helps cool whatever fire Talia lit inside me.*

He could hear her below singing with Elliott, and the sound of their voices made him smile. It seemed the only time the two didn't fight like rabid dogs was when they were involved with music. *Or,* he amended silently, *when she was in danger from someone other than Elliott himself.* The time Elliott had stepped between her and the shadowspawn in Yucanter Forest was a perfect example.

He shook his head. It seemed an older brother's love meant Elliott could threaten to skin her alive one minute and be willing to die to protect her the next. It was one of the mysteries of sibling love and rivalry, he supposed. Odd, yet beautiful.

"That young lady has a great voice," the driver said, and Jase glanced over at him with raised eyebrows.

"Yes, she does," he agreed, wondering if the man was finally coming out of his self-imposed silence. "Kind of makes you want to join in doesn't it?"

The driver shrugged. "I s`pose," he said and fell silent once more. When it became apparent that he intended to remain silent, Jase went back to watching the trees.

Well, at least I know he can talk, he thought with a bewildered shake of his head. He had started to wonder if the man was a mute.

Talia's singing faded, and Jase sighed. He still didn't know what he was going to do about her. He was extremely attracted to her. He had told her in a letter that he loved her. But did he? How did one know something like that for sure? He simply couldn't say since he'd never actually been in love before. True, he loved Tana. But that was different; they had grown up together — practically as brother and sister. He and Tana were as close as two people could be without actually having romantic ties.

A sudden thought jarred him, and he had to stifle a groan. Tana was in Kindel's Grove, and she and Talia didn't like each other. Sure, they had only met once, but that single encounter resulted in a fight that could rival some of the conflicts he'd seen the past few weeks.

He ran his fingers through his hair and grimaced. Spending the night in Kindel's Grove meant the chances were pretty good that Tana would learn he was there and she and Talia would run into each other again. As perceptive as Tana was, she was bound to pick up on the fact that he and Talia liked each other. *Why didn't I see this coming?*

He must have spoken aloud because the driver was watching him. "Girl trouble?" he asked.

Jase put up his own barrier of silence by pursing his lips tightly and turning away. *This would be the time he chooses to start talking,* he thought irritably.

Fortunately the driver chuckled but said no more.

He had to think this through. The warders would most likely stay at *The Lazy Gentleman,* so it was possible Tana would be too busy tending to her guests. If he could get Elliott and Talia and a few others to stay at his house, the two girls might never meet. He hoped so. He didn't want a repeat of their last meeting. He hadn't even liked Talia back then, and Tana had been prepared to run her off as she did all the girls who showed any interest in him. And Talia certainly did little to hide her interest in him now. He wondered if his feelings for her were as noticeable to others as hers were to him. Probably, or Elliott wouldn't act so disgusted all the time. Even if he tried to hide his attraction to Talia, Tana would pick up on it. Girls had an uncanny knack for things like that.

He exhaled sharply, blowing out his cheeks. If getting involved with a girl made life so complicated, he wondered if Elliott might be right in his belief that women were ruinous. He squashed the thought as soon as it came, and a smile washed over his face. He enjoyed being with Talia, sitting next to her where he could feel the warmth of her body and smell the sweet scent of her hair. It was the thought of *not* being with her that tied his stomach in knots.

He closed his eyes in defeat. He was in way over his head here.

Pushing the thoughts away, he glanced at Seth riding a few horse-lengths ahead. The captain sat straight and alert in the saddle, scanning every inch of the forest around them as if he expected an attack at any moment. He held the reins loosely in his left hand, while his right rested on the hilt of one of the twin *kamui* swords crossing the small of his back. In spite of an atmosphere so relaxing that many of the warders looked lulled into complacency, Seth looked on the verge of violence. After the incident in Yucanter Forest, Jase couldn't really blame him. The group's desire to relax that day had very nearly gotten them all killed. It seemed Seth wasn't going to let it happen again. Captain *I'll-relax-when-I'm-dead* was back to stay.

As they neared the lane leading to his home, Jase sat forward anxiously and scanned the trees ahead. He'd never been so glad to see the narrow road in his life. He just hoped he would find his house still standing, since there was no telling what might have happened while he'd been away. As if reading his thoughts, Seth moved his horse alongside the coach and looked up at him. "I'd really appreciate it if you would get back inside the coach," he said. "Considering the circumstances surrounding your departure, there is no telling what might still be lurking around in the chance you or Gideon might come back."

Jase leveled a stare at him. "This is my home," he said fiercely. "I won't be afraid to approach my own home."

Seth scrutinized him for a moment, then nodded. "I guess you have a right to that," he said.

They were still in the shelter of the lane when Seth spoke. "I smell smoke," he said, his eyes narrowing.

"It's coming from the chimney," Jase said, pointing to the thin column visible through the trees. "Someone is cooking."

"It seems your mother is back from Seston," Seth said, then glanced at the warders. "I wonder how pleased she will be when she sees the number of guests she now has."

"She'll be all right," he answered. "I'm more concerned with how she's going to react toward me."

"I'm sure she'll be thrilled to see you," Seth told him. "Why wouldn't she be?"

"Well, like you said, I didn't exactly leave under the best of circumstances."

They exited the lane, and Seth's eyes fell on the porch. The damage was even worse in daylight, and Jase grimaced at the sight. One of the pillars was completely burned away and the section of the roof it once supported was sagging slightly. Two more pillars were scorched, as was the front of the house next to the window. The window, he noted with surprise, had been boarded up.

"What did you do?" Seth asked with a sidelong glance.

"I didn't do that," he insisted. "That was the K'rrosha."

The statement turned the head of every warder within earshot, and he flinched. The looks they gave him were skeptical, but there was a trace of uncertainty as well, as if they could almost believe what he said was true.

Seth raised an eyebrow. "And the apple trees?"

"Ah..." he hesitated. "That I did do. I had a little trouble with the Shadowhounds."

He saw the looks that passed between the warders and sighed. When was he going to learn that it wasn't wise for his guardians to be more afraid of him than they were of those they were protecting him from? It was bad enough that he was afraid of himself most of the time.

The coaches stopped in front of the house, and Jase climbed down. He'd only taken a couple of steps when the front door of his house flew open and Tana raced out with a squeal of delight. He was so surprised to see her that he barely had time to brace himself before she leapt into him, throwing her arms and legs around him in a hug that threatened to squeeze the life out of him. The impact of her body slammed him back against the coach and nearly made his knees give out.

With little regard for those watching, she covered his face with a barrage of kisses, interspersed with laughter and a dozen or so breathless *welcome backs*. He was aware of the shocked stares of the warders, especially Seth's, and tried unsuccessfully to unwind her legs from around his waist.

It was at that exact moment that Talia exited the coach.

He saw the look in the Chellum Princess' eyes and panic filled him. *Ta'shaen* flared at the edge of his Awareness, and he nearly embraced it, though he had no idea what he would do with it when he did. As it was, he wished he could make a hole in the Veil and step through to a place a thousand miles away. This was worse than any of the scenarios he'd imagined on the way here.

Talia's eyes burned with fury, but Tana, oblivious to everything but him, continued with the hugs and kisses. "I know you told me not to come out here," she said, "but I couldn't let the place — especially your mother's flowers — just rot away. So, a few days after you left, I came out here and found the porch half burned down, and the front window broken, and the living room clawed to pieces, and I've worried sick about you every day since." She slapped him in the head to show her disapproval, then went right back to hugging him even more fiercely than before.

He glanced at Talia and found that her eyes had narrowed to slits. Her teeth were clenched and both hands were knotted into fists. If he didn't end this now, the warders would really get a show.

Firmly — probably more firmly than was truly necessary if the confused look in Tana's eyes meant anything — he unwrapped her arms and legs and moved her back to arm's length. He thought he saw hurt in her eyes, but it vanished so quickly he wasn't sure. Then Tana spotted Talia standing a few feet away, and the space between them turned frosty cold.

"Tana, you remember Talia Chellum," he said, trying for civility in light of the hostility he could sense brewing between them.

Tana inclined her head in a barely perceptible bow. "Your Highness," she said, "I almost didn't recognize you. It's been some time since I saw you last, and you have grown more... beautiful."

Jase wasn't sure how Tana did it, but the word *beautiful* had all the feeling of a curse. It was obvious from the muscles tightening in Talia's jaw that she thought so as well. She was quiet a moment before flashing her most charming smile. "Thank you. You haven't changed a bit."

Tana frowned, and from the corner of his eye Jase saw Seth close his eyes and shake his head resignedly. Clearly, the captain thought a fight was about to erupt. Thankfully, Talia had more to add. "You're just as lovely as I remember."

Tana's frown transformed into a smile, but Jase could tell it was forced. She turned back to face him. "I took the liberty of patching things up around here, since you and Gideon Dymas left things in such a mess." Her eyes flicked to the coach. "I assume he's with you."

"I am," Gideon answered, climbing from the coach. He offered his hand in greeting and she accepted it warmly. "It's good to see you again," the Dymas told her, "in spite of the promise you broke to stay away from here."

"Sorry about that," she said with very little sincerity, "but it's not every day that the village's golden boy up and vanishes. I felt it might be a good idea to see to the place before somebody else in town let their curiosity get the best of them. All hell would have broken loose if they had seen the mess you two left behind." She looked back at Jase. "Especially since it had already broken loose when I informed the Village Council that your 'funeral' was a fake and that you had left with Breiter. Reapandry Villicks and Mayor Rhead are so mad about the deception they have threatened to put you over their knee. They've got Jukstin and the others who were in on it walking on eggshells."

Gideon laughed at the comment and moved to join Seth on the porch. The two began talking quietly, and Gideon gestured to the south while Seth shook his head.

"How long have you been staying here?" Jase asked. "Really." He could still feel Talia's eyes on them, and it made the skin on the back of his neck prickle. When Tana stepped right up next to him, lowering her voice as she spoke, he risked a quick look at Talia and found her looking like she wished she had a knife.

"I came out the very day you left," she told him. "I had — " she cut off as Elliott climbed out of the coach. Her mouth hung open, her words lost, and she followed Elliott with eyes filled with bedazzlement. She recovered quickly and jerked her gaze back to Jase's. It was too late, though; he knew what he'd seen in her eyes — it was the same intense look Talia had for him. Apparently, Talia had seen it as well because she was looking back and forth between her brother and Tana, a sudden light of understanding in her eyes.

"I had my father hire a couple of girls to look after the tavern so I could come tend to things here. As mad as the Village Council was at you and Breiter, they would have gone to Trian looking for you if they'd seen what your fight with the shadowspawn did to the house." Her eyes slid back to Elliott, and she watched as he stretched his back near the porch. "Is that Elliott?" she whispered.

Jase heard uncertainty in her voice, but there was something else there as well — a tremor of nervousness he couldn't quite define. With her thus occupied, he was able to study her face, and he saw right off that he'd been right about the intensity of her gaze. Her eyes traveled the length of Elliott's body, and an appreciative smile tugged at the corners of her mouth.

A momentary wave of jealousy washed through him, but he was able to push it away when he realized what all of this meant. He had tried for months to convince her that he didn't love her romantically, and she had dismissed it out of hand each time. For her to be so suddenly smitten with Elliott was a godsend. It meant she had finally accepted what he'd been saying all along. Perhaps coming home hadn't been such a bad thing after all.

"He's grown up," she said, and the tone of her voice let him know he was right. She turned and smiled at him. "The last time I saw him he was laughing hysterically while Daris switched my behind."

Talia gave a little laugh and stepped near. "Actually, I think his laughter was a carryover from Seth switching mine." She shot her brother an angry frown. "He didn't let up until we reached Drusi Bridge."

Jase poked Tana in the shoulder. "That reminds me of something I've been meaning to ask you ever since that day," he said. "Why were you mad at me for so long? I'm not the one who switched you."

Tana raised her eyebrows as if she didn't understand the question and looked at Talia. She seemed equally baffled. Without answering, Tana offered her arm to Talia. "Do you think you could introduce me to your brother?" she asked, and just like that the tension between the two girls evaporated.

"I'd love to," Talia answered, and they moved away arm in arm.

Jase watched them go, completely bewildered with the exchange. *One second they look ready to knife each other, and the next they are as chummy as childhood friends.* He ran his fingers through his hair. Had he missed something here?

He watched as Talia introduced Tana to Elliott, and his jealousy spiked anew. It was completely stupid of him to feel such a thing, but he couldn't help it. She really was his closest and dearest friend. *And because of that,* he admonished himself silently, *you should be happy for her.*

The thought made him sigh. He supposed in a way he was. But for some reason he couldn't begin to fathom, it pained him as well. He told himself this was exactly what he had always wanted — for Tana to find someone else to love — but now that it seemed to be happening, all he could think about was how much he would miss her. *I really am an idiot,* he thought. *And a selfish one to boot.*

Shaking his head at his own stupidity, he turned to see Thorac and Endil approaching from the other coach. The warders, now that the show was over, began dismounting to stretch their tired muscles.

Seth turned from his conversation with Gideon. "Tend to the horses and unload what you need for dinner," he ordered. "We will be staying here tonight."

Jase studied Tana and Talia a moment longer, then moved up the steps to his house, truly amazed by what he was witnessing. The two appeared to be the best of friends, though how that could be possible so quickly, or how long it would last, he couldn't say. He took a deep breath and let it out slowly. It would be interesting to see how all this played out.

As the coach pulled up in front of Jase's house, Elliott put up his guitar and readied to exit. Gideon's musical talent had been a most pleasant surprise, making for a rather enjoyable trip. He never would have imagined the Guardian of Kelsa would turn out to be such an accomplished composer. Six or seven of the songs he'd played for them he claimed to have written. It was truly amazing.

Still, their arrival in Kindel's Grove had him eager to get out and move around. It had been two years since he'd been able to explore the woods behind Jase's home, and he was eager to do so again. Hopefully there would be time.

A loud squeal of delight sounded from the direction of the house, and he peeked out of the window to investigate. He caught sight of a sun-browned girl with long brown hair and large pretty eyes darting down the steps toward them. She was grinning from ear to ear as she disappeared from his line of sight. A heartbeat later he heard a grunt as something thumped loudly against the outside of the coach.

He started to rise, but Talia shoved him back into his seat and exited the coach with a very determined look on her face. He let her pass, then leaned forward so he could look through the open door. He grinned in amusement when he found Jase trying to disengage himself from the pretty girl who had very thoroughly wrapped herself around him and was kissing him repeatedly. Suddenly his sister's demeanor as she exited the coach made much more sense. *She is jealous,* he thought with a smile. *Serves her right for the way she is always drooling over him.* This was going to be fun to watch.

He chuckled at the horrified look that washed over Jase's face as he caught sight of Talia, then watched as Jase firmly, perhaps even a bit forcefully, disentangled the girl's arms and legs and pushed her gently away. *Very fun to watch indeed,* he decided.

It was then that he got a better look at the girl's face, and his eyes went wide in wonder. *Tana Murra,* he realized. *Jase's childhood friend.*

He swallowed hard and sat back in his seat, not quite sure what to make of the jolt of energy which was so powerfully washing through him. It left his mouth dry and his palms sweaty. His heart was doing somersaults in his chest.

He felt Gideon's stare and looked up to find the Dymas grinning as if he knew some great and marvelous secret. The grin was almost as unnerving as the feelings he was having because of Tana.

"Something wrong?" Gideon asked.

"No, not at all," Elliott answered, lifting the guitar case from the seat. "I was just thinking about the last time those two young ladies met. They tried to strangle each other."

Gideon leaned forward, his eyes intense. "It never ceases to amaze me how time can change the way one feels about others. I wouldn't worry too much about them."

Elliott frowned. "You think they'll be friends?" he asked incredulously.

Gideon's chuckle made the hair on his neck stand on end. "Oh, I'm certain they'll be much more than just friends," he said. Grinning, he left the coach.

Elliott gripped the handle of the guitar case firmly. Smoothing his pants, he stepped nonchalantly from the coach and casually strode toward the porch. Without looking in Tana's direction, he began stretching his back, realizing as he did, just how stupid he was acting. Realizing one's stupidity, however, rarely did much to stop it, and he continued to act as if he hadn't seen her. He didn't dare look at her for fear of staring and letting everyone know what he was thinking.

And therein lay the irony, because he wasn't sure himself.

"Elliott," Talia said from behind him, and he turned to find her approaching with Tana on her arm. The two were smiling, but where Talia's smile was one of satisfaction, Tana's was nervous. "You remember Tana," his sister continued, presenting the other girl with a gentle nudge forward.

Elliott took Tana's hand and raised it to his lips, kissing it gently as he bowed. "It's a pleasure to meet you again," he said. He had gone through this exact ritual with hundreds of girls over the past few years — as Crown Prince he was always having to attend social functions where girl after scatterbrained girl would seek him out and try to be noticed — but now, as he spoke the words to Tana, he was startled by the level of his sincerity. It truly was a pleasure. He just hoped no one noticed that his heart was trying to pound its way out of his chest. He glanced past her to where Gideon stood next to Seth. The Dymas still wore the same knowing smile, and his eyes glittered with delight. Seth, on the other hand, wore a mask of disgust.

"My, don't we have nice manners this time," Tana said, drawing his eyes back to hers. "The last time we met, I remember you laughing at the expense of my very tender bottom."

Elliott flashed his most charming smile, trying desperately to maintain some sense of composure as he was swallowed by the depth of her gaze. "You seem to have recovered from your injuries nicely," he replied, pleased to see her blush. Then he realized that his comment could be misinterpreted as a reference to the niceness of her bottom, and his cheeks grew hot as well.

Seth saved them all from the awkward moment when he shouted for the warders to unload for the night.

Elliott smiled at Tana and turned away, grateful for the respite. He wasn't used to this. He was usually the one to embarrass others, not *be* embarrassed. He also wasn't used to having his wits scrambled by a girl. It was something he had sworn would never happen. So why was he already missing the sight of her face? What was going on here?

Standing on the porch, Gideon watched the exchange between Tana and Elliott and smiled in satisfaction at knowing another piece of the puzzle had fallen into place. He couldn't say for sure how this would affect the war against Maeon, or even if it would. But he knew the reason he'd felt compelled to come to Kindel's Grove had been fulfilled.

He marveled once again at how past, present, and future sometimes converged for brief, but very precise, moments in time to form the intricate web of fate. He had wondered all day what he would witness here. It wasn't until he'd felt the rippling tendrils of Earthpower settle and solidify around the two young people, binding them together in a way neither of them could possibly imagine, that he had understood what he was seeing was the will of the Earthsoul.

It was nice when stirrings in the Power turned out to be something pleasant. More often than not his premonitions of things to come involved something catastrophic, usually involving blood and loss of life. He could still sense one such future disturbance, but he couldn't pin it down to a specific time or place. He had tried meditating on it last night, but had received no insights. It was frustrating, but as the Earthsoul weakened, so did his ability to see into the future.

He sighed. There had been a time early in his life when he had been able to see almost anything before it happened. Now, most of what he received by way of revelation was not much more than confirmation that certain events were meant to be. Not quite as useful as having the eyes of a Seer, but he was grateful for it anyway.

Sometimes, simply knowing he was traveling the right path was sufficient.

When Seth called for the warders to unload the coaches and Elliott turned away from her, Tana shook herself mentally and the spell was broken. Temporarily at least. That something had just happened was undeniable. She flashed a quick smile at Talia and turned away. She was glad the animosity between them was gone. It would make figuring out what had just happened easier.

With her thoughts still jumbled with images of the Chellum Prince, she had to concentrate to keep her voice smooth. "Captain Lydon," she said, moving to stand before him and Gideon. Jase stood in the doorway behind them, but she forced herself to keep her attention on Seth. "If you'd prefer, the warders can stay at my father's inn. I'm sure there are rooms enough for them."

Seth glanced at Gideon who nodded. "Thank you," the captain said. "I'm sure they will appreciate it."

"I'll go into town and arrange it then," she told him, then glanced at Jase who was still watching from the doorway. His face was smooth, but the look in his eyes showed he was wrestling with many of the same feelings she was. She knew him well enough to know if she didn't say something to put him at ease he would give himself fits trying to come to terms with it all.

Her eyes returned to Elliott, and she wondered if she understood any of it herself. Elliott caught her gaze briefly — no more than a second or two at most — but it was enough to let her know what she had to do.

She turned back to Jase. "Will you escort me into town?" she asked. "I think we need to talk."

His eyes darted to Talia, then back to her. He seemed torn between the two of them, unable to make a decision. For a moment, she thought he would refuse. To her surprise, and more obviously to Jase's, Talia came up the steps.

"Go with her, Jase," she said, and Tana smiled gratefully. Talia returned the smile, but there was uncertainty in her eyes. She was nervous about letting them go off together, and Tana admired her for having the courage to do so.

Jase still looked uncomfortable, but he agreed.

Tana gestured to Seth. "If you and your men would like to rest for a bit, I'll have things ready at the inn in an hour or two."

Seth looked as if he was about to disagree with the arrangement, but Gideon headed off the outburst. "That will be fine," Gideon replied. "Jase can bring back whatever supplies you think we will need. There will be six or seven of us who will be staying here."

Tana turned to Jase. "Your wagon is in the barn," she told him. "I'll help you hitch up the horses."

Jase moved down the steps without speaking, and she saw the look that passed between him and Talia. *The sooner we talk about this, the better,* she thought, trying unsuccessfully to suppress the feeling of dread rising within her. She had always known this day would come — that someday she would have to openly acknowledge that Jase didn't love her the way she had always dreamed he would. Still, knowing something was inevitable didn't make it any easier to accept. If anything, throwing Elliott into the mix only made things more awkward.

She took a deep breath, her heart still fluttery, and followed him to the wagon. She couldn't deny that something had passed between her and the Chellum Prince. Laying eyes on Elliott had been like a signal flare to her heart that it was time to let Jase go. She had held on to him much longer than she should have. Acknowledging that truth, however, did nothing to alleviate the fear swelling inside her. She loved Jase too much to let him be hurt.

Side by side in the wagon, Jase and Tana sat without speaking as the wagon rumbled down Forest Road. When Tana finally broke the silence, Jase jumped at the sound of her voice even though he'd been waiting for her to speak. He'd had a pretty good idea what she would say, but actually hearing her voice tied his stomach into knots.

"So have you finally fallen *in* love with someone?" she asked, her eyes searching his face as if she might find the truth there.

"I don't know," he hedged. "I'm not sure what I'm feeling."

"But you do have feelings for the Chellum Princess?" she pressed, and he could sense how desperately she needed to know. He knew better than to lie to her, so he nodded.

"I do."

She leaned closer and her face grew mischievous. "Do you have *thoughts* about her," she asked, and he flinched with embarrassment at what she was implying.

"What kind of question is that?"

She elbowed him hard in the ribs. "Just answer the question."

He felt his face flush. "Sometimes," he admitted, looking away to hide his embarrassment. Her giggling made him go on the offensive. "There were times when I had the same kinds of *thoughts* about you," he said.

Surprisingly, she looked pleased. "Well, it's nice to know my efforts weren't a complete waste of time," she said, sounding extremely satisfied.

Shaking his head, he looked up at the sky. "Will I ever understand women?" he groaned.

"I doubt it," she answered. "But if it makes you feel better, we don't understand ourselves most of the time either."

They were quiet for several minutes, and Jase found himself watching her from the corner of his eye. She stared straight ahead, seemingly lost in thought, but he could tell she was waiting for him to continue the conversation.

He considered for a moment, unsure what to say. "Do you remember when we were kids and used to sneak out to the beaver ponds to go swimming?" he asked. She nodded, turning to regard him as he spoke. "For the longest time, you used to swim topless like you were one of the boys. We were young enough that it seemed quite natural, and I never gave it a second thought. Then one spring, you kept your shirt on, and for the first time it occurred to me that you weren't like all my other friends. That because of gender, you had the potential to be something more. At first I was fascinated by the prospect. It was intriguing."

He smiled at her, trying to put a little levity into the moment. "For one thing, you were much better-looking than the rest of my friends."

"And a better swimmer," she added. "Go on. I'm curious to see where you are going with this."

"From that moment on," he told her. "I couldn't help but look at you differently. You were my best friend *and* a girl. A very pretty girl who only grew more beautiful every year. I was proud to be seen with you. To have the entire village think we were... well, whatever they thought."

He paused and searched for the right words. "But it changed things between us in a way that's hard for me to explain. The expectations and assumptions of others seemed to steal away the earlier, less awkward relationship we enjoyed as kids. The older we grew, the more difficult it became for me. I felt like I was living some kind of a lie. And then at New Year's..."

"The kiss," she said, nodding to herself.

"My love for you has grown stronger every day," he said. "And I do love you, with all of my heart. You are my dearest and most trusted friend, but..." he trailed off, unable to continue.

"But you aren't *in* love with me," she finished for him, and he cringed.

When she remained quiet, he risked a peek at her and found her eyes intent on his face. "I know that, Jase," she said. "I've known it for years." She looked out through the forest and pursed her lips. "I've just never wanted to accept it." She turned to regard him once more, and her eyes were soft. "But it's okay," she said. "I can see now that I was the one being foolish. I'm sorry for all the emotional turmoil I caused you."

"Actually, I think it was for the best," Jase admitted. "It kept all the other girls in Kindel's Grove from bothering me. In a way you freed me to do all the things I wanted to do without emotional attachment."

"I freed you to meet someone like Talia Chellum," she said, leaning over to kiss him on the cheek. "And I'm freeing you now from the past years of my selfish stupidity. I think you two make a lovely couple. I wish you well."

He put his arm around her and hugged her close. "Thank you," he said, pressing his cheek against the top of her head. "And you have my permission to chase after Elliott."

She jerked out of his arm, and he laughed at the surprise evident in her eyes. "Oh, come now," he said. "Don't you think everyone noticed how you two were oogling one another?"

"I was not oogling," she said defensively.

He widened his grin, and she smiled with embarrassment. "Okay, maybe a little," she admitted. "But I'll bet it was nothing like when you noticed Talia."

"I wouldn't know," he said. "I couldn't see my face."

They laughed then, and Jase realized that everything was going to be all right between them. With a simple conversation, they had been able to step back across the years to that time when life was simple and they could just be friends. No expectations. No awkward feelings. Just friends.

After a moment, she looked over at him and smiled. "I'm not in love with you, Jase Fairimor."

"Good. Because I'm not in love with you either," he answered and kissed her gently on the cheek.

"Well, now that everything is settled," she began, and he knew by her tone of voice what was coming, "I want to know what in hell's name is going on to cause you to come back here with a dozen Elvan warders and a Dymas."

Back to normal, he thought with a smile. "Of course," he said.

Starting with the night he and Gideon fled Kindel's Grove, he told her everything that had happened to him over the past two weeks. He left nothing out, and by the time they reached town her eyes were troubled and her jaw was set. She was horrified by what she'd heard, but she handled it better than he thought she would, and even gave words of encouragement and offered to help any way she could.

And that's what friends do, he thought. *Good friends, anyway. True friends.*

CHAPTER 11

Apologies and Explanations

By the time Jase brought the wagon to a stop in front of *The Lazy Gentleman*, word was spreading like wildfire that he had returned to town. And while his friends greeted him with a wave and smile, most of the older folks narrowed their eyes at him and frowned disapprovingly. Tana, it seemed, was right about their unwillingness to forgive him for deceiving them and running off to Chellum.

"Don't mind them," Tana told him as she climbed down from the wagon. "They'll understand why you had to leave once they learn the truth about what's been happening."

Jase wasn't so sure. "Well, they won't learn it from me," he told her. "I'm heading home before the Village Council calls a special session to interrogate me. Facing the Kelsan High Tribunal was scary enough. I don't think I'd live through an encounter with Reapandry Villicks and the Mayor."

Tana smiled at him. "You'll do fine," she told him. "You are a Dymas, after all. And if that doesn't work, you could always play the royalty card."

As if that would mean anything to Reapandry, he thought. "Just the same," he told her, "I'm leaving."

"Not without having a drink with your friends first, you're not," a voice said from behind him.

He turned to find Bornis and Jukstin moving up behind the wagon. Jukstin's little brother Mathin was with them.

"Mathin will take your wagon to our place and hide it behind the barn," Jukstin said. "Kip Adomen and the Alvear boys and a few others are already spreading rumors that you are at the mercantile or at the church or headed back to your place — everywhere except where you will be — so that Reapandry won't know where to look."

"But this is only going to work if you get your rear end out of that wagon and into the tavern where it belongs," Bornis said with a grin. "Those spreading the rumors will be along shortly." His grin widened. "And they'll be thirsty."

Jukstin's eyes grew mischievous. "We told them you were buying."

Jase chuckled. "I suppose that's the least I can do considering all you guys have done for me." Jumping down from the wagon, he turned to Tana. "Are you coming?"

"No. I need to make the arrangements for your escorts like I promised. Besides, if I go in the tavern, the patrons will expect me to work." She flashed him a smile. "Don't spend too long at the tavern," she warned. "Remember, you still have someone waiting to talk to you back at your place." Giggling, she moved up the steps to the inn. "When I see you tomorrow you can tell me how things went."

Mathin climbed into the wagon, and Jase and his friends cast a quick glance to see that no one was watching as they used the departing wagon as a cover to scurry across the street and into the tavern.

Once inside, they moved to a table in the far corner and took seats where they could watch the door. Both Bornis' and Jukstin's faces were expectant, their eyes filled with curiosity. It was obvious that they had many questions for him, but to their credit, they waited until the rest of Jase's friends arrived before starting in on him.

Galam Frestrem and Corom Phipps were the first to arrive. Both slipped in the back way and moved directly to the table. Helem Mertom came in the front a few minutes later, and Heril Kinsten arrived a few minutes after that. They had just settled in around the table when Gilium Hresdom slipped in the back way with a broad smile on his face.

"The Transtin boys are loving this," he told them as he sat down. "Seril and Mikka especially." He gave a laugh. "But I fear they may grow up to be professional liars."

Galam snorted. "I think they have already achieved that status," he told them. "I've heard some of the tales they've told the schoolmistress as to why they were late for school."

"Still," Gilium countered, "we shouldn't encourage them."

"In light of how the Village Council reacted the last time we deceived them," Jase said, "you shouldn't be doing any of this."

"We were under oath from Brieter," Jukstin said with a smile. "We *had* to lie to them."

Jase leaned forward and looked him in the eyes. "But this time *you* took the initiative. Reapandry and the Mayor — not to mention your parents — are going to be furious when they find out what you've done."

Jukstin shrugged. "Let them. Most of us won't be here much longer anyway."

"What do you mean?" Jase asked.

"We're going to Trian to enlist," Corom answered. "We are going to help fight this war against Shadan."

Jase frowned. "How do you know about him? My uncle only addressed the High Tribunal three days ago concerning his return."

"There have been rumors about the army massing in Melek since you left," Helem said. "If you listen to the stories passing through the ranks of the Highwaymen, you can usually piece together what is going on."

"And then there are the prophecies," Bornis said. "The other night... the light that filled the northern sky... Elder Previnser called the village together to tell us we were witnessing the fulfilling of prophecy."

"He rang the church bell," Gilium offered. "Scared the life out of me at first, coupled with the light and all — I thought maybe the world was coming to an end."

"He read to us from an Elvan book of scripture," Corom added, pulling a scrap of paper from his pocket. "I wrote it down — as best as I could anyway. My mind was a bit jumbled and my hands were shaking from the excitement of it all." He unfolded the paper and began to read.

> *And in that day shall ye know that the sons of the birthright have come, for behold the house of Fairimor shall be crowned with Fire; yea, Fire and Light shall throw back the night, even to the lifting of the Veil of Darkness cloaking the lands of thine inheritance.*
>
> *Watch ye, therefore, for the time of Elsa's awakening, and prepare to join the keepers of the sacred trust in their fight against the Hand of Darkness. Yea, verily I say unto you: gird on thy armor and take up thy sword and go forth into battle, yea even the fiery battle of cleansing.*

"And so we will go," Jukstin told him firmly. "We must."

Jase felt an icy gauntlet take him by the heart. This was his fault. They were answering a call to arms he'd issued by fulfilling a bloody prophecy he'd had no intention of fulfilling. And when they went to battle and bled and killed and died, that would be his fault too. Their blood would be on his conscience along with all the others who had died for the sake of the Fairimors since this whole thing started. The deaths of career soldiers sworn to the Fairimor line was bad enough; he didn't think he could bear it if these — his childhood friends — were to be killed as well. He opened his mouth to tell them just that, but they'd already read the look in his eyes.

"We know what you are going to say," Corom said. "And you can stick it in your ear. This isn't your burden alone. Not anymore. The call has been issued. We will answer." His voice and his face abruptly softened, and he leveled a stare at Jase. "What? You think we aren't up to the task?"

"It's not that," Jase said, looking around from face to face. They all looked as determined as Corom. Even Bornis. Jase couldn't believe he was the same young blacksmith who had vomited at the sight of the shadowspawn-slaughtered sheep — what was it... a month ago now? He pushed the thought away and continued. "But you see... I... I was the one who lit the sky."

None of them looked surprised. "I told you it was Jase," Bornis said, slapping Gilium on the back. "You owe me a drink."

Jase stared at him. "What made you suspect *that?*"

Bornis shrugged uncomfortably. "I've known you were a Dymas since the day you killed the thieves out on the lane leading to your home. I know I pretended like I didn't see what you did, but I did."

"And then there was the firestorm north of Drusi Bridge the night after you left for Chellum," Helem added. "Like I said, there have been rumors."

"But there was no way you could have known that was me," he told them.

Helem smiled. "I didn't," he said with a chuckle. "I just wanted to see if you would admit to it."

"I think," Jukstin said, waving for the serving girl to bring them a second round of drinks, "that maybe you should tell us what you've been up to since you left. If we are going to answer a call to battle, it might be nice to know what exactly it is we will be facing."

"Okay," Jase said. "But you aren't going to like what you hear."

And he was right. The longer he talked, the darker their expressions became. By the time he finished, their faces could have been carved from stone.

They were quiet for a long time, and he studied each of them intently. His heart sank when he saw the fire burning in their eyes. Contrary to his initial hopes that he was talking them out of going to Trian to enlist, he saw that he'd only strengthened their resolve to help him fight this battle.

Jukstin finally broke the awkward silence. "It sounds as if we are indeed needed in Trian," he said, and the others nodded. "And sooner than later."

Jase knew then that there was nothing he could say to change their minds. He shook his head in resignation. "When you get to Trian," he told them, "go see Breiter. He will have a spot for all of you in the Trian Home Guard. He's already mentioned it to me, and it will certainly be better than marching all the way to Zedik Pass. Besides...." He stopped and his face hardened into a frown. "...the war will be coming to Trian before too long anyway." He hesitated a moment before continuing. "I saw it in a dream."

"You *saw* it?" Bornis asked.

Jase nodded. "Sometimes a Dymas can see the future."

"And...?" Jukstin asked.

"It didn't look good," he told them. "But the future is never certain. What I saw will not come to pass. I'm not going to let it." He took a sip of his drink and forced a smile. "When I join you all in Trian it will be to celebrate the destruction of Shadan and the rejuvenation of the Earthsoul."

"How can you be sure?" Gilium asked.

"Because I'm on my way to retrieve a Blood Orb of Elsa," he answered. "With it I will do what my Uncle Areth failed to do twenty years ago. If we're lucky, none of you will have to fight at all; I will end the war before it has a chance to get started."

They talked for a half hour more before Seril and Mikka burst through the front door of the tavern. Their faces were red from running and excitement.

"Quick," Seril shouted, hurrying up to the table, "the council knows you're here. They'll be here in a few minutes."

Jukstin rose and glanced at the doorway leading through the kitchen and out to the back of the tavern. "Come on, Jase," he said. "Time to go."

It was tempting, but Jase waved them off. "You guys go ahead," he told them. "As unpleasant as it will be, I think I need to speak with the council. I owe them an explanation. At the very least they deserve an apology. If I don't do it here, they'll come out to my house, and that will make the others in my group very angry. Especially Seth."

"Well, it's your hide," Jukstin told him, then motioned to the others. "Come on, let's get out of here." The rest of his friends rose and started for the door, and Jukstin called over his shoulder. "I'll have Mathin take your wagon to the mercantile," he said. "You can pick it up there after you've done battle with Reapandry and the Mayor."

"Thanks," Jase told him, then added, "If I don't see you again before I leave, remember what I said about Breiter having positions for you. I'll expect to see you wearing Fairimor blue when I return to Trian."

"Sure thing, Jase," Jukstin told him, then slipped out the door.

Jase watched Helem, Corom, Gilium leave, then turned to find Bornis still standing beside him. The young blacksmith's face was creased with worry.

"You be careful, Jase," Bornis said, extending his hand in farewell. When Jase took it, Bornis pulled him forward and hugged him so tightly Jase thought he felt some of his ribs crack. Smiling, Jase hugged him back.

When Bornis released him, Jase clapped him on the shoulder. "Go on," he said. "Get out of here before the council arrives."

Bornis looked as if he would say more but didn't. After one last nod, he left.

Jase paid the tavern girl for the drinks, then moved to the front door and stepped out onto the boardwalk. A large group of people was coming down the street toward him. Reapandry, white hair shining in the sun, led them, and next to her strode Mayor Rhead, his face red and blotchy from the effort of trying to keep up with the older woman. Behind him came the rest of the council. This was going to be interesting.

Jase started toward them, opening his arms in a gesture of welcoming. It was met by a hardening of faces.

"You have some explaining to do," Reapandry growled, and behind her the rest of the council nodded.

Jase smiled disarmingly. "Yes, I suppose I do," he told them. "But I don't think the middle of the street is the best place for that. Neither is the tavern." He gestured back down the street. "Perhaps we could go to the schoolhouse or the church." *Preferably the church,* he thought. *They can't kill me if we are in the church.* Keeping his smile in place, he strode past them without slowing. He didn't need to look back to know they were following; he could hear them grumbling at him under their breath. Reapandry sounded particularly irritated.

The large procession drew the attention of the other members of the community, and most stopped what they were doing to join Reapandry and the council. Businesses and shops were hurriedly closed. Tools were put away. Children too young to be left to play on their own were scooped up and brought along. By the time they reached the church, Jase thought the whole of the village proper had gathered. He even spotted Jukstin and Bornis and the others hanging back out of Reapandry's line of sight.

He took a deep breath and let it out slowly, then moved up the steps into the church. There were as many people behind him as what had filled the five tiers of Trian's lesser councils, and it terrified him even more than facing the High Tribunal had. Trian's politicians had only a name by which to identify him — the people of Kindel's Grove had watched him grow up. They *knew* him.

He sighed. *At least they used to,* he added silently. It made him wonder how they would react once they realized he wasn't the same young man who'd left here two weeks earlier.

He moved to the front of the room and took a seat next to the pulpit.

Reapandry and the council filled in the first two rows and the rest of the townsfolk crowded in behind them. Jase cringed when he found that near the back it was standing room only.

Elder Previnser moved forward through the crowd and took a seat next to Jase. With his eyes still on the congregation, he leaned toward Jase and whispered. "This is the second time this week our church has been this full. Why do I get the feeling you were the cause of the other meeting as well?"

Jase cringed inwardly but somehow managed to keep his face smooth. "Because I was."

Elder Previnser studied him quietly for a moment. "I thought so." He made a slight gesture toward the congregation. "Would you like me to welcome them, or do you want to get right to the point?"

For his answer, Jase moved to the pulpit. As he did, a profound silence fell across the room. Behind him Elder Previnser muttered, "Why aren't they that quiet for me?"

Jase ignored him. Instead, he let his gaze travel across the room. Every face was a mixture of curiosity and a quiet but obvious anxiety. Even those who were angry at him for faking his death and running off to Chellum looked nervous.

He cleared his throat. "First let me apologize for the trauma I may have caused you because of my bogus funeral. Had there been any other choice, believe me I would have taken it. Considering, however, that the assassination attempt at the tavern was only one of many such attempts, Captain Lyacon felt it wise to give the enemy an excuse *not* to come back. Second, let me say I'm sorry for leaving without any explanation other than the one Tana may have given to you. Again I had no choice."

Mayor Rhead raised his hand. "Why don't you just tell us what is going on, Jase. After we know that, we'll decide if we are going to forgive you or not."

"Fair enough," Jase told him. "But I guarantee you aren't going to like what you hear." He motioned to the back of the chapel. "Those of you with young children might want to take them outside. I don't want to be responsible for causing them nightmares."

When no one moved, he shrugged. "Suit yourself," he said, then began. "The Earthsoul is still dying, and Throy Shadan has been refleshed once more. Even now he masses an army on the Meleki side of Zedik Pass. K'rrosha Shadow-lancers, Shadowhounds, and tens of thousands of Darklings and other Power-wrought creatures stand to march with the cultist armies, all of which will be led by a host of Agla'Con. Death's Third March is underway." He paused to let his words sink in.

"Four days ago the enemy launched a brazen attack on Fairimor Palace, and dozens of innocent people were killed. I was there. I took part in the battle. It was another in a long line of battles I've experienced since leaving Kindel's Grove, but I don't tell you this to boast. Anyone who boasts about being in a battle is a fool. I tell you because I want you to understand that when I do things you may not like, there's a bloody good reason for it, not the least of which is keeping myself and those I care about alive."

Taking hold of the edges of the podium, he continued. "As a friend of mine told me recently: we are at war with the dark side. Death is coming for us. Time is against us. And since it is my job to keep us alive, I will do whatever is necessary to do just that." He paused, letting his face harden into a mask of determination. "I've gone into hiding to keep us alive. I've killed to keep us alive. The shadowspawn I don't mind so much, but killing men is something I hope I never have to do again. And yet I will if I need to, because we are at war. I've accepted who and what I am in order to keep us alive, and I will continue to develop the Gifts bestowed upon me until I can crush the enemy once and for all."

He stopped and studied the congregation. The curiosity and anxiety were gone from their faces. Now he saw only fear. Fear because of what they were hearing, certainly. But he realized some of their fear might be directed toward him personally. *And why not?* he thought. *I am a walking disaster most of the time.*

Finally Reapandry broke the silence. "You mentioned Gifts," she said softly. "What kinds of Gifts?"

Jase met her gaze without flinching. "Gifts of *Ta'shaen*," he answered. "Like many Fairimors before me, I have become a Dymas."

The reaction was far less than he had expected. Yes, there were a couple of audible gasps, but for the most part, the people of Kindel's Grove were unfazed by the announcement. Even old Luecas Sabhin, the man who had throttled him years earlier for mentioning Brysia's Gift, sat quietly.

He realized then that the fear present in their eyes was *for* him, not because of him. What happened next wasn't a surprise.

"What can we do to help?" Reapandry asked, and beside her Mayor Rhead nodded.

Jase was quiet as he tried to get a handle on his emotions. The question was so simple and yet so heartfelt that tears threatened to spring up in his eyes. It was several moments before he could speak. He knew what he had to say even if it nearly killed him to say it. He looked at Jukstin and the rest of his friends standing in the back of the chapel and forced the words from his throat.

"You can let those who are willing and able answer the call of prophecy," he told them. "It is time, as the scriptures tell, 'to join the keepers of the sacred trust in their fight against the Hand of Darkness.' I and those with me are on our way to retrieve a Blood Orb of Elsa. With it we hope to rejuvenate the Earthsoul and lock Shadan and his K'rrosha away for good. The armies of flesh and blood, however, will need to be met with the sword."

"And for those of us too old to go to war?" Reapandry asked.

"Pray for those of us doing the fighting," Jase told her. "And pray for the Earthsoul." He raised his hand to still any further questions. "I know you have much more to ask," he told them, "but I need to get back to my place before Gideon Dymas starts to worry about me."

There was a collective gasp of astonishment at the mention of Gideon, but Jase ignored it. He'd already given them enough to think about; he didn't need to elaborate on his traveling companions. He stepped away from the pulpit, but Elder Previnser caught his sleeve.

"Since the congregation is already gathered," he said, "I would like to conclude with a prayer — for your success and safe return."

Jase smiled. "I would like that," he said. "I think I'm going to need all the help I can get."

When Jase returned home a short while later, he found the *Bero'thai* ready to go into town. They were gathered in front of the barn, some standing, some already in the saddle. Seth was speaking to them, and Jase overheard the captain's orders for them to return before sunup.

Jase glanced across the yard to see that the rest of the horses had been unsaddled and unhitched and put into the pasture. The coaches were parked in front of the house.

He steered the wagon alongside the coaches and climbed down. After unhitching Tana's horse, he led it to the pasture, then returned to the wagon to get the food he'd picked up from Zander's Mercantile. Seth joined him at the wagon as the *Bero'thai* started away in a rumbling of horses' hooves. Jase caught sight of Elliott riding among them and turned to Seth.

"Where is he going?" he asked.

Seth's eyes sparkled with anger as he watched Elliott ride away. "To town," the captain replied. The frown beneath his mustache was obvious. He started for the house. "Did you and Tana have a nice talk?" he asked.

"Yes, but it wasn't as nice as the talk I had with most of the village at the church," he said darkly. "Once they learned I was there, there was no leaving without speaking to them. Doing battle with Darklings was less intimidating."

"Well, I hope you still have some courage left," he said, the anger in his voice spiking sharply, "because someone else would like to speak with you." He gestured toward the porch where Talia was seated in Brysia's swing. "Let me know if you need any help," he added with a smirk.

For a reply, Jase tossed a bag of supplies at him.

Seth caught it easily and continued toward the front door while Jase moved to join Talia on the swing. Before Seth went inside, he shot one last warning look at both of them.

"What's gotten into him?" Jase asked, leaning back in the swing.

"For one thing, he's angry with Gideon for stopping so early in the day," she answered. "But really, I think he is irritated with Gideon for allowing young people to go off unsupervised."

"If he's worried for our safety, he could always order a warder or two to tag along," Jase suggested.

"The kind of danger Seth perceives isn't the kind that can be countered with sword or bow." She studied him for a moment before asking, "Are you and Tana going to be all right?"

He smiled. "Things are back the way I've always wanted," he told her, then explained in detail what he meant. She listened carefully, and he could tell she was relieved by what she was hearing. He sensed she had been worried things might turn out differently. For her to have let him go off alone with Tana showed her faith about the strength of their budding relationship.

Without saying a word, she leaned forward, drawing him in with eyes so green and bright they took his breath away. He found himself leaning as well, and their lips met in a kiss that awakened every fiber of his being and lit a forest fire in his soul. When she encircled his neck with her arms and the moment lengthened, he understood what she had meant by a real kiss.

The following morning, a loud knocking on his bedroom door pulled Jase from a very pleasant dream, and he groaned — as much from losing the image in his mind as from the earliness of the hour. Seth, it seemed, wanted to make up for lost time. Jase rolled over and looked at the window. It was still dark. The only light came from the lamps the warders were using to hitch up the teams.

He flopped back down and sighed at the loss of the dream. He had been back on the swing with Talia, reliving the moment of the kiss. It had played out a dozen times during the night, but for the first time in a long time, he actually felt refreshed. It made him wish he could dream like that every night. It had certainly been better than watching Trian go up in flames or destroying the Shadan'Ko. He closed his eyes to try to picture the dream once more, but Seth banged roughly on the door.

"Get up now, Jase," he barked, "or I'll haul you to Seston in your small clothes."

"I'm up!" Jase shouted. "Geeze, don't you ever sleep?"

"I'll sleep when I'm dead," came the harsh reply.

Frowning at the door, Jase threw off the covers and rose to dress. The only consolation for having to get up so early was that Talia was even prettier in real life than she was in his dreams. He looked forward to spending another day with her.

When he joined the others downstairs, he noticed right off that Elliott was missing. He didn't have to ask where he was; he could tell by the smile on Talia's face and the frown on Seth's that the Chellum Prince had spent the night in town. They ate a quick breakfast, secured the house, and moved to the coaches. Before he climbed inside, Jase cast one last look at his house and frowned. *Why is it always so hard to leave?* he wondered.

Talia was waiting for him inside, and he took a seat next to her. Thorac sat opposite them and his eyes sparkled knowingly. He grinned at each of them but didn't speak. It was the only time Jase could think of where the little man had stayed silent about anything.

By the time they reached town, it was light enough to see, but Jase wished it was still dark. He wished even more that Seth hadn't ridden past the window to tell him he ought to look outside. There were some sights that could tear a man's heart out. This was one of them.

Lining both sides of the street from the church to the school to Adomen's livery, the residents of Kindel's Grove stood to see the procession off. If their faces hadn't been so somber, Jase might have felt they were watching a parade. Instead they looked as if they were gazing at a funeral procession.

Only his friends showed any excitement at his passing, and Jukstin and Bornis trotted out to the coach to wish him well.

"We'll be waiting for you in Trian," Jukstin told him. "Make sure you come back."

He assured them he would, and they passed out of sight.

When the coaches finally stopped at *The Lazy Gentleman* to pick up Elliott, they found him standing at the front door with Tana. She wore a robe over her nightgown, and her hair was a mess, but it didn't look like she had just woken up. She held a bouquet of roses. A closer look showed them to be made out of paper.

As Jase watched, Elliott took Tana's hand and kissed it, bowing as he did. Tana smiled and waited for him to stand straight before stepping forward to kiss him on the cheek. Then she stepped over to the coach and opened the door.

"You be careful," she told them. "And you better stop here on your way back north or I will have something to say about it." She reached in and took each of them by the hand. Jase's she held the longest, and the look she gave him was warm.

"Don't do anything stupid," she warned.

Tana stepped back as Elliott approached, and they stopped to gaze at each other one last time. Jase grinned when he saw the look that passed between them.

Talia saw it too.

"We are going to have fun today," she whispered, and Thorac chuckled.

Elliott climbed in and noticed all of them staring at him. "What?" he asked hotly.

Oh, yes, Jase thought. *Very much fun indeed.*

At a farmhouse ten miles south of Trian, Falius Tierim stood at a fence surrounding a midsized pasture and gazed up at the stars. Borilius stood beside him, mumbling under his breath, as agitated as Falius had ever seen him. Gwuler stood a short distance away, a motionless statue of black-robed calm. He'd been a Shizu once, Falius knew, a long time ago, before he had come to understand his abilities in the Power. Tonight, though, Gwuler had taken hold of the Shizu persona once more — a silent, patient shadow just waiting to erupt into deadly motion.

Falius had always admired the Shizu, had on several occasions recruited one or more squads from various clans to tend to matters of business. He wondered if Shizu were the 'contacts' Gwuler had promised to bring, though why the Riaki would bring them out to watch the sky in the cover of darkness, he couldn't begin to fathom.

Judging from the sound of his muttering, neither could Borilius.

They stood there for almost an hour before Borilius' impatience finally got the best of him. "This is ludicrous," he snarled in Gwuler's direction. "Gideon and his party have been gone four days, and so far all we have done is ride out to this country hellhole and mingle with the livestock. When are these mystery friends of yours going to arrive?"

"Patience," Gwuler replied, his Shizu calm obvious.

Borilius' anger spiked sharply, and Falius had to clench his teeth to keep from smiling. The Zekan had very nearly seized the Power.

"They will be here soon," the Riaki soothed. If he was aware of how close Borilius had come to striking him with the Power, it didn't show.

Another hour passed, and even Falius' patience started to wear thin. Gwuler, however, remained unperturbed as he continued to watch the night sky. It was difficult, but Falius held his tongue. A short time later the Riaki spoke.

"They are here."

Instinctively Falius turned to watch the road leading in from the highway, but a sound above drew his attention back to where Gwuler's gaze had remained all along. Giant winged shapes, a dozen at least, and as large or larger than K'ressh, dropped out of the sky and began landing silently in the pasture before them. Numerous black-clad shapes leapt from the baskets the creatures had borne and fanned outward. Slender, slightly curved swords glinted in the darkness. Falius didn't have to use his Awareness to know that he and the others were already surrounded.

Two of the figures strode toward them. When they were close enough, Falius saw that his assumptions had been correct — *koro* hood-masks marked the men as Shizu.

"Shozen Hom," one of the men said. "Deathsquad Valhei is at your service."

CHAPTER 12

A Change of Power

Crouching in the shade of a small Kairus tree on a hillside above the outskirts of Gahara City, Shavis Dakshar and his men watched Derian Oronei make his way up the dry streambed toward them. Without his Shizu uniform and black *koro* hood-mask, Derian might look like an ordinary Riaki citizen to the casual observer; but to the trained eyes of a Shizu he may as well have been wearing his sword. The plainest *kitara* robes in the country couldn't hide that kind of deadly grace. A leopard from the Iga'rala Mountains would have been easier to conceal.

Shavis frowned. He hoped Derian had done a better job of blending in while he was in the city. If not, he may have been followed. He dismissed the thought as soon as it came. He'd been with Derian long enough to know the young Shizu had probably made himself no more threatening than a mouse. A mouse that would have eliminated anyone who showed even the slightest interest in him beyond what the simple *kitara* robes should inspire.

He let his eyes move from Derian to the Iga'rala Mountains rising in the distance. Even with the horses they had finally secured from a village in Hattori Prefecture, it had taken them two days to make their way through the Pass of Merishal. With all the soldiers moving north to take up positions near Capena, he was surprised it hadn't taken them longer than that. Half the northern clans had sent troops — ordered to do so by the Imperial Clave. The war against Kelsa was already well underway.

He glanced back at the leafy green of Gahara City spreading the full length and width of the valley and fought to suppress a frown. With war so imminent, it seemed odd that none of Gahara's troops had been called up — they were the finest warriors in all of Riak. For them to have been ignored by the Emperor was an insult to their collective pride. And yet, he was starting to wonder if there was more to it than a simple political slap in the face. It was implausible, but he was starting to wonder if the Imperial Clave was hoping Gahara would erupt into leif warfare and had left all its troops here to ensure a bloody and destructive outcome.

It was a foolish thought, and a far-fetched one, but he couldn't shake the feeling that the Imperial Clave was pretending to ignore Gahara the way a carrion bird would ignore a wounded animal, keeping its distance, feigning indifference, but ready to feast as soon as the opportunity arose.

And Gahara was wounded, he decided. Things had changed here since he and his men had left on the Deathstrike.

"It is as we feared," Derian said, climbing the hillside toward them. "Leif Iga has been voted down. Leif Tsuto now holds the Highseat of Gahara."

Shavis nodded. He'd suspected as much when they'd found Tsuto's banner waving above the arched gate-towers marking the boundary of Gahara Prefecture. Seat changes in Gahara weren't uncommon — the six rival leifs were forever vying for control of the clave — but the next clave assembly wasn't for another two months. That Iga had been voted down meant a special assembly had been called by one or more of the leifs and sufficient cause presented for them to strip Iga of the Highseat.

"Do we know the reason behind the other leifs taking action against us?" Shavis asked.

Derian shrugged. "Word on the streets is that Tereus Dromensai was found guilty of treason. But no one I talked to seems to know what the charges were. Iga's central estates are deserted, and the Flag of Transgression flies above the assembly hall. It looks as if we have been disbanded." He looked down at his clothes. "It was good advice to go dressed like this. I saw the bodies of several of Iga's nobility still being displayed in different locations throughout the city. Evidently, some from our leif didn't go quietly."

"Something isn't right," Shavis hissed, aware of how obvious the statement was. "Tereus Dromensai is no traitor. I'd bet my life on it."

"But after what we learned of Clan Samochi's involvement with the Con'Kumen, might not Gahara also have fallen victim to that evil?"

"Not Iga!" Shavis snarled, surprised by his own vehemence. "Not Tereus!" He forced himself to be calm. "Even if Highseat Dromensai was guilty of treason," he continued, his tone only slightly moderated, " — and I for one believe he isn't — there is no cause to disband the entire leif." He paused to glance at each of the others in turn. Railen, the youngest of the three, stood grim-faced and determined. Keries wore a contemplative frown. Derian, only a year Keries' senior, appeared eager. All three would follow him no matter what he decided. He just hoped he would do the right thing.

"Something else is at work here," he told them at last. "I intend to find out what."

"How?" Derian asked, and Shavis heard excitement in the young man's voice.

Shavis started down the slope to the streambed. "I'm going to go ask the new Highseat."

Shavis strode past the two leather-armored Sarui guardsmen keeping watch at the entrance to Gahara castle and moved into the courtyard beyond. Neither guard tried to stop him, and both did a fair job of feigning indifference. Only their eyes gave away the lie — a glimmer of surprise mingled with curiosity. And they weren't alone; all around him, people stopped to stare.

He wore his black *komouri* uniform and *koro* mask and carried his sword in his left hand. The symbol of Leif Iga was in plain view on his chest. But it was neither his sword nor the fact that he wore the insignia of a disbanded leif that drew so many stares; it was the red sash tied around his right arm. The red sash — sign of a failed Deathstrike.

It guaranteed his passage in to see the Highseat regardless of the state of affairs in the city. Shizu honor was at stake, and nothing could interfere with his reckoning before the Highseat. It mattered little that Iga had been disbanded; the red sash told all who saw him that he was already without leif or clan. It was the mark of honor lost. A mark that required his blood be shed to atone for failure. Not even clan warfare was of a higher priority than a Shizu reckoning.

He glanced at the red sash briefly, then turned his gaze back toward the entrance to the castle. *Not far from the truth,* he thought darkly. Honor *was* at stake. Not just his, but that of Iga's as well. Perhaps even that of Gahara. He set his jaw determinedly. Only it wouldn't be his blood that flowed to make this reckoning. It would be the blood of the Con'Kumen and any who aided them. If he had to turn the other Gaharan leifs on their heads, he would find the truth he sought.

He crossed the bridge of the dry moat and started down the narrow lane leading to the steps of the inner gate. The dark, narrow slits of arrow nooks slid past the edges of his vision as he walked, and he briefly wondered how many eyes followed his passing from within their depths. *How many arrows are pointing at me?* he wondered. *How many would have already been loosed if not for the red sash?*

Two more Sarui in ceremonial leather armor stood at the top of the stairs, and both stepped aside to let him pass, their eyes glued to the death mark on his arm. Sarui and Shizu may be bitter rivals when it came to guarding leif and clan, but both groups understood the importance of the sash. The grudging respect in the Sarui's eyes was evident as they watched him. Sarui understood honor — their method of reckoning was even more drawn out and painful than that of the Shizu.

He reached the door to the castle foyer and stepped inside. The twenty or so people in the room — all civilians from Gahara's various leifs — fell silent as he moved through them. He pursed his lips grimly. They knew what the sash meant, too, and watched him with the morbid fascination of people watching someone going to the headsman. Ignoring their stares, he moved into the long hallway leading to the Clave Chamber and pushed past several startled nobles of Tsuto.

Eager for the upcoming confrontation, he shoved the chamber doors open and strode inside. What he found surprised him, and he slowed. The chamber, normally bustling this time of day, was empty save for a smattering of guards stationed at the doors and five men gathered in the center of the room. One was the newly appointed Highseat of Gahara. The other four were Leiflords wearing the mark of Clan Samochi. They stood before the dais of the Highseat in a manner indicative of entreaty, and Shavis realized that they had just arrived themselves. Whatever business had brought them to Gahara had likely not yet been addressed.

Their presence tripped an alarm inside his head, and he was suddenly grateful that his reckoning required him to come with his sword. The Samochi lords were not going to like what he had to say.

Good, he thought grimly, *perhaps their reckoning begins today as well.*

He glanced again at the man Leif Tsuto had placed as Highseat and recognized him as Gariel Tobdana, former Sarui warrior raised to Leiflord. He was an ambitious but likeable man who had built himself quite a reputation over the years. It wasn't surprising to see that he'd been appointed Highseat. Finding him giving audience to four Leiflords from Samochi so soon after being raised as Highseat, however, doubled the alarm already sounding in Shavis' mind. Luckily, his *koro* concealed whatever emotions may have shown on his face.

From where he sat atop the dais, Tobdana spotted him as he entered, and his eyes momentarily widened in surprise. Shavis wasn't sure if it was due to the sash on his arm or the symbol of Iga on his uniform, and right now it didn't matter. Everyone not of Leif Iga was his enemy until he knew what was going on.

The four Samochi Leiflords watched disdainfully as he approached, obviously upset at having their meeting with Tobdana interrupted.

Shavis ignored them and, true to the protocol of the reckoning, crossed the room to the circle of black stone set in the floor at the foot of the dais. He went to one knee. "Shavis Dakshar of Leif Iga returning from failed Deathstrike on Croneam Eries of Kelsa," he said formally, pleased to see a glimmer of recognition flash across the faces of the Samochi four. He bowed his head in what he hoped they would take for shame but was really to cover his thoughts. If they saw the look in his eyes, they would know he was itching to draw his sword.

"Your leif has been disbanded," Tobdana said. "Iga no longer has a voice on the clave." Shavis looked up to see Tobdana motion for the Samochi Leiflords to join him on the dais. They took seats to Tobdana's left and watched him grimly.

"Do you wish me to hear your report?" Tobdana asked.

"My honor demands it," he answered formally.

Tobdana nodded. "You may proceed."

Shavis glanced pointedly at the Samochi Leiflords. Now that they faced him, he could see that one of them, an older gentleman with a weathered face and slashes of grey at his temples, wore the gold knot of Highseat on his left breast. *So the Samochi Highseat is involved, is he? So much the better.* "With all due respect," he said softly, "I'd prefer my reckoning not be done in front of them."

Tobdana shook his head. "They are my guests, Dakshar. If you wish to report, you will do so at this time."

"As you wish," he replied evenly, "but Clan Samochi isn't going to like what I have to say." Then, with blatant disregard for Shizu etiquette, he rose and removed the red sash from his arm. Tossing it at the feet of the Leiflords, he hissed, "That belongs to you! This failure lies with Clan Samochi."

He expected some kind of outburst from the four, but they said nothing. All they did was lift their eyes from the sash to regard him with contempt. Tobdana, however, exploded into rage.

"How dare you speak to my guests that way!" he growled, lunging to his feet. "You violate more than Shizu honor in this, Shavis Dakshar!" He gestured to the six Sarui posted at the doors. "Guards, arrest this man. No! I want him executed! Immediately!"

With a hiss of steel, Shavis unsheathed his sword and leapt up the steps of the dais before anyone else in the room could even move. "Stop where you are," he ordered the Sarui. "Unless you think you can close the distance before I kill your pretend Highseat." His sword tip sparkled inches from Tobdana's chest.

Reluctantly, the guards stayed where they were.

"I haven't finished yet," Shavis told Tobdana menacingly.

To the surprise of all, it was the aging Samochi Highseat who spoke. "Go ahead, we're listening," he said. The comment drew a glare from Tobdana.

Keeping his sword at Tobdana's chest, Shavis gave his report. He started with Sallen Zeph and how the rat-faced fool had assumed Deathsquad Alpha were members of the Con'Kumen simply because those in the Samochi Deathsquad were. He told of how he had killed Sallen and then moved to stop the Samochi strike, killing all six members of the strike team to save the children. His interaction with Calis Hurd and the details concerning Tey Eries being left in Kelsa with Raimen and Tohquin he kept to himself.

When he finished, Tobdana was trembling with barely controlled fury. "Lies!" he shouted. "This is a ploy of Leif Iga to regain their standing. It was Tereus who was found guilty of treason. Perhaps he was guilty of more than we first thought. Perhaps it is he and Leif Iga who are Con'Kumen."

"Careful," Shavis warned, edging forward. "I killed the last man who thought I was Soulbiter's servant." He glanced at the Samochi four. "You are awfully quiet," he told them. "Why?"

"Because I believe you," the Samochi Highseat replied.

Tobdana's head whipped toward the man, but he was too stunned to speak.

"Why is that?" Shavis asked.

"Because I ordered the strike," the Samochi Highseat whispered, and a glow of red appeared in his fist.

Something unseen clamped down on Shavis' hands, jerking him forward so suddenly he barely had time to blink. Tobdana had no time to do anything but gasp as Shavis' slender blade took him square in the chest, plunging nearly to the hilt. The red light vanished from the Samochi Highseat's fist, and the invisible grip holding Shavis vanished.

Horrified, Shavis glanced up to find Tobdana staring at him in disbelief. Blood trickled from the corner of his mouth as he mumbled something unintelligible, and then he slumped to his knees and died.

"Guards!" the Samochi Highseat shouted. "Your Highseat has been murdered. Kill this man."

Outraged by what he knew had happened, Shavis jerked his sword free and turned to meet the attacking guards. It would be no use denying the murder they had just witnessed. Trying to convince them that the Highseat of Clan Samochi was an Agla'Con would be just as futile. But he didn't want to kill these men either. They had done no wrong. They were victims of this treachery as much as he or Tobdana.

He met their attack and tried to inflict as little harm as possible while still putting them out of action. The first two were the hardest; both were strong and quick. The third approached him hesitantly, casting uncertain glances in the direction of the Samochi Highseat and only half-heartedly raising his sword. Shavis put him down easily with a kick to the head, then spun to meet the final three. It was unconventional fighting — with them trying to kill him while he did his best not to hurt them too terribly — but when the last guard dropped unconscious to the floor, he was pleased with the fact that no one had died.

That accomplished, he turned to face the dais. There would be no restraint here. The Agla'Con was going to die.

The Highseat of Clan Samochi smiled, and the red of corrupted Earthpower flared in his hand. "It wasn't exactly what we had planned," he said, sounding very satisfied. "But it will do."

"What will?" Shavis asked, taking a few slow steps forward.

He knew he could never reach the dais before the Agla'Con brought the Power to bear. He knew also that he would not survive whatever it was the Agla'Con would hurl his way. Then again, if he could get a few steps closer, a well-placed bladestar might disrupt the Agla'Con's attack long enough for him to finish the man off. He'd read in an Old World text that many of those who corrupted *Ta'shaen* couldn't do more than one thing at a time — if he could get close enough, he still might have a chance. Carefully, he pressed the release button on the hilt of his sword and felt the two-ended dagger detach itself from the handle.

"Drop your sword," the Agla'Con warned, raising his fist to display his talisman.

Shavis did as he was told, and the silvery blade clattered noisily to the floor.

"Gahara will be ours," the Agla'Con purred. "With Iga disbanded and now guilty of the murder of Tsuto's appointed Highseat, leif warfare is bound to break out. We will wait until the dust settles and then Samochi will move in to take control."

"Don't you mean the Con'Kumen?" Shavis asked, and from the corner of his eye he saw one of the guards stir, a slight lifting of his head that showed he was conscious. He experienced a faint glimmer of hope when he realized it was the guard who'd been reluctant to engage him.

"I know the truth of your clan," he continued, keeping their eyes focused on him. If the guard survived, then perhaps...

The Samochi Highseat's smile held no amusement. "The truth can be dangerous," he said. "You of all people should know that."

"I am dangerous," Shavis hissed and hurled the dagger.

Instinctively the Agla'Con struck, and something unseen slammed into Shavis so hard he heard the snapping of bone as he was hurled backward across the room. There was a whirling of color as he tumbled head over heels through the air, and then light flashed inside his head as he struck the floor and slid another fifteen paces to slam into a stone pillar.

He knew he should be dead, but the fact that he wasn't gave him hope. Fighting the waves of dizziness and pain threatening to overwhelm him, he opened his eyes and blinked toward the dais.

The Agla'Con was clutching at the dagger buried in his chest, his face a mask of surprise and pain as he wondered how it had gotten there.

Shavis smiled. It seemed the stories he'd read were correct. The Agla'Con had been able to attack almost without thinking, but he'd been unable to stop the hurled blade. He watched as the man's head sagged forward and he toppled from the chair and down the stairs.

A moment later the doors burst open and a dozen Sarui guards rushed in, fanning out across the room. Shavis forced himself to his knees and watched them come. He was still smiling when they took him.

Watching from the third story window of Togaru Temple, Derian Oronei frowned as dozens of Sarui guards swarmed the entrance to Gahara Castle a half block to the west. Like fish swimming up a strong current, the Sarui plowed through the hundreds of panicked people trying to flee whatever mayhem had erupted inside the castle proper.

"This isn't good," he said, and from the corner of his eye he saw Railen move to the other window and pull back the curtain for a peek. "Shavis has caused quite a stir."

Railen grunted but said nothing as he stared at the scene below. The young Shizu was a good ten years younger than any of the other members of Shavis' squad and newly raised to the sword. And, as they had learned on their journey to Kelsa, he was also newly Gifted with *Ta'shaen*. Like Raimen and Tohquin, Railen's talent was with Light, and he could make himself vanish from sight as they could. But, and this was the part that really had Derian concerned, Railen could also *feel* when others used the Power. Not just Light, but any of the Seven Gifts. Obviously Railen was something more than simply *Dalae*. Shavis had even commented that he thought the youngest member of Deathsquad Alpha might be on his way to becoming a Dymas. Derian gazed at his young friend in awe. *A Dymas*, he thought. *It doesn't seem possible.*

"What do you suppose he did?" he asked, watching to see how Railen would respond. The young Shizu didn't like to speak of his Gifts, especially the one that involved feeling when others used the Power.

"Who knows with Shavis," Railen replied. "But with that much commotion,

I'm thinking it had something to do with..." he hesitated, "with what I felt earlier."

Derian nodded. *The Power.*

He looked back out the window. Fifteen minutes earlier Railen had jumped up and rushed to the window to look toward the castle. His actions had been so startling that Keries had drawn his sword and cast about for an enemy. Derian had been startled as well, but for an entirely different reason. For Railen, so newly come into his Gifts, to have felt the Power being wielded likely meant it had been something powerful.

"We need to find out what happened in there," Derian told him.

Railen let the curtain drop. "I'll go," he said excitedly. "I can go places the rest of you can't."

Derian moved away from the window and fixed the young Shizu with a hard stare. "It will be dangerous," he cautioned, knowing he was going to let Railen go anyway. "If what you say is true, then whoever used the Power may be able to feel you as well."

"I won't use the Power unless I have to," Railen said. "My true gift of invisibility is my youthful face." He grinned. "No one ever considers me much of a threat."

"Only fathers with daughters," Derian muttered dryly, and from where he stood watching the door, Keries chuckled. Derian reached into the inner pocket of the nondescript *kitara* robe he wore and withdrew a pouch of bladestars. "Take these," he said, handing them to Railen. "I don't want you to be completely weaponless." He watched Railen tuck the bladestars away into the drab brown robes of a *Jiu* monk's apprentice, then continued. "Don't do anything except find out what happened. Once you learn that, join me at Tendomi Shrine."

"Yes, Derian," the young Shizu replied. "It will be as you say." He turned to go but stopped at the door. He looked back, his eyes troubled, and for a moment it looked as though he might speak. Pursing his lips tightly, he nodded and slipped silently out the door.

The thudding of booted feet receded down the hallway, and Railen Nogeru rose from where he'd crouched against the wall in an act of deference. He glanced at the backs of the departing Sarui of Leif Shochu and smiled. A dozen strong and armed to the teeth, they had paid him little mind as they'd moved past. Only one had even spared him a second glance. Sarui looked at servants the way they might view a mule or an ox, and, in all likelihood, esteemed the animals of greater value. Their indifference had given him the opportunity to study them carefully.

They'd borne the limp form of a Shizu in their midst, and, while it didn't take a genius to decide it had been Shavis, it troubled him that Sarui from Leif Shochu had taken him when it was Leif Tsuto that held the Highseat. Whatever Shavis had done to elicit such chaos should be addressed by those who sat in judgment.

He watched them vanish around a corner, then turned his gaze in the direction they'd come from. He had only been into Gahara Castle once, but he was pretty sure this corridor led to the Clave Chamber. Glancing around to make sure he was alone, he started down the hallway.

A short distance further on, several young women in green livery moved out of an intersecting hallway, and he flashed them his best smile as he stepped to the side to let them pass. Gesturing grandly with a sweep of his arm, he dipped his head in a bow. The girls smiled back, then quickly pressed their heads together to whisper as they continued on down the hallway.

When they were gone, Railen started forward once more, his apprehension growing with each step. He was nearing the Clave Chamber now; anyone else he encountered from this point on wouldn't be fooled by his boyish smile. The only inhabitants this deep inside the castle would be clave members from Tsuto and the Sarui who guarded them.

He reached the doors of the Clave Chamber and eased one open just enough to peer inside. The room was filled with Sarui bearing the mark of Tsuto, but three more squads from Shochu were visible near the dais. And there, standing among them, were three men wearing the symbol of Clan Samochi.

Railen frowned. *Why am I not surprised?* He knew instinctively that this was tied to the strike on Croneam Eries, but how and why were questions that would have to wait. A squad of Sarui, all of them looking worse for wear, was coming toward him.

He eased the door shut and hurried away down the hall. He'd gone only a short distance when a chorus of angry voices sounded from around the corner ahead of him, cutting off his escape. Frantically he looked around for a place to hide. There was a side passage back near the entrance to the Clave Chamber, but he would never reach it before the Sarui came out into the hall. He tried the handle of the door on his left, but it was locked. The only recessed nook in this section of the hall was occupied by a small table holding a vase of flowers.

He glanced in the direction of the voices and saw the lengths of men's shadows coming into view along the floor. Behind him, the hinges of the Clave Chamber door creaked loudly as someone pulled it open. It was risky, but he had no choice. Calmly, he opened himself to the Power and cloaked himself with invisibility.

Careful not to make any noise, he pressed himself close to the wall and went still.

The angry voices grew louder as half a dozen men, clave representatives from Tsuto from the look of it, rounded the corner and strode past him toward the Sarui leaving the chamber. One came dangerously close to bumping into him, and Railen flinched at the near miss. When they were past, he disengaged himself from the wall and started away.

He rounded the corner only to find a squad of Shizu racing down the long corridor toward him. Cursing under his breath, he moved to the opposite wall and pressed himself into a small enclave fronting a door. Hopefully none of the approaching Shizu were Gifted with Spirit. If so, the bladestars Derian had given him would be needed after all.

The Shizu passed without incident, and Railen thanked the Creator for allowing things to go right for a change. A moment later the squad of wounded Sarui rounded the corner from the opposite direction and moved past. One, an older man with an injured arm and an eye as swollen and purple as a plum, turned and looked right at him. His good eye sparkled brightly.

Railen held his breath, but when the Sarui slowed, he knew that he'd been discovered. He was reaching for the bladestars tucked in his robe when the man called ahead to his companions.

"I forgot my helmet," he told them. "Go on ahead. I'll catch up to you in a moment." He stood there quietly, watching them go. When they vanished into a side passage farther down the hall, the Sarui turned his attention back to Railen.

"I feel you standing there," he said softly. "And I am not your enemy." To show that he meant it, the Sarui moved his hand away from his sword. A moment later he embraced the Power.

CHAPTER 13

Seeds of Rebellion

Tendomi Shrine wasn't much of a shrine, Derian decided. At more than six hundred years old, it was all but forgotten, and its buildings had crumbled into worm-riddled heaps of rotten wood. Most of the symbols carved in the stone markers lining the lane leading in had been worn away by wind and time. The once beautiful gardens and well-trimmed trees were tangled and overgrown with briars and buwalla vines. What had once been the smooth paving stones of a courtyard were broken and cracked, and in many places the stones were tilted upward by Kairus saplings working to reclaim the space. Only a few bars of sunlight angled through the leafy canopy, slender fingers of white that did little to brighten the gloom.

Leaning on one of the marking stones, Derian turned his attention back to the nine Deathsquad leaders from Leif Iga sitting on the short wall across from him and considered what he should do next. The faces of all nine men were pinched into contemplative frowns, and it was clear to Derian that they were wondering what they were doing here. Their collective mood was as dark as the atmosphere of the forgotten shrine. Frankly, he was surprised they had agreed to come here at all.

Meeting once a leif was disbanded constituted treason to the clan — a crime punishable by death should they be discovered. That only nine of the thirty-six Iga squads had sent a representative showed what the majority of the leif thought of treason. Still, he was encouraged that this many were willing to risk their lives to listen to what he had to say. As for the other twenty-seven squads... well, he hoped their refusal to come meant they had decided to wait until the year of transgression was ended so they could be absorbed into the other leifs, and not that they believed the charges against Tereus.

The nine who sat before him were certainly skeptical of his claims that Samochi served Soulbiter and might be behind the removal of Tereus Dromensai as Highseat. Fortunately, they were willing to listen further if he could provide proof. The problem was, he didn't have any. Railen hadn't yet returned from Gahara Castle with word of what had transpired there, and Derian could tell by the faces of the nine seated before him that their patience was starting to thin.

"Even if what you say is true," Akota Tynda said at last, his dark eyes troubled, "and I'm not yet ready to say it isn't, we will have a difficult time convincing the other leifs. They have waited long for the fall of Iga." He rubbed at his silver-flecked hair. "Without proof it will be hard enough convincing the rest of Iga's leaders."

Derian studied Akota a moment before speaking. He was pleased that Akota was among those who'd come. As head of the six strike teams comprising Deathsquad Alpha, Akota was the oldest active Shizu in Gahara and as deadly with sword and bladestar as any Shizu to ever live. It was that skill which had allowed him to reach an age most members of a Deathsquad never would. For the Shizu of Leif Iga, Akota Tynda was a legend. His influence would go a long way in convincing others to join in the search for truth. *If I can convince him.*

"We will find proof," Derian assured them. "And then we will crush Samochi and any others who serve Soulbiter. Leif Iga will be vindicated."

"But what you are suggesting," Madrel Tokasa piped in, "may very well spark a war with Samochi that will swallow all of Gahara. Is the reinstating of Iga worth the risk?"

"Letting servants of Maeon go unpunished threatens all of Riak," Derian countered. *Leave it to Madrel to be the voice of opposition,* he thought. The man was a dyed-in-the-wool pessimist. "They are like Railus Bark Beetles," he told them, hoping the analogy would give them pause for thought. "Ignore the infected branch and the whole tree will become sick."

"But remove too large a branch and the rest of the tree goes into shock," Akota said. "Samochi seats nearly half the Imperial Clave. Empty those seats and Riak will erupt into clan warfare unlike any in the past three hundred years."

Endaman Leir, the youngest of the nine, leaned forward and glanced down the line of men to Akota. "If what I've been reading in the *Holdensar Prophecies* is true, we may be going to war soon anyway. Holdensar spoke of an army of darkness coming forth from the Nine Lands to help Maeon wage war against the Light of Creation. Perhaps these Con'Kumen are part of that army."

"Prophecies," Tokasa scoffed, but fell silent when Akota frowned darkly at him.

"Dalarus Pemaru's squad recently returned from a Deathstrike in Melek," Akota told them. "Talk there was of the return of Shadan and the army his cult is massing to invade Kelsa. With Sagaris massing an army as well, it makes me wonder who we have united with, Melek or Shadan?"

Endaman's voice was somber. "There are many who believe Shadan is nothing more than a myth the cult uses to further its cause. But if he is a long-dead Agla'Con come back to wage war against Kelsa, he would most certainly be evil. Would he not?" He paused to let his words sink in. "Where would a figure such as Shadan — if he is real — get his power? Certainly not from the Light of Creation. I realize Kelsa is our enemy for their treachery in taking the lands of our First Fathers, but don't you think these groups who have sworn allegiance to Maeon are more of a threat to our way of life? Perhaps the 'tides of darkness' referred to in the *Holdensar Prophecies* are these Con'Kumen."

Tokasa eyed him levelly. "Are you saying you believe Derian's claim that the Con'Kumen and the Shadan Cult are connected to the treachery behind Iga being disbanded?"

"If Derian's account of what happened on the Eries Deathstrike is accurate," Endaman began, "yes."

That set off a debate that lasted for over an hour.

Derian listened to them as they went back and forth, discussing things they had heard, asking questions and presenting ideas on this topic or that. They haggled over Sagaris' reasons for sending troops to the northern border to take up positions near Capena. They questioned the motives the Imperial Clave might have had for not calling upon Gahara's armies to join the rest of their countrymen in that mobilization. They frowned at how Clans Vakala and Maridan, two of the most bitter enemies in all of Riak, had suddenly united and sent emissaries to Sagaris seeking the favor of the Emperor as they laid claim to lands controlled by Clan Premala.

But mostly they talked about how there had been no trial for Tereus and no explanation for the severity of Iga's punishment. They were troubled that the Flag of Transgression had been raised without approval from the Imperial Clave and angry that the other five Gaharan leifs had so hastily dispatched nearly their full contingent of Shizu and Sarui to see that Iga was scattered to the wind. Samochi's possible involvement was the hottest topic, and truly fanned the flames of their anger.

Derian let them talk, the first traces of hope rising in his chest as he realized that, slowly but surely, they were convincing themselves to rise up in rebellion against this injustice and fight for the honor of Iga.

七

It was dark when Shavis finally came to after being pummeled by the angry Tsuto Sarui, and he blinked uncertainly for a moment, trying to figure out where he was. The air was close about him, and he was cramped and sore. His first thought was that he'd been thrown into one of the many cells in the lower levels of Gahara Castle; but then he caught a glimpse of starlight visible through the bars directly overhead and realized it was much worse than that.

Great, he thought, shaking his head with disgust, *they dropped me in a* shoari.

Gahara Castle didn't have *shoari,* so he'd probably been taken to one of Leif Tsuto's estates. He looked up at the bamboo poles of his *shoari* prison. The opening was small, barely large enough for a man to fit through, and low enough that he could reach it from where he sat. Just enough moonlight slipped through the poles for him to see that this *shoari* was a scant four feet square. It was constructed of roughly hewn Kairus slats, and he had to be careful not to get sliced by any of the sharp edges.

He tried to push himself into a sitting position, but his right arm screamed in pain. He sagged back against the wall with a hiss. His hand was swollen, and he couldn't move his fingers. Gingerly, he probed the area above his wrist and found that it was broken. He closed his eyes and breathed slow and deep, trying to think past the pain.

When it finally subsided, he clenched his teeth in anger. *Shoari* pits were the lowest, most unsanitary form of imprisonment in Riak, often doubling for garbage bins or latrines. Sometimes prisoners had been left in a *shoari* until they were swallowed by their own waste and died. For Leif Tsuto to dishonor the rank of Shizu by casting him into one showed how much he'd angered them with his supposed killing of their Highseat.

Then again, he was lucky Leif Tsuto hadn't simply killed him — especially considering how vehemently the other three Samochi Leiflords had screamed for his blood. All things considered, this wasn't the worst thing that could have happened.

He shifted his legs to try to remove a cramp, and a pungent odor strong enough to make him gag wafted up from the muck he'd disturbed in the far corner. He quickly amended his thoughts of being lucky. Evidently there were some things worse than death.

He rose up on his knees and peered sideways through the bamboo bars of the *shoari* entrance. He could see several buildings to the right and an open stretch of land to the left. A wall rose behind both and bent around and out of sight. A *leif stronghold,* he decided. *But whose?* He glanced at the banner hanging limply on the pole of the largest building but couldn't make out the symbols. Gingerly, he sat back down and tried his best to ignore whatever it was that squished beneath his weight. There was nothing to do now but wait.

A scuffling sounded in the *shoari* next to him, and he listened carefully, trying to decide if it was a person, a rat, or something worse. Whatever it was fell silent, and Shavis leaned against the wall to think. His arm was starting to hurt again, and even with the stench assaulting his nose, he was hungry.

There was no way of telling how long he'd been unconscious. Hours or even days could have passed. After witnessing the anger in the faces of the Sarui who'd beaten him, he knew he was lucky to have awakened at all.

In the cell next to him, someone coughed.

"So I do have company," he said loudly enough for the other to hear.

"You're the company," the man replied. "I've been here for a week."

The voice was familiar, and Shavis sat up in surprise. "Dromensai?"

"Who asks?" the voice said back.

"Shavis Dakshar of Deathsquad Alpha," he said, trying to keep the excitement from his voice. It wasn't the best of circumstances, but at least he knew Iga's Highseat still lived.

"Dakshar," Tereus said. "Yes, I know you. You were Hardlin's son, yes?"

"Yes," he replied. "I thought you might remember me."

"How did you find your way down here with me?"

Shavis laughed ruefully. "Simple. I uncovered a plot by Clan Samochi to take over Gahara and killed the Agla'Con responsible."

"Doesn't sound like a crime to me," Tereus said.

"Yes, well the Agla'Con was the Samochi Highseat." He paused, waiting for a reply. When Tereus remained quiet, Shavis continued. "The bad part is that before I killed him, he killed Gariel Tobdana, the man who replaced you, and made it look like I had done it."

"I see," Tereus said, his voice tight with anger.

"There's more," Shavis offered. "The Samochi Highseat was a member of a group who call themselves the Hand of the Dark. Con'Kumen in the Old Tongue."

There was a long silence before Tereus spoke. "Are you sure?"

"He told me himself. You've heard of them then?"

"I have," Tereus said. "I was investigating rumors of their organization when I was brought up on false charges and tossed in here."

"The Samochi Deathsquad that accompanied me and my team on our strike in Kelsa were also of their group," Shavis said, frowning at the memory. "I killed them and terminated the strike."

"Why don't you tell me about it," Tereus said, and a loose board rattled near Shavis' head. "There's a crack you can speak through so you can keep your voice down and not anger the Sarui guards. I'm sure you've seen they can be very temperamental at times."

With one last look at the stars visible through the entrance, Shavis put his face close to the crack and began his tale.

と

Sitting beneath the canvas tarp he'd strung between two trees, Derian Oronei looked up from the small fire flickering in front of him as movement at the edge of the camp caught his eye. A Shizu guard materialized from the darkness of the lane leading into Tendomi Shrine and started toward him. A light rain had been falling since midday, and the guard's *komouri* uniform was glistening. From where he sat near a fire of his own, Akota Tynda rose and moved to join Derian beneath the tarp.

The guard stopped short of the makeshift shelter. "Two men are coming this way," he announced, his voice only slightly muffled by his *koro*. "One wears the *kitara* robes of a beggar, but there is no doubt he is Shizu. The other, a Sarui, wears the mark of Tsuto. We have men within striking distance if you think it necessary to have them eliminated."

"No," Derian said. "Let them pass."

The guard nodded and made his way back out into the surrounding forest. When he was gone, Akota spoke. "Why would your man Railen bring a Tsuto Sarui here?"

He'd been wondering the same thing, but didn't have an answer. He motioned Akota to sit. "Let's wait and see."

A short time later two men moved out of the darkness and came purposefully toward them. Behind them moved a half dozen Shizu, hands on weapons, eyes narrowed in mistrust.

Derian sighed in relief when he saw that the one dressed as a beggar was indeed Railen, then he turned his attention to Railen's Sarui companion. He wore his armor, but with one arm bandaged and in a sling and one of his eyes blacked and swollen shut he looked a little worse for wear. His other eye, however, was quick and alert as he studied the three dozen Shizu watching his approach.

"I've brought you the key to Samochi's undoing," Railen said, gesturing to the man at his side. "An eye witness to the events surrounding Shavis' capture and alleged act of murder."

"Alleged?" Akota asked, and the Sarui nodded.

"Shavis Dakshar is innocent of Gariel Tobdana's murder," the man began. "I am Kalear Beumestra, and I was there." He hesitated, looking at Railen for a moment before continuing. Derian saw Railen nod encouragingly, and the Sarui continued. "I was witness to more than those from Samochi are aware," he said, averting his eyes as if he were embarrassed.

"He is Gifted," Railen broke in excitedly. "More so than me. He, too, can feel when others use the Power."

"The Samochi Highseat that Dakshar killed was an Agla'Con," Kalear said with a hint of disgust in his voice. "He is the one who killed Tobdana. I saw... felt... him guide Shavis' sword into Tobdana's chest. It is a simple trick of Air —" He stopped, and Derian realized he'd said more than he'd intended. "The Agla'Con tried to kill Dakshar as well but underestimated him." Kalear dipped his head and added. "You Shizu are resourceful."

Derian dipped his head at the compliment, silently impressed that Kalear had given it. It was no secret that Sarui and Shizu didn't like each other. Even those working for the same leif rarely associated with one another. For Kalear to give such a compliment, especially to a Shizu of a rival leif, was no small thing.

"Does anyone else know of this?" Derian asked.

"Only myself and the three Samochi Leiflords who were with the Agla'Con. As you can imagine, they were very upset with Dakshar. But with Tobdana and the Agla'Con both dead, they weren't in a position to do anything about it."

"Where is Dakshar now?" Akota asked, moving farther back under the canvas and inviting Kalear and Railen in out of the rain. They seated themselves near the fire.

"Sarui from Shochu took him to one of their compounds. I do not know if he still lives."

"Why Shochu and not your leif?" Derian wondered aloud. When Kalear turned to face him, he continued. "Tsuto held the Highseat. It was your right to take him."

"I do not know why Shochu involved itself with Tobdana's murder," Kalear admitted with a shrug. "But it was Shochu who brought the charges of treason against Tereus and pushed to have your leif disbanded. Perhaps they view what Dakshar did as retaliation from Leif Iga."

"Even then it would be Tsuto's right to take him," Derian said, looking to Akota for help. The aging Shizu's face was creased with thought, but he didn't have an answer either.

"There is more," Railen added, his tone darkening. "The three Samochi Leiflords are staying at the same Shochu compound where Shavis was taken."

"But what dealings would Samochi have with Shochu?" Akota grumbled aloud. His eyes narrowed, and his face darkened with anger. "Unless..." he trailed off, unable to continue.

Derian felt his own calm melt away as he realized what Akota was suggesting. Forcing his voice to remain soft so as not to alarm the rest of the camp, he finished Akota's thought. "Unless Shochu has ties to the Con'Kumen as well."

"It would make sense," Kalear told them. "Shochu pushed hard to have your leif disbanded, but only after they lost out on obtaining the Highseat for themselves. It was a very close decision. Tsuto won by a single vote."

Endaman Leir had moved in from the shadows and was listening nearby. When Kalear finished speaking, the young Deathsquad captain took a step closer and spoke. "So your motivation then, Sarui, is to see Tobdana avenged?"

If Kalear was offended by Endaman's tone, he didn't show it. "Dakshar already did that," he said. "But it would please me if the others from Samochi were brought to justice. If what Railen told me of these Con'Kumen is true, then all of Gahara is at risk. Besides," he said, gesturing with his wounded arm, "Shavis Dakshar could have killed me. Very easily, in fact," he added with a grudging frown. "But he didn't. I owe him for that."

"If what Shavis has uncovered is true," Akota said solemnly. "All of Gahara — all of Riak — will owe him."

"Then we attack Shochu and see if Shavis still lives?" Railen asked, his eagerness evident in his voice.

Akota's eyes narrowed grimly. "It pains me to say it, but leif warfare in Gahara has begun."

亡

"Croneam Eries," Tereus whispered, sounding impressed. "I wasn't aware he had returned to the position of First General."

"No one did," Shavis admitted. "It only recently happened. His absence in Greendom is what saved his life."

"Forgive me for saying so," Tereus said, "but I'm glad the strike failed. A man like Eries deserves to die in battle and not from assassination."

Shavis frowned. "But I thought you were aware of the strike. The messenger who brought the order from Sagaris hinted as much."

"No," Tereus replied, anger evident in his voice. "This is the first I've heard of it."

It was Shavis' turn to be angry. "But why would the Imperial Clave send a Deathsquad from an outlying clan without the knowledge of their Highseat?

They would have to know you would find out about it."

"Unless they had already decided I wouldn't be around when you got back," Tereus countered. "I'm starting to think there is more to Samochi's plot to overthrow Gahara than meets the eye."

"And you think the Imperial Clave is involved?" Shavis asked, stunned by what Tereus was suggesting.

"I don't know," Tereus said, but the way he said it told Shavis that he did indeed believe Sagaris was involved. "Perhaps after they sent you on the strike they realized they made a mistake about you being one of the Con'Kumen and this was their way of rectifying the error."

"By destroying the entire leif? Even they couldn't be that bold."

"They've done worse things," Tereus replied. "The question now is what they plan to do next. With Iga disbanded, Clan Gahara is more vulnerable than they've been in three hundred years. It wouldn't take much to bring us down now."

They fell silent as a Sarui guard strode past the openings of the *shoari*. Shavis waited for him to move out of earshot before speaking once more. "I just don't see a connection between the Deathstrike on General Eries and a plot by Sagaris to take Gahara. It might simply be a coincidence."

"It could be," Tereus countered. "But I want you to stop thinking with your head for a moment and tell me what your instincts are telling you. What do you *feel*, Dakshar?"

Shavis was quiet as he considered. Tereus was right. No matter how much he tried to reason this through logically, he couldn't ignore the cold pit of dread that formed in his stomach every time he thought of the Con'Kumen. If they existed in Kelsa, they could certainly be in Riak as well. Maeon didn't recognize the differences of the races. His only concern was the state of a person's soul. That, and destroying every person he could, any way he could.

Though it pained him to admit it, he leaned toward the crack and whispered his answer. "I feel Soulbiter has a hold on the hearts of many throughout our nation, including the hearts of those on the Imperial Clave. What better way to destroy a country than to do it from within."

"But you say a high-ranking official in Fulrath was involved as well?"

"A colonel named Calis Hurd," Shavis said, feeling his anger rise anew. "Apparently, he was as surprised by General Eries' return to duty as we were. Reinstatement for a retired general does not bode well for an upstart colonel. I think he hoped to profit from Croneam's death. He is the one who sought the aid of the Imperial Clave to carry out the assassination. And he provided the guide who turned out to be Con'Kumen."

"Then I suspect this man Hurd is a member of the Hand of the Dark as well," Tereus said.

Shavis nodded. "That's what I came back to Riak to investigate." He shifted his weight, careful of his injured arm, and added, "I believe him to be sworn to Maeon. When I find proof, I will return to Fulrath and kill him myself."

"Taking this personally, I see," Tereus mused.

"A strike ordered by the Con'Kumen isn't valid," Shavis hissed. "Without the honor of the Shizu code, it is nothing less than murder. Innocents were killed, Tereus. I owe it to General Eries — and his grandchildren — to uncover the truth."

"Well, you've certainly uncovered something," Tereus whispered. "The problem now," he added in a stronger voice, "is to find a way to do something about it. We certainly aren't in a position to do much."

Shavis had been considering that since he'd arrived, and it led him to his next thought. "They haven't killed you yet," he whispered. "Why?"

"I'm not sure," Tereus replied. "I've gone before their questioners six times now, and each time all they ask about are the disappearances of clave members from clans I've never had dealings with."

"They think you are responsible?"

"Obviously. Only I have no idea what they are talking about. They don't believe me, though. Probably the reason I'm still alive."

"I still don't see what Tsuto hopes to gain from keeping you. Me, on the other hand..."

"Tsuto?" Tereus asked. "We are in Shochu hands."

Shavis frowned. Now he was really confused. Why would Shochu have taken him? Tobdana was not of their leif. Why would they involve themselves with his murder? It was Tsuto's right to punish him for his crime; they should have taken him. None of it made sense.

He sat thinking for a time, trying to piece it together. Tereus had fallen silent, so he was left to grapple with the mystery on his own. When the guards passed by a half hour later, he still hadn't come to any conclusions.

One of the guards stopped above the *shoari* window, a dark shape in bulky armor that blacked out the background of stars. Shavis knew the man couldn't see down into the pit any better than he could see out of it, but the Sarui's stance was arrogant. He obviously relished the dishonor such accommodations brought upon his Shizu captive. In all honesty, Shavis couldn't say he would feel any different if their roles were reversed. For a Highseat to be treated like this, however, was an abomination. What Shochu hoped to gain by keeping Tereus captive was anybody's guess.

A thought came to him, and he sat up in surprise, shocked and more than a little worried. If the sudden insight were true, things were worse than he'd first thought. He waited impatiently for the guard to move on so he could confirm his suspicions.

When the Sarui finally left, Shavis leaned toward the crack. "Who provided the evidence of your supposed treason?" he asked.

"Shochu did," Tereus answered. "Why?"

"Because I think I know where they obtained it," he said. "I think *they* are the ones working with Samochi."

He could almost hear Tereus thinking.

CHAPTER 14

Strike for Truth

It took two more days for Derian and Akota to contact and convince the other twenty-seven Iga Deathsquads to join together in defiance of the High Clave's order to disband. It was a day and a half more before Iga's Sarui could be convinced of the rightness of the cause. The delay had cost them valuable time, but it had also opened the way for an even bigger rally to the cause. Tokasu Romari, Iga's Leiflord, had come to Tendomi Shrine, and he'd brought members of five of Iga's wealthier families with him. Three had sat on Gahara's High Clave before Iga had been disbanded.

The arrival of Lord Romari was fortuitous, to be sure, but Derian was still angered by the amount of resistance he and Akota had encountered while making their case to the rest of Leif Iga. Even with Kalear's testimony to support it, several members of the ruling class had refused to believe the accusations made against Samochi and Shochu. The situation had worsened when Akota, fearful that those in opposition would leak news of Iga's uprising to the other leifs, had detained them all. *They will be released,* he had assured the other Shizu captains. *When the truth is brought to light.*

Looking at the grounds of Tendomi Shrine now, Derian thought Akota's actions had been wise. The forgotten shrine looked nothing like the vine-choked ruins he'd found four days earlier. A good portion of the encroaching vines and brambles had been cut back. The courtyard area had been cleared of rubble, and tents and makeshift shelters stood everywhere. To one side of the crumbling remains of a centuries-old building, a practice area had been set aside and dozens of Shizu were practicing forms with their swords. On the other side, time was being devoted to bladestars, bows, and other weapons.

Iga had mobilized a small army. Formidable in its own right, but one the other five leifs would crush if they learned of it. One they might crush anyway once the fighting started. The thought made him more than a little nervous. It would be best if they struck Shochu soon. With each passing hour the risk of being discovered increased dramatically.

He glanced over as Akota moved up beside him. The aging Shizu's eyes followed those engaged in mock battle. "The leif representatives just voted," he said, fastening Derian with his dark eyes. "There were enough votes to support a strike on Shochu."

"When do we go?" he asked.

"Tonight," Akota said. "If we leave as night falls, we can follow Adgawa River through Tsuto lands and strike Shochu shortly after dark. Depending on what we learn from those at the Shochu estates, we will then be in a position to strike either Tsuto or Tihou as well if necessary."

"And you are sure the way through Tsuto will be clear?"

"No," Akota admitted with a shake of his head. "But that Sarui friend of Railen's seems trustworthy enough. Unless Tsuto has suddenly altered their patrols, the map he drew should allow us to pass through without incident. If we do run into any..." he trailed off meaningfully.

Sarui friend of Railen, Derian thought with a smile. It was true, of course — the two men had formed an instant friendship. Due mostly, he decided, to their shared abilities with the Power. He didn't mention his thoughts about the two men to Akota, but focused instead on the last comment. "I hope there isn't trouble," he admitted. "Tsuto isn't the enemy here. They are victims of Samochi's treachery as well as us."

Dalarus Pemaru, captain of the six teams who comprised Deathsquad Amai approached from where Lord Romari and the clave members were still clustered together. "That went well," he said when he neared. "But we'll want to act before they can change their minds. Lord Romari still isn't convinced this is the right course of action."

"We will act," Akota assured him. "Everything is in place. We wait only for nightfall."

"Good," Dalarus said with a firm nod, then turned to face Derian. "You'd better be right about this, Oronei," he warned darkly. "Or Iga is finished."

七

Shavis Dakshar gave up trying to work the cramps from his sore muscles and sat back against the rough-hewn walls resignedly. Five days in a *shoari* holding pit was starting to take its toll on his body. He ignored the ache in his arm and tried not to think about the burning rash and sores on his legs and feet or the unsanitary filth which caused it. Save for the beating he'd received for mouthing off to a guard two days earlier, he hadn't been taken out of the *shoari* at all. He was weak from hunger, and usually got sick even when he did manage to eat. The only good thing to happen to him so far was that his sense of smell had given out after the first night. And thankfully so; the stench was unbearable otherwise.

After nearly two weeks in the same conditions, it amazed him that Tereus even had the will to continue living. At first he'd suspected the trips to the Shochu questioners might be offering the Highseat a respite from the vileness of the pit; he soon realized it was merely swapping one kind of torture for another. Today they had beaten him so badly they'd had to carry him back to the *shoari*. When they dropped him unceremoniously back into the filth, Tereus had remained quiet for so long that Shavis had feared him dead. But, as he'd done every other time they'd questioned him, Tereus pushed himself into a sitting position and unleashed a string of curses at those standing watch above.

Shavis admired him for his strength — it was a testament to the power of the Shizu. And Tereus had been outstanding as the leader of Deathsquad Boli before he'd given up the sword to become a bureaucrat. Still, things were starting to look grim, and he wondered how much longer Tereus could survive under such conditions. He feared the Highseat might die before the week was up.

He snarled silently. And what of himself? How much longer could he take it? If it wasn't for his anger and his obligation to Tey Eries, he might have given up already. Somehow he would find a way to fulfill his debt to her.

He rose unsteadily to his knees and peered up through the bamboo poles at the darkening sky. Stars were beginning to appear, and the moon hung large and round above the eastern horizon. The rains of the last few days had finally moved on, but he doubted he would ever be dry again.

He glanced to the left and found a pair of Sarui standing a few paces away. Another pair stood near the well. He hadn't seen a Shizu the entire time he'd been a prisoner, but that didn't mean they weren't around. He had spotted the three Samochi Leiflords moving between buildings yesterday morning, though, so his suspicions about their involvement with Shochu had been confirmed.

He stayed on his knees for a while, letting the cool night air bathe his face as he gazed out across the compound. He was staring distractedly at the outer wall of the compound when a flicker of motion atop the wall caught his attention. It was the barest whisper of black-clad movement, but he knew instantly what it was. A heartbeat later the four Sarui guards stationed around his *shoari* collapsed into heaps, and a dozen black-clad Shizu flowed out of the shadows. When they began pulling up the lids of the *shoari*, he didn't know whether to be relieved or fearful. Crouching down in the shadow of his cell, he listened as the locks were broken loose in a splintering of bamboo. The covering was pulled away, and two shapes loomed above him.

"Dakshar is that you?" a familiar-sounding voice asked.

He sighed in relief and rose, extending his good arm. "It is," he said, allowing himself to be hauled up into the night. His rescuers steadied him, and he pointed. "There, in that one: Tereus Dromensai."

The Shizu who'd lifted him from the *shoari* hissed in surprise. "He lives?"

Shavis nodded. He'd been right about the voice, and it brought a smile to his face. "Yes, Akota. But he is in worse shape than I am. Be careful with him." Several more Shizu removed the lid to Tereus' cell and pulled him up into the night.

"Highseat," Akota said formally. "It pleases me to find you alive." He took Tereus by the hand in greeting. "The area has been secured, and Leif Iga's warriors are assembled and waiting your orders."

From between the two Shizu supporting him, Tereus asked weakly, "How many are here?"

"All of us," Akota replied.

"Excellent," Tereus said. "The Shochu clave is assembled in the main hall. There." He pointed to a building at the far end of the compound, then turned to Shavis. "Your friends from Samochi are still with them." He released the shoulder of the Shizu supporting him and stood on his own, and once again Shavis marveled at Tereus' strength of will.

"Take as many men as you need in order to capture them," Tereus continued, "but kill only if you must. I want to have a few words with the Shochu Leiflord."

Akota bowed and turned to go, but Tereus stopped him. "When they are safely in our custody," he added, his voice tight with anger. "Burn this place to the ground."

From a hilltop a mile to the south of the Shochu estates, Shavis Dakshar watched as a raging inferno engulfed the Shochu clave hall and its surrounding compound in a maelstrom of fire that could probably be seen from anywhere in Gahara. A building collapsed in on itself, and a column of angry sparks whirled into the night sky. By morning all of Gahara would know what had happened.

Iga had lit the flames of war.

Behind him stood the captured Shochu clave members and their allies from

Samochi. Bound and gagged, they watched the destruction of their estates with looks of fury. He studied them a moment longer, then moved to where the Healer was attending to the Iga warriors who'd been injured in the battle.

His own wounds had been healed, but with it had come a renewed sense of smell. It wasn't a pleasant experience. Both he and Tereus smelled like an animal that had been dead and moldering in the sun for weeks. No wonder the other Shizu were keeping their distance. Before he did anything else he would need to find a clean uniform and take a vigorous bath in the river.

Tereus Dromensai stood with the Healer, and the two were talking to Akota. The Highseat had already managed to change into fresh clothes, and color had returned to his face. Except for the exhaustion evident in his eyes, he looked as if nothing had happened. Amazing, considering how close to death he had been. The Healer had commented that Tereus would have been beyond his ability to heal if he'd spent even one more day in the *shoari*.

"It's unanimous then?" he heard Tereus ask as he neared.

"Yes, Highseat," Akota answered. "Every squad has spoken."

Tereus turned to face Shavis. "You're just in time, Dakshar," the Highseat said. "It seems Iga is impressed with your recent deeds and wishes to honor you."

Shavis bowed deferentially. "Thank you, Highseat. But that is not necessary. I work only for the honor of Iga."

"Then continue to do so," Tereus said, "as Shozen of Lief Iga."

Shavis blinked in surprise as Akota slapped him on the back. "Congratulations, Shozen Dakshar," he said loudly. "Iga awaits your orders."

"You did this?" he asked, and Akota nodded.

"Shozen Galasei never returned from his summons to Sagaris. After everything else that has happened lately, it is our fear he isn't going to. Iga needs a leader right now, and the men and I feel you are the perfect replacement."

"With all due respect," Shavis told him, startled by the unexpected promotion. "You are the one who should — "

Akota cut him off with a wave of his hand. Stepping close he spoke in a whisper. "I'm getting too old for all of this," he said, glancing around to make sure no one else could hear. "Once we crush Samochi, I plan on giving up the sword. I want to fight the rest of my battles on the political front."

Shavis wanted to protest, but Tereus spoke before he could. "Do what you need to, Shozen Dakshar, to bring Iga back into honorable standing in Gahara."

It was difficult to force his apprehension aside, but Shavis conceded. "As you wish, Highseat," he said, then turned to Akota. "Select our six best strike teams," he ordered, "and I'll tell you what we are going to do."

七

Sitting tall in the Myrscraw's saddle, Shavis let the cold air of high altitude wash over him and sighed deeply as the briskness awakened his senses. The whispering hiss of the bird's wings as they caught the swift air currents blowing out into the expanse of the Drinisis Ocean made him smile. With a speed unimaginable on the ground, the giant birds were bearing them toward their destination and Iga's next strike for truth.

Stealing the six Myrscraw from Gahara's aviary had been easy; the other leifs had been so busy trying to find out what had happened at Shochu that they'd left the pens relatively unguarded. Using the giant birds without authorization from Sagaris was a serious crime in Shizu society, but it was a drop in the bucket compared to the additional birds he planned to steal from the aviary on the Island of Myrdyn. That act would bring the wrath of every Shizu in Riak down on them once it was known. *But only if we fail in uncovering the truth.*

The thought made him frown. If they did fail in their efforts to expose the Con'Kumen, it wouldn't matter that Lief Iga, disbanded and dishonored, was acting independently from the rest of its clan; Gahara would be finished. In the eyes of Riak, Iga's transgressions would be Gahara's. His beloved city would be destroyed.

He looked up at the sparkling canopy of stars spreading above, then down at the dark gloss of the sea visible beneath the clouds below. The white, reflected image of the moon seemed to move with them as it appeared and disappeared behind the cotton-like masses. The sharp smell of sea salt filled the air.

There was no other place he enjoyed as much as a Myrscraw's saddle. There was nowhere else a person could see the world as it was meant to be seen — the way God must see it.

Surrounded by the seemingly endless black of night, and with nothing below him but the emptiness of several thousand feet of open sky, he felt momentarily isolated from the rest of the world. It was a serenity he truly enjoyed, but one that would be short-lived. When they reached Myrdyn, he and those with him would loose a stone that might bury all of Riak in an avalanche of destruction.

He glanced at the other birds riding the night around him. Each bore the weight of six members of a Deathsquad. Two rode high on the bird's back in the saddle, the other four in light-weight baskets secured to the bird's feet. It was risky, but thirty-six Shizu should be enough to overwhelm those who guarded Myrdyn's main aviary. Especially since they wouldn't be expecting it. The tricky part would be not killing those on duty. Yes, he needed the birds, but he wasn't willing to shed innocent blood to get them. Hopefully the guards would be regular military and not Shizu or Sarui.

Several minutes passed, and Myrdyn Isle came into view, a rugged chunk of black against the shimmering expanse of the ocean. Shavis raised his arm and the other five birds moved into formation around him. When they were all in place, he gave the signal and watched as they dropped from view, feathery blades of death knifing toward the ocean below.

When they were lost from view, Shavis nudged his Myrscraw into a slow descent, angling toward the island as was Shizu protocol. With any luck, the spotters would see him coming and would be ready at the aviary to receive him. By then, Akota and the other five squads would be in position.

The main aviary was located in the mouth of a rugged canyon fronted by an Imperial stronghold. That stronghold, with its walls and battlements lining the shoreline of Myrdyn Bay, had been designed to repel a naval attack. Apparently, no one had ever considered the possibility of an attack coming from the air. The Myrscraw were the property of the Shizu, after all. And the Shizu belonged to the Imperial Clave.

Not any more, he thought darkly. *Those ties are about to be severed. Forever.* Because regardless of the outcome of his search for the Con'Kumen, Leif Iga was about to commit an unpardonable act of treason.

The lights of the watchtowers came into view, and Shavis angled the Myrscraw toward them. When he passed by one of the towers a moment later, a spotter was swinging an oil lamp in welcome. The green flame inside showed that all was well.

Grinning, Shavis turned the bird toward the massive dome of the aviary and began his final descent. As he sailed over the rooftops of the stronghold, he was pleased to find everything dark. Except for the watchtowers and the guardhouse at the aviary's entrance, the inhabitants of Myrdyn Isle were asleep.

He glanced at the lattice of the aviary dome and pursed his lips admiringly. From a distance, it bore the appearance of an overturned wicker basket, one that was loosely woven with gaps to allow in air and sunlight. The supporting tines were not wicker, but fully grown senfer trees. The lashings were buwalla vines. Even dried, most were thicker than a man's leg; some were as long as a city block. The dome itself could shelter an entire village, or, as was the case here, an entire army of Myrscraw. At capacity, Myrdyn's aviary could hold as many as three hundred of the giant birds. He doubted there were that many in here tonight — unfortunate since he planned on taking them all.

He guided his bird toward the ground-level entrance of the aviary, taking in the scene before him. He was pleased to see that only a dozen guards were on duty. None of them were Shizu.

There was a deep *swooshing* of air as the giant bird hovered long enough for the passenger basket to be unloaded, then it settled gently to the paving stones and waited for the basket to be unlashed. Shavis climbed from the saddle and turned to face the guards. The puzzled expressions on their faces were obvious.

"What business have you with Myrdyn?" one of the men asked, eyeing the rest of Shavis' squad curiously. "We've received no word of a Deathstrike." He glanced again at the bird. "You aren't returning it are you?"

Shavis shook his head. "No. We aren't returning it."

"Then state your purpose," another man said, suddenly wary.

A flickering of black coalesced around them, and the guards found themselves staring at the glittering points of two dozen Shizu swords.

Akota moved up out of the darkness. "The area is secure, Shozen," he said. "What shall we do with these?"

Shavis kept his eyes fastened on the guards. Their faces were pale and frightened. They fully expected to be killed. "Bind them and tuck them away some place where they will be found in the morning. As long as they are quiet, don't harm them. If they try to raise an alarm, silence them."

He moved to the first man who had spoken and held out his hand for the man's sword. "Our fight is not with you," he said, looking him in the eyes. "No one here needs to die." Keeping his hand extended, he waited.

Reluctantly, the man handed over his sword, then motioned for his men to do the same.

Shavis nodded to Akota, and the guards were led away. When they were gone, he turned to Derian. "Open the flight doors," he ordered. "We take every last bird."

七

Akota Tynda watched Shavis riding the night sky ahead of him and smiled with admiration. He had indeed been the right choice for Shozen of Leif Iga, he decided. No one else would have been willing to make a decision so monumental. Or so far-reaching. By taking ninety-seven birds from Myrdyn, Shavis had, in a symbolic gesture at least, declared war on Riak. By tomorrow, Riak would be ready to declare war on Shavis.

He let his eyes move across the aerial armada filling the sky around him. A hundred and three birds — nearly a quarter of all the Myrscraw in Riak. Nowhere else would they be found in such numbers. Even Sagaris had no more than ten or twelve. By taking so many, Shavis had not only made it easier for Iga to carry out its hunt for the Con'Kumen, he had effectively crippled an aerial retaliation against Gahara. At least until Sagaris united enough clans and acquired enough birds to launch an assault. And that was assuming they didn't use the winged shadowspawn he'd heard tale of. If the Agla'Con got involved, five thousand Myrscraw wouldn't be enough to save Gahara.

He thrust the thought away. Below him, the Iga'rala Mountains were dropping away to reveal the broad valley of Gahara. It spread before them in a sea of mottled shadow. Most of the outlying valley still slept, the residents of the various leifs unaware of the turmoil ready to engulf them.

Nestled in the center of the valley some distance ahead, however, the city proper glittered brightly. The attack on the Shochu compound had undoubtedly roused every last member of the High Clave. They wouldn't know who the enemy was, of course, but he knew they would be prepared to meet it. *Good. It will keep them busy until we can finish with...* He stopped, realizing that he didn't know *what* Shavis planned to do next. Not that it mattered. He had complete confidence in the newly appointed Shozen's abilities.

Around him, the riderless birds banked right, following Shavis' lead, and Akota and the others urged their own birds to follow. Moving along the foothills to the northern end of the valley, they turned into a narrow forested canyon. There, they descended to the heavily fortified compound that was Iga's secret stronghold.

Tereus Dromensai was waiting for them in the courtyard as they landed. Moving up to them, the Highseat surveyed the Myrscraw approvingly. "You have big plans, I see," he said.

"Yes," Shavis replied. "But we must move quickly if we are to achieve our next objective."

"Which is?"

Shavis' face darkened. "To hunt the Con'Kumen in Samochi."

Surrounded by the Shizu of Deathsquad Alpha, Shavis Dakshar checked the stars to see the Flower Constellation dipping near the western horizon. It would be light in another hour. The trip to Gahara with the stolen birds to pick up the rest of Iga's Deathsquads had taken more time than he'd anticipated. Akota's insistence that they fly back east to the ocean and approach Samochi from the direction of Myrdyn Isle had cost them valuable time as well. Still, Akota's plan was good. Now if they were spotted by anyone on the ground or in the air, they would be mistaken for an envoy from the Riaki Isle. It would take time for news of the stolen birds to reach Sagaris, so the deception should work.

Another positive to Akota's plan was how it had allowed them to avoid Sagaris' air space and the winged creatures that filled the sky over Sagaris at night. Rumor said the creatures were shadowspawn controlled by Agla'Con.

Shavis frowned. The shadowspawn had been news to him, but he wasn't going to doubt anything where the servants of Maeon were concerned. If Soulbiter's influence had spread beyond Clan Samochi, he and the rest of Iga would hunt it there as well. He clenched his teeth in anger. *Even if we have to hunt in Sagaris itself.*

Pushing the thought away until later, he scanned the coastline visible through a break in the clouds, a thin ribbon of white crashing on jagged rocks. He urged his bird to angle a bit more to the southwest. Around him, the rest of the giant birds matched his movement.

Samochi lay ten leagues inland, nestled in the heart of a broad river valley used mainly for growing crops. The clan's wealth had come as a result of being the leading producer of rice in all of Riak. *But*, he thought darkly, *they've been sowing other seeds as well.*

When they crossed the shoreline and moved over land, Shavis guided his bird down until they were only a few hundred feet above the trees lining the river. He made a quick count to see if all the birds were still with him, then scanned the darkness ahead for the lights of Samochi. They came into view a few minutes later, a scattering of pin pricks against the predawn darkness.

Most of the city still slept, it seemed, completely unaware of the wave of death winging toward them. As expected, the signal towers ringing the city were dark. Even if the Myrscraw handlers of Myrdyn Isle had somehow managed to send word of the theft to the mainland, there was no reason for anyone in Samochi to believe they would be the target of a massive strike. Any message would have been sent to Sagaris to inform the Imperial Clave of the tremendous crime. He imagined the Emperor calling the clave members together at this very moment to discuss the theft and speculate on the thieves' motives.

He smiled. A day or two more, and all of Riak would know what those motives were.

They crossed the boundary marking the outskirts of the city, and buildings streamed below them in a blur of angles and lines, occasionally broken by a grove of trees marking a shrine or temple. A moment later Samochi Castle came into view, its five-story keep looming above the stone fortifications of its foundation.

Pyramid in shape, but with jutting eaves at each level, the keep was a rugged-looking building, its sharp angles at odds with the smooth stone of the walls and battlements below. A few watch lights burned at intervals throughout the castle compound, small pools of light that did little to throw back the gloom.

The windows of the uppermost part of the keep were lit as well, but it was more for display than for security.

Sitting up in the bird's saddle, he raised his arm and gave the signal. Death-squads Amai and Boli broke north and south in a flanking maneuver while Deathsquad Alpha and the others went straight in.

The members of the Samochi clave would most likely be housed in the keep itself, but there were a few mansions and homes on the castle grounds that might be home to some as well. None would be spared attack; he wanted them all.

As was the custom, those of the ruling class would be guarded by Sarui, so he and his men shouldn't have trouble overpowering them. They would, however, need to act quickly if they hoped to secure the gates of the inner compound and avoid an onslaught by the Shizu stationed without.

If we can close the gates, he thought with a smile, *it will take an army to recapture the keep.* Samochi Castle had an odd layout, but one that would work in his favor. Iga's Deathsquads could hold it for several days if needed. It should be enough time to find what he was searching for.

He didn't want to fight a battle with Samochi just yet — or at all, if it wasn't necessary. His war was with the Con'Kumen. If he could learn the truth of their organization, he could loose the entire Riaki nation against them.

He heard a shout from the ground as they passed over the inner wall of Samochi Castle, but whatever alarm the man might raise would be too late. In a flurry of giant, grey-black feathers, the Shizu-laden Myrscraw plunged into the heart of Samochi like a knife.

Standing on the battlements of Samochi Keep, Shavis gazed down at the army assembling below and waited for Derian to bring him word. Rays of morning sunshine bathed the battlements in a sheen of orange, but the swarming mass of men gathering below was still locked in shadow. He could see clusters of Shizu in their black *komouri* uniforms and *koro* hood-masks standing beside groups of leather-armored Sarui. All seven Samochi leifs were present but stood apart from one another according to leif.

A good sign, he decided. It meant they mistrusted one another, perhaps suspecting that a leif from Samochi was responsible for the capture of the keep.

He studied the cluster of men nearest the gate leading into the inner compound and was able to get a glimpse of their banner. Byoten — the leif whose Highseat he'd killed in Gahara. He'd learned during the fighting this morning that Byoten had retained control of the clave and had already appointed a new Highseat.

He shook his head in disbelief. That one, too, had been Agla'Con as evidenced by the gaping hole in the side of the second story of the keep. He wished he would have considered the possibility the Agla'Con he'd killed in Gahara would have surrounded himself with others like him. The oversight had cost Keries and six other good men their lives. Their deaths pained him. So did the damage to the keep.

He wondered how many in Leif Byoten knew that the two men they had elected to represent them had sworn themselves to Maeon. He hoped it wasn't many. He wanted to believe that the majority of Riaki citizens were still a righteous people. They had to be. He refused to believe Maeon could have gained such a hold over them. Deceived them, perhaps, but not converted them. The Con'Kumen were simply a disease that needed to be eradicated before they could spread further.

And he certainly didn't want to fight those gathering below if their crime was nothing more than being misled by the Hand of the Dark. Enough innocent lives had already been lost due to their scheming. There was no need to add to the bloodshed. He needed to root out those responsible and bring their dark works into the light. And he needed to do it before the Samochi leifs organizing below lost their mistrust of one another and decided to attack. Because they would attack, he knew, as soon as they realized it was an outside force who had captured the keep. They would attack in spite of the written warning he'd tossed down earlier that the Highseat and the rest of the clave members would be killed if those outside the keep didn't cooperate.

Since the Highseat was already dead, it wasn't much of a threat. But the Samochi leifs didn't know that. If he had to, he could toss the Highseat's body into the courtyard below to show he meant business. They wouldn't risk the lives of the other clave members after that. Maybe.

He turned and glanced at the shattered corner of the keep and frowned. He suspected the gaping hole left by the battle with the Agla'Con was part of the reason the Samochi leifs hadn't attacked. They knew what had wrought the destruction and weren't eager to involve themselves in a battle where there was no defense against their enemy's power.

Returning his attention to the massing army, he spoke to Akota standing silently beside him. "We don't have much time before they decide the lives of their clave members are less valuable than the honor of Clan Samochi. When they do, they will attack."

"That is how I figure it as well," Akota said, then fell silent once more.

Leaving Akota to his silence, Shavis returned to his study of the army milling below.

It was almost an hour later before Derian came for him. The young Shizu's eyes were wild, and his voice was breathless as he hurried up to them. "Shozen," he said excitedly, "we've found something."

Shavis glanced at Akota, and they followed Derian as he jogged across the rampart and into the keep. The young man kept looking back to make sure he hadn't lost them, and Shavis wondered what could have so completely disrupted his Shizu calm.

They followed him up four flights of stairs and down a narrow passage. At the far end was an opening where a thick door had been chopped from its hinges. No, he decided, not a door but rather a false wall which could be swung aside, probably with a hidden lever or catch. That axes had been used showed that Derian and those with him had been unable to find the release. That they had realized it wasn't a real wall in the first place was nothing short of a miracle. He wondered how they had discovered it.

"In there," Derian said, pointing through the gap.

Shavis cast a quick glance at Akota, then moved inside. What he found turned his blood to ice.

An altar of black stone stood in the center of a large room, dull rivulets of what appeared to be dried blood streaking the sides. The windows at the far end of the room had been darkened with something that could have been blood as well, and the morning light filtering through was a tainted hue of amber. Scrolls of canvas and thick parchments bearing the complex characters of the Ancient Language hung on opposite walls.

Behind the altar stood a small shrine with a two-foot-high carving of a man inside — a man dressed in crimson and black robes with a crown of fire shaped from pure gold. That alone would have been enough to send a chill up Shavis' spine. Combined with everything else, it caused the hair on his arms and neck to stand on end. He turned to find Akota scanning the scrolls.

"You can read them?" he asked, and the greying Shizu nodded.

"They are prayers to Maeon," he said, his voice filled with disgust. "And those," he said, pointing to the parchments, "are the words to their sacrifice." He met Shavis' gaze and his eyes narrowed in rage. "A blood sacrifice."

Shavis frowned at the altar. He'd been right about the streaks.

Derian moved up beside him, a look of revulsion on his face. He pointedly ignored the altar and gestured to the far corner.

"There's a cabinet in the corner, Shozen Dakshar," he said formally. It was an obvious attempt to hide his disgust for what they'd found. "We thought you should be the one to open it."

Shavis moved to the large wardrobe-like cabinet. It was locked, and he doubted the key was anywhere to be found. He turned to ask for the axe Derian had used to open the wall, but the young Shizu was already retrieving it for him.

Hefting the axe, Shavis took one last look at Akota, then smashed the lock in a single stroke. He pulled open the doors and moved to one side as Akota held up a pair of glowstones.

Four black robes with crimson lightning bolts sewn into the shoulders hung on hooks, and an assortment of wicked-looking daggers sat on a shelf above them. The jeweled hilts threw back the light of the glowstones in an array of multicolored prisms.

The real discovery, though, was a black, leather-bound book tucked in behind the daggers. Shavis eased it from the shelf and opened it.

"This is it," he said, thumbing through the pages. "This is what we came for."

On a page near the back of the book he found the date of the Deathstrike on Croneam Eries. And there, on the list of Con'Kumen contacts in Kelsa, was the name of Calis Hurd.

CHAPTER 15

The Enemy Within

The messenger saluted and left, and Elam Gaufin and Taggert Enue stared at one another in surprise. Elam looked at the note once more and raised his eyebrows. Croneam had been back from Trian for two days now, and this was the first communication they'd received from him since meeting him in the Tunnel.

"Why would Croneam want us to attend this meeting?" he asked. "It doesn't have anything to do with us."

"I don't know," Taggert shrugged. "Perhaps there is more to it than just a discussion of new trading policies."

"I hope so," he said. "I hate discussing things I know nothing about." He glanced across the compound to where the two thousand men of the Chellum Home Guard were being housed in squat, red-bricked barracks. The practice field was visible between the rows of buildings, and he could see a large number of his men engaged in physical exercise and weapons practice. The activity was a result of the daily routine he'd set for them in order to keep them focused on the upcoming war.

He heard shouting and laughing mingled with the sounds of practice swords clacking and nodded to himself. That was the other reason he'd ordered the physical routines — the main reason, really — since he wanted to keep them all from going stir crazy. Let a man linger too long on what he was missing back home and there were bound to be problems. So far, his plan seemed to be working.

"I never thought I'd say this," he told Taggert. "But I hope Croneam has an assignment for us. I'd hate for my men to lose their focus."

"Is sending them into battle your answer?" Taggert asked.

"We're going to fight eventually," he replied. "Why not sooner than later? More of us will live through it if we are alert instead of complacently lazy."

"Your men look sharp enough to me," Taggert said in their defense. "Perhaps your expectations are too high."

"A result of having to answer to Seth Lydon," Elam muttered. "For him, nothing short of perfection will do." Mentioning the Chellum captain made him wonder where Seth and the others were and if they were well. He hoped they were safe in Trian, but he suspected Gideon Dymas had whisked them off into harm's way once more. He had the greatest respect for the warrior-prophet, but Gideon drew shadowspawn and other evils the way a lamp drew moths. He hoped Gideon's party fared well in their quest to heal the Earthsoul. Success for them in that endeavor meant fewer lives lost out here on the front lines.

He tucked the note in his pocket, and he and Taggert started for the fortress.

"Seth Lydon is a remarkable man," Taggert mused softly as they walked. "Too bad he made himself an outlaw in Capena. We could have used him on the southern border. His knowledge about Riak would have been invaluable. In all honesty, Riak scares me more than the shadowspawned armies of Shadan."

Not me, Elam thought silently. Aloud he said, "Seth is more valuable where he is. From what I understand, our only hope of defeating Shadan is to rejuvenate the Earthsoul. And the only two who can do that are Endil and Jase Fairimor; keeping them alive is priority one."

"I thought Gideon Dymas was with them."

"Precisely why they need protection," Elam muttered. "Seth will keep an eye on all of them, Gideon included."

They reached the end of the cluster of barracks assigned to the Chellum Home Guard and turned up a wide, tree-lined lane. Manor homes belonging to the High Command and others associated with the governing of Fulrath lined both sides of the street. Children played on the shaded lawns between the homes, and their laughter filled the air with its sweet sound. It was a smattering of normality in an otherwise rigid environment.

He glanced up at the fortress looming overhead and sighed resignedly. And yet it was difficult to forget that Fulrath was a city built for war, no matter how normal life might appear on the surface.

At the fortress gate they returned the salute of the grizzled veteran seated in the shade of the guard tower, then moved through into the courtyard beyond. A pair of warders on their way out of the fortress proper passed them, and Elam caught a piece of their conversation.

"I don't understand it either," one of the men said, "but it has the Governor's signature on it. Orders are orders."

Elam watched them over his shoulder for a moment before following Taggert into the domed foyer leading to the council chambers. As always, he was impressed with the statue of Fulrath's Fighting Lion. For something carved from stone to look so real was truly remarkable. That it faced the entrance in a stance which undoubtedly caused many first-time visitors to flinch in surprise, showed the craftsman had a sense of humor as well. There were a handful of people in the room, but all of them avoided his gaze as he and Taggert moved through their midst. They passed a pair of custodians mopping the floor near the lion, then nodded to the pair of guards who stepped aside to allow them into the hallway leading to the council chamber.

The room was packed with people eager to hear what Croneam had to say, so he and Taggert took seats on the back row near the door. *That way,* Elam thought, *I can make a quick exit if the meeting should prove too long or boring.* He looked to the front of the room and found most of the military council already present and seated on the stand. Governor Prenum's chair was noticeably empty, however. So was Croneam's.

Joneam Eries spotted him and Taggert and motioned for them to join him on the stand. Elam declined with a wave of his hand, then glanced at Taggert. "I'd rather stay out of the collective line of sight," he told his friend. "This council stuff isn't for me." Taggert shrugged his indifference, and they squeezed in on the back row.

Elam studied the crowd for a moment before leaning back in the bench and resting his head against the wall. The murmur of voices filling the room was loud, but he was still able to hear what the two women seated in front of him were discussing. It wasn't very complimentary of Croneam or the military, so he cleared his throat loudly enough to get their attention.

They turned to look at him, noticed his uniform, and hurriedly faced forward once more, red-faced and silent.

Taggert laughed. "I see you haven't lost your touch with the ladies."

Elam frowned at him but said nothing.

"I'm only teasing," Taggert said, elbowing him in the ribs. He fell quiet for a moment, then asked, "I've been meaning to ask you... how is your wife going to get along while you're away?"

"She'll do fine," he replied. "Her mother came to live at our house so she can help Jaina with the baby."

"I didn't know you were a father."

"I'm not, yet. The baby isn't due for another month or so."

"I see," Taggert said, and something in his voice made Elam look at him. "I know becoming a father can be a scary experience for some men," Taggert continued, "but it's not worth killing yourself over."

Elam raised his eyebrows. "What are you talking about?"

"This sudden eagerness you seem to have for fighting Shadan's armies. If it were me with a child on the way, I'd do everything I could to avoid battle. You've been talking like you want to orphan your child before it's even born."

"Wrong," Elam replied flatly. "It's because of my wife and child — and all the other wives and children in Chellum — that I'm eager to engage the enemy. I *am* thinking of them when I risk my life." He gave Taggert a flat-eyed stare. "I have sworn to preserve Chellum, but I certainly intend to stay alive while doing it."

When Taggert looked skeptical, he continued. "You weren't there so you didn't hear what I heard — didn't *feel* what I heard. Gideon Dymas *prophesied*, Taggert. He said that if I and my men would do all we could, even to the extent of leading the charge if necessary, then Chellum would be spared."

"So the Home Guard is to be the sacrificial lamb?" Taggert asked, raising a questioning brow.

Elam shook his head. "There's more. He told us that we are the finest Chellum has to offer. He said that because we are part of Chellum — the Chellum he said would be preserved — if we would put our trust in the Creator, we would be preserved as well."

"I see," Taggert said, his tone just as dark as before. "So you aren't reckless because you are afraid of becoming a father, you're reckless because you're indestructible."

"I never said that," Elam snapped. He could see where this was going, and he wasn't about to be drawn in. Taggert loved to philosophize, and this was the kind of topic he loved most. If he didn't put an end to this right now, the old general would drag it out for days. "I said if we trust in the Creator we will be preserved. If we don't...." He shrugged. "The faith of men is a fickle thing. I don't call that being indestructible."

"Yet your faith is strong," Taggert said. "Do you think to carry all two thousand of your men on your shoulders?"

"I'll bloody well do my best," he growled, hoping to make clear by his tone that he was done discussing the matter.

Before Taggert could reply — and it was clear he was going to — the doors opened and Colonel Hurd stepped into the room. He glanced around briefly, and his eyes fell on Elam and Taggert. "Please, come join us at the front," he said, motioning them to rise.

"No thanks," Elam said. "We're comfortable right here."

"Oh, but you must," Colonel Hurd insisted. "You are part of Fulrath's military now. It will be good for the merchants, and especially the bureaucrats, to see Chellum and Fulrath united under Military Law."

Taggert rose, but Elam leaned back against the wall. "I prefer to keep a low profile," he said.

"A low profile? After everything you just told me?"

Elam scowled at him for a moment, then rose to join him, gesturing for him to follow Hurd who was moving up the aisle ahead of them.

It was then that he heard a muffled sound, far away down the hallway toward the foyer. It was swallowed almost immediately by the murmuring of voices all around him, but for that one brief moment it had been clearly audible. And it had sounded like a scream.

Frowning, he stopped and turned back to the door, cocking his head to listen. He couldn't say for sure, but he thought he could hear the dull ring of clashing steel.

Taggert stopped. "What is it?"

Elam lifted a hand to shush him and reached for the latch. "I'm not sure," he said, pulling open the door.

The clash of steel on steel sounded loudly, and someone howled in agony. Without waiting to see if Taggert was following, Elam drew his sword and bolted toward the sounds of battle.

"Because I told Gideon Dymas I'd be ready to march to Zedik Pass within the month," Croneam told Lenea as they walked down the hallway leading from his study, "that's why."

"But is closing the city to trade necessary for you to accomplish your objectives?" she demanded angrily.

Croneam held the door for her, and they passed into the antechamber of the private stairwell leading to the bureaucratic section of the fortress. The guards in the antechamber stiffened and kept their eyes fixed on the wall, pointedly minding their own business. He smiled at their wisdom. Most of the soldiers in this part of the fortress knew of Lenea's temper. A few of the unfortunate ones had been on the receiving end of one of her tongue-lashings.

"I'm not closing trade," he told her patiently, pleased with how calm he kept his voice. It was the one tool he had that could soften her wrath, and he tried to use it whenever he could since she had a hard time fighting with him unless he shouted back. "I'm tapering it down a bit. We need to encourage the residents of the surrounding communities to take their business elsewhere for the time being. Fulrath is a military establishment, after all, and one with an extremely large bull's eye painted on it at the moment. What good will trade do any of our people if Shadan's armies fill up the Free Zone?"

"I still think you're being too abrupt," she said without looking at him. Her tone had softened considerably, so he knew his plan of not fighting back was working. "Two weeks isn't enough time for most of them to relocate their merchandise, let alone find a new place to do business."

"Merchants are resilient," he said, shrugging. "They'll do fine. Besides, I've offered to purchase a lot of their goods myself for the upcoming war. Soldiers need supplies you know."

"And I suppose you'll be paying military prices," she muttered darkly.

"Wars are expensive," he countered. "If they don't like what I offer, they can always transport their goods to Tradeston or Trian. I'm sure they could get more money from either place."

"But transporting anything that far means a loss of profit worse than selling to you," she snapped.

He sneaked a glance to find her face red with anger.

"Convenient, isn't it?" he said.

She scowled but said nothing.

He reached over and gently touched her arm. She met his gaze, her eyes angry.

"I'm not trying to rob our people," he told her softly. "True, they will lose money on their goods. But money is the least of things at stake right now. They will most likely lose everything they own, their homes included, if the Meleki armies lay siege to the fortress. The sooner we rid them of what will only weigh them down and get them far away from here the better. They don't have to lose their lives as well."

"They'll remember you as a cheat if you don't handle things right," she warned.

He reached up to stroke his mustache. "Possibly," he said, pushing open the door at the bottom of the stairs and gesturing Lenea into the narrow hallway leading to the foyer. "But I intend to be remembered as the man who saved their homes from destruction."

They passed an empty sentry nook, and Croneam frowned. Reaching into his pocket for his watch, he found that it was only two o'clock. The sentry change wasn't due for another hour. He slipped the watch back into his pocket and made a mental note to scold whomever had left their post unattended. Even in the heart of Kelsa's largest military establishment proper protocol must be strictly adhered to. Especially in the heart of —

He let the thought die as they reached the foyer.

There should have been two guards fronting the private corridor, but he and

Lenea moved into the high-domed room through an empty doorway. The statue of the Fighting Lion faced an empty doorway as well; the main entrance was unguarded.

The foyer, normally a hive of activity, was quiet, the benches mostly empty. Only ten people waited for their chance to speak to a council member or judge — only ten; when thirty or forty usually had appointments. If anything, the foyer should have been even more crowded than usual since he hadn't given the council enough time to cancel their appointments for the rest of the day. The lack of people hoping for audience didn't make sense.

"Did you send word to the council to halt all regular duties?" he asked Lenea.

"No," she said. "Why?"

An alarm went off in his head, and he slowed, taking a closer look at their surroundings. Two guards — men he didn't recognize — blocked the entrance to the council chamber, and it didn't take a genius to realize they were agitated about something. In addition to the patrons, two custodians stood near the statue of the Fulrath Lion. Croneam knew most of the staff in this part of the fortress, but he had never seen either of the men before. He couldn't tell what they were working to clean up, but their mops, he noted curiously, weren't wet.

He glanced at a man seated on a bench. With his head down and his arms folded, he appeared to be asleep. Only the nervous tapping of a finger gave away the lie. Farther down the bench, a woman in a blue dress with a shawl hanging about her shoulders was fumbling with the contents of a basket she had sitting in her lap. The basket was much too large for any practical use, and the woman appeared nervous. Next to her stood a man studying the mural hanging on the wall before him. His riding cloak was long and heavy — odd considering how warm it had been lately — and there was a bulge near his hip.

Croneam reached over and took Lenea's arm, bringing her to a stop. She glanced at him, her face still angry from the argument they'd been having, but the anger vanished when she saw the look in his eyes.

"What's wro — " She cut off as the room erupted into movement.

Both custodians stepped on the ends of their mops and pulled, revealing steel-tipped spears cleverly concealed as the shafts. The foot-long blades flashed brightly as they raised them and started forward. The man feigning sleep and the one studying art pulled swords from under their cloaks and moved forward as well. The woman pulled a crossbow from her basket and leveled it in his direction.

It all happened so fast that Croneam barely had time to shove Lenea behind him and draw his sword before the two custodians reached him.

The wooden shafts were no match for the Power-forged steel of a Dragon-blade, and he severed both with ease, then hissed in pain as one of the severed spear blades came spinning into his side. The pain was excruciating, but he clenched his teeth and ignored it.

With one broad sweep he removed one man's head, then killed the other with a thrust through the center of his chest.

When the rest of those seated around the room screamed and dove for cover, Croneam breathed a sigh of relief — it meant they weren't part of the attack. More importantly, it meant there were only three left to deal with.

Make that five, he amended silently, watching as the two guards drew their swords and moved to stand with the others.

A crossbow bolt whistled past his head and shattered against the far wall, and he saw the woman in the blue dress working to reload her weapon. He could count on one hand the times he'd faced a female enemy in battle, and although part of him cringed at the notion of killing her, he had very little forgiveness for assassins. Reaching to his side, he yanked the spear blade free and hurled it in her direction. His blood mingled with hers as the blade took her in the chest and she collapsed with a gasp. The crossbow clattered uselessly to the floor beside her.

Aware of the growing patch of blood at his side, he moved forward to engage the remaining four. He grimaced when he saw the look in their eyes — a kind of frenzied light that told him they fully expected to die and weren't afraid of doing so. Normally he would take comfort from an enemy realizing they were overmatched, but this was different. These four looked eager to die, perhaps believing they would die as martyrs for some cause only they understood. He slowed. An enemy who didn't care about dying was a formidable opponent, dangerous and unpredictable.

They came at him as one, and he was forced to give ground. He parried every thrust, his sword a flashing streak of silver as it flicked first one way, then another. From the corner of his eye he saw Lenea gliding around the outer edge of the room, shushing the terrified witnesses while she kept an eye on the battle. She reached the woman in the blue dress and retrieved the crossbow.

Croneam didn't see if she was able to load it because his opponents grew bolder and it was all he could do to keep from getting his head chopped off. One of the guards slashed him across the forearm and blood welled forth, darkening the grey of his sleeve and wetting his wrist.

The pain sparked his anger and he whirled, dropping to one knee and slicing the man's legs out from under him. He collapsed with a gut-wrenching howl and lay writhing in a rapidly spreading pool of blood.

In one smooth motion Croneam came back up and managed to clip the other guard across the cheek. The man slapped a hand to his wounded face only to gasp in shock as a crossbow bolt took him squarely in the back. Lenea, it seemed, was a better shot than the woman in the blue dress.

The remaining two, seeing their comrades dropping like leaves before the wind, grew desperate and attacked in a frenzy, swinging with a fury he could barely hold back. Even worse, they separated and moved to squeeze him in between them.

He tried backing toward the statue to keep them from surrounding him, but they saw what he intended and rushed him. He managed to deflect their swords but was unable to strike a blow in return. He was growing tired now, and they knew it.

The doors of the council chamber flew open and Elam Gaufin raced down the hallway toward him. General Enue was close on his heels, and behind him came Colonel Hurd and several guards.

Elam Gaufin fell upon the nearest assassin and killed him easily, then turned to stand with Croneam against the remaining assassin. Alone now, the man flailed his sword desperately, though uselessly, unable to make contact with even the outstretched swords surrounding him.

Seeing that the man no longer posed a threat, Croneam motioned for his men to back off. He wanted this one alive.

Colonel Hurd obviously missed the signal. Snarling in rage, he took a crossbow from one of the guards and shot the man dead.

"You fool," Croneam shouted. "I wanted him alive."

Before Hurd could respond, Lenea's voice broke into the silence. "Croneam," she said softly. "This one still lives."

He moved to where Lenea knelt over the woman in the blue dress. Her breathing was shallow, her eyes distant and unfocused.

"This isn't how it's supposed to be," she said as if talking to some unseen person. "I served you well. I was promised a place of glory at your side. The Hand of the Dark — " She gasped, and her body jarred as if struck. A heartbeat later she died.

"The Hand of the Dark," Croneam hissed. "So they rear their ugly head in Fulrath now, do they?"

"What's the Hand of the Dark?" Colonel Hurd asked.

Before Croneam could answer, Lenea gasped. "Croneam, you're bleeding!"

She scowled at Hurd. "We can discuss the Con'Kumen later," she told him. Taking Croneam's sword, she handed it to Elam, then led Croneam to a bench where he could sit. "Captain Gaufin, if you would please run to the front gate and report this to the guards, they will send someone to fetch a Healer."

"Yes, Governor," he said and sprinted away.

Croneam watched him go, then turned back to find Lenea's eyes fastened on his face. "I'd tell you that you are not as young as you used to be," she said, "but you'd get mad at me." Folding a wad of cloth she'd taken from the dead woman's basket, she pressed it to his side. "So instead I'll say that old or not you are a skilled warrior, Croneam Eries, and I owe you my life." She hesitated as tears sprang to the corners of her eyes. "How did this happen?" she asked, her voice bitter. "How did these people get so close to you?"

"I don't know," he said, putting his hand on hers and helping to apply pressure to the wound. He had lost a great deal of blood, and he felt weak. But he was angry too. "But I'd say they had help." He looked at the two dead guards. "And if I find out there were more people involved than the few here today, I will open the flood gates of my vengeance. There will be a reckoning of blood so great even the Con'Kumen won't be able to stomach it."

Taggert chuckled softly. "Hard to stomach, indeed, since it will be their blood that flows."

Nodding emphatically, Croneam waited for the Healer. No one spoke as soldiers arrived and began hauling the bodies of the would-be assassins away, and Croneam took advantage of the silence to close his eyes and lean back against the wall. *How had this happened?* he wondered. *How had these parasites gotten so close?* He winced as Lenea increased the pressure on his wound.

And they were parasites, he decided. *Filthy creatures living off the good of their host.* That Fulrath could be infected was infuriating.

Elam Gaufin returned a few minutes later with Resaline Groben, one of Fulrath's many Healers. She took Croneam's head in her hands, and the healing flows of Earthpower surged into his body. When Resaline released him, Croneam rose to his feet and surveyed the foyer, pointedly ignoring the *tisking* sound Resaline made as she eyed him up and down.

Custodians — real ones this time — were mopping up the blood slicking the tiles and were doing their best to remove all traces of the battle. The merchants and members of Fulrath's council were still gathered in the council chamber, and he didn't want them tracking blood through the fortress once they were dismissed.

They would know something had happened, of course. His delay and the way Captain Gaufin and the others had stormed out of the council chamber a short while ago would tip them off. *But,* he thought grimly, *they don't need to see the aftereffects of the battle.*

He rubbed at his newly healed side and marveled at Resaline's ability. She was new to her assignment, only four years on the job, but her skill nearly equaled that of old Joselyn back in Greendom. He'd have to ask Joneam where he'd found her.

Taking a fresh shirt from the soldier who'd run to fetch it for him, he pulled it on and began buttoning up the front while he gazed down the hallway toward the council chamber. When he finished, he checked his watch and was surprised to see that less than ten minutes had passed since the attack began. Perhaps he would be able to downplay the incident after all.

"Lenea," he said, "if you're up to it, I think we should still address the council."

"Do you think that is wise?" she asked, searching his face with her clear blue gaze. He knew what she was thinking and made a placating gesture.

"I'm all right," he assured her. "Just a little tired." Ignoring Lenea's skeptical look, he glanced in the direction the Healer had gone. "That young woman has great skill," he said, then turned to Taggert and Elam who stood off to one side. "Thanks for your help as well," he added. From the corner of his eye, he saw Hurd frown, angry at being left out of the thank you. *Bloody fool*, Croneam thought. *We could have used the last one alive.*

He pulled on a new jacket and met Lenea's gaze once more. "I will not let this feeble attempt on my life disrupt my efforts to win this war. It will take more than two-bit assassins, Con'Kumen or otherwise, to end what I plan to accomplish."

"And what about an investigation?" Lenea asked. "Don't you want to find out who arranged all this?"

"Of course I do," he told her. "But first things first. Let's address the merchant issues and then we'll hunt the Con'Kumen. If what I experienced in Trian is any indication, hunting them won't be an easy task. They are elusive and shrewd. Elison Brey has been trying to root them out of Trian for months. Only lately has he had any success." He frowned at the memory of the battle inside the Dome. "And his efforts have come at great cost. Knowing what the enemy is capable of makes ridding the city of all non-military personnel that much more important. After seeing the resources the Con'Kumen brought to bear in Trian, this really was a pathetic attack."

"But one that still almost succeeded," she countered. "Next time you might not be so lucky."

"There won't be a next time," he replied. "I plan on doubling the guards with men I choose myself."

Elam Gaufin stepped forward. "It might not mean anything," he said softly. "But on the way in I overheard two guards, warders actually, discussing an order they'd received from the Governor. I didn't hear what the order was, but I think they may have been pulled from duty here in the foyer."

Croneam turned to Lenea, but she shook her head. "I issued no orders," she said.

Croneam frowned. "Two other pairs of guards weren't where they were supposed to be either," he said softly, glancing around the room at those milling about. "Perhaps there is more to this than simply a bunch of cultist fanatics."

"You think the guards were involved in a conspiracy of some sort?" Lenea asked.

"Those two were for sure," he told her, indicating the bodies being hauled away. "The others..." he hesitated, "I'm not sure. Most likely they were issued bogus orders so they wouldn't be here when the attack came."

Elam nodded. "That is my theory as well," the young captain said softly. "But you know what that means?"

"Yes," Croneam said. "We already suspected there was a traitor in our midst. Someone with a lot of authority and clearance."

"Any ideas?" Elam asked.

Croneam glanced to where Colonel Hurd was talking quietly with Taggert. "No," he lied, then lowered his voice to a whisper. Only Elam and Lenea could hear his words. "But whoever it is covers their tracks very well." He pulled at his mustache thoughtfully. "Still, there may be a paper trail we can follow. Those orders came from somewhere. After meeting with the merchants, we'll interview those who received them and see if we can trace it back to the source." He gestured them forward. "The sooner we finish with the new trading policies, the sooner we can investigate."

CHAPTER 16

The Will of the Earthsoul

"Well, that went better than expected," Joneam commented as the last of the bureaucratic council members filed out of the room. "I thought the Merchant's Guild would put up more of a fight."

"How could they?" Lenea commented darkly, "with Croneam being so..." she paused for emphasis, "*blunt.*"

Taggert snorted a laugh. "He certainly was that. I don't know who was more surprised, the merchants or the bureaucrats."

Standing to one side with Teig Ole'ar, Elam listened as Croneam issued orders to the High Command concerning the tapering off of trade and the eventual evacuation of all non-military personnel and wondered for the hundredth time why he and Taggert had been summoned to the meeting. Neither of them were members of Fulrath's military tribunal. Perhaps it was nothing more than an act of courtesy — Taggert was a general after all — and he supposed it wouldn't be polite to invite the leader of one of Chellum's forces and not the other. Still, it was pretty boring stuff, and he hoped it didn't go on much longer.

From talk of trade, the conversation turned to the assassination attempt and how best to investigate it. Governor Prenum stayed quiet, but Elam could tell she was angered by Croneam's downplaying of the incident. Elam had to agree with the general, though. After the attacks that had taken place in Chellum Palace and Fairimor Dome, things could have been much worse.

Croneam ordered a doubling of the guards at every station — an order that drew a bitter look from Colonel Hurd since he would be in charge of carrying it out — and Lenea requested a full contingent of warders be assigned to Croneam at all times. The aging general scowled, but when the rest of the tribunal nodded their agreement, he conceded.

When talk finally turned to the war with Melek, Elam perked up. At last, something that might concern him and the two thousand he led.

"Phase one," Croneam said, "will be to recapture Zedik Pass and fortify it against the time when the main body of Shadan's army begins their march."

"How do you know they aren't there already?" Colonel Wyndor asked.

Croneam smiled. "I have it on the best authority that their main army is still in the Plains of Criet. And I doubt the group holding the pass is of any size. Once we retake it, a couple thousand men could hold it for weeks if they set their defenses at the narrows."

Colonel Hurd leaned forward. "What about the Agla'Con rumored to be with this army? One or two of them could retake the pass without much help from those they lead."

"The Agla'Con are more than just a rumor," Croneam said, glancing at Teig. The Elvan spy stood unflinching beneath his stare. "My Master of Spies has informed me that they number five hundred or more."

"Five hundred!" Hurd shouted. "What need have they of an army with those kind of numbers?"

"And how would you expect regular soldiers to stand against them?" Wyndor asked. "Defending the pass or otherwise. We have none who can use the Power as a weapon."

"That might not be entirely true," Elam said, and all eyes turned to regard him. "One of my men has ability with *Ta'shaen*. True, he is young and has little idea what he is doing. But if he is Gifted, others may be as well."

"Unfortunately," Joneam said, "very few have answered Lord Fairimor's call to come forth and be trained."

"More will come," Croneam insisted, but his son seemed unconvinced.

"Is there some way we can facilitate this gathering?" General Gefion asked.

"Not unless you can eradicate the irrational prejudice most people have toward those who can wield Earthpower," Taggert said. "Until the fear the Gifted have of war outweighs their fear of the public's reaction toward them, they will be hesitant to come forth."

"All we can do is continue to spread the word," Croneam said at last. "People who are Gifted have a special connection to the Earthsoul. She will bring them forth when the time is right."

The comment made Elam smile. It was nice to see someone have faith in things larger than himself. Perhaps if more people exercised that kind of faith, victory wouldn't seem so out of reach. He noticed Taggert's skeptical frown and let his smile fade. For as philosophical as Taggert seemed to be, Elam was starting to wonder if the man even believed in God at all.

"Back to the problem of Zedik Pass," General Chathem said. "Assuming the Agla'Con don't get involved, a very unlikely prospect if you'll pardon my opinion, there will still be a sizable force there, shadowspawn included. You said yourself that Shadowhounds destroyed part of the caravan."

"That is true," Croneam conceded. "But only Shadowhounds were used, not Agla'Con."

"And your point?" Gefion asked.

"Gideon Dymas told the High Tribunal that the Agla'Con aren't so much warriors as they are shadowspawn leash-holders. They will fight when they have to, I'm sure. But it won't be until Shadan thinks it's necessary, and it won't be in Zedik Pass."

"How can you be so sure?" asked Colonel Hurd.

"Because if they start blasting things with Air and Fire and Earth in a place like the narrows," Croneam said, "they'll bring the cliffs down on their own heads as well; not a very convenient thing to have happen if you're needing to move an army through there. No. They'll fight that much of the battle with conventional soldiers — at least as conventional as an army made up of shadowspawn can be."

As Croneam and the others talked, Elam felt a tickling on his skin, a faint whisper of unseen energy that caused the hair on his arms and neck to stand on end. Puzzled, he rubbed at the goose pimples popping up, but the feeling only grew stronger. The very air around him seemed to come alive with power. It was warm and soothing even as something icy cold tickled his mind. Those around him seemed unaware of whatever it was he was feeling, so he tried to dismiss it.

"Who shall we send to retake the pass?" Joneam asked, and Elam flinched as the energy gathering around him intensified, a sudden surge of warmth that flowed into him in a rush and caused his heart to burn. It was the same feeling he'd felt when Gideon Dymas had prophesied about Chellum's involvement. He knew what it meant — what it was telling him to do.

"I'll go," he told them. "And take the two thousand I command." As the words left his mouth, the burning in his chest intensified sharply, then vanished. All that remained was a faint whispering in his ears, not truly audible, but enough to fill him with a feeling of absolute calm.

Croneam reached up to stroke his mustache thoughtfully, while Joneam and the other two generals raised questioning eyebrows. Taggert sat with his mouth hanging open in shock.

"What makes you think it should be you?" Croneam asked at last. His eyes burned with intensity, but his voice was soft.

"I felt something just now," Elam explained, his voice firm with conviction. "I volunteer because it is the will of the Earthsoul that I should." He knew how crazy it must sound to the others, and the look Taggert exchanged with Hurd confirmed it. They thought he was out of his mind.

Croneam's gaze, however, remained unchanged.

"Your men are Palace Guards," Joneam said into the silence. "I know they are well-trained defenders, but what experience do they have with attacking a fortified location? I mean no offense, but I wonder if they have the skills necessary to launch this kind of attack. Do they have any combat experience at all?"

"Practically none," he told the younger Eries, his eyes still locked on Croneam's. "Except the skirmish in Talin Pass, most of my men have never fought. But like you said, they are well-trained, and their skills involve combat in tight quarters as would be necessary for fighting inside a castle or fortress." He paused and turned to Joneam. "The narrows, they are restrictive to a lot of movement?"

"No more so than the hallway of a fortress or the back alley of a city," Croneam answered.

"Or a wagon rut," Taggert muttered dryly.

Elam ignored him. So did Croneam.

"Forty years experience as a general and every shred of common sense I possess are screaming for me to say no to this," Croneam said. "But I can't. I open my mouth to form the words and they die on my tongue." He leaned forward and his hazel eyes glittered. "Because I believe you about this being the will of the Earthsoul. I felt something just now as well. Therefore, I grant your request."

"What?" Taggert gaped, and generals Chathem and Gefion turned equally surprised looks on Croneam.

The aging general's face was set. "You heard what I said. Elam Gaufin and his men will retake Zedik Pass for us. Two thousand is more than enough to accomplish the task. And they will be able to hold it for us until we can move more of our army into place."

"This is madness," Taggert hissed. "Sending him to Zedik Pass is only going to fulfill the death wish he so suddenly seems to have. For a week now, all his talk has been of things that make me think he is deliberately trying to get himself killed."

To everyone's surprise, Croneam laughed. "We all die eventually," he said.

"Perhaps it's best to do so on one's own terms." He grew serious once more, and his gaze returned to Elam. "Zedik Pass is yours," he said. "Don't disappoint me."

Elam gave a slight nod. "I won't."

Back in his study, Colonel Hurd stood in front of his liquor cabinet and cursed steadily. Too angry to drink, he held the empty glass and shook his head in disbelief at how miserably the assassins had failed. Either they were completely incompetent or Croneam hadn't lost as much of his skill as a man his age should have. Either way, the attack had been a disaster.

He poured a glass of brandy but didn't drink it. And that bloody Captain Gaufin. Bloody meddling do-gooder with his bloody talk of the will of the Earthsoul... what a bunch of rubbish!

He took a calming breath. So Elam felt compelled to try to retake the pass did he? Well, it wouldn't be hard to get a message to those who held it, warning them about the Chellum Home Guard. One or two Agla'Con should be able to wipe them out without too much trouble, so long as they did it outside the narrows. Croneam was right about the cliffs collapsing if a battle were to be fought with the Power.

He took the shot of brandy in a single gulp. Elam and his men were a minor problem and could be easily dealt with. Croneam, on the other hand, was proving much more difficult. And he had less than two weeks before the Satyr returned to... he'd rather not think about what.

He poured himself another shot of brandy. There was still enough time to come up with another plan to eliminate Croneam. Worst case scenario: he'd kill Croneam himself. It would mean getting him alone, and striking before the general knew any better — a must if he were to succeed. He had no illusions of being able to take Croneam in a fair fight; the man had earned a Dragonblade for a reason.

But if he killed Croneam himself, he would have to flee Fulrath and most likely Kelsa as well. It would free him of his obligation to the Brethren and keep the Satyr from coming for him, but it would mean the loss of everything he'd worked so hard to gain.

He moved to the window and looked out at the city. Dusk was approaching, but men still practiced in the yards, and there was movement in the streets. In Merchant's Quarter, however, things had already quieted down for the night. In the courtyard below, soldiers moved about on patrol. Not a full hour had passed since Croneam issued the order, and already a full doubling of the guards was in place. And Governor Prenum's order for warders to attend Croneam at all times only made matters worse.

Calis turned the tiny glass in his fingers and smiled. If it did become necessary for him to kill Croneam himself, being in control of fortress security would make it feasible. But where to flee to once the deed was done? Certainly not Riak. He'd had enough of Shizu and their odd ways. Zeka then? Or perhaps one of the many islands they controlled?

He knew it was time to start planning an escape. It didn't matter if he hired the deed done or did it himself; with Shadan's armies coming, his days in Fulrath were numbered anyway.

Elam Gaufin stood on the observation tower in the practice yard assigned to the Chellum forces and gazed down at his men assembling below. Many were bare-chested, having already started preparations for bed. Others, on their way to wash up when they'd heard the order to assemble, held towels.

Taggert stood next to him, mumbling about the lunacy of this course of action. Elam ignored him as best he could and waited for the rest of his men to gather. When they were in place, he raised his hand for silence.

"Men of Chellum," he said loudly, "we have our first assignment. One that will surely put us in harm's way, but one I'm confident we can perform with honor." He expounded the assignment in detail and watched as looks of concern sprang across the faces of those nearest the tower. If theirs was any indication, the rest of his men were probably equally alarmed. When a whispered ripple of dismay washed across the group, he knew he'd been right. Taggert heard it as well and muttered something about 'always being right' under his breath.

Elam wanted to shove him over the railing.

"Though this fight is far from our home," he continued, keeping his attention fastened on his men, "the peace and safety of Chellum is at stake. When Fulrath is threatened, the rest of Kelsa is threatened with it. Chellum has never suffered an assault from an invading army. Let's keep it that way." He paused and weighed his next words carefully, not completely convinced he should share them. But anything that could build their confidence was worth the risk.

"On the night we left Chellum, Gideon Dymas told me that the Home Guard had a special role to play in this war. He said that when the time came, I would know what we were supposed to do. This is it, gentlemen; Zedik Pass is ours. If we fight honorably, Chellum will be spared."

He had expected some kind of reaction, but there was only silence. It made him wonder what they were thinking. "Dismissed," he called and turned away. It was a three-day journey to Zedik Pass; perhaps he would know their thoughts by then.

CHAPTER 17

Children of Ta'shaen

Elison Brey studied the list of names of the Con'Kumen he'd captured during the raids on the chapter houses and frowned in frustration. It was a short list — too short for the number of people captured — but there was simply no way to identify those who refused to talk. If not for the cooperation of a handful of young people newly recruited to the so-called brotherhood, as well as a select few like Cheslie Brandameir, he wouldn't even have the names he did. And he certainly wouldn't have uncovered the locations of two additional chapter houses. He blew out his cheeks in frustration. Two hundred and twelve people in custody, and he had names for only forty-three. The Hand of the Dark kept their secrets well.

A knock at the door startled him, and he looked up as Breiter stuck his head into the room.

"Sorry to interrupt you," the young captain said, moving into the room, "but we are needed at the palace's main gate."

Elison rose. "Is something wrong?" he asked, tucking the list of names away and buckling on his sword.

"I don't think so," Breiter answered, but he didn't sound sure. "There is a small group of people claiming to be Gifted who want admittance into the palace. They say they have come in answer to the crowning of Fairimor Dome with Fire." He shifted his feet uncomfortably. "Without Gideon or Jase here to verify it, though, we have no way to be sure. They could just as easily be Agla'Con for all either of us would be able to tell."

Elison joined him at the door, and they started down the passage leading to the Fairimor home. "I wouldn't put it past those conniving vermin to attempt such a trick," Elison told him. "Especially with Zeniff somewhere here in the palace."

He looked over at Breiter to find his face lined with concern. Reaching out, he clapped his young friend on the shoulder. "But my heart tells me this is something good for a change. Gideon told me this might happen. He said Jase's fulfilling of prophecy had likely opened the floodgates for other prophecies to be fulfilled as well. The Gifted answering the call is one of them."

"I hope you don't mind if I hold onto my paranoia until we know for sure," Breiter said. "It's what's been keeping me alive."

Elison eyed his friend for a moment without speaking. Breiter's face was set, and there had been no trace of levity in his voice. After all the young captain had been through lately, Elison couldn't say that he blamed him for his suspicions about the arrival of those claiming to be Gifted. "I suppose it wouldn't hurt to have a contingent of archers close by in case these people turn out to be hostile," he said. "We can never be too careful when the situation might involve Agla'Con."

Breiter nodded. "I'm glad you think so," he said, sounding relieved, "since I already instructed Captain O'sei to see to it."

Elison gave a hearty laugh. "I should have known your paranoia would have already gotten the best of you."

Breiter tried to look offended, but it didn't last; a heartbeat later he smiled. "My paranoia has gotten the best of the last five people who have tried to kill me," he said. "As long as it works..." he trailed off meaningfully.

"Has Lord Fairimor been informed of the arrival of these people?" Elison asked.

"Yes. He was also optimistic about what it might mean but cautioned me to be careful. If they are what they claim, Lord Fairimor wants them brought into the inner palace so he can welcome them. He wants to know if there are any among them who can use the Communicator Stones and ward the links. He received word this morning from Governor Drastin that several Dymas have come forth in Tradeston."

"That's good news," Elison replied. "With the arrival of Gifted here in Trian, I was hoping the other cities may have had some come forward as well." He shook his head. "And it's about time," he added. "I was starting to wonder if there were any Gifted left in the world."

"They're out there," Breiter said. "They simply needed something to get their attention. Something to let them know they aren't alone."

"Well, Jase certainly did that," Elison commented. "But in all likelihood, he caught the attention of every Agla'Con in the country as well."

"Good. I hope it scares the life out of them," Breiter said, reaching up to scratch at the goatee he was letting grow back. "After Randle finishes meeting with the Gifted," he said, returning to the topic at hand, "I suppose we'll have to find them a place to stay until we can decide what to do with them. We really need Gideon here to train them for battle."

"That would be nice," Elison agreed, "but I'd rather have Gideon where he is, looking after Jase. The boy scares me worse than anything Shadan or Maeon might throw at us."

They entered an antechamber and started down the stairs leading to the dining hall. The pair of Elvan *Bero'thai* standing guard nodded to them as they passed, and he and Breiter returned it without speaking.

"We've identified three more of the Con'Kumen taken in yesterday's raid," Breiter told him as they made their way down the stairs. "Cheslie Brandameir recognized one as a young lady from her neighborhood. The other two gave up their names voluntarily. All three seem ashamed by what they have done and are hoping their cooperation will afford them a lighter sentence. I think some of them really didn't know what they were getting themselves into until it was too late. Even if they'd wanted to leave the organization, they wouldn't have been able to. The Con'Kumen aren't very forgiving toward those who betray them."

Elison let a frown harden his face. "Seth told me they would have killed Miss Brandameir if we hadn't interrupted their meeting. It makes me think the sharp rise in the number of murders over the past few months is a direct result of people trying to leave the Con'Kumen after learning its true purpose. They're being killed to keep them quiet."

"I thought the same thing," Breiter said. "But what troubles me even more than that is the number of people who didn't leave the organization even *after* learning the truth. What kind of a person gives himself over to Maeon?"

"One who deserves death," Elison growled. "And if I get my way, I will exterminate them all."

Breiter grunted in agreement.

They reached the dining hall, and Elison blinked in surprise when Elder Nesthius rose from the table to meet them. The aging Prophet rarely came into the Fairimor home anymore. It had, in fact, been months since his last visit.

Elder Nesthius smiled knowingly, his aged face a maze of wrinkles. "I had business up in the temple," he told them by way of explanation. When he chuckled, Elison realized he'd let his disbelief show in his face.

"I'm not *that* old and feeble," the elderly Prophet said. "Besides, I had a pair of your *Bero'thai* help me to and from."

Breiter glanced around as if looking for someone. "Where is Elder Zanandrei? I should think he would have liked to have gone with you."

It was Nesthius' turn to be surprised. "Young Jendus is at the church holding services," he said, then raised a snowy eyebrow at them. "You didn't know today was Church Day?" he asked, the disappointment heavy in his voice.

"We've been busy," Elison replied, unable to hide his embarrassment. "I guess I lost track of what day it is."

"I should think you two, of all people, would be seeking a little divine help to strengthen you in your war against the dark side," Elder Nesthius chided.

Elison and Breiter turned to look at one another, both of them at a loss for words.

Elder Nesthius nodded emphatically. "Good. I can see that you regret your negligence toward the Creator and that you will not let it happen again." He started toward them, his pale blue eyes sparkling brightly. "You will be pleased to know," he said, taking them each by the arm and leading them toward the doors exiting to the Dome, "that I have some information which should lift your spirits in light of your negligence."

"And that is..." Elison prompted.

"The Children of *Ta'shaen* are returning."

Holding the aging High Priest's arm to support him as they moved through the outer palace, Breiter listened to Elder Nesthius tell of his trip to the Temple of Elderon. He was glad in his heart that the aging Prophet was still with them; he was glad that he was still able to hear the voice of the Earthsoul. Ninety-five years had taken its toll on his body, as evidenced by his need of support to walk, but his mind and his will were as sharp as the day he was anointed High Priest of the Church of Elderon. And his eyes, bits of polished blue agate, shone with the intensity of a forest fire.

"I was carried away in a vision," Elder Nesthius told them as they walked, his wrinkled face tight with emotion. "In it I saw many things that will shortly come to pass. Some are good. Others... not so good. The one that concerns me most is where I beheld the Hand of the Dark rise up and try to take control of Trian."

"You said 'try to take'," Elison said, motioning for the warders stationed at the door ahead to open it for them. "Does that mean we put the attempt down?"

"Honestly," Elder Nesthius replied with a shrug, "I don't know. That vision faded into another before I could see the outcome."

"That could mean the outcome is uncertain," Breiter offered.

Elder Nesthius shrugged. "The outcome of most prophecies is uncertain," he said. "It is the paradox of prophecy. On one side is the Prophet who sees the events of the future. On the other side is the person in that future who, in spite of what some long-dead man has said, has agency to act as they wish. And while it is true what we do today can prepare the way for those prophecies to be fulfilled, it is that moment yet in the future that tips the balance one way or the other."

"What else did you see?" Breiter asked, turning the conversation back to where it had started.

"That the people who have come to the palace claiming to be Gifted will play a part in the upcoming war against the Con'Kumen."

"Well, that's good news," Elison said with a grin.

"It would be," Nesthius said, "if I knew what part they are to play. That's the other problem with prophecy," he said turning to glance at Breiter. "Just because someone has a part to play in something doesn't mean the rest of us are going to like what they do."

"I thought you said you had learned something good," Elison said, the exasperation evident in his voice.

"The return of the Gifted is good," Nesthius told them. "It heralds the return of the *Mith'elre Chon*."

Breiter frowned. "But doesn't the coming of the *Mith'elre Chon* mark the beginning of the Third Cleansing and a series of battles prophesied to forever alter the Nine Lands?"

Elder Nesthius turned to study him for a moment. "You're a bit of a pessimist, aren't you?"

Elison laughed heartily. "No. He's just paranoid."

Elder Nesthius gave a little shrug. "Not a very good way to live."

Breiter was about to respond on how it was paranoia that had kept him alive all these years, but they reached Elder Nesthius' apartments before he could form the words.

"Thank you for escorting me," the elderly church leader said, taking hold of the door latch to support himself as he turned to face them. His face grew solemn as he continued. "One other thing I saw," he told them, his voice as solemn as his face. "One that concerns you both directly." He paused, his eyes moving back and forth between them for a few moments. "Not many days hence, arrows shall hiss around you as thick as hail from a summer storm. One of you will pass through the storm unscathed. The other..." he said, his voice and eyes sad, "will fall."

"Now *I'm* going to be paranoid," Elison said after Elder Nesthius closed the door in front of them. He glanced at Breiter to find the young man's face pinched into a frown. It made him wonder what his friend was thinking. *Probably the same thing I am,* he thought darkly. *Is it going to be me or him?*

Breiter turned to meet his gaze. "Well, this is rather awkward," he said uncomfortably. "I don't want to be the one to die, but I don't want it to be you either."

"It's not going to be either of us," Elison told him firmly. "Elder Nesthius said the outcome to most prophecies is uncertain. We'll just have to do what we can to keep it that way."

"If that's true," Breiter countered, closing his eyes and taking a deep breath, "then why tell us about it at all?"

"So that we can thwart it," Elison answered. He didn't really believe it was possible, but he wanted to say something to put his friend at ease. He had learned from watching the recent events unfolding in Jase's life that attempting to stop fate was equivalent to trying to stop an avalanche by throwing rocks at it. He put his arm around his friend's shoulders. "Come on. We have people waiting for us at the main gates."

When they arrived at the vaulted foyer on the palace's main level, they found Taka O'sei waiting for them at the doors leading to the courtyard. A dozen Palace Guard, dressed in ceremonial armor, stood to one side of the doors, while a contingent of Elvan *Bero'thai* in their mottled greys stood on the other. The two groups were eyeing one another with looks that showed how deeply the riff between them had become. He'd been right when he'd told Gideon that the Palace Guard viewed their reassignment to the outer palace as a demotion. That they had been replaced by men not of their own country had likely made the insult that much worse.

He was pleased to see that Taka didn't share his men's discontent. The dark-haired captain stepped forward to greet them. "Are you two all right?" he asked. "You look like you just drank a glass of sour milk."

"We're fine," Elison lied. "Are your archers in place?"

"Three dozen line the top of the courtyard wall," he answered. "If these Gifted turn out to be more than what they claim, I'll have them turned into pin cushions."

Elison nodded. "Great. Let's go see who they are." He started to follow Taka but stopped when Breiter took him by the arm.

"If it's okay with you," the young captain said quietly, "I think one of us should wait in here." He glanced around guardedly. "I might be wrong, but I took Elder Nesthius' vision to mean that we would be together when the storm of arrows came. If we stay separated, the prophecy can't be fulfilled."

Elison studied Breiter's face for several moments, trying to gage his emotions.

This went way beyond his friend's normal paranoia, he realized. This was a deep and genuine fear. And it wasn't just the fear of dying either. Breiter was terrified by the notion that he may no longer be in control of his own destiny.

"You stay here," he said and watched Breiter relax. If trying to thwart the prophecy gave his young friend the feeling that he still maintained some measure of control over his life, then so be it.

Clapping Breiter on the shoulder, he turned and followed Taka out the door.

The courtyard was empty save for the half dozen Palace Guard already on duty and fifteen or sixteen individuals of various ages and backgrounds standing together near the fountain. Most were young and wore the inexpensive clothes of the working class. One, a middle-aged noblewoman if the pearls sewn into her dress meant anything, stood beside an old beggar woman dressed in rags. Next to them stood a uniformed Highwayman, sword still buckled around his waist. A quick glance at the top of the courtyard walls found a bristling row of razored arrow points.

"You must think we are extremely dangerous people," the old beggar woman said as he drew near. "But then I would expect nothing less from the man appointed by Gideon Dymas to watch over the city in his absence. Especially since I raised my hand to support that appointment."

Elison's eyes went wide as he took a closer look at the old woman.

"Lady Korishal?" he asked, unable to contain his surprise.

His shock was due in no small part to her being dressed in rags — something he would never have thought possible for one of the most influential people to ever sit on the Kelsan High Tribunal. Even more astonishing was the fact that she was still alive.

Shortly after supporting his appointment to Chief Captain, she had resigned her position on the tribunal and vanished from Trian. Some on the council believed she'd had enough of politics and had left in search of a quieter life. He knew better. Marithen Korishal had gone with the rest of Kelsa's Dymas to Greendom to stand against the armies of Shadan. When she hadn't returned, he and many others on the council had assumed she'd died in battle. He was glad to find out that assumption had been wrong.

Smiling, she reached up to touch his cheek. "I'm pleased that you remember me," she said.

It was difficult for him to keep his voice level. "Where have you been?"

She glanced at those who'd come with her. "Here and there," she answered, "watching over my children."

"Your children?" he asked, more than a little confused.

The woman in the pearled dress took a step toward them. "That's what she calls those of us who are Gifted," she offered. "At least those of us whom she's taken under her wings to teach and to train." She gazed at Marithen fondly. "Many of us wouldn't be alive if it wasn't for her. We'd have died in a mishap of our own making, been burned at the stake by our terrified neighbors, or killed by an Agla'Con after refusing to join their cause."

Marithen smiled happily at the comment. "My children need their mother," she said.

Elison stared at her for a moment, unsure what to think. He knew this was the same woman who'd sat on the tribunal, but something about her was different. Something felt... wrong.

Noticing his odd look, the woman in the pearled dress took his arm and led him a few steps away from Marithen. "The Battle of Greendom changed her," the woman said. "She survived the battle unscathed — physically at least — but her mind has never been the same. It's hard to explain, but she came away from that nightmarish day scarred." She touched the side of her head meaningfully. "She's not the same person she was when she left Trian."

"How do you know all this?" Elison asked.

The woman glanced briefly at Marithen, then fastened her gaze on his once more. "Because I was there, too," she said, a sadness washing over her face. "And I was unable to heal the wounds inflicted upon her mind."

"You're a Dymas then?" he asked.

She nodded. "When occasion permits," she answered.

He indicated the others. "And them?"

"Four have the potential to be Dymas," she replied. "The others have but singular Gifts. Thanks to Marithen, however, they are very skilled with what they can do."

"Very well," he said, then raised his voice so the others could hear. "Children of Ta'shaen," he said, letting his eyes sweep across them, "on behalf of Lord Randle Fairimor, High King of Kelsa, I welcome you to Trian. If you will please follow me, I will show you into the palace."

Randle set the stack of messages on the table, then looked up to find Cassia watching him from across the rug. Even with the lines of age starting to show up on her face, she looked young — much younger than he did anyway — and he marveled at how well she was cheating aging. Considering the worries associated with her position as High Queen of Kelsa, the fact that she looked the way she did was nothing short of a miracle.

He wished he could say the same about himself. In the few weeks since learning of Shadan's return, the number of gray hairs on his head seemed to have doubled. He realized that if it wasn't for Cassia's calm and steady presence, his hair would be as white as Elder Nesthius'.

Cassia smiled at him, and he knew he'd let something of his thoughts show on his face. "What is it?" she asked.

He looked into her eyes for a moment before answering. "I was just thinking how lucky I am to have you in my life," he told her softly. "I can't imagine having to bear the weight of the throne alone."

"And yet if you had to, you would do fine," she said, getting up from her chair and moving to join him on the sofa.

"How can you be sure?" he asked, taking her hand.

She leaned over and kissed him gently on the cheek. "Because you are a Fairimor."

He took a deep breath and let it out slowly. "But one who was never meant to sit on the throne. Areth should be here right now instead of me. He is the one who was trained for this."

"The real training comes from doing," Cassia countered. "You have filled your brother's shoes nicely. Areth did what was required of him so the prophecies could be fulfilled. We must do the same."

They fell silent, and Randle found himself thinking about Areth. His brother had been a wise and noble King, loved and respected by all who knew him. It was odd that he'd never taken a wife. And unfortunate. They could have used another firstborn son to go in search of a Talisman of Elsa. *And if Areth had had a son,* he thought longingly, *he would be on the throne right now instead of me.*

He closed his eyes wearily. But even Areth had been nothing more than a steward of Trian, sitting on a throne that rightfully belonged to another. And he wasn't alone. For three centuries, the Fairimor Kings had been living a lie, waiting for the rightful heir to reclaim what was his.

"I know what you are thinking," Cassia said softly. "And you know as well as I that it won't happen until the Earthsoul is rejuvenated. Maybe not even then." She squeezed his hand tightly, and he looked up to see her eyes shimmering with intensity. "He walks the path fate placed before him. Just as you must walk the one before you."

She was right, of course, but hearing it didn't make it any easier to accept. Eager to change the subject, he pointed to the stack of messages he'd placed on the table.

"Walking the path, as you call it, may have just gotten a little bit easier," he told her. "One of those messages was from Governor Drastin. It seems several Gifted have come forward in Tradeston as well. One in particular is someone we know."

She sat up excitedly. "Who?"

"Erebius Laceda," he answered, watching her eyes go wide. *As well they should,* he thought. Erebius was a veteran of the Battle of Capena and, now that they knew he had survived, the Battle of Greendom as well. His knowledge and skill would be most valuable in the upcoming war. "There's more good news," he said before she could speak. "His daughter Junteri is with him."

"That's wonderful," she said. "What are you going to have them do?"

"I want them to stay in Tradeston for another week or so to gather any other Gifted who might be in the area, and then I want them to go to Fulrath. General Eries will need them there."

"And the Gifted who come to Trian, what will you do with them?"

"Any Dymas I will keep here," he told her, "to counteract the threat the Con'Kumen are becoming to our city. Everyone else will be sent to Fulrath to be trained by Erebius."

Cassia's face grew worried. "But might not the presence of Dymas here in Trian provoke another attack by the Con'Kumen?"

Randle let his face harden into a frown. "I certainly hope so," he answered firmly. "Because this time I will be ready for them."

Cassia opened her mouth to reply, but the door leading to the Dome opened, cutting her off.

Elison strode in, followed closely by Breiter and two women, and Randle felt a rush of excitement when he recognized the older of the two as Lady Korishal of House Korishal. He was on his feet instantly and moved to take her hand.

"By all that's holy," he said, looking her over and shaking his head in disbelief at seeing how poor of shape she was in. "I thought you had perished."

She reached up and patted his cheek — a gesture that was surprising to say the least — but it wasn't until she spoke, calling him by his first name, that Randle realized something wasn't quite right. Marithen had been the most proper and refined member of the Kelsan High Tribunal; to act so casually here was odd.

"My dear young Randle," she said, smiling fondly, "I died many deaths during the Battle of Greendom, but the real conflict is yet to come." She started for the library area, keeping hold of his hand as she walked. He had no choice but to follow.

"It is why the Earthsoul has summoned me and the others here to Trian. We have come to protect you from the Hand of the Dark."

"How do you know about them?" he asked, stopping to study her face intently.

"Because they've been hunting me for the past twenty years," she told him, an odd smile on her face. "And because I've read the prophecies. It's the reason I worked so hard to gather my children together. Death's Third March is coming, my dear young King. The Children of *Ta'shaen* will rise to meet it."

Randle glanced over his shoulder at Elison.

Frowning, the captain touched the side of his head and shrugged imperceptibly.

"And who is your lovely counterpart?" Randle asked Marithen. "Is she your daughter?"

"My daughter?" Marithen asked, turning to look at the woman in the pearled dress. "Yes, yes. My daughter. My lovely daughter. She's a Dymas, you know. And a skilled one at that."

"I am Beraline Hadershi, my Lord Fairimor," the woman told him. "I'm originally from Chellum, where my father was a merchant, but I've been living in a village on the Chellum Highway since the Battle of Greendom."

"You were there?" Randle asked.

Beraline nodded solemnly. "Yes, and I, too, died many deaths during that battle. Figuratively speaking, of course."

"Welcome to Trian, Beraline Dymas," Randle told her. "Your presence here is most welcome."

"The remainder of the Gifted who came with them," Elison offered, "have been shown to rooms in the outer palace. I figured you would want to speak with Ladies Korishal and Hadershi."

"Yes, indeed," Randle said, then guided Marithen to one of the sofas. He took a seat across from her, next to Cassia. "Marithen Dymas," Cassia said, "why didn't you come back to Trian before now? We could have offered you protection from the Con'Kumen."

"I was waiting for the sign," she said simply, then gestured to Elison. "My dear Captain Brey," she said, "I'm thirsty. Will you please have some wine brought up?"

"Certainly," Elison answered, shooting Randle an odd look.

Randle said that it would be all right, but Beraline spoke up. "Marithen Dymas will do better with water," she said, giving the older woman a disapproving look. "Or juice or milk. Wine has a tendency to bring back unwanted memories about Greendom."

Randle glanced worriedly at Marithen, but if she was offended by the younger woman's intervention, it didn't show. "What sign were you waiting for?" he asked.

"Why the Crown of Fire, of course," she said, then closed her eyes. Rhythmically, she began to recite:

And in that day shall ye know that the sons of the birthright have come, for behold the house of Fairimor shall be crowned with Fire; yea, Fire and Light shall throw back the night, even to the lifting of the Veil of Darkness cloaking the lands of thine inheritance.

Watch ye, therefore, for the time of Elsa's awakening, and prepare to join the keepers of the sacred trust in their fight against the Hand of Darkness. Yea, verily I say unto you: gird on thy armor and take up thy sword and go forth into battle, yea, even the fiery battle of cleansing.

She opened her eyes, and Randle found them sparkling with frightening intensity. "Where is the young man who fulfilled prophecy?" she asked. "Where is the young lion who issued the call for our Cleansing Hunt?"

Randle was quiet a moment before answering. "He has gone to retrieve a Blood Orb of Elsa," he said at last. Marithen may be a bit odd in her old age, but he knew instinctively that he could trust her. "With it, we will end this war with the shadow once and for all."

"Once and for all," she repeated, rocking slightly from side to side. "Once and for all. He'll die more than once and he'll do it for all. If he doesn't die wisely the world will fall."

Beraline Dymas leaned forward to look into Marithen's face, then turned to Randle. "I think Lady Korishal could use a good night's sleep," she said. "The road to Trian has been long for her. As you can see, her illness becomes worse when she is tired."

Randle nodded and turned to Elison. "Captain Brey, would you show Lady Korishal to her room in the south tower?" he said. "And make sure a pair of *Bero'thai* are assigned to her door. I want to make sure she is kept safe." *From herself,* he added silently.

Elison moved to Marithen and extended his arm for her. "Lady Korishal," he said politely, "if you would be so kind as to accompany me..." he trailed off as she rose to take his arm. Together, they made their way across the dining hall and disappeared into the tower.

When they were gone, Randle turned to Beraline Dymas. "What happened to her?" he asked. "That is not the same woman who sat as a member of the High Tribunal."

Beraline frowned. "No, she is not," she replied sadly. "The Battle of Greendom changed her. It scarred her emotions, somehow disrupting her mind. She is still a good person — and an extremely powerful Dymas — but there are moments when she becomes... how should I put this...?" She hesitated and met

Randle's stare levelly. "...unstable."

"What do you mean 'unstable'?" Breiter asked. "Is she dangerous?"

"Only if you are a shadowservant," Beraline said. "When battling the enemy, Marithen Dymas is the most efficient killer I have ever encountered. But..." again she hesitated, "...she sometimes gets carried away. I've seen her do things to shadowspawn that I thought only shadowspawn were capable of doing. I would use the word 'brutality' to describe her dealings with Darklings, but it seems too mild a term for what she does to them." She shuddered. "I emptied my stomach the first time I saw her kill one."

"Good for her," Randle said. "I hope her reputation scares the life out of those godforsaken scum."

"Oh, it does," Beraline answered softly. "Among our enemies, the only name mentioned with more fear than hers is Gideon Dymas." She paused, her eyes and face expectant. "I've heard rumors that he is alive. Are they true?"

"Yes," Randle answered. "It is he that guides the *young lion*, as Marithen called him, to retrieve the Blood Orb."

"And this young lion, he is a Fairimor?"

"My nephew," Randle replied. "Jase. He is Brysia's son."

"I have felt him," Beraline said. "And I hope you will forgive me for saying that he scares me to death."

"Then you are a wise and knowing Dymas," he told her. "Gideon Dymas has said the same thing."

Beraline studied his and Cassia's faces for a moment, and Randle could tell that she was debating whether or not to continue. It was obvious that she had more to say. Finally, she spoke.

"It troubles me to admit it, but what sounded like so much babble from Marithen a moment ago was in fact a snippet of prophecy. It, as well as the longer one — which she recited perfectly, by the way — come from the *Eved'terium*. The line *if he doesn't die wisely the world will fall* is assumed by most scholars to be a reference to the *Mith'elre Chon*."

"There are many prophecies concerning the *Mith'elre Chon*," Randle told her. "While most hint at his — or her — death, many give the impression that death itself will be vanquished by this person. Take the *Cynthian*, for example. It says, and I hope I say this right, that *the very foundations of Death and Hell will tremble at the appearance of The One Who Comes Before*."

Breiter coughed to get everyone's attention. "I hate to interrupt such an interesting discussion," he told them, "but I'm more than a little concerned by Lady Korishal's admitted and very obvious instability. Such an instability coupled with her tendency toward brutality while in battle leads me to believe she may pose a threat to Trian."

Beraline Dymas opened her mouth to speak, indignation in her eyes, but Breiter held up a hand to silence her. "Let me finish," he said. "And believe me when I say that I mean no offense. It is my job, however, to protect Lord Fairimor and his family from harm and to ward them from any perceived danger. Lady Korishal strikes me as dangerous. What assurance do I have that when the next battle comes she won't turn on us in a moment of delusion?"

Beraline's shoulders sagged and she sighed deeply. "None," she said and Breiter nodded.

"That's what I thought," he said, turning to Randle.

"However," Beraline snapped. "I believe her heart to be pure. Yes, she kills Darklings in horrific ways. I've seen her pull their arms off with the Power and then beat them to death with their own severed limbs. I've seen her blast them into a bloody mist. I've seen her slice their legs off with blades of fire and then walk among the wounded, killing them with a real blade so she could conserve her strength in *Ta'shaen*. I've seen her do things so brutal that I wondered why the Earthsoul didn't rescind her Gift."

She leaned forward and looked Breiter in the eyes. "All I can tell you is this: the Power that she wields is pure and undefiled. She is a Dymas, Captain, not an Agla'Con."

Breiter remained unconvinced. "But the fact remains that she could turn into one. And what really scares me is that in her state of mind she might not even know it."

"That is the very attitude which has kept me and all the other Gifted in hiding the past twenty years," she said angrily. "And one that will need to change if we are to win this war. How can you expect us to fight at your side if you refuse to trust us?"

Randle had heard enough. "Breiter," he said before the young captain could speak, "your concern has been noted. But Beraline Dymas has a point. We need them. They are answering the call of prophecy. So, do us all a favor and rein in that paranoia of yours. That is an order."

Breiter's face was smooth, but anger burned in his eyes. "Yes, my lord. It will be as you say."

"Good," he said, then turned back to Beraline. "I am no Dymas," he said gently, "but I have learned enough from Gideon to know that a lack of control over one's emotions is a sure path to the dark side. Lady Korishal's heart may be pure, but we have to acknowledge that Breiter has a point as well. As unstable as Marithen is, the possibility exists that she could turn against us. Correct me, if I am wrong."

Beraline shrugged imperceptibly. "The possibility exists," she admitted. "But I will not let it happen."

"And if it does?" Breiter asked.

"Then I will deal with her the way I deal with all Agla'Con," she answered. "Rest assured, Captain, that if Marithen becomes an Agla'Con, I will kill her." Her voice broke then, and tears formed at the corners of her eyes. "It wouldn't be the first time I've had to kill someone I loved. You see, I know my duty as well. My allegiance is to Kelsa, and more importantly, to the Earthsoul."

There was an awkward moment of silence before Breiter rose to his feet and moved to stand before Beraline. "Lady Hadershi," he said, extending his arm, "if Lord Fairimor is finished speaking with you, I would be honored to escort you to your room. The walk should allow me enough time to properly apologize for my mistrust."

Beraline looked to Randle who nodded. "That will be fine," he told them. "I'll have one of the *Bero'thai* bring by a detailed report of all that has been happening lately. I'd like you to look it over, and I welcome any insights you may have about things."

"It will be my pleasure, Lord Fairimor," she said, then took Breiter's arm. The two started for the door.

"Oh, I have two more things to ask of you," Randle said, waiting as Beraline turned back to face him. "Can you use a Communicator Stone?"

"I've used one before."

"Excellent," he told her. "We'll make use of one tomorrow to contact the other cities."

"And your other question?" she asked.

"Will you inform me if you feel the corruption of the Agla'Con that resides somewhere within the palace? You'll be reading about him in the report."

Beraline's eyes widened momentarily, but then her face set determinedly. "Certainly, my lord," she answered. "Right after I rip the fiend's filthy heart out."

Standing beside her, Breiter grinned. "I'm liking her more by the minute," he said, then motioned toward the door. "Come, Lady Hadershi. I'll show you to your room."

After Breiter finished speaking to Beraline Dymas, he went to his own apartments in the north tower. It had been a long day — a long month, actually — and he hadn't spent more than an hour with his wife in the past several days.

Zea looked up from the book she was reading as he entered, and a wry smile spread over her face. "Excuse me," she said. "Do I know you?"

Breiter lowered his head in apology. "I'm sorry I haven't been around as much as I should," he told her. Moving to the cushioned sofa, he sat next to her and gently took the book from her hand. Then, with even more care, he placed his hand on the growing mound her stomach had become. "How's our little angel today?"

"She was asleep until she heard your voice," Zea answered, flinching. "There. Did you feel that? She rearranged herself."

Breiter raised an eyebrow at her. "So it's a girl now, is it?"

She nodded. "The Healer who came to check on me this morning said so. She was doing a probe with her, her... the Power and found out."

"They call it their Awareness," Breiter told her, his mind only half on what he was saying. The baby was still moving inside the womb, and he was fascinated to see the ripples it created across Zea's stomach. Lowering his face toward her navel, he spoke to the baby. "Hello in there," he said. "This is your daddy speaking. You need to hold still or you're going to crack your mommy's ribs."

Zea pushed him away playfully. "You're getting her even more riled up," she told him, then studied him quietly for a moment. Smiling, she added, "The Healer says it won't be much longer. A couple of weeks is all. And then you can play with her all you want."

"I can't wait," he said, hearing the tremor in his own voice.

Zea heard it too. "What is it?" she asked.

He looked away, unable to answer.

She reached up and put her hand on his cheek, turning his head toward her. "Breiter, what's wrong?"

"Something bad is coming," he told her. "And it's coming soon."

"Bad things have been happening for weeks," she told him. "Why are you so troubled now?"

"Because this one is going to involve me and Elison," he told her, then looked away uncomfortably. "Elder Nesthius had a vision," he continued, but it was difficult to force the words out. "In it, he saw that one of us is going to fall in battle."

Zea's face grew pale as she pondered his words. "But he didn't say which one of you it would be?"

Breiter shook his head. "No." He looked around the room for a moment, then returned his gaze to Zea. Her eyes had filled with tears. "Hey," he said softly. "I'm not going to let it happen. Elder Nesthius said that Elison and I would be together when the battle came. If we stay apart, the vision cannot come to pass."

Zea nodded, but Breiter could see in her eyes that she wasn't so sure.

CHAPTER 18

Acceptance and Denial

Gazing down at the army gathering in the outer compound of Samochi Castle, Shavis Dakshar smiled as, one by one, the seven leifs raised the Flag of Negotiation. It had taken less time than expected — he'd ordered the Flag of Negotiation raised above the keep less than an hour ago. For the seven Samochi leifs to have responded so quickly showed a united desire to resolve things peacefully if possible. He wondered if that would change once they learned of the Con'Kumen worship chamber.

"Instruct the Leiflords to come to the needle gate," he told Akota. "Leif Byoten may send up to four representatives if they wish. I want them to see what their elected officials have been up to. Allow them each a single bodyguard."

"Yes, Shozen," Akota said, then moved to where Derian stood with paper, ink, and pen. The aging Shizu dipped the pen and quickly wrote the instructions. After a cursory check for accuracy, he pressed a piece of soft leather to absorb the extra ink, rolled the paper, and tied it with a ribbon. With a flick of his wrist, he tossed it to those waiting below.

Shavis turned to Railen. "Come. We'll wait for them in the lower courtyard." He eyed the young man as they walked, taking his measure. "You'll let me know if you feel any use of the Power?"

After a slight hesitation, Railen nodded.

"Good," Shavis said. "If necessary, you have my permission to do whatever it was you did to kill the Agla'Con."

Railen flinched and glanced over sheepishly. "To be honest, Shozen Dakshar, I don't know *what* I did."

Shavis studied him quietly for a moment. He'd wondered how much control Railen had over his newfound abilities. Half the damage to the keep had been from him. Still, the fledgling Dymas — he could be nothing else considering how he could wield four of the seven Gifts — had saved the lives of a dozen men when he'd killed the Agla'Con. Shavis glanced at the gaping hole in Samochi Castle. "If anyone asks," he told his young companion, "you can tell them it was the Agla'Con who blew off the front of the keep."

Railen smiled gratefully. "Thank you, Shozen."

"I should be thanking you," he said, patting him on the back. "You saved at least two squads with your... with whatever you did."

"I think it had something to do with Air," Railen offered. "If it had been Spirit...." He blew out his cheeks in frustration. "I need somebody to teach me what I'm doing."

Shavis smiled. "I won't argue with that."

They made their way down an open stairway and into the courtyard fronting the castle's main level. Akota joined them, and they watched as a dozen Shizu with bows took up positions around and above the door. Shavis pursed his lips grimly at the sight. *Just in case those gathering outside change their minds about negotiating.*

He and the others stopped several paces short of the narrow iron door and waited. From the battlements above, Derian shouted, "They approach, Shozen."

Shavis waited a few moments longer, then gestured to Akota. "Open it."

The slit of light at the far end of the needle gate did little to illuminate the narrow interior, but Shavis could see shadowed movement. A moment later the Samochi Leiflords and their bodyguards began slipping out one at a time. Sixteen in all, they filed into the space cleared for them and looked around at the archers guardedly. They all wore traditional *kitara* robes, but Shavis knew some of the men were Shizu. His suspicion was confirmed when the iron clang of the door slamming shut made eight of the sixteen men flinch.

The Leiflords, he thought as he studied them. *The rest, the disciplined ones, are the Shizu.* He stepped forward and bowed formally.

"Representatives of Samochi," he said, "I am Shozen Dakshar of Leif Iga of Clan Gahara." He saw a flicker of recognition on the faces of the men from Byoten, but what it meant, he couldn't say. "I am glad you have answered the invitation to talk, as it is not our wish to war with Clan Samochi."

"You have a strange way of showing it," the Byoten Leiflord growled, looking pointedly at the shattered corner of the keep.

From the corner of his eye, Shavis saw Railen cringe.

"I regret the damage done to Samochi Castle," he told them, hoping his sincerity showed. "It is a magnificent structure. If it is any consolation, I can assure you the man responsible for the destruction is dead." When the Byoten Leiflord stiffened, Shavis frowned. *He knows who I'm talking about,* he thought. *He knows the Highseat was Agla'Con.* It wasn't a comforting thought. He hoped Railen was on his guard. If any of these men could use the Power as well.... He didn't finish the thought.

"And since we wish to avoid any further abuses of the Power," he continued, "you will submit to a quick search before we proceed."

Akota started forward, but the eight men Shavis knew to be Shizu shifted into a defensive stance. It was a subtle movement, but one that gave them the appearance of leopards ready to attack. Even in the *kitara* robes of a civilian they looked deadly.

The creak of two dozen bowstrings being drawn filled the air, and a hush fell over the courtyard. Shavis glanced at his men approvingly, then returned his gaze to the Samochi Leiflords. "Gentlemen, please," he said. "We wish to negotiate. Let us have no violence here." He made a gesture of peace with his hands. "However," he said, letting his voice chill. "If I find that any of you are Agla'Con, you will be dealt with in the same manner as the last two who challenged me."

Akota moved through them, patting each man down. He confiscated an assortment of daggers and several pouches of bladestars, but found nothing that resembled the talismans an Agla'Con might use to control the Power. When he was content with his search, he nodded to Shavis.

"Now that you know none of us can wield the Power of the Agla'Con," the Byoten Leiflord said, "why don't you tell us why Clan Gahara has attacked Samochi?"

"First, let me make it clear that Iga is acting independently from the rest of our clan," he told them. "Know also that Leif Byoten was our target and not all of Samochi. And it was our second target at that. Our first strike was against Leif Shochu of Clan Gahara. Their main compound has been destroyed and the Flag of Transgression raised." He saw another flicker of recognition in the Byoten Leiflord's eyes as Shochu's name was mentioned... recognition that quickly turned to worry.

"What we found there led us to Samochi Castle. What we found here leads me to believe the conspiracy of evil is far larger than any of us first thought."

"Explain yourself," the elderly looking lord of Leif Reisten demanded.

"Perhaps if I show you," Shavis said, starting for the keep.

The sixteen men of Samochi fell in behind him, while Railen and a dozen armed Shizu brought up the rear. Akota moved up beside him, and Shavis glanced over to find his jaw set determinedly.

Shavis led them through the arched doorway of the keep and into a large receiving room lined with wooden benches. There he stopped, surprised to find a *komouri*-clad Shizu sitting in the corner. His *koro* mask was in place, and the red sash of a failed Deathstrike was tied around his arm.

Shavis turned to Akota. "What is he doing here?"

"He has been here all morning," Akota answered with a shrug.

"Since last night actually," Railen added. "Apparently he wants to see the Highseat so he can make his reckoning."

"I see," Shavis said, turning to regard the solitary figure.

One of the Samochi Leiflords stepped forward. "He is from my leif," the man said. "I will address this if you wish."

Shavis waved him off. "That won't be necessary," he answered, moving to stand before the masked Shizu. "What is your name?" he asked.

The slitted *koro* hood-mask turned upward, and the man's dark eyes regarded him for a moment before he answered. "I am Javan Galatea of Leif Kashi," he said. "Leader of failed Deathstrike against one Jase Fairimor of Kelsa. I await the Highseat of Samochi that I may make reckoning for my failure." He noticed the insignia on Shavis' shoulder and his eyes narrowed. "Who are you?"

"I am Shozen Dakshar of Leif Iga, Clan Gahara," he answered. "Temporary holder of Samochi Keep. Your orders... they came from Fendomeir Osoren of Leif Byoten, former Highseat of Samochi?"

The Shizu nodded.

"Then remove your mark," Shavis told him. "Osoren is dead. There are none here to condemn you."

Javan looked around uncertainly, reaching up to finger the sash on his arm.

"Do it," Shavis insisted. "That your strike failed is just as well. Those who gave you your orders were servants of Maeon. There is no dishonor in not doing his will."

"This is outrageous!" the Byoten Leiflord snapped, but Shavis cut him off.

"Silence," he hissed, pleased to see the man flinch. "You will have proof soon enough. And though I do not wish a war here, if you speak to me again, I will kill you." He turned back to Javan. "Return to your leif, Galatea, and speak no more of your failure."

After only a moment's hesitation, Javan rose and removed the mark, tucking it away inside his uniform. He pulled off his *koro* mask. "As you wish, Shozen Dakshar," he said, but uncertainty filled his voice. He started to leave but stopped. "I was asked by the man who was to be my target to deliver a message. He said Riak should leave off trying to kill members of his family or else the Leiflords and other nobility would suffer a reprisal the likes of which hasn't been known since Dunkin's Ghost."

"Thank you," Shavis said, "the warning has been noted." He turned to Railen. "See that Strikecaptain Galatea is let out of the keep."

"Yes, Shozen," Railen said, escorting Javan back the way they had come.

When they were gone, Shavis gestured toward the stairs. "Gentlemen," he said, "your proof awaits."

Two squads of Shizu with bared swords lined the hallway leading to the chamber, and Shavis acknowledged them as he passed, then stopped short of entering the chamber.

"This is it gentlemen," he told the Samochi Leiflords. "You're not going to like what you see."

He moved into the room and stepped to one side, allowing those from Samochi to move into the nightmare he and his men had found. A handful of Iga Shizu followed them inside as well and took up positions in the corner. If there was going to be a confrontation, he knew the sight of the altar and the prayers to Maeon would spark it. The sixteen from Samochi stopped in the center of the room and looked around in dismay.

"Blood of Maeon," the Kashi Leiflord whispered. Near him two others swallowed in disgust.

The four from Byoten cast about for a moment, then turned to face Shavis and Akota. "What treachery is this, Gahara?" the Leiflord asked. His face was a mask of rage, and his lips were drawn back in a silent snarl. "Do you think us so foolish as to fall for such an obvious attempt to discredit our clan?" He looked at the altar with disgust. "I can see what you are trying to do, and it will not work. It is Gahara who serves Maeon, not Samochi."

No sooner had the words left the man's mouth than Shavis took a step forward and punched him squarely in the throat. With a choking gasp, the Byoten Leiflord dropped to his knees, his eyes wide with shock and pain.

In hindsight it wasn't the most proper way for a Shozen to respond to such a statement, but Shavis' anger had gotten the best of him before he could consider another option. "Two others have accused me of being Maeon's servant," he hissed at the man. "And both are dead."

He glanced at the other fifteen and found most of them on the verge of retaliation. The Samochi Shizu looked like tightly drawn bow strings waiting to loose their arrows. He definitely needed to work on his negotiation skills if he hoped to remain a Shozen for any amount of time. It was his job to diffuse a tense situation, not spark the conflict. He softened his voice.

"Everything you see is as we found it. We knew to come look here because of similar treachery in Gahara." He paused for emphasis. "The Hand of the Dark

— the Con'Kumen as they call themselves — are like a cancer. No clan, not even Gahara, is immune."

"So you attack our keep and kill our Highseat?" the Leiflord of Vantoru spat sarcastically. "Who made you Emperor of Riak?"

Akota stepped forward. "Actually, we suspect the Emperor as well."

"That's blasphemy," the Vantoru lord hissed. Behind him several others muttered their agreement.

Sensing that things were about to erupt into violence, Shavis held up his hands in a placating gesture. "I know this is difficult for you to accept," he said calmly. "I, too, was angry when I learned that Maeon had gained a hold on some from my clan. But ignoring it won't make it go away. I've given you proof that there are those in Samochi who are using your clan to further Maeon's purposes." He glanced pointedly around the room. "Use your eyes, gentlemen. This room and its contents have been here for a long time. Even if we had captured the keep a month ago instead of just this morning, we could not have replicated the evil that is in this room, and you know it."

He paused, letting his words take affect. "And one thing more you should know. Your former Highseat, Fendomeir Osoren, was an Agla'Con. He thought to kill me with the Power, was so confident that he could in fact, that he admitted to being a member of Maeon's order before I killed him."

"Lying filth," the Byoten Leiflord croaked from where he knelt clutching his wounded throat. Fists swinging, he launched himself at Shavis.

Shavis dropped him on his back with a single punch, then turned to face the rest of the group as they sprang into action as well. The Leiflords themselves didn't present much of a problem, but their Shizu bodyguards fought ferociously. If not for the Shizu of Iga standing guard throughout the room, he and Akota would have had their hands full.

As it was, his jaw ached terribly, and at least one tooth had been knocked loose before they could subdue those who challenged them. He rubbed the side of his face and glanced at the five Leiflords who had been foolish enough to fight. All five were doubled over trying to regain their wind. Three were wiping blood away from the corners of their mouths.

So much for negotiating, he thought sourly, then waited for them to regain their composure. They glared hatefully at him, but without their Shizu body-guards — who were being held at swordpoint against the wall by Railen and the others — they would probably think twice before lashing out again.

He turned to regard the two Leiflords who hadn't fought, those from Kashi and Asahi. They stood to one side, frowning disapprovingly at their Shizu bodyguards. At first he thought they were disappointed with the poor performance of their men. He quickly realized they were angry because the negotiations had deteriorated into violence.

The Kashi Leiflord stepped forward. "Shozen Dakshar," he said politely, "we apologize for the behavior of our Shizu. And though we can't speak for them," he added, scowling at the other Leiflords, "we regret their actions against you. As for myself, I'm not sure how much of this I am willing to believe, but I'm not going to discount it either." He turned and looked at the altar. "It pains me to think that Riak could be a pawn of Maeon, but you are right when you say ignoring the possibility is dangerous."

The Asahi Leiflord nodded. "There are rumors coming from places near Sagaris. They speak of creatures other than Myrscraw that are patrolling the skies above the Imperial Palace. I don't want to make assumptions as yet, but the only other creatures with a Myrscraw's size are shadowspawn." He paused meaningfully. "And the only people who can control shadowspawn are the Agla'Con."

"Rumors and lies," the Byoten Leiflord snarled. "Are you willing to risk clan warfare because of rumors and lies?"

"More than just rumors," Shavis said, pulling the black book from his pocket. "I have a list of names of Riaki men and women who have sworn an oath to Maeon, as well as a record of their dealings with members of their order who reside among the other nations — Kelsa and Melek included. I found it in this room. I'm sure it wouldn't be too difficult to match the handwriting with other documents that your past two Highseats have written."

He opened the book and began thumbing through the pages. "But what makes me most curious right now," he said, looking pointedly at the Byoten Leiflord, "is if I'm going to find your name in this book as well."

He smiled when he saw the blood drain from the man's face.

Akota Tynda watched while Shavis Dakshar spoke with the Leiflords of Kashi and Asahi. The newly appointed Shozen of Leif Iga stood before the two men with his arms folded, looking relaxed while they thumbed through the book. One would never know that only moments before he had defeated two Shizu with barely any effort at all. The man was as hard as steel and as deadly as a spotted viper. He was the perfect choice for Iga's military leader. *Especially with how complicated things seem to be getting,* he thought. *But,* he added, *if anyone has the mettle to save Gahara and the rest of Riak from this evil, it is Shavis Dakshar.*

He breathed out wearily. When they'd started down this path of hunting the Con'Kumen, none of them could have anticipated how wide-spread the organization had become. Nor would they have expected to find the names of the Emperor and several members of the Imperial Clave alongside the names of

Calis Hurd and others from Kelsa and Melek.

In addition to the Emperor and members of the Imperial Clave, the book held the names of several of Samochi's most prominent citizens. All were near the front of the book, the date of their oath nearly twenty years old. When Shavis had read them aloud, the Byoten Leiflord and his two Shizu bodyguards had flown into a second rage. All three had managed to get past the Shizu who'd been guarding them and had launched themselves at Shavis.

He glanced to where the two Shizu lay unconscious, their eyes rolled back in their heads, and pressed his lips into a frown. As hard as Shavis had hit them, Akota was surprised to see them still breathing. The rest of the Samochi lords, save the two from Kashi and Asahi, were being led out at swordpoint. Their Shizu, already bound against further aggression, were well on their way out of the castle. Negotiations with the bulk of Samochi were at an end.

"This will complicate things," Akota said as he gazed down at the Byoten Leiflord laying bound and gagged at his feet. The man's eyes were wild with fury, and his jaw muscles contracted as if he were trying to chew through the rag wedged between his teeth. His name wasn't in the book, but Akota was convinced he was just as guilty as those whose names were.

Shavis turned at his comment. "On the contrary, I'd say things have gotten easier. With this book we can hunt the Con'Kumen at will."

"I meant for Samochi," Akota countered. "With the leadership of Byoten either dead or suspected of having membership in the Con'Kumen, leif warfare is all but guaranteed. The other leifs, whether they truly believe what we've told them or not, will tear Byoten apart. And most likely each other as well." He turned to the two Leiflords. "With all that has happened here today, your leifs will be especially targeted."

"I don't think so," Tamind Roliar of Leif Kashi said, stepping around the Byoten Leiflord to face him.

Akota met his gaze and waited for him to continue, silently impressed with how the man had responded to the situation. After the Byoten Leiflord and his two Shizu had been subdued, Tamind and the Leiflord of Asahi, Agaro Domei, had given their names and pledged their support of Gahara's drive to rid Riak of the Con'Kumen. Tamind had even helped bind the Byoten Leiflord's hands before stuffing the rag in his mouth to silence his outbursts. "I can speak for Agaro and myself when I say our leifs are with you in your hunt. But Samochi is a proud clan. The other four leifs will likely side with Byoten." He paused and looked down at those who were bound. "Byoten will deny involvement with the Con'Kumen, and the other leifs will believe them because they will want to believe. Admitting that members of your clan have given themselves over to

Maeon is difficult for the proud of heart to do."

"What about Kashi and Asahi?" Akota asked. "What will they believe?"

"Our clave members will believe what we tell them," Tamind said, turning briefly to look at Agaro who nodded agreement. "We will withdraw to our estates and let the rest of Samochi do what they will. Whether they choose to accept the truth or not will be up to them."

"They may see your withdrawal as a threat to the clan and might take action against you," Shavis warned. "They will think you are in league with Gahara."

"We *are* in league with you," Tamind said firmly. "Leif Kashi will help hunt the Con'Kumen, Shozen Dakshar. With the evidence placed before us, to do anything less is to be in league with Maeon."

"Asahi is with you as well, Shozen," Agaro said. "And don't worry about us. Our leifs are more than a match for the rest of Samochi. They will think twice before taking action against us."

Akota smiled, pleased to see his thoughts about Dakshar had been right. The man had an air about him that commanded respect. His very presence drew honorable men the way a rally flag would draw the brave of heart in a battle. And they were in battle, he knew, warring with an enemy that suddenly seemed to be everywhere.

Shavis turned to him. "Akota, return the Samochi Leiflords to their leifs and prepare to vacate the keep." To Tamind and Agaro he added, "You are free to go or stay as you wish. And thank you for your support."

"Thank you, Shozen Dakshar," Tamind said, "for exposing the evil among us." He extended his hand and Shavis accepted. "After I meet with my clave I will come to Gahara and add my testimony to yours on what has transpired here in Samochi."

"Thank you," Shavis said. "That will help matters in my clan considerably." He turned and motioned for Railen to lead the Samochi lords away.

Akota smiled again. Shavis was indeed the right man for the task. If the way Asahi and Kashi had pledged support to him was any indication of the influence he could have on other clans, then perhaps the ancient Prophet Kallenia Trepenskar's vision of Riak unified under one leader wasn't such a stretch after all.

Akota blinked. The tingling he felt at that last thought made him wonder if he was looking at the man who would bring Trepenskar's vision to pass.

With a shiver of disgust, Railen released the Power and turned his back on the smoke rising from the outer courtyard. He tried to ignore the startled look on Derian's face as they started back to where Shavis and the others were waiting with the Myrscraw, but it was difficult. His friend was all but gaping at him. Embarrassed by what he had done, Railen quickened his pace.

The events inside the worship chamber had played out pretty much the way he had expected. He'd figured most of the Leiflords would reject the information and proof concerning the Con'Kumen presence among the Byoten leadership. Still, he was pleased that Kashi and Asahi had believed. They were powerful leifs. Their withdrawal from the Samochi High Clave until things could be investigated further would be hard-felt by the rest of Samochi.

He was surprised by Tamind Roliar's offer to go with them to Gahara. With how volatile things would be in Samochi the next few weeks, it was a tremendous risk for him to leave his leif. But Tamind was a hard man, and very obviously knew what he was doing. He reminded Railen of Shavis.

As surprising as Tamind's offer was, however, it was nothing compared to the shock the High Clave of Gahara would feel when Shavis — Shozen Dakshar, he amended — dropped in on them with the might of Iga's Deathsquads.

He knew the High Clave would be gathered to discuss last night's raid on Shochu and the theft of the Myrscraw. He knew also that they would be reeling from the magnitude of the crime, and that they were divisive enough to still be trying to come to a consensus on what should be done about it.

He grinned. But the turmoil they felt over the strike against Shochu was a drop in the bucket compared to the chaos that would erupt when Shav — Shozen Dakshar arrived.

He hoped their shock at the unorthodox nature of Iga's arrival and the presentation of evidence didn't cloud their reasoning when it came time to accept the truth. If the leifs of Gahara reacted in the same manner as the five from Samochi had, things would get ugly really fast. Highseat Dromensai would do more than simply withdraw Iga's support — he would lead them into battle. Gahara would be torn apart.

He shook his head in irritation. Unfounded and unnecessary worrying would do him no good. Shozen Dakshar would convince Gahara of the truth. He would. He must.

He and Derian reached the rear courtyard where the Myrscraw were being readied for flight, and he paused to look around. The large birds seemed restless and ready to fly as they tilted their heads to watch the Shizu milling around them.

Even though he'd ridden them more times than he could count, he still couldn't help but marvel at their size and power. Seeing so many gathered into one place was a bit unsettling even for him. Thankfully, they had mild temperaments.

He'd seen what the birds could do when forced to fight, or when they hunted for food over the oceans, sometimes catching sharks and other large fishes. With talons the length and sharpness of a Dragonsword and beaks large enough to clutch a grown man like a minnow, they were the most fearsome predators known to man. Or at least, he amended silently, to those men who knew about them. Since their discovery two millenia ago the Shizu had kept the giant birds a secret. But that secret was about to be revealed.

He pursed his lips into a frown. If there was one thing he didn't agree with Shavis on, it was flying out of here in broad daylight. Too many people would see the Myrscraw and wonder. The mystery behind the Shizu mystique would be broken. It was a crime greater than anything Iga had done so far. *But why would Shavis stop now? Everything else he's done since returning to Riak has been unconventional.*

He sighed. Things were definitely spiraling out of control.

Derian took the lead as they made their way to where Shavis and Akota were readying their birds, and Railen let him move on ahead, not at all eager to face Shavis now that he'd had another blunder with the Power.

Slowing his pace, he skirted around several Myrscraw who were preening each other and ducked as another stretched its large wings. One yawned and ducked its head as he passed, and he reached up to scratch the bird above its eyes before moving in the direction Derian had gone. This was not going to be pleasant.

Shavis looked up as he neared. "Have the Leiflords returned to their men?" he asked.

"Yes, Shozen," Derian said, then cast an amused look at Railen. "But it might be awhile before the five leifs move to attack the keep."

"I'm surprised they haven't done so already," Shavis replied, casting a quick glance toward the front of the castle grounds.

Railen read the look in Derian's eyes and shook his head in warning. His friend ignored it. "I suspect they hold back for fear of the Dymas we have with us."

Railen scowled at him, but when he felt Shavis' eyes on him, he smoothed his features and did his best not to cringe under the Shozen's gaze.

"What did you do?" Shavis asked flatly.

"Nothing much," he answered, trying not to sound defensive. "At least I didn't mean to do much."

Shavis' eyes narrowed. "Go on."

"I was watching from the battlement as the Leiflords exited the needle gate. That fool from Byoten had only been clear for a few seconds before he ordered those closest to him to kill the lords from Kashi and Asahi. I couldn't let that happen."

"What did you do?" Shavis asked again, and it was obvious by his tone that his patience was starting to slip.

Before he could answer, Derian came to his rescue. *And a fine thing too,* Railen thought, *since he's the one that started this.*

"Let's say whoever replaces the Byoten lord and the dozen or so archers he commanded will think twice before attacking either Kashi or Asahi."

"You killed them?" Shavis asked, raising an eyebrow.

"I couldn't let them strike down the only two who supported us," Railen told him. "Especially since Tamind is coming to Gahara to testify of what we found here. He wishes us to pick him up at his compound in the northern district."

"Then it's just as well," Shavis said. "The Byoten lord was Con'Kumen even if his name wasn't in the book. And Kashi and Asahi may turn out to be powerful allies. You did well, Railen."

Railen breathed a sigh of relief and went to find his bird. He had been worried Shavis would be angry at his striking with the Power. Especially since he had no idea what he had done. He hadn't known living flesh could be incinerated in such a manner. In fact, he hadn't known he was Gifted with Fire at all — this was the first time it had shown itself. Until today he'd only been able to wield Spirit, Light, Water, and Air. This fifth Gift was a bit disturbing. *But not nearly as disturbing as Derian calling me a Dymas,* he thought.

It had to be true, though. No one else he knew had five Gifts. Apparently, the situation with the Con'Kumen wasn't the only thing that was spiraling out of control.

He reached his bird and climbed into the lightweight saddle. A quick stop at Kashi's central compound to pick up Tamind, and then it would be home to Gahara. Hopefully things in his beloved city were still relatively normal, because in a few short hours, chaos would be the word of the day.

Standing guard in the Clave Chamber, Kalear Beumestra listened to the din of voices as Gahara's five active leifs discussed what to do about the attack on Shochu and the theft of the Myrscraw by Leif Iga. That disbanded Iga had no representation to deny or defend the accusations was probably just as well. He sensed that those arguing the issue were ready for blood, even in the supposedly neutral setting of the Clave Chamber.

Gahara still hadn't elected a new Highseat to replace Gariel Tobdana, but

Kalear thought that was probably just as well also. Tereus Dromensai was the rightful Highseat. The charges brought against him had been false. His imprisonment by Shochu was an outrage against all honor and decency. Iga's strike against Shochu had been fully justified.

He clenched his teeth as he studied the newly appointed clave representatives from Shochu. They'd been chosen this morning to replace those taken by Iga in last night's raid. They seemed more than a little confused by what was going on, but angry nonetheless. *Stupid men, and cowards,* he thought. Their behavior only confirmed his belief that guiding Akota Tynda's men safely through Tsuto territory to facilitate last night's attack had been the right thing to do.

That he would be killed for treason if his involvement with Iga were discovered mattered little; he had helped strike a blow against a little-known evil, and he didn't regret his actions in the least. If anything, it gave him a sense of pride. Iga was an honorable leif, and he hoped they would be able to regain their standing in Gahara. It was toward this goal that he was working now as he stood guard at this emergency session of the High Clave.

Tereus Dromensai hadn't said when Iga's Deathsquads would return from Samochi, but he'd seemed certain it would be soon. Shavis Dakshar had hinted it might be as early as today. With all the Leiflords and their clave constituents gathered to discuss Iga's perceived treachery, today would be the perfect time for Iga to present itself. He hoped he was here to see it.

He smiled. It was because he suspected it might be today that he had made a few arrangements of his own. All the other Sarui on guard were his men, handpicked and instructed as to Iga's whereabouts and dealings. They knew that Dakshar was innocent of Tobdana's death. They also knew of Shochu's involvement with the Samochi Agla'Con. It hadn't taken much to convince them — they knew of his ability with the Power and that he would never lie about it being misused. Being related to most of them through marriage or by blood had helped as well.

He let his gaze sweep across the five dozen members of the five leif claves seated below the raised dais of the High Clave. The lesser claves used no chairs — a nuisance to move around every time the Clave Chamber was needed for something other than a meeting — but instead used a thick cushion and sat directly on the polished stone floor. They sat according to leif, each group forming a cluster where they could discuss amongst themselves the matters being addressed by the High Clave.

The eleven members of the High Clave did use chairs, and sat in a semicircle facing those gathered below. In the center, the throne-like chair of the Highseat was markedly empty. With the matter of what to do about Iga occupying most of their attention, it seemed the leifs had decided replacing Tobdana wasn't a priority. Kalear suspected that solving the Iga situation had become the platform many of them would use to try to capture the Highseat for themselves.

Sorry to disappoint you all, he thought, *but Gahara has a Highseat. And a good man he is, too.*

The time allotted for individual leif discussion ended, and the issue of what to tell the Imperial Clave in Sagaris was due for a vote. He listened as each leif explained their position and was disgusted by their reasoning. If Leif Tizin got their way and Iga's transgression was expounded in uttermost detail, Gahara would look like the foolish child who had cut off a finger and then instead of trying to stop the bleeding, held the finger up for everyone to see. Leif Waga's proposal was even worse. They didn't want to acknowledge that the finger had even been removed.

Something had to be done, though, or Sagaris would see Gahara's inability to unify after this crisis as a weakness and would most likely start plans to conquer the coveted mountain valley.

He listened for almost an hour before he finally gave up and forced the rumbling of voices to the far corners of his mind. Focusing instead on his Awareness of *Ta'shaen,* he let the comforting, peaceful waves of Earthpower tingle along the edges of his mind as he slipped deeper into the meditative state he'd learned by accident about six years earlier. It was both calming and refreshing. It also made him less aware of the physical world around him, a welcome relief since he was sick of listening to the fools babbling in front of him.

Thus immersed, he felt Railen slipping silently toward him.

The young Shizu had wrapped himself in the invisible cloak of bended Light, but Kalear could see him with his Awareness. "So, you are back from Samochi, are you?" he whispered, keeping his eyes straight ahead.

"Yes," Railen's voice said from the air beside him. "And we found what we were seeking. Now Samochi is experiencing as much chaos as what I see here."

"You have no idea what mayhem you caused by the destruction of Shochu's estates. It is a good thing they believe the Shizu of your leif acted alone or every man, woman, and child in Iga would have been scourged and exiled from Gahara forever."

"If they still feel that way after Shozen Dakshar and Highseat Dromensai make our case to them, Iga will leave on its own. Dakshar's patience for fools is running thin."

"Where are your men now?" he asked, checking to see if those nearby were still paying him no mind.

"They will be arriving any minute now," Railen assured him. "I came ahead to clear the way."

"You didn't..."

"Kill anyone?" Railen finished for him. "Of course not. They might have a headache when they come to, but they'll be fine. Having your men wear a white wristband was a good idea, by the way. I had to whack far fewer heads than I thought I would."

"I'm glad I could help," Kalear muttered dryly. "So what did you find in Samochi?"

"You'll see," Railen whispered, and there was a faint tremor in *Ta'shaen* as he moved away.

The minutes passed slowly, and Kalear began to cast about nervously. He made eye contact with his men stationed at each of the doors and flashed a quick hand signal. *Be ready*, he told them. *Iga has returned.* Each of them nodded and eased out of the way of the door they guarded, offering Shavis and his men a clear path into the Clave Chamber. They didn't have to wait long.

Iga's warriors poured into the room in such numbers that the five leifs were overwhelmed in seconds, unable to do anything but watch as two hundred Shizu and half that number of Sarui archers swarmed in from all directions to surround each leif cluster in a wall of silvery blades and steel-tipped arrows. The hush that fell over the room was palpable as the High Clave tried to come to terms with the enormity of the situation. Kalear looked about approvingly. Not a drop of blood had been shed.

It was into this shocked silence that Shozen Dakshar and Highseat Dromensai came. They were followed closely by several members of Clan Samochi as they made their way purposefully toward the raised dais of the High Clave.

"At ease," Dakshar barked, and the Shizu and Sarui lowered their weapons. They remained where they were, however, so the threat of violence was only slightly less than before.

Dakshar and Dromensai reached the top of the dais and turned to study the room's occupants. Kalear could have sworn no one was even breathing.

"Representatives of Gahara," Tereus Dromensai said loudly. "Pardon the interruption, but there are a few matters that need to be discussed."

CHAPTER 19

Iga's Return

Even without the Iga Deathsquads and their Sarui counterparts standing over the five leif claves with weapons drawn, Tereus Dromensai would have had a captive audience. Everywhere he looked mouths hung open in shock. Here and there a head shook slowly in disbelief — disbelief which was rapidly turning to an acceptance of the truth, if the looks being cast in the direction of Shochu meant anything. Those twelve, newly selected as they were, looked ready to sick up. Their faces were white. Their postures made them look like animals ready to flee.

Tamind Roliar of Clan Samochi's Leif Kashi had just added his testimony to the tale he and Shavis had laid before the Iga leifs. *The alliance between Shochu and the Agla'Con leader of the Con'Kumen in Samochi is real,* he had told them. *Gahara had been threatened from within. But,* he had insisted to his captive audience, *the real danger is to all of Riak.*

Tereus still saw doubt in the eyes of those from Tsuto — not surprising since they stood to lose the Highseat now that he had returned to refute the charges brought against him by Shochu — but he desperately needed their support. Their vote would tip the balance in Iga's favor. He glanced toward the doors where the Tsuto Sarui stood. It was time to tip that balance.

"I have one more person I would like you to hear from," he told them. "Kalear Beumestra, Sarui of Leif Tsuto, was on duty the day of Tobdana's murder."

The Sarui guard came forward and moved up the steps to stand beside him and Shavis. He seemed a little hesitant as he looked at those seated below, but after a moment he nodded to himself and began.

Tereus, eager to see how Tsuto and Shochu would react, watched them as Kalear gave his account. He couldn't say for sure, but the Tsuto leif members looked as if they believed what the Sarui was telling them. Shochu on the other hand looked outraged.

"I've heard enough," Pachus Lemorin growled. He was the eldest of the two representatives Shochu had placed on the High Clave and was by reputation a loud and confrontational individual. Tereus wasn't surprised by the outburst. "Why should we believe the word of one who claims ability with the Power?" Pachus snarled at Kalear. "In my opinion, you are no different than this Agla'Con you *claim* killed Tobdana."

"You are mistaken," Kalear replied, his voice remarkably calm considering the insult he'd received. "To be Gifted means my ability with *Ta'shaen* comes from the Earthsoul *freely*." He took a few steps toward Lemorin and stopped, resting his hands on his sword hilt. "Agla'Con were Gifted once," he said, his tone conversational, "but they had their Gift rescinded because of transgression. Now whatever Power they wield is stolen from the Earthsoul, corrupted in its use so that it is ruined and becomes a sickness to Her. I felt this corruption when the Samochi Highseat killed Tobdana."

He paused. "It is well documented that an Agla'Con must use a talisman of some kind if they are to harness *Ta'shaen*, a crystal perhaps, or a gem, set in any number of metals. Tell me, when Shavis Dakshar was arrested and the Samochi Highseat's body removed, was such a thing as I have described found on his person?"

"Yes," Anosar Problain of Tsuto said. "Exactly as you have said. A crystal dagger, it was, and still clutched tightly in his dead fist."

"That proves nothing," Lemorin snarled. "Many people carry such trinkets."

"Of course they do," Kalear answered. "I merely make mention of talismans to show you that when I do this..." he motioned with his finger and Pachus' chair violently upended itself, dumping the startled clave member on his head, "...you'll see that I do it without the aid of one." He took another step forward. "I do not steal and corrupt the Power as they do. It comes to me as a Gift from the Earthsoul."

He held out his empty hands for Pachus to see. "I am no Agla'Con!" he said fiercely. "Compare me to them again and you'll find out what other Gifts I have."

He turned to face the congregation. "There are only two reasons for someone who is Gifted to lose their Gift and be forced to steal *Ta'shaen*, to corrupt it as the Agla'Con do. Reason one is greed. They want more than what the Earthsoul has allotted for them, so they spurn Her kindness and take what they want." He shrugged. "An action without honor, to say the least, and evil as well. But reason number two is more evil still. They lose their Gift and become Agla'Con because they pledge themselves to Maeon."

He turned and looked at Shavis. "Shozen Dakshar has uncovered something that I'll admit is not pleasant to consider, but he has the proof to support his claims and witnesses to back him. To what he, Highseat Dromensai, and the Kashi Leiflord of Clan Samochi have spoken, I add my testimony as well."

He let his eyes move across the faces of those assembled before him. When he spoke, his voice was hard. "I am not a learned man," he told them. "But I do know this: the name Con'Kumen is of ancient date. It translates as Hand of the Dark. And Agla'Con, in case you've never taken a history lesson, means Heart of Darkness. A more literal translation would be Vessel of Darkness. Think on it, gentlemen, before you cast all reason to the wind. Whether you like it or not, the evil is among us. What Gahara does about it is up to you."

He moved down the steps and returned to his post as if nothing had happened.

Tereus studied Kalear a moment, considering the words he'd spoken. The Sarui had said a great deal more than expected, much of it concerning things only one with his abilities would know anything about. Movement at the corner of his eye caught his attention and he turned to see Pachus Lemorin picking himself up and returning to his chair. *Kalear* did *a few unexpected things as well,* he added silently, a smile creeping across his face. It had given them all food for thought.

"Gentlemen of Gahara," Tereus said. "Without actually letting you see each name in the oath book which Shozen Dakshar discovered in the Samochi worship chamber, I've given you all the proof I have. The decision is yours. You can either join with Iga in our hunt for evil or you can sit back and wait to be swallowed by it. We are not here to force your hand. My leif will retire to our estates where we will await your decision. If you wish to join us, we will welcome you as brothers. For me, the only desire stronger than hunting these so-called Con'Kumen is the desire to see Gahara united, to see that we do not self-destruct as a clan. If you do not wish to join us, Iga will withdraw from Gahara so as to avoid any further tensions between leifs."

Pachus rose and started toward him, fury burning in his eyes, but Shavis moved to intercept him. The Shozen's sword flashed brightly, and the startled clave member had to stop or else risk cutting his own throat.

"That's close enough," Shavis hissed.

Pachus took a hasty step backward, his eyes filled with rage. For a moment, it looked to Tereus as though he might move against Shavis anyway. Instead, he turned and vented his anger on the audience.

"Do not be fooled by all these lies!" he shouted. "Remember that we gathered to address the crimes committed by Iga, not to be forced to listen to their propaganda. What of the destruction of my leif's estates and the taking of our clave members? What of the theft of the Myrscraw? These crimes cannot be allowed to go unpunished."

Tereus had heard enough. "Crimes?" he growled, stepping around Shavis to face Pachus. He didn't need protection from this pompous fool. He hadn't lost that much of his Shizu skills since giving up the sword to lead Gahara. If Pachus opened his mouth again he'd stuff a bladestar in it. "Crimes," he said again, laughing derisively. "I am taken without trial and dumped in a *shoari* for weeks, and you have the nerve to speak to me of crimes."

He took another step forward and was pleased when Pachus backed up. "I am still Highseat of Gahara," he hissed. "Shozen Dakshar acted on *my* order when he destroyed the Shochu estates where I'd been imprisoned. He took the Myrscraw with my blessing. If I ask him to remove your head for insubordination, clave member Lemorin, it would be my right." He paused to let his words sink in. "But I am not here to shed the blood of those loyal to Gahara." His eyes narrowed. "You are loyal to Gahara, aren't you, Lemorin?"

Without waiting for an answer, he moved down the steps. "As I said earlier, Iga will be at our estates. If you wish to keep Gahara in one piece, feel free to join us in our hunt for the Con'Kumen." He made a motion with his hand, and the Shizu and Sarui of Iga began moving toward the doors. He joined them but stopped in the door and glanced over his shoulder.

"Don't wait too long to make your decision, gentlemen," he told them. "Because Sagaris will hear about matters in Gahara soon, and then the real danger will start. For it is the Emperor himself who leads these so-called Con'Kumen. He *is* the Hand of the Dark in Riak."

The silence that fell over the congregation was suffocating.

Shavis watched Tereus leave, then let his gaze sweep across the stunned inhabitants of the Clave Chamber. They were thinking deeply, he knew. Tereus' words had stung them all to the core.

He slid his sword back into its ironwood sheath and started toward Kalear, crossing through the center of Leif Waga's members on his way to speak with the Sarui. They flinched nervously away from him as he passed.

Kalear looked up as he approached. "That went well," the Sarui said, indicating the gathering with a nod of his head. "I've never seen them so quiet."

Shavis nodded. "Yes, it did. I especially appreciated your testimony on things." He paused and searched the Sarui's face for a moment. "Tell me," he said softly, "why you didn't strike me with the Power that day when the Samochi Highseat killed Tobdana. After seeing what you did to Pachus Lemorin, I think you could have killed me easily if you had chosen to."

Kalear met his gaze squarely. "Had I used the Power to subdue you, the Agla'Con would have felt my use just as I felt his. He would have known I knew what he was and very likely killed us all to cover his secret. If I was to be of any help in bringing to light the true nature of Tobdana's murder, it was necessary to keep my abilities a secret."

"So you stood by and let me take you out? What if I had killed you instead of just removing you from the fight?"

Kalear smiled. "First, let me say that I didn't *let* you do anything. I fought as well as I could. You are simply more skilled than I am." His smile deepened, and Shavis felt a gentle pulling at his hip. He looked down to see his sword easing itself out of its sheath. "At least with traditional weapons," the Sarui added, and the sword snapped back into place. "Second," he said, his voice serious once again. "I could see in your eyes that you weren't going to kill me. But I'm glad you didn't knock me completely senseless. Hearing the Agla'Con admit to being a shadowservant was most enlightening."

The last of Iga's Shizu and Sarui left the Clave Chamber, and the spell Tereus had cast on the gathering began to dissipate. An angry muttering of voices sprang up, and Shavis didn't have to turn to know that the eyes of many were watching him and Kalear. He decided it would be best for the Sarui to come with him to Iga's estates.

"Walk with me," Shavis said, moving into the hallway beyond. "I know you are a loyal member of Tsuto," he told the Sarui, "but with all that has transpired, I think it would be wise for you to come with us." He dipped his head politely to the two Tsuto Sarui who stepped aside to let them pass, then continued. "How long have you known of your Gifts?" he asked, trying to keep the conversation relaxed.

"Almost twenty years. Why?"

"You've met my young friend, Railen?"

"Yes," Kalear answered. "He is tremendously powerful for one so young."

"Yes, he is," Shavis replied. "But he's as clumsy as a drunkard when it comes to doing anything with his newfound Gifts." He cast a sideways glance at Kalear. "He could really use someone to teach him what he is doing."

"I would like that," the Sarui answered. "I think there are things he can teach me as well."

"Good," he said, clapping Kalear on the shoulder. "I'll talk to Tereus about having you assigned to the soon-to-be-formed Deathsquad of the Gifted."

"The what?"

"Something I've been thinking about lately," he answered. "For now, just keep Railen from setting anyone else on fire. We'll worry about you mentoring others when we find them."

Kalear seemed truly taken aback. "What makes you think I can mentor others?"

"Call it a hunch," he told him. "And if I'm right, we'll need more like you if we are to destroy the Con'Kumen."

It was dusk when Shavis and Kalear finally arrived at Iga's estates. The first lights had appeared in the windows of some of the buildings, and several young men in blue *kitara* robes were moving from lamppost to lamppost, lighting the wicks within.

Shavis was pleased to find the Flag of Transgression gone and the blue and gold banner of Iga flapping gently in the evening breeze once more. Dozens of people from Iga's most prominent families had arrived from their respective estates to discuss what to do next, and he could see in their faces that they were happy to come out of hiding. With the charges of treason dropped — at least as far as Tereus was concerned — the dignitaries and other members of Iga's leif clave could meet once more.

He passed a half dozen men and women exiting a coach and uttered a greeting to them. Their smiles were warm, and they wore brightly colored *kitara* robes as a sign of rejoicing for Iga's return. Many had brought their children with them, and the youngsters were running about the shaded gardens. Their laughter filled the air like music.

At first glance, everything seemed to have returned to normal. To the trained eye, however, the merriment of being reinstated as a leif was superficial at best. The threat of war was still very real. The ordinary citizens of Iga wouldn't notice, of course. To them the Shizu would appear to be on errands as they delivered packages and messages between buildings. Shavis knew better. There was a regularity and orderliness to their movements that belied random errands. These were patrols.

A closer inspection of the estates revealed a host of archers in camouflaged tree posts and on the roofs and balconies of buildings. And the closer he moved to Highseat Dromensai's dwelling, the more Shizu there seemed to be — nearly half of Iga's contingent unless he'd forgotten how to count.

"It seems Highseat Dromensai isn't taking any chances," Kalear observed. "If the other leifs do choose foolishness over reason, it looks as if Iga will be ready to fight."

"I pray it doesn't come to that," Shavis told him. "I didn't return from Kelsa to have Gahara torn apart by civil war. I came to hunt the Con'Kumen."

Kalear frowned. "It pains me to think how much innocent blood will be shed before this is over. The web of deception those miscreants have spun over Riak is far-reaching. Many eyes have been blinded by them. Many hearts have been hardened against the truth."

"I fear you may be correct in that," Shavis told him. "And it pains me as well. Still, it is a war that must be fought. To do nothing is to surrender everything to Maeon." He gestured toward the training yard where several Myrscraw were being kept. "Come, I need to take care of something."

They reached the holding yard and were met by Derian. The young Shizu clapped his fist to his chest in salute. "All is ready, Shozen," he said formally. Dropping his salute, he cast about guardedly for a moment before continuing. "Are you sure about this?" he asked, his tone much less official.

Shavis saw Kalear flinch. Apparently, the Sarui wasn't used to having the orders of a superior questioned. *He'd better get used to it*, Shavis thought. *Because Deathsquad Alpha is far from conventional.* Nothing they had done since returning to Riak had been by the Code. Derian's next assignment wouldn't be either. *Things change*, he thought. *Sometimes they have to.*

"Yes, I'm sure," Shavis said. "She will be safer here. With all that has happened concerning the uncovering of the Con'Kumen, the chances of word reaching Hurd are great. I will not risk that. Hurd is a coward. He would probably panic and take action against Raimen and Tohquin and Tey Eries. I want her where I can assure her safety."

"It will be as you say," Derian answered, his formality returning. "Railen has asked if he may accompany me on this mission."

"That will be fine," Shavis told him. "But make sure the little one is dressed warmly. I don't want her catching cold."

"Yes, Shozen," Derian said as he started away.

Shavis watched him go, wishing that it was he who was going to retrieve Tey Eries instead of Derian and Railen but knowing that this was for the best. If he went, he would be tempted to kill Hurd, and it wouldn't do to have Kelsa thinking Riak was assassinating its military leaders. He suspected that even someone like Calis Hurd would be missed.

He breathed out his frustration. Yes, he needed to see to Hurd's crimes, but he needed to address the crimes of the Con'Kumen in Riak first. He still had plans for the black-hearted colonel, of course. If he was able to see them through to fruition, it might lessen the tension growing between the two nations.

He looked at the Shizu of Iga moving about their business, and his resolve deepened. *Yes*, he decided, *the Con'Kumen have to come first.* Even if it meant war with Sagaris, he would see their evil crushed.

Colonel Hurd stood in the doorway of his study and stared at the empty room in shock.

Gone!

There was no doubt about it. The house was empty. The Shizu and the child they protected were gone. The realization slammed him like a fist, a jarring surge of uncertainty that sent a chill up his spine and caused him to run from room to room looking for his unwelcome guests.

It galled him to admit it, but he had gotten used to having them here. Their presence meant Shavis hadn't found anything to connect him with the Con'Kumen. As long as they were here, it meant their Shizu leader wasn't going to return for blood. And as long as they were here, it was possible he could kill the two Shizu warders and use the little girl to further his own ends. He had even made contact with half a dozen of the Brethren in Fulrath to help him accomplish the feat. This sudden disappearance changed all that.

He cast about nervously. What did it mean? Had Shavis found something to incriminate him? If so, it was possible he'd removed the girl to avoid having her witness any more violence. He resisted the urge to reach up and rub the spot on his chest where Shavis' sword point had drawn blood the night he'd dropped the girl off. He shuddered. If the Deathsquad captain had somehow connected him to the Con'Kumen, he would surely return. And death would come with him.

He moved to the shelves where he kept his brandy, forcing himself to remain calm. Even staying in his study in the fortress wouldn't be enough to stop Shavis from coming for his head — Raimen and Tohquin's ability to vanish would make reaching him easy. One or both of them could be here right now. He cast about nervously, spilling his drink.

He glanced down at the mess and poured himself another glass, taking it in a single shot as he closed his eye and tried to reason it all out. That he still had his head made him think Shavis hadn't found anything. As quick-acting and impulsive as the man seemed to be, Fulrath would be short one colonel if the Shizu knew the truth.

That could only mean that Shavis had found nothing and had withdrawn his Shizu simply to keep their involvement in all of this a secret. The Con'Kumen kept their secrets well, so the likelihood of Shavis finding anything was remote. If it hadn't been for the blabbering fool Sallen Zeph, none of this would have happened in the first place. It was fortunate for the Brotherhood that Shavis had removed the man's head. The Con'Kumen didn't need members with big mouths.

He moved to his chair and sat down, trying unsuccessfully to ignore the uncomfortable silence. It was strange, but as badly as he hated the little brat, he had gotten used to hearing her laughter as she teased the kitten or played a game with one of the two Shizu.

He frowned. That was a sight he'd never gotten used to — assassins playing cards with a child. After all he'd heard about Shizu and their role in the Riaki military, their fondness for the child seemed somehow wrong.

He took another shot of brandy. Blood of Maeon, but Shizu were odd. He'd make it a point never to involve himself with them again. And since it seemed they'd gone for good, and more importantly that he'd been allowed to keep his head, it was time to put some of his plans into action.

With Croneam back in Fulrath, the time the Satyr had given him to have the general eliminated was ticking away. Only nine days remained before it would return to see if he had fulfilled his obligations to the Brotherhood. If he hadn't, the Satyr would carve him into pieces. The memory of it appearing in his study flashed unbidden through his thoughts and he shuddered. Shavis and his Shizu may be gone, but things were still dangerous. Probably more so. If he had to choose, he'd prefer to die at the hands of a Riaki Deathsquad than a twisted shadowspawn.

Fortunately, he hadn't been idle while Croneam was away. And it was a good thing, too, since the first attempt had been such a disaster. *Burn that bloody Elam Gaufin and his bloodly do-goodiness.* If not for the Chellum captain's quick intervention, Croneam would be dead, and calling upon the second group of assassins wouldn't be necessary — at least not for Croneam. They could have been used on Joneam or even on Governor Prenum. He puffed out his cheeks angrily, then took a calming breath.

On a bright note, the second group of assassins was ready and awaiting his orders. It had actually been quite easy; the number of Brethren present in Fulrath was staggering. And though they knew they wouldn't survive the attack on the general and his warders, they had agreed to it anyway. The low-ranking fools actually believed Maeon would give them honor in the world of the dead for their deeds. *Let them die,* he thought smugly. *It means more room in the world of the living for me.*

All he had to do now was fulfill his promises to the Brethren and avoid a second meeting with the Satyr, and he may even be raised to *Mae'rillium*. Add to that a promotion to general, and he would be powerful indeed.

He smiled. Both promotions were attainable. All he had to do was eliminate Croneam and a few others on the military council, and a move up the chain of command in both organizations would be his. Croneam had to be the first target, though. The others would have to wait. With the aging general trying to sniff out who had orchestrated the first attempt, the time to act was now. If he waited too long, there was a chance Croneam might trace the first order back to him.

Once Croneam was dead, he would see what could be done about Governor Prenum. The woman was a nuisance. And far more powerful than any woman had a right to be.

Turning from the liquor cabinet, he moved down the hall to his room. With the girl and her Shizu gone, he'd sleep well for a change. He wouldn't have to hear her wake up crying for her parents or listen to the Shizu comfort her. It was such an odd combination — her crying and an assassin's soothing words to help her go back to sleep. On several occasions one of them — Tohquin he thought it was — had even sung to her. *Singing! From a Riaki Deathsquad member!*

He shook his head in bewilderment. Their unpredictable, uncharacteristic behavior had been as disturbing as the threat of violence they could have unleashed on him at any moment. *Thank Maeon they are gone*, he thought and began stripping off his uniform.

He climbed into bed, and the softness of the mattress swallowed him. Forcing himself to relax, he let his mind wander ahead a few days to envision the moment when the blood of Croneam Eries would stain the floor of Fulrath's main fortress.

Wrapped warmly in her blankets, Tey Eries nestled back against Tohquin Nagaro and closed her eyes. She'd sat in wide-eyed wonderment for nearly two hours as the Myrscraw soared southward through the darkness, so captivated by the experience of flying that Tohquin had wondered if she would ever fall asleep.

He pulled her a little closer, still paranoid that she might somehow slip out of the bird's saddle, and glanced down at her face. She was a vision of serenity, her tiny face smooth with the kind of calm only a child could demonstrate. She trusted him to keep her safe. She *knew* he would.

The thought made him smile. If more people had her kind of faith, the world truly would be a wonderful place.

He touched her cheek with the back of a finger. She reminded him of his own daughter. It was the reason he was so fond of her. Both were mild and even-tempered. Both showed a genuine concern for others. And both were observant and quick to learn. They would make friends instantly, he knew. It was the reason he planned on asking Shavis if Tey could stay at his house until it was time to return her to her grandfather.

He knew his wife wouldn't object. Kailei loved children. She'd take Tey in and treat her as her own. It would be nice for Aimi to have someone to play with, too. Having the laughter of little girls fill his home would do them all some good.

Assuming, of course, that he'd be around to hear it. He had no idea what Highseat Dromensai and Shavis — Shozen Dakshar now, according to Railen's report — had been up to, but it sounded as if Shavis was on the verge of attacking Sagaris in his hunt for the Con'Kumen.

He sighed. He may very well be taking the sleeping bundle in front of him into a country on the brink of civil war.

No matter. A couple of weeks at the most and it would be time to return her to Fulrath. He just hoped war wouldn't be rearing its ugly head there as well. If Melek was truly mobilizing its armies to invade Kelsa, Fulrath was sure to be a target.

He adjusted the blanket around her face to keep the cold air of high altitude from chilling her nose and cheeks. It was odd, but when he had her in his care, it was easy to forget that he was a Shizu Deathsquad member. And one who had been sent to kill her grandfather at that.

Blood of Maeon, but things have changed, he thought, glad in his heart that they had. If not for Tey Eries, he'd have returned to Riak with the rest of his squad to await the next strike, continuing on as he always had. Now, however, he was considering giving up the sword — at least as far as Deathstrikes were concerned. The only killing he planned to do from now on would involve strikes against the Hand of the Dark.

A sudden updraft rocked the Myrscraw, and Tohquin clutched his precious cargo a little tighter to him. She was, after all, responsible for the redemption of his soul.

The tap at the door was soft, but Shavis came awake instantly, throwing off the blanket and snatching his sword as he moved to see who it was. The room was dark save for a pale halo of orange light cast by a stubby candle burning on the table, but Shavis moved easily through the shadows. When he pulled open the door, he saw that night still held. Only the faint rim of grey above the eastern horizon showed that morning was rapidly approaching.

Raimen stood before him, looking eager and alert, but with faint lines of weariness tugging at the corners of his eyes.

Shavis motioned him in. "Welcome back," he said, taking up an oil lamp. He struck a match and set the flame to its brightest. When they were both seated across the table from one another, Shavis poured them each a cup of spice root tea and motioned for Raimen to begin his report.

"Tey Eries has been taken to Tohquin's home," he said. "Kailei was more than happy to take her in and care for her until this is all over. And Tey was excited to be able to play with someone her own age."

"I'm glad," Shavis said, relieved that they had arrived safely. "What news of Colonel Hurd?"

"That man plots more than the Imperial Clave," Raimen muttered darkly. "If not for either Tohquin or I employing our Gift whenever he was around, I'm certain he would have tried to eliminate us. Not knowing where one of us was at all times dissuaded him."

Shavis took a sip of his tea. "His days of plotting are nearing an end. As soon as I finish here, I intend to pay him a visit."

"I thought you might," Raimen said. "Railen told us you found evidence that proves Hurd is Con'Kumen. As if there was ever any doubt," he added disgustedly. "The man is vermin scum."

"All the Con'Kumen are," Shavis replied. "Which is why a quick strike against them is such a priority. The sooner we eliminate them all, the better. Hurd included."

"With the Shozen's permission," Raimen said, and Shavis was amused by the young Shizu's use of the title. If he didn't know any better, he'd say it was Raimen's way of coming to terms with his squad leader being so highly promoted. "I'd like to volunteer to accompany you when you return Tey Eries. I want to meet her grandfather."

Shavis saw through him. "And a crack at Hurd, unless I miss my guess."

Raimen smiled and shrugged.

"Sorry," he told his young friend. "The privilege of removing the Colonel's head belongs to Croneam Eries. If he doesn't take the opportunity to do so, I will do it for him."

"Still a little bitter, I see."

Shavis showed his teeth in a smile. "You have no idea."

They talked of other things, then. Raimen told of the kitten Tohquin had found for Tey and the games the three of them used to play. Shavis spoke of his confrontation with the Samochi Highseat and the events leading up to Tereus

Dromensai's return to power. He told Raimen of Kalear and his remarkable abilities with *Ta'shaen,* and how he hoped the Sarui could teach Railen some control.

"I'd like to meet him," Raimen said.

"You will," he told him, setting his cup on the table. "I'm adopting him into our leif until things cool down with Tsuto and the others."

There was a knock at the door, loud and frantic, and Shavis sprang to his feet in alarm. Snatching his sword from where it was propped against the table, he drew it in one smooth motion. Raimen vanished without having to be told, and Shavis knew the young Shizu was positioning himself for a strike.

Staying where he was, Shavis called to the door. "Enter."

The nob turned, and a wide-eyed servant girl in blue-green *kitara* robes stepped in. "Pardon this early intrusion, Shozen Dakshar," she said breathlessly, "but Highseat Dromensai requests your presence at once. Urgent matters of business, he says."

"Thank you," Shavis said, then dismissed her.

Pulling on his *komouri* uniform and soft *kotsu* boots, he spoke to the seemingly empty room. "You can accompany me if you wish," he said. "But stay concealed until we find out what this is all about."

"Yes, Shozen," came the whisper.

Shavis took a bag of bladestars from the table and tossed them in the direction of Raimen's voice. They disappeared with a slight metallic clinking.

"Come," he said and moved outside.

The streets were quiet and empty. So was the main compound when they cut across the northern corner on their way to the Highseat's mansion. A few armed Sarui patrolled the perimeter, highly visible in their ceremonial leather armor and fan-tailed helmets, and Shavis nodded to them. Their presence made the citizens of Iga feel safe and secure, but the true guardians of the estates were the Shizu. They weren't visible, but Shavis knew they were within striking distance should they be needed.

As he and Raimen neared Dromensai's mansion, Shavis slowed to study things carefully. The windows were lighted, and several men were visible in the receiving room. Two dozen Shizu squatted in groups in the shadows of four carriages parked near the front of the mansion. They appeared relaxed — at least as far as Shizu ever relaxed — but as he approached, some of them tensed, studying him warily. They didn't wear their *koro* hood-masks, but they were armed.

When he was close enough to see their insignia he found that they were from Gahara's other leifs. Shochu, he noted, was not among them. Raimen whispered a farewell, but Shavis knew he would stay nearby until he was certain there was no danger. Passing through the midst of the Shizu, Shavis moved up the steps to the door, rapped lightly, then pushed it open and moved inside. He'd already guessed the purpose of his summons — the Shizu escorts waiting outside had given him the clue. But he had expected to find delegates from the four leifs, not the Leiflords themselves. Yet here they were, Lughat Muli of Tsuto, Tauro Sigura of Waga, Simaru Hasi of Tizin, and Orito Nagusa of Tihou.

He stopped in front of them, hoping his surprise didn't show on his face.

"Welcome, Shozen Dakshar," Tereus greeted. "Thank you for joining us."

Shavis dipped his head but said nothing.

"Please sit down," Tereus said, motioning to an empty cushion in the circle.

Shavis did as he was told, laying his sword across his knees. He looked at each of the Leiflords as he waited for Tereus to speak. They appeared anxious, but determined. He could tell by the glint in Tereus' eyes that this was good news. He knew what they had decided before the Highseat spoke.

"Gahara is united, save Shochu," Tereus said. "The hunt for the Con'Kumen begins."

Lord Muli leaned forward. "We discussed the evidence you laid before us for most of the night," he said, directing his comments toward Shavis. "There were many of our respective claves who tried very hard to find reasons *not* to accept what you told us. In fact, there were several... arguments," he paused and glanced at Lord Sigura of Waga. "Let it suffice to say that Lord Sigura had to teach clave member Pachus Lemorin a second lesson."

Sigura ignored the comment. "In the end, Shozen Dakshar," the Waga Leiflord said, obviously changing the subject, "it was your testimony that was most convincing, although the evidence you gave was disturbing. I'll admit I didn't believe at first because I didn't want to believe."

"Nor I," said Lord Muli. "Learning that those around you, men you trusted, are servants of Maeon is like eating the bitter herb. I, too, had difficulty at first."

"Yet you're here," Shavis said, gesturing to the other two as well.

"Because your words ring true," Lord Hasi said. "As incredible as they may be, they resonate with truth."

Lord Nagusa, who had thus far remained silent, leaned forward. "We suspected there were some among us who were seeking for power," he began, then turned to Tereus, lowering his head in apology. "The reason we were so willing to believe the charges brought against you, Highseat," he said, his tone sincere. "And for that we beg your forgiveness. We realize now that the only glory you seek is for Gahara. Unlike this new enemy who seeks glory for Soulbiter."

Shavis let his eyes move from face to face. "It's good to see that your eyes are open to the truth," he said. "I have encountered many whose eyes have been blinded against it." He shook his head sadly. "There are many who serve Soulbiter simply because they do not believe he exists."

Tereus nodded. "I think that is the state of many in Shochu. I refuse to believe that there are very many who knowingly allied themselves to Maeon."

"But even one is too many," Sigura snarled.

"I agree," Tereus said. "But regardless of how many exist, Shochu's alliance with the Agla'Con of Leif Byoten constitutes a transgression for which they must be punished."

"I agree," Lord Muli agreed. His face was angry as he massaged one clenched fist with his other hand. "Their punishment should be the same as what they enforced upon Iga."

"If I may say something," Shavis offered. When Tereus motioned for him to proceed, Shavis fingered his sword thoughtfully for a moment before speaking, trying to find the right words. What he planned to say next would likely offend all who listened.

"Since all of this started, I have seen far too many innocent people suffer, usually women, their children, and the aged. The actions which bring about such suffering must please Maeon greatly." He hesitated and looked each of them in the eyes. "For this reason, I urge restraint in whatever punishment you devise for Shochu. I admit those who have dishonored Gahara must be punished. I only ask that you consider the ramifications, the potential for future evil, should we act as has been our tradition. Consider the innocent lives that will be affected."

He fully expected the Leiflords, and maybe Tereus as well, to rebuke him, but instead of chastisement there was a thoughtful silence as the five men looked at one another.

Tereus grinned openly. "I told you he was worthy to be made Dai'shozen of Gahara," he said.

Shavis blinked. "Excuse me?"

"Dai'shozen," Lord Muli said, taking on the tone of a teacher lecturing a student. "Chief General of Gahara's armies." He glanced at Tereus briefly, flashed a smile, then continued. "The position was held by Moratsu Heeda of Shochu, but since he was the one to call Shochu to arms against the rest of us..." he trailed off meaningfully.

"Surely the honor should go to one greater than I," Shavis began, but Tereus cut him off.

"Shavis," the Highseat said softly, emphasizing the use of his given name. "In the eyes of the leaders of our clan, there is *none* greater than the man we see seated before us. You are as deadly skilled a Shizu as has ever served our people, but you are wise with your power. You look beyond the boundaries of the conflict and consider all the lives at stake, not just those bearing steel. If Gahara — if Riak — is to be saved, it will come from a man who values life more than death, justice more than vengeance. You are that man, Dai'shozen Dakshar. That is the truth I know. That is the truth I see before me."

CHAPTER 20

The Rose of the Forest

Borilius Constas closed the book of names, then tossed a small bag of gold to the hawk-faced *Mae'rillium* who led the Con'Kumen chapter in Seston. The man tucked it away with a smile. "It's a pleasure to do business with one such as yourself," he said conversationally.

Borilius waved him off, returning the book of names to him and starting for the door. "Where can I find this Iveera Silliam?" he asked curtly.

He was glad Seston had its own chapter — a city this size should — but it didn't mean he had to rub elbows with the Con'Kumen underlings who comprised it. They served a valuable purpose in keeping track of membership and recruiting and such, but it didn't give them the right to be chummy with him. He was an Agla'Con, after all, not some money-grubbing fool whose only link to the true Power in the Brotherhood was an oath to serve the dark.

"Two streets over," the man replied, obviously stung by the harshness of the question. He pointed west. "On First Street. Big blue house that doubles as the Mayor's office. You can't miss it."

"I'm sure I can't," Borilius told him and left.

For Iveera Silliam, morning tea with her friends and chatting about the latest news in town was her favorite part of the day. Hayshi Grimmis was in the middle of a particularly interesting piece of gossip when a knock at the door interrupted her. Frowning, Iveera set her cup down and rose to investigate. No one but her friends used the side door — and they were all here. If it was another council member coming to bother her at her home instead of going to her husband's office, she would hit him with the broom leaning in the corner.

She pulled the door open, a scathing rebuke ready on her lips, but blinked in surprise when she found a man she didn't recognize standing before her. That he was Zekan was shocking enough. When he flashed a quick hand signal identifying himself as a member of the Brotherhood, her heart nearly stopped.

"Good morning, sister," he said casually, stepping past her into the room. His eyes fell on the women gathered at the table and he hesitated. "Oh, am I interrupting something?"

"Not at all," she said, taking him by the arm to hide her shock. "Ladies, I'd like to introduce my brother Dreksin," she said smoothly, hoping for an air her friends would perceive as genuine affection. It was difficult to hide her awe at having an Agla'Con come to her house. The sign he'd flashed had identified him as such; the red crystal dangling from a cord around his neck proved it.

"You never told us you had a brother," Hayshi said, smiling coyly as she eyed the new arrival.

"Oh, I'm sure I must have mentioned him at some time," she insisted, showing the Agla'Con to a chair. "He runs a trading company out of Zabrisk." She patted him on the arm. "A very well-to-do company, I might add." She took a seat across from him and leaned on her elbows. "So, Dreksin, what brings you to Seston? Did you finally realize it was time to visit your baby sister after so many years?"

The Agla'Con smiled, but his eyes showed that he was not amused. She couldn't tell if it was because of the alibi she had created for him or because so many women were present, but it didn't matter — displeasing an Agla'Con was a short path to the grave. The initial awe she had felt quickly turned to a cold knot of fear.

"Bad news I'm afraid," he said, looking pointedly at the rest of the women.

Bwendelin Eue understood the look and hastily stood. "Come on, ladies," she encouraged. "Iveera and her brother need to be alone. I'm sure they have a lot of catching up to do... in addition to whatever the bad news is. We'll check back with you tomorrow, dear. Let us know if there is anything we can do to help." She smiled pleasantly at the Agla'Con. "It was a pleasure to meet you, Dreksin."

The Agla'Con inclined his head. "The pleasure was all mine."

When the last of her friends had filed out, Iveera waited expectantly for the Agla'Con to speak. His features had hardened considerably now that her hastily created facade was no longer necessary. He was a very dangerous man, she realized, and she knew instinctively that if she wanted to go on living, she would need to give him exactly what he wanted.

"I am looking for a woman," he said, and there was an edge to his voice that made her want to run for her life. Not that it would do any good — she had seen what an Agla'Con could do with the Power. "She isn't a native of Seston," he continued. "In fact, she isn't fully Kelsan. She has Elvan blood and most likely a contingent of warders and servants."

Iveera nodded, eager to provide the Agla'Con with what he wanted so he would leave. "She is staying at *The Rose of the Forest*," she blurted. "Her name is Relaiya Wyndor, and yes, she does have warders."

"I thought she might be using an alias," the Agla'Con mused aloud, then fastened his gaze on her once more. "Which way is this inn?" he demanded.

She pointed south. "On Main Street. Two blocks down."

"Thank you," he said, rising from his chair. "You have been most helpful."

By the time he reached the door, her curiosity had gotten the best of her. "Agla'Con," she said, putting as much reverence in the title as she could. "Who is this woman really?"

He hesitated as if he might not tell her, then shrugged. "Everyone in town will know by nightfall. I suppose you may as well know now. Her name is Brysia Fairimor. She is the Sister Queen of Kelsa."

Her eyes went wide, and the Agla'Con chuckled at her. "If you wish to continue serving Maeon," he advised, "you would do well to stay out of the streets until my colleagues and I depart. Things are about to get very messy."

The door banging shut startled her so badly she thought she might faint.

The Rose of the Forest was a nice inn even by Trian's standards, Borilius decided. Large and well built, but aesthetically pleasant as well. The garden in the center of the structure was unlike any he had ever seen at an inn. It seemed a shame that most of it probably wouldn't survive the attack.

"So will you be staying with us, Master Dreksin?" the innkeeper asked, and Borilius had to make a conscious effort to answer him. He hated the name the Iveera woman had chosen for him, but he couldn't risk not using it now that so many of her friends had already heard it.

He forced himself to meet the innkeeper's expectant gaze. "Yes, I think I will," he answered. He could feel someone using the Power in a room upstairs, and though he couldn't tell what the wielder was doing, it felt like the Gift of Earth. "Do you have a room with a view of the garden? On the top floor perhaps?"

"Ah, I'm sorry," the innkeeper hesitated. "The top floor is not available. One of my guests has it all to herself. A bit eccentric, I know, but she has paid well for the privilege."

"That's quite all right," Borilius assured him. "A room on any floor will be fine. Let me go and retrieve my luggage from my sister's house and I'll be back shortly."

"Your room will be ready for you when you return," the innkeeper said, then moved away as if he intended to see to it himself.

Borilius remained where he was and stretched out with his Awareness, probing the layout of the rooms above. Whoever had been using *Ta'shaen* had stopped, making it impossible for him to determine who it had been. But there were two women in a room on the top floor, one Elvan-looking, one not. Both were pretty. Several warders stood guard at various points throughout the building, but the women were the only two on the top floor.

He probed the only stairway leading up to that level and found several more warders guarding the way. Well-defended under normal circumstances, he conceded, but this evening's attack would be far from normal. He smiled in satisfaction and pulled back his Awareness. This was going to be easy.

Two young warders appeared on the stairs and Borilius stiffened in surprise when he recognized one of them as the *Mae'rillium* who had sent the message to Zeniff. He'd seen the young man's face clearly in Droe Strembler's thoughts.

He watched as they crossed the common room and left, then moved to follow, eager to see where they were going. If he could, he wanted to let the *Mae'rillium* know of the impending attack. Anyone who could rise to such a high rank in the Brotherhood at such a young age was deserving of information that might keep him alive. And not only that, if the young man was one of the Sister Queen's warders, he might be able to help pull this off. At the very least, a warning would keep him from interfering. If the young man didn't know this was in response to the message he'd sent to Zeniff, he would probably fight to protect the Sister Queen.

Borilius stepped out onto the boardwalk and watched as the two warders crossed the street to *Tate's Mercantile*. A sign in the window advertised drinks and pastries, and the warder with the *Mae'rillium* was pointing to it and nodding his head enthusiastically. When they entered the store, Borilius cast about casually to see that he wasn't being watched, then followed them across the street. He found them inside talking to the store's owner.

"Put it on our bill with the rest of the stuff, Tate," the *Mae'rillium* was saying. "Mistress Wyndor will see to it when we leave."

"Sure thing," Tate replied, handing them the pastries. "Will there be anything else?"

"Probably," the other young man said. "Who knows with Mistress Wyndor."

"When you see that warder captain of yours," Tate told them, "let him know the sharpening stone he requested has arrived."

They said they would and turned to go. That was when Borilius gave the hand signal. The *Mae'rillium's* eyes flashed with understanding then concern as he looked to see if his companion had seen. When he found him busy juggling the pastries, he very discreetly gave the confirmation signal.

"Excuse me, gentlemen," Borilius said, including the storekeeper in his words. "But could you tell me where I can find the Silliam residence? Iveera is my sister. It's been so long since I last came to Seston that I can't seem to find my way around anymore."

He listened politely as Tate gave him directions, then thanked him and turned back to the two young warders. "I noticed you came from the inn across the street," he said. "Is it a nice place? I will be staying for only a short time so I want my time here to be memorable."

"It is," the *Mae'rillium* answered, and his companion nodded. "Zeka is a long way from here," he continued. "Are you here just to see your sister? Or do you have business as well?"

Borilius feigned a guilty smile. "Does it show that badly?" he asked. "I hope my little sister doesn't see through me as easily as you have." He gave a laugh. "Truth is, I'm meeting several of my colleagues here tonight and we've got a celebration planned. If I do end up staying at *The Rose of the Forest*, I'll try to make sure we don't cause you too much trouble."

The *Mae'rillium* nodded his understanding. "Well, in case you do, we'll send our complaints to...?"

"Zeniff," Borilius replied. "Master Zeniff. He is the one who'll be paying our bill." Using Zeniff's name was risky, but he decided to chance it. As far as this young Con'Kumen knew — as far as he needed to know — his message had been answered. Nevermind that it wasn't by whom he thought.

"Well, I'll be on duty this evening," the other warned lightheartedly. "So try to keep things under control."

"Of course," Borilius replied, then turned back to the store owner. "Up this way you say?" he asked, pointing in the direction of Iveera's home. When Tate nodded, Borilius excused himself with one last *thank you*.

He made his way down the street in the direction of Iveera's and didn't stop until he was sure they could no longer see him. At a road leading east into the forest, he glanced back to make sure he wasn't being followed, then headed to where Falius was waiting with Gwuler and his small army of Shizu.

Maira and Brysia were in the rose garden enjoying the coolness of the shade when Daris finally joined them. He'd been over to the Waypost again, helping Brant interrogate the Con'Kumen escapees Brant's men had recaptured in Kerns.

In spite of threats of execution, the men had not divulged who had set them free. Daris' frustration was starting to show in his face.

Maira watched him come into the gardens and smiled as he bent to smell one of the roses. It seemed even his frustration couldn't keep him from enjoying the simpler things of life, and for that she was glad. Too many of the men she knew were so caught up in their work they simply wouldn't take the time.

He saw her watching him and returned her smile. "I thought I might find you two out here," he said. "What better place for two roses than in a garden full of them."

Maira exchanged glances with Brysia and they both laughed.

"Where did that come from?" Brysia asked. "Have you been out in the sun too long today?"

"The sun pales in comparison to the warmth I feel from you," he replied dryly.

"Did you or Brant learn anything yet?" Brysia asked.

"No. And we aren't going to either. I had them executed after they started chanting praises to Maeon again. Filthy scum. What do they think they will earn in the afterlife from serving Soulbiter?" He moved to a bench to sit next to a rose bush sporting peach-colored blooms. Taking a calming breath, he picked a fallen petal from the bench near his hip and rubbed it lightly between his fingers.

His enjoyment of the silky feel of the petal while wearing his sword was such an odd contrast that Maira once again marveled at the difference between his rugged appearance and his warm heart. It was yet another witness that a battle raged inside him between his fierceness as a warder and the gentleness of the man she had grown to love. Unfortunately, it was starting to look as if the warder in him would win out. Especially in light of the recent executions.

She thought about their dinner together weeks earlier and sighed inwardly. She had been so certain he would turn his duties over to someone else that she had lain awake all night thinking about the possibilities of a life with him. Whatever had happened to change his mind must be something dire indeed — his whole demeanor had changed overnight. Where he had once looked upon her with eyes that made her pulse quicken, his gaze now held nothing but a detached, professional watchfulness. That, and a hint of sadness.

She glanced at Brysia and found her studying Daris. The Sister Queen's eyes were as intense as Maira had ever seen them, and made her wish she could hear Brysia's thoughts. She'd overheard an argument between Brysia and Daris two nights ago, and it pained her to know they had been talking about her. That argument had escalated to shouting when she'd arrived at the door of Brysia's room, and she had stood in the hallway in shock, fearing to knock, but unwilling to leave because of curiosity. She'd caught only the tail-end of the argument, and part of what she'd heard had been in the Ancient Language when Brysia tried to throw Daris off, so she hadn't heard much. But she suspected Brysia's sudden withdrawal of comments concerning Daris' retirement was a result of Daris having won the argument.

He dropped the rose petal and met Brysia's gaze. "I've been thinking that it might be wise to return to Trian," he said, and Brysia shook her head.

"Let's not go through this again," she warned, and Maira wondered if this was the part of the argument she'd missed. Daris' response confirmed it. He held up his hands in a placating gesture and smiled.

"I don't want to fight," he said gently, then reached into his pocket and pulled out a piece of paper. "But I just received word from your brother that the Kelsan High Tribunal met and Military Law and Power has been invoked. Kelsa will indeed be going to war against the Shadan Cult. Randle is hoping to have you at his side when it comes time to make some of the decisions regarding the war."

"I don't think — " she began, but cut off as a thunderous boom rocked the entire inn, rattling the glass in the windows and causing the rose bushes to sway.

Daris was on his feet instantly, his sword drawn, his face etched in stone. Four more of Brysia's warders materialized from the rear of the garden to stand beside him. Greig and Tomlin appeared in the door leading to the common room.

"What was that?" Greig asked, and Daris motioned him into the garden.

"I don't know," he replied. "I'll go check it out. The rest of you stay here and watch the ladies. Keep them here in the garden until I return."

Maira and Brysia moved closer together as the warders formed a protective circle around them, and Maira watched Daris move up the steps and into the inn. She hoped it was nothing serious and put her hand on her chest to try to calm the beating of her heart. It pounded wildly against her palm, and the sound of it thumping in her ears made her think of war drums.

Daris had barely stepped from the boardwalk when a second boom rattled the entire street. He flinched as a shockwave ripped past him, overturning potted plants on window sills and cracking the glass in the windows. He turned in the direction of the blast to see fragments of what was left of the Waypost's main building raining down into the street. One of the barracks was already a shattered heap and bodies littered the compound. The junction in front of the ruined Waypost was a mass of confusion as Highwaymen fled the destruction, shouting for those citizens who had rushed forward to help to run for cover.

All along the street, people rushed out of shops and businesses to investigate the sound, while those already outside on the boardwalks and in the streets stopped what they were doing and stared in horror at the ruined buildings. An eery, shocked silence fell over the town.

Daris took one look at the shattered buildings, and a wave of dread filled him. Only an Agla'Con could wreak such destruction, and only one who felt he had a point to prove would do it so openly. That the Waypost had been targeted made him suspect this was retaliation for Captain Fenian's uncovering of the Con'Kumen.

He moved cautiously down the street, keeping his attention mostly on the Waypost, but searching the alleys and rooftops as well. No, he decided, there was more to this than an Agla'Con whose pride had been bruised. The Con'Kumen preferred to work in secret. This was something else entirely.

He glanced back at *The Rose of the Forest*, and the reason the Agla'Con had come to Seston hit him like a hammer.

Even as he bolted for the inn, he heard Maira's scream.

Daris had only been gone a few moments when a second boom sounded, rocking the inn and the eight who stood in the gardens. Flinching, Maira took hold of Brysia's arm, and they stood close, casting about anxiously and throwing numerous glances at the doorway. The warders held their positions, swords raised, faces and eyes alert. A heavy silence followed.

The rear of the garden erupted into movement as Shizu after black-masked Shizu poured over the rear wall and into the gardens. The heavily thorned trellis did little to slow them, and their swords flashed as they landed lightly among the bushes and began advancing toward them. She counted eight, and more were still coming over the wall.

The warders turned to face the Shizu, and Maira's heart sank when she saw the fear in the young men's eyes. They'd heard stories about the Shizu, and it was clear from their expressions that they believed themselves to be overmatched. They were certainly outnumbered.

Maira's breath came in ragged gulps as the young men moved forward to defend her and Brysia, and she was so terrified she couldn't make herself back away from the scene before her. All she could do was scream for Daris.

"Run!" Tomlin shouted over his shoulder. "There is no need for all of us to die."

The sound of his voice jarred her into movement, but Brysia remained where she was. Her green eyes glittered fiercely as she watched the assassins coming toward them.

The two nearest Shizu threw something, and two of the warders staggered, clutching at their chests and crying out in pain. Something hissed past Maira's head, and she heard the *thump* of it striking a pillar behind her. She turned to see a six-pointed bladestar embedded in the wood.

"Run!" Tomlin shouted again, then turned to Maira. "Get her out of here!"

Maira took hold of Brysia's arm. "Please, my lady," she begged. "We must run." She looked up to find the last of the Shizu landing in the garden. At least she hoped there were no more; the fifteen or so making their way forward would be more than enough to overpower the six warders. Another warder was struck by a bladestar, but the valiant young man pulled it free and dropped it among the flowers. His sword stayed trained on the enemy.

Brysia shook her head fiercely. "I will not flee from this scum," she snarled and pulled her arm loose. Kneeling, she shoved her fingers into the soil and closed her eyes.

The garden erupted into a flurry of leaves and petals as a dozen rose bushes lashed out at the Shizu, catching them in a writhing, whipping mass of thorned stems that grew and twisted around them in choking grips of death. Thorns sprouted into daggers six inches long and the startled shouts of the assassins changed to cries of pain.

Several Shizu tried hacking their way free of the growing entanglement, but the rose bushes fought like something alive, sprouting and growing a new stem for every one that was chopped down. Two Shizu managed to break through, but they were met by the warders. The angry young men fell on them, and the clash of steel filled the garden.

As Maira watched, a wall of thorns sprouted in the center of the melee, twisting in on itself until the Shizu attempting to fight their way forward were lost from view. Brysia pulled her fingers from the soil, and the writhing, lashing movement of the roses stilled. The Sister Queen rose unsteadily to her feet, and Maira caught her arm to help. Cries of pain were audible behind the thorny barrier, but so were the sounds of Shizu hacking their way through.

Greig and Tomlin appeared at Brysia's side. "My lady," Tomlin said, "we must get you out of here." Beside him, Greig nodded.

"Daris told us to stay here," she replied, but she didn't sound too certain. Maira followed her gaze to where the wall of thorns was shaking as several Shizu threatened to break through.

"He will understand," Greig assured her. "Tomlin's right. We need to get you to a place more easily defended."

Brysia hesitated a moment longer before answering. "Yes, of course," she said, but instead of moving, she reached for Tomlin's sword. "Just let me borrow your sword."

His face was puzzled, but he complied. With a couple of swipes, she severed a dozen long-stem roses from their bushes and handed Tomlin his sword. "Help me gather these," she ordered. "And I will help you fight."

CHAPTER 21

"Death Dulls Not My Sword"

"Did you feel that?" Borilius asked, halting his appraisal of the destruction he had wrought on the Waypost.

"Yes," Falius answered, starting in the direction of the surge of Earthpower. "It felt like the Gift of Earth. I will go check it out. Finish your work on the Waypost. Remember we want to leave some of them alive to tell Gideon Dymas what happened here."

"Of course," Borilius replied, and Falius felt him ready another strike. He hoped the Zekan didn't get too carried away with things. He was known to take a bit too much pleasure from killing. *Ta'shaen* jolted in protest as another corrupted lightning bolt exploded into the garrison compound, shattering another building and scattering bodies like leaves in the wind. He supposed it really didn't matter how many Borilius killed. So long as enough of them lived to point Gideon in the right direction. And as long as the Sister Queen survived, he added. Gwuler's Shizu better not harm her.

He walked down the street in the direction he'd felt the Power being used. All around him, people ran about in confusion, screaming in fear and pain as Gwuler's Shizu poured into their midst, springing from the alleys and rooftops like giant black insects. Several dozen Highwaymen rushed to engage them, but most were no match for the Deathsquad's deadly skill.

Ignoring the struggles around him, he reached out with his mind and began searching for the one who had fought with the Power. Perhaps there was more to gain in Seston than just bait for the Fairimor lad. If this Gifted was someone he could recruit, it would serve Maeon's cause nicely. If not... Borilius wasn't the only one who could take delight in killing.

Facing the empty common room, Tomlin stood at the bottom of the stairs and waited for Greig to return from Brysia's room. He could hear the clash of steel in the gardens as warders battled the Shizu still trying to cut their way into the inn. The sounds of battle came from the front of the inn now as well.

He was starting to think he might not survive this attack but decided it really didn't matter. He had taken a pledge to serve, and that was exactly what he intended to do. He slid his sword back into its scabbard and hooked his thumbs behind his belt. Taking a deep breath, he tried to calm himself as best he could. All he could really do now was wait.

Booted footsteps sounded on the steps behind him, and he glanced over his shoulder to find Greig coming down. His friend's face was pinched with determination. "The ladies are secure in Brysia's room," Greig told him. "And Matail, Hend, and Robil are blocking the door."

He nodded. "Let's see what we can do to keep them out of the fight."

"That shouldn't be a problem," Greig replied.

It was the kind of cocky reply Tomlin would expect from his friend, but he heard something more in the words as well. He turned to find Greig looking at him. "What is it?" he asked.

"I want you to know it is nothing personal," Greig told him.

Tomlin frowned. "What are you talking about?" he asked. Then he noticed the blood dripping from his friend's sword, and the horror of what it meant struck him like an axe. A half second later so did Greig's sword.

Daris had only gone a few steps toward the inn when the street was suddenly swarming with Shizu. They seemed to come from everywhere; the alleys, the rooftops, even from the backs of several wagons. Then, because he was armed, they converged on him from all sides.

He met the attack and tried to clear his mind of everything except for how many Shizu he would kill. He wanted to know how good he had been in his old age before they finally got him. And they would get him, he knew; there were too many to stand against them for long.

Time and motion seemed to slow as he wove his way among them, becoming one with his sword. Four... five... six... he kept count of his kills and realized it was almost perfectly synchronized with his heartbeat. Another beat, another dead Shizu. One more beat, one more killing blow. Maybe he wasn't as old as Brysia thought.

And then time and motion returned to normal, and he found himself on the defensive, barely managing to keep from getting his head taken off as the Shizu blocking his way to the inn slashed and twirled with more skill than any opponent he'd faced in his life. He could sense other Shizu rushing in from behind and frowned grimly. He was going to die now, he knew. His only regret was that he wouldn't get to say goodbye to Brysia.

Then reinforcements arrived — three of his warders and a half dozen soldiers from the garrison — and he let them engage the lesser Shizu while he focused his attention on the Blademaster before him. For that was what the man was, he realized. There were no etchings on his blade to prove it, but it didn't matter. Only skill mattered. And right now it appeared the Shizu had more.

Daris continued to counter every move, but was unable to launch an attack of his own. The Shizu must have sensed he had the upper hand, because he pressed forward with even more ferocity, and it was all Daris could do to keep from being slashed to pieces.

The glass doors of Brysia's balcony shattered outward in a crystalline spray, and a black-clothed figure plummeted into the street. If the fall hadn't killed him, the thorny stem tightening around his neck certainly would. A second Shizu staggered out of Brysia's room, clutching at a similar stem entangling itself around him. The thorns turned to dagger-length spikes in a flash, and the man's corpse toppled over the balcony and into the street.

The realization that Brysia was fighting for her life caused him to falter slightly, and the assassin's blade grazed his thigh, leaving a bloody slash. He growled in pain and forced himself to concentrate. The pain in his leg woke him, but it was the danger to Brysia that fueled his attack. He lunged forward, turning the Shizu's sword away with his own, then viciously slammed his forehead into the man's face.

The Shizu staggered backward in pain and tried to regain his stance. Daris howled in rage and whirled, bringing his sword around in a sweeping arch that sliced the Shizu completely in two. From within the narrow slit of his mask, the man's eyes went wide as he toppled into two separate heaps.

Daris was already racing past, his eyes fixed on the door of the inn, his heart burning with the fear that he might already be too late to save Brysia. A Shizu tried to bar his way, but Daris left him standing armless in his wake, not even bothering to kill him. There would be time for that later. Right now, all that mattered was reaching Brysia.

He rushed into the inn but slowed when he found Greig standing over the lifeless body of Tomlin. The young warder's eyes were filled with pain as he looked up, and though Daris shared his grief, this wasn't the time for mourning. They still had a job to do.

He didn't know how many others had reached Brysia's room in addition to the two she'd killed with the Power, but there was the sound of clashing steel in the garden area, so he knew more Shizu were on the way. That Greig had remained by the side of his dead friend was touching, but it showed that the young man didn't have what it took to become a warder. His first duty was to Brysia. Mourning for a friend had to wait.

"Why aren't you upstairs with Brysia?" he growled. "Don't you know the enemy has already reached her room?"

"I'm sorry," Greig stammered, hanging his head.

As Daris shoved past, he glanced at Tomlin's lifeless body and noticed that his sword was still in its scabbard. The blood pooling on the floor as it spilled from the wound in his throat was far too fresh to have been done by any Shizu who'd already made it upstairs. The look in his rapidly glazing eyes was that of surprise, not pain or fear.

Daris noticed all this in the time it took to complete the step, and an alarm went off inside his head — that sixth sense he had learned to trust over the years, and one which had never failed him. Whirling, he brought his sword up just in time to stop the blow that would have removed his head.

Greig seemed startled that his sword hadn't found its mark, but he recovered quickly, bringing his foot up to kick Daris squarely in the chest. The force of the blow slammed him back into a table and he went down in a tangle of chairs as the table collapsed.

He was on his feet instantly, kicking a chair away and moving to engage his pupil. "So you've betrayed us to the Con'Kumen," he snarled. "I suspected it was someone on the inside. I just hadn't considered it might be someone so close to me. Someone I trusted enough to let him replace me as Brysia's warder." He attacked in a fury, but Greig turned it aside easily.

"As I told Tomlin before I killed him," Greig replied, and it seemed to Daris as if the young man was concentrating more on what he was saying than he was on his sword — a bad sign considering that his movements were so effortless; it meant the young man was even more skillful than the Shizu Blademaster he'd faced outside. "...it's nothing personal. I have the greatest respect for you as a warder. You have served Brysia well, and the training you gave me was, as you can see, exceptional."

Daris' eyes narrowed. "I didn't teach you everything I know," he spat, but he was starting to wonder if it mattered. In addition to his tremendous skill, Greig had the added benefit of youth. And he hadn't already fought a dozen Shizu either.

"I will feel bad about killing you," Greig replied with mock sincerity. "But my master has set me on a different path. I hope there are no hard feelings."

"I'll decide that after I finish cutting your heart out," Daris told him and Greig laughed.

"Enough talking," he said, and Daris found himself facing an onslaught he couldn't fully defend. He took hits on both arms, his shoulder, and one across the cheek. None of them were very serious, and he didn't know whether to credit it to dumb luck or to the last reserves of his skill. He didn't want to consider the possibility that Greig might be toying with him.

Four Shizu slipped in from the garden and started toward them, then paused, obviously confused by the sight of two warders fighting.

"The Sister Queen is upstairs," Greig told them. "I will handle this one."

The black-masked heads nodded, and the Shizu moved past and on up the stairs.

A moment later a man howled in pain, and Daris knew Brysia was defending herself with her Gift. He hoped she could hold them off long enough for him to reach her.

Greig slashed him across the shoulder again. *If I can reach her*, he amended and continued to fight for his life.

Greig's smile was confident and mocking as he continued to draw blood, and Daris felt himself growing weak. If he didn't do something soon, it would be over for him. And for Brysia as well.

Gritting his teeth in determination, he feigned a loss of concentration and opened himself for attack. Greig took the bait and lunged, thrusting straight forward in a move that was meant to take him in the chest. Daris managed to catch enough of the blade to turn it down and away from the killing thrust Greig intended. Pain flashed white-hot through his mind as Greig's blade plunged through his hip.

Howling, Daris twisted his body violently, using the solid mass of bone to bind Greig's sword and tear it from his grasp. The surprised young man had time to blink only once before Daris finished the spin and lopped his head off.

Grimacing against pain more exquisite than any he had ever felt, Daris hobbled past Greig's headless form to the doorway leading to the kitchen. He anchored the hilt of Greig's sword against the inside of the door frame, closed the door, and lunged backward as hard as he could.

As the sword tore free, he clenched his teeth to keep from screaming and landed heavily on his back. The room whirled around him in a flash of color, and he nearly passed out from the pain. A great fountain of blood welled from the wound, and he pressed his palm against it. A wound that deep couldn't be stopped completely. Not without a Healer.

Gripping his sword with his other hand, he forced himself to his feet and did his best to run up the stairs.

Standing in the center of her room, Brysia Fairimor channeled what little strength remained of her abilities into the wall of thorns she'd woven in the doorway. Two Shizu were hacking their way through, and it would only be a few moments more before they were inside. With the stems no longer connected to the earth, there was only so much she could do to enhance them, and she was quickly running out of the necessary elements to rebuild the sections they had already cut away. Beside her on the floor, the Shizu who'd made it into the room still thrashed against the stem choking the life out of him, and she redirected enough of the Power into it to finish him off.

Maira huddled in the far corner, her face ashen, her eyes wide with hopeless terror. Brysia frowned sadly at her, then returned her attention to the door. One of the Shizu was forcing himself through a rent he'd made, and the only thing slowing him was the thorns tearing at his clothing. She tried to spike them into lethal daggers but didn't have the strength.

She sighed resignedly. She wouldn't be the first Fairimor to die at the hands of assassins. She just hoped her story would be told accurately.

The Shizu gasped sharply and slumped forward, and Daris' voice sounded from beyond.

"Brysia," he called, pain heavy in his voice. "It's me."

She rushed forward and pulled the dead assassin through, shoving the body out of the way. She turned to find Daris' face filling the opening. He was covered with blood, and his eyes were filled with pain — horrible pain for him to show it so openly.

Tears welled up in her eyes. "Sword of My Heart," she said in the Old Tongue and touched a section of the thorn wall, withering it into nothing with the last of her strength.

She helped him into the room and guided him to a chair. He gingerly sat down, and she began checking his wounds. There were many. And the one in his hip was bleeding so profusely she couldn't believe he was still standing.

Rough voices sounded down the hallway, and Daris rose to his feet, gripping his sword tightly with one hand and moving her around behind him with the other. He swayed, and she had to catch him to keep him from falling. He looked over at her with eyes already starting to dim with death, and she bit her lip to keep from weeping.

"Sit down," he told her gently, taking her hand and guiding her to a chair. He knelt at her feet and rested his head on her knees. "Rose of my heart," he said, and tears welled up in her eyes when he repeated it in the Old Tongue, "*Antanami en koires.*"

"I have failed you," he continued, still using the Old Tongue. "And I beg forgiveness for my weakness."

"*Atanami en 'liott,*" she said, tenderly stroking his hair. "You have given your life to me. There is no failure in that." She brushed at the tears on her cheeks and continued. "Your place in the Halls of Eliara is assured. Go there in peace, my brave guardian. You have earned your rest."

He sagged into her then, and she pressed her head to his, weeping.

In the corner, Maira wept as well.

She heard a rustling and looked up to see two Shizu slipping into the room. Behind them moved a third man — Kelsan from the look of him — who motioned with his hand, causing the rest of the thorn barrier to crumble into dust. She didn't need to see the glow of red in his other hand to know him for what he was.

"How touching," the Kelsan said mockingly, motioning the two Shizu to each side of her. He moved to stand before her, but his face was uncertain as he studied Daris. When he seemed satisfied that the warder was dead, he turned to regard her for a moment before speaking. "Your Gift is quite impressive," he said. "You will make a better prize for Aethon than we first thought."

Her contempt must have shown in her face because the Agla'Con smiled. "You know the name, I see," he said, then turned to Maira. "Don't you forget to mention that name to her son when he arrives," he ordered, and Brysia jerked in surprise. Her shock at hearing that Jase was coming was so great that she had to take hold of Daris' uniform to keep him from sliding unceremoniously to the floor. He had done too much for her to let him slump over like a sack of wheat.

She cradled his head in her hands, and her heart skipped a beat when she felt a pulse still beating in his neck. *He's alive! By all that's holy, he is still alive!* It was a realization that was both heartening and heartbreaking in its implications, and she didn't know how well she covered either emotion.

Fortunately, the Agla'Con attributed the look on her face to hearing about Jase. He chuckled malevolently. "He's turned into a very powerful young man, your son," he said. "A full-fledged Dymas, unless I miss my guess."

She felt Daris press his head into her lap slightly and braced herself when she realized what was coming. The Agla'Con must have sensed something as well, because he shouted a warning to the Shizu. It came too late to save him.

With one last burst of strength Daris spun and buried his sword deep into the man's chest. The Agla'Con's eyes went wide with pain and shock, and he gasped as he staggered backward. Daris pulled his sword free and managed to kill one of the Shizu before the second one struck him a savage blow in the side. Daris barely noticed. He chopped the assassin's arm off, then finished him without so much as a second look. He glanced around the room, a satisfied smile spreading across his face, then he turned back to face Brysia.

She looked into his eyes, and the hope she'd had that he would live was swept away.

He pressed his sword hilt to his forehead and uttered the words, *"Keishun en 'liott krentis."* With one final act of strength, he thrust his sword into the floor boards at her feet and collapsed.

She caught him as he fell, and felt the last breath leave him as he died. She laid him on the rug, then knelt to take his head in her lap once more. She looked at his sword swaying gently back and forth, and her heart burst as she echoed his final words. *"Keishun en 'liott krentis,"* she whispered. "Death dulls not my sword."

CHAPTER 22

Premonitions Fulfilled

Holding Daris' head in her lap, Brysia wiped at the tears streaking her face and looked up as Maira moved to kneel across from her. Her friend's face was a mask of grief and shock as she tenderly placed her hand on Daris' forehead. Instinctively Brysia placed her hand on Maira's to comfort her. Outside the window, the sounds of battle raged on.

"It is believed by some," Brysia said softly, ignoring the chaos in the street below and forcing the trembling from her voice by sheer will, "that certain noble spirits remain here long after the death of their body. Legend tells of heroes killed in battle, who were seen fighting for good long after their burial." She glanced at Daris' sword standing upright in the floor near his head. "My heart tells me Daris may be such a hero. His last words were the pledge uttered by Galadorian Stromsprey when he fell in battle during the First Cleansing."

"What did he say?" Maira asked, heartache heavy in her voice.

"That death..." she choked on the words and took a deep breath to steady herself. When she regained her composure, she continued. "That death dulls not his sword."

Maira pressed her face to Daris' chest, and her body jerked with sobs. Brysia bent and pressed her cheek against Maira's. "I know he didn't let it show near the end, but he loved you very much. He will be waiting for you on the other side of the Veil."

Maira nodded but said nothing.

They were still kneeling with their heads lowered in sorrow when the Agla'Con entered the room flanked by two Shizu. At the sound of his booted feet, Brysia looked up and glared hatefully at him. To her credit, Maira added a contemptuous look of her own.

"Sorry to disturb the tender moment, Miss Fairimor," the Zekan said, "but we must be on our way. Come peacefully, and I won't use the Power to bind you, or..." he looked pointedly at Maira, "harm your friend."

Brysia rose and stepped away from Maira and Daris. "Certainly," she said, trying to put as much dignity in her words as she could. "But I must warn you, there are those who will come for me."

"I'm counting on it," he said, his smile chilling. He looked down at his dead companion. "Although, his death," he said, nudging the corpse with his toe, "will make things a bit more challenging." He turned his gaze back to her. "Your son has grown extremely powerful. Especially since he now enjoys the tutelage of Gideon Dymas."

She inhaled sharply, and the Agla'Con looked at her curiously.

"You didn't know?" he mused. "Most interesting. After the events that have been taking place in Trian, I was certain you would have received word. No matter. Gideon and your son will follow, and I will finish what was started." He motioned to the door. "After you, my lady."

The two Shizu fell in behind her as she moved to the door, but she stopped when the Agla'Con paused to address Maira. "When Gideon and his party arrive, be sure to tell them all you can. I want them to fully appreciate what was done here today."

Maira's eyes narrowed angrily, but she nodded. Brysia caught her gaze, and they exchanged one last look before the Shizu led her away.

Down in the common room, the remaining Shizu — perhaps twenty in all — were holding off an assault by a large group of soldiers and the citizens who had taken up arms to help them. The windows had been broken out, and several Shizu armed with bows were skillfully shooting anyone who got too close to the inn.

"Time to go," the Agla'Con announced, then turned to Brysia. "Shield your eyes," he said, and there was a blinding flash of light in the street. The Shizu poured from the inn, and she and the Agla'Con followed. The Riaki assassins formed ranks around them, swords ready, but after the Agla'Con's strike with the Power, there was no need. All along the street, the soldiers and townsfolk were holding their hands to their eyes and shaking their heads in pain.

Brysia's eyes narrowed in anger as she stared at the Agla'Con's back. *If only I had a knife.*

Two blocks up the street, they ran into a group of Highwaymen returning from patrol, and swords hissed from scabbards as they moved to bar the way. The

Shizu readied themselves to attack, but the Agla'Con's talisman flared red before they could advance. The ground beneath the riders' feet exploded upward in a wall of dirt and rock, and men and horses alike were thrown in all directions. The terrified horses fled, trampling several riders and dragging away others who had become entangled in the stirrups. Those not killed were too stunned to fight, and the Agla'Con and his Shizu passed them without further conflict.

They encountered two more groups of Highwaymen before they reached the edge of town, but both times the Agla'Con brushed them aside with the Power the way Brysia might rid troublesome insects from her garden. And yet it was better than letting the Shizu address the resistance. The Agla'Con's way of dealing with things might look horribly violent, but when she passed those he'd struck, she found that most were only stunned. Few of the injuries were life-threatening. The Agla'Con was in a hurry, she decided. Gideon and Jase must already be close.

A short distance into the forest, they joined more Shizu tending enough horses to carry the entire group. She noticed a one-armed man sitting among them whose face wasn't hidden by a *koro* mask. A red crystal hung from a gold chain around his neck.

"It took you long," the Riaki told his Zekan counterpart. "Did you run into trouble?"

"Nothing I couldn't handle," the other replied, "but Falius is dead." He motioned toward the horses. "Why these? I thought we had use of..." he hesitated when he saw that Brysia was listening, "other means of travel."

The Riaki glanced at her as well. "I had to send them back before my clansmen grew suspicious," he said. "Besides, we don't want to outdistance those who will give chase."

The Zekan frowned his displeasure but accepted the reins offered him by a Shizu. Brysia did the same, but she had to pull her skirt to her knees to sit comfortably in the saddle. She felt the eyes of some of the men on her and cast about defiantly. *Look all you want,* she told them silently, *but touch me and I'll kill you.*

She still might, if the chance presented itself. They were in a forest, after all. A little time to regain her strength, and she would show these devils what else she could do.

Sitting atop the coach with the driver Jase had named *The Mute,* Elliott listened to the laughter of those riding below. Laughter at his turning into a pudding-brained fool unless he missed his guess. *Well, aren't I?* he scolded himself. *I take one look at a pretty girl and start acting like an idiot.* He shook his head in disgust. He'd always said girls were ruinous. This proved it.

Talia said his name loudly enough for him to hear, and the laughter started up again. He knew he shouldn't have teased her and Jase so much. They were paying him back with a vengeance.

The Mute glanced sideways at him. "A lovely young lady," he said at last.

Elliott looked at him in confusion. "Which one?"

The driver smiled. "Which one are you thinking about?" he asked, then started to chuckle.

Great. Now even this guy is getting in on the teasing. It made him wish he had his own horse so he could get away from everyone. He would be free to ride at his own pace, explore some of the side roads under the pretense of scouting, and.... He stopped, shaking his head in disgust. *And think about Tana.*

He couldn't help it, but every time he closed his eyes he could see her face. A lovely, slender, smooth face, with large, luminous blue eyes that —

He slapped himself in the face, then did his best to ignore the startled look The Mute was sending his way. *Stop it,* he told himself. *You'll probably never even see her again.*

With everything he and the others would be facing in the near future, it was very likely he'd wind up killed in battle. Which, as he'd said all along, would be the only way he would ever lose his head.

Too late, a little voice whispered. *Tana took your wits when she took your heart.* It was a truth he couldn't deny.

He noticed how quiet it had become in the coach and pursed his lips thoughtfully. He wondered if he were to admit to liking Tana if it would help his sister and the others stop the teasing. It took less than a second to decide that wouldn't be the case.

Realizing he couldn't fight it, and knowing that it was no fun trying, he closed his eyes and called up the image of her face. He had gotten a very good look at it two nights ago, when they'd spent half the night talking and laughing. He could see every angle and curve, right down to the tiny dimple on her left cheek when she smiled. And then there was the rest of her, soft and strong at the same time. Scurrying about all day waiting tables had given her an excellent shape.

A thought struck him, and he cringed. How would his father react when he found out the next King of Chellum had fallen in love with a tavern maid? Perhaps it was best not to know.

Thinking about how the members of the Chellum Council would react, however, made him grin. The sooner he and the others finished this mission, the sooner he could find out if his assumptions about the political upheaval his relationship with Tana would cause had any substance to it. He certainly hoped it did.

Sitting next to Talia, Jase sat quietly and gazed out the window at the trees slipping by. He saw the marker for the turnoff to Jersil's Hollow and sighed wearily. They had left Kindel's Grove yesterday, spent the night at a dump called *The Yellow Oak*, and had been riding since daybreak. He'd heard Seth tell Gideon that they would be staying in Ordin, which, now that he had seen the marker for Jersil's Hollow, was still ten miles away. He had forgotten how boring things can get when all you do is travel. He'd give anything to get out on a horse and maybe hunt down a forest hen or two.

"How much farther to Seston?" Talia asked him a short time later, and he turned to look into her eyes. If Thorac hadn't been sitting across from them, he may have been tempted to give her a kiss. She must have read his thoughts because she bit her lip and smiled knowingly. "I'm anxious to meet your mother again," she added, "and see if I can clear up any past misconceptions about me."

"We should arrive sometime tomorrow afternoon," he told her. "Seth won't be happy about it, but I'm pretty sure my mother will insist that we stay with her at *The Rose of the Forest*. With so much daylight left, he'll want to continue on to Scloa twenty miles further on."

"Is he still angry at our stopping in Kindel's Grove?" she asked.

"I don't think it was the stopping so much as what happened during the stopping," Thorac piped in. "First Elliott slips off to see Tana, then you two end up alone on the front porch. While you were out there smooching on the swing, I heard him tell Gideon, rather angrily I might add, that 'Love has no place in any of this'."

"We weren't smooching," Talia retorted, but her blush gave away the lie. "We only kissed once."

Thorac leaned forward. "Yes, but how *long* was that one kiss?"

"What was Gideon's reply?" Jase asked, trying to turn the conversation back to something a little less awkward.

"Gideon told him to tend to his job and he would tend to his."

"What do you suppose that means?" Talia asked.

Thorac reached up to pull at his beard. "Gideon can see things that need or are meant to be," Thorac told them. "Some people, and I'm not saying Seth is included in this group, would call Gideon eccentric because of his erratic, and often unexplainable behavior. But if you accept him for what he is, a Prophet and

Seer, then you don't need to question his actions."

Jase was quiet as he considered. "He calls it 'Finding a piece of the puzzle'."

Talia looked from him to Thorac and back. "Are you saying Gideon had us stop in Kindel's Grove so Elliott could fall in love with Tana?"

Thorac grinned. "Well, I don't think it was so you two could smooch on the swing."

"We weren't smooching!" Talia said, biting off each word sharply.

Thorac burst out laughing, and Jase had to put a hand up to cover a smile of his own. Talia looked at both of them for a moment, then started to laugh as well. When things quieted once more, Jase went back to watching trees slip past the window.

Time seemed to drag on, and he found his eyes growing heavy. Last night's inn truly had been a dump, and he was feeling the effects of a poor night's sleep. He closed his eyes and leaned back. Opening himself to the Power, he immersed his Awareness in the shimmering aura the way Gideon had taught him to. There, in the life-giving essence of *Ta'shaen*, he could find rest without sleeping.

He was deep into his meditation, when he felt a tremor in *Ta'shaen*. It felt weak, the point of origin still so far off that it was nothing more than a pin-prick to his Awareness. Still, it was something he hadn't felt before, so he was curious. Reaching out with his mind, he began tracing the lines of Earthpower back to the point of origin the way Gideon had shown him.

He had only stretched his Awareness over a short distance when he felt the second disturbance. This time, because he was already focused, he felt the tremor as it spread out from the wielder. He also felt the corruption. It took only a moment longer to discover it was coming from Seston.

His eyes snapped open, and he threw open the door. "Stop the coach," he yelled, and the horses bellowed in protest as the driver pulled hard on the reins.

Without waiting for the coach to come to a complete stop, Jase jumped down and raced back to the second coach. Gideon had exited as well and was waiting for him. Jase took one look at him and knew Gideon had felt the disturbance also.

"I've known for three days that something bad was coming," the Dymas said. He closed his eyes, and Jase felt him stretch out with his mind.

Seth rode up and frowned at them both. "What's wrong," he asked, his eyes scanning the trees around them. Snorting, his mount tossed its head in response to its rider's agitation.

"There is an Agla'Con in Seston," Jase blurted, and Gideon put up a hand to silence him.

"And an army of Shizu," Gideon said, his eyes still closed, "They are attacking an inn called *The Rose of* — "

" — *the Forest*," Jase finished for him, not needing his Spirit-enhanced insight to make the connection. "Where my mother is staying."

Gideon's eyes snapped open. "Your mother is *there?*" he asked.

For his answer, Jase moved to a warder. "I need your horse," he told him. When the man hesitated, Jase took him by the foot and shoved him out of the saddle.

Gideon's hand on his shoulder stopped him before he could mount. "Jase," he said softly, "I know what you are thinking, but you would never reach Seston in time to help."

"So I just abandon her to the Shizu?" he growled, knowing even as he said it that Gideon was right.

"Of course not. But you must be reasonable. Seston is still fifteen leagues away."

Jase nodded and handed the reins back to the warder he'd upended. The man scowled as he took them and climbed back into the saddle.

"We can't do anything to stop what is happening there, but we may be able to help mend the damage. And while we should worry about your mother, my senses tell me there is more to this than just a Riaki Deathstrike."

"Can we at least hurry, then?" Jase asked, knowing how much it sounded like a plea.

Gideon turned to Seth. "You heard him, Captain. I don't care if you kill the horses in the process, just get us to Seston by morning."

"Yes, Dymas," he said and began shouting orders.

Jase ran back to his coach, but instead of getting in with the others, he climbed the ladder to the driver's seat. "Get out of the way," he growled. "I'm driving now."

Startled by the vehemence in his voice, the driver complied without even checking to see if Seth approved of the change. Jase settled into the seat next to Elliott and slapped the reins sharply. The coach lurched into motion, and the ousted driver howled his displeasure as he scrambled to climb inside.

Jase barely noticed. If anything had happened to Daris or his mother, he thought grimly, there would be some very serious hell to pay.

CHAPTER 23

The Chase Begins

Gideon's group rode through the night, pushing the horses as hard as they dared, urging every last bit of strength they could out of them in their haste to reach Seston. When the animals started to falter, Gideon called for a brief halt so he and Talia could heal them.

Refreshed, the animals ran anew, showing no evidence of their previous weakness. Jase held the reins and urged them on, listening to the rumbling of the coach beneath him.

"Gideon says we can only renew them once," Talia said from beside him. "If we were to heal them again, they would feel refreshed but they would die within the hour. As it is, we'll have to swap them for other horses when we reach Seston. These will need weeks to rest before they will be back to normal."

Jase nodded but didn't respond. Talia had traded places with Elliott during the stop so she could be here to comfort him. Her presence was soothing, and hearing her voice was nice. He simply didn't feel like talking.

He had no idea what they would find once they reached Seston, but from what little he had been able to perceive through *Ta'shaen*, he knew it was going to be bad. The only thing that kept him from despairing completely was his determination to get to his mother. He focused on Seth riding ahead of them with a bundle of glowstones to light the way and urged the horses on.

She will be all right, he thought. *She has to be all right.*

As the miles passed, the outline of trees grew gradually distinguishable as night began to wane. Before long, the soft grey of morning was upon them, and Seth put the glowstones away. The first rays of orange were clipping the tops of the trees when they cleared the last dense section of forest and Seston came into view. Jase felt his chest tighten with apprehension as they neared. When they reached the main part of town, he found that his dread had been justified.

Bodies lined both sides of the street, and most were covered with sheets or towels to hide their identities. Hundreds of people milled about, each wearing the same stunned look of loss and confusion. Women and children knelt beside many of the bodies, and their sobs could be heard even above the sound of the wagons.

Jase looked at the bodies that had not been covered and saw they didn't need it. The black of their *koro* masks hid their features. *So many*, he thought. *How could there have been so many?*

They stopped in front of *The Rose of the Forest* and Jase climbed down and moved to where Seth was speaking to a group of Highwaymen. Gideon and Elliott joined them also.

"This is Captain Callison," Seth told them when they were all together. "He heads the Waypost here in Seston."

"Call me Brant," he said, extending his hand in greeting. "After this debacle, however, I think my military career is over."

Gideon waved the comment away. "You mustn't blame yourself for this. Shizu Deathsquads are a formidable enemy. And Agla'Con are a force in and of themselves."

Brant did little to hide his surprise. "How did you know about them?"

"He is Gideon Dymas," Seth said. "Now, if you will excuse me, I have some looking around to do." Jase watched the Chellum captain make his way toward a pile of Shizu corpses. Elliott went with him, and together they examined the insignia on the uniforms.

Jase returned his attention to Brant and listened while he explained what had happened. "I lost a third of one garrison, and half of the other," he said bitterly. "Nearly a hundred men, and only a few of them killed by Shizu."

"What news of my mother?" Jase asked. "And what of Daris Stodd, her warder?"

Brant's face grew solemn. "Daris is dead."

Jase shook his head in denial, a cold fist clutching at his heart. Tears formed at the corners of his eyes, but he ground his teeth and willed them away. "And my mother?"

"I'm sorry, Master Wyndor, the Deathsquad took her with them."

"Wyndor?" Jase asked incredulously. "You mean you didn't even know who she was?"

"Jase," Gideon warned, but he brushed him off.

"My name is Fairimor," he snarled, taking hold of Brant's uniform and pulling him roughly forward. "Miss Wyndor was an alias. Her real name was Brysia." His anger took him and he shook the man. "You let them take the Sister Queen of Kelsa, you fool!" Without thinking, he took hold of the Power and seized the startled captain's throat in an invisible grip of Air. Brant's eyes boggled as he struggled for breath.

"Jase," Gideon shouted, slapping him so hard in the head it made his teeth rattle. "That's enough."

Jase released Brant and forced *Ta'shaen* away. "I'm sorry," he grumbled, turning away in embarrassment.

"Uhh... that's all right," Brant replied, reaching up to rub his neck. He sounded sincere, but Jase could hear fear in his voice as well.

"The boy is a Dymas," Gideon told Brant. "But sometimes his emotions overpower his wisdom."

"No," Brant said again, "it's okay. I would react the same way if it was my mother they'd taken."

"Where is Daris?" Jase asked, eager to change the subject. He knew Seth would discover what happened to his mother. The Shizu were good, but they weren't good enough to hide their trail from Seth. Now was the time to pay respect to Daris.

"He's still up in your mother's room," Brant said. "Maira Aulious is watching over him." In a gesture of good will, he took Jase by the arm. "I will go with you. He was my friend, too, you know. I have never met a man so brave or dedicated in my life. Or as skilled." He gestured to the Shizu. "We have counted fifty-three dead Shizu. By our accounting, Daris killed a third of them himself."

Jase nodded. He had expected nothing less from his mother's guardian.

"And your mother," the captain continued with awe in his voice, "killed almost as many as Daris. Come, I will show you to her room."

Jase let himself be led toward the inn, trying desperately to steel himself for what he would find inside.

Gideon watched Jase enter the inn with Brant Callison, then turned to regard Talia. Her eyes were on those milling about in the street, and her face was solemn as she shared their grief.

"Go and heal those you can," he told her. "Send someone to get me if you find any that require more than you can give. I'll be here at the inn."

She nodded, and he could see that she was grateful for something to do. He knew how she felt. Keeping busy meant you had less time to dwell on the depth of the loss. He waited until he felt her embrace the Power, then moved to the boardwalk and sat down. He caught Thorac's eye and motioned the Chunin over.

"Keep people from disturbing me," he told him. "I'm going to see if I can get a look at what happened here."

Thorac nodded and took a protective stance in front of him.

Gideon took a calming breath and immersed himself in the Power. Viewing the past was always easier than seeing the future. The future was ever-changing, made so by the choices and actions still not yet taken; but the past was solid. With how recently these events had occurred, the path to them would be short. The strength of the disturbance and the added benefit of being where it happened would also facilitate his seeing things clearly. Power and proximity always made investigating through the eyes of *Ta'shaen* easier.

He slowed his breathing and slid deeper into the Power, tracing the threads of fate's fulfillment back in time. Like so many other catastrophic events, the webs of fate were complex. So many people had been affected by this attack that the potential for future repercussions was tremendous. The branching threads were innumerable. He ignored the lesser threads and their myriad possibilities and concentrated instead on getting to what had already come to pass. It grew brighter as he drew near, a luminescent tangle that coalesced into the vision he sought.

Once there, the perfect eye of *Ta'shaen* enabled him to see things from every angle, to hear every sound, to feel every emotion. He fought for breath as the absolute completeness of understanding offered by this spiritual perception threatened to overwhelm him. Aware of the sweat beading on his forehead, he clenched his teeth and kept himself immersed in the vision, riding it through to its conclusion.

When it finally ended, he opened his eyes only to cover his face with his hands. The brutality of what he'd witnessed sickened him, but it was the valor and bravery he'd seen by Daris and those who'd fought alongside him that made him want to weep. The warder had fought like a dragon, ignoring wounds that would have killed any other man. He couldn't begin to guess how he had endured long enough to reach Brysia. The warder had died a hero's death indeed.

And Brysia, bless her heart, had been just as fierce.

He rose to his feet and let his eyes travel south. And she was alive.

Hold on, Sister Queen, he told her silently. *We are coming.*

He turned to Thorac. "Keep an eye on things here until I return. I'm going to pay homage to one who fell with honor."

When he reached Brysia's room, he found Jase kneeling at the side of the bed that held Daris' body. The warder had been covered with a sheet to hide his numerous wounds, but his head was visible on the pillow. His eyes were closed. His face, in spite of a wicked gash on his cheek, was calm. A slight smile creased his lips. To one who didn't know better, he might appear to be sleeping.

Jase looked up as he entered but remained kneeling. The boy's eyes held a mixture of anger and anguish that Gideon found frightening. Once again, he realized how vulnerable Jase was to the enticings of the Dark One. Inability to control one's emotions was as sure a path to becoming Agla'Con as was having an evil heart.

Gideon left Jase to his mourning and turned to the young lady sitting in the chair by the window. Maira. He knew her from the vision. Her face was tired, her eyes red from the tears she had long since quit crying. He had felt her anguish at Daris' death as well. And he had seen enough to know just how deep a love they'd had for one another.

She rose and bowed a greeting. "Gideon Dymas," she said. "If you'll allow me, I have arranged for Daris' burial in the plot set aside for my family. I know he deserves to be laid to rest in the Fairimor Gardens with all the great ones who've gone before him, but..." she trailed off, unable to finish.

Gideon took her in his arms and hugged her close. "No," he said. "He deserves to be here under the care of the woman he loved." He felt her body shaking as she sobbed, and he smoothed her hair with one hand. "He would want to remain here."

"I think so, too," Jase said. "And I thank you for making the arrangements."

Maira stepped back and Gideon let her go. "Oh, Jase," she said, moving to embrace him. Jase held her, putting his cheek on her head and whispering words of comfort while she cried anew.

"They knew you were coming," Maira told them between sobs. "The Agla'Con who took Brysia told me to give you a message. He said that Aethon would be pleased with her as a prize."

"I know," Gideon told her, seeing his anger reflected in Jase's eyes. "I saw it in my Viewing." He slammed his fist into his open palm. "One more thing to add to my list of regrets for not killing that maggot when I had the chance."

"There's more," Maira said. "They know you will follow them. They are *counting* on it."

Gideon nodded. "I know."

Jase released Maira and stepped forward, his eyes burning with intensity. "So what do you intend to do?" he asked.

"We will see to things here as quickly as possible," he said, looking at Daris. "And then we will get your mother back and send those who took her to join

Maeon in hell." He didn't even try to cover his rage.

He glanced back at Jase, suddenly worried that he'd let too much of his anger show. The smile spreading across the boy's face was chilling.

"I'll be downstairs," Gideon told him. "Join me when you're ready."

After Gideon left, Jase turned back to Maira. "Thank you for all you have done for Daris," he said. "I will inform the rest of our group about the arrangements. Do you need help getting him to the burial plot?"

"Captain Callison will see to it," she told him, her eyes going once more to Daris.

Jase studied her for a moment when she wasn't looking, and his throat tightened once more with sadness. He could see how much she loved Daris, could tell from her eyes that something had happened between them during the last month to make that love even stronger. Something which made the loss that much more painful.

He took her arm to guide her out of the room but stopped when he noticed Daris' sword. He had been so preoccupied with his grief that he hadn't noticed it sticking out of the floor. He released Maira's arm and moved to stand before the sword. "He did this?" he asked and she nodded.

He took hold of the hilt and pulled the sword free. Moving to the bed, he took Daris' sword arm from beneath the sheet and forced fingers stiff with death around the hilt, then set the blade crossways across Daris' body. Stepping back, he smiled in satisfaction.

He turned to Maira. "Come," he said, beckoning with his hand. "Let's go make ready to honor him."

She took his arm, and they made their way down to the common room. They found Gideon standing in the doorway leading to the garden and moved to join him. Jase took one look at the nightmarish sight beyond and grunted his pleasure. "I'll bet they weren't expecting that."

Gideon cast a sideways glance at him and smiled. "No, I don't think they were. Perhaps they'll be more cautious the next time they attack a Fairimor."

Jase looked at the tangled, thorn-laden wall of roses and the assassins impaled in their midst and tried to picture what it had been like for his mother in those moments before she was taken. That she had been angry was certain. He just hoped she hadn't been afraid. Knowing her, she wouldn't have shown it even if she was. He took one last satisfied look, then turned away. Her captors had no idea what they were in for.

There were several bodies laid out on the floor near the dining tables, and Jase moved toward them. Their faces were covered, but he could see by their uniforms that they were the rest of his mother's escort. Hend, Matail, Robil, and next to them Greig and Tomlin — they'd all died a hero's death trying to protect his mother. He bowed his head in a moment of silence for them, then turned to Maira. "Would you see that Captain Callison honors them as well?"

"Yes, of course," she answered, but Gideon stepped up next to her.

"Except that one," he said. "You can toss him in with the rest of the assassins."

"But Greig fought most valiantly to protect us," Maira countered, obviously confused by Gideon's comment.

"He is Con'Kumen," Gideon growled. "It was he who delivered Daris' most serious wound."

"How do you know this?" she asked, seemingly unwilling to believe what she heard.

Jase shared the sentiment. He'd known Greig for several months, and they'd had some good times together. He was odd, yes, but very eager to serve. Daris had spoken often of the young man's potential.

Gideon turned his blue eyes on them both. "I saw it," he said, and there was venom in his voice. "If Daris hadn't taken his head, I would have."

Maira stared at the corpse in shock, unable to speak.

Jase was speechless as well, unable to do anything but take Maira's hand and lead her outside.

Thorac and Endil were waiting for them, their faces grim. They had been helping where they could, and Endil, Jase noted, looked like he might vomit at any moment. *He's not used to this sort of thing,* Jase thought, then caught himself as the full import of the thought struck him.

But I am.

In a few short weeks, he had seen more death and carnage — had *caused* more death and carnage — than he had ever thought possible.

And he had become accustomed to it.

So accustomed, in fact, that it barely registered anymore. He glanced down the street at the shrouded bodies and those who mourned them. He may have grown used to the sight of blood, he decided, but he would never grow used to the pain. He would never grow that callous.

Seth came down the street toward them, his silver hair shining in the morning sunlight, his sword hilts glinting at his hips. Both paled in comparison to the fire burning in his eyes.

"There were at least twelve strike teams, and I found insignia from six different squads," he told them. "All were from the same leif, which is odd. A strike this large is usually shared with the rest of the clan."

"What does that mean?" Endil asked.

Seth frowned. "It means whoever organized the strike wanted to keep it a secret from the rest of Riak."

"Or from someone else," Gideon muttered. "Who were they?"

"Deathsquad Valhei of Clan Vakala," Seth answered, and it was obvious from the tone of his voice that it was a name he knew. He pointed south. "They went down Tetrica Road, but less than four strike teams remain."

"Good work," Gideon told him, then motioned toward the Waypost. "Get fresh horses from Captain Callison, then meet us back here. I'll finish tending to the wounded."

As Seth moved past, Jase caught his arm. "Help me get her back, Seth."

The captain's face was hard. "By my life or my death, I will," he answered fiercely, then moved off.

Jase watched him go, then cast about for his other friends. Elliott was speaking with two Highwaymen, while Talia was helping Gideon heal the wounded. Thorac and Endil were helping some of the warders unhitch the horses from the coaches. Maira was speaking with the two Highwaymen who would be taking Daris' body to the burial plot.

He knew he should do something to help as well, but couldn't bring himself to move. The full weight of what had happened was settling in on him, and he felt as if he was being crushed by it. The urge to sit, cover his head with his hands, and weep nearly overpowered him, and he stood there for a long time just watching, wishing there was something he could have done to prevent all of it from happening. He knew now the meaning of despair.

A wagon moved past with several bodies laid out in the back, and Jase shook himself out of his trance. Two grim-faced soldiers rode in the wagon, and the handles of several shovels were sticking out the back. Hurrying over, he asked for one of the shovels, then turned and followed Maira and the Highwaymen to the burial plot.

He'd found how he could help.

Seth stood at the side of Daris' grave and watched sadly as the casket was lowered by Jase, Elliott, Endil, and Thorac. Jase was covered with dirt, and tears streaked his cheeks — white lines against a layer of dark. He had dug the grave himself, attacking the ground with a seriousness that had kept the others in the group from offering to help. Gideon could have dug the hole with the Power in a matter of seconds, but the Dymas had sensed that it was something the boy needed to do. Seth hoped he would receive such an honor when it was his time to go.

He watched Maira for a moment, and thoughts of Cheslie Brandameir crept into his mind. Is this what she would have to go through for him some day as well? To watch as he was lowered into the ground at her feet? He hoped not, but he couldn't deny the fact that he lived the kind of life that made it a very real possibility. Perhaps it would be best if he didn't see her anymore. After witnessing the agony on Maira's face as she watched Daris be lowered into the ground, he didn't want to cause Cheslie the same kind of pain.

Only he couldn't deny that he was attracted to her. That night they'd stood on the Overlook together was one of the only pleasant memories to come out of the past few weeks. He could still see her delight as she'd gazed out over Trian. She reminded him of Elisa, and it was both wonderful and agonizing at the same time.

Agonizing, because in his heart he knew if he let himself love her it would be the death of him. Or her, as it had been with his beloved Elisa.

The casket settled gently to the bottom of the grave, and Seth looked up as his four friends stepped back.

Gideon stepped forward, and in his hands he held the *Book of Halek*. He opened to a page near the back and began reading.

> And lo, the angel of death calls all men, and none escape. But grieve not for the righteous, saith the Lord God of Creation, for they are mine, and I take them unto myself in glory.
>
> Yea, verily I say unto thee, a work I have for them which could not be done in the flesh. Therefore rejoice at their transformation, for my work has only begun.

He closed the book and took Daris' sword from Jase. The blade flared blue as Gideon wrought upon it with the Power. It grew so bright that those watching had to shield their eyes. Gideon moved to the large stone Maira and Jase had selected for Daris' headstone and took the sword in both hands, raising it above his head. There was a loud *sching* and a brilliant flash of light as the Dymas plunged it into the rock.

When Seth's vision cleared enough for him to see, he found Daris' sword buried half its length in the stone.

Gideon turned back to face them. "Daris' final words were *Keishun en 'liott krentis*," he told them. "Death dulls not my sword." He put the book away and glanced briefly at each of them. "And so it shall not." His eyes settled on Jase. "Pay your last respects," he said quietly. "And then we must be on our way. It's time to hunt those who did this."

As Gideon moved away, Seth joined him. When they reached the short fence separating the graveyard from the rest of Maira's residence, Gideon stopped and looked back at the group. Seth could see that he was troubled, and he had a pretty good idea what it was about.

"What now of the Talisman?" he asked, his eyes momentarily stopping on Jase. "Are we going to abandon it and go in search of Brysia?" He reached up and rubbed at the stubble on his cheeks, then continued. "I mean no disrespect, but is one woman worth the risk to the Earthsoul if we fail to retrieve the Talisman?" Seth knew by the anger flashing in the Dymas' eyes that he'd taken offense to the question.

"Of course not," Gideon hissed, then quickly lowered his voice. "You and Jase will go after Brysia. I'll take Endil to Thesston where he can retrieve the Talisman."

"And what of the others?"

"Let them choose their path," Gideon told him. "But for now we ride together. Those who took Brysia are going south. If we hurry, we may be able to overtake them."

Seth nodded his approval. "That was my thinking as well."

"I'm glad we finally agree on something," Gideon muttered, some of the heat fading from his voice. He looked over then, and his face softened further. "I'm trusting you to find her, Seth. Don't let me down."

Moved by the desperation he heard in those few words, Seth bowed deeply. "I won't," he said, then left to finish preparations for their departure. *If I have to walk into Con'Jithar itself,* he vowed silently, *I will see Brysia safely home.*

CHAPTER 24

Brothers of the Dark

The canal that separated the outlying areas of Tetrica City from the densely populated city proper was as wide as a city street and deeper than a castle moat. Staring down into it from atop a high-arched bridge, Borilius Constas breathed a sigh of relief that he and the others had finally reached their destination. Blood of Maeon, but he hated horses.

He was even more relieved when he found the guardhouse at the opposite end of the bridge untenanted. Not that it would have mattered to Gwuler's Shizu — they would have opened the way for them without any trouble. He simply didn't want to alarm the residents of Tetrica until he could make contact with the Con'Kumen stationed here; and killing a squad of City Guardsmen would certainly draw the wrong kind of attention.

He turned to study his lovely prize, silently impressed to see her looking as good as she did. Her long, honey-colored hair was in disarray, and there were dark circles under her eyes from lack of sleep, but aside from that, she didn't look like she had spent three days in the saddle. He hadn't used the Power to rejuvenate her strength as he had the Shizu, since a tired prisoner was easier to guard. It was a good thing, too. Even in her tired state she had been more troublesome than he or Gwuler had anticipated.

They had stopped for only one night of rest, riding straight through the first night and all of the following day before stopping outside a small village called Draiplin. No sooner had they moved from the road and started dismounting than she had attacked them with *Ta'shaen*, whipping up a writhing tangle of tree branches that had killed eight of Gwuler's Shizu before he could stop her.

He was thoroughly impressed with her strength, of course, both in spirit and in the Power. But the loss of so many men vexed him sorely, and he was in no mood to lose any more. They needed to get her somewhere without any vegetation so he could loose the shield he'd been forced to put around her. Maintaining it as long as he had was starting to wear on him as much as the hasty ride and lack of sleep.

They crossed another bridge into the downtown district of Tetrica and kept right on going until they reached the section of the city known as the Waterfront. The smell of the sea and the pungent odor of fish grew gradually stronger as they rode down one of the narrow streets and into an open-air market. He wrinkled his nose in disgust. Even being from Zeka, he had never gotten used to that smell. It was one of the reasons he'd left his native country and gone to Melek to serve in Maeon's armies.

He called for a stop and surveyed the plaza before him, searching for the building he hoped was still here. He had only been here once, several years earlier when he'd come to test new recruits for Gifts in the Power. A short wall at the far side of the plaza overlooked the shipping yards, but besides that not much looked familiar, especially in the dark.

He urged his horse forward again, studying each building carefully, looking for the red and black emblem of the Con'Kumen that should be in the corner of one of the windows. He found it in the window of a two-story building to the left of the short wall. It was small, no more than a few inches tall, and he would have missed it if not for the lamps glowing brightly within the house. He was glad someone was still awake at this late hour.

Motioning toward the building with his free hand, he urged the others to dismount. They did so without speaking, and joined him on the porch of the chapter house. As usual, Brysia Fairimor was glaring at him. He looked past her and found that Gwuler's Shizu had disappeared into the shadows around the building. Their horses were already tethered to railings and lampposts.

Gwuler joined him, his face uncertain. "Are you sure this is the best course of action?" he asked. "Aethon — "

"Said nothing of our using the Con'Kumen," Borilius said, cutting him off. "If we are to reach Thesston ahead of Gideon, we are going to need some help. And since you thought it necessary to return your Riaki transportation, I don't see that we have much of a choice."

Gwuler's eyes narrowed, but he said nothing. The Fairimor woman, however, smiled at them both. "You'll find that you'll have fewer and fewer choices as time goes on," she said. "Right up until Gideon Dymas cuts your black hearts out."

Borilius ignored her, moving instead to knock on the door. The sound of footsteps neared, and a young woman opened the door. She was no more than fifteen or sixteen, but the wicked scar on her cheek and the glint in her eyes killed any innocence that may have otherwise been associated with her age.

"Yes," she asked suspiciously. Her eyes moved from him to Gwuler before stopping on Brysia. "Can I help you?"

Borilius flashed a hand signal identifying himself as one in the Brotherhood, then offered a quick bow. "I'm very sure you can, Sister...?" he trailed off, waiting for her name.

She didn't give it, but she did open the door to let them in. "I'll summon my father," she told them, her eyes narrowing. "You can wait here." She indicated a couple of sofas before disappearing down the hallway.

"A feisty one," Gwuler commented as he moved across the room to examine a painting on the far wall.

Borilius motioned for Brysia to sit. When she didn't comply, he seized her with the Power and plunked her firmly onto the sofa. "I grow tired of your attitude," he growled.

She smiled. "Already? We've only been together for three days."

Gwuler chuckled, and Borilius had to force himself to keep from scowling at them both.

The scar-faced young woman returned a few minutes later. A tall, hard-eyed man with greying hair came with her. He pulled his Con'Kumen robes close around him and studied them all carefully for a moment before speaking. "I am Shaloth," he told them. "I am keeper of the chapter house in Tetrica. And you gentlemen are?"

"Gwuler Hom of Clan Vakala and Borilius Constas of Zeka," Borilius replied. "We are on the errand of The First and are in need of assistance from the Brotherhood."

The man's eyes widened slightly at hearing Aethon's title but then narrowed just as quickly. "If you are truly on his errand as you claim, then it strikes me as odd that you would need help from the ranks of the Con'Kumen. Where are your shadowspawn? Certainly they would prove more useful than we."

"Do not play games with me," Borilius snarled, seizing the man in an invisible grip of Air. He yanked him across the room toward him, and their faces stopped inches apart. "I care nothing for your precious little chapter, nor will I think twice about crushing your head if you do not cooperate with me and my companion fully. Do you understand?"

Terrified, the man nodded.

"Good," Borilius said, but he didn't release the man. "Now, I will explain what it is we need, and you and your people will provide us with it. Fair enough?"

Again the man nodded.

Borilius let him go, and Shaloth staggered backward, rubbing at his throat. "Forgive me, Agla'Con," he stammered, "but I had to be sure you were who you said. Randle Fairimor has called for the extermination of our order and the government of Tetrica is aggressively seeking to root us out."

Borilius waved him off. "That is not my problem," he told him. "Let me tell you what *is* my problem."

Taking mental notes of all that was said, Brysia listened as Borilius informed, insulted, and then threatened the leader of this so-called chapter house. He would not escape Gideon's wrath for what he had done. And if Jase had become a Dymas as Borilius claimed, the man was even dumber than she thought he was. Jase was a force to be reckoned with even without any Gifts in the Power. Daris and Seth had trained him well.

The knowledge that her son had been trained in the art of killing had always made her uncomfortable. Now, though, it gave her hope. She didn't doubt he would come for her. And Gideon would come with him.

She listened to Borilius prattle on and set her jaw to keep from sneering at him. Borilius' plan to lure Gideon into a trap was foolhardy. But then she had decided long ago that Borilius was a fool, albeit a very dangerous one. He was as cold-hearted and unstable emotionally as any person she'd ever met. He could address tumultuous situations with the utmost calm, only to fly into a rage at trivial and insignificant things. It had become her new pastime to do what she could to use that instability against him — without getting her head cut off, of course.

He noticed her watching and scowled. She raised an eyebrow in challenge and let the barest of smiles creep across her lips. It had the desired effect, and he stuttered, momentarily losing his train of thought. His scowl deepened, but all he could manage to do was glare at her.

"Will the Sister Queen be going with you to Thesston?" Shaloth asked, apparently eager to fill the uncomfortable silence.

"Of course she will, you idiot," Borilius growled. "She is the whole reason Gideon and his lackeys are after us."

"But we want them to think she is still here in Tetrica," Gwuler advised. "At least for a day or two. It will buy us the time we need to accomplish our goals in Thesston."

"So my people are to provide Gideon and his group with false information," Shaloth said with a nod. "Yes, I understand. And I assure you it is something they are very good at."

"There's more," Borilius said, and Brysia listened with barely controlled rage as the Zekan outlined a plan for the murder of as many of Gideon's group as possible, Jase excluded. If she hadn't still been bound and shielded, she would have tried to kill him with her bare hands.

"If we can separate Jase Fairimor from Gideon," Borilius continued, "we will have a better chance of taking him. He may be powerful, but he is very clumsy. If you cannot kill the Dymas, then let the Sister Queen's whereabouts be known to them. Jase will undoubtedly want to go after his mother, while Gideon will feel compelled to retrieve the Talisman."

When he finished speaking, he leaned back in his chair and smiled at her. It was so smug, so self-satisfied, that she really did try to get him, struggling against the invisible grip that held her.

Borilius shook his head, and his tone was that of a grownup scolding a child. "Now, now. We can't have any of that. It's a long way to Arkania, and you'll need your strength." The invisible grip tightened until she had trouble breathing. Grudgingly, she quit struggling.

"That's better," he purred, and the pressure lessened.

The door at the rear of the room opened and four men strode in. They moved purposefully toward the three at the table, and their fists sprang to life with the red of Agla'Con fire. They'd been drawn by Borilius' use of the Power, Brysia knew, and had come to investigate. If she hadn't been so terrified by the sight of them, she may have been able to appreciate the look of surprise that swept across Borilius' face, a look that thoroughly washed away his earlier smugness.

"Identify yourselves," one of the newcomers hissed, and Brysia followed his haughty gaze to Borilius.

The Zekan had his composure back, and he stood to greet them with a bow. "I am Borilius Constas, General in the Meleki armies of Aethon Fairimor," he told them politely. He made a small gesture with one hand, and the red of the newcomers' talismans winked out. "And as you can see, I far surpass you in strength and skill."

The four Agla'Con were so startled by what had just happened that they could only stand and stare. Gwuler leaned over and rapped his knuckles on the table to get Borilius' attention. "Aethon would not be pleased with you terrorizing those he sent us here to enlist," the Riaki said meaningfully. Brysia saw the look that passed between them and recognized the deception.

"You're right," Borilius said, congenial once again. "Forgive me," he apologized. "It's been a long week."

He made another slight gesture, and the four Agla'Con visibly relaxed. She had no way of knowing for sure, but she decided Borilius had released them from the same kind of grip he held her with.

"You were sent by The First?" one of the men asked. He was older than his three companions, but years younger than Borilius or Gwuler. His deferential tone showed that he was more than willing to take an apprentice's role in light of Borilius' strength.

Borilius reseated himself, a very satisfied smile spreading across his face. "That is correct."

The four younger men inclined their heads in obeisance. "How can we serve?" they asked as one.

Gwuler and Borilius exchanged looks and the Riaki gave a slight nod. "We need K'rresh," Borilius answered. "And passage for the rest of our men on the fastest ship you can find."

"I mean no disrespect," the older Agla'Con said, keeping his voice neutral. "But don't you have K'rresh of your own?"

Borilius' smile vanished. "They were destroyed by the adversary we seek to ensnare," he told them harshly, and Brysia knew the matter would be dropped. "Like I said," he continued, his tone friendly once more, "it's been a long week." He motioned to some chairs in the corner, and four slid across the floor toward the table. "Have a seat," he ordered. "And we'll tell you what you need to know."

Brysia listened to the explanation Borilius offered and weighed the inconsistencies of what he said with what she already knew. He glanced at her once with warning in his eyes, and she looked away. She knew better than to argue the differences in front of the newcomers; they wouldn't believe her anyway. But it did lend insight into what her abductors were faced with. They were desperate, and they were making things up as they went. It gave her the distinct impression that Aethon had no idea they were doing any of this. It was all valuable information, assuming she could find a way to exploit it.

The seven men talked for quite some time, Borilius issuing orders and the four Agla'Con and the man Shaloth nodding with eager compliance. Brysia made mental notes of all they said and memorized the names of the four new Agla'Con. Jelm and Quinton — the strongest of the four — were to accompany Borilius to Thesston and help with the theft of the Talisman, while Derbis and Nathal went with Gwuler and the rest of the Riaki by boat to Gyllas. Shaloth and his Con'Kumen would wait for Gideon's party to arrive so they could eventually drop the hints necessary to point them in the right direction.

Brysia filed everything away, knowing that the time would come when she would be able to put the knowledge to use. Right now, knowledge was the only weapon she had.

When everything was settled, they rose to carry out their assignments: Jelm to retrieve the K'rresh — whatever those were — and Nathal to secure passage by ship. Borilius pulled her to her feet with the Power and turned her over to Derbis.

"Keep her shielded at all times," Borilius warned the younger Agla'Con. "She is very capable of killing you with her Gift. If she annoys you in any way, you have my permission to hurt her however you like. But don't damage her too severely. We need her alive if we are to lure her son into our trap."

Brysia glared at him but decided to keep her retort to herself. Borilius gave an emphatic nod to show he thought her silence wise.

The six Agla'Con formed a circle and each put one hand in the middle. Shimmering red filled the space between them, casting odd shadows on the walls and giving the entire room a hellish glow. "We are one in purpose," they said in unison, "Brothers of the Dark. May the Hand of Darkness uphold us as we go forth in this great cause to bring all glory to Maeon."

The light faded and Borilius and Gwuler faced one another. "We'll see you in Gylass," Borilius said, then he, Jelm, and Quinton left the room.

Brysia studied the three who remained and pursed her lips grimly, fighting the nausea growing within her from the evil she'd just witnessed. She had known all her life that the Agla'Con were servants of Maeon, but witnessing their dark pledge firsthand turned her stomach. For the first time since her capture, a small part of her was starting to wonder if escaping from this madness might be impossible.

"Come," Derbis said and led her out into the night.

Talia's hand on his arm and a gentle, "Wake up," brought Jase out of the dream he'd been having, and thankfully so — he'd been doing battle with the Agla'Con who had taken his mother; and they had been hurling deadly bolts of lightning at each other with little regard for those around them. Several of his friends had been killed, and he couldn't say for sure if it was he or the Agla'Con who had done it. He pushed the images from his mind and looked over at Talia.

"We've stopped," she said, gesturing out the window.

He followed her gaze to the wall of trees looming tall and dark along Forest Road. It was evening, two days out from Seston. At Seth's insistence they had journeyed through last night and all of today without stopping in order to keep pace with Brysia's abductors. There had been no sidetracks, and Seth hadn't found signs of them stopping to rest. It showed how determined the Agla'Con were to reach the coastal city quickly.

The long ride wouldn't have been so bad if they hadn't already missed an entire night's sleep in their efforts to reach Seston. One night with no rest was an inconvenience; two was downright murderous. Groaning, he forced his tired muscles to respond and climbed out of the coach to investigate. His eyes fell on the *Bero'thai* sitting straight-backed but weary in their saddles, and he immediately regretted his earlier thoughts. Where he had enjoyed the relative comfort of the coach, the warders had been forced to ride most of the time, their only respite coming during the brief moments they had ridden atop the coach. And that had been more to rest the horses than themselves. He moved through their midst with a new appreciation for what they were doing for him.

And Seth, he knew, had not left the saddle at all, often scouting miles ahead to make sure the Agla'Con and their Shizu hadn't left the highway to head out through the forest. How he was able to distinguish their tracks from all the others on the highway was almost as amazing as his being able to go almost a hundred hours without sleep.

Jase found the Chellum captain standing beside his horse a short distance ahead of the first coach, and he moved to join him. Gideon was already there, and he and Seth glanced at him as he drew near, seemingly surprised to see him.

I'm not that lazy, he told them silently, then frowned worriedly. "What did you find?" he asked, suddenly apprehensive about the answer.

"Perhaps you'd better come and see," Seth told him and started into the forest.

A hundred paces from the road, they found a clearing. It looked to have been cleared by people preparing to build a home, but there, near the center, stood an odd-looking grove of saplings reaching skyward. A closer look at the saplings caused him to hiss in surprise.

Crushed to death in limbs gone wild with some unnatural frenzy were the limp forms of eight black-clad Shizu.

"Good for her," Jase said proudly. "But it's a shame one of them isn't an Agla'Con."

"They spent the night here last night," Seth told Gideon, ignoring Jase's comment. "Perhaps we should rest now as well. I know we are still only a day behind them, but overtaking them will serve no purpose if we are too exhausted to fight."

Gideon inhaled deeply, then let the breath slowly out. "Yes, I suppose you are right," he admitted, sounding displeased with the idea. His tone gave Jase the impression the Dymas had considered not stopping until the Agla'Con were in sight. "But not here. Draiplin is only a few miles ahead. We can replace some of the horses and get a good meal." He looked pointedly at Seth. "And a good night's sleep in a bed won't hurt you either."

Seth's smile held no humor. "But not a full night," he countered. "I want to be on the road again by four. Otherwise we'll never catch them before they reach Tetrica." He glanced back to the Shizu. "What about them?"

"What *about* them?" Gideon asked darkly.

"Are you just going to leave them there?"

The Dymas nodded. "Let them rot. After all, it's better than they deserve."

Seth shrugged, and he and Gideon started back for the coaches.

Jase let them go. Moving closer to the grove, he studied the nightmarish scene his mother had wrought with her Gift. A month ago such a sight would have horrified him. Now... now he found himself wishing that more of them had died. It was several minutes before he turned his back on their scarecrow forms and hurried to catch up with Seth and Gideon. Only then did it occur to him how hardened he had become.

CHAPTER 25

Choices in Tetrica

The street is narrow, too narrow for the throng passing through, and people shove and shoulder their way along with little regard for those around them. Buildings rise on each side of the street, a wall of dilapidated ruins stretching so high the upper levels seem to converge into one. The dark openings of windows and balconied doorways gaze down on the throng of people like so many empty sockets, thousands of depthless holes frozen in a rictus stare. The buildings look as if they might collapse at any moment.

One end of the street glows red as huge columns of fire swirl skyward, twisting fingers of fury rising out of sight. The other end is cloaked in a seething mass of darkness — a tangible, shadowy wall that ripples as if alive.

Jase stands in the midst of the throng and watches as thousands push first one way and then the other, unable or unwilling to choose which way to go. Many venture into the buildings and are not seen again. Those who stray too close to the darkness are swallowed without a trace as well. Those who brave the fiery end of the street flash from existence as brilliant specks of white.

Thousands are perishing at both ends of the street, but the number of people around him doesn't diminish. He doesn't know how it is possible, and right now he doesn't care. His only concern is finding Talia. He'd seen her a moment ago, venturing toward the fire. He tries calling to her, but she remains hidden from view. He continues to cast about for some glimpse of her, but she is gone.

Then he spots Elliott. His friend is only a short distance away, but he doesn't look when Jase calls to him. He stands unmoving, his eyes fixed upon the wall of blackness. Jase follows Elliott's gaze and blinks in surprise when he finds how close the darkness has crept. A quick glance towards the fire shows that it has advanced as well. Both are

closing quickly now, and except for the entrances into the buildings, there is nowhere
to go. He looks into the doorway of a nearby building and knows instinctively that it
and all those like it hold a death worse than those advancing from each end of the
street.

Thousands of people continue to vanish as fire and darkness advance, and he can
feel the heat of the flames on one cheek and the cold of winter on the other.

He looks first one way and then the other. Fire and void. Light and darkness.
Death and death. He closes his eyes for a moment, and when he opens them again, the
street is empty. Elliott, Talia, and the thousands upon thousands of people have
vanished. The walls of darkness and fire loom over him, stretching so high they
converge into one.

There is no sound now save for his own breathing. Even the buildings vanishing in
the wall of flames make no sound as they are consumed.

He turns toward the wall of fire even though the heat is starting to sear his flesh.
Behind him, the cold of the darkness is numbing. If he remains where he is, they will
reach him together. It seems so simple a thing — this waiting for death — but he knows
if he makes no choice at all, it will be the dark which claims him.

Taking one last breath, he steps into the fire...

Jase jerked awake with a start, the heat from the fire still on his skin.

Blinking against the darkness, he fought the confusion which always held fast each time he had one of these dreams. Gradually his senses came back to him, and he felt the cushioned seat and gentle sway of the coach beneath him. The warm press of Talia's body as she slept at his side was soft and reassuring.

He leaned close to the window so the cool night air could wash over his face and tried to make sense of the dream. It was the third time he'd had it. The first time had been in Draiplin. The second, this morning when he'd dozed off. And each time it had been the same. Two deaths. Two choices. What did it mean?

From the seat across from him, Seth spoke quietly. "Are you all right?" It was a simple question, but Jase could hear the bitterness present in the older man's voice. Seth was angry that they'd been unable to catch the Agla'Con before they reached Tetrica. Jase shared the sentiment, but he was glad Seth had finally decided to ride in the coach and get some much-needed rest.

"I'm fine," Jase replied. "I just had another strange dream."

"Just a dream?" Seth asked.

Jase knew what he was asking and frowned. "I'm not a prophet," he told his friend. "I'll leave those kind of dreams to Gideon."

For his answer, Seth grunted.

"We should be nearing the outskirts of Tetrica any time now," Seth said a few minutes later. The thin sliver of moonlight coming through the window illuminated the inside of the coach enough for Jase to see he was shaking his head. "I really thought we could overtake them, Jase. I'm sorry."

"We'll catch them," Jase said. He knew how badly Seth hated failure, especially his own; but this wasn't over yet. "If we have to track them all the way to Riak, we'll catch them."

Seth leaned forward, and his eyes reflected the moonlight like agates. "You've changed," the captain said. "And I like what I see."

Jase blinked, surprised by the sudden compliment. Seth didn't give praise freely. To do so now meant something — especially in light of all that had gone wrong of late. And then it occurred to him that this was more than simple praise. The captain knew something he wasn't telling.

A moment later Jase realized what it was.

"We're splitting up, aren't we?" he asked, feeling Talia stir beside him. He lowered his voice. "Aren't we?"

Seth seemed to consider. "We have two missions now," he answered. "Retrieving the Talisman is of utmost importance — the fate of the world is at stake should we fail in that." His eyes narrowed. "But we will not abandon your mother to the Agla'Con. To do so risks the outcome of the first mission as well."

Jase didn't have to think too deeply to know what Seth was implying. The captain — and Gideon as well — were worried about his ability to do what was necessary if his mother were to be lost. They were worried his anger and grief would cause him to abandon his duty to the Earthsoul and seek revenge. It was frightening to consider, but he realized they might be right.

"So who goes where?" he asked, steeling himself for the answer he feared and telling himself that he would accept whatever Gideon and Seth had decided.

"You and I will find your mother," Seth answered, and Jase let out the breath he didn't realize he'd been holding. "Gideon and Endil will retrieve the Blood Orb of Elsa."

"And the others?"

Seth shrugged. "That will be decided once we reach Tetrica Palace."

Jase leaned back into the cushioned seat and considered this new turn of events. He wasn't pleased with the idea of separating himself from Gideon. The Dymas was the one stable force in an unseen storm of darkness and corruption so vast Jase couldn't even begin to understand it. His guidance was more critical now than ever. *How can I go on without Gideon around to mentor me in my quest to master* Ta'shaen? he wondered. *What if I'm not up to the task?*

Seth must have perceived his thoughts because he chuckled. "You will do fine," he said. "Like I said earlier, I like the changes I see in you."

"Yes, but it's those you can't see that worry me," Jase muttered, then added more strongly, "If it comes to battling Agla'Con, I don't know if I have what it takes."

"When the time comes, you will. And you'll do it for your mother."

Jase looked out the window at the lights glittering beyond a distant hill. *I hope so,* he thought, *for all our sakes.*

Tetrica Palace wasn't so much a palace as it was a keep. Riaki in design, it was a single, five-storied structure with peaked roof and jutting eaves. It was surrounded by one main wall adorned with the usual guard towers and battlements, but the true defense lay in the four lesser walls and a series of moats and bridges. If the outer wall were breached, the attacking army would have to repeat the task four more times in order to reach the keep.

And since the bridges could be destroyed, the invaders would be faced with the challenge of scaling a wall without the benefit of dry land beneath their feet. It made moving in and out of the palace troublesome for those who lived there, but Jase decided it was a small price to pay in light of how easily it could be defended, by a small number of soldiers if necessary.

The coaches thundered across the last of the bridges and into the main courtyard. They were met by six palace guards. Jase followed Seth out of the coach and stopped to offer his hand to Talia as she came out behind him.

"I've always wanted to see this palace," she told Jase. "It's the only one like it in all of Kelsa. Henisor Tetrica built it in A.S. 1161 for his wife. She was Riaki, you know. He thought it would make her feel more at home."

"It must have done just that," Seth commented from behind them. "She let an entire leif of her clansmen in one night and had her husband murdered."

Talia turned to regard him with wrinkled brows. "Are you sure? I never read anything about that in the history books."

Seth shrugged. "Some things are conveniently omitted for fear of corrupting the young," he muttered. "Or some such nonsense like that."

Talia continued to study the keep as they entered, but Jase could tell she was bothered by what Seth had told her.

Elliott and Gideon moved to join them. They were followed closely by Endil and Thorac. Jase looked at each of his friends and noted how tired everyone looked. Traveling nearly three hundred miles in four days could do that to a person. He was just glad they had made it here without any mishaps. It was as long a stretch of time without someone or something trying to kill him as he'd had in a month.

But they were in a city again, and the cities of Kelsa had veins of evil he hadn't known existed until all of this started. If they didn't learn what they needed and get out of here quickly, there was no telling what might happen. He was confident the Agla'Con had arranged some sort of a surprise for them.

One of the guards stepped forward and addressed Gideon with a bow. "Dymas," he said politely. "Welcome to Tetrica. I am First Captain Eli Omasil of Palace Security. I hope your journey thus far has been pleasant."

Jase and the others exchanged looks, but Gideon was unfazed. "As well as could be expected," he lied. "I know it is late, but I need to see Lord Tetrica immediately. There are some urgent matters I need to discuss with him."

"Of course, Dymas," Captain Omasil answered. "Lord Tetrica wasn't expecting you for another day or two, but I will see that rooms, food, and baths are prepared for all in your party."

"Thank you," Gideon said, then motioned toward the palace. "Please, lead the way."

Jase and Seth fell in behind Gideon, and the others followed. As they walked, Gideon asked questions about those they were chasing, but Omasil only shook his head. "I have heard of nothing unusual," he said. "Riaki people are not uncommon in our city, but a group the size you describe would draw attention."

"Not Shizu," Seth whispered, and Jase glanced over to find a scowl on the Chellum captain's face. Seth looked at him and added, "They are only seen if they want to be."

Jase thought of the Deathsquad which had attacked him at his house and nodded. Without *Ta'shaen* he would never have known they were there. *Without Ta'shaen,* he added, *I would never have survived.* The image of them bursting into flames came unbidden into his thoughts, and he pushed it away in disgust. It hadn't been the first time he'd used his Gifts to kill, but it had been the beginning of a streak of uncontrolled brutality. Without really meaning to, he tallied his strikes with *Ta'shaen* and watched as those he'd killed flashed through his mind. It was a long and bloody list.

He sighed with horrified resignation. And that list had only begun.

They entered a large chamber on the main floor and were asked to wait while Omasil fetched Lord Tetrica. When the captain disappeared into an adjacent room, Jase looked around in surprise. He had expected Lord Tetrica's residence to be on one of the upper floors.

When he thought about it, though, he realized that having the King on the main floor where he could be evacuated quickly was wise. If his quarters were on one of the upper floors, an enemy would only need to capture the ground floor to capture the King.

He glanced around the room and noticed the recessed nooks in the shadowed corners of the room and the guards standing alertly in them. Pairs of guards stood at all the main doorways. There were slits in all four walls through which arrows could be fired from adjacent rooms. Any enemy that stormed into this room would have their hands full.

In addition to the military adornments, the room was well-furnished, and lavish tapestries and other expensive artifacts adorned the walls and tables. It reminded Jase of the museum in Trian, if a bit more heavily guarded.

Lord Tetrica arrived a few minutes later with his wife. They were young by nobility standards, the youngest of all Kelsa's monarchs, in fact.

"Gideon Dymas," Lord Tetrica said, rushing forward to take Gideon's hand in his. "I am so pleased you made it here safely. And with such speed as well."

Gideon shook his hand firmly, then bowed to Lady Tetrica as she moved up next to her husband. "My lady," he said politely, then returned his attention to the King. "Some things have happened to make haste necessary," Gideon told him. His eyes darted around the room before returning to Lord Tetrica. "I assume this room is secure?"

The King's face grew serious. "Yes," he answered, then gestured to several sofas. When they were all seated, he continued. "This is something serious," he said. It wasn't a question.

Gideon glanced at Jase before speaking. "The Sister Queen was abducted from Seston by two Agla'Con and a small army of Shizu. We tracked them here to Tetrica, but as you might have guessed, we lost them. We do not know if they are still here or if they left for Riak. If they left, it was most likely by ship. I need you to help locate them if they are here, or provide a fast ship to pursue them if they are not."

"Of course," Lord Tetrica said without hesitation.

Gideon nodded as if he'd expected no other answer. "I'll also need a ship to take me to Thesston," he said. "And I want to leave immediately if possible."

Talia broke in before Lord Tetrica could respond. "You're leaving?" she asked, her tone bordering on indignation. "What about Jase's mother?"

"If you'll let me finish," Gideon said firmly, then turned back to the King. "Seth Lydon and Jase Fairimor will be staying to search for the Sister Queen. Please provide whatever assistance they may require. Don't worry about the Agla'Con. Jase will handle them if it comes to that. What I need most from you is information gathering. Find those who took Brysia, and Seth and Jase will do the rest."

Lord Tetrica turned to study him for a moment, and Jase was tempted to look away from the intense scrutiny. Lord Tetrica may be young, but he was every inch a King. When he spoke, however, his voice was sympathetic. "My heart goes out to you, Lord Fairimor. Whatever I can do to help find your mother, I will."

"Thank you," Jase told him. *And I'll try not to wreck too much of the city if it comes to a battle.*

"What about the rest of us?" Talia asked. "Where do we go?"

There was the trace of a smile on Gideon's lips as he turned to study the Chellum Princess. "Wherever you want," he said. "Except for Endil. I'll need him to remove the Talisman from the temple in Zeka. And I'll take the *Bero'thai* as well. They would be too conspicuous here anyway. You'll need to blend in if you are to spy out Brysia's location."

"I'm staying here," Talia said, her tone decisive.

Gideon looked to Thorac. "What about you?"

The Chunin shrugged as if the choice involved nothing more than which type of cheese he preferred on his bread. "If you'll let me take a bath first, I think I might want to see this lost Temple of Elderon. Oh, and I think I would like something to eat."

Gideon pursed his lips. "Elliott?" he asked.

The Chellum Prince was silent for a moment, his eyes darting back and forth between Talia and Gideon. Jase was surprised to see him struggle with the decision, since he was certain that Elliott would choose to stay with his sister. They may fight nearly every minute of the day, but next to Seth, Elliott was Talia's fiercest protector.

Finally Elliott spoke. "I'm coming with you," he told Gideon, and the look he gave his sister was apologetic. To her credit, Talia looked concerned.

Seth, on the other hand, looked ready to explode. The look he shot Elliott was scathing.

Jase expected an outburst from him, but Seth noticed the look Gideon was directing his way and the anger subsided, at least to the point where Elliott was no longer in danger of bodily harm.

"It is decided," Gideon said with finality, then turned back to the King. "How soon can you have the ship ready?"

Captain Omasil stepped forward. "Pardon my interrupting," he said, "but *The Arrow of the Sea* is due to set sail tomorrow for combat exercises. Give me an hour to rouse the crew and she is yours."

Gideon smiled his appreciation. "Thank you, Captain," he said, then turned to Thorac. "You had better hurry if you want that bath."

With their decisions made, they rose and let themselves be guided to their rooms so they could clean up. A short time later they reconvened in the main hall and were ushered to seats around a large banquet table where food was being laid out by servants in green livery.

Jase studied the food curiously, alarmed by what he saw. Fish meat of various colors adorned one platter, and it didn't take a genius to tell that very little of it had been cooked; most had simply been sliced raw. There were odd-looking vegetables, and steaming piles of shellfish, and dark-colored sauces in which to dip things. He looked up to find Elliott and Talia studying the food with the same mixture of curiosity and alarm that he felt. He tried not to smile. If he had looked that stunned, their hosts had most likely been offended.

Seth and Gideon, however, were already eating. The Chellum captain's plate was piled high with slices of the raw fish, and he was drizzling a dark greenish sauce over the entire batch. Gideon was splitting shellfish and seemed to be enjoying every bite. Jase didn't have to look at Thorac to know the Chunin was eating like it would be his last meal; he could hear the little man's satisfied humming.

Following Seth's lead, Jase took several slices of the raw fish and was pleased with what he found. The meat was sweet and not fishy-tasting as he had thought it would be. The greenish sauce, however, burned his tongue and throat, and if he breathed wrong, his nose as well. He wiped away tears and glanced at Seth. "How can you stand that?" he coughed.

Seth grinned around a piece of fish and shrugged. "It's an acquired taste."

Jase shuddered and began experimenting with some of the other foods. Most were good — better than he'd thought they would be — but there were a few things he nearly gagged on. Oddly enough, those were the foods Seth seemed to enjoy most. He also seemed to enjoy the newfound torture of making sure Jase was watching when he ate them.

When everyone started to slow, Gideon leaned back in his chair and addressed them all solemnly. "It is almost time," he told them. "Jase and I will keep in touch by Communing." He glanced at Jase. "You do remember how to do that, right?"

"I think so," he answered honestly.

"It will come back to you," Gideon said. "I will check in with you each night to see how you are faring. We will have to be careful, though," he warned. "If our enemies realize what we are doing, they can eavesdrop on us. We'll have to keep things short."

"What do you want us to do once we have recovered my mother?" Jase asked. He knew it might sound presumptuous, but in his mind, there was no alternative *but* to recover her.

"Return here and wait for me to rejoin you. If we obtain the Talisman before you find your mother, we will join you in your hunt for the Agla'Con."

"You make it sound so easy," Talia muttered, shaking her head. "What if we can't — " she cut off, her face going red as she realized what she had been about to ask. "I'm sorry, Jase," she said. "I didn't mean to... I mean I was..." She cut off again, and tears welled up in her eyes. "I'm sorry," she said, wiping at her tears. Her chin trembled, and the tears flowed more freely. "I guess I've been holding everything back for so long that it's finally breaking free." She wiped at the tears fiercely. "I know we will find your mother," she said and glanced at Seth. "We have the best tracker in the Nine Lands with us."

Jase was moved by the show of emotion and had to fight to keep his own tears in check. He didn't like considering the possibility that they wouldn't find his mother — he refused to consider it. "We will find her," he soothed, as much for himself as for Talia. Then he turned back to Gideon, and his voice took on a ferocity he didn't intend. "You just make sure you get the Talisman so we can end this war with Shadan once and for all."

CHAPTER 26

Meeting Death

The street is unusually crowded for such a late hour, but Breiter forces his way through the mass of bodies determinedly. He needs to reach the Con'Kumen chapter house before the brethren who have escaped from prison can alert those gathered there that they are about to be attacked by Elison and a host of Elvan Bero'thai.

He looks over his shoulder to urge his men to hurry, but they are gone. So is everyone else. The street is empty. The only thing visible in the quickly gathering shadows is a pair of feral green eyes staring out at him from a narrow alley.

When he raises a crossbow at them, the eyes vanish.

Lowering his weapon, he turns and runs toward the chapter house once more. If he doesn't reach Elison in the next few minutes, his friend will walk into an ambush.

He rounds a corner and finds himself once again surrounded by a mass of people. Ignoring their protests, he shoves his way through them, offering apologies as he goes but not really caring if the people hear. Right now only Elison matters. He has to reach Elison.

The street empties into a plaza fronting a bridge that spans the Trian River, and Breiter slows, casting about in confusion. He's already been through here. Somehow, he has made a wrong turn and doubled back on his route.

Cursing, he starts for the bridge once more. He crosses the bridge, forces his way down unusually crowded streets, and turns into a plaza fronting the Trian River.

Three more times this happens, and each time the panic he feels at not being able to reach Elison increases ten-fold. He stops in the center of the plaza and looks around in bewilderment. The mass of people has vanished. He is alone save for a pair of feral green eyes staring out at him from a dark alley.

He remains motionless, and the plaza seems to move and shift around him. Buildings change shape — some stretching taller, others shrinking away into the distance. The feral eyes multiply in the dark spaces between the buildings until every avenue is closed to escape.

He casts about nervously. Behind him, standing as the center-point of the plaza, is a fountain. And there, sitting at the water's edge, is a young girl in a blue dress. She holds a small birdcage on her lap, oblivious to the danger surrounding her. Lazily, she dabbles her fingers in the water.

Something moves at the edge of his vision, and he turns to see Elison and his Bero'thai exiting one of the buildings. They seem unaware of the danger lurking in the shadows around the plaza, and Breiter raises his hand in warning.

The plaza goes white with a flash of lightning, and thunder rocks the buildings. A moment later the skies open, and everything vanishes beneath a storm of arrows.

Breiter jolted upright, the last vestiges of the nightmare still clear in his mind's eye. Pressing his palms against his face, he willed the awful images away. It was the second time tonight that this had happened. The second time tonight that he or Elison had died. He lay back on the pillow, blowing out his cheeks wearily. He wished he could remember the part of the dream that led up to the storm of arrows. If he could do that, he might be able to find a way to keep it from happening.

Beside him Zea stirred. "Did you have another nightmare?" she asked softly.

"Not another one," he told her. "The same one." He pulled the covers aside and moved to the window. He threw open the curtains to let the early morning light stream in, then moved to the wardrobe to dress. "The bloody storm of arrows Elder Nesthius told us is coming." He frowned. "There was more, but I can't remember any of it." He tugged on his shirt. "I wish Nesthius had never said anything."

Zea rose and moved up behind him. The hard mound of her stomach pressed against his lower back as she took him in her arms. "But if he hadn't told you about it, then there would be no way for you or Elison to prepare to meet it."

"That's true," he told her. "But the very thought of it happening at all is making me more paranoid than I've ever been in my life."

"But I thought it was your paranoia that's kept you alive all this time," she teased.

"This is different," he told her. "This time I *know* something bad is going to happen. And if Nesthius is right, there isn't a bloody thing I can do about it."

Zea turned him around so she could look him in the eyes. "That's what really scares you isn't it — the idea that you might not be in control of your life anymore?"

"That's certainly part of it," he replied. He reached up and brushed a lock of her hair behind her ear. "The thing that scares me most, though, is that I might not be here to help raise our daughter."

She leaned forward and kissed him on the mouth. "Then by all means," she whispered, "see what you can do to keep Elder Nesthius' vision from coming to pass."

Beraline Hadershi looked up from the book she was reading and watched Captain Lyacon exit the north tower stairwell. His face was pinched with worry, and his eyes were troubled. He was halfway across the dining hall before he noticed her.

"Oh, good morning, Lady Hadershi," he said, smiling sheepishly. "I didn't see you there."

She set the book on the table. "Please, Captain," she said, "call me Beraline." They'd had a very nice chat last night as he'd escorted her to her room. After apologizing for his mistrust of her being a Dymas, he had brought her up to date on all that had been happening in Trian the past few weeks. He had even told a little about his wife and the baby girl they were expecting. He was an extremely likable man, and she believed they were well on their way to becoming friends. What he said next confirmed it.

"Of course," he said, stopping near the table and eyeing the tray of fruit Allisen had brought in earlier. "But then you must call me Breiter."

"Breiter it will be," she told him, studying his face intently. Something was definitely troubling him. There was a weariness in his eyes that told her he hadn't slept well.

She was about to ask what was wrong when *Ta'shaen* tickled her Awareness, a faint whispering of energy that she recognized as the Gift of Discernment. She had only experienced the Gift a handful of times, but she knew better than to ignore the feeling. Immediately she opened herself to the Power, and Breiter's thoughts sounded loudly inside her mind.

Arrows... thick as hail from a summer storm. A bloody storm of arrows. One of us will pass unscathed. The other will fall. Burn fate and all its bloody foretellings. Burn Nesthius' vision. Elison and I will be fine. I won't — Breiter's thoughts cut off, and Beraline blinked when she realized he was staring at her. The tingling of Discernment vanished.

"Are you okay?" he asked. "You look like you've seen a ghost."

"Or a vision," she said, releasing the Power and rising from the chair to face him. It was presumptuous, but she stepped close and took him by the hand, searching his face intently. She knew now what was troubling him, and she didn't like what she saw in his eyes.

"I know about Elder Nesthius' vision," she told him. "Or part of it anyway. Just now, the Earthsoul let me see into your mind."

His face could have been carved from stone. "And..." he prompted.

"And I think you and Captain Brey better start preparing to meet it."

"How do you prepare to meet an attack that could come anywhere at anytime?" he asked. "How do you defeat an enemy that seems to be everywhere?"

"Perhaps," she offered softly, "the kind of preparation Elder Nesthius expects from you two doesn't involve a sword or a bow."

Breiter studied her for a moment without speaking. "What are you saying?" he asked at last.

"That maybe," she said, her voice soft, "the enemy you and Elison need to prepare to meet is death."

"Sorry," he told her. "I've got someone more important to meet first. She should be here in a couple of weeks."

"Breiter, I'm serious. If Elder Nesthius saw it in a vision, it is going to happen. Maybe not tomorrow, maybe not even next year. But the fact remains that you and Elison are in danger. One of you is going to die."

"Not if I have anything to say about it," he told her, pulling out of her grasp. "If you will excuse me, I have an appointment with some of the prisoners in the dungeon." He crossed the dining hall to the doors leading to the Dome and waited while the *Bero'thai* opened them for him. Before he left, he cast a quick look over his shoulder. His face was set, his lips tight with determination.

She could see in his eyes that he believed Elder Nesthius' vision was real — that wasn't the problem. The problem arose from his belief that he could keep it from happening.

He disappeared through the doors, and she shook her head sadly. She would help him any way she could, of course. And Elison Brey too. She prayed that it wouldn't be to their deaths. Glancing at the scars still slightly visible on her arms, she frowned. *Or mine.*

She knew from experience that trying to rewrite the books of fate was akin to kicking a sleeping Shadowhound with the hope of scaring it away. Sooner or later the bite would come.

Randle watched as those he'd called together for this special session of the Core Council took seats around the table. He'd called only as many of the Core as he'd dared — of the twelve current members, there were only five he trusted.

Andil and Cassia sat next to Elder Nesthius. Elison sat next to the Communicator Stone that would be used for General Eries.

Two more stones had been placed on the table. Those would be used to include General Crompton and Governor Drastin since they had found Dymas to ward their ends of the links.

The others — Breiter, Judge Zeesrom, and Ladies Hadershi and Korishal — he'd invited to bring the number of participants to twelve as required by law. He trusted them, and he needed their help and advice. They sat opposite Elison, their eyes thoughtful as they waited for him to speak.

He turned to Marithen. "Lady Korishal," he said, "if you would be kind enough to ward the room against eavesdropping, we will begin."

She smiled fondly at him. "My dear young Randle," she began, and beside her Judge Zeesrom blinked in surprise at the familiarity of her words, "I would be honored."

Since he couldn't tell if she had actually done anything with the Power, Randle looked at Beraline Dymas. She nodded that the ward was indeed in place.

"Activate the stones," he told her and watched as the blue luminescent images of Governor Drastin and Generals Eries and Crompton flared into being.

"Welcome, Gentlemen," Randle said. "Are your ends of the links warded?"

When they nodded, he continued. "Excellent. I'll get right to it then." He cleared his throat. "The Con'Kumen are becoming a very great threat, as dangerous as the army Shadan is massing to march against us. In some ways they are more dangerous. And while it is true that we need to send men to Zedik Pass to meet Shadan's army, we cannot neglect the enemy that has already massed among us. They are many, they are well organized, and they have resources that can only be countered by Dymas."

He paused and looked around at those assembled before him, flesh and luminescent images alike. "And those Dymas are starting to come forth. In Kelsa, at least. Some are responding to the proclamation I issued last month. Most, like Ladies Hadershi and Korishal, are answering the call issued by my nephew six nights ago when he lit the skies over Kelsa's heartland. Apparently, Jase's actions that night were the fulfilling of prophecy."

"One of many to come," Croneam said. "According to what I've been reading in the scriptures, the crowning of Fairimor Dome with Fire is not much more than a pebble tumbling down a rocky slope." His shimmering image leaned forward, and he smiled beneath his mustache. "But it is a pebble that will loose the entire mountainside as it gains momentum. Soon the entire world will feel what that boy is capable of." He leaned back, his face thoughtful. "I just hope we like the outcome."

"Amen to that," Elder Nesthius said.

Randle ignored the comment and tried to suppress the dread that rose inside him every time he was reminded of what Jase was capable of. "Returning to the point at hand," he began, "the Dymas are answering the call. We need to decide what to do with them as they arrive."

"What to do with them?" Governor Drastin said with a frown. "You speak as if they were trespassers guilty of causing a disturbance."

Lady Hadershi laughed. "We tend to think of ourselves as a valuable commodity. One that needs to be shared and distributed as best suits the needs for which prophecy has summoned us." She turned her gaze on Randle. "Lord Fairimor understands this. As do all those who have and will come forward." She returned her attention to Governor Drastin, but her words were for everyone. "I heard no disrespect in the High King's words. The Gifted have come forth to do what he requires. We are here to engage the Hand of the Dark in battle."

Governor Drastin nodded, but the hardness of his face remained unchanged. "Of course," he said. "But since it is the Gifted who will be wielding the Power in battle, perhaps we ought to ask them where they think they should go. Who knows better than they — than you Lady Hadershi — where their Gifts will be of the most benefit?"

Randle reached up to rub the bridge of his nose. "Which once again brings us to the point at hand," he said irritably. "It is no small thing that I have asked Ladies Hadershi and Korishal to sit in on this council. True, I needed their abilities with the Power to operate the stones, but the real reason I invited them is because I have asked them to oversee the creation of an Army of the Gifted." He glanced at the image of Governor Drastin. "Along with Erebius Laceda. He is there, is he not, warding your end of the link?"

Governor Drastin nodded. "He is."

"Erebius Dymas," Randle said, "I know you can hear me. Widen the range of the Stone so we can see you."

The shimmering halo around the image of Governor Drastin pulsed outward in a flash of bluish white, and two more figures came into view behind the chair that held Governor Drastin's image. Erebius sported a bit more white in his shoulder-length hair, but other than that he didn't appear to have aged much over the past twenty years. If anything, he looked even more fierce than he had before he'd vanished after the Battle of Greendom. His daughter didn't look to be more than twenty-five or thirty, but considering how the Power enabled a wielder to cheat aging, she could be sixty for all Randle could tell.

"Welcome back," Randle said warmly. "I take it the last twenty years have been largely uneventful for you."

"Hardly," Erebius said, with a wry smile. "While the rest of the world has been resting on its laurels, those few Dymas who survived the massacre you call the Battle of Greendom have been preparing for the arrival of the *Mith'elre Chon*."

Croneam's image leaned forward. "Preparing? How?"

"By staying alive," Erebius replied. "And by gathering in all the Gifted we could find before they could be recruited or killed by the Agla'Con."

"But if you knew you would be needed again," Andil began, "why didn't you come forward sooner?"

"Yes," Judge Zeesrom said. "And why didn't you return to tell us that the Earthsoul had not been rejuvenated and that Shadan had survived?"

Lady Hadershi answered for him. "Would you have believed us?" she asked softly.

The room was quiet as they considered.

It was Croneam who finally broke the silence. "Without proof, probably not," he answered. "I was at Greendom when Shadan vanished into flame and void. I saw it with my own eyes. And when the K'rrosha exploded into fiery bits a short time later, I was convinced that Areth Fairimor had been successful in the rejuvenation. The Refleshed have no place in this world as long as the Earthsoul is strong."

"I was at Greendom as well," Lady Hadershi said. "And like you, I believed Shadan's destruction meant the Earthsoul had been rejuvenated. It wasn't until recently that I learned differently. But it is clear that something happened in the Soul Chamber to thwart Shadan's armies. Areth Fairimor must have used the Talisman of Elsa."

"It wasn't Areth," Randle told her. "He was killed before they ever reached the chamber. It was Gideon Dymas who used the Talisman's power to strengthen the Earthsoul. The entire mission — including its failure — was nothing more than what Gideon calls another piece of the puzzle."

"What puzzle?" Andil asked.

Randle shrugged. "Fate. Prophecy. The will of the Earthsoul. Who knows? The whole bloody thing gives me a headache whenever I think about it."

"Did Gideon know that Areth was doomed to fail?" Croneam asked, his face thoughtful as he twisted one end of his mustache.

Randle was quiet a moment before answering. "He did."

Judge Zeesrom leaned forward slightly. "Did *you* know it was destined to fail?"

Randle sighed deeply. "I did."

"And for twenty years you said nothing about it?" the Chief Judge asked in disbelief. "How could you do that?"

"He had no choice," Cassia told them. "Gideon put him under oath not to speak of it, and he bound the oath with the Power. Only recently did he release Randle from the binding."

"But even if I could have told you," Randle began, "would you have believed me any more than you would have believed any of the Dymas?" Their silence told him they wouldn't have.

"Why would Gideon do such a thing?" Judge Zeesrom asked. "What did he hope to accomplish?"

"He was fulfilling prophecy," Elder Nesthius said. His face and voice were calm, but his eyes told a different story as they glittered brightly. "Gideon is more than simply another Dymas warrior. He is a Prophet and a Seer. The Earthsoul speaks to him through *Ta'shaen*, and when Gideon learns what must be done, he does it, without hesitation or reservation. His erratic behavior is questioned by those who aren't privy to what he knows, but I can assure you that Gideon's only concern is for the welfare of the Earthsoul."

"But how could staying quiet about the failure of the mission to heal the Earthsoul be for Her benefit?" asked Governor Drastin. "What did we gain from such a deception?"

"Twenty years in which an entire generation of Gifted could come of age," Randle told them. "After the heavy losses we suffered during the Battle of Greendom, we needed time for those numbers to increase."

"And we needed time to train those we gathered in," Erebius added. "We knew this day would come even if we weren't sure when it would happen or who the enemy would be. We didn't even know if it would happen in our lifetime. For all we knew, Death's Third March might not have come until the end of the next six thousand years of the Earthsoul's existence."

"Earlier you mentioned the *Mith'elre Chon*," General Crompton said, "and that you have been preparing for his arrival. What can you tell us about that?"

Everyone at the table turned to regard the aging general. He'd been so quiet during the discussion that Randle had forgotten he was there. Normally the man had a comment for everything. For him to have remained silent meant he was thinking deeply about something.

"Now that it is clear that Death's Third March is indeed upon us," Erebius began, "we believe the *Mith'elre Chon* may have already come."

Lady Korishal nodded her head enthusiastically. "*For out of the wasteland shall he come,*" she quoted, "*the* Mith'elre Chon, *a son of thunder with fire in his eyes and lightning in his hands. And though he shall be a man of death, healing and salvation ride in his wings."*

Erebius smiled at her before turning his attention back to Randle. "It took twenty years, but Gideon returned from Mount Tabor. He returned from the wasteland of the Shadan'Ko. It is my opinion, and the opinion of many of the Gifted, that Gideon is the *Mith'elre Chon*."

"Then someone needs to tell Gideon," Randle chuckled, "because he thinks it is someone else."

"Does he have a particular person in mind?" Croneam asked.

Randle regarded him quietly for a moment before answering. "I'm sure he does," he told him. "But until the prophecy is fulfilled, we can only guess."

"What makes you think it hasn't already come to pass?" Erebius asked, his brow lined with doubt.

Elder Nesthius turned to study Erebius, and the aging Prophet's wizened face was bright with the light of understanding. "Too many prophecies remain unfulfilled," he told them all. "Do not let your hope for a swift victory against the enemy cloud your judgment. Gideon Dymas is indeed a son of thunder, but he is not the *Mith'elre Chon*. Not yet at least. When the One Who Comes Before does indeed appear, the entire world will resonate with the sound of his coming. And the ranks of the Army of the Gifted will be filled."

"Which," Randle said with a bewildered shake of his head, "once again brings us back to the purpose for this meeting." He turned to Erebius. "I want you and your daughter to remain in Tradeston for a few more days to gather in what Gifted are coming forth now, and then I want you to go to Fulrath. The main body of our army of Gifted will be organized there. I want you to head them, Erebius. I need you to. Until Gideon returns, you are the oldest and most experienced of Kelsa's Dymas."

Erebius dipped his head. "It will be as you request, my lord."

"Thank you, my friend," Randle said, his heart filled with gratitude for the man. Turning to Beraline Dymas he continued. "I need you and Marithen Dymas to stay here in Trian for a time," he told her. "Your presence will cause the Con'Kumen to reconsider their course of action. If they continue to rear their ugly head, I will have you remove it."

"You will be working with me and Breiter," Elison told them. "Together we will exterminate the Con'Kumen and free the city of their threat."

"When that is finished," Randle said, "you may go to Fulrath if you wish and join the Army of the Gifted. They will need your knowledge and experience as they confront the armies of the Agla'Con."

"Do we know how many we will be facing?" Erebius asked.

Randle hesitated a moment before answering. "At least five hundred," he said. "Maybe more."

Beraline Dymas pursed her lips grimly. "We will need at least three hundred Dymas," she said and Erebius nodded. "And as many Gifted as are willing to come forth to be trained for battle."

"And we will need Healers," Croneam added. "Every one we can find."

Randle rubbed his eyes. "I can only issue the proclamation so many times," he said wearily. "We need something more to get their attention."

"Trust in the prophecies," Croneam soothed. "The Children of *Ta'shaen* will answer the call of the *Mith'elre Chon*."

"Of course," Randle said. "You are right. We simply need to be patient." He fastened his attention on Elison Brey. "As for the Con'Kumen, however, I want swift action. I want them eradicated from our city, and I don't care how you go about it."

Elison's face was hard as he spoke. "That is my sentiment as well. We have learned all we are going to from many of the vermin. They are nothing more than so much trash filling up our prison." He hesitated, looking briefly at Cassia before returning his attention to Randle. "You know that I do not glory in the shedding of blood. I have spent my entire career trying to avoid it." His eyes narrowed. "But I cannot overcome the feeling of dread I experience every time I consider what might happen if the Con'Kumen were somehow able to free the prisoners we've taken. Those lost to the cause of darkness would surely try to bring down the government."

"What are you saying?" Randle asked. "Do you want to execute them?"

Elison's eyes narrowed. "Yes. If anyone deserves death it is the Con'Kumen." He looked around the room at faces lined with disbelief. "Not all of them, mind you. Just those whose souls have been taken by Maeon. There are many, I believe, who would repent of their crimes if given the chance."

"And so what do you propose?" General Crompton asked.

"Perhaps if I showed you," Elison said, placing a brass urn filled with oil on the table and gesturing to Lady Korishal.

The elderly Dymas smiled, and a small orange flame sprang up. "Look into the fire," she told them, "and I'll show you what your young captain has been up to."

The chamber in the Trian dungeon was long and rectangular, with two iron-bound doors facing each other across its narrow width. Several oil lamps hung in brackets along the walls, but the far corners of the room were cloaked in shadow. Sparsely furnished, the room had a single table with chairs at one end and two rows of benches at the other. The benches were empty, but Taka O'sei of the Palace Guard and Breiter

Lyacon of the Fairimor Home Guard sat at the table with Lady Korishal. An area of sand five inches deep and a dozen feet square covered the floor in front of them. Eyes and faces hard, they watched Elison Brey lead a Con'Kumen prisoner through one of the doors and into the center of the spot of sand.

The young Con'Kumen kept his head down as Elison forced him to his knees. His eyes stayed fastened on the chains binding his hands in front of him. "What is the sand for?" *he asked. His voice held no defiance or bitterness.*

"To catch your blood," *Captain O'sei answered darkly.* "I won't have your Con'Kumen filth defiling the floor of the dungeon."

The young Con'Kumen nodded but said nothing.

Elison drew his sword. "The time has come," *he said,* "for you to meet death." *Using the point of his sword, he drew the symbols for Con'Jithar and Eliara in the sand in front of the young man's knees.* "What you find beyond the Veil depends on you."

A tear slid down the young man's cheek. "I understand."

Gripping his sword hilt tightly with both hands, Elison raised it above his head. "By the authority vested in me by the people of Kelsa, I hereby sentence you to death for treason against the Blue Flame. Should you wish to repent of your crimes against your countrymen and forsake your allegiance to the Hand of the Dark, I will send an epistle to your family informing them of your change of heart and allow them to collect your body for burial. In addition, your name will not be included on the proclamation which is to be sent throughout the city of Trian announcing the names of those who have been executed for this treachery."

He paused a moment to let his words settle into the young man's mind. "If, however, you choose to die with the oath of the Con'Kumen still on your lips, your name will go before the public and your family will suffer humiliation. The choice is yours, Con'Kumen — anonymity in death with the possibility of mercy in the afterlife, or public shame and a sure descent into the depths of hell." *He tightened his grip on the sword.* "What say ye?"

The young man's shoulders shook as he began to sob, and tears rolled freely down his cheeks. "I am sorry for what I did," *he whispered.* "I know the Con'Kumen are evil. I know what I did was wrong. I never intended to betray Kelsa, but I accept the punishment as dictated by the laws of our country."

He looked up then, his eyes filled with desperation. "But you don't understand... I have to keep my oath to protect my family. The Con'Kumen aren't content with only killing those who betray them; they go after our families. Please, you must protect my family. You must put my name on the list so the Con'Kumen will believe that I died loyal to them. They are murderous scum who will harm those I love if they know that I have forsaken their oath."

Elison studied him intently for a moment. "Have you forsaken them?"

"Yes," the young man said. "I wish I had never heard of them." He lowered his head once more. "After you take my head," he whispered. "Protect my family."

The sound of Elison's sword sliding into its scabbard caused the young man to look up in surprise. When Elison offered his hand, the surprise deepened.

"You want to protect your family?" Elison asked, helping him to his feet. "Then help me eradicate the Con'Kumen. Show your loyalty to Kelsa by helping me give death to those who truly deserve it."

The young man blinked away tears. "It will be as you say," he said, "and thank you."

Elison whistled and two Bero'thai entered the room from the door leading out of the dungeon. "My men will show you to your new residence," Elison told the young man. "You are no longer a prisoner, but you must understand that until the Con'Kumen are destroyed I cannot let you leave the palace grounds. If any in their organization were to see you, our plan would be ruined."

Nodding, the young man let himself be led away.

Elison smoothed the sand, then exited the room to fetch the next prisoner. He returned with a middle-aged man with light brown hair and a thin mustache. He resisted Elison's urging enough to show his disdain for the captain but not enough to provoke harsher treatment. His face was arrogant, his eyes hard and hate-filled. His smile was mocking as he studied those seated at the table and the patch of sand spread before them.

"On your knees, Con'Kumen," Elison barked as they reached the center of the sand. When the man refused, Elison struck him on the back of the knees with his sword hilt, dropping him with a grunt.

Elison drew his slender blade from its scabbard. "The time has come," he said, "for you to meet death." Using the point of his sword, he once again drew the symbols for Con'Jithar and Eliara in the sand. "What you find beyond the Veil depends on you."

"I know what I will find," the man hissed. "And I shall receive glory far beyond anything you pathetic — " he cut off as Elison backhanded him across the face.

"I didn't give you permission to speak," Elison snarled. "Interrupt me again and I'll remove your tongue." The point of his sword hovered dangerously close to the man's face. The Con'Kumen's eyes narrowed angrily, but he didn't speak further.

Raising his sword, Elison spoke the same words he had said to the younger man. When he finished, he tightened his grip on the sword. "What say ye?"

"Glory be to Maeon," the man snarled. He opened his mouth to say more, but Elison removed his head in a single stroke.

The Viewing faded and those around the table turned their attention to Elison. He sat stone-faced before them, his eyes glittering.

"With the council's permission," he said, "I would like to give all two hundred prisoners a chance to forsake their oath to the Con'Kumen."

"And if they don't?" Judge Zeesrom asked.

"Then we'll need more sand," Elison answered. "But I do not believe that will be the case."

"You have my permission," Randle said, letting his eyes move around the room. "What do the rest of you think?"

"I support it as well," Croneam said, and the rest of the council nodded their agreement.

"Very well," Elison said. "I will begin interviewing the remainder of the prisoners first thing in the morning."

Randle turned to Croneam. "General Eries," he began, "what news from Fulrath? Have you made plans to retake Zedik Pass?"

"Yes," Croneam replied. "Two thousand of the Chellum Home Guard led by Elam Gaufin left yesterday. Lord Nid and a small number of Gifted who were already among Elam's men went with them, as did Taggert Enue. I gave Elam the name of a powerful Dymas living in Greendom who will undoubtedly join them as well. I instructed Elam to start an evacuation of Greendom."

"Very good," Randle said. "But why troops from Chellum and not the Roves of Fulrath?"

Croneam was quiet a moment, thinking. "Captain Gaufin volunteered," he said at last. "And the spirit of the Earthsoul whispered to me that it was the right course of action. There were those who argued against it, of course, including General Enue. Which is odd, because as soon as Taggert realized Elam would indeed be leaving, he turned command of Chellum's main army over to Nemean Leva so he could go with Elam. Don't ask me why, but he was most insistent on tagging along. It was my decision to let him and Elam go. I didn't feel it wise to hold back those who are willing to walk fate's path."

"I trust your decision," Randle told him. "And thank you for your efforts. When Erebius Dymas arrives, begin work on the creation of the Army of the Gifted."

Croneam brought his fist to his chest in salute. "It will be as you say, Lord Fairimor."

"If there is no other business," Randle said, "then we will adjourn for the time being. I will keep the stones here in the inner palace. If you need to communicate with me, and have a Dymas to ward the link, please contact me at any time."

They assured him that they would, and the links were severed. He turned to those that remained. "We all know our duties," he told them. "For the honor of

God, the Flame of Kelsa, and the liberty of the people, let us fulfill them."

"Amen," Elder Nesthius said, and everyone began filing from the room.

Randle caught Elison by the arm and then motioned for Breiter to join them. They moved away from the others. "Thank you for your work, my friends," he said. "Trian would be lost without you."

"We are just doing our duty," Breiter told him. "We live to serve the Blue Flame."

"Precisely why I don't want either of you dying any time soon."

Zeniff removed his dark blue judge's robe and hung it in the wardrobe next to the crimson and black robe he wore as an Agla'Con. Both were symbols of his power. Both would allow him to take control of the ancient city and reign in Randle Fairimor's stead. Eventually.

First he had to stop Elison Brey and halt the extermination of the Con'Kumen. And he would certainly need to find out where the bloody captain was keeping those who were forsaking their allegiance to the Brotherhood. Their betrayal could not go unpunished.

He closed the door of the wardrobe and moved to a chair across the room. Thumping himself down, he tried to reconcile the situation. He'd lost more than two hundred members of the Brotherhood, and while it was but a fraction of those he commanded, their capture had made the rest of the organization nervous. Recruiting had been put on hold, since it was impossible to tell if the person they were trying to seduce was actually interested in joining the Hand of the Dark or if they were one of Elison Brey's spies.

He rubbed his eyes wearily. And Ladies Hadershi and Korishal would make another reprisal difficult to carry out. Both were extremely Gifted Dymas and more than a match for any of the Agla'Con he had in his command. He hated admitting it, but Korishal was powerful enough to squash him like a bug if she ever learned who he was.

Brooding, he sat in silence until the Changeling Shadan'Ko grunted in agitation. Zeniff flinched. He had forgotten the creature was still waiting for orders. He turned an appreciative eye on it and smiled. It was proving far more useful than he'd ever anticipated and was one of the reasons he knew as much about Elison Brey's plans as he did.

"Continue on as you have," he told it. "I want regular reports about Captain Brey's activities. And see if you can learn the names of any who have forsaken their oath to the Brotherhood. I need to show them what happens to those who betray me."

"It will be as you say," the Shadan'Ko replied evenly, its speech and mannerisms perfectly Elvan. Beneath the fair exterior, however, was the soul of a wild animal, bloodthirsty and ferocious.

Zeniff frowned as a sudden apprehension washed through him. If the Shadan'Ko ever turned on him, he would be forced to kill it without the aid of the Power lest he alert Hadershi or Korishal to his presence. He would do well to remember that. It would also be advisable to keep a sword or dagger close at hand.

He gestured dismissively toward the door. "You have your orders, my pet," he cooed. "Fulfill them and there will be flesh to eat." *The flesh of Elison Brey and Breiter Lyacon,* he added silently.

Dipping its head in a bow, the Changeling spun on its heel and left.

Zeniff returned to his contemplation, fingering the talisman hidden beneath his shirt. As much as he longed to seize the Power, the time for that kind of action would have to wait. He was going to have to rely on more traditional forms of weaponry to kill the pesky captains — and Ladies Hadershi and Korishal as well if he could manage it.

And now that he knew of the offer Elison Brey was making to those foolish enough to forsake their oath to the Brotherhood, he knew how it could be done. *Very soon,* he thought with a smile, *the blood of my enemies will stain the streets of Trian.*

CHAPTER 27

Greendom

With the morning sun in his eyes, Elam Gaufin brought his horse to a stop on the final hill overlooking Greendom and squinted down at the town below. Riding beside him, Teig Ole'ar and Taggert Enue did the same.

People were visible moving about in the streets, and there were people and animals working in the surrounding fields. On the main roadway leading out of town, a squad of Highwaymen was leaving a trail of dust as it moved up the slope toward him. He watched the men come for a moment, then turned his attention back to Greendom.

Sprawled amid the grassy swells of the Allister Plains, it was larger than most towns dotting Kelsa's highways and was comparable to Seston or Drusi. It even had its own Waypost at the eastern end of town overlooking the river. It was clean and well-kept, with bright hues of paint on all the buildings and well-groomed flower gardens in many of the yards. Trees just now reaching maturity provided shade for children to play in. It was a far cry from the smoking remains of twenty years ago, and a testament to the perseverance of people who, having claimed a place as their own, would rebuild it no matter the extent of the destruction.

He wondered if they would return to rebuild this time. He frowned. Would there even be anyone left to return?

"It's a shame that none of that will survive the invasion," Taggert said. "Greendom is even more beautiful now than it was before Shadan and his Agla'Con destroyed it." He gestured to the sight below. "It's going to be difficult to convince people that they will need to evacuate."

Elam cast a sideways glance at the aging general and smiled. For all his grumbling that this was nothing more than a suicide mission, he sure seemed interested in being involved. He'd surprised them all yesterday morning at departure when he'd shown up on his horse, sword at hip, and muttered something about being bored with Fulrath, and how it might be nice to ride on over to Greendom, and, since Elam and his men were going, mightn't he ride along with them? *Someone,* he'd added, *needs to look after these impetuous youngsters.* Even with the general's ceaseless philosophizing, Elam was glad he had come.

The squad of Highwaymen drew near, and Elam raised his hand in greeting as they reined in their horses. They took a moment to study the Chellum army stretching westward before addressing him and Taggert. "That's quite a number of horsemen you've brought with you," the man in the captain's uniform said. "General Eries must have decided to try to retake the pass."

"Yes," Elam nodded, nudging his horse forward so he could offer the man his hand. "I am Elam Gaufin. And this," he added, indicating Taggert, "is General Enue. We will be leading the attack. Our Elvan companion is Teig Ole'ar, Master of Spies for Croneam Eries. The Meleki you see over there is one of the Dymas who will be assisting us."

"I am Crismon Pelias," the captain replied, glancing at each of them in turn, "commander of the Waypost here in Greendom." He gestured at the insignia on Elam's uniform. "You are from Chellum?" he asked, sounding puzzled. "I was certain General Eries would send Roves from Fulrath."

"It's an interesting story," Elam told him, shooting a warning glance at Taggert. The last thing he needed right now was another one of the general's extrapolations about this being a fancy way to commit suicide. "But one that will have to wait for another time." He handed over a rolled parchment. "This is from General Eries. It contains the details of our mission and the list of supplies we will need from your Waypost. It also contains an evacuation order for Greendom. The Fulrath High Command wants the town emptied of civilians by week's end."

"I had a feeling it would come to that," Captain Pelias said, tucking the parchment in his pocket and turning to look down at Greendom. "And that will be easier said than done. There are many who will want to stay and fight."

"If that is their choice, then they should be allowed to do so," Elam told him. "But I intend to make the nature of the enemy quite clear to them. If they decide to stay after that — "

" — then they are as crazy as we are," Taggert finished.

Elam chuckled. "That's not what I was going to say, but I guess it works."

"It certainly does," Teig muttered. "I've seen Shadan's army, remember?"

Captain Pelias turned a surprised stare on Teig, and for a moment it looked as if he might inquire further. A quick glance at the column of horsemen stretching away down the hill waiting to move on changed his mind. He turned his horse toward Greendom. "If you will follow me, gentlemen, I will escort you into town."

It took only a few minutes to reach the outskirts of Greendom, but even in that short amount of time, people had stopped what they were doing and had come to the road to watch the procession pass. And they were still coming. Hundreds at first, and then thousands, they lined both sides of the road and stared at the small army in awe. Everywhere he looked, Elam found faces filled with wonder and excitement, nervousness and fear.

He cocked his head toward Taggert. "Do you still think it will be hard to convince them to leave?" he asked.

The old general shrugged. "Probably," he said. "Especially now that they've seen the magnificent army you've brought to protect them. Look at their faces. They think we are a force to be reckoned with. They have no idea how insignificant we are compared to what awaits in Melek. We can tell them about Shadan's armies, of course, but they won't believe us. People only want to believe what they can see."

Elam frowned. As much as he hated to admit it, Taggert was right. He and his men were but a drop in the bucket compared to the horror poised on the other side of Zedik Pass. He pushed the thought away. "Then we'll make them believe," he said, looking down at the line of faces staring up at him. "You said yourself that they will believe only what they can see. I plan to show it to them."

Taggert regarded him quietly for a moment. "And how are you going to do that?"

Elam glanced over his shoulder to where Lord Nid was riding next to Idoman and the other young Dymas he had taken as apprentices. "You'll see," Elam told him. "And I promise it will be a sight none of these people will ever forget."

Idoman listened in wonder as Lord Nid continued his lecture on *Ta'shaen*, only half aware of the fact that the Chellum army had reached Greendom. He glanced absently at the line of people watching him and the others ride past, then fastened his attention back on the Meleki King, eager to hear more. Around him, the other nine Gifted did likewise.

"Of the Seven Gifts of *Ta'shaen*," Lord Nid told them, "Spirit reigns supreme. It is the overlord, the patriarch, the head. With Spirit, a Dymas can wield Fire in ways that a person Gifted only with Fire could never even imagine. It is the same with Water, Light, Earth, any of them. As a Healer, a person Gifted with

Spirit can heal the kinds of shadowwounds that might kill an ordinary Healer; and by shadowwounds I mean those inflicted by shadowspawn and the demons of Con'Jithar. If a person loses a limb or an eye through accident or battle, a Dymas can restore what was lost if treated in a timely manner."

He paused, and his face grew nostalgic. "Some Old World writings mention Dymas who could heal blindness, give hearing to those who were deaf, and restore lost limbs regardless of when the injury occurred." He turned and looked at Idoman, and a shiver ran down the young man's back when he saw the fire glittering in the Meleki's eyes. "It is written that some could even heal death."

Behind them, Sereth Herisham, the newest member of Lord Nid's apprentices, shook his head in disbelief. "Heal death?" he scoffed. "I've never heard of such a thing. Unless you count Shadan and the other Refleshed."

"The Refleshed are different," Lord Nid countered. "They are the spirits of the dead refleshed into bodies vacated by others. Those who are restored to life by Dymas are reunited with their own earthly bodies. Though healed, they are still subject to death. Eventually, every person must pass through the Veil and on to the next life."

"I overheard Captain Gaufin talking about the Veil," Idoman began. "He said that unless the Earthsoul is rejuvenated by the Fairimors, the only life that awaits us beyond the Veil will be one of darkness and misery."

"He's right," Lord Nid said. "And we'll speak more of that later. Right now, we need to finish discussing the Gift of Spirit." He rubbed his copper-colored cheek. "Where was I?"

"Healing death," Idoman reminded.

"Oh, yes," the Meleki King said, nodding his head in wonder. "There are only a few accounts of it being done, all in Old World writings, but I refuse to believe that such a marvelous working of the Power is gone from the world. It really only requires two things: a tremendous amount of skill as a Healer, and the blessing of the Earthsoul. If the healing isn't in line with Her will, all the Dymas in the world couldn't bring a person back from the dead. Oh, and I don't think the person can be dead for more than two or three days. It has something to do with their soul becoming too accustomed to the afterlife, or something like that."

"Not to mention the fact that they will have started to stink," Sereth muttered.

Lord Nid acted as if he hadn't heard. "As for my statement that Spirit is the overlord of the Seven Gifts, consider this: A person may have multiple Gifts of *Ta'shaen*, but unless one of them is Spirit, that person will never be able to wield more than one Gift at a time. Spirit also allows a Dymas to combine two or more of the Gifts into a... a..." he hesitated, and Idoman could tell he was searching for the right word, "into a superweapon."

"What do you mean by superweapon?" asked Heppil Sourish, the sandy-haired lieutenant who had come forth after the attack in Talin Pass. "Is it something like what Gideon put in the center of the Chellum camp to destroy the Darklings?"

"Perhaps," Lord Nid replied. "Why don't you tell me what Gideon's weapon did? What did you feel?"

Heppil turned to Idoman. "Ask him. He saw the Shadowhounds trigger it."

Idoman nodded. "I did see it," he said. "With my eyes and my Awareness." He paused a moment, considering. "It was primarily Spirit," he said at last, "tightly woven together with Light and Air."

"And Fire," Sereth added. "A little bit, anyway. I felt it."

Lord Nid smiled. "Four Gifts woven together into a superweapon," he said, then laughed heartily. "Gideon Dymas does it better than anyone I know." He sobered immediately. "But without Spirit as his primary Gift, Gideon could not have done what he did. Remember that." He glanced sternly at each of them, then fell silent so they could consider this latest teaching. Urging his horse to move faster, he joined Elam and the others at the head of the procession.

Idoman glanced at the other Gifted and found their eyes still fastened on the Meleki King. "He's something else, isn't he?" he said, and they nodded.

"Do you think he is going to teach us how to craft a superweapon?" Heppil asked.

"Eventually he will," Idoman replied. "But I heard him tell Elam that his first priority is to make sure we don't accidentally kill anyone. Ourselves included."

Gerish Vomanei, the youngest of Chellum's Gifted, turned an amused grin on Sereth. "Do you think Lord Nid's sudden fondness for lecturing has anything to do with last night's mishap with Fire?"

Sereth's face reddened with embarrassment, and he scowled. "I was only trying to help get dinner prepared a little more quickly," he snapped.

Idoman couldn't stop himself from joining the teasing. "I wouldn't worry about it," he said conversationally. "I heard Lord Nid say he likes his food well-done."

Hulanekaefil heard a chorus of laughter rise from his new apprentices and glanced over his shoulder to find a scowl on Sereth's face and grins on the faces of the others. They were teasing the lad again, he realized. Probably about last night. He snorted a laugh. Well, it wouldn't be long before the shoe was on the other foot. Every one of the young men was as clumsy as a drunkard when it came to doing anything with the Power. Sereth would be laughing at them all soon enough.

He faced forward again and sighed resignedly. *Now, if only I could find some humor in the situation.*

Elam moved his horse close and looked over at him. "Are you all right?" he asked. "You look tired."

"I'm worried," Hul replied, shooting a glance over his shoulder at the fledgling Dymas, "about them."

Frowning, Elam followed his gaze. "In what way?"

Hul chuckled, a low sound, without humor. "Every way," he said. "Their youth, their inexperience, their lack of understanding about their potential... take your pick." He realized he was raising his voice, and looked around sheepishly. Fortunately, no one seemed to have noticed. The townsfolk were too busy gawking at the number of horsemen streaming by, and the soldiers were preoccupied with reaching the Waypost at the far end of town so they could rest.

Hul lowered his voice. "I know Croneam believes they can help us in the upcoming conflict, but right now they are as dangerous to us as they are to the enemy. I am going to need help training them if I am to have them ready to face Agla'Con."

"Then I have a surprise for you," Elam said, smiling. "Croneam gave me the name of a Dymas who resides here in Greendom. He said she is someone you know."

"I know many Dymas," Hul told him, "but most of them are dead." He waited expectantly for the name, but Elam remained quiet, suddenly preoccupied, it seemed, with looking at the line of faces watching him and the others ride past. Hul's curiosity finally got the best of him.

"Well," he said irritably, "are you going to tell me her name?"

Elam blinked at him. "What? Oh, sorry," he apologized. "I was just thinking about how much these people stand to lose." He shook his head as if to force the thoughts away. "The Dymas is Joselyn Rai."

"Joselyn," Hul said with a smile. "So, she survived the Battle of Greendom, did she? That is wonderful. I've never met a more talented Healer in all my life." He turned to Elam and added, "Or a more gifted teacher of young Dymas." A sudden wave of sadness swept through him, and he glanced away, looking instead at the Death's Chain Mountains rising in the distance. When he was finally able to speak, his voice trembled with emotion. "She taught both of my sons."

Elam opened his mouth to speak but cut off as Captain Pelias called over his shoulder to them. "My men will lead your army to the Waypost," the captain said, nudging his horse to the side of the road and bidding Elam and Taggert to follow. Teig went with them also, and they stopped in front of a two-story inn and turned their horses about so they could watch the men of Chellum move by.

Motioning for Idoman and the rest of the Gifted to continue on, Hul nudged his horse from the procession and moved alongside Elam and Taggert. As he did, he glanced up at the sign above the entrance. *The Final Stand* was lettered in blue in the center and had the image of a sword beneath and blue flames on each side — symbols of the weapons used during that monumental stand against Shadan's army. Hul smiled appreciatively. It was a fitting name.

The stream of men and horses continued to move by, and Hul and the others watched without speaking as Elam returned salutes and offered words of encouragement to many of the soldiers. When the last of the army had passed, Captain Pelias dismounted and tethered his horse to a hitching post. Hul and the others followed suit.

"Most of the Highwaymen stationed at the Waypost have homes in Greendom," Captain Pelias told them as he started for the inn, "so we have room in the barracks for many of your men. I'm afraid the rest will have to pitch tents. You four are welcome to stay here at the inn if you wish."

"Tents are fine," Elam told him as they moved into the common room and took seats at a table near the window. "For those of us who spend our nights surrounded by the stone of palace walls, it's actually nice to be able to hear the wind blowing or birds chirping." He laughed, but it sounded forced. "For many of my men, the younger ones at least, this is all still some kind of grand adventure. Too bad it's going to turn into such a nightmare."

"And you have no idea how awful that nightmare will be," Taggert muttered, motioning for the serving girl to bring him a drink. "I fought in the Battle of Greendom. I remember."

"Things were every bit as bad in Melek," Hul told them. "Before Shadan's armies could march into Kelsa, they had to go through my army. And they did. Quite easily, in fact." He shuddered at the memory. "Tens of thousands of Meleki died trying to keep Shadan from leaving my country. Thousands more died trying to keep the remnants of his army from returning." He pointed eastward. "The only consolation came from how deeply Zedik Pass flowed with a river of cultist and Darkling blood."

Taggert nodded his agreement. "We had them bottled up nicely, didn't we?" He took off his hat and scratched the top of his head. "I don't think more than a handful of cultists escaped. The Darklings were killed to the last. I don't know how many Agla'Con escaped, but I imagine they were few in number as well."

"Actually, they numbered in the hundreds," a voice said from the kitchen doorway, and they looked up to find an elderly woman in a light blue dress watching them.

Hul hurried across the room and took her hands in his, squeezing affectionately. "Joselyn Dymas," he said with a smile. "Light of Heaven, but it is good to see you again."

Joselyn made a tisking sound as she looked at her hands. "You can do better than that," she said, then threw her arms around him, hugging him tightly.

He hugged her back, surprised by the affection but pleased as well. As High King of Melek, hugs were something he didn't experience very often because his warders never used to let people get so close to him. It had been for his safety, of course, but he'd always considered the lack of contact with the people he loved as an emotional casualty of the pomp and grandeur associated with his position. For a moment, he didn't want to let go.

But Joselyn released him and stepped back to gaze up into his face. "You look well," she told him. "Considering all the rumors I've been hearing lately, you look better than I thought you would. If truth be told, I thought you were dead."

"I had a few close calls," he said, smiling down at her.

"How are those boys of yours?" she asked. "My goodness, but they must have children of their own by now."

"They're dead," he replied, his earlier sadness returning with a vengeance. He didn't know why it was suddenly so intense, but it pierced his heart like a dagger and made him squeeze his eyes shut to hold back the tears. Perhaps the sorrow in Joselyn's eyes had triggered it. Or maybe he'd been holding his grief back for so long, he simply couldn't do it anymore. Whatever the case, he felt as if he couldn't breathe.

Joselyn took him by the hand, and he felt the brush of her Awareness with his mind. He opened himself to her touch and let the Communal link form between them. As it did, he felt the intensity of her sadness. She had loved his sons as dearly as if they were her own. Her teaching had made it possible for them to become the powerful Dymas they had been.

Show me what happened, she said through the link, *and I will grieve with you.*

He did as she asked, and Joselyn watched without speaking as Krosefil and Galafin covered his and Gideon's escape from Shadan's fortress. When the memory faded, Joselyn looked up into his face. He felt her sadness, as deep and powerful as his own, but there was another emotion washing through the Communal link that was just as powerful. Joselyn, he realized, was proud of what her two apprentices had done. And deep down inside, so was he.

Focus on those feelings of pride, she told him, *and let their sacrifice be glorious in your heart. They died honorably. Glory is theirs in the afterlife.*

"Thank you," he whispered.

Smiling, she embraced the Power and sent flows of Spirit washing through him. It didn't heal the emotional wounds he bore. It couldn't. But it did lessen the pain of those wounds and buried them beneath the feelings that mattered most.

Hul breathed out a relaxed sigh when she finished. He hadn't been lying when he'd told Elam that Joselyn was the most talented Healer he knew. Taking her by the arm, he led her to the table where Elam and the others waited expectantly. They had no idea what had passed between him and Joselyn, and he decided to leave it that way.

"Gentlemen," he said, "I would like to introduce Joselyn Rai, Dymas General from the Battle of Greendom."

Dymas General? Elam thought, rising to offer his hand in greeting. *How did Croneam forget to mention that?* "It's a pleasure to meet you," he told her, hoping his surprise at her title hadn't shown on his face. "General Eries told me a great deal about you." *Just not the part of you being a general,* he added silently. He could tell by Captain Pelias' stare that he'd had no idea either. The man was actually gaping.

"Did he now?" she asked, her blue eyes twinkling. "And who might you be that Croneam is telling you my secrets?"

"Elam Gaufin," he answered. "Captain of the army that is going to retake the pass."

"You're going to need more than two thousand men," she said, then turned to Taggert before Elam could respond.

"You look familiar," she said. "Have I healed you before?"

"Twice," Taggert replied. "Both times were during the Battle of Greendom."

"Leg wounds," she said with a nod. "Each time it was a different leg, if I remember correctly." She looked at the insignia on his uniform. "You've been promoted since then. You were a captain, were you not?"

Taggert seemed impressed. "You have a good memory."

"For some things," she said. "I forgot your name."

Taggert gave a hearty laugh. "Taggert Enue," he said, offering a bow. "And I'm pleased to remake your acquaintance."

"How did you know I brought only two thousand?" Elam asked. "Did you count them as they rode by or was it a really good guess?"

Joselyn smiled. "I received a letter from Croneam," she answered. "He told me about what you are planning to do and asked me to help. I understand you have a group of young men in your army who are in need of some training."

"Are they ever," Lord Nid replied, then looked embarrassed when Elam turned to stare at him. The Meleki King shrugged apologetically and continued. "Don't get me wrong," he told Joselyn. "They all have the potential to become very powerful wielders of *Ta'shaen*. Five will undoubtedly be Dymas someday. But they are all newly Gifted and understand practically nothing about their Gifts. In a single day of riding from Fulrath to Greendom they've already had several..." he hesitated, "mishaps."

"Well then," Joselyn said matter-of-factly, "I guess I will have to ride along with you to Zedik Pass."

Elam stared at her in wonder. Yes, he would be glad to have another Dymas in the ranks, but he couldn't help but think she was too old to be in a saddle. Especially considering that once they left Greendom, they would be avoiding the roads and riding cross-country to approach Zedik Pass from the small forest along the foot of the mountains.

The frown that stole across the old woman's face told him she'd read his thoughts. "Don't worry about me," she told him firmly. "I've forgotten more about riding a horse than you have ever learned."

Elam inclined his head. "My apologies, Dymas," he said. "Having you ride along with us will be an honor."

"And an adventure," Lord Nid added, smiling fondly at the older woman. "Between the two of us we might actually be able to turn those young Gifted into a force to be reckoned with."

"First things first," Elam said. "General Eries was very specific in his instructions about the evacuation of Greendom. He wants the town emptied of civilians by week's end. He doesn't care where they go, so long as they are not between him and Shadan's army come time of battle."

Captain Pelias frowned at him. "Even with an order from the High Command, it won't be easy to convince people that the danger is extreme enough to warrant an evacuation."

Elam fastened his eyes on Joselyn. "On the contrary, I believe it will be quite easy."

CHAPTER 28

A Nightmare Remembered

Seated on the stand behind the podium, Taggert studied the multitude assembled in the Greendom church and pursed his lips grimly. Similar crowds were gathered in the schoolhouse, the tavern, the inn, and every other building large enough to hold more than a few dozen people. They were eager to hear the reason for the Chellum army's arrival, but he could tell they were growing impatient. A conversation from a couple seated on the front pew confirmed it.

"The Mayor and the council better get things going soon," the man said, "or I'm heading back to the fields. What's so important that they couldn't wait for my workday to end?"

The woman, bouncing a young child on her knee to keep it entertained, frowned. "I want to know why they thought we all needed to be here. I had to wake Kelvin from his nap. He's going to be a handful for the rest of the night."

Seated next to the couple, an older woman snorted irritably. "I was getting ready to bake bread," she grumbled, "and had to leave it still rising on the cupboard. I'll be up all night finishing it now. Especially since I'll have to rebuild the fire in my stove."

Taggert listened a moment longer, then shut their complaining from his mind. Baking bread and restless babies would be the least of their concerns once they got a look at what was coming their way. And they would get a look, he knew, as soon as Elam and Joselyn finished visiting the other buildings so the Dymas could weave the flows of Spirit that would link each location together. Elam's plan was good, even if it was taking longer to set up than he had anticipated.

The minutes dragged on, and the din of voices grew gradually louder as people's agitation increased. Taggert looked across the room and found himself the focal point of many angry stares. *It's not my fault,* he told them silently. Narrowing his eyes, he scowled right back at them.

Just when it appeared to Taggert that the congregation was about to exit en masse, Elam strode through the door with Joselyn and Lord Nid. They moved purposefully down the aisle toward the stand, and all conversation died in their wake. By the time Joselyn and the Meleki King took seats next to Taggert, the room was quiet save for the fussing of several babies.

Moving forward, Elam removed a small bluish stone from his pocket and placed it on the podium in front of him. It flared to life with the light of *Ta'shaen,* and a halo of blue enveloped Elam and those seated on the stand behind him. Taggert didn't know whether it was Joselyn or Hul who had activated the stone, but he suspected the Meleki. Joselyn would be doing her part soon enough.

"Sorry for the delay," Elam told the congregation, "but we wanted to ensure that we would only have to do this once. This stone, along with the others I distributed to each of the other meeting places, is allowing me to address every group in the village simultaneously. As you may have guessed, I have enlisted the help of Dymas to accomplish this task."

Elam's use of the word Dymas sent a murmur of concern through the crowd, and Taggert imagined that there had been similar reactions in the other congregations as well. He let his eyes move across the faces seated before him and found fear in the eyes of many. Elam saw it too.

"Oh, come now," he chided. "You of all people should appreciate the importance of those who can wield the Power of the Earthsoul; this town is here today because of them." He pointed at Joselyn. "For the past twenty years this sweet woman has lived among you, healing you and your children with the Power. What fear do you have of her?"

He let his gaze travel across the room. "None whatsoever," he said, "because you know and love her. Well, she is more than a simple Healer, ladies and gentlemen; she is a Dymas, a veteran of the Battle of Greendom. And not just a veteran, a hero. One who fought side by side with other Dymas to hold back an army of shadowspawn."

It was difficult for Taggert to stifle his grin as he watched the reaction of those in the crowd. Everywhere he looked, people were gaping in wonder at the woman they thought they knew. And the most amazing thing about it, he decided, was how their fear had melted away. When he cast a sideways glance at Joselyn, he found her sitting as calmly as if Elam were discussing something as simple as the weather.

"Good," Elam said. "I can see in your faces that you are better people than some I've dealt with recently. But enough about Joselyn Dymas. The real reason I gathered you together is to read you this." He held up a rolled parchment for them to see. "It is from General Croneam Eries of Fulrath and concerns the evacuation of Greendom."

A loud murmuring swept through the crowd, and Elam held up a hand to silence them. "Bear with me," he said firmly. "If you still have questions as to why this is important when I am finished, I will gladly answer them." Unrolling the parchment, he read:

> *Citizens of Greendom, it is with heavy heart that I, Croneam Eries, issue this evacuation order for the town of Greendom and its surrounding areas. Were there some other option, I would gladly take it. Unfortunately, the Shadan Cult has amassed an army and is preparing to invade our country once more. What is worse, Throy Shadan himself leads this army and brings with him a host of Agla'Con and shadowspawn.*
>
> *Fulrath is preparing to meet this threat, but the High Command can no longer guarantee the safety of any town or village east of Talin Plateau. Therefore, under authority of Lord Randle Fairimor, High King of Kelsa, I order all inhabitants of Greendom to vacate the city by week's end. Persons who fail to evacuate do so at their own risk and will no longer be under the protection of Kelsa's military.*
>
> *For the honor of God, the Flame of Kelsa, and the liberty of the people, it shall be so.*

A chorus of angry questions rose up immediately, but Elam raised a hand to silence them. "Hold your questions," he shouted. "We aren't finished yet." He motioned for Joselyn to join him, then retrieved the brass urn from the floor at his feet and set it up on the podium. "Idoman," he said into the stone, "if you and the others will please light your urns, we will turn the time over to Joselyn Dymas." He stepped aside, and Joselyn moved up to the podium.

"Still think you don't want to leave?" Joselyn asked as fire sprang up in the urn in front of her. "Perhaps this will change your mind. It is a glimpse of the nightmare I faced twenty years ago on this very spot. It is a glimpse of what is coming our way once more. And this time it is much, much worse." She gestured with her hand, and the drapes at all the windows drew closed, throwing the room into sudden shadow. Only the stone and the urn remained to give light. "Gaze into the fire," she commanded, and the Viewing came to life.

Idoman stared at the shimmering blue image of Joselyn Dymas standing behind the podium in the schoolhouse and shook his head in awe. There were dozens more like it scattered about the village. And every one was showing the same image to its crowd as what he saw before him here. He'd had no idea so many marvelous things could be done with the Power. Casting about the room, he found that the congregation was spellbound by what they were seeing.

"Gaze into the fire," the image of Joselyn said, and the fire in the urn Idoman had placed next to the small Communicator Stone shimmered brightly. His eyes went wide with wonder, and like everyone else in the room, he was drawn into the Viewing.

Fire fell from the sky in waves, spiraling fountains of red-hot death that hammered into the Power-wrought shields of Kelsa's Dymas with the sound of an avalanche. Lightning stabbed down as well, flashes of silvery blue that shook the invisible barriers with resonating booms before crackling away down their curving lengths.

Clustered beneath those shields, the combined armies of Kelsa, Elva, and Chunin stood on the western slopes overlooking Greendom and watched grimly as tens of thousands of shadowspawn swarmed through the ruined town and started up the slope toward them.

A second barrage of lightning hammered into the shield Joselyn was helping to hold in place above the forces led by Croneam Eries, and she felt it weaken as one of the Dymas fainted from exhaustion. The soldiers around her flinched nervously with each corrupted strike, but they held their ground. There would be no retreat this time — with so few Dymas remaining to cover their escape, they had retreated as far as they were going to.

"Archers ready!" Croneam Eries shouted from atop his horse, and Joselyn watched a young female Dalae weave a stream of Air to amplify Croneam's voice and carry it to the far reaches of the dome. The white-haired general turned to the small group of young people standing nearby and nodded. Each wore a blue armband signifying the Gift of Air. "Speed the volley," he told them, then turned to the Dymas maintaining the front part of the shield. "On my mark," he said, "open the shield."

Turning back to face the enemy, Croneam watched them come. So did Joselyn.

Most were two-legged Darklings, but those were slower than the heavy-bodied wolf-like creatures and Shadowhounds leading the charge, and they quickly fell behind. And that was just the way Croneam wanted it. Grinning, he gave the order. "Fire!"

Arrows hissed away down the slope as thick as locust, then blurred into nothingness as the Gifted at Croneam's side urged them forward at speeds no bow alone could ever achieve. They plunged through the first line of shadowspawn in sprays of greenish brown and on into the second, then the third. Many didn't come to a stop until the fifth or sixth body. Like wheat hewn with a sickle, the misshapen beasts fell to the earth in a swath a hundred paces wide. A second volley removed the stragglers.

Finding themselves at the forefront of the cultist army, the legions of Darklings hesitated, momentarily confused, it seemed to Joselyn, by the sudden loss of their more ferocious counterparts. By the time they recovered, it was too late.

On Croneam's command, a squad of Gifted wearing red armbands stepped to the front edge of the shield. A hole opened for them, and they turned the area below into a sea of fire. When it faded a few moments later, all that remained of the Darklings was a charred expanse littered with melted, misshapen helmets, armor, and weapons that glowed red from the intense heat.

A cheer rose from Kelsa's armies, and swords were raised and shaken at the enemy. Several men called for a charge down the slope to retake Greendom, and it was taken up by others until the inside of the shield thundered with the call. But there would be no charge, Joselyn knew. Croneam wasn't a fool. The destruction of this wave of shadowspawn was but a finger-chopping compared to what was marshaling itself in the streets of Greendom. Any kind of offensive would only hasten Kelsa's defeat.

She followed Croneam's gaze to where the front line of Shadan's army was reforming on the edge of town. K'rrosha Shadowlancers had moved forward to issue orders, and the tips of their lances flared red as they gestured to those they commanded. Joselyn spotted Satyrs, Wohlvins, Quathas, and a dozen more she didn't have names for. Among the unnamed were scores of what looked like giant insects, multi-legged monstrosities with glossy blue-black plating and an array of spikes, pinchers, and stingers. As the grotesque wall of creatures started up the slope toward them, the sky above Kelsa's shields fell silent.

Croneam turned to Joselyn. "Why have the Agla'Con stopped attacking with the Power?"

"I don't know," she told him. "Perhaps they feel the next wave will be more than enough to destroy us without help from them."

Croneam grunted. "I was hoping you would tell me it's because they are tired."

"That is a possibility, I suppose," Joselyn said, forcing a laugh. "They certainly can't expend all their strength fighting us lest they lose control of the shadowspawn."

"How many Agla'Con are left?" Croneam asked.

Joselyn stretched out with her Awareness to feel for the corruption all Agla'Con spawned while wielding the Power. "At least three hundred, but most are at the rear of Shadan's army. I can feel them driving the shadowspawn forward."

Croneam reached up to pull at his mustache. "How many Dymas remain?"

"Less than a hundred," she told him, "but nearly every one is helping to maintain

the shields. We cannot spare them for battle without losing our defenses. As for the Dalae... I don't know how many remain. Sixty or seventy, perhaps. The battle at the river was costly."

Croneam watched the enemy move up the slope. "So this is it," he said softly, "the final stand." He turned to look at her, and his eyes were fierce. "Let's make it something the enemy will never forget."

Joselyn nodded. "What would you have me do?"

"Make Communal contact with our Dymas," he told her. "Have them raise the edge of the shield and allow the shadowspawn to advance. Once my men and I have engaged them, all Dymas are to release their shields completely and kill as many of the Agla'Con as they can. I want their first strike to be on those at the rear of Shadan's army where they won't be expecting it. Those near the front will undoubtedly think the attack is aimed at them and will weave shields to ward it off. That should allow you to pinpoint their location and keep them from entering the fight."

"What of the K'rrosha?" Joselyn asked.

Croneam's eyes narrowed as he glanced down at the black-cloaked riders. "I've already made arrangements for their destruction," he told her. "Assuming Marithen Dymas still lives." He turned to face her. "Let me know when the Dymas are ready."

Joselyn opened her Awareness and touched the mind of the nearest Dymas who then touched the mind of the Dymas closest to him, and so on until the Communal link was a vast spider web of linked minds. She quickly informed them of Croneam's plan, then severed the link. "It is done, General," she told him.

Nodding to the young woman assigned to amplify his voice, Croneam drew his sword and turned to face his army.

"The battle for Greendom is lost," he shouted, "but the war with Shadan is not over. It will never be over so long as the Earthsoul lives and men remain who are willing to stand against this evil. You have fought well," he told them. "There is no shame in losing to a superior force. You have earned a place of honor in the history books and glory in the life to come." He turned his horse to face the enemy and raised his sword. "They think we fear them," he continued. "Let's show them how wrong they are."

The shouting that erupted from the united armies was deafening. Everywhere Joselyn looked men and women from three nations were hefting weapons in a show of support for the beloved general. This would be a battle remembered for all time. Too bad it was going to end with Kelsa's defeat.

Taking a deep breath, Joselyn opened herself more fully to the Power and watched the horde of evil flow up the slope toward them. Through her Awareness, she saw that thousands were moving to the north and south in a flanking maneuver. Thousands more of the winged varieties had already flanked them and were preparing to attack *from behind. Fortunately, the Elvan archers had spotted them and were readying a volley that would bring many of the creatures crashing to earth.*

Those marching at the forefront of Shadan's army reached the edge of Kelsa's shields, and the Dymas holding the shields in place raised them to let the shadowspawn continue their approach.

"For the Flame of Kelsa!" Croneam Eries shouted, and his voice echoed beneath the dome of Spirit like a thunderclap. Spurring his horse, he plunged into the midst of the shadowspawn with Dragonblade flashing. Thousands of Fulrath's finest followed, and the work of death commenced on both sides.

"For the Honor of God," Joselyn whispered, then she and the other Dymas let the shields go completely. A heartbeat later, the rear of the cultist army vanished beneath a barrage of lightning and fire.

Just as Croneam had predicted, the Agla'Con scattered along the front lines cast up shields to ward off the attack, thinking that it had been meant for them. Their positions revealed, they became easy targets for Kelsa's Dymas. Dozens died in the first strike, and the Dymas suddenly found themselves on a more equal footing with the enemy. While a few of the more powerful Dymas kept the Agla'Con busy, the remainder attacked the shadowspawned army.

Lightning hammered into knots of spike-backed Shadowhounds, exploding some, hurling others limply through the air. Streamers of Fire ripped through the midst of the insect-like monsters, bursting them apart in fountains of blue-green blood. Fists of Air pummeled Darklings into heaps of twisted armor and ruined flesh.

Croneam and the Rove Riders of Fulrath cut their way deep into the swarming mass of shadowspawn, and on the slope to the north, a legion of axe-wielding Chunin did the same. The Elvan archers cleared the skies of the winged shadowspawn, then turned to launch volley after volley into the enemy trying to cut its way past Croneam.

Joselyn couldn't believe her eyes; the army of shadowspawn was starting to fall back. With so many of the Agla'Con dead, there was nothing to force the Darklings to keep fighting. The thought gave her an idea.

Wending her way down the slope, she searched the front line with her Awareness, looking for any Agla'Con who still lived. When she found them, she killed them with sharp, narrow thrusts of Fire. Every time an Agla'Con died, the legions of shadowspawn grew that much more disorganized. Joselyn smiled. A few more minutes of this, and we will have them on the run.

She had scarcely finished the thought when corrupted fire began falling from the sky once more, river-wide torrents that poured into the midst of Kelsa's armies and burned thousands of men and shadowspawn to ash. At first she thought the Agla'Con had combined their strength to launch the strike, but when she focused her Awareness on the Fire, she found that it had originated from a single source. Throy Shadan had taken a hand in the battle.

Joselyn felt him take control of the talismans of the remaining Agla'Con, binding them together into one. When he struck again, lightning hammered into the battlefield, and the lifeless bodies of men and shadowspawn somersaulted through the air. In several places the earth exploded upwards in sprays of dirt and grassland sod. An entire column of Elvan archers vanished beneath a wall of flames. A squad of Chunin soldiers blew apart into sprays of blood and tattered flesh.

Everywhere Joselyn looked, men and women were dying at the hand of the refleshed Dreadlord. A few more moments and there wouldn't be a single person left alive. Pushing the thought away, she sliced the head off of a Darkling who'd risen to block her way, then burned a hole through a Satyr before it could lunge at her. Strike after strike, she cleared a path in front of her, making her way down to where Croneam, horseless but still very much alive, fought viciously. She hoped she could reach him before one of Shadan's strikes found either of them.

A sudden, gut-wrenching shriek filled the air, and every head on the battlefield turned to see Shadan framed by a fiery-edged void. He moved through into the darkness beyond, and the void collapsed in on itself with a deafening boom. A heartbeat later the K'rrosha Shadowlancers exploded into balls of incandescent fire.

A heavy silence fell across the area as soldiers on both sides of the battle considered what they had just witnessed. For a moment, no one moved.

Then Croneam raised his sword. "Praised be the Fairimors," he shouted. "Victory is ours." Whirling, he spun into the midst of a band of Darklings and resumed the work of death. Thousands of soldiers joined him, and within minutes, the entire cultist army was in full retreat.

Joselyn let them go, turning instead to gaze up the slope to where the united armies had stood. Tens of thousands lay dead. Thousands more were wounded. She had no estimate for how many had been burned from existence by the fires of Shadan. Not since the Second Cleansing had so many good men and women died in battle.

Sighing wearily, she started up the slope in search of those who could be healed.

When the Viewing faded, Elam stepped up to the pulpit and looked out into faces pale with fright. Some looked on the verge of sicking up. Several women were weeping openly. Several more had fainted and were being fanned by their concerned husbands. Elam could tell that whatever questions or arguments they may have had were gone. Only a fool would want to stay here now.

"Now you know what hell looks like," he told them. "Well, it is about to pay a return visit. Therefore, the evacuation order from Croneam Eries is effective immediately. Take your families and whatever belongings you deem necessary and get as far away from here as you can. Don't go to Fulrath — it, too, is being cleared of civilians. You have until week's end."

He stepped from the pulpit and strode through a congregation stunned to silence.

CHAPTER 29

Crossing Over

"They want to be found," Seth said as he stepped into the shade of the building where Jase and Talia were waiting. He glanced back the way he had come and frowned. "There is no other explanation for how many people know they were here."

Jase nodded. This wasn't the first time he or Seth had considered that the Shizu were deliberately leaving a trail. The Agla'Con with them had certainly gone to great lengths to taunt them back in Seston — attacking so openly and then telling Maira to deliver a message to Gideon. The thought that Brysia's abductors wanted him to find them tied his stomach into knots. It made him wonder if splitting from Gideon had been a good idea after all.

He glanced back to Seth. He still wore both swords at his hips, but his clothes were the same nondescript grey of those who lived and worked near the docks. It made him look more like a mercenary than a warder, albeit a very deadly one.

"You said *were*," Jase told him. "Have they left then?"

Seth continued to stare down the street. "Most of the rumors hint along those lines," he replied, turning to regard them with furrowed brow. "But two people I spoke with reported seeing them this morning in the Waterfront District."

"Do you believe them?" Talia asked, and Jase turned to study her. She, too, had adopted local fashion in order to blend in and wore a light blue skirt with matching shirt tied at the waist with a strip of green. On her feet were a pair of open-toed sandals but no stockings. Her hair, a tightly wound bun held in place with a polished piece of bone from some sea creature, had her looking like any number of Tetrica's female residents. It also exposed a fair portion of her lovely neck.

When he realized he was staring, he looked away. Fortunately, Seth hadn't noticed. His eyes had returned to something down the street. "I'm not sure what to believe," he replied, "but my instincts tell me we're headed for trouble."

"So what else is new?" Jase muttered, then followed Seth's gaze. "What are you looking at?" he asked.

"Someone has been following us," Seth answered. "Ever since we left the palace this morning. I haven't gotten a good look yet, but I think it might be a woman."

"What do we do next?" Talia asked.

"We go to the Waterfront District," Seth replied, casting about to make sure the warders Lord Tetrica had provided for them were in sight. When all were accounted for, he rubbed the side of his nose with one finger — the sign to stay close — and started down the street.

Tetrica was similar to Trian in that all its roads had been paved with slabs of stone, a necessity because of the frequent rains that would mire dirt roads for weeks. Curbing and ditches guided the rains out of the streets into hundreds of canals crisscrossing the city, then on into the harbor. Small boats of every color and design filled the canals, and in some places the waterways were even busier than the streets above. Bridges, some as wide as a city street, others nothing more than a single plank, linked the different sections of the city.

They started across one of those narrow planks, and Jase looked down and found a group of children using poles to guide a makeshift raft. They were laughing and shouting and splashing, and seemed to be having a great time. As he watched, one young girl pushed a boy into the water. When he didn't immediately surface, Jase grew worried. A moment later, though, the lad appeared on the opposite side of the raft and grabbed the back of the little girl's dress, pulling her backward into the canal. Children in Tetrica, it seemed, were as comfortable in the water as the children in Kindel's Grove were on land.

When Talia murmured an indignant, "Did you see what he did?" Jase realized she had missed the first half of the scuffle. The look she directed at the little boy was angry.

Jase gazed at her with mock seriousness. "Some boys just don't know how to treat a lady," he told her, then let the smile he'd been holding back slip across his face.

Talia's eyes narrowed, and she punched him in the arm.

Seth glanced over his shoulder, and his scowl needed no words.

Stifling their amusement, they fell dutifully silent and waited for Seth to turn back around. When he did, they looked at one another and grinned. Impulsively Jase leaned over and kissed her on the cheek.

For what had to be the hundredth time today, he counted himself lucky to have her with him. Her presence was comforting and helped lessen the fear and anxiety he felt because of the abduction of his mother. She made him feel that finding Brysia wouldn't be so difficult after all.

A sudden shriek filled his ears, so piercing and loud he threw his hands to his ears to ward it off. It tore at his very soul, a cry of grief and loss so terrible it threatened to overwhelm him. He embraced the Power and prepared to lash out at whatever evil had caused the suffering. As *Ta'shaen* filled him, so did the realization that it hadn't been a scream at all, at least not a human scream — it was something else altogether, something far greater and far more powerful. He had no idea what, but *Ta'shaen* itself resonated with the disturbance. It was a pulsating tremor of Spirit-sound that bombarded his Awareness from every side.

He realized he had stopped and looked up to find Seth standing with his swords drawn, casting about for an enemy. The sight of bared steel sent the city folk scurrying for cover, and the street around them rapidly cleared. The warders moved in from all sides.

Talia took him by the arm, her face lined with concern as she spoke urgently to him. Her mouth moved, but her words were muted by the cry sounding in his head.

Then, as quickly as it had come, the shriek cut off, fading to nothing more than a ghostly echo at the very edge of his mind.

He released the Power and reigned in his Awareness, flinching in surprise as his spiritual perception vanished and his physical surroundings rushed in on him like a wave. There were the frantic calls of people as they rushed away from the sight of Seth's blades, Talia's urgent words of concern for his well-being, the sound of his own labored breathing — all of it a new kind of sensory overload that caused him to squeeze his eyes shut to steady himself. "I'm all right," he managed, opening his eyes once more. "I'm okay, really." He reached for Seth's arm. "Put your swords away," he said. "There is no enemy here."

"What the blazes happened?" Seth growled, motioning for the warders to resume their positions. "You gasped as if you'd taken a knife in the back."

"I don't know," he replied. "It was a disturbance in *Ta'shaen*, but it was unlike any I've ever felt." He glanced around at the frightened and confused looks of the townspeople. Some had started to venture forth from their hiding, but many were still crouched behind benches or huddled in doorways. "Let's get out of here," he said and started walking. "I'll tell you on the way to the

Waterfront."

七

Elliott leaned back from the rail of *The Arrow of the Sea* and wiped his mouth with the back of his hand. He hadn't thought he'd had anything left in his stomach after a long morning of vomiting, but apparently he did. He heard Endil and Thorac laughing and made a fist at them behind his back. He'd never been on a ship this size before. How was he supposed to know it would turn his guts to —

He gagged again, heaving over the railing.

When the wave of sickness passed, he straightened, did his best to ignore the snickers behind him, and continued his thought. If anything, a ship this size ought to be smoother than the smaller crafts he and Jase used on the lakes near Chellum. The waves didn't look all that big. So why did he feel like he wanted to die?

He glanced at Gideon sitting near the rear of the ship — the 'stern' one of the crew had called it — and did little to hide his scowl. Last night when he had first started to vomit, he'd asked the Dymas to do something about it, but Gideon had shrugged him off, saying that there wasn't anything actually *wrong* with him. Seasickness, he'd said, wasn't something that could be healed with the Power. And then he'd suggested it might all be in his head.

Elliott frowned at him. *All in my head, indeed! It's my stomach that's angry!* As if to prove his point, his stomach knotted once more, and he leaned for the rail.

When he finally finished discoloring the water below, he walked unsteadily to the crates where Endil and Thorac were playing cards and flung himself down on a pile of rigging. "I've never felt so horrible in my life," he muttered in their direction.

Thorac answered with a chuckle. "You're not the first man to have his guts turned to mush on one of these," he said. "I've seen men so sick they couldn't even stand. You're handling it better than most."

"And I can't tell you how good that makes me feel," Elliott muttered sarcastically. He was quiet a minute as he watched them play cards, then asked, "How long of a trip is it to Thesston?" He hoped he didn't sound like he was whining.

Thorac glanced at Gideon for a moment, then shrugged. "If Gideon maintains the wind he's created with the Power, we should arrive sometime tomorrow morning."

Elliott pinched his eyes shut and groaned. "I'll be dead by then."

"You know," the little man said conversationally, "I've heard tell of an herb that can take the edge off of seasickness. It grows in Arkania. I've also heard that Zeka, because they're such a seafaring group of people, began importing this special herb for those passengers who are — how shall I put this — of a more delicate nature."

"Why are you telling me this?" Elliott asked. "Do you actually like seeing me suffer?"

Thorac feigned innocence. "Me?"

"The captain has some if you want it," Endil said, and the look he directed toward Thorac was amused.

"Why didn't you tell me sooner?" Elliott growled, pushing himself from the pile of rigging. It was lucky for them both that he felt as badly as he did. Otherwise he'd be tempted to string them up with the sails.

"Relax," Thorac told him. "The herb can only be taken on an empty stomach." He leaned forward meaningfully. "Your stomach is empty now, isn't it?"

Before Elliott could answer, Gideon cried out in horror.

"No! Not the Talisman! Not the Talisman!"

The Power-wrought wind died and the sails sagged. The sudden loss of momentum caused the ship to settle deeper into the water, and everything was thrown forward. The crunch of wood and creak of riggings echoed across the deck. Shouts of anger and alarm filled the air, and men began running to and fro to right toppled crates and to secure riggings. Someone was shouting that a man had fallen overboard. Through it all, Gideon sat with his hands pressed to his face, howling with beastly fury. Lightning crackled overhead, and dozens of bolts stabbed the ocean around the ship.

Endil drew his dartbow, and Thorac leapt to his feet, hefting his axe and casting about in alarm. Believing that they were under attack from an Agla'Con, Elliott forgot about his sickness and drew his sword as he made his way toward Gideon. If the Dymas had been struck, he had to see if he could do something to help. As he neared the big man, Gideon lowered his hands and looked up.

The lightnings ended, but fire still raged in the Dymas' eyes. "The Blood Orb of Elsa," Gideon said through clenched teeth, "has been defiled." He rose to his feet and strode up the deck to where the captain was helping pull one of his men from the water. The rest of the crew watched Gideon with a mixture of fear and anger at the trouble he had caused.

When the wet sailor had been hauled back in, Gideon checked to see that everything else was in order, then returned to the stern. "Hold on!" he shouted, and the sails filled once more. Within minutes they were plowing through the water at a pace nearly double that of before.

Timbers groaned from the stress, and the entire ship sounded as if it might come apart at any moment, but Gideon's face was determined as he pushed the ship onward. Elliott glanced around and found every crew member's face masked with fear.

He turned his attention back to Gideon, and his stomach knotted when he saw despair present in the big man's eyes. Pursing his lips, he rushed to the railing once more. This time, however, the urge to vomit had little to do with seasickness.

Jase leaned on the railing of Green Dolphin Pier and gazed out across the vastness of Tetrica Harbor. The blue-green waters were relatively smooth, protected from the roughness of the sea by a natural spine of rock running from the hills on the east of the city to one of two small islands several miles away. From the second island, a thirty-foot-high wall completed the barrier as it stretched around to butt into the rocky shoreline below the palace. The wall, constructed from blocks of stone the size of wagons, was a marvelous display of Tetrica's determination to control the sea.

He watched fishing ships of various sizes return from a day's labor on the open seas and marveled at the orderly way they maneuvered into position along one of the many docks jutting from the piers of the different districts.

Camoth District, he had found, was mainly for the shipping of goods, but there were still people fishing along the docks and piers. Earlier he'd watched a group of children on the other side of Green Dolphin Pier catch a bucket-full of greyish eels by lowering homemade hooks baited with fish meat on pieces of string. On this side, he watched with fascination as a little girl and her grandmother used a small net baited with bread to haul up dozens of shimmering little fish called Silver Darts.

Talia stood next to the girl and her grandmother, watching in wonder as they repeated the process again and again. She glanced at him and smiled with delight as the little girl handed her the rope and let her pull up the next net of fish. She set it on the pier, and the little girl clapped enthusiastically, then she and Talia knelt to put the fish into a basket.

Jase's pleasure at watching them was interrupted by someone stopping beside him. He glanced over to find a young woman staring at him. She leaned on the railing and smiled mischievously, looking him up and down in a manner that made his cheeks go red. Even with the wicked-looking scar on her cheek she was pretty, but there was a hardness in her eyes that told Jase whatever beauty she had was on the surface only. She wore pants like a man and her hair was cut short. She had a pair of daggers tucked behind her belt.

"I hear you're looking for a group of men," she said simply.

"That's right," he said casually, not really sure if he could put much trust in anything she might tell him. He had dealt with her kind for most of the afternoon; thieves and other lowlife scum who had heard of their search and were only too happy to provide information — for a small fee of course — whether it was true or not. They had been guided here by a beggar who claimed to have seen a group of black-clad men and a woman who may have been Elvan board a ship on the Green Dolphin yesterday.

He looked to the end of the pier where Seth was speaking to the owner of one of the ships moored there, and watched as the man shook his head and pointed across the harbor to a different pier. Seth nodded. When he started back down the pier, Jase could tell by his walk that he was angry. Another false lead.

Jase turned his attention back to the girl, ready to dismiss her as another street urchin looking to make some quick money when she added, "These men, they are a group of Shizu perhaps?" Her smile twisting into a satisfied smirk told him she'd seen his surprise. None of those whom they had questioned had been told the men they were searching for were Shizu. If she knew it, it had to be because she had seen them.

He looked away again. If he didn't play this right, he would end up paying whatever outrageous price she thought her knowledge was worth. "They are Riaki," he admitted, not willing to meet her dark gaze for fear she would see the hope in his eyes.

Her laugh was neither amused nor genuine. "You can brush me off if you wish," she said darkly. "But then how will you find the pretty Elvan lady and her Agla'Con escort?"

His shock was so complete that he could only stand and stare at her.

"I thought that might get your attention," she said with satisfaction. Her eyes moved to Talia briefly before returning to his. "I'm not as pretty as that tramp you're with," she said, "but now you've got no choice but to pay attention to me, do you?" She took a step closer. "Does my scar bother you?" she cooed. "I have scars in other places as well. I could show them to you if you'd like."

Jase took an unconscious step back. "I just want to find those I'm searching for," he told her, "and I'm willing to pay whatever you want. Just name your price."

"Money?" she scoffed. "Is that what you think I'm after?" She was about to say more when Talia noticed them talking and came to investigate. She didn't look jealous, Jase noted, just concerned.

The scar-faced girl took on the appearance of a caged animal. Her eyes flicked back and forth between him and Talia, and she looked on the verge of fleeing.

"This young lady," Jase told Talia in as calm a voice as he could muster, "might know something of those we are looking for."

"That's wonderful," Talia answered, but she sounded doubtful.

"You don't believe me?" the girl snapped, her earlier bravado returning. She huffed herself up, and for a moment it looked as if she would leave. Instead, she glared at Talia contemptuously. "I might not live in a fancy house or have fancy clothes," she growled, "but I've earned what I have. Not like you lazy nobles who are what you are because of nothing more than blood!"

Her shouting drew stares from everyone within a hundred feet, and Jase found himself looking around self-consciously. Most people had stopped what they were doing and were watching to see what would happen. Talia was rendered speechless by the unexpected tirade and looked to Jase for help. Unfortunately, he was as stunned as she was.

"Uh, look," he began uncertainly, "we can work something out. Just name your price." He looked past her to Seth. The warder had noticed the situation and had quickened his pace to join them.

"You don't get it, do you?" she said derisively. "We don't want money. We want your heart." She lunged so quickly that neither he nor Talia had time to react. He saw the blade flash, heard Talia gasp, then stared in horror at the hilt sticking from her stomach. She collapsed at his feet.

"No!" he shouted, seizing the girl in a fist of Air and hurling her against the railing so violently he heard bones break as she crumpled into a heap. He looked up as three men he hadn't noticed earlier came at him with daggers similar to the one the girl had used. He brushed them aside like gnats, hammering them with an invisible fist of Air. It sent them through the railing in a splintering of wood and cracking bone, and they fell lifeless into the water below.

All around him people screamed and tried to flee, though where they intended to go, Jase didn't know. Farther down the pier Seth had drawn his swords and was locked in battle with five men who had suddenly appeared in front of him. The captain killed two and wounded the other three as he fought his way forward. Others rose to block his way, coming over the railing from somewhere below. Several more were rushing down the pier from behind him.

Furious, Jase sent a stab of lightning into those behind Seth, and the entire pier rocked as the searing bolt shattered wood and scattered bodies like leaves before a gust of wind. When the flash of light faded, Jase was pleased to see that none of those he'd hit were moving from where they had fallen. Seth barely broke stride as, stroke after killing stroke, he felled those in front of him.

Jase heard the sound of clashing steel behind him and turned to see the warders engaged as well. The entire pier, it seemed, had come alive with this unknown enemy. Several warders rushed up to him, but he shouted for them to help Seth instead. The area around the captain had become too congested for another strike with the Power, and he didn't want to risk hitting Seth or any of the innocent people caught in the madness.

Knowing that the fight was out of his hands, he knelt next to Talia.

She lay on her back, and a circle of blood was rapidly spreading around the knife. Her breathing came in quick, shallow gasps, and her face had gone white. Her eyes were pinched tight against the pain. He placed his hand on hers, and she looked at him, blinking away the tears that welled up when she saw him.

"Jase," she said, her teeth clenched tight with pain. Taking his hand, she placed it on the knife hilt. "You are going to have to pull it out before you can heal me." Her voice held so much trust that he wanted to throw his head back and scream in agony. He didn't know how to heal! He'd had nothing more than a few rudimentary lessons and had killed most everything he had tried to heal. The image of the starling with the broken wing bursting into flames came unbidden to his mind and he shuddered. He couldn't do this. He didn't dare.

"Jase," she said again, drawing his eyes to hers. "There is only you. I can't heal myself. It doesn't work that way. Please, Jase. The first step is to remove the knife."

"I can't," he told her, tears of his own filling his eyes at the admission of weakness. "I'm liable to kill you instead of making things right. I — " He cut off, unable to continue.

"And I'd rather die knowing you tried than that you did nothing," she said, tightening her grip on his hand. "Now remove the knife."

Her tone left no room for argument. Nodding, he pulled the knife free and then pressed his palm on the wound to slow the flow of blood. Her body tensed, and she gasped, but she placed her hands on his.

She looked up, her emerald eyes watery. "Hurry, Jase," she breathed, and he could hear that she was growing weaker.

He closed his eyes and tried to clear his mind of everything but Talia and her wound. It was a difficult task considering that Seth and the warders were still locked in battle with the attackers and people were screaming and running for cover all around him.

He forced it all away determinedly and carefully opened his Awareness to look through the eyes of *Ta'shaen*. The wound was deeper than he had thought, the loss of blood extreme. He saw where the knife had severed an artery, and he realized she was bleeding to death internally.

He focused his mind on the artery and opened himself to that part of the Power that was *Sha*, the Gift of Flesh. It shimmered on the edge of his Awareness, a white river of luminescent life. Carefully, he reached toward it...

And watched in horror as it drew back, recoiling away from him as if it realized he had no business trying to wield it. He tried again and once more *Sha* withdrew, sliding to the furthermost edge of his Awareness.

After the third attempt, he gave up and returned his Awareness to Talia. Her lips were turning blue and she was shivering, so close to death that he could see the Veil that would soon open to let her pass into the world beyond. It shimmered in his mind's eye, a thin translucent curtain just inches from her head. She was going to die unless he did something to stop it.

He grew desperate then, and angry. In a panic he reached out with all the force of will he possessed and seized the Power, all seven Gifts, drawing in as much of each one as he could hold. Focusing on the wound once more, he tried to direct a flow of healing toward it.

Talia's body jerked and she cried out, digging her fingers into his hand so deeply that she drew blood. Terrified at what he had done, he released *Ta'shaen* and opened his eyes. She was looking at him with eyes beginning to cloud with death. "Thank you for trying," she whispered, and her eyelids fluttered a moment before closing.

"Talia?" he whispered.

No answer.

"Talia?" he said again, gently touching her face.

Still no response.

Not knowing what else to do, he gently lifted her head and cradled it against his chest, fighting back the sobs as he held her close. A moment later he felt her stir.

"Did you use the Talisman?" she asked weakly.

He was so surprised to hear her speak he could only gape. A heartbeat later her words registered in his mind. *The Talisman!*

Without intending to, he drew in enough of *Ta'shaen* to level half the city and had to forcefully push it down to a trickle. When he had control, he reached into his shirt and withdrew the Talisman.

It flared to life in his fist, and he pressed it against Talia's stomach, stretching inward with his Awareness and willing the Orb to help. The ancient blood of Elsa heard his call, and Talia gasped. Her eyes went wide in surprise as the warmth of *Ta'shaen* flowed into her, mending the severed artery and closing the wound. Jase saw it in his mind's eye, a brilliant flash of green that vanished as quickly as it had come.

Talia sagged into him, overcome with exhaustion but very much alive.

Jase didn't know whether to laugh or cry. His joy at having her healed was overshadowed by the realization that he'd had little to do with it. Without the aid of the Talisman, without its ability to act of its own will, he would have lost her. He was sickened by the idea that he had very nearly let her die, and he hated himself for his lack of ability to heal. The only thing he could do was hug her close and kiss her tenderly on the head.

Seth appeared at his side, laying his swords on the pier and reaching to inspect the wound. Jase put his hand on the captain's arm. "She's all right," he said. "She's been healed."

"You?" Seth asked, and Jase flinched at the disbelief in his voice. Seth, it seemed, had as little faith in his abilities to heal as he did. And justifiably so.

"No," Jase told him. "It was the Talisman."

Seth waved it off. "So long as she's alive," he said. "That is all that matters." Then his face turned into a mask of death. "Who did this?" he asked, taking up his swords once more.

Jase motioned for the warders to come stay with Talia and took one of their cloaks to make a pillow for her head. "Keep the sun off her," he told them, then turned to Seth. "Over there."

As they crossed to where the young woman lay crumpled against the railing, Jase looked down the pier. The people who had been caught in the unexpected conflict still huddled against the rail or behind crates. Their eyes were filled with horror as they studied the scene before them. More than a dozen men were scattered across the pier, all of them dead. Three of the warders lay motionless as well, and Jase didn't need *Ta'shaen* to see their life blood dripping between the planks and into the sea below.

He caught sight of the elderly woman holding her sobbing, terrified granddaughter, and his anger deepened. Their fishing net, abandoned on the pier behind them, still shimmered with the little girl's catch. She didn't deserve to see such violence. No child did. It was a robbing of innocence that could never be rectified. And the little girl wasn't alone. All along the pier people who had been doing nothing more than enjoying their simple lives had been victimized by these nameless assassins. It made him want to scream.

They reached the young woman and stopped. She lay face down on the pier, and for a moment Jase thought she was dead. When he knelt beside her, she groaned, turning her head and reaching for her second dagger lying on the pier in front of her. Seth kicked it away with the toe of his boot, and it slid beneath the railing and fell away into the water.

Jase took her by the shoulder and rolled her over onto her back. Her face was lined with pain, but he ignored it. There would be no pity here, and no sympathy. She had tried to kill the woman he loved, maliciously, and without provocation. If anything, she deserved death herself. The look on Seth's face showed he thought so as well.

"My legs," she moaned. "I can't feel my legs."

He had broken her back when he'd thrown her against the railing, he realized, but he hardened himself against her pain. No sympathy. No remorse. He leaned forward and looked into her face. "Who sent you?" he asked coldly.

She stared up at him, her eyes glittering with rage. "Go to hell," she hissed, spitting at him.

Something inside Jase snapped, and all the emotion he'd been trying so desperately to contain the past several days broke loose. Fear, frustration, anger, and every ounce of hatred he possessed overwhelmed him. Hissing, he grabbed the front of her shirt with both hands, jerking her toward him.

"Tell me," he yelled, shaking her. He felt Seth's hand on his shoulder, heard him shout to release her, but he ignored it. "Who sent you?" he shouted again. Then he seized *Ta'shaen*.

It fought him, unwilling to come while he was so out of control, but he harnessed it anyway, pulling in as much as he could stand and bending it to his will. "Tell me," he snarled, and the world around him grew dim.

The girl's eyes went wide with shock and revulsion as images began flickering through Jase's Awareness. He saw the world through her eyes and watched the knife plunge into Talia's stomach. Through her ears, he heard Talia's gasp of pain. He felt the girl's satisfaction at what she had done.

Focusing on her thoughts, he pressed himself deeper into her mind and watched as she followed Seth as he moved through the streets of Tetrica. He saw her leave a large building with the group of assassins. Hundreds of images, thousands of thoughts.

She was Con'Kumen, three years into her dark oath. She had received the scar on her face from an Agla'Con whom she'd talked back to. She was jealous of anyone she thought prettier than herself. She was the daughter of a man named Shaloth who headed the Con'Kumen chapter house in Tetrica.

That last...

He focused on her thoughts of the chapter house and pressed his Awareness deeper, forcing himself into her mind, searching every flickering image. The face of a man came into view. Her father, the man Shaloth. *Lead them along for a while, Shaloth said. And when we're ready, we'll isolate them on one of the piers. Do what you want with the others, but do not harm the boy. The Agla'Con want him alive. They want him to despair. They want him vulnerable and weak so he will be easier to take. Once this is accomplished we can reveal where they have taken his mother and our duty to the Agla'Con will be fulfilled.*

He was so stunned by what he saw that he lost his hold on the Power. The images vanished from his mind, and the girl's face came back into focus before him. Her eyes were wide with horror, and she was stammering unintelligibly. A red glow painted her face. Points of red light reflected in her eyes.

He blinked in confusion and looked down to find Seth pulling on his arms in an attempt to remove his grip from the girl's shirt. Seeing that he was finally getting a response, Seth slapped him hard across the face, and Jase staggered backward, relinquishing his hold on the girl. She slumped over and covered her face with her hands, sobbing uncontrollably.

Jase rubbed at his stinging cheek and looked up to find Seth looming over him. The captain's face was livid, and he was gripping one of his swords so tightly his knuckles were white. "What did you do?" he demanded, lowering the tip of his sword toward Jase's chest. "What happened inside you to cause this?" He thrust the sword to within an inch of the Talisman.

Jase looked down to find the red glow of Agla'Con corruption just beginning to fade. He grabbed the Talisman and stuffed it into his shirt. Rising, he scowled back at Seth, every bit of his anger still with him. "I did what I had to," he snarled. "She is Con'Kumen." He pointed to the others. "All of them were Con'Kumen. This attack was ordered by those who took my mother."

"You invaded her thoughts," Seth said, a mixture of fear and loathing in his voice. "That is why the Talisman went red. You did what is forbidden! Such action makes you no different than them." His voice had risen to a shout by the end, and he slammed his sword point down into the pier.

Probably to keep from using it on me, Jase thought, but he refused to back down. "I learned who set this up," he shouted, his fury still raging. "And he knows where they took my mother." He turned from Seth to address the warders. "Take her back to the palace and have a real Healer look her over," he ordered. They looked to Seth to see if he would confirm the order, and Jase followed their gaze.

Seth's eyes were hard as he studied him. After a moment he nodded to the warders. Pulling his sword from the pier, he slammed it back into its sheath. "I know what you are thinking," he said, "and you are not going without me."

Jase shook his head. "There are Agla'Con involved in this," he countered. "You will only get in my way."

Seth started to object, but Jase held up a hand to silence him. "I'll restrain you with the Power if I have to," he warned and watched Seth's eyes narrow to slits. The captain didn't take kindly to threats, and it was evident by his scowl that he wouldn't forget this one for a long time. *So be it,* Jase thought. He wasn't going to risk Seth's life in a battle with Agla'Con.

Leaning forward, he looked his friend straight in the eyes. "This is my fight," he said fiercely. "This is personal."

CHAPTER 30

Truth in Error

Seth watched Jase disappear into the crowd, then turned his gaze on two of the warders. "Follow him," he ordered. "Do what you can to keep him alive, but don't get in his way." *Because he's as dangerous as the enemy right now.*

Turning, he moved to kneel next to Talia. The smile she gave him was tired, but color had returned to her face. He ran a finger down her cheek.

"I thought we'd lost you," he said softly, and the notion of how close to death she had been was like a firebrand through his heart. She was his responsibility — had been since her birth. With her strong will and often rebellious attitude, no person in the world caused him as much grief as she did. And yet it only served to endear her to him further. Next to Elisa, he had never loved any one person as much as he loved Talia. She was the daughter he'd never had. If he were to lose her as he had lost Elisa, he would fall on his sword in shame.

She placed her hand on his and turned to kiss his palm. "Not yet," she replied, and he pulled her close and hugged her.

"If you ever scare me like that again," he whispered just loudly enough for her to hear, "I'll switch your backside so hard you won't sit for a month."

He felt her body start to shake and thought for a moment that she was laughing at his false threat. When he leaned his head back to smile at her, however, he found her eyes brimming with tears. "What's wrong with Jase?" she asked, fear heavy in her voice. "I saw the Talisman. Is he turning into one of *them*?"

"Of course not," he answered firmly, but he wasn't so sure. Gideon had warned that this kind of thing might happen. It was the Dymas' greatest fear.

Maeon wanted Jase badly and would stop at nothing to claim him as his own. It was a terrifying and terrible thing to have to watch for, and it scared him to death. But it was nothing compared to the horror of what he was duty-bound to do if it did happen. *Don't do it, Jase. Don't make me have to kill you.*

Hoping he'd kept his thoughts from showing on his face, he helped Talia to her feet. He was about to pick her up and carry her when she stepped away, moving in the direction of the girl who had stabbed her. He watched as she knelt and looked into the young lady's face. It took a moment before the injured girl realized who was kneeling beside her. When she did, her eyes took on a look of terror comparable to what she had shown Jase.

"You," she rasped. "You are dead. You have to be dead." She covered her face with her hands and began sobbing again.

Talia reached out and touched the girl's hands, drawing them away from her face. Seth knew what Talia was considering and moved to stand beside her. Frowning, he rested his hand on his sword hilt. The injured girl looked like a caged animal ready to bite the one trying to free it.

"You don't have to do this," he told Talia quietly.

"I know," she replied without looking at him. "But if I don't, who will?"

He had expected nothing less from her and sighed resignedly. "Okay," he said. "If you must." He supposed he should try to learn from her example of compassion, but he kept his hand on his sword anyway. Compassion was good, but it sometimes got people killed.

Talia placed her hand on the girl's head and closed her eyes. A heartbeat later the girl's body stiffened, and her eyes went wide with surprise. When she relaxed, the pain was gone from her face. She still looked wary, on the verge of flight or attack, but she lay still and studied Talia with a look that was both wondering and fearful. Talia moved to stand but swayed weakly. Seth grabbed her to keep her from falling.

The girl started to sit up, but Seth's sword tip at her throat stopped her. "Don't make me undo what she did for you," he warned, then motioned for the warders to take her into custody.

Drawn by all the commotion, two squads of City Guardsmen poured from the streets above the Waterfront and blocked off the end of the pier. Their stances were wary as they watched Seth and the warders approach, and their hands strayed to their weapons. It took Seth several minutes to explain the situation and several more minutes to convince the men to let him and the others pass.

When they were finally cleared to go, Seth took one last look at the scar-faced girl and found her staring at Talia. He couldn't tell what she was thinking, but if he had to guess, he'd say it had something to do with how confused she was about the compassion and mercy she'd received. Knowing of her involvement in the Con'Kumen made him think it was probably a first-time experience for her. He hoped it was enough to change her path in life. After she was released from prison, of course. Which, unfortunately for her, wouldn't be for a very long time.

Turning to Talia, he scooped her up in his arms and carried her from the scene. He knew she probably preferred to walk, but that was too bad. He didn't intend to put her down until they reached the palace.

The door exploded inward in a spray of shattered wood, and Shaloth threw his hands up to shield his face. The force of the explosion sent him tumbling backward out of his chair and upended the desk he'd been sitting at. He pushed himself to his knees and looked up to find a young man filling the doorway. He knew who the lad was, but he hadn't expected him for several more days. Something must have gone wrong with the attack at the pier.

He tried to rise, but some unseen force seized him in a vice-like grip and hurled him across the room. Specks of light filled the inside of his head as he struck the wall. His breath left him in a rush. Before he could fall to the floor, the unseen fist had him, and he was hurled across the room to slam into the other wall.

He raised his hands in surrender and tried to speak. "Pl... pl... pl ...ease," he choked, but he was thrown across the room once more. This time he felt ribs crack, and the lights flashing before his eyes grew so bright he thought his head was on fire. He was dragged away from the wall and dropped in the center of the room. When he was finally able to look up, he found Jase Fairimor standing over him.

The boy's grey eyes were as cold and hard as steel, and his teeth were bared in a snarl. "I know who you are," Jase hissed. "I know what you've done."

The unseen fist clamped around his throat, and Shaloth found himself looking Jase in the eyes. He couldn't feel the floor beneath his feet. "My not killing you depends on whether or not you tell me what I want to know," Jase told him, then lowered him back to the floor. "I know you had contact with the Agla'Con who took my mother. I learned it from your daughter. Tell me where they are and I won't do to you what I did to her."

The grip lessened, and Shaloth nodded. He had planned all along to point the boy in the direction of his mother; he just hadn't thought it would be so soon. Or under these circumstances.

He fought for breath. "They... took her... to... Gylass," he wheezed, reaching up to rub at his damaged throat.

"Liar," Jase shouted, and Shaloth tried to brace himself as he was hurled across the room once more. It did little good. He slammed into the wall with such force bones cracked and the plaster on the wall crumbled into powder. Over and over it happened, and he began to think the boy meant to pummel him into mush.

Suddenly the grip released him, and he sagged into a heap. He could hear the sound of voices above the pounding in his head and opened his eyes to investigate. Several of his men were storming in to help. He tried to warn them off, but he was unable to find his voice. He could only watch as they rushed the young man with swords raised.

Jase made a motion with his hand, and the sword blades shattered into deadly shards of steel that caught the men full in the face and dropped them screaming at his feet.

Jase glanced down at them the way he might glance down at a pile of dung he wished to avoid stepping in, then fastened his attention on Shaloth once more. "I will ask you one more time," he said darkly. "Where is my mother?"

"I told you," Shaloth answered. "They have taken her to Gylass."

He didn't need to see the look in the boy's eyes to know what was coming. The red glow of Agla'Con fire shining beneath his shirt said it all.

Seth and the others were within sight of the palace when an explosion a few blocks away rocked the entire district. People screamed and dove for cover, and horses reared, throwing their riders to the street. Pigeons took flight from the roofs and eaves of buildings in a terrified flurry of feathers. Glass from a dozen broken windows tinkled loudly across the paving stones. Seth tightened his hold on Talia and whirled in the direction of the sound.

He found a plume of dust billowing skyward, a grey-white maelstrom of boards and fragments of wood, ceramic shingles, and bits of glass. A moment later it began raining debris onto the rooftops of adjacent buildings.

Jase.

Pursing his lips grimly, he handed Talia to one of the warders. "Take her to the palace," he ordered, then headed in the direction of the destruction.

He had trouble getting there when he couldn't find a bridge to cross one of the blasted canals, and he leapt onto a passing boat in frustration. Offering a quick apology to the startled occupants, he leapt to a ladder rising from the water on the other side. Back on solid ground, he raced down one last street and into the plaza beyond.

He wasn't prepared for what he found.

A crowd had gathered in front of the remains of what had once been a two-story building, and many of the people were staring at it in fright. The roof and upper floor were gone, as was the front and most of one side. Several of the surrounding buildings had sustained damage as well. Nearly every window in the plaza had been shattered, and debris lay scattered everywhere. A cloud of dust hung heavy in the air.

He spotted several men pulling a body away from the rubble, while a half-dozen others still searched for whoever else might have been inside.

Jase knelt in the middle of the plaza, his head down, his shoulders shaking with the sobs he wasn't even trying to hold back. A man lay in the street next to him, but Seth couldn't tell if he was dead or alive. He approached cautiously, his hand straying to his sword.

Jase looked up as he neared, and Seth lowered his hand away from his sword. The boy's eyes were haunted, but his earlier malice was gone. He looked lost and scared. And there was something else in his eyes that Seth had never seen before. Loathing perhaps? Remorse? It didn't matter. Right now, Jase needed help.

He dropped to one knee and reached out to touch Jase on the arm. "Are you all right?"

"He spoke the truth," Jase moaned. "He spoke the truth, and I didn't believe him." He slumped forward and pressed his face to the street, covering his head with his hands. "I'm no different than any of them," he groaned. "No different."

"Yes, you are," Seth told him firmly. "Because you recognize that what you did was wrong. Now you must make certain to never do it again."

Jase kept his head down for a while longer, and Seth let him. He stood above the boy protectively, giving any who strayed too close a look that told them it would be best if they minded their own business. They were content to do just that.

When Jase's grief finally ran its course, he wiped the muddy tears from his cheeks and rose to his feet. "They've gone to Gylass," he said. "And they are only two days ahead of us."

Seth put his arm around him. "Then let's fetch ourselves a ship."

When Seth released him, Jase moved to stand above the man who called himself Shaloth. It wasn't his real name — he'd learned that when he'd invaded the man's thoughts. His real name was Piera Kalmara, and he was a Con'Kumen twenty-five years into his oath. He'd spent his entire life here in Tetrica, working to overthrow the rightful government, and he had recruited hundreds of people into the brotherhood.

Jase frowned. It was the kind of knowledge that made him wish he'd simply killed the man along with all the others when he'd obliterated the chapter house. If not for the fact that Shaloth might be useful in uncovering the rest of the Con'Kumen, he would have incinerated him with the Power. Fire, he decided as he looked at the rubble littering the plaza, was cleaner than whatever he'd done to destroy the chapter house.

He sighed inwardly. He wasn't even sure what he'd done, but he thought it may have been a fist of Air interwoven with Spirit. Whatever the case, he was glad the warders Seth had sent to watch over him had kept their distance. It had likely kept them alive.

They were keeping their distance now as well, and he motioned them forward.

"Fetch or fasten a litter and bring this filth with us," he told them. "But be careful. I don't want him dying on the way to the palace." *Because I want him healed and healthy for Lord Tetrica to interrogate.*

Reaching beneath his shirt, he pulled out the Talisman of Elsa and ran his thumb over the smooth golden orb gripped in the eagle's talons. He was unworthy to possess such an item, he knew, and it sickened him. He was unworthy to be called a son of the birthright. He had transgressed the laws of the Earthsoul and violated the blood of the woman Elsa. He would accept his punishment.

Turning to Seth, he handed over the Talisman. "I'll need you to keep this for a while," he told the captain. "Let's pray it isn't forever."

Seth's eyes narrowed worriedly. "You've lost the ability to wield *Ta'shaen*," he said. It wasn't a question.

Jase cringed. "No. That I could still do..." he hesitated, "if I wanted to wield after the manner of the Agla'Con." This was something he didn't like having to admit, especially to Seth. "When I open my Awareness, I find myself in a void absent of the Power. It is a void I have felt before, on other occasions when I've done something I shouldn't have. *Ta'shaen* is still there — I can still sense it. But it's out of reach unless I force the issue."

"And the Talisman gives you the ability to reach beyond the void and seize the Power without the approval of the Earthsoul," Seth said with a nod. "I understand. And I will keep it for you until you are ready for it."

"Thank you."

Seth tucked the Talisman away in a pocket. "How long have you had to wait for the Earthsoul to forgive you?" he asked. "Because I don't exactly relish the thought of pursuing a group of Agla'Con without the aid of a Dymas. I will, of course, with or without your abilities to help me. It's suicidal, I know, but I promised Gideon Dymas I would rescue your mother."

It might be suicidal anyway, Jase thought, but he knew better than to say so. He shrugged uncomfortably. "A few hours. A day at the most." He looked away, unsure if he should continue. "But I've never done anything quite this bad."

Seth grunted. "I'll say," he said, then added, "But at least you know what you did was wrong and are willing to make it right. Giving up the Talisman was the first step in that, and it is a gesture that won't go unnoticed by the Earthsoul."

Jase nodded, but he wasn't so sure.

The warders finished making a litter for Shaloth and were in the process of loading him on it, when several squads of City Guardsmen entered the plaza from one of the side streets. They fanned out across the area with swords drawn and crossbows raised.

The crowd gathered in front of the destruction hurriedly dispersed, leaving behind the bodies of those killed and the few who were still searching for survivors.

"Please tell me the dead are Con'Kumen," Seth said.

"Every single one," Jase replied.

"No innocent people were killed?"

Jase shook his head. "None. I could sense everyone in the area with my Awareness. The only people who died were the enemy."

Seth exhaled his relief. "Thank the Creator," he muttered softly, then added, "Because this is going to be hard enough to explain as it is. Quiet now. Let me do the talking."

A squad of City Guardsmen surrounded them, swords and crossbows at the ready. One of the men stepped forward, his eyes hard as he studied Seth suspiciously.

"This is the second time today you've been at the scene of a rather large disturbance," he said, then glanced pointedly at the remains of the chapter house. "A disturbance that is obviously a result of the Power being wielded. Care to add to your explanation before I have you arrested?"

Seth tucked his thumbs behind his belt. "As I told you at the pier, we are on the errand of High King Fairimor — with Lord Tetrica's blessing as well, I might add — and our mission is to destroy the Con'Kumen wherever we find them." He glanced at the shattered building. "Well, we found them."

The guardsman glanced at Shaloth lying on the litter. "You mean to tell me that Judge Kalmara is a member of the Hand of the Dark?" he asked. Clearly he was doubtful.

"That's what *I'm* telling you," Jase answered before Seth could say anything.

A flicker of surprise washed over the man's face, but it quickly turned into a mask of indignation. "And who the blazes are you?" he growled.

Jase took a step forward. "Jase Fairimor," he said, then let his voice drop to a menacing whisper. "And unless you want me to do to you what I did to the Con'Kumen chapter house, you will stop this ridiculous line of questioning and let us get on with our business."

He felt Seth's hand on his arm and looked over to find a glimmer of amusement in the captain's eyes. "Easy, Dymas," Seth soothed. "The man is only doing his job. Have him come with us to the palace, and Lord Tetrica will sort everything out."

"You're bloody right we're going to the palace," the guardsman replied, but Jase could tell the anger was forced. He no longer seemed certain that he wanted to see all of this through to the end, but he likely didn't want to lose face in front of his men either.

Jase had more important things to worry about. Turning away from the man, he gestured to the warders. "Bring Judge Kalmara," he told them. "He and Lord Tetrica have things they need to discuss."

He turned back to the guardsman. "And we've got an appointment with the rest of the Con'Kumen that I fully intend to keep. You're welcome to join us, of course. Just don't slow us down or get in our way."

Not surprisingly the man decided he had more pressing matters to attend to. He and his men moved to inspect the ruined chapter house.

Seth chuckled. "You're starting to remind me of Gideon."

"Except for the part where I cross into the realm of the Agla'Con and lose my ability to wield the Power," he grumbled. "Gideon has certainly never done that."

"There is much you don't know about Gideon," he said. "Much that gives me hope for you, even when you do stupid things."

Jase didn't know how to respond. *Gideon wielding the power of the Agla'Con?* It didn't seem possible.

Seth clapped him on the back. "Come. We need to speak with Lord Tetrica."

The way back to the palace was crowded, and Seth hissed his frustration at how long it was taking them to make their way through the throngs of people. "It looks like every person in the district intends to investigate your handiwork," he told Jase. "Word spreads fast, it seems. By nightfall, every person in Tetrica will know that a Dymas went to war against the Con'Kumen."

Jase flinched but said nothing, and Seth studied him intently.

It had taken a tremendous amount of courage for Jase to admit that he'd lost the ability to wield *Ta'shaen.* Even more impressive was how conscientious he had been about his own weakness and had given up the Talisman to keep from misusing it. It gave him hope that the Earthsoul would forgive the boy and reinstate his Gifts. He didn't want to think about how difficult things would become if Jase had lost his birthright for good.

Shaking the thought away, he continued. "I wouldn't worry too much about it. You've done Tetrica a great service by removing those scum." He glanced at the litter the warders were bearing and frowned. "I just hope Shaloth doesn't die before we can get him to the Healer. His knowledge about their organization will be invaluable. It's likely that he knows every member of the brotherhood in the city."

"But will he talk?" Jase asked, his face skeptical.

Seth reached up to stroke his mustache. "Oh, I think he will," he said with a smile. "Once Lord Tetrica lets him know that you're standing by to enter his thoughts again." Jase's mouth dropped open in shock, but Seth continued before the boy could speak. "Shaloth doesn't know that Thought Intrusion is forbidden," he said. "Even if he does, it won't matter. He thinks you are an Agla'Con."

Jase reached up to rub his eyes wearily. "Until the Earthsoul forgives me," he said sadly, "I am."

The pain in Jase's voice spoke volumes, and Seth put his arm around the young man's shoulders. "One of the keys to overcoming weakness," he said softly, "is to never forget how it feels to fail."

Tetrica Palace was quiet. Captain Omasil, fearing that the Con'Kumen might be capable of an attack similar to the one that had taken place at Fairimor Dome, had sent the servants to their quarters and placed the Palace Guard on a heightened state of alert. Those stationed here on the main floor stood rigidly at their posts and looked to be carved from stone. Scattered amidst the museum-like collection of paintings, carvings, and weapons, they could have been just one more kind of decoration — mannequins sporting armor. Only their eyes, ever watchful within the face-plates of their helmets let Talia know they were alive.

Lying on a cushioned sofa in the middle of the room, she closed her eyes and listened to the heavy, oppressive stillness. It was difficult not to picture herself in a mausoleum.

The thought made her cringe, and she hurriedly pushed it away. She didn't need a reminder of how close she had come to really being in one. If not for Jase — if not for the Blood Orb — she would have died. She placed a hand over the spot where she'd been stabbed and marveled at the miracle of Ta'shaen.

Annarie, the Healer for Tetrica Palace, spoke and Talia jumped in surprise. She'd forgotten the aging woman had stayed to keep watch over her.

"Is my lady all right?" she asked. "You aren't experiencing any pain are you?"

Talia smiled tiredly. "No. I was just thinking about how lucky we are to have *Ta'shaen.*"

"Luck has nothing to do with it," Annarie said. "The Power is a gift from God."

Talia nodded but said nothing. Instead, she closed her eyes once more and thought about Jase.

Jase, who had healed her and then turned to the power of the Agla'Con in his anger. Jase, who was Gifted beyond any to walk the earth, if Gideon's claim was true, but who had stolen the Power the way the enemy did. Jase, the one who held death and salvation in his hands.

She took a long, slow breath. She hoped he was all right. It had been two hours since the attack on the pier, two hours since he'd gone in search of the Con'Kumen. She suspected that he had caused the explosion she and Seth had seen, but she had no way of knowing. The destruction could just as easily have been wrought by an Agla'Con. She was starting to worry that something had gone wrong. He and Seth should have returned by now.

She felt a hand on her forehead and opened her eyes to find Annarie looking at her. "If you wrinkle your forehead like that for too long," the elderly woman said, rubbing gently, "you'll ruin that lovely skin of yours."

Talia smoothed her features. "I know," she said. "But I can't quit worrying about Seth and Jase."

"Jase," Annarie said. "He's the one who healed you?"

Talia smiled. "Yes."

"And a skilled Healer he is," Annarie said, sounding jealous. "I couldn't have done a better job myself."

"Actually," Talia said, "it was his first time."

Annarie stared at her in shock, obviously at a loss for words. It was just as well, because a moment later Captain Omasil entered the room followed by Seth and Jase.

Talia rose to meet them, leaning on the arm of the sofa to steady herself. She was still weak from being healed, and the sudden rise made blood rush to her head.

Jase crossed the room in a few quick strides and took her in his arms, hugging her close. She hugged him back, ignoring the layer of dirt and grit covering his hair and clothes. He was alive, and that was all that mattered. Besides, with half her dress stained dark with blood, she didn't look much better than he did.

Captain Omasil spoke to Annarie. "There is a man in the antechamber who needs your attention. After you heal him, come back here and check on these two." He indicated Seth and Jase.

The aging Healer started away and Omasil turned to Seth. "I'll fetch Lord and Lady Tetrica," he said. "They will be interested in what the young Dymas has been up to."

Talia felt Jase cringe, and she stepped back. Looking up into his face, she took his hand and squeezed it gently. "Don't worry," she told him. "I'm sure they will be pleased that you have eliminated so many of the Con'Kumen from their city."

Seth grunted, and he and Jase locked gazes. Talia knew from the look in Seth's eyes that it would be best if she didn't ask what had happened. Suddenly weary, she sat back down. Jase and Seth remained standing.

Annarie came back a few minutes later, her face as dark as a thunderhead. The look in her eyes as she studied Jase was one of disgust. Crossing the room to Seth, she placed her fingertips on his temples and closed her eyes as she opened her Awareness and probed him for injuries. Seth waited quietly while she did.

"There's nothing wrong with you," she said, lowering her hands, "unlike that poor fellow I healed out in the foyer. I've never seen a man beaten so close to death." Her lips twisted into a frown as she turned to face Jase. "That was your doing, wasn't it?" Talia flinched at the harshness in her voice. Jase, however, didn't even blink.

"That filthy cur is the head of the Con'Kumen here in Tetrica," he told her evenly.

"Even so," Annarie said, "he is still a man." She took a step forward and raised her hands toward Jase, but he put up a hand to stop her.

"I'm fine," he told her. "I don't need healing."

The aging Healer's eyes narrowed. "I wonder," she muttered, but she didn't press the issue. She turned an angry frown on Seth. "I don't know what this young whippersnapper did to save the girl," she said, "but I'd say he got lucky. After witnessing his handiwork on the man I healed, he's obviously a better butcher than a Healer."

Talia's anger spiked at the comment, but Jase laughed. It was a harsh sound, without humor. Before he could respond, however, Lord and Lady Tetrica entered the room.

The King's face was set, but Talia thought he looked uncertain as he crossed the room toward them. "I sent Captain Omasil to ready a ship for your departure," the young King told Seth. "I assumed you would want to leave as soon as possible now that you know where the enemy has taken the Sister Queen."

"Thank you," Seth said with a bow. "And yes, we do want to be on our way."

Lord Tetrica fixed Jase with a stare. "Then Lord Fairimor had better speak quickly if he is to tell me all he has done to my city."

It took Captain Omasil less than an hour to ready a ship, and Jase found himself scrambling to pack his things. He was in the act of stuffing everything into a leather bag when he felt a tickle along the edge of his Awareness. Relieved, he cleared his mind and opened himself to the Power, letting it wash through him in a river of cleansing heat. The Earthsoul had forgiven him. And for that, he was grateful.

Releasing the Power, he took one last look around to make sure he hadn't forgotten anything, then left his room on the jog. His hair was still wet from a quick bath, and it was the first time all day he'd felt cool.

He'd spent most of the last hour talking to Lord Tetrica about the day's events and had apologized a dozen times for the mayhem his destruction of the chapter house had caused.

The King had been troubled to learn the Hand of the Dark was in his city, but he had vowed to finish rooting them out. He was certain Judge Kalmara and his daughter would provide the information necessary to destroy the rest. If not, they would be executed.

Both Lord and Lady Tetrica had thanked him for eliminating so many of the Con'Kumen in today's conflict, and the look in their eyes showed they meant what they said. Still, it was obvious that they would be glad to see him and Seth be on their way. It would mean no more explanations to Tetrica's bureaucracy about why parts of the city were being destroyed.

Jase blew out his cheeks resignedly. After the bloodbath on the pier and the devastation unleashed on the chapter house, he understood full well why they would be glad to see him leave. In one day, he and Seth were responsible for more chaos than Tetrica had seen in a very long time.

He rounded a corner and found the elderly Healer, Annarie, coming down the hallway toward him. Smiling in spite of how he felt about her, he called a *hello*. She dipped her head in reply but remained silent, her eyes narrowing as she watched him draw near. She'd waited until he and Lord Tetrica were finished discussing the Con'Kumen before starting in on him again with a diatribe that could have stripped the bark off a tree. *By all rights*, she had said, *this young woman should have died from such a loss of blood, and I'll never know how a butcher such as yourself managed to heal her.*

He didn't know if her animosity was due to his treatment of Shaloth, or if she was envious of how completely Talia had been healed. In the end, though, it didn't matter. She had taken a dislike to him — he had seen it in her eyes.

The way she looked at him now was no different, and it irritated him to the point that he couldn't help acting on his next impulse. He stopped and waited for her to reach the far end of the hallway, then embraced *Ta'shaen*. Weaving a slender tendril of Air, he poked her firmly in the bottom.

With a squawk that sent several servants running for cover, she whirled to glare at him.

Flashing a broad smile, he bowed grandly, then turned and strode away.

Seth and Talia were waiting for him in the main hall with Lord and Lady Tetrica. Both had bathed and were wearing a fresh change of clothes. Seth looked as impatient as Jase had ever seen him. Apparently, learning where the Con'Kumen had taken Brysia had whetted the captain's appetite for the hunt.

"Sorry to keep you waiting," Jase said as he joined them.

Seth shrugged it off. "As long as you're back to your normal self," he said, bending to pick up his bundle. Before he could take it, Jase embraced *Ta'shaen* and lifted it toward the captain's outstretched hand.

"I am," he said. "But I want you to hold onto the Talisman awhile longer." Seth nodded.

Talia stepped near and put her arms around his waist, pulling him close in a hug. "Thanks again for what you did," she whispered in his ear, brushing his cheek with a light kiss.

He reached up and touched her cheek with the back of his fingers. "You're welcome," he told her, his voice catching in his throat. He'd nearly lost her today, and the thought was almost more than he could handle. He wondered if she realized how close he'd come to letting her die, that without the Talisman's uncanny ability to react to his need he would have. The very thought put a stranglehold on his heart.

Lord Tetrica cleared his throat, and Jase and the others turned to face him. "Captain Panos and his crew are at your command, Lord Fairimor," he said, "for as long as you need them." He stepped forward and offered his hand. "I wish you luck in your journey and God's speed in recovering your mother."

"Thank you," Jase told him, then offered his hand to Lady Tetrica. "And once again I am sorry for all the chaos I caused today. I know the destruction of the chapter house won't be an easy thing to have to explain to the city council."

"On the contrary," Lady Tetrica said. "I think most will be pleased that such an evil has been removed from their midst. And having our enemies think we have a Dymas who might deal with them in like manner will be most advantageous. It may even encourage those Gifted who are afraid to answer the proclamation to come forward to serve."

"I hope so," Jase told her. "I need all the help I can get."

"I'll say," Seth muttered.

Jase gave him a dirty look, but Seth acted as if he'd said nothing and bowed to the King and Queen. "We appreciate all you have done for us," he told them. "And I will do my best to see that your ship and crew are returned to you safely." With that, he started for the door. "Come on you two," he said over his shoulder. "Let's get moving."

Jase followed the silver-haired captain with his eyes for a moment, then sighed and bent to pick up his and Talia's bags. With one last bow to Lord and Lady Tetrica, he offered his arm to Talia, and they followed Seth out into the courtyard where they were joined by an escort of Tetrica Palace Guard.

One of the men offered to carry their bags, and Jase handed them over. Taking Talia's hand in his, he found comfort in her grasp. She smiled at him, and he returned it, realizing as he did, that a casual observer might confuse them for two young lovers on a holiday instead of two people desperately pursuing Agla'Con. It made him appreciate how deceptive appearances could be.

The guards led them along the wall of the keep around to an arched gate framed by twin guard towers. There, a long set of steps set into the cliff face descended to the waterfront. At the bottom lay a heavily guarded pier and the ship that was to carry them to Gylass.

Jase took one look at it, and a knot of dread tightened in his stomach. He had never sailed before, and the horror stories he'd heard about what the sea could do to some people made him worry he would spend the entire time bent over a railing. Gylass was half again as far as they had already come, so even if he managed to speed the ship along with the Power as he'd seen Gideon do last night when he and the others had come down to see the Dymas off, it would still take days to get there.

He was growing weary of travel by any means, he decided. None of it was as exciting as the stories he'd read made it out to be. If anything, it was nothing more than a day-to-day hell that kept changing the form of misery as it gradually worsened. If not for the image of his mother's face firmly set in his mind's eye, he would have given up already.

Guards stepped aside to let them pass, and they moved down the pier to the ship. Once there, he held Talia's hand as they climbed the ramp to the ship's deck, then turned to look around. Above them, Tetrica Palace glowed orange in the last rays of the setting sun, but most of the city and all of the waterfront already lay in shadow.

A few ships still dotted the waters, but they were moving toward the docks where they would be tied down for the night. After the multitudes he'd seen earlier in the day, the docks and piers seemed almost deserted. Only a scattering of fishermen were still visible dropping lines into the water below.

He turned back to the city and let his eyes travel its length, suddenly disconcerted to be leaving Kelsan soil. It was something he had never thought he would do.

His boast to Seth of how he would track the Agla'Con all the way to Riak if necessary sounded in his mind, and he let it steel his resolve. He would go further than Riak if it meant getting his mother back. Looking out over the shadowed harbor, he pursed his lips determinedly. For his mother, he would walk into Con'Jithar itself.

Settling himself on a crate, he watched the crew unfasten the moorings and push off from the dock. There was little wind in the harbor this time of night so oars were used instead. He knew he could fill the sails with *Ta'shaen*, but the number of ships still in the harbor would make steering tricky, and he didn't want to be responsible for a collision. He wouldn't risk using the Power to drive the ship until he was certain there was nothing to crash into.

They were nearly to the mouth of the harbor when he felt a tickle at the edge of his Awareness. With it came a soft, almost imperceptible sound like the whispering of a voice. He closed his eyes and shut off the world around him as he stretched into his Awareness of *Ta'shaen*. The sound came again, still faint but understandable. *Jase?*

I'm here. On a ship in the mouth of the harbor.

The tickle at the edge of his Awareness grew, and a moment later the sound of Gideon's voice filled his head, as loud and clear as if the Dymas were standing before him.

There you are, he said. *I've been probing the palace. What are you doing on a ship? Did you locate your mother?*

The Agla'Con are taking her to Gylass. He felt a ripple of surprise but knew immediately that it wasn't due to the mention of Gylass. Gideon had seen into his thoughts just then — he knew what he had done to gain the information. Disappointment mingled with revulsion flowed from Gideon's mind, and he obviously didn't try to stop either one.

What you did is forbidden, he scolded. *It makes you no better than our enemies. Compulsion is the way of the Agla'Con, Jase. It is vile.* He paused, and Jase could almost see him shaking his head. *What chance of victory do we have if you become one of them?*

I'm sorry. I lost control. He knew it was a feeble excuse even before Gideon responded.

Tell that to the Dainin when they invoke a cleansing hunt for you, Gideon told him darkly. *I'm surprised the Earthsoul decided to give you back your gifts.*

Jase bristled at the comment. *I thought we needed to keep this short,* he said.

Yes, we do, Gideon replied, the heat fading from his voice. *Our enemies already know an awful lot about our dealings. They removed the Talisman of Elsa from the temple this morning.* He paused. *I see you felt the defiling as well.*

Yes. But I didn't know what it was.

We have been betrayed, Jase. First your mother, and now the Talisman. Our enemies know what we are about, and they are seeking to use it against us. If I probe for it, I can feel the presence of the Talisman somewhere to the south, so it is possible that whoever took it is looking to join with those who have your mother. Go to Gylass and look for her. But be careful. Act only if you must. I am almost to Thesston so I will stop at the temple and see if I can learn anything of value. I'll join you in Gylass if I can, but if I'm wrong about these incidents being related, you'll have to recover Brysia on your own. My first responsibility now is to find the Talisman. We cannot allow it to be used as a weapon of evil. Even defiled, the reservoir of Ta'shaen *it can access is great.*

Jase shook his head. *But I can't —*

Yes, you can, Gideon interrupted. *You have to. You are strong enough to handle any Agla'Con in the world if you will control your emotions. Trust in yourself, Jase. I'll be in touch.*

Gideon's Awareness withdrew, and Jase opened his eyes to find Seth and Talia standing over him.

"Are you all right?" Seth asked.

Jase nodded. "I just Communed with Gideon," he told them. "And things are worse than we thought. The Talisman of Elsa has been stolen, and Gideon is going to try to recover it." He took a deep breath and let it slowly out. "It's up to us to get my mother back."

CHAPTER 31

Hunting Solo

When Gideon severed the Communal link with Jase, he couldn't help but worry that he was making a mistake by sending the boy on alone. *But what choice do I have?* he asked the darkening sky. He couldn't let the Talisman of Elsa be used for an evil purpose. Any Agla'Con with the right knowledge could tap into enough of *Ta'shaen* to finish bringing down what remained of the Veil. If that happened, the war with Maeon would be over. Con'Jithar would swallow the world without a fight.

He ran his fingers through his hair angrily. But they couldn't abandon Brysia to the Agla'Con either. If they were to lose Brysia, Jase might lose his soul to anger, and Maeon would win anyway. As difficult as it was, he would just have to trust that the boy could handle things. He was certainly strong enough. It was his control that was worrisome. That and the fact that he had already slipped into the realm of Agla'Con on more than one occasion. What he had done in Tetrica was sure to draw the attention of the *Nar'shein Yahl*. He was too powerful a wielder for them not to take note of the possibility that he could become corrupted. They simply wouldn't allow it to happen.

And neither will I, he thought grimly.

He glanced at the coast of Zeka visible along the horizon, a thin line of uneven black rimmed with red from the setting sun. It had been necessary to turn the driving of the ship back over to the natural wind while he'd been Communing with Jase. Now that they were so close to Thesston, he thought he might leave it that way. He was tired from his sustained use of the Power and needed to rest. Too bad he couldn't find rest from his worry.

Thorac, Endil, and Elliott were watching him from where they stood near the rail, and he moved to join them. They knew of the loss of the Talisman, of course. He'd told them as soon as he'd learned of it. After his display of anger, he'd had to. Jase wasn't the only one who lost control of his emotions. Unlike Jase, though, he no longer slipped into the realm of the enemy. The last time he had done that was nearly three hundred years ago.

"I just finished Communing with Jase," he told them. "The Agla'Con have taken his mother to Gylass, and he has already set sail in pursuit."

"Gylass?" Thorac wondered aloud. "Why would they go to Gylass?"

Gideon shrugged. "I'm wondering the same thing," he admitted. "One of the Agla'Con is Zekan. Perhaps he is taking her to his chapter house or something." He glanced down at the waves slipping past the hull and frowned. "It makes me believe they are trying to lure Jase into a trap. It is the only reason they would have taken Brysia."

"And you let him go?" Thorac asked.

"I had no choice," Gideon replied, realizing that his frustration had made it into his voice. He glanced down at the little man and added. "Would you want to be the one to tell him he couldn't go after her?"

"Not for my own kingdom," Thorac replied, then added, "So we hunt those who took the Talisman?"

"*I* will hunt them," Gideon told them, putting enough of an edge in his voice to stifle any objections. "As soon as we reach Thesston, you three will take the first ship back to Tetrica." He locked eyes with Endil. "The Talisman has been defiled, so it is no longer necessary for you to remove it from its resting place. And I will not risk you in a battle trying to recover it from those who took it. We may need you if — *when* a second Blood Orb is found."

He turned to Elliott. "And you," he said before the Prince could object. "Your sword will be no good against the enemy I face now. Those who took the Talisman are probably Agla'Con. If it comes to a battle, I will be too busy trying to kill them to protect you." Elliott started to protest, but Gideon silenced him with a wave of his hand. "I don't want to hear it, Elliott. You will return to Kelsa with the others."

For once the boy didn't argue. Scowling, he stomped away. Gideon heard him mutter, "I knew I should have gone with the others."

Gideon snorted a laugh, then turned to Thorac. "You and the *Bero'thai* will be in charge of getting Endil safely back to Trian. The Fairimor bloodline must be preserved."

Thorac's frown was as large as Elliott's, but Gideon wasn't surprised when the little man nodded his acceptance. "It will be as you command, Dymas."

Gideon patted him on the shoulder. "Thank you, Thorac. I knew I could count on you."

He glanced back at the Zekan coastline and frowned. *Now, if only I had as much confidence in Jase.*

と

Brysia stood near the rail and listened to the sound of the Con'Kumen ship as it sliced its way south toward Gylass. Every now and then, the bow struck a wave with a resonating boom and a spray of white mist jetted skyward to sparkle in the moonlight. She stood near enough to enjoy the coolness of the mist but not so close that she truly got wet. She had found out yesterday how cold the inner sea was this time of year when she'd jumped overboard. Their ship had crossed the path of a boat going west toward Zeka, and Gwuler hadn't been paying attention to her. She'd decided to risk the swim.

The Riaki had been so angry when he realized what she had done that he hadn't immediately pulled her from the water, choosing instead to drag her through the waves with the Power for at least a mile. Her hair was still stiff with sea salt because of it.

They were two days out of Tetrica, but she sensed Gwuler's Power-wrought breeze had driven them as far as the ship normally would have covered in three or four. At this rate, they would arrive in Gylass sometime tomorrow.

Something large and black flickered at the corner of her eye, and she glanced up to see a monstrous, leathery-winged creature dropping to the deck of the ship. Borilius climbed from its back and held up a leather bag for Gwuler and the others to see. The bag glowed so brightly that beams of white light shone through the seams. It had to be the Elsa Talisman, she decided. Nothing else could radiate such power. Behind him, the massive creature — she thought it must be a K'rresh — lifted back into the night and was gone.

"I got it," Borilius said, sounding extremely pleased with himself.

Gwuler looked from the pouch to the sky. "Where are the others?"

The glow of the Talisman lit Borilius' smile as he answered. "I left them behind to kill Gideon."

"They are not strong enough to do the job themselves," Gwuler countered. "Gideon will destroy them."

"They are expendable," Borilius said with a shrug, "but Gideon won't have as easy a time as you think. Our efforts at the temple alerted every Agla'Con within fifty miles of Thesston. We hadn't even left the temple grounds before the first one arrived. Four more arrived within an hour, and it's very likely more came after I left."

Brysia gasped. Even Gideon couldn't stand against so many Agla'Con alone, especially in ambush. He would be killed, and Jase would be on his own. When she realized Borilius was looking at her, she glared at him with a hatred deeper than any she'd ever felt.

"Gideon Dymas is going to have quite a surprise when he reaches the temple," Borilius said, and his feral chuckle made the hair on Brysia's neck stand on end.

"And the boy?" Gwuler asked.

"He did a thorough job of destroying the chapter house in Tetrica," Borilius said somewhat grudgingly. "I've been probing the city with my Awareness since I left the temple, but I couldn't find any of those we had talked to. Shaloth was either killed or thrown in prison." He shook his head. "The boy is dangerous. We will have our hands full with him."

"He's coming then," Gwuler said. It wasn't a question.

"Yes," Borilius answered. "This is working out better than any of us planned. Aethon will be very pleased with the gifts we have for him. So pleased in fact, he may even let me keep the Sister Queen for myself."

Brysia stiffened, then turned away so he wouldn't see the fear in her eyes. She had to grip the rail with both hands to keep from shaking. The thought of being turned over to an Agla'Con for a plaything was enough to make her wish she had a sword to fall on. She would rather die than be defiled in such a way. The thought that it might be Borilius who kept her made it even worse.

For the first time since her capture, true desperation crept into her heart. *Oh, Jase,* she thought, *even if you have to destroy me yourself, don't let them have me.*

The Port of Thesston boasted the largest collection of ships anywhere on the Inner Sea and was second in size only to Thion, its sister port on Zeka's western coast. From his vantage point at the bow of the *Arrow of the Sea*, Gideon gazed at the strings of lamplight marking the piers and docks and marveled. Add to that the number of bobbing twinkles marking the ships still moving about, and the waters of the bay seemed to glow. Even in the middle of the night the number of ships moving in and out of port was impressive. It was nothing short of a floating city.

Two military vessels passed to the north, and Gideon traced their outlines against the glow of the moon. The *Arrow of the Sea* was a large ship by Kelsan standards, but it was tiny compared to the ships in Zeka's armada. Some of the privately owned trading vessels were larger still. It made him glad Zeka was an ally. No nation in the world could compete with such a navy.

He watched the glimmering ocean of ships a moment longer, then made his way to his cabin to collect his things — a single bag which consisted of nothing more than a second pair of pants, a dark grey cloak, and a copy of the *Book of Halek*. He didn't need much more than that. Lord Pryderi would provide everything else necessary to reach the temple.

With bag in hand, he returned to the stern and stood with Thorac near the helmsman. The number of ships around them slowly diminished until they were one of only three ships moving into the mouth of Thesston River. A short time later, those two pulled into sheltered coves, and lines were tossed to men on stone piers. The *Arrow of the Sea* continued upstream alone.

A short distance further on they passed between two massive stone towers marking the entrance to the city, and the ship moved out of the river's current into the calmer waters of Thesston's Interior Harbor.

Gideon glanced around appreciatively. It was just as he remembered. Walls thirty feet high stretched away from the entrance towers in both directions, encircling Interior Harbor and giving it the feeling of a giant bowl. Docks jutted from the walls like the spokes of a wheel and lamps burned at the ends of each. The soft glow was enough to show that the dozens of ships moored here all bore the flag of Zeka's Royal Armada.

He motioned to a dock near the stone staircase rising to the top of the wall, and the helmsman nodded. Turning the wheel, he guided the ship smoothly in. When they neared, the crew members working the riggings lowered the sails and began tying them down, while eight or nine others leapt to the dock with ropes in hand and began tying the *Arrow of the Sea* in place.

A squad of Harbor Guardsmen descended the stairway from the city and moved to investigate the new arrival. Their breastplates glinted in the moonlight as they drew near.

Gideon turned to Thorac. "I'm sorry to have dragged you all this way for nothing, my friend."

Thorac shrugged. "What else would I have done?"

Gideon glanced toward the cabins. "I have already spoken with Captain Diam," he continued. "He wants to wait until morning before starting back to Kelsa so the crew can rest and gather whatever supplies you'll need. Don't wake Endil or Elliott, they'd only want to argue my going on alone." He knelt so he could look his small friend in the face. "If I don't return, you'll need to inform Lord Fairimor and the council of what happened. Don't let them give up on this. Without a Blood Orb of Elsa, winning the war against Melek is meaningless.

Don't let them forget that. Maeon is the real enemy. He is the one who must be defeated."

Thorac offered his hand and Gideon took it, feeling the strength in the little man's grip. "Be careful, Dymas. Kelsa needs you."

"Kelsa needs the Fairimors," Gideon said as he stood. "Keep Endil safe."

He moved down the ramp and was met by the Harbor Guardsmen. After identifying himself to them, he followed them to the stairs. He didn't need to look back to know Thorac was still watching from the railing.

He smiled at the memory of how pleased he'd been to learn Thorac was in Chellum when he and Jase had arrived. He hadn't told anyone, but *Ta'shaen* had whispered to him that Thorac's presence was another piece of the puzzle falling into place. What exactly the little man was supposed to do, however, was still a mystery. Perhaps it was nothing more than what he was doing now, what he had done all along. Perhaps his call was simply to lend strength to others by being there for them. Who could say? The only thing he knew for certain was that they were no closer to fulfilling their mission than when they had started. If anything, they had even further to go. And things were getting worse by the minute.

Elliott waited until Gideon disappeared through the archway into the city beyond, then slipped from his cabin and moved cautiously toward the front of the ship. From behind the forward mast, he watched Thorac move to the stairs leading below deck and waited until he was sure the little man had retired for the night. Glancing around the deck one last time, he moved to the ramp and descended to the pier. Nodding politely to the crew members who were securing the ship, he made his way toward the stairs leading up out of the harbor and was met by the Harbor Guard.

"Where do you think you are going?" one of them asked.

"With Gideon Dymas," he answered truthfully, keeping his voice as soft as possible. "I wasn't quite ready when he left so I told him I'd catch up." It was a lie, of course, but they didn't know that. *Unless,* he thought with sudden apprehension, *Gideon warned them I might try to follow.* He told himself they were only doing their job, but the longer they studied him, the more he was starting to think they weren't going to let him pass. Most likely they had seen how sneakily he'd left the ship and were suspicious of his actions.

He decided to risk another lie. "Look," he said. "I'll be honest with you. I've never been to Thesston before, but I hear the taverns here serve a really great rum. I'm traveling with a grumpy little Chunin who thinks he's my mother and who would never let me go near such a place. Come on, can you help me out or what? I'll be back before he wakes up."

When the squad captain shook his head, Elliott thought it was to say no. "Kids are the same in all countries," he said with a soft chuckle, stepping aside to let Elliott pass. "Take the third street on your left once you pass the guard tower. Look for the tavern called *Lailies*. Just don't get so drunk that you can't find your way back. I don't want to have to explain this to the Chunin."

"Thanks," Elliott said, moving past with a mischievous grin. At the top of the stairs, he took one last look to make sure Thorac hadn't been roused, then slipped into the city. With any luck, Thorac wouldn't realize the bulges in his bed were nothing more than pillows until the ship was well out to sea. By then it would be too late.

Gideon could play at being invincible all he wanted, but Elliott knew better. The Dymas needed help whether he wanted it or not.

With a string of his best curses filling the air, Thorac crumpled the note in a fist and punched the pillows stuffed under Elliott's blankets. Was everyone in the Chellum family crazy? If the Agla'Con didn't kill him, Gideon certainly would for disobeying his orders. He moved out of Elliott's cabin and was met by Endil.

"I take it he's not sick," Endil said.

"He's gone with Gideon," he growled, tossing the note away in disgust. He glanced past Endil to the Zekan coast already diminished to a thin line in the distance. *And there isn't a bloody thing we can do to change that now*, he thought. Even if they returned to Thesston, they'd never find him. *Con'Jithar!* He knew he should have checked on Elliott before they left. He just hadn't expected the young Prince to do something so stupid. He began swearing again, but stopped when he noticed Endil's disapproving frown.

"He better not get himself killed," Thorac said. *Because I don't want to have to answer to Seth.*

Gideon reached the grounds of the temple shortly after midday. He knew it when his horse stepped over the remains of a stone wall and a subtle change in *Ta'shaen* tickled his Awareness. He reined the animal in sharply.

It had been more than five thousand years since Elsa's blood had sprung forth as a Talisman of power, yet the spirit of that moment remained. He could feel it in his soul — a warm, vibrant sensation that awakened him to a sense of the true power of God. The spirit of Elsa had survived the destruction of the Old World, had lingered even after the temple itself was forgotten. The area ahead looked no different than that stretching behind him, but one thing was certain: This was hallowed ground.

He followed the line of cream-colored stone with his eyes and spotted the bodies of several warders sprawled in the forest loam. One was partially covered by ferns, but he could see the hole burned through the man's chest.

Without embracing the Power, he opened his Awareness and let the currents of *Ta'shaen* speak to him. The spirit of Elsa was strong, but he could feel tendrils of corruption still scattered about the area from the Agla'Con attack on the warders. He probed the area cautiously, feeling for some sign of life, warder or otherwise, but there was nothing. He pressed further, searching for some sign of ambush or treachery, but the forest and the temple grounds were empty.

Closing off his Awareness, he dismounted and tethered his horse to a tree that had grown up through the crumbled remains of the wall. He picked his way quietly through the trees, ignoring the bodies of the warders as best he could. He'd known he would find them dead. It was the reason he had come alone — he simply wasn't willing to risk any more of Pryderi's men in the chance the Agla'Con were waiting for him. If Brysia was the bait for a trap to ensnare Jase, he had reason to believe there might be a trap here as well. He could sense no trace of the Agla'Con or the Talisman, however, so maybe his fears were unfounded. They might have simply taken it and left.

Gathering his cloak around him, he continued on toward the remains of the temple. He would still be careful, though. He hadn't lived as long as he had by being careless.

The wall of the inner courtyard was in a similar condition to the outer, but to his surprise, most of the temple itself still stood. Pyramid in shape, it consisted of three levels with a wide landing at levels two and three and a single spire rising from the top of the third. The outside was almost completely overrun with vines and creeping ivy, but the opening where the front doors had stood was visible. The doors themselves had long since crumbled to dust.

Part of one wall on the lower level had collapsed, but the opening was overgrown with vines so dense it was hardly noticeable. The remains of a statue and a fountain stood at the foot of the steps leading to the second level. The mass of foliage surrounding the fountain showed it still had at least a partial flow of water.

He scanned the area with his Awareness once more in search of enemies but found nothing. Cautiously, he moved up the steps and through the door into the middle chamber. He didn't know where the altar was, but the seething mass of

Spirit left behind by the defiling of the Talisman led him to the third floor. He paused a moment to let his eyes adjust, then moved up a set of stairs. Using the disturbance as his guide, he passed down a wide corridor to a small, well-lighted chamber at the rear of the temple.

He stopped in the doorway and let his eyes move across the room. Four more warders lay dead, their faces burned away by the Power. A fifth lay sprawled in a patch of dried blood. Slender bars of light streamed through two vine-choked windows high in the ceiling, making pools of white on the floor next to the remains of the ruined Altar of Elsa. The blue crystal block had been cleaved in two by corrupted *Ta'shaen*, and the words *Glory to Maeon* had been written in blood across one half.

Shocked by the vileness of the blasphemy and desecration, Gideon clenched his teeth in outrage and moved toward the altar. They would pay for this, he vowed. If he had to hunt them for the rest of his life, they would pay. With an effort, he calmed himself, and placed a warder's cloak over the bloody scrawl so he wouldn't have to look at it. He would need all of his concentration in order to view what had happened here. If he was lucky, he would be able to learn where the Agla'Con were going.

Kneeling next to the other half of the altar, he worked at clearing his mind, then focused his Awareness on the residue of corruption so he could trace time back to the moment of the defiling. When he was calm, he opened himself to *Ta'shaen*.

Fire engulfed the room in a surge of corrupted Earthpower so sudden and powerful he managed to block only part of it. Staggering blindly backward, he threw up a shielding barrier of water and dove through the door into the corridor, rolling several times to extinguish his burning clothes. Behind him, lightning hammered through the ceiling into the altar chamber, and chunks of rock and burning lengths of ivy sprayed in all directions.

He cast up a shield of Air and Spirit and raced away from the attack. Thunder shook the temple, and everything around him went red with fire. The far end of the corridor exploded, and chunks of rock and a cloud of dust billowed toward him. A section of the roof collapsed and stones large enough to crush an ox fell in front of him, smashing through to the level below. One massive chunk struck the edge of his shield, and he was knocked backward.

The air around him continued to burn, and he felt the heat through his shield. It quickly became difficult to breathe. He glanced at the sky through the hole in the roof and tried to pull in a wave of Air to push the flames back down the corridor when something large and black sailed across the opening. Now he understood why he hadn't sensed the Agla'Con when he'd probed the area earlier — they had K'rresh. They were attacking from the sky.

And judging from the amount of *Ta'shaen* they were hurling his way, there were at least six of them. Maybe more. He didn't stand a chance against so many. At least not on the defensive.

With effort, he released *Ta'shaen* and dove through the recently opened hole in the floor, tumbling headlong to the level below. He struck so hard the wind blasted from his lungs and light filled the inside of his head. When he rose to flee the inferno raging above him, he realized he'd broken a bone in his shoulder. Ignoring the pain as best he could, he opened his Awareness and began searching for his enemies.

Without *Ta'shaen* filling him, the Agla'Con could no longer feel his presence and would either have to search with their Awareness or strike blindly. If they searched for him, the advantage would be his. Of course, it was possible they would tire of their game and decide to collapse the entire building on his head, but he didn't think so. Bragging rights for the one who killed him were at stake here. Undoubtedly, each Agla'Con wanted the glory of that moment badly. It wasn't self-flattery for him to think such a thing — the Agla'Con had put a price on his head two centuries ago. Every time he escaped one of their attacks the price grew. Whoever these men were, it was likely they would stop at nothing to collect it.

The booming of thunder and collapsing stone still sounded on the floor above, and he could see his own shadow stretching out before him as he ran. It was a thin line of black outlined by the inferno spilling through the opening behind him. As long as they lashed at him, he thought with a grim smile, there was a chance he could kill a few of them before they got him.

He stopped in a broad, high-vaulted chamber to catch his breath and focused his Awareness on the strongest of the channels of Power stretching out into the forest. It was like a giant red finger in his mind's eye, a bright conduit of corrupted Earthpower pointing right at the Agla'Con who wielded it. The man was a fool to think he could gain anything by such an unrestrained use of the Power.

Knowing he would have to act quickly, he opened himself to *Ta'shaen* and unleashed a torrent of flame. The satisfaction of feeling the Agla'Con die was short-lived, though, and he barely managed to get a shield up before the room around him blew apart in a spray of rock. A heartbeat later everything went red with fire.

By sheer force of will he held a shield in place around him and raced away down another corridor, away from the retaliatory strike. The Agla'Con weren't terribly strong, but there were enough of them to make up the difference. And now he had made them mad.

He released the Power once more, and had to shield his face with his hands as he plunged headlong through a wall of flames and splintering stone. The temple trembled as the entire corner of the building behind him collapsed under the onslaught. Apparently, they were no longer concerned with individual bragging rights. He had to get out of the temple before they brought the entire structure down on his head.

Half running, half falling, he plunged down a flight of stairs, searching the path ahead with his Awareness, desperate for a way out. It took him longer than he'd hoped, but he finally found the room where the wall had collapsed, and he raced toward the daylight streaming in through the tangle of vines. He was nearly there when they found him.

CHAPTER 32

Unexpected Allies

Elliott watched as Gideon disappeared among the trees, then lowered the spyglass he'd taken from the *Arrow of the Sea* and urged his horse forward once more. He didn't want to get too close in case Gideon was using one of his Dymas tricks to search the area for enemies, but he didn't want to lose him either. Tucking the spyglass in his pack, he hung it on the saddle horn opposite the quiver of arrows and bow he'd purchased from a fletcher on the outskirts of Thesston. He'd bought the horse there as well, but the fletcher had demanded a king's ransom for it. *The bloody thief.*

Still, the man had known his craft, and the bow was one of the finest Elliott had ever seen. So were the arrows. They would allow him to help Gideon and still keep his distance from the Agla'Con. The Dymas had been right when he'd said a sword wouldn't be much use in a battle with Power-wielders, and he had no intention of getting any closer than he had to.

The horse slowed as it picked its way carefully across a rocky streambed splitting the meadow, and Elliott steadied himself while it did. When it reached the other side, he relaxed and returned to his contemplation. Agla'Con may be mighty in their own way, but he was a terrific shot with a bow. And as Thorac had so ably demonstrated with Shalan Ras, the black-hearted vermin bled and died just like everyone else.

When he reached the spot where Gideon had disappeared among the trees, he slowed his horse, surprised by the density of the forest. He couldn't see more than a few dozen yards, and he was suddenly nervous he might ride up on the Dymas without knowing it. Dismounting, he kept his eyes on the tracks left by

Gideon's horse and moved as quietly as he could. He'd only gone a short distance before he spotted Gideon's dappled grey tethered to a tree. The Dymas had gone ahead on foot.

He tethered his own horse to a nearby tree and took the bow in his left hand. He slung the quiver over his shoulder, notched an arrow, and began picking his way carefully through the trees. His skill as a woodland hunter made following Gideon's tracks easy.

He spotted the body of a dead warder sprawled next to the remains of a wall and dropped to one knee, raising the bow and casting about nervously. The gaping black hole in the man's chest showed that he'd been killed with the Power. Beyond the wall, the bodies of three more warders were visible. All of them had been killed in the same manner. For a moment, he questioned the sanity of following Gideon here, but pushed his fear away. Keeping the bow raised, he continued forward.

The trees grew even more dense, and for a time his vision was limited to twenty or thirty feet. He was starting to worry if the bow would be of any use after all, when the trees began to thin once more and the large pyramid shape of the temple came into view. Several smaller buildings surrounded the temple, but most had collapsed into heaps of rubble and were covered with a dense tangle of ivy and other vines. Except for a few large trees, the area was open to his view.

He decided it was as good a place as any to wait. For what, he didn't know. But he didn't think he would have to wait long.

A flickering above the trees caught his attention, and he glanced up to see a massive bat-like creature sail silently overhead. Before it disappeared, he caught sight of a man riding on its back. *An Agla'Con and his K'rresh.*

Keeping one eye on the sky and the other on the forest around him, he moved to where he had a better angle should the creature reappear. He was still watching the sky when the top of the temple erupted into fire. Even from such a distance he felt the heat on his face. A heartbeat later the ground trembled as lightning pummeled the spire, and deafening peals of thunder shattered the silence. Shards of superheated rock filled the sky. If Gideon was inside — and he probably was — he was in serious trouble. *Con'Jithar, but I hate being right all the time.*

The Agla'Con and his winged mount came into view again, and Elliott drew fletching to cheek and released all in one motion. The arrow struck the creature in the joint where leathery wing met body, and the K'rresh howled, rolling to the side and throwing its rider clear as both plummeted to the earth. The beast struck with a bone-shattering thud and lay still. The Agla'Con, dazed but clearly alive, tried to rise. Elliott loosed a second arrow and watched the man topple into the undergrowth, as dead as his mount.

Part of the temple collapsing rattled Elliott's teeth, and he glanced up to see a second K'rresh dive past the hole in the roof. It sailed out over the line of trees only to return a moment later to land in the clearing in front of the temple. *This is too good to be true*, he thought, taking aim at the man's back. Eyes narrowing, he let the arrow fly.

It struck the Agla'Con high in the shoulder, and he cried out in pain. Staggering, but still alive, he whirled, and Elliott found himself running for his life as the forest around him blew apart under a barrage of lightning.

Jelm Cloema directed every bit of *Ta'shaen* he could muster into the upper level of the temple and reveled in his strength as he felt the stone of the temple begin to melt. Fire was his forte. Not just the massive gouts he was using on Gideon, but the killing tendrils he'd used on the warders earlier. Fire was the only weapon worth using if one wanted to enjoy the pain of the enemy. And he'd felt Gideon's pain — it was a pleasure he wanted more of.

Gideon's hold on the Power cut off, but Jelm doubted the Dymas had been killed so easily. None of the clumsy fools who'd been drawn here by the theft of the Talisman were skilled enough to kill him. Not without a great deal of luck. And if they knew what was good for them, they would leave the actual death blow to him. Gideon was his. Borilius had put him in charge of this attack. Of the seven with him, he was strongest. By right of strength, Gideon's head was his.

He continued to pour a torrent of fire into the temple, knowing it was only a matter of time before he felt Gideon writhe in agony. This was the moment the Agla'Con society had anticipated for more than three hundred years. He felt fortunate to be the one to accomplish it.

He felt something brush his Awareness but shrugged it off, attributing it to one of the other Agla'Con. A heartbeat later he realized his mistake as the air around him turned to fire and agony unlike anything he'd ever known consumed him.

Turning to study the glare through the trees, Elliott listened until the Agla'Con's screams faded into silence. *Way to go, Gideon*, he thought, then picked his way through the trees once more.

The lightning attack had ceased, but the Agla'Con was still behind him somewhere, angry at being wounded and with revenge on his mind. The random stabs of lightning in the general area seemed to be an attempt to flush him out. Elliott smiled grimly. *You may have the Power, you filthy cur, but you're on my playing field.* Keeping his eyes on the forest to his right, he circled behind a dense stand of trees and knelt among the ferns. Measuring time with the pounding of his heart, he waited until the Agla'Con came into view.

He raised the bow to his cheek and let the arrow fly. *I never miss twice in a row.*

The razored shaft struck the Agla'Con below the collar bone and sunk clear to the feathers. Howling, the man staggered forward, and the forest around him exploded into fire and lightning as he lashed out with the last of his strength. Elliott loosed another arrow and the tumult ceased.

"Nice shot," came a whisper from behind him.

Elliott whirled, the Sword of Chellum in hand as he cast about in all directions. "Who's there?" he whispered, but the forest remained silent. He took a couple of steps forward, and his eyes picked up movement as something large disappeared among the trees. He continued to scan the dappled shade but saw nothing.

Nice shot, the voice had said. A compliment to be sure. Coupled with the fact that he was still alive, and it wasn't hard to decide whoever had spoken meant him no harm. He shook his head. Not even Seth could move so quietly. It was a thought as unnerving as it was encouraging.

He sheathed his sword and picked up his bow. Notching another arrow, he glanced in the direction the shape had gone. *Who are you?* he wondered, then set off to find another Agla'Con.

Laying beneath the dome of Spirit he'd thrown between him and the flames, Gideon used a lever of Air to lift the heavy block of stone from his crushed leg. The pain was excruciating, but he pulled his Awareness away from it and concentrated on breathing. The air inside his protective barrier burned his lungs, but he ignored that as well. The temple was beginning to collapse. If he didn't get outside soon, he was a dead man.

Pouring every bit of his remaining strength into his shield, he pulled himself across the floor toward the charred remains of the ivy. The torrent of fire opened enough for him to see blue sky through the gap in the wall. The huge trees that had caused the wall's collapse still stood, but their rough bark smoked from the heat escaping the room. It wouldn't be long before they, too, burst into flames.

He could tell by the differences in the flows that there were at least two Agla'Con still striking at him. There had been more earlier, perhaps as many as seven or eight. Except for the one he'd killed, he couldn't account for why the others had broken off their attack. Not that it mattered. These two would be enough to finish him unless he did something soon.

They were attacking so relentlessly that he couldn't launch an effective counterattack and still maintain his shield. Frustrating, since he could feel where both men were. Infuriating, because he could feel that neither man came anywhere near his level of ability. If not for the earlier attacks taking such a toll on his strength, he could have killed them both easily. Now, however, he didn't stand a chance against even the most pathetic of their group. It made the notion of dying all the more bitter.

He edged his way closer to the opening, aware that the stones above him were beginning to crack with heat. Beneath him the floor was hot enough to cook on. Part of his shield slipped, and his cloak burst into flames. Hissing, he snuffed them with a spray of Water.

The resulting distraction was enough to allow his shield to slip further, and a white-hot finger of lightning streaked through the opening in the wall and slammed into the floor beside him. The explosion threw him backward across the room, and he tumbled down a stairwell to a lower level.

He struck the floor so hard that *Ta'shaen* slipped away and his Awareness collapsed in on itself. The spots of light filling his head were quickly swallowed by darkness.

The thundering of the Agla'Con attack on the temple suddenly cut off, and Elliott dropped to his knees in defeat at what the silence implied. *They've killed Gideon,* he thought, gripping the bow so tightly his knuckles hurt. He wanted to howl his anger but knew it would only alert the Agla'Con.

A moment ago he had managed to sneak close enough to another one to peg the scum squarely in the back, but he didn't know how many more remained. Obviously enough to kill Gideon, so he'd better be careful. Forcing himself to remain calm, he rose and ghosted through the trees in search of his next target.

He heard voices ahead and picked his way carefully toward the sound. Once he spotted them, he stayed behind a couple of large elms until he was close enough to get a shot. They stood just off the edge of the trees and were studying the temple intently. They seemed to be waiting for something. If he was fast enough, he might get the second arrow off before the first man could cry out and alert his companion. At least he hoped so. If not, he would be dodging lightning for the rest of his short life. He refused to think about what might happen if he missed the first shot.

He stopped behind one of the elms and notched an arrow. Taking a deep breath to steady his nerves, he raised the arrow to his cheek. He could hear the Agla'Con congratulating themselves on what they had done, and their brazen laughter only solidified his desire to shoot them both. He took aim at the one on the right and prepared to let the arrow fly.

It was then that he realized he wasn't alone. Slowly, since any sudden movement would likely draw the attention of the Agla'Con, he turned and looked behind him... right into the chest of the largest man he had ever seen. He followed the green and brown-cloaked frame up to a deeply weathered face with dark brown eyes and a mouth large enough to bite off his head. Ten feet tall at least, with arms and legs the size of tree trunks, the man looked strong enough to uproot a tree. His dirty red hair was cut short, and his feet were bare. He held a shield that looked to be made of bark in one hand and a green net in the other.

He glanced past Elliott to the Agla'Con then back to Elliott. Raising a finger to his lips, he signaled for silence, then pointed to the Agla'Con.

Elliott turned to see two more of the giant men slipping silently through the trees toward the Agla'Con. When they had closed to within a dozen feet, they attacked, bursting from the foliage with such speed the Agla'Con had no time to react.

Green nets enveloped the Agla'Con in a crackling flash of green-white energy, and they fell writhing to the earth. The glow of red flaring in their fists winked out.

"Come," the giant man said. "Let us see if Gideon Dymas still lives."

Elliott looked from the giant face to the nets and back to the face. "You're Dainin," he said, completely awestruck by what he had just witnessed.

"Yes," the other replied. "I am Ammorin. Chief Captain of the *Nar'shein Yahl*. And they," he said, pointing at the two who had captured the Agla'Con, "are Pattalla and Sharrukin." He glanced off through the trees. "Shaalbin and Bettashin will be along shortly." He put a massive hand on Elliott's shoulder and guided him around the tree. "We thank you, young lord, for your assistance in our hunt. Now, however, we must hurry to see if *El'kali* still lives."

They crossed the clearing to the temple and were joined by two more Dainin. Each carried a net with an Agla'Con struggling inside. "The one we seek is not among these," Ammorin told them. "Our Cleansing Hunt continues."

When they reached the temple, Ammorin gestured toward the smoldering south wall. "Come with me," he said to Elliott, and they picked their way carefully through the charred vines. It was dark inside, so Ammorin produced two glowstones to light the way.

After a few minutes of searching, they found Gideon at the bottom of some stairs in the far corner of the shattered room. His clothes were badly burned and blood streaked his face. Worse yet, he didn't appear to be breathing.

Ammorin knelt beside Gideon and placed a large finger on his neck to check for a pulse. "He still clings to life," the Dainin said, and Elliott exhaled sharply in relief. "But barely," the Dainin added. He handed Elliott the glowstones, then gently lifted Gideon and cradled him protectively in his arms. "We must leave before the roof falls. Quickly now, I will heal him outside."

Elliott held the stones for Ammorin to see where he stepped, and they rejoined the others. Ammorin laid Gideon on a cloak shed by one of the other Dainin, then closed his eyes and began running his fingers lightly over the Dymas' still form.

"I do not know how he still lives," Ammorin said, admiration evident in his voice.

Elliott knew instinctively that the Dainin was a Healer and was examining Gideon's wounds with the Power so he could heal them properly, but it didn't make the waiting any easier. He glanced at Gideon's pale, blood-streaked face and hoped the Dainin was Gifted enough to heal him. *For the love of creation, hurry.*

When Ammorin seemed satisfied, he placed one huge palm on Gideon's head, and the Dymas stiffened as the Power flowed into him, bringing renewed life and strength. Gideon inhaled sharply and his eyes snapped open. A moment later he relaxed and raised a hand, placing it on Ammorin's arm.

"Ammorin, my friend," Gideon said softly. "It's good to see you again."

"You are making a habit of this," the Dainin said with a grin. "Last time was near Capena, I think."

Gideon sat up tiredly. "Yes. That's two I owe you now?" He noticed Elliott, and his face darkened. "What are you doing here?" he growled. "You are supposed to be on your way back to Kelsa."

"Easy, my friend," Ammorin said, making a placating gesture. "The Chellum lord very likely saved your life when he killed three of the Agla'Con who were attacking you."

"You did what?" Gideon asked, obviously surprised.

"And you thought I would get in the way," Elliott said, shaking his head and making a tisking sound. His pleasure at Gideon's reaction vanished when he realized what Ammorin had said. "How did you know who I was?" he asked, glancing up into the weathered face.

Ammorin's brown eyes glowed with amusement. "I recognized your sword," he said, pointing to Elliott's hip. "That blade was forged in the fires of *Aarin'sil.* It is one of the finest ever made."

"I'm kind of fond of it," Elliott replied, trying unsuccessfully to hide his surprise.

Gideon took Ammorin's hand and rose unsteadily to his feet. He looked at the Agla'Con imprisoned within the Dainin nets and frowned. "Am I right to assume they aren't the focus of your hunt?" he asked.

Ammorin nodded. "The one we seek has escaped us once more." He paused and pointed south. "But now we can track him more easily. It is he who has taken the Talisman of Elsa."

"Then we hunt together," Gideon said, following Ammorin's gaze southward. "But we must hurry. I fear there is more this man wishes to accomplish."

"Does it involve the Sister Queen?" Ammorin asked. When Gideon blinked in surprise, he added, "We tracked him to Seston as well."

"We'll talk on the way," Gideon told them, motioning Elliott and Ammorin forward.

"What of these?" Sharrukin asked, indicating the captive Agla'Con.

Gideon's eyes were full of contempt as he studied the nets. "Execute them."

CHAPTER 33

'Keepers of the Earth'

Walking next to the Dainin reminded Elliott of what it was like to be a child walking next to a grownup. For every step they took, he took two or three; and even then he had to hurry to keep up. No wonder they were able to move about so quickly. One glance at their effortless stride made him think they could outrun a horse.

That last thought made him regret the loss of his and Gideon's horses even more. Both had broken loose and bolted during the battle, scared senseless by the booming thunder and lightning. He and the others had followed their tracks for a time, but when it became evident the horses were determined to run all the way back to Thesston, they'd resigned themselves to walking.

Ammorin and his men had offered to carry him and Gideon, but neither he nor the Dymas felt like accepting the offer. That really would make him feel like a child. No. Unless he was dead or dying, he would use his own legs. Keeping his attention on the ground ahead of him, he did his best to keep up.

Ammorin noticed him watching his feet and slowed his pace. "Sorry, Lord Chellum," he apologized. "Sometimes I forget myself."

"That's all right," Elliott said breathlessly. "I can handle it." He glanced back at Gideon starting to lag behind and added, "But I think Gideon Dymas could use a rest."

Ammorin turned to regard Gideon. "We should rest a moment," he said, stopping so the Dymas could catch up.

When Gideon joined them, he bent and rested his hands on his knees, breathing heavily. Elliott had never see him so exhausted. "I had forgotten how draining... that kind of a battle... can be," Gideon said between gulps of air. "Either that, or I'm getting old."

"Let's sit by the brook," Ammorin said to Gideon. "Speed will grant us nothing if you die along the way." He reached into his cloak and withdrew what looked like a shriveled carrot. "I will make you *harrolia* tea. It will take the edge off your weariness. Come. We can talk while you rest."

Using Pattalla's cloak for a pillow, Gideon lay on his back in the shade of a tree and closed his eyes. Elliott and the others sat in a circle around him, and Elliott gazed down the canyon to where it opened onto the coastal plains stretching toward the Inner Sea. The water shimmered brightly in the afternoon sun, but it would be dark before they reached the plains. If they didn't obtain horses, it would be morning before they reached Thesston. And from what Ammorin had said, the Talisman was already days away. Most likely, the Agla'Con had flown south on K'rresh.

Ammorin produced a small wooden bowl from his pack and crushed some of the *harrolia* root between his fingers, sprinkling it in the bottom of the bowl. When the bowl began filling with water, Elliott blinked in surprise when he realized what it meant.

"If you are Dymas," he began, "why didn't you use the Power on the Agla'Con instead of all that sneaking around with nets?"

Ammorin seemed shocked by the question and looked to the others for help. They were as stunned as their leader and looked at Elliott as if he were insane.

"The Dainin," Gideon said, his eyes still closed, "don't believe in using *Ta'shaen* as a weapon." There was no ridicule or scorn in his voice. If anything, Gideon sounded as if he admired the Dainin for their choice. Elliott gaped at him. Coming from a man who had spent most of his life wielding *Ta'shaen* in battle, it was more than a little odd.

Ammorin nodded. "*Ta'shaen* is the power by which all things were and are made. Using it to kill goes against the charge we received from the Earthmother to keep and sustain life."

"Yet you chopped the heads off those you captured without any reservation," Elliott countered.

Ammorin shrugged, the movement of his massive shoulders like the rearing of a horse. "I didn't use *Ta'shaen*."

Elliott frowned at him. "Killing is killing," he said.

"Not to the *Nar'shein Yahl*," Gideon said, sitting up to accept the bowl of tea. After a sip, he continued. "I know it isn't easy for you to understand; it took me many years to terms with their belief." He paused as if searching for the right words. "Part of their charge as Keepers of the Earth is to preserve the sanctity of the Earthsoul. And in the eyes of the Dainin, there is no quicker path to violating Her trust than using *Ta'shaen* for destructive purposes. With what She has asked of them, using *Ta'shaen* to kill would be... hypocrisy."

"But you do go into battle," Elliott said to Ammorin. "I heard what you said about the Battle of Capena."

"Our Cleansing Hunt happened to coincide with what Gideon was doing," Ammorin replied, motioning for Gideon to drink more of the tea. "So we joined with him to defeat the Agla'Con. We are permitted to defend ourselves with *Ta'shaen*, but if there is to be any killing, it must be done another way." He grinned, and the deep lines on his cheeks changed angles. "Mostly we let *El'kali* do the killing. It makes the return trip to Dainin easier." He paused and leaned forward conspiratorially. "After we heal Gideon, of course. You wouldn't believe the trouble he can get himself into."

"Oh, I can believe," Elliott told him, pleased with the scowl that spread across Gideon's face. "But I'm still not sure I understand the whole Cleansing Hunt thing. I mean, I know you hunt Agla'Con who are doing extraordinarily rotten things — but my question is: Why not hunt them all?"

"Agency," Ammorin said as if that explained everything. When Elliott just stared at him, he continued. "Good or evil. God or Maeon. Men have the right to choose the path they follow. Simply being Agla'Con is not enough to merit a Cleansing Hunt. But when an Agla'Con does something extraordinarily evil, the Earthsoul calls for justice and we must act." He hesitated and looked at Gideon. "Aethon Fairimor's name was called again," he said. "Those who went after him did not return."

"That maggot has Maeon's own luck," Gideon grumbled. "And if we don't stop those who took the Blood Orb, he'll have Power none of us will be able to stop." He handed the empty bowl to Ammorin with a thanks, then rose, much more steady than before.

While the others gathered up their cloaks, Elliott moved close to Ammorin and looked up into his large face. "You only partially answered my question," he said. "I understand the notion of agency, but Agla'Con are evil. I'm sure the Earthsoul wouldn't mind a drastic decrease in their numbers, regardless of what they have or have not done."

Ammorin's large eyes fastened on his face. "There are many people in the world who have no ability with *Ta'shaen* who are as dark of heart as any Agla'Con. I ask you young Prince, why do you not hunt them?"

Elliott considered, but Ammorin answered for him. "Because there are too many of them and not enough of you. It is the same with the *Nar'shein Yahl*. There aren't enough of us to hunt them all."

Elliott turned to go, but Ammorin stopped him. "More I have to say," he said gently. "It is easy to confuse personal vengeance with justice. The Dainin despise the Agla'Con above all living flesh, and it is for that reason that we do not hunt them unless we are called to do so by the Earthsoul. We do not want our hatred of them blinding our eyes to Her purposes. Hatred clouds judgment. Hatred confuses vengeance with justice. Hatred destroys."

He paused and looked down the canyon to the coastal plains spreading below. "The reason there are so few of us to hunt so many," he continued softly, "is that not many of my people are willing to risk exacting our own personal vengeance instead of justice for the Earthsoul. We catch those we can, as we did this morning. You were right about the Earthsoul not minding when we lessen Agla'Con numbers. But remember, it was Gideon who pronounced judgment on them, not us. We would have taken them back to Dainin and turned them over to the tribal elders for sentencing."

"Yet at Gideon's command you executed them," Elliott said, still confused by the obvious contradiction. "Why?"

Ammorin put a massive hand on his shoulder and leaned in close, his large brown eyes sparkling with conviction. "Because he is *El'kali*. The Soldier of God. His calling differs from ours, though we are one in purpose. In the eyes of my tribal elders, Gideon Dymas is chief among the *Nar'shein Yahl*."

Gideon leaned forward in the saddle of the horse he'd borrowed from a farm near the mouth of the canyon and looked over at Ammorin who was matching the galloping animal stride for stride. He'd forgotten how quick the Dainin were, and how strong. Thirty miles into this sprint and they didn't even look winded.

He looked over his shoulder and found that Elliott's borrowed horse had started to lag behind again. Its lathered coat appeared slick in the moonlight, and its eyes were half closed. Its nostrils flared with labored breathing. Gideon frowned. Ammorin had already healed the animal once; to do so again would likely result in its death when they finally stopped running. Too bad there hadn't been better animals to choose from.

He sat up and motioned for the group to slow. Thesston was only a few miles away now. If they had to, they could ride double the rest of the way.

Elliott guided his horse close. "I knew I should have taken the mule," he muttered angrily. "This old boy's had it."

"We should have stopped at that ranch like I wanted and borrowed fresh horses," Gideon told him. "We could have been in Thesston by now." He used the word *borrow* instead of *steal* since he fully intended to have Lord Pryderi repay the farmer whose animals they'd taken. If only Elliott had thought to bring more money, they could have purchased decent horses from the ranch. *If only I had thought to bring some of my own.* He sighed. As the Guardian of Kelsa he was so used to having everything provided for him that he hadn't thought he'd need any.

"*Stealing* one was bad enough," Elliott countered, putting more emphasis on the word than was truly necessary. "In Kelsa it's a crime you can be executed for, you know? I don't know about Zeka, but I'll bet they don't think too highly of it either."

"The farmer will be more than compensated," Gideon told him. "So it isn't stealing." He brought his horse to a stop and motioned for Elliott to dismount. "Get your things and climb on," he said. "We'll ride double."

Elliott did as he was told but grumbled under his breath the entire time. When he finally slapped the old horse on the rump to send it on its way, his words had become audible. Gideon thought he heard *not so much as a thank you* as the last line.

Ammorin offered to carry Elliott's things for him, and the young Prince handed them over, then lifted a hand toward Gideon for help up onto the horse. Grinning, Gideon lifted him with the Power and dropped him into place behind him.

The cold silence that fell over the young man made Gideon glad he couldn't hear what he was thinking. Elliott had picked up some pretty rough language from Thorac during the past few weeks, and he didn't seem shy about using it. The fact that he was silent now was amazing.

To smooth matters between them, though, he spoke over his shoulder, "I appreciate what you did back at the temple. I would not have survived if you hadn't disobeyed my orders and come to help."

"You're welcome," Elliott grumbled, then began mumbling under his breath once more.

Gideon spurred the horse forward, and Elliott had to grab hold of him to keep from falling off. A string of curses filled the air, and Gideon saw Ammorin cringe at the words Elliott chose to use. Knowing he would hear about it later, Gideon directed a small flow of Air into the young man's mouth to shut him up. He fell silent with a choking gasp, but Gideon could feel the angry stare Elliott directed at the back of his head.

Ammorin and the other Dainin laughed for nearly a mile as they continued their run through the dark.

彳

When the second group of people they encountered fled at the sight of his Dainin companions, Elliott decided that moving through Thesston at night was for the best. He didn't want to imagine what kind of commotion they would have caused in the daytime. It was even more enjoyable that those who'd run away in fear had been people of questionable nature, cut-purses and harlots, and the like. Perhaps it would deter any future crimes they might have been contemplating. If not forever, then at least for a week or two.

They continued on in silence, their solitude interrupted only twice more by people running away in fear. When they were within sight of the palace, Ammorin and his four companions vanished.

Elliott blinked and reached up to rub at his eyes. *It has to be fatigue,* he thought, but when he looked for them again, they were nowhere to be found.

He was about to ask Gideon for an explanation when Ammorin's voice sounded from somewhere nearby, "We're still here, young Prince."

The Power, he thought and shook his head. He didn't know why he kept forgetting they were Dymas. They were certainly as powerful as Gideon; Ammorin might even be more so.

He listened for them, but their bare feet made less noise than a mouse as they ghosted unseen through the city.

They reached the palace gates and were stopped by a squad of six guards. Elliott let himself slide off the rear of the horse and waited for Gideon to dismount as well. The Dymas handed the reins to one of the guards, ignoring the startled look on his face, then turned to the captain. "I need to see Lord Pryderi at once."

The captain held up his hand to stop him. "No one is allowed onto the grounds this time of night," he said, looking at Gideon's tattered clothing with contempt. "Especially not someone like you."

Elliott tucked his thumbs behind his belt and stepped forward. He made sure they noticed the Sword of Chellum hanging on his hip. "I don't think you realize who you are talking to," he said, aware of how on edge the six men had become, "but this is Gideon Dymas. And Lord Pryderi is expecting him."

"What proof do you have of that claim?" the captain asked suspiciously. His gaze, still fastened on Gideon, showed he didn't think the legendary defender of Kelsa would be so poorly dressed.

"How is this?" Gideon asked, and the captain flailed wildly with his arms as he was moved out of the way by the Power. Without waiting for a response from the man, Gideon glanced at the others who hastily moved aside. With a nod of his head to show he thought them wise, Gideon moved through the archway and into the courtyard beyond.

Elliott bowed his head to the captain. "Thank you for your cooperation," he said, then followed Gideon through the arch.

When they were out of earshot of the guards, Ammorin whispered from somewhere to his right. "Gideon hasn't lost his way with people, I see," he said, amusement heavy in his voice.

"You should have seen the way he handled the Chellum bureaucracy," Elliott told him, glancing to where he thought Ammorin was.

"He gets things done," Ammorin replied, and Elliott flinched in surprise when he heard Ammorin's voice somewhere on his left.

"Would you stop that?" he said.

"Stop what?" Ammorin asked, his voice once again to the right.

"All that moving around," Elliott told him darkly. "It makes me nervous."

"Don't worry, young Prince," Ammorin whispered from directly behind him. "I won't step on you."

Great, he thought, reaching up to rub the bridge of his nose with his thumb, *a Dymas with a sense of humor.* Impulsively, he jumped to his left and collided with one of the unseen Dainin. From the sound of the grunt, he thought it was Ammorin.

"Oops," he said, "I didn't see you there."

Gideon glanced over his shoulder. "Stop fooling around," he growled. "We're in a hurry."

Elliott sighed wearily. If Gideon didn't lighten up, it was going to be a long journey to... to...

He glanced at the lights glowing in the windows of the tower and frowned. He had absolutely no idea *where* they were going, and it was not a comforting thought. They were certain to go by boat, though, so he hoped Lord Pryderi could provide more of that seasick herb. If not, he *would* hear Gideon laugh. He'd learned firsthand that when it came to someone else's misery, the Dymas did indeed have a sense of humor.

The dining hall of Thesston Palace was large enough for five Dainin to sit comfortably, but only after much of the furniture had been pushed out of the way to make room for them all. Too large for any of the furniture anyway, the five *Nar'shein Yahl* sat on the floor around the table, enjoying the mountain of food brought out by Pryderi's servants. And it was a mountain, Gideon decided as he watched them eat enough to feed twenty men. The poor servants were scrambling to keep up.

Pryderi seemed amused by the sight. "I knew my father had those oversized utensils made for a reason," he commented as he watched Ammorin lift the fork he'd used to skewer an entire ham. "I just never thought I would have the honor of seeing them used."

"The honor is ours, Lord Pryderi," Ammorin said from around a mouthful of food. "You are a most gracious host." The other four nodded their agreement.

Gideon finished with his own plate and pushed it away before one of the servants could fill it again. Beside him, Elliott was still picking at his food. It didn't appear that he had eaten any of it.

"Why aren't you eating?" he asked.

Elliott cast a sideways glance that held as much irritation as resignation. "Because I don't feel like feeding the fish," he said, then glared at Pattalla and Sharrukin when they started to chuckle.

"Once the herb is in your blood," Pryderi said for what Gideon counted as the third time, "it is safe to eat other foods. Please, don't pass on such a fine meal."

"Yes," Ammorin said with a mischievous smile, "because if Lord Pryderi is wrong, we can always use what you eat as bait."

Gideon listened with amusement to the banter between the Chellum Prince and the *Nar'shein Yahl*, and raised an eyebrow in surprise. He didn't remember Ammorin being such a tease, but it was good to see someone giving Elliott some of his own treatment. The Prince had been less than kind in his teasing of Talia and Jase. Perhaps this was a little bit of that Dainin justice Ammorin was always talking about.

After awhile, though, he shut their banter from his thoughts and returned to the task at hand. "I'll need a ship," he told Pryderi. "And make sure the crew is free from ties here in Thesston. I don't know when I will be sending them back, and I don't want to deprive any more families of their husbands and fathers if I can help it." He paused a moment before continuing. "Once again, I am sorry for the lives lost at the temple. They were all good men, I'm sure."

"They were some of my best," Pryderi said, sounding tired. "I'm sorry they weren't up to the task."

Gideon heard the guilt in the King's voice. "This isn't the first time the Agla'Con have known my plans," he told Pryderi. He could do nothing about the King's weariness, but he would not let this self-imposed guilt weigh him down as well. It was foolishness for him to think he was somehow responsible for the loss of the Talisman.

"It seems a member of the Kelsan High Tribunal is a traitor," Gideon continued, aware that Ammorin and the rest of the Dainin had ceased their ribbing of Elliott to listen. "At first, I suspected one of the lesser members, but it appears this person is one of the Core."

"The dangers of a democratic government," Ammorin said. "There is always someone who puts their own desires above that of the common good."

"Yes," Gideon said, "but when they put the desires of Maeon above what is right is when I say to hell with the council and start making the decisions myself. When another Blood Orb is discovered, the tribunal will be the last to learn of its whereabouts."

"Actions like that might be seen as a dictatorship," Pryderi warned.

"I prefer to think of it as executive privilege," Gideon told them. "I've made decisions without the tribunal before. I'll do so again. At least where a Talisman of Elsa is concerned."

"Speaking of which," Pryderi said. "Do you know where they've taken it?"

"South," Gideon told him and left it at that. The time for executive privilege had begun.

"How soon do you need that ship?" the King asked.

Gideon looked at Ammorin and the rest of the Dainin. "As soon as they are finished eating," he said, then looked questioningly at Ammorin.

The Dainin set his fork down and rose. The rest of his men were only a heartbeat behind.

Gideon glanced back to Pryderi. "It seems we are ready now."

The King nodded. "The crew will meet you at the docks," he told them, then motioned for one of the guards standing at the door. "Summon Captain Eridel," he ordered. "Have him and his men report to *The Sea Blade* at once."

"Yes, my lord," the man said and trotted from the room.

Gideon took Pryderi's hand in farewell. "Have my message delivered to Randle Fairimor as quickly as possible," he said, "and then continue your preparations for war. Without a Talisman of Elsa, we may have to fight it after all."

CHAPTER 34

The Voice of Elsa

Brysia Fairimor watched until the lights of Gylass faded into the distance, then picked her way across the deck toward her cabin. She ignored the stares of the Vakala Shizu assigned to watch her but cast a wary glance in the direction of Borilius. The man was worse than a rabid animal — unpredictable, dangerous, and with no regard for the pain he caused others. This newest turn of events proved it. Destroying those ships in Gylass harbor had served no purpose. If all he'd really wanted to do was attract the attention of other Agla'Con, he could have used the Power on the sea or a stand of trees — anything but ships full of innocent fishermen.

But Borilius liked to kill. It gave him some kind of twisted pleasure.

He stood now with the six Agla'Con who'd come in response to his attack on the fishing boats, issuing instructions to them in his usual condescending manner. She didn't understand how the others, especially Gwuler, put up with the man. Borilius must truly sit high in the eyes of Maeon for the others to be so submissive in light of his abusive nature.

In spite of his bravado, however, she was starting to think he might not be as confident about his plans to capture Jase as he seemed. That he had enlisted the aid of more of his brethren hinted that he didn't think he, Gwuler, and the two from Tetrica were strong enough to carry out this plan.

Neither Jelm nor Quinton had returned from their ambush of Gideon at the temple — a fact she liked to remind Borilius of on an hourly basis — so perhaps Borilius was worried the Dymas had survived. Gideon was sure to come in search of the Talisman if he had.

She pulled open the door to her cabin and let it slam shut behind her. There, in the dark, she let the facade of anger and defiance she always put on for Borilius fall away. It was easy to imagine that this was how it must be in Con'Jithar, for if her life this past week was any indication, hell truly was a place without hope.

Feeling her way to her bed, she lay down and pulled her knees up to her chest, cradling them with her arms. *Be careful, Jase,* she thought.

Then, like every night before, she let the tears she'd been hiding from her captors flow freely down her cheeks. She wept for Daris. She wept for Gideon. She wept for the villagers in Seston, the guards of the temple, the innocent fishermen, and all the others murdered by the beastly men who were her captors. But mostly she wept for her son who, win or lose, would be changed forever by what the next few days would bring.

Sitting at the table in the captain's cabin, Seth felt the sudden shifting of weight as the ship settled deeper into the water, then braced himself against the lag and deftly caught the lamp that had started to topple. *Will the boy ever learn?* he thought angrily, rising to investigate this newest mishap. Jase had already caused three fires by cutting the Power-wrought winds too quickly. If the frantic shouts coming from the cabin next door were any indication, he had just caused another.

Jase better have a good reason for cutting off so sharply or Panos was liable to hang him from one of the masts. And that was if the crew didn't get him first. They were already nervous, and probably a little envious, too, of how fast Jase was pushing the ship. It didn't help that he had dumped them all on their backsides half a dozen times. With Captain Panos close on his heels, he stomped up the stairs and onto the deck, ready to give the boy a good scolding.

His anger vanished when he found Jase lying motionless on the deck. Talia knelt over him and several of the crew had gathered as well. Seth rushed forward to investigate.

"What happened?" he asked, kneeling next to Talia.

"I'm not sure," she answered. "One moment he was sitting there focused on the sails like always, the next moment he collapsed. I've checked him over, and there doesn't seem to be any injury. I did feel his exhaustion, though." She looked up and her eyes were frightened. "If I hadn't buoyed up his strength just now, that exhaustion may have been great enough to kill him. It still might if he doesn't get some rest."

"I knew he was overdoing it," Seth growled. "But you can't tell a Fairimor anything." Groaning with the effort, he lifted Jase into his arms and started across the deck. *Good heavens, the boy has grown.*

He squeezed through the door to Jase's cabin and laid him on the bed, then pulled off his boots and stepped back as Talia covered him with a blanket.

"You can keep an eye on him if you wish," he told her, "but I think you need to get some sleep as well. Even without the Power, we'll reach Gylass sometime tomorrow morning." He glanced down at Jase again. "If he is as tired as you say, he'll sleep at least that long." He shook his head. "I don't know what good he thinks he will do us if he kills himself before we catch up to those who took Brysia."

"He's frightened," Talia replied. "He's afraid what he might find when we do catch up."

Seth looked into her eyes and pursed his lips grimly. "So am I."

The jungle is thick with mist. Shadows hang heavy beneath the dark canopy of trees, and what little light exists is tainted with the decay of rotting leaves and moss-covered limbs. The muddy ground clings to his boots. Snake-like vines snag his feet with every step. A look back shows his footprints filling with fetid water, a string of tiny pools of muck and slime.

Every step is more difficult than the last. Every step threatens to pitch him headlong into the writhing undergrowth. His legs feel as if they are made of lead, their strength gone. His lungs burn with labored breathing.

And yet he runs.

He runs because he has to. He has to catch up to those who have taken his mother. He has to escape the danger close on his heels. He is trapped between what might be and what will be, and no matter which way he goes, he sees no escape.

The jungle begins to close in on him, a writhing, whipping mass of vegetation so dense that shadow overcomes light and everything disappears into darkness. He can feel the vines as they coil around his arms and legs. He pulls desperately at those winding around his neck — those iron-hard cords trying to strangle him — but they only entangle his fingers as well. It quickly becomes difficult to breathe.

He reaches for the Power, but it slips away like mist because he is too weak to embrace it. He struggles desperately then, breaking some of the vines with his hands and biting through others with his teeth. As quickly as he severs one, a dozen more move in to replace it. It isn't long before he can't move at all. A numbness begins to seep into him, and he quits struggling.

So this is death, he thinks, *and everything around him explodes into light.*

Jase.

At the sound of the voice, he tries to open his eyes, sure that the dream is over. His exhaustion is still too great, and his body refuses to respond. The numbness remains, but he can't say if the vines still hold him in their choking grasp. He isn't sure if he is still even in the jungle. There is a sensation of movement, but it takes a moment for him to realize that it is he who is moving and not the writhing mass of killing jungle.

He tries again to open his eyes, and this time they respond.

He finds himself sailing through a blackness so vast and deep that it seems to go on forever. If not for the points of light far ahead in the distance, he would think himself alone. He glances down and finds that he can see himself; odd since there is no light save the small points in the distance.

As he watches, the points of light draw closer, but they don't increase in size or brightness. Once again, the discovery seems odd.

Jase.

It is the same voice as before, but now he knows it isn't coming from a person. It is sounding inside his head.

I'm here, *he thinks back.* Who calls?

I am Elsa, *the voice replies.* I am she who was slain by Maeon. I am she whose blood waits for the joining of old and new so salvation may come. I am she whose blood has been stolen by those who would corrupt it for evil purposes.

The points of light coming toward him increase in brightness, and he is forced to shield his eyes against them. You have faltered, my son, *Elsa scolds.* You have done what is forbidden. Several times now you have crossed into the realm of the Agla'Con. To do so again is to risk becoming one of them. Do not fail me, blood of my blood. The Earthsoul needs you.

For a moment, a deep and terrible sadness fills him, piercing his heart and threatening to crush him. It is Elsa's sorrow, he realizes. The sorrow of a doomed world should he fail. I know the hearts of those who have taken the Blood Orb, *the voice of Elsa continues.* They will use it to bring down the Veil. You must stop them lest Con'Jithar swallow us all.

I don't know where they are, *Jase replies.*

Look, *Elsa commands, and the points of light flare like the sun. When they fade, Jase finds himself looking at the Inner Sea from a thousand feet in the air. To the west, lights from the port of Gylass twinkle on a stretch of black that is the Zekan coast, but the vision turns his eyes southward, pulling his Awareness toward a ship sailing into the mouth of Illiarensei, the Arkanian river known as 'The Mother of all Waters.'*

The people on the ship come into focus, and he sees them all — a crew made up of Con'Kumen from Tetrica, a dozen Shizu, ten Agla'Con, and... his mother. He sees her sitting alone near the front of the ship watching the jungle coastline of Illiarensei slide by.

His joy at finding her alive and well is stifled by the shock of what else he finds. There, wrapped in a leather bag and glowing like the sun, is the stolen Talisman of Elsa.

Don't let them have me, Elsa says, and everything vanishes in a flash of white.

Sitting in the chair beside Jase's bed, Talia found herself dozing as she waited for him to wake up. When he finally did, he jerked upright so suddenly that she let out a surprised squawk before throwing her arms around him in a hug. She had started to wonder if he was ever going to wake at all. A couple of times during the night he had stopped breathing, and she had been forced to use her Gift to get his lungs working again. He'd been so close to death that it came as a shock when he gently pushed her away and rose unsteadily to his feet.

"I know where my mother is," he said. "I saw where they have taken her."

She knew from the certainty in his words that he'd had a vision, and she offered her arm to support him as he moved to the door. "Seth will want to know what you saw," she told him, pulling open the door and guiding him out into the morning sunlight.

She knew what it was like to have a vision, how powerful the images could be. Her own vision of Jase's certain death if she didn't accompany him on his journeys was still as fresh in her mind as if she'd had it this morning. One look at Jase's face told her that whatever he had seen was just as haunting. Probably more so.

They found Seth near the helmsman, studying the Zekan coastline. The port of Gylass was directly south, still some ten miles away, but she could hear Seth already giving instructions for when they arrived. He looked over as they neared, and some of the tension in his face vanished when he saw Jase walking under his own power.

"How are you feeling?" he asked, stepping down from the platform.

"Tired," Jase answered. "But I'll be fine."

"You nearly died, you know," Seth said, some of his usual harshness returning. "I told you not to use so much of the Power for so long."

Jase nodded as if he'd heard it all before and put up a hand to silence Seth. The captain's eyes narrowed with anger at being brushed off, but he fell silent. "I know where my mother is," Jase said, then cast about to make sure no one else was listening. As an added precaution, he stepped close and lowered his voice to a whisper. "They have sailed to Illiarensei, and..." he hesitated, "they have the Talisman of Elsa."

Seth studied him for a moment. "How do you know this?"

"I heard the voice of Elsa herself."

Seth reached up and pulled at his mustache. After a moment he asked, "What else do you know?"

"Nothing," Jase replied, but Seth raised an eyebrow at the obvious lie. "Fine," Jase hissed. "There are a few Agla'Con in their group."

"How many?"

"Ten."

"Too many," Seth said without hesitation. "We'll wait for Gideon at Gylass."

Jase's face hardened into a mask of determination. "No we won't. We're going to Illiarensei. They intend to use the Talisman to bring down the Veil, Seth. I cannot let that happen."

"And your mother?"

"I intend to get her back as well."

Seth was quiet for so long that Talia thought he might not speak again at all. His eyes were fastened on Jase's as if he were trying to size up his ability to see this through. Finally, he turned to the helmsman.

"Helm to port, sixty degrees," he ordered, ignoring the startled look on the man's face. "We're going to Arkania."

Elliott gazed down at the bow of *Sea Blade* as it sliced through the dark waters of the Inner Sea and decided the ship was well-named. It was a slender craft, long and narrow, with triple masts that caught so much air the craft almost seemed to fly. Though it could certainly be used for combat, its strength was its speed and maneuverability. He suspected it was used mainly for gathering intelligence.

Lord Pryderi had boasted of the ship's speed on the way to the harbor, but what had seemed like lavish embellishment then seemed inadequate now that he was witnessing the speed firsthand. And with Ammorin using *Ta'shaen* to fill the sails, it really was the fastest ship in Zeka's fleet.

They were only a day out of Thesston and already the port of Gylass was in sight. But the best part, he decided, was how he hadn't spent the entire trip slumped over the side of the ship puking his guts out. The sea really was quite lovely when you weren't so sick you couldn't see straight.

He studied the Zekan coastline a moment longer, then made his way over to Gideon. The Dymas sat with his back against the center mast. His eyes were closed, and his face was lined with concentration. It was the third time today he had attempted to make contact with Jase, but so far there was no sign of him anywhere. Judging by the frustration on the Dymas' face, it wasn't going well this time either.

Elliott waited quietly, entertaining himself by trying to fold the shapes of shadowspawn with some of his colored paper. It took two sheets to make a Quatha — one for the head and arms and one for the legs and tail — but a K'rresh was really only a variation of the bat and was easier to figure out. It took only a single sheet. He was working on folding a Shadowhound when Gideon's eyes opened and he exhaled his frustration.

"He's not in Gylass," he said, and Elliott heard a touch of fear in his voice. "If he was, I would have found him. And the only ships in the harbor are Zekan." He hesitated and Elliott could tell he was debating whether or not he should continue. "I did sense the residue of corrupted Earthpower in the harbor," he said after a moment. "So it's possible he already engaged the Agla'Con in battle. The only problem with that theory is that there was no trace of Jase's ability with the Power. Either the corruption I felt is completely unrelated or — " he broke off, unable to finish.

"Or they got Jase," Elliott said, swallowing the knot rising in his throat. If Jase had been killed or captured, then Talia would have been as well. He crushed the paper Shadowhound in a fist. "No," he said. "I refuse to believe that."

"So do I," Gideon agreed. "But it still doesn't change the fact that he is not in Gylass."

"What do we do now?" Elliott asked, still warring with the notion that his sister had been harmed or killed. *She's fine,* he growled at himself. *She has to be.*

"The only thing we can," Gideon replied. "We go after the Talisman."

He rose and Elliott followed him to where Ammorin stood with his hands on the helmwheel. He had insisted on steering while he filled the sails, claiming it made his job easier when someone else wasn't plowing through swells unnecessarily. The Dainin looked down at them as they drew near, and Elliott saw a frown creep across his face when he realized Gideon was bringing bad news. "Did you find the fledgling Dymas?" he asked.

Gideon shook his head. "Forget about going to Gylass," he said. "Let's finish the hunt."

CHAPTER 35

Fate's Path

Standing on the edge of the small forest nestled at the base of the Death's Chain Mountains, Elam Gaufin gazed north toward Zedik Pass and frowned. Teig Ole'ar and the other scouts had just returned with a very unpromising report. Both ends of the narrows were guarded by sizeable forces of men and Darklings of approximately a thousand each. The presence of Darklings meant Agla'Con were likely nearby as well since only they could keep the shadowspawned creatures from turning on one another in their thirst for blood. Bad news indeed.

Worse still, Shadowhounds had been sighted in the cliffs above. And Sniffers were certain to be accompanied by Shadowlancers. This was going to be harder than he had thought, even with the help of Dymas. Particularly because the young ones seemed determined to kill themselves in the process of learning.

He pulled his eyes away from the narrow slit of the pass and made his way back through the trees toward camp.

Fortunately, Joselyn Rai and Lord Nid had an uncanny knack for unlocking each students' potential as they taught them how to properly embrace the Power. Those with the potential to become Dymas had already learned to call upon three or four of the Seven Gifts of *Ta'shaen* and were learning new things each day. And while it was true they'd had as many mishaps as successes, he couldn't deny that they were quickly becoming a force to be reckoned with. He just hoped they didn't set any more of the tents on fire. It had rained again last night, and some of the men were angry at having to sleep in the wet grass.

He reached camp and picked his way through tents and lines of horses, returning salutes and greetings as he walked and issuing instructions and encouragement wherever he saw it was needed. The men were in good spirits, and there were plenty of smiles and pats on the shoulder as he passed. They were trusting him to see that they made it through the next few weeks alive. He hoped he wouldn't disappoint them.

He reached his tent and found Taggert studying a map at a makeshift table some of the men had lashed together out of logs. He couldn't stop himself from grinning as he watched the old general so engrossed in his planning. It made it easy to forget how badly Taggert had grumbled about the lunacy of this mission. It also took the sting out of the general's grim predictions that not a single one of them would return alive.

"Did you hear Teig's report?" Elam asked.

Taggert nodded. "I dismissed him a few minutes ago. This is worse than even I imagined," he said with a shake of his head. "Sniffers, Shadowlancers, and Agla'Con. Even if we do retake the pass, I don't imagine we'll hold it for very long."

"We'll hold," Elam said, moving to study the map. "I've got some ideas once we retake it."

"*If* we retake it," Taggert muttered, but Elam knew the old wardog wouldn't even be considering an attack if he didn't believe there was a chance of success.

"Let me know what you decide," Elam told him, moving past the table toward his tent. "I'm going to meditate on this new information."

"Meditate?" Taggert asked, raising his eyebrows in question.

Elam shrugged. "Maybe pray would be a better word."

"Say one for me," Taggert said, turning his attention back to the map. "I'm going to need it."

Elam watched quietly for a moment, then went into his tent.

乇

The following morning Elam stepped from his tent into the deep shade the Death's Chain Mountains cast over the small forest. Mist rose in pockets around clumps of ferns, and the sounds of birds and squirrels filled the air.

Much of the camp was already awake and moving about, and narrow tendrils of smoke from cookfires wafted up into the canopy above. Elam stretched his back for a moment, then inhaled deeply, enjoying the mingled smells of wood smoke, trees, and earthy loam.

He'd lain awake most of the night, but oddly enough, he wasn't tired. He had indeed offered a prayer, a long one in fact. If he was going to lead two thousand men into battle, he wanted to make sure he had God on his side. Several things had occurred to him during his supplication, not the least of which was the belief that he and his men were here because they were meant to be. And he didn't believe the Creator intended for them to be some kind of sacrificial lamb. If they went forth with faith, trusting that what Gideon had told them was true, the Creator would carry them through this. He believed that. He needed his men to believe it as well.

He spotted Idoman and the other fledgling Dymas a few tents away sitting in a semicircle in front of Joselyn Rai and Lord Nid. He couldn't hear her words, but the stern look on Joselyn's face showed she was once again lecturing them on the dangers of embracing the Power without complete control over one's emotions. She glanced at him as he passed, and he inclined his head politely. She gave him a quick smile, then fastened her wrinkled face back on her pupils.

Lord Nid excused himself from the group and moved to join him. Together they picked their way through the trees toward the area set aside for cooking and eating. "I heard the report about what we will be facing," the Meleki King said. "And I hope you will forgive me for saying that we are going to need more than a dozen newly trained Gifted to defeat battle-hardened Agla'Con and the shadowspawn they command."

"All we can do is our best," Elam told him.

"Our best," Lord Nid said, a trace of sadness in his voice, "isn't always good enough."

Elam grunted but said nothing more.

When they reached the cooking area, they found Taggert already into a bowl of bread pudding.

"How did your meditation go?" Taggert asked from around a mouthful of food. He shook his spoon at him and added, "Several of your men informed me that your tent was lit most of the night. How are you going to lead them into battle if you stay up all night reading?"

Elam took a seat next to him and accepted a bowl offered by a young soldier. "I wasn't tired."

"You will be," Taggert huffed.

"I'd like to address the men," he told the aging general. "All of them. We can do without sentries for a little while." He took a spoonful of the bread pudding and chewed slowly. "As soon as everyone is finished eating," he continued, "have them come to that meadow south of camp, the one with the large rock in it. It should be large enough to hold everyone, and the rock will give me a place to stand while I address them." He finished off the pudding and stood. "I'll be waiting for you there."

Taggert studied him a moment before speaking. "Is it time for battle then?"

Elam nodded. "As soon as you and Lord Nid finish the plan, we will attack." He started away but stopped after a few paces and glanced back at the two men. "Don't hold back on anything," he told them. "Playing it safe will cost us the battle."

"What are you up to?" Taggert asked suspiciously.

"You'll see," Elam replied, then turned away. If Taggert and the Dymas did what he wanted them to, the men of Chellum would be plunging into the jaws of hell itself come time of battle. Skilled though they were, they would never survive unless he did something to strengthen them against their own fears and doubts. Those would be the most dangerous enemies they would face.

He'd spent half the night thinking of what he would say to boost his men's spirits. He had written several different speeches, read and researched a dozen scriptures, and pondered stories from history to see if there was some kind of wisdom or inspiration he could impart to them. But the morning light had come, and he still had no idea what he was going to say — at least as far as flowery speech was concerned.

His message to them would be simple: Have faith.

Two words that might just determine the outcome of the war.

Taggert Enue stood next to the large rock Elam had chosen for his speech and looked across the sea of faces assembled before him. They ranged in age from twenty-five to fifty, but the majority of them were young. Too young to be faced with what was coming in the days ahead. All but the very oldest among them had never fought a real battle — the night in Talin Pass aside — and he had serious doubts about their mettle. He pushed the thoughts aside and looked up at his younger counterpart.

Even though he outranked Elam, the young Captain was the true leader of these men, and it was to Elam that they looked for guidance. He had known that would be the case when he had relinquished command of the ten thousand he led in order to tag along here. He didn't begrudge Elam the burden he bore, and he didn't question his ability to lead. But he was concerned with his friend's state of mind.

Something about Elam had changed during the past few weeks, and Taggert wasn't sure he liked what he saw. Either his friend truly had the kind of faith he claimed, or he was crazy. Whatever the case, it was going to be an interesting ride.

Elam stood on the rock above him, looking out over the gathering. His arms were folded across his chest, and he held a book in one hand, but the intensity of his gaze was at odds with his calm stance. Taggert needed only to look into the eyes of those nearest the rock to see the effect Elam had on the gathering — they were awestruck by the sight of the young captain. Taggert had to admit he had never heard this many men so quiet.

"Thank you for assembling so quickly," Elam said, and Joselyn used the Power to send his words to the far edges of the crowd. "I will keep this short. In two days we will be attacking a force equal in size to ours but one which has the added advantage of Shadowhounds and other creatures of the dark. There may or may not be Agla'Con among their ranks as well." He paused to let his words sink in.

"I do not tell you this that your hearts may be troubled, but instead to call up a remembrance of what sets us apart from our enemies. They have forsaken the Light of Creation and turned their backs on Him who gave them life. In the dark time that will soon be upon us, let us not do the same. Instead, let us go forth with faith in Him who made us. Let us trust in His strength to preserve us."

He unfolded his arms and opened the book he held. "Let me read to you from the *Cynthian*. The Prophet Esielliar said, '*Let not your spirits be troubled, neither your hearts be weary. But let your hearts be drawn out in prayer and thanksgiving to that God who created you and who upholds you from day to day. For behold, saith the Lord, I am with thee until the end of the world, and in my hands are ye sheltered. Trust in me and ye shall be delivered.*'"

He closed the book. "Brethren," he began. "I call you brethren because we are — all of us — sons of Him whose words I just read. I call you brethren because we are a family united in the cause of defending our nation against an evil so vast we cannot even begin to look forward to victory unless we are united in our faith in God and our trust in one another. Remember that it was Elderon who created our great nation. It was He who solemnized the union between the Kelsan Lord Imor and the Elvan Princess Temifair and anointed their son as ruler of this nation. It is through that sacred lineage that the Earthsoul will be made whole. The Fairimors are the keepers of that sacred trust. We are the keepers of the Fairimor blood. We are a choice nation with a sacred trust."

He paused again and seemed to be taking measure of his audience. "It is time to uphold that trust."

Taggert looked around at the faces of the men nearest him. Not an eye blinked. Not a lip moved. Elam couldn't have had their attention any more firmly if he had used the Power. Even the forest around them had grown quiet, as if nature itself were listening.

"I do not know what the next few days or weeks will bring," Elam continued, and Taggert was drawn back in as completely as the rest of the men. "I do not claim to see the future. I do not claim to be a prophet, a preacher, or for that matter, even a great leader of men. But one claim I do make, and I make it before God as well as before you: We are here because we were chosen by God to walk this path. We are here because He sees in us the strength to carry us through to the end."

He stopped, and an embarrassed smile crept across his face. "I told you I would keep this short," he said, "so I will. But one last claim will I make." He held the *Cynthian* before him and continued. "If you will put all of your trust in God as He has requested, He will preserve you."

He drew his sword and raised it toward heaven. "Oh, Lord God Almighty," he said, "we, some of the sons of Kelsa, commend ourselves into thy hands. Go with us as we face our enemies. Strengthen our arms and our swords in the time of battle. Let not our hearts be weak, nor our spirits faint. Guide us in our path." He touched the hilt to his forehead. "For the Flame of Kelsa, the liberty of our people, and for *thy* honor, oh God, let it be done."

He lowered his sword, and two thousand voices said in unison, "Amen."

Taggert caught Elam's gaze and bowed his head in admiration. In all his years of serving in the military, he had never heard words as powerful. There was only one thing he disagreed with in all of Elam's speech: the man was indeed a great leader of men. A very great leader. Perhaps they would make it through this after all. Fate, it seemed, was at work.

七

Breiter blinked in surprise as the stack of papers in front of him was moved aside by a tray of food. He looked up, expecting to find Allisen, and blinked again as Zea smiled warmly and bent to kiss him on the cheek.

"You got up too early this morning," she scolded. "How are you going to have energy to play with your daughter if you don't sleep?"

Breiter smiled sheepishly. "I couldn't help it," he said, pulling a chair out for her and helping her ease herself into it. She sighed with the effort, then took his hand and placed it on her stomach.

"Can you feel that?" she asked. "Your baby girl says hello. She recognizes your voice."

Breiter smiled. "Of course she does," he said, putting his face close to Zea's stomach. "Hello in there. This is your daddy speaking. It's time to stretch those legs and kick your mommy in the ribs."

Zea slapped him playfully in the head. "Would you stop? She doesn't need any encouragement."

They were still laughing when Beraline Dymas exited the north tower stairwell and joined them at the table. She wore a light green skirt and white cotton blouse, and her long, dark brown hair was wound up in a bun that was held in place with a pair of laquered sticks. For the first time since arriving at Fairimor Palace, she actually looked on the verge of relaxing.

"Good morning," she said, offering her hand to Zea. "I'm Beraline. And you must be Mrs. Lyacon."

Zea smiled. "Please, call me Zea."

Beraline moved to the chair next to Zea and sat down. "I've heard about you," she said. "And the little one you carry. The time is close, yes?"

Zea nodded. "Yes."

Beraline gestured toward Zea's stomach with her hand. "I can check on her if you wish."

"You're a Healer?" Zea asked, sounding surprised.

"She's a Dymas," Breiter told her. "This is Lady Hadershi, the one I've been telling you about."

Zea smiled warmly. "Then by all means."

Beraline placed a hand on Zea's stomach and closed her eyes. A moment later she smiled. "You have a healthy young daughter in there," she said. "Do you want to know what she looks like?"

"Yes," Zea said even as Breiter answered, "No. I want it to be a surprise."

They looked at each other for a moment without speaking. Finally, Breiter laughed. "I suppose it wouldn't hurt to know a little bit about her. Unless she looks like me, of course. Tell me she doesn't look like me."

Beraline shook her head. "Well, she isn't going to have a goatee, if that's what you mean."

"Tell us," Zea said excitedly, "who does she look like?"

"She has your eyes, Zea, and her father's chin. Minus the goatee. But she does have a full head of hair, light brown from the looks of it."

Breiter took Zea's hand and winked at her. "She sounds beautiful," he said. "Just like her mother."

Beraline opened her eyes and sat back in her chair. "I understand the Healer who has been looking after you has gone to Fulrath with the others, so if there is anything I can do to help you with the delivery just let me know."

"Thank you," Zea answered. "I will."

The doors leading to the Dome opened, and Elison strode in followed by a pair of *Bero'thai*. "Good news," he called, coming toward them. "We've uncovered the location of another chapter house. Two of those who foreswore their allegiance to the brotherhood gave up its location."

"Are you sure the information is reliable?" Breiter asked.

"It has to be," Elison answered, taking a seat. "The two were being questioned separately from one another but gave the same description of the place. I told you there would be those willing to cooperate with us." He noticed the tray of food sitting on the table. "Are you going to eat that?"

Breiter grinned. "Yes. Go get your own."

"I'll fetch you something," one of the *Bero'thai* said. "What would you like?"

"Whatever Allisen will give you," Elison answered. "And have her send something for Lady Hadershi as well."

"Yes, Captain Brey," the warder answered and disappeared into the kitchens.

"So," Elison asked, "do you want to come with me on the raid?"

Breiter's eyes darted to Zea's briefly before returning to Elison's. "No," he answered, trying to keep his voice casual. "I need to finish interviewing my half of the prisoners."

Elison shrugged. "Suit yourself," he said. "But sooner or later we are going to have to work together again. It might be best if it was on our own terms and not according to the scheming of the enemy."

From the corner of his eye Breiter saw Beraline purse her lips thoughtfully. She had said much the same thing several days ago regarding death, and the words had stung him then too. Both she and Elison were right. It was foolish to be so paranoid about Elder Nesthius' prophecy. And yet he couldn't abandon the idea that he would be able to keep the prophecy from coming to pass. He had to, for all their sakes.

He glanced at Zea to find her staring uncomfortably at her hands, and he wondered what she was thinking. Was she worried that he might say yes to joining Elison? Or was she starting to believe that Elison and Beraline were right, and that he should face the prophecy down and let fate have its way? Whatever his wife's thoughts, he wasn't going to ask her about it here in front of the others. He might not like what she had to say.

Beraline broke the awkward silence. "I will accompany you if you wish, Captain," she said, and Elison nodded his thanks.

"You will be most welcome," he told her. "And Lady Korishal as well, if she wishes."

"I'll let her know what you are planning," Beraline answered. "But I think she will probably decline. She is busy testing and training several young *Dalae* who arrived at the palace early this morning. Besides, she prefers to hunt shadowspawn. It might be best if we wait until her skills as a warrior are truly needed."

"When are you planning to attack?" Breiter asked.

"As soon as they gather for one of their meetings," Elison answered. "I have men already in place within striking distance. We will be ready to hit them the moment they are all inside."

Zeniff studied the Changeling Shadan'Ko silently for a moment before speaking. *This is too good to be true,* he thought. And it had happened far sooner than he could have hoped for. Maeon must really be watching out for him.

"Are you sure?" he asked at last.

"Yes, my master," the creature mewed. "I heard it from Captain Brey himself. He plans to attack the chapter house as soon as your people gather for a meeting. He has several men watching the place and several squads of soldiers stationed within striking distance."

"And you are sure it is the one in Aldea District?"

The Changeling nodded. "I was with him when he went there this morning to study the area in order to plan his attack."

Zeniff grinned. "Then we better make sure someone is there to meet him, don't you think?"

"Shall I go?" the Shadan'Ko asked, its bright yellow eyes hungry with anticipation.

"No," Zeniff answered with a smile. "I will see to it myself. I want you to continue on as you have been. If you learn anything more, let me know."

"Yes, my master," it mewed, then morphed once again into the form of an Elvan warder. Turning, it left the room.

Zeniff reached up to scratch his cheek. What a fortuitous turn of events this was. With Elison still offering amnesty to all those willing to forsake their allegiance to the Brotherhood, the way had opened for him to lay a deadly trap for the captain. And Breiter Lyacon as well, if he could figure out a way to get the two men together. He didn't know why, but they had begun working independently of one another several days ago — at least when they were outside the palace. Even within the palace, they were seldom together for very long. He didn't believe they'd had a falling out; the two men were like brothers. Perhaps they felt they could accomplish twice as much in their fight against the Con'Kumen if they each headed a strike team. Whatever the reason, he needed to get them together for a single attack. Killing one and not the other would make any future attempts nearly impossible.

He exhaled his frustration and moved to the window to stare out at the city. He hated relying on luck to get things done. Luck was fickle. Unfortunately, it would take luck to get the two men together for an attack. He would just have to trust that Maeon would continue to take a hand in things. Otherwise he would have to be content with killing only one of the men. But which one?

It was Breiter who uncovered the location of the first chapter house, opening the way for the others to be discovered. It was Breiter who had warned Jase Fairimor of the impending assassination in Kindel's Grove before cheating death in Tri-fork on his way back to Trian. The man was as lucky as he was meddlesome.

And yet his activities were nothing more than minor nuisances compared to the vengeance Elison Brey had unleashed upon the Con'Kumen. The man was as dangerous as a Shadowhound and as crafty as a Satyr. And he had taken it upon himself to hunt the Brotherhood into extinction. Breiter may be a thorn in the Con'Kumen's side, but Elison Brey was a Dragonsword.

If he could get them both at once, excellent. If not, and he had to make an attempt on just one, it was going to be Elison Brey. He nodded in satisfaction, his decision made.

"Goodbye, Captain," he whispered to the city. "Your time has finally come."

He smiled. And then it would be time to prepare to meet Gideon when he returned with the Blood Orb. With that kind of power in hand, the Con'Kumen's conquest of Trian could begin in full. Glory would be his as he seized the throne in the name of Maeon.

But first things first. Right now he needed to pay a visit to some of his Con'Kumen and set things in motion for the assassination of Elison Brey.

The hallway leading to the outer palace was more quiet than usual, and Breiter paused a moment to look around, suddenly apprehensive about continuing on. He shouldn't have come without an escort of *Bero'thai.*

Behind him, three servants in blue livery rounded a corner and started toward him. One of them pushed a wheeled cart bearing fresh linens. The other two held feather dusters and talked in whispers as they walked. They stopped at the door to one of the apartments — he thought it might belong to one of the Wyndors — and rapped lightly on the door. After they'd entered, Breiter turned his attention to the domed rotunda marking the exit from this part of the palace.

It, too, was quiet. At least the part he could see. Most of the large room was lost behind the curvature of the walls as they stretched around to the far door — a door that should have been guarded by a pair of *Bero'thai,* but was instead manned by two Palace Guards. The attempt on his life a couple of months back flashed through his thoughts, and his hand strayed to his sword. What were they doing here? Elison had assigned them to the outer palace when he'd brought the *Bero'thai* in to watch the Fairimor household. Had he made some new arrangement with Captain O'sei that he had forgotten to mention?

"You look like you just spotted a Darkling," a voice said from behind him, and he jumped in surprise. Whirling, he had his sword halfway from its scabbard before he realized the voice belonged to Judge Bresdin Zeesrom. Bresdin wore dark grey pants, a blue-grey tunic, and a wide-brimmed hat; and without his judge's robes, he wasn't readily recognizable.

Bresdin's hands came up in a warding gesture. "Easy there, Captain. It's only me." He took a cautious step forward. "Are you all right? You seem a little jumpy."

Breiter eased his sword back into its scabbard. "I've got a lot on my mind," he mumbled. "And, yes, I'm jumpy. Especially when people sneak up behind me."

Bresdin chuckled. "I wasn't sneaking," he said, then changed the subject. "How are things going with the Con'Kumen prisoners? Are there many willing to accept amnesty in exchange for forsaking their oath?"

"More than I thought there would be," Breiter answered, starting forward. Bresdin came with him, and together they entered the rotunda. Feigning disinterest, Breiter glanced around the room. It was empty save for two more sets of Palace Guard stationed at the doors on the left and right. The doors were open, making the contrast between the *chorazin* of the inner palace and stone of the outer palace that much more noticeable. He turned his gaze on Bresdin. "And those who are willing to join us are providing some valuable information. Information that should allow us to crush the Con'Kumen once and for all."

"I hope you are right," the Chief Judge replied. "The sooner we free the city of their influence the better."

They chatted idly as they walked, and Breiter found himself relaxing for the first time all day. There was something in Bresdin's manner that was soothing, a confidence that made it easy for Breiter to let go of some of his apprehension. It wasn't until they moved through an open-aired courtyard bridging two of the towers that Elder Nesthius' words echoed through his thoughts. Instinctively he quickened his pace. With so many windows overlooking the area, it would be the perfect spot for an ambush.

Judge Zeesrom hurried to keep up. "Hey, what's the hurry?"

"Sorry," Breiter answered, once again slowing his pace. "I was thinking of something else." He had to force himself not to look up at the windows.

They reached a large antechamber with hallways branching off to various locations in the outer palace, and Breiter slowed in surprise when Bresdin started for the hallway leading to the stables. "Are you going out of the palace alone?"

The Chief Judge smiled guiltily. "I am," he answered. "It's much easier to look at the artwork at Jyoai College when I don't have a pair of *Bero'thai* standing behind me calling attention to the fact that I might be someone important. Last time I went to the museum, a group of law students learned I was there and ruined the entire afternoon with a bunch of silly questions their professor could have answered for them." He shrugged. "I know it's foolish to go alone in light of the trouble with the Con'Kumen, but I need a little anonymity from time to time. I might go insane without it."

"Well, be careful," Breiter told him worriedly. "House Fairimor needs you."

Bresdin waved dismissively. "Don't worry about me," he answered. "I do this all the time."

Breiter watched him go, then shrugged and continued on to the apartments where they were holding those who had foresworn their oath to the Con'Kumen. It was time to get some more information and hunt the Hand of the Dark into extinction.

The Grenser Chapter House in Trian's southeastern district was the largest in the city, its members the most loyal. Many had been in the Brotherhood since its inception, some thirty years earlier. Even those new to the cause had a lust for power that made Zeniff think he could trust them with this assignment. The look in their eyes showed they were excited about what a visit from him might mean. They were eager to strike back at those who were threatening their organization.

"The time has come," he told them, taking a seat in one of the cushioned sofas, "to take the heart out of Randle Fairimor's campaign to exterminate the Brotherhood." Smiles crept across their faces as he continued. "We will strike them hard, killing Elison Brey and as many of the *Bero'thai* as possible, and we will do it soon. But first we will need to get them somewhere that will make a massive strike possible. Somewhere that will show the citizens of Trian that we are a force to be reckoned with. I want the entire city to feel our wrath."

"Are we to move against the Dome again?" one of the men asked excitedly.

"Not this time. But don't worry, the Brotherhood will pay another visit to Fairimor Palace soon enough. This time we are going to let Captain Brey come to us." He grinned wickedly. "He has learned the location of the Aldea House, and he is watching it, waiting for us to gather for a meeting. We are going to give him what he wants."

Vin Shilsum, the oldest of the group, frowned thoughtfully. "But the Aldea House is small," he said. "And the surrounding neighborhood is too confined to allow any kind of a large-scale strike."

"Precisely why I need you to let Elison and his *Bero'thai* capture the Aldea House," he said, then put up a hand to still the protests forming on their lips. "Elison is offering amnesty to all those willing to forsake their allegiance to the Brotherhood and join him in his cause. I want you to do just that. After he throws you in the dungeon for a few days, he will bring you forth for interrogation. When he offers you the chance to forsake your oath, do it. Show him how sorry you are for your actions and offer to help him. Give him the location of the River Plaza Chapter House and tell him he is going to need plenty of help to take it because of how heavily fortified it is."

"But Master Zeniff," one of the young women said, "the River Plaza House has been vacant for months."

"And it will remain vacant," he told her. "The objective here is to get Elison to an area where we can launch a massive assault against him and his men. I want them all dead."

"When would you like us to stage a meeting at the Aldea House?" Vin asked.

"Tonight," Zeniff told them. "And make your resistance convincing. If Elison captures the place without a fight, he might become suspicious. If we need to lose a few lives in the process, so be it. But make sure enough of you survive to give Elison the information he will need to plan his attack on the River Plaza House. When he and his men arrive, we will be ready for them."

七

Standing in the darkness of an alleyway adjacent to the Con'Kumen chapter house, Elison Brey watched a pair of *Bero'thai* neutralize the last of the guards stationed about the property. When they signaled that all was clear, he turned to Beraline Dymas.

"Let's go," he said, then moved out of the shadows and across the street. Flickers of grey appeared from every direction as dozens of *Bero'thai* slipped from their concealment to join him. Moonlight glinted off drawn blades and the razored heads of arrows as the Elvan warders swarmed through the gardens and took up positions around the door and windows. Around back, Taka O'sei and his men were doing the same.

When Elison and Beraline Dymas reached the front porch, Beraline drew upon the Power and blew the front door inward in a spray of shattered wood. *Bero'thai* poured through the opening, and the sound of clashing steel sounded within. Drawing his sword, Elison followed. Moments later it was over.

Six Con'Kumen lay dead. A dozen more were wounded. The rest, some twenty or so, had surrendered without harm. Now, in the process of being bound by the *Bero'thai*, they showed the same look of surprise and fear that those taken in previous raids had shown.

"They never think it will happen to them, do they?" Beraline said, moving to stand beside him. "They believe they can simply do as they please and nothing will ever come along to stop them."

"I suppose it's human nature," Elison began, "to believe that one is exempt from the workings of a higher power, whether it be the laws of men or..." he paused, thinking of Breiter. Turning to meet Beraline's gaze, he continued. "Or the will of the Earthsoul."

She eyed him curiously. "And what do you believe?" she asked.

He hesitated a moment, considering. "I believe in walking the path that fate has placed before me."

CHAPTER 36

To Kill a Dragon

The vaulted corridor inside the Imperial Palace echoed hollowly with heavy-booted footsteps, and Shavis Dakshar and those who'd come with him pressed themselves deeper into the darkness among the columns and went still. Clothed in *komouri* black, they vanished into shades of lethal shadow and watched a squad of Darkling soldiers draw near.

Shavis frowned inside his *koro* mask as he studied the twisted, beastly shapes. These were different than the three groups he'd seen in the upper levels of the keep. They were half again as large and much more heavily muscled. Thick, blood-blackened armor formed a hodgepodge of protection around an array of spikes and horns, scales and bristly fur.

As the creatures filed past where Shavis hid, one paused to sniff the air, its boar-like snout working furiously as it cast about in alarm. It grunted something unintelligible to the other five, but they snarled their irritation and continued on, leaving the boar-face to confront the shadows alone.

Shavis held his breath as the creature hesitated, seemingly unsure what to do. It looked at its quickly departing comrades, then turned to peer into the shadows for a moment, its nose still working furiously. Finally, it shook its head and hurried to catch up with the others.

When they were gone, Shavis stepped out of the shadows and was met by Railen.

"What were those?" the young Shizu asked, his eyes fixed in the direction the Darklings had gone.

"Very large shadowspawn," Dai'shozen Kamishi of Clan Avalam said as he moved out of the darkness. "Fortunately, they didn't appear to be very bright."

"Or they were in a hurry," Kalear Beumestra said as he and Dai'shozen Balasei of Clan Derga slipped from the gloom, "to find out what is happening deeper inside the palace." The Sarui's rugged face creased into a frown, and his eyes narrowed to slits. "The Power draws shadowspawn the way light draws a moth, and right now, it is being wielded by several Agla'Con."

"He's right," Railen said, his voice only slightly muffled by his *koro* mask. "And we are close. I can feel it."

Shavis nodded. He'd brought Railen and Kalear for just such a reason, knowing that they would alert him to any use of the Power. His suspicion that Sagaris was under Agla'Con control had just been confirmed.

"Perhaps we should leave," Dai'shozen Balasei said softly. "We've learned what we came here to learn."

"Not all of it," Shavis said softly. "There is more to all of this than merely a resurgence of the Agla'Con. Come, I want to know what it is." Taking the lead, he started down the corridor. The others had no choice but to follow.

A short time later, the vast expanse of the palace's center rotunda came into view, and they stopped within the shadows of the corridor that had taken them there. Going to his belly, Shavis slithered forward to the railing to investigate.

He was on a second-level balcony overlooking the high-domed room, directly across from the entrance to the Emperor's audience chamber. And there, guarding the door to that chamber, stood a pair of K'rrosha.

Shavis motioned for the others to come and have a look, then they all moved back into the relative protection of the corridor. When they were out of earshot of anything that might overhear them, Shavis turned to face the others.

"Why do Greylings guard the way into the Emperor's audience chamber?" he asked. He already knew the answer to his question — or thought he did. He just wanted to hear it from someone else. That way he could be sure his fears weren't running away with his imagination.

"Because," Dai'shozen Kamishi whispered, "Sagaris is in league with those who serve Shadan."

Shavis studied each of them quietly for a moment before speaking. "Perhaps we should go find out."

⺅

Tohquin Nagaro stood in the doorway of his daughter's room and watched with a smile as she and Tey Eries played with a pair of dolls. They were pretending the dolls were mommies taking care of their baby, and moved them about the room acting out the various things mommies do. Their baby, four times larger than the dolls and with four legs, a tail, and stripes, was Tey's kitten. Wrapped snugly in a blanket and lying in a tiny wooden cradle, the little feline seemed oblivious to the girls' play. Only the occasional opening of one of its eyes to check on the little girls' whereabouts showed it was even alive.

He envied the children's play. He envied the peaceful little world they lived in. They were as oblivious to the conflicts raging in Riak as the kitten was to them. They were two, tiny, innocent people in a world full of strife. He was thankful for the gentleness of their actions. For him, listening to their laughter was an escape — a moment of refuge that buoyed his spirit and renewed his resolve. *They* were what he was fighting for, he reminded himself. And he would do everything he could to ensure they had a future. Even die if necessary.

He watched a moment longer, then turned and went down the hall to the kitchen.

Kailei stood at the counter chopping herbs for one of her soups, and he watched quietly for a moment, unwilling to interrupt her at her work. He enjoyed watching her even more than he enjoyed watching the children. He may be willing to die fighting for the children's future, but it was for Kailei that he lived. She was his life.

She turned and found him standing in the doorway, and a smile spread across her face. "I didn't hear you come in," she said, her dark eyes shining. "How long have you been back?" She moved to him and put her arms around his neck, pulling him close for a kiss.

"Just a few minutes," he answered, touching her cheek with the back of his hand. "I've been in watching the girls play."

"How did things go with Shochu?"

"The rest of the Con'Kumen received their punishment," he said, sidestepping the details. Kailei knew the punishment was death, but even after all these years, he was still uncomfortable discussing violence in her presence. "On a brighter note," he continued, "the citizens of Shochu were allowed to remain a leif. Highseat Dromensai decided against raising the Flag of Transgression, insisting that they had been deceived. Those who swore allegiance to Gahara were allowed to remain. Those who didn't were exiled. As you might imagine, there were few who didn't take the oath."

She led him to the table and they sat down. "How long do I have you for this time?" she asked, still holding his hand across the table.

He gazed into her eyes and sighed. He should have known she would sense he was only stopping by on his way to his next assignment. "About an hour," he replied. "Shavis has returned from Clan Hasho and has called for the High Clave to assemble. Apparently, Hasho wishes to join the alliance."

"Hasho," she said with a nod. "That is the fifth clan this week, is it not?"

He traced the back of her hand with his fingers, trying to understand where this sudden interest was coming from. She almost never asked him questions about the Shizu. She was, in fact, not supposed to. The potential for security leaks was one of the reasons Shizu were discouraged from marrying. Taking a wife wasn't expressly forbidden, but men who did were duty-bound to keep quiet about their assignments.

Tey Eries had changed all that. From the moment he had returned from Kelsa with the little girl and asked Kailei to care for her, his wife's interest in what he did had grown. He supposed her right to know the truth had grown with it. "Shavis is quite persuasive," he told her. "His method of dropping in with an entire legion of Shizu and exposing the Con'Kumen worship chambers has a way of getting people's attention."

"He did what?" Kailei gasped.

"It's unorthodox, I know. But it worked so well with Samochi, he's done the same thing in each of the clans since. Once the evil is exposed, the Highseat and the rest of the clave find it difficult to refute. There is still opposition, mainly from those who have been exposed, but with eight clans already pledged to this new alliance, the resistance grows weaker each time."

"How does he know where to go?" Kailei asked.

He hesitated only a moment before answering. She deserved to know the truth. All of it. "He discovered a book of names in Samochi, a kind of Con'Kumen address book, I guess you could say. Since then, he's found two more. There is enough information in those books to keep him busy hunting these vermin for a very long time."

She studied him intently for a moment before speaking. "How many of these raids have you gone on?" she asked, and he heard something in her voice he couldn't identify. Not fear exactly, and not worry. Was it resignation perhaps? After all the years they'd been married, was she just now preparing herself for the day when he wouldn't come home from a strike? Or was it because these were no longer ordinary strikes but precursors to all-out civil war?

"Three," he answered with a shrug, attempting to downplay both her question and his own thoughts. "The other clans are starting to take a more active role in the hunt, so I think my turn might be over."

"Until Sagaris," she said, and for a moment he was unable to cover his surprise.

"What makes you think we will attack Sagaris?" he asked, his features smooth once more.

"Shavis told me," she said, and he realized she knew more about what had been taking place over the past few days than she was letting on. "He and Railen stopped by to see Tey," she added. "Shavis felt it wise for me to know about his plans. If something should happen to all of you, he asked me to make sure Tey is returned to her grandfather."

Tohquin smiled. He shouldn't have been surprised by this. Shavis was breaking every other rule and tradition he came across; why not this one as well? He leaned across the table and kissed Kailei gently on the nose. "Welcome to Deathsquad Alpha, Kailei Nagaro," he said. "It sounds like Shavis has made you Gahara's first female Shizu."

She giggled and rose from the table. "About an hour, you say?" she asked, taking him by the hand. "That means we had better hurry."

His confusion lasted only until he realized she was leading him toward their bedroom.

Rocking on his heels impatiently, Raimen Adirhah knocked a second time, then leaned to the side to peer through the window of Tohquin's kitchen. Where was everyone? The clave was meeting in less than ten minutes and it was a fifteen-minute walk. If they left now, they would have to run. He shook his head in agitation. And with dusk approaching, the streets would be crowded with people on their way home for the evening, so it might take even longer than that.

The door opened, and he looked down to find Aimi and Tey. "Raimen!" they squealed in delight, and he bent to take them in his arms. They hugged him tightly, then patted his cheeks with their tiny hands.

"How are my two favorite girls?" he asked, smoothing their hair as he stood.

"Good," Tey answered and Aimi echoed her.

"Aimi," he asked, "where is your dad?"

"He's taking a nap with mommy," she answered. "Do you want me to wake him?"

"I'm awake," Tohquin said as he came into the room with an embarrassed smile on his face. Behind him, came Kailei. She was wearing a *kitara* of red silk that failed to cover as much of her legs as it should have. Her face was as red as her robe.

Raimen looked down at Aimi. "Looks like that nap did your mommy and daddy some good," he said, and from the corner of his eye he saw Kailei flinch with embarrassment.

"Girls," she said, beckoning them out of the doorway, "run into the kitchen and set the table. Dinner will be ready soon." She folded her arms beneath her breasts, and Raimen looked away when he realized the robe was the only thing she had on.

He coughed uncomfortably. "We'd better hurry," he told Tohquin. "We're going to have to run if we're to make it to the chamber on time."

Tohquin turned and kissed Kailei, and Raimen busied himself with his feet. It was amazing how quickly their embarrassment had turned into his. When Tohquin joined him, Raimen bowed a farewell to Kailei without looking at her and hastily slipped out the door.

When they were out of earshot of the house, Raimen started to chuckle. "A *nap*," he said, shaking his head in amusement.

Tohquin shrugged. "You have to tell the children something."

"I guess you do," Raimen agreed, but it occurred to him that he really wouldn't know. Unlike Tohquin, he hadn't married, choosing the safety of the Shizu code instead. History was full of accounts where the wives and children of Shizu had been taken or killed by rival clans seeking to exploit some weakness or exercise control over their enemies. The practice wasn't all that uncommon today, and it angered him that innocent women and children would be used in such a way.

He cast a sideways glance at Tohquin. He admired his friend for his choice to marry in spite of the dangers. He admired Kailei even more for being able to deal with how often Tohquin was away. It must be difficult for her to know that each time Tohquin left he might not be coming back. They were both very strong people. Much stronger than he was.

He had often wondered what it would be like to have a family of his own, but each time he thought he might actually want to see what married life was all about, his fear had gotten the best of him. He knew deep inside that if something ever happened to those he loved, he wouldn't be able to deal with the loss. And so he avoided the risk altogether, as was the Shizu way. It was a cowardly approach, to be sure, but a realistic one.

"Have you spoken to Railen recently?" Tohquin asked, and Raimen pulled himself out of his thoughts.

"No. I haven't seen him since the night he came to fetch us from Hurd's."

"He's changed," Tohquin said. "But it is a good thing, I think. He and that Sarui friend of his are heading up Shavis' new Deathsquad of the Gifted."

"I've heard about that," Raimen replied. "Not a bad idea considering how Agla'Con seem to be sprouting like weeds all over our nation. I don't mind fighting men like myself, but going against someone who uses *Ta'shaen* as their weapon is something I can do without."

Tohquin turned to look at him. "You'd better get used to the idea," he said, "because we've both been recruited."

Raimen was unable to hide his surprise. "We've what?"

"We are Gifted," Tohquin answered with a shrug. "That means we are in."

"But our abilities are nothing spectacular," he argued, not at all pleased with the idea of going to battle against those who could hurl any number of destructions at him. "Neither of us can do more than bend light, and only around ourselves at that."

"Because that is all we have learned how to do," Tohquin countered. "Kalear — he's the Sarui — says we have only harnessed a small portion of *Shiin*, and that with his guidance, we can learn to do much more than just make ourselves invisible."

"Is that so?" Raimen asked. He was still nervous that he might have to face an Agla'Con, but the possibility of increasing his abilities with *Ta'shaen* was intriguing. "That would be something."

Tohquin nodded his agreement. "I thought so too."

They hurried on, weaving their way through the crowded streets, bowing apologies to those whom they startled and nodding their recognition to those they knew. When they rounded the corner of Togaru Temple and Gahara Castle came into view at the far end of the street, they were forced to slow their walk. The line of people waiting to enter the castle stretched nearly a block. There were clave representatives from each of the eight clans Shavis had rallied to the alliance, as well as squads of Shizu and Sarui who had come as escorts.

Raimen was impressed. "I didn't realize that all the clans had been invited," he said, and Tohquin shook his head to show he hadn't either. "Maybe there is more to this than just the welcoming of Hasho into our union," he added, letting his eyes move down the line to the castle entrance. "Looks like it's going to be standing room only."

"There you two are," a voice said from within the crowd, and they turned to find Railen coming toward them. "You're late," he scolded playfully, punching each of them in the arm. "Shavis, uh, I mean Dai'shozen Dakshar, sent me to find you. He wants you to wear this." He handed them each an armband. "It is the insignia for our new squad. Come with me. I'll take you to where the rest are gathered."

"How many of us are there?" Tohquin asked.

"Eighty-three," Railen answered, the excitement in his voice evident. "Ten or so from every clan. Fifteen have the potential to become Dymas."

"And you?" Raimen asked.

"I have the potential as well." He motioned for them to follow. "Come. Highseat Dromensai wants us all present when the other Highseats arrive."

"Is that what this is for?" Raimen asked. "To present this new squad for approval?"

"That's part of it," Railen answered, looking as if he'd say more. A quick glance at the crowd silenced whatever else he had been about to say. "You'll have to wait for the rest. It will be better coming from Shav — from Dai'shozen Dakshar."

Raimen exchanged looks with Tohquin and shrugged. Knowing Shavis, it undoubtedly would. He adjusted the armband so the insignia — a flaming sword framed by a circle of blue — would be visible to those he passed. The curiosity of those who saw it, he noted, was almost as great as his.

The Clave Chamber of Gahara Castle was as full as Shavis had ever seen it, a shoulder-to-shoulder throng of Shizu black and Sarui leather interspersed with patches of brightly colored *kitara* robes. He let his eyes travel across the faces in the densely packed room, and the feeling of pride for what had been accomplished during the past eight days warred with his apprehension over what lay ahead.

Nine clans had united in the cause to destroy the Con'Kumen. Nine clans with the possibility of two more joining in the next few days. And still it wasn't enough. Sagaris was surely aware of the alliance, and the Imperial Clave had more than nine clans at their disposal. Soon they would decide this alliance was too big a threat to ignore. Especially with what he had planned.

"Honorable representatives," Highseat Dromensai said loudly, waiting as the noise in the room faded into silence. "Gahara welcomes you to the first assembly of our newly formed alliance against the Con'Kumen. And a special welcome to you, Clan Hasho, as the newest member of this union." He inclined his head toward the Hasho Highseat before continuing. "Not since the Battle of Sekigaroga, have so many clans come together in one cause. We have cleansed ourselves of the evil discovered in our midst, and we are continuing to reach out to other clans to help them do the same. It is a worthy cause, an undertaking that may very well mean the salvation of our nation as we know it."

Tereus paused, and Shavis studied the faces of those nearest him, finding in them the same grim determination he himself felt. Tereus saw it, too, and smiled. "It does my heart good to know the majority of our citizens still walk openly in righteousness as opposed to slinking through the darkness of corruption. But," he said loudly, pausing for emphasis, "it only takes a few men of power and influence to blind the eyes and cloud the minds of the many."

He made a fist and shook it angrily. "We will continue to fight this evil by exposing the Con'Kumen and their vile worship chambers. We will continue to hunt those whose names are listed in their book of names. But, as important as those tasks are, as necessary as it is for us to continue doing them, they amount to nothing more than pinpricks when compared to the size of the wound we must inflict if we hope to defeat the monstrous beast of the Con'Kumen. To kill the Dragon, one must cut off its head."

A ripple of murmurs flowed through the crowd as many in the audience followed the Highseat's words through to conclusion. "Yes," Tereus said. "We must attack the source of this corruption. We must attack Sagaris."

The murmuring erupted into full-fledged shouting, and it took several minutes for things to quiet down. "I know how you feel," Tereus told them. "The Highseats of our alliance didn't come to this decision lightly. But information has come to us recently which has sealed our course of action. If there were any other choice, believe me, we would take it." He turned to Shavis. "I have asked Dai'shozen Dakshar of Clan Gahara, Kamishi of Clan Avalam, and Balasei of Clan Derga to tell you what we know."

Shavis and the other two stepped forward. "Two nights ago," Shavis began, "I, along with Dai'shozen Kamishi and Balasei, and a few others, went by Myrscraw to Sagaris. What we found there was worse than anything we could have imagined. The city itself is patrolled by Shizu and Sarui as it should be, but in numbers we found hard to believe. The night skies are filled with creatures the size and likes of which I have never seen." He paused, not even trying to hide his frown. "But it is what we found inside the walls of the Imperial Palace that is most alarming."

He hesitated a moment before continuing. "We infiltrated the Imperial Aviary and managed to slip far enough into the palace to find that it is mostly deserted. The inner and outer walls are manned by Darkling warriors, and creatures unlike any I have ever seen patrol the palace corridors. We spotted Shadowhounds in one of the courtyards. The only people we saw were Agla'Con."

He let his gaze sweep the crowd. "We managed to sneak as far as the rotunda but had to stop there. The entrance to the Emperor's audience chamber was guarded by a pair of K'rrosha. Neither I, nor those with me, felt like taking our chances with them."

A hand went up near the front of the assembly, and Shavis recognized the man as Shozen Hattoku of Leif Iso of Clan Ieous. Shavis liked the man and trusted him to ask a relevant question. He motioned for Hattoku to speak.

"Rumor has it that only Shadan can authorize the use of the Refleshed," he said. "The presence of K'rrosha in the Imperial Palace suggests an alliance between Emperor Samal and the Shadan Cult."

Kamishi nodded. "Dai'shozen Dakshar and I thought likewise," he told the congregation. "For that reason we journeyed to Melek last night to see if there was indeed a connection." He paused and looked to Shavis.

"What we found there," Shavis said, picking up the lead, "was worse than anything we found in Sagaris. The Shadan Cult has massed an army larger than any since the Second Cleansing, and they are on the verge of entering Kelsa. I know many of you are thinking, 'So what? Kelsa is our enemy. Let them fight it out, and then we can go in and claim what is ours.'"

He made a conciliatory gesture. "Normally I would agree with you. But this army is more than a group of enraged cultists seeking to invade their neighbors to the west. It is led by an army of Agla'Con. There are Darklings, Shadow-hounds, Shadowlancers, and dozens of other creatures I don't have names for."

He took a calming breath. "My point is this: Kelsa is doomed. Even if Riak were so inclined to lay claim to the land of our First Fathers, there won't be anything left to claim. And it matters not that Sagaris is in league with this army, because those in Sagaris care nothing for our nation. Neither Riak nor Melek will gain anything from this invasion because they are nothing more than pawns to a secretive evil."

He was becoming so angry that he had to tuck his thumbs behind his belt to keep his hands from shaking. "Shadan Cult. Con'Kumen," he growled, spitting both names like a curse. "These names matter little. Both are subject to Soulbiter. *He* is their master. He is the power that drives them. He is the only one who will benefit from such a war."

He paused and looked out across the sea of faces. He had touched a collective nerve, he realized — shocking, frightening, and probably offending every person in the room. They didn't like what they'd heard, but he could tell they weren't going to shy away from it either.

"The Emperor and the members of the Imperial Clave have given themselves over to Maeon," he shouted, and his voice echoed off the far walls. He held up the book of names for them to see and shook it in his fist. "Their names are here with the rest of the Con'Kumen. They have been selling out our countrymen to Soulbiter for decades." He lowered the book and let his gaze sweep the crowd before continuing. "You want to cleanse this evil from Riak? Give me permission to remove its head."

The silence that followed lasted only a few moments before Shozen Hattoku raised his sword above his head and rattled the scabbard. "Death to Sagaris," he shouted, and a thousand voices took up the call. As Shavis watched, a bristling sea of swords was raised and the rattling of scabbards grew deafening.

He turned to Tereus, and the Highseat nodded grimly. Shavis brought his fist to his chest in salute. *Two days to finish preparations*, he thought grimly. *Two days before Riak plunges headlong into civil war.*

After the cheering subsided, Tohquin listened as Shavis introduced the Deathsquad of the Gifted. He called them *tres'dia* — Fire Sword in the Riaki tongue — and explained their purpose in the upcoming conflict. When he finished, he asked for all Shozen and Dai'shozen to stay so they could begin planning the attack on Sagaris. Everyone else was dismissed.

Kalear Beumestra called for the members of *tres'dia* to follow him, and Tohquin fell in behind Railen and Raimen as they filed through the doors leading to the rear of the castle. He glanced down at the armband Railen had given him and marveled at how quickly life could change.

A little more than a month ago he had been an ordinary Shizu sent to carry out a routine strike against a Kelsan enemy. Such a small act to have snowballed into such a maelstrom of conflict. Such a small thing to have turned life in Riak upside down.

That one strike had led to the uncovering of the Con'Kumen, started Shavis' investigation into the source of the evil, and ultimately put Riak on the brink of civil war. It was amazing how something which seemed so trivial at first could have such far-reaching ramifications.

And then there was Tey.

Thinking of her brought a smile to his lips. If anyone would have told him that the Eries Deathstrike would result in his caring for the general's granddaughter until she could be safely returned to him, he would have said they were crazy. If they'd told him that bringing Tey into his home would light Kailei's desire for more children, he would have laughed in their face.

The procession slowed, then stalled altogether as those near the front began funneling through the single door leading to the rear courtyard. Raimen and Railen turned to face him. The older of the two was shaking his head.

"Railen's been holding out on us," Raimen said, shooting the fledgling Dymas an accusatory stare. Tohquin raised a questioning eyebrow at Railen and waited.

"It's not my fault," Railen said defensively. "I only got back from Hasho a little while ago. And besides, Shavis told me to keep quiet."

Raimen looked at Tohquin. "He accompanied Shavis to both Sagaris and Melek," he said, shaking his head in awe. "Just *listening* to Shavis was enough to turn my blood cold."

"It was much worse in person," Railen said. "Let me assure you."

"Do we have a chance?" Tohquin asked.

Railen exhaled slowly. "To be honest," he said, casting about to make sure no one was listening, "I don't know. Shavis must think so or he wouldn't risk it."

He reached up and ran his fingers through his hair. "As for Kelsa...." He paused, shaking his head. "It will take an act of God to save them."

CHAPTER 37

A Storm of Arrows

The morning breeze blowing down from the mountains behind Fairimor Palace was cool and refreshing, and Randle Fairimor breathed it in appreciatively as he and Cassia made their way through the gardens of the Overlook. The mountains to the east were rimmed with gold. The tops of the tallest trees of the garden were painted a deep golden-orange, their leaves shimmering and flickering like fire as they rippled in the breeze. The top of the Dome and surrounding towers shone brightly as well. Only the grey-green shapes of *Bero'thai* slipping among the foliage ruined the perfect beauty of the moment.

Randle did his best to ignore them, trying instead to focus on the serenity of the gardens. For the hundredth time this week he wished he could send the warders away so he and his wife could have a moment to themselves. The life of a king, he decided, was not nearly so grand as people imagined it to be. The lack of privacy was maddening.

Cassia noticed his frown and squeezed his hand reassuringly. But considering all that was troubling him right now, it didn't help much.

They reached the eastern edge of the Overlook and gazed down at the waking city. Still cloaked in shadow, it spread before them in a patchwork of greys and browns. It was a maze of streets and buildings as vast as any in the world. It was prosperous, peaceful, and civilized. And yet it was beginning to destroy itself from within, thanks to the Con'Kumen.

But not for much longer, he vowed. *Soon the Con'Kumen will be no more.*

The line of sun creeping down the face of the Dome reached him and Cassia, and they squinted at the brightness. Within minutes, the whole of the city was bathed in the soft, orange light.

"There is much worth fighting for down there," Cassia whispered.

Randle cast a sideways glance at her. "But will there be anything left once the fighting is over?" he asked.

Cassia frowned worriedly. "Precisely why I'm starting to worry that sending all the Gifted to Fulrath is a mistake. If things do turn ugly, we are going to need more than Ladies Hadershi and Korishal to fight alongside our troops. We are going to need our own Army of the Gifted."

Randle considered. She was right, of course. But there was nothing he could do about those he'd already sent to help Croneam. He would just have to hope that more arrived to replace them. He put his arm around his wife's shoulders. "You are right," he told her. "And so any others who arrive will be apprenticed to Beraline and Marithen."

"Thank you," she said, then turned to gaze out at the city. A short time later she pointed to a squad of *Bero'thai* moving across the courtyard below the Overlook. "Isn't that Breiter and Lady Hadershi there with the warders?"

Randle held his hand up to his eyes to block the sun-glare. "Yes, it is," he answered. "You've got good eyes."

Cassia smiled at the compliment. "It's nice to see Breiter getting some fresh air," she said. "I was starting to wonder if he would ever set foot outside the palace again."

"He goes out all the time," Randle told her. "Just not with Elison."

Cassia frowned at him. "Why? Did they have a disagreement?"

Randle hesitated a moment before answering. "No. They are still the very best of friends. Breiter is just..." he broke off, shaking his head, "he's trying to avoid the fulfilling of prophecy."

"What prophecy?" Cassia asked, her eyes narrowing with concern.

Randle watched Breiter and his *Bero'thai* move through the palace gate and disappear into the inner city. When they were gone, he turned to look at Cassia. Her face was expectant as she waited for him to answer. Taking her hand, he turned back toward the Dome. "It's a bit complicated," he said. "Come, I'll tell you on the way back inside."

The doors leading in from the Dome opened, and Elison looked up to find Randle and Cassia coming in with a contingent of *Bero'thai* on their heels. As they did almost every morning, they'd gone out to the gardens of the Overlook to have a relaxing moment together before facing the burdens placed upon them by their positions as King and Queen. The look in Cassia's eyes told him something had ruined the moment.

He rose from his breakfast and moved toward them. "What is it?" he asked. "You look troubled." He glanced at the *Bero'thai* for an answer, but Lourin, the eldest of the five, shrugged.

Cassia stopped in front of him, her eyes searching as she looked up into his face. "Randle told me of Elder Nesthius' prophecy concerning you and Breiter," she said.

Elison chuckled. "Oh, that," he said, turning and gesturing her and Randle toward the table. "I keep forgetting about it until someone brings it up."

Cassia's eyes went wide with surprise. "How can you forget about something like that?" she asked incredulously.

"You look hungry," Elison told her. "Come, have some breakfast." He gestured to Lourin. "Would you tell Allisen to bring something up?"

"Yes, Captain Brey," the Elvan warder replied, starting for the kitchens.

When they were seated, Cassia leaned forward and fixed him with a stare. "You haven't answered my question," she said pointedly.

Elison shrugged. "I guess I don't ever truly forget about the prophecy," he told her, setting his fork down and leaning back in his chair to look at her. "I've just quit worrying about it. I'm not going to let it interfere with me doing my job. If it happens, it happens."

"I've never considered any prophecy from Elder Nesthius to be an *if*," she retorted. "Elison, you and Breiter are in danger!" Realizing that she was on the verge of shouting, she took a moment to compose herself. When she continued, her voice was much softer. "Aren't you going to do anything?"

Elison sighed. He'd had this exact discussion with Breiter a dozen times already — and Randle and Zea and Lady Hadershi as well — and no amount of talking was going to change a bloody thing. He glanced briefly at Randle before looking Cassia in the eyes. "What am I to do?" he asked softly. "You said yourself that this is not an *if*. It is a *when*. It is going to happen no matter what Breiter or I do. Accepting that fact allows me to focus on the present and what needs to be done right now to exterminate the Con'Kumen."

"And Breiter?"

"Breiter is as jumpy as a cricket on a hotplate," he told them. "But he is still getting his job done, so I can't complain. If anything, his paranoia about the future is sharpening his focus on the present. Right now, nothing is escaping his notice."

Cassia didn't seem convinced, but she let the topic die. "Where was he going just now?" she asked, changing the subject.

"To the art museum at Jyoai College," Elison said, shrugging. "He didn't say why, but I got the feeling it has something to do with our hunt for the

Con'Kumen."

"At the art museum?" Randle asked.

"I know," Elison said. "It didn't make sense to me either." He shrugged. "But if Breiter thinks it is important, I trust him. I just hope he doesn't take too long. I need him to help interview the prisoners captured during the Aldea raid."

"Have you learned anything from them yet?" Randle asked.

Before Elison could answer, Allisen came in bearing a tray of food. He waited until she returned to the kitchens before speaking. "I haven't actually spoken to any of them yet. I wanted them to get a feel for what life in the dungeon might be like before I offered them amnesty for information. Free them too quickly, and the information might not be as reliable."

"When will you start?" Randle asked.

"As soon as I finish my breakfast," Elison replied. "Our spies have already determined which of those taken in the Aldea raid are the most likely to give us valid information, so we will start with them."

"Spies?" Cassia said, sounding surprised. "You have spies in the dungeon?"

Elison nodded. "Many of those who forsook their allegiance to the brotherhood taught us the hand signals and other secret signs the fiends use to communicate and to identify one another. We taught them to a few of our most reliable warders and put them in among the prisoners. They listen to them talk amongst themselves and identify those most likely to repent. It was Breiter's idea, actually. And so far it has worked well for us." He laughed. "Breiter may be paranoid, but he thinks of everything." He pushed his plate aside and rose. "Now, if you will excuse me, I have some interrogations to perform."

The guard handed the sketch of Judge Zeesrom back to Breiter. "Yeah, I know the man," he answered. "He's a pretty nice fellow for a judge. But I haven't seen him in the museum in over a month. Are you sure he said he was coming here?"

"That's what he said," Breiter answered. "But he was also dressed in such a way as to avoid notice. Said he didn't want to be recognized because the law students pester him."

"Now, that's true," the guard replied. "It happened the last time he visited, now that I think about it. But like I said, that was over a month ago. He hasn't been back since, at least through this entrance. You could try the private entrance at the far side of the building. It's to the right of the oil paintings. Small door, comes in from a courtyard near the dormitories. It's possible he came in that way. A person of his status would have clearance to use it."

"Thank you," Breiter said, tucking the sketch into his pocket. "We'll check it out." He and Beraline started across the museum, and his escort of *Bero'thai* fanned out around them. They moved nonchalantly, as if they were looking at the hundreds of sculptures displayed on the stands and pedestals, but Breiter knew better. The *Bero'thai* were looking at everything *but* the exhibit.

Beraline, on the other hand, seemed preoccupied with the art, pausing occasionally to study this piece or that. A large bronze statue of a wild boar caught her attention and she ran her fingers along the backbone, tracing the ridge of bristly fur. "Looks very much like a Shadowhound, doesn't it?" she said. "Minus the spikes, of course. And the claws."

Breiter raised an eyebrow at her, and she hurried to catch up. They started walking, and she looked over at him. "They are related, you know. Boars and Shadowhounds. Most shadowspawn stem from creatures native to this world, creatures that are taken and twisted by the power of the Agla'Con, or bred with demons from the realm of Con'Jithar."

"I've always thought of Shadowhounds as more like a wolf," Breiter told her. "Especially considering how long their legs are. Not to mention their teeth."

"They have wolf in them as well," Beraline said. "And probably several other things I don't know about." She blew out her cheeks resignedly. "But it is their demon blood that makes them so vicious. It is their demon blood that gives them the ability to walk up stone walls, and kill with nothing more than a scratch."

Breiter glanced over at her. "You know a lot about this, I see."

She smiled. "Marithen taught me."

He was quiet a moment, considering. Truth be told, Marithen Korishal frightened him as badly as shadowspawn did. *And almost as much as Nesthius' prophecy,* he added, then pushed the thought away. "She is a good woman," he said at last and meant it. What scared him was the knowledge that even good people could do bad things if they didn't possess a full state of mind.

They reached the private entrance, and Breiter showed the guard the sketch of Judge Zeesrom. "Do you know this man?" he asked.

The guard looked at the sketch for a moment, then nodded. "He's come to the museum from time to time. He's a judge, isn't he?"

"He is," Breiter answered. "Has he come here in the last week? It would have been four days ago, specifically."

"Not that I remember," the guard said. "The only people who come through this door are the professors and a few of their privileged students."

"Thank you," Breiter said, and he and Beraline started away.

When they were out of earshot of the guard, Beraline asked softly, "Now what?"

"We put a *Bero'thai* on him," he told her. "I want to know where he is going when he leaves the palace. It's obvious he didn't come here like he told me he was going to."

"And...?"

Breiter narrowed his eyes. "I don't like being lied to."

"It's possible he simply changed his mind and did something else instead."

"I know," Breiter whispered. "And that's what scares me."

The Con'Kumen prisoner looked up in surprise as Elison sheathed his sword. Like all the others before her, this one, too, had fully expected to die and had been willing to do so if it meant saving her family from those she'd forsaken.

He offered the young woman his hand. "You've proven your loyalty to your family," he told her. "And I will do my best to protect them. Now, prove your loyalty to Kelsa by giving me information that will lead to the destruction of the Con'Kumen."

She looked at him in disbelief for a moment, but finally took his hand and let herself be helped to her feet. "You're not going to kill me?" she asked.

"Not if you are sincere about forsaking your oath to the Con'Kumen," he told her.

"And..." she hesitated, "and you will protect my family from retaliation?"

"Yes."

She looked briefly at Captain O'sei sitting at the table, then fastened her eyes on his once more. "I will tell you whatever you want to know," she said.

Elison smiled at her, then motioned for the *Bero'thai*. "Take her to the interview room," he told them. "Allow her to bathe and give her something to eat. I'll be along shortly."

"Yes, Captain Brey," they said, motioning for the woman to join them.

She started forward but stopped and turned back to face him. "What day is it?" she asked.

Elison stared at her blankly for a moment. "It's the eighteenth, I believe," he said, looking to Taka for confirmation. The captain nodded.

"Then you are in luck," she told them. "The Con'Kumen in the northeastern quadrant gather on the eighteenth at the River Plaza Chapter House for their monthly meeting." She shook her head. "Only the eighteenth," she said in wonder. "It felt like I was in here longer than two days."

Elison gave her a sympathetic smile. "Not being able to see the sun go down throws off your sense of timing."

She returned the smile. "Be careful if you go after them," she cautioned. "There will be Con'Kumen from five or six chapter houses in attendance. And they may have as many as five Agla'Con with them."

"Thank you..." he said, waiting for her name.

"Zephira."

"Thank you, Zephira," he told her. "I'll be along shortly to have you draw me a map of this place."

Nodding, she let the *Bero'thai* lead her away.

Elison turned his gaze on his friend. "Finally," he said, making a fist, "the break we have been looking for."

Taka rose and moved from behind the table. "This is going to be big," he said. "Do you think Ladies Hadershi and Korishal will be up to the task? Five Agla'Con might be more than they can handle."

"They'll handle it," he said, then punched Taka in the arm excitedly. "This is it, my friend. Tonight, we bring the bloody brotherhood to its knees."

A knock on the door of his study brought Zeniff out of the book he was reading, and he glanced at the clock in surprise. It was just after eleven; he wasn't due at the courthouse for another three hours. *This had better be important,* he thought irritably, pulling his robe around him as he moved to the door.

"Yes," he called. "Who is it?"

"One who serves," came the reply.

Zeniff grinned in satisfaction and pulled open the door, motioning the Shadan'Ko inside.

Like a well-trained dog, it moved to its customary spot in front of his chair and waited for him to sit down.

Adjusting his robes, he studied the creature without speaking. It met his gaze, its Elvan eyes unblinking, and once again he found himself marveling at the creature's abilities. If he didn't already know better, he would have sworn he was looking at a real Elvan *Bero'thai*. Changelings were rare to begin with — one so cunning and disciplined was nothing short of a miracle. "You have news for me?" he asked.

The Changeling nodded. "Captain Brey has learned the location of the River Plaza Chapter House as you wished, my master," it said. "He plans on raiding it this afternoon."

"This afternoon?" he asked, a wave of surprise washing through him. "Don't you mean this evening?"

The creature grunted. "No. The one called Zephira told him that your people are already assembled, and Elison plans on attacking before they can leave. He said it was just as well to attack while it is still light. He wants the general public to see what happens to those who turn against their government. And he believes that since all the other raids have happened at night, the

Con'Kumen won't be expecting a strike during the day."

Blood of Maeon, he thought darkly. *Now I'm going to have to hurry.* His fingers tightened on the arm of the chair in irritation. He hated hurrying. It always led to mistakes and missed opportunities. "Did he say what time?" he asked, doing his best to shake off his displeasure.

"Five," the Shadan'Ko answered promptly.

Zeniff relaxed, a smile creeping over his face. *Plenty of time to get my men into position*, he decided, then looked up at the Shadan'Ko. "You have done well," he told it. "And your actions merit a reward. Tonight, when I return from the attack, you will feast on the flesh of Elison Brey."

Breiter dismissed the Con'Kumen prisoner and waited while two of the *Bero'thai* escorted him away to the interview room. When they were gone, he turned to Gavin, the blonde-haired warder who'd helped with today's interviews. "So, what do you think?"

Gavin's eyes narrowed, and he pursed his lips distastefully. "I think he was lying."

"Good," Breiter said. "So do I." He scratched at his goatee thoughtfully. "But what was he lying about? The River Plaza House or forsaking his oath to the Con'Kumen?"

"I'd say both," Gavin replied. "I don't pretend to be Gifted with Discernment, but everything about that man resonates deception."

"I think so, too," Breiter said, pulling his watch from his vest pocket and flipping open the cover. Three o'clock. He blew out his cheeks wearily. He and Gavin had been at this for most of the afternoon. "And I don't think he is alone in his deception," he said, tucking his watch away. "Has Elison learned anything from his half of the prisoners?" he asked. "If so, I would be curious to know if it had anything to do with this River Plaza House."

Gavin shrugged. "I haven't seen Captain Brey since early this morning," he replied. "I know he came to the dungeons to do interrogations, but he wasn't here very long. He left with Captain O'sei while you and Lady Hadershi were still at the museum."

"Did he say where he was going?" Breiter asked.

The warder's head swivelled from side to side. "I didn't have an opportunity to ask, but judging from how many *Bero'thai* went with them, I'd say he and Captain O'sei were preparing to conduct another raid."

Breiter made a fist. "Good. It's about time we hit those mongrels again. This time I hope it hurts them badly enough to make them reconsider their cause." He glanced at where the Con'Kumen had knelt in the sand, then smoothed the area with the toe of his boot. "I know Elison wishes to keep the beheadings to a minimum, but too little of their blood has been shed by my reckoning. Especially after the destruction they wrought that night in the Dome."

Gavin nodded in agreement. After a moment he gestured to the door through which the Con'Kumen had just exited. "So, what do we do about our dishonest friend?"

"We give him a chance to talk," Breiter said. "But not in the way he or the others think. Come. I'll explain on the way to the interview room."

Zephira looked up as the door opened and Vin Shilsum was ushered inside by a pair of Elvan warders. The two bowed politely to her, then exited the room, locking the door from the outside and leaving Vin to stare in surprise at her and five other members from the Aldea Chapter House.

She understood what he was feeling. She'd only just arrived herself, after having spent the day in a room in the outer palace guarded by a pair of *Bero'thai*. This room, with its walls and ceiling constructed of *chorazin*, was somewhere in the inner palace. It was also well-furnished, with several plush sofas, a half dozen chairs, a table with food, and two large mirrors on adjacent walls. She never would have imagined that she and the others would be treated so nicely.

Vin must have been thinking the same thing as he moved to the table and picked up a slice of ham. Turning to face the rest of them, he smiled. "Things went exactly as Master Zeniff said they would," he told them. "That fool Lyacon offered me amnesty for nothing more than an oath forsaking the Brotherhood. And he was so excited by the news of the River Plaza Chapter House, I wouldn't be surprised if he is on his way to raid it right now." He glanced at the clock on the wall and laughed. "If he hurries, he might reach it in time to see Elison and all of his bloody *Bero'thai* walk into our trap."

Zephira smiled appreciatively. "Master Zeniff is cunning. But I want you to make sure you tell him who divulged the information to Elison Brey. It was quite a bit of acting, if I do say so myself. Perhaps after they let us out of here, I will go back to the university and rejoin the theater."

Vin snorted. "Once Master Zeniff finds out what you have done for the Brotherhood, he may very well give you the theater as a gift. He may even — " he cut off as the door flew open and a dozen *Bero'thai* swarmed in with swords drawn. Their faces were set, and there was death in their eyes.

Zephira's heart froze in her chest as she watched them come for her. *They know,* she realized. *Somehow they know.* Turning to face them, she forced her fear away and did the first thing that came to mind. "Glory be to Maeon," she snarled, and then they took her.

Standing in an adjacent room, Breiter Lyacon watched through the trick mirror as the *Bero'thai* bound the Con'Kumen prisoners and led them away. When they were gone, he turned to Gavin. "Take them back to the interrogation room in the dungeon and execute them," he told the warder. "When you finish there, put their heads on pikes in front of the Aldea Chapter House. I want Master Zeniff to know I am on to him." He started for the door.

"Where are you going?" Gavin asked.

Breiter hesitated as the nightmare he'd had every night for the past week flashed through his mind. *It's coming true,* he thought resignedly. *The bloody thing is actually coming true.* Taking a deep breath, he forced his dread away. "To warn Elison."

The assault on the Con'Kumen chapter house was swift, the show of force impressive. All across the plaza, stunned citizens stood in stupefied wonder as seventy-five Elvan *Bero'thai* poured from surrounding alleyways and took up positions around one of the plaza's three-storied buildings. Behind them came two hundred City Guardsmen, blue-laquered armor shining, swords forming a bristling line of steel that cordoned off the entire southwest corner of the plaza and closed off the streets running behind and parallel to the building.

Standing at the fountain in the center of the plaza, Elison Brey gazed upon the juggernaut and smiled with grim satisfaction. *This is it,* he thought excitedly. *The beginning of the end for the brotherhood.*

He glanced at Ladies Hadershi and Korishal and found faces pinched with determination. Neither woman would embrace the Power unless it was necessary, but if it did come to that, each was an army unto herself. Their eyes met his, and he nodded.

Together they started across the plaza.

The rooftop cafe of the *River Plaza Inn* was one of the finest cafes in all of Trian. The serving girls were beautiful, the food was delicious, and the dappled shade of its arching, ivy-covered trellises provided a cool, comfortable place for patrons to sit and sip their drinks while they enjoyed a commanding, third-story view of the plaza below. For Zeniff, that view was even more important than ever as he watched Elison and his two Dymas move across the plaza toward the chapter house.

This is it, he thought eagerly. *Time for Elison to die.* He would love to simply strike the man down with the Power, but he feared discovery by Marithen Korishal. The woman was as skilled as Gideon and had the temper of a

Shadowhound when provoked. Truth be told, she frightened him more than any Dymas alive. No. He would just have to kill Elison and his men the old-fashioned way.

Rising, he moved to the wrought-iron banister at the edge of the roof to study the scene before him. Elison's men had moved into position around the chapter house, Bero'thai in the front, City Guard in the back. The way they were deployed showed Elison's desire to take as many prisoners as possible while minimizing the loss of life on both sides. It was a good plan, he conceded, and would have been successful, if the captain's target were legitimate. He chuckled. Disappointing his enemies was always such a pleasure.

He glanced at the other six rooftop cafes surrounding the plaza and smiled grimly. A dozen archers were stationed at each — men and women who had begged for the opportunity to strike back at the man who was hunting them. Bows in hand, they stayed in the shaded areas beneath the trellises, back out of Elison's line of sight. A dozen more men waited on the ground level of each building with swords and shields in hand. Their orders were to attack any who survived the initial volleys, civilians included. He wanted all of Trian to feel the pain of this attack.

Elison reached the chapter house, and Zeniff felt a surge of Ta'shaen as Lady Korishal blew the door from its hinges with a fist of Air. He watched the Bero'thai swarm inside, then moved away from the banister as Elison and the Dymas went in after them. Grinning, he took a seat at a table in the shade and watched his archers edge into position at the edge of the cafe. A couple of minutes for Elison and his men to discover that they'd been duped, and the Brotherhood would paint the plaza red with blood.

Shouting for those ahead to move aside, Breiter urged his horse onward, weaving his way down Trian's main avenue with little regard for those he sent scurrying for safety. Horses reared in fright, throwing riders and rocking carriages. Women dropped baskets or packages as they scooped up frightened children. Here and there, an angry curse was hurled his way as people barely managed to avoid being run down. Somewhere behind him, three squads of Bero'thai were trying to keep up but were finding it difficult to do so. One man could speed through the streets this way; sixty needed a bit more room.

Breiter leaned forward in the saddle and rode for all he was worth, ignoring the chaos he was causing. He would apologize to people later. Right now he needed to reach Elison.

The clock tower of Trian's Central Plaza came into view, and Breiter's throat tightened with fear when he saw the time. If the report he'd gotten from the

Bero'thai was correct, Elison would be attacking in the next five minutes. Offering a silent prayer, he urged the horse to run faster — but even at this speed, he was still ten minutes away.

He angled across Central Plaza toward the cream-colored arch marking the entrance to North Road. People scattered at his approach, but he barely noticed. Streaking past the arch and on down the street, he rode like a madman. Minutes later, he reached the street that would take him to River Plaza.

Expecting to find the way choked with people, he slowed his horse as he turned the corner and was surprised to find the way ahead virtually empty. There were so few people, in fact, he wondered for a moment if he had taken a wrong turn. A quick glance at several storefronts told him this was indeed the right way, and he urged his mount into a gallop once more, free to make a straight line down the center of the street without fear of trampling someone. He held his breath. This was going to be close.

Two blocks short of the arch marking the entrance to the plaza, things went horribly wrong as a wagon exited a side street in front of him. Its young driver, obviously unskilled at handling the team of horses, barely managed to halt them before they thundered up onto the boardwalk in front of them. The heavily laden wagon closed off the street like a wall.

With no time to stop, Breiter's mount tried to jump the wagon and slammed into the mound of goods with the force of a battering ram. The crunch of broken crates and shattering glass was followed by the gut-wrenching sound of snapping bones as the horse broke both its front legs. Breiter was thrown violently forward, glanced off the back of the horse's head, and somersaulted forward into the street beyond. He struck the ground with his shoulder, and light filled the inside of his head as he rolled to a stop. Dazed, he lay still for a moment and tried to figure out what had happened.

Drawn by the horrible sound of the collision, people rushed from the surrounding buildings to investigate. Several knelt at his side to see if he was all right, and he gazed up into faces lined with concern. One elderly woman put a hand on his forehead and made a tisking sound.

"You military boys are always in such a hurry," she said. "And look what it got you. Whatever business you had certainly couldn't be worth risking your life over."

Breiter pushed her hand away and rose to his feet. "It certainly is," he told her, then pointed to the wagon and his dying horse. "Get that bloody wagon out of the way so the rest of my men can get through here," he shouted. "And somebody put that horse out of its misery." Without waiting to see if they obeyed, he started running.

Two blocks, he thought angrily. *Two bloody blocks. If not for the fool in the wagon I would have been there already.* Grinding his teeth in frustration, he ignored the pain in his shoulder and ran.

Elison stared at the vast assembly hall on the second floor of the chapter house and shook his head in disbelief.

The room was empty.

The whole bloody building was empty, in fact. Oh, there were a few robes and medallions, and a jeweled dagger or two scattered about, but the place looked to have been abandoned months ago.

He snorted in disgust. "The girl Zephira must have had the wrong information," he said at last. "Or..." he hesitated, unable to finish the thought.

"Or she lied to you," Beraline finished for him.

Elison frowned. "That would be a very bad mistake on her part," he said darkly. "I will only offer amnesty to these vermin once." He took hold of a chair and tossed it across the room. It slammed into the black-laquered podium in a crunch of wood. "Come on," he said. "The sooner we return to the palace, the sooner I can have a little chat with Zephira."

Movement at the arch caught Zeniff's attention, and he turned to see a lone figure running into the plaza. He held his sword in one hand and was waving at the soldiers surrounding the chapter house with the other. He was shouting to them, but his words were lost in the clamor of civilian voices.

With a quick glance at the chapter house to see that Elison and the Dymas were yet inside, Zeniff opened his Awareness just enough for a quick, searching thrust in the direction of the running figure. It was Breiter Lyacon.

"Glory be to Maeon," he said with a grin, then turned to his archers. "Let the others handle Elison," he told them. "I want you to kill that one." He pointed to Breiter. "I have a thousand gold marks for the one who brings him down."

As Breiter neared the fountain in the center of the plaza, the world around him seemed to slow. Everything came into sharp focus — both sight and sound — and he had the sudden, unmistakable feeling that this had all happened before.

His eyes fell on a young girl in a blue dress, sitting on the fountain's edge. She held a small birdcage on her lap, clutching it protectively as she watched the soldiers surrounding the chapter house. She flinched as he ran past her, her eyes going wide with fright as she heard what he was saying.

"It's a trap," he continued to shout, his voice raw with the effort. "Ready for attack."

Those soldiers closest to him turned to regard him curiously, then brought up their shields and cast about in alarm. He raced past them and on toward the chapter house. He was nearly there when Elison and the two lady Dymas strode out into the light.

A heartbeat later the entire area came alive with arrows.

Elison took one look at Breiter racing toward him with sword drawn and knew instinctively what was coming. As much as his friend had tried to avoid it, fate, it seemed, had come calling.

He shouted a warning to Ladies Hadershi and Korishal, but it came too late. The sickening *hiss-shump* of pierced flesh sounded all around him, and he turned to find Lady Korishal clutching at an arrow protruding from her stomach. A second arrow had pierced her thigh. Beside her, Lady Hadershi was blinking in surprise at an arrow that had taken her high in the chest. Elison caught her as she staggered to one side, then shielded her body with his as arrows continued to fall all around them, kicking up sparks when they hit paving stones, drawing Elvan blood when they hit home. Already a dozen *Bero'thai* lay dying.

Several who weren't wounded rushed to his side, and he handed Beraline over to them. Her eyelids were fluttering, and her eyes were rolled back in her head. "Get her inside," he ordered, then rushed to Marithen Dymas.

Still clutching at the arrow in her stomach with one hand, the elderly Dymas made a warding gesture with the other, and the hail of arrows plunging toward them clattered loudly against an unseen barrier a few feet above their heads. He caught her in his arms and started for the doorway, eager to get her to safety.

"No," she hissed, "not until I stop the archers."

Nodding, he turned her toward the plaza. A moment later the rooftop cafe of a nearby inn was torn apart by several stabs of silver-blue lightning. Bodies tumbled through the air, flailing, rag-doll forms that thudded onto the paving stones and went still.

Marithen struck a second roof, and then a third, reducing them and their inhabitants to smoking fragments of flesh, wood, and ivy. The storm of arrows lessened dramatically, but the angry Dymas wasn't finished. She buried a fourth cafe beneath a red-hot ball of fire that set the remainder of the building ablaze and blew out the windows of nearby buildings. A fifth exploded upward in a spray of wood, plaster, glass, and bodies — a plume of destruction that rained debris on the area like ash spewed from an erupting volcano.

Before she could strike again, the shield she held above them rocked beneath a stab of lightning that rattled Elison's teeth and made his hair stand on end.

Marithen snarled like a wild animal, her eyes flashing with a killing intensity that had lost all traces of sanity. "Agla'Con," she hissed, then pummeled another cafe with stab after stab of lightning, crushing it right down to its foundation.

As the last peel of thunder faded into silence, Marithen sighed wearily and collapsed unconscious into his arms. The protective barrier above him vanished, and arrows fired from the only remaining rooftop hissed around him once more. Shielding Marithen's body with his, he took her inside the chapter house and laid her on the floor next to Beraline. Drawing his sword, he moved back outside.

A large group of *Bero'thai* had taken up positions around the remaining cafe and were shooting down every archer foolish enough to show his or her head. The rest of the plaza was in chaos, a tumult of clashing steel and armor as *Bero'thai* and City Guardsmen cut down the dozens of Con'Kumen who had rushed from the buildings to attack, but who had found themselves outnumbered because of Lady Korishal's quick and thorough destruction of the archers. The battle, it seemed, was all but over.

Not that it matters, Elison thought.

Steeling himself, he moved through the carnage in search of the body he knew he would find.

CHAPTER 38

Springing the Trap

Normally the kind of curses Borilius was hurling into the air would make Brysia frown with contempt. Now, however, she could barely hold back the smile threatening to steal over her face and had to turn away to keep the Agla'Con from seeing her satisfaction. He was angry enough as it was. No need to aggravate him further.

They'd been anchored along the bank of Illiarensei since early morning, and the Shizu that Gwuler had sent to search for the location of the Veilgate had not yet returned. It was now late afternoon and Borilius' temper was as hot as the jungle air. He was especially frustrated that they had been forced to sit here, fully exposed to any Power-sensitive Arkanians who might be in the area.

She knew enough of their odd religion to realize his fears were founded. Those Arkanians who were Gifted to the level of Dymas usually set themselves up as village priests. Once in power, they used their abilities to offer people of lesser abilities to the demon gods they called *Con'droth*. She wasn't sure, but she suspected the demons were creatures from the realm of Con'Jithar. The hypocrisy of it all made her shudder. It also made her glad that Borilius had decided to be cautious.

"I knew I should have gotten the exact location of the Veilgate from Falius before he got himself killed," Borilius growled. "An army couldn't find anything in that mess." He spat at the dense mass of foliage overhanging the banks of the river for emphasis.

"The Shizu will find it," Gwuler said, making a placating gesture with his hand. "We must be patient. It is a large area to search."

"Precisely why I wish Falius had told us more than he did," Borilius yelled. Throwing his hands in the air, he stomped away down the deck. Con'Kumen scattered at his approach, but he ignored them the way he would a gnat. "What if he lied about this place?" he shouted, then turned around and moved back to face Gwuler. "It's a long way to travel for nothing."

"We have the Talisman and the Sister Queen," Gwuler replied softly. "If we have to, we can sail to Vakala and return to Melek from there."

Brysia was amazed at how calm the Riaki remained in spite of Borilius' ranting. If she could, she would have slapped the Zekan's face several hours ago. Still, it was good to see him so out of sorts. The greater his anger and frustration, the more clouded his judgment. One or two little mistakes, and Gideon or Jase would crush him.

Borilius shook his head. "Not without our main prize we can't. Remember, Aethon sent us to capture the boy. None of our other accomplishments will mean anything to him if we fail in that. This is our last chance to please him, Gwuler. If we fail we are finished. Knowing Aethon, he'd probably feed us to Shadowhounds."

"He isn't that strict," Gwuler said, but he didn't sound convinced.

Pleased with the tension between them, Brysia listened awhile longer, then moved to where she could be alone. One of the Agla'Con — she thought it might be one of the new Zekans — still maintained the shield between her Awareness and the Power, but twice now she had felt it tremble when he had let his concentration momentarily slip. With such a mass of plant life just waiting to be used as a weapon, she was tempted to try to push through the shield and see how many Agla'Con she could kill before they stopped her. She could probably get two. Three if she was lucky.

But it wasn't time yet. Jase was coming for her. And Gideon, too, since she refused to believe that the Dymas could have been so easily killed, even in ambush. And since the Agla'Con were leaving a trail a blind man could follow, it wouldn't be long before Jase and Gideon caught up. When the time came for her to join the battle, she would know.

She gazed eastward across the river, amazed by the sheer volume of water flowing into the Inner Sea. It had to be fifty miles to the other bank, and there was still a noticeable current. She'd read somewhere that the number of rivers and streams feeding Illiarensei numbered in the tens of thousands, and many were larger than either of Kelsa's two largest rivers. The rainfall in Arkania's Storm Mountains must be something to behold.

A clamor of voices brought her out of her thoughts, and she turned to find several crew members standing near the ramp that stretched to the bank. They were calling for Borilius and Gwuler as a lone Shizu moved up the ramp toward them. The *komouri*-clad warrior stopped when he reached the deck and brought his fist to his chest as he addressed Gwuler.

"We found it," he said.

"Finally," Borilius breathed, exasperation fully evident in his voice.

The Shizu ignored him, keeping his attention fastened on Gwuler. "It is only a mile inland from the river," he told them, "but it is nearly ten miles farther upstream. My men and I found a place suitable for the ship. I left them to watch for our arrival."

"Excellent work," Gwuler told him, then turned and shouted for the crew to hoist the anchors. They responded in a flurry of movement, and a few minutes later the ship pulled away from the bank, its sails once more filled with corrupted Earthpower.

Brysia watched the wall of jungle foliage slip past, and a knot of fear tightened in her stomach. *It is close now,* she thought grimly. *The Agla'Con are about to spring their trap.*

She saw the grin on Borilius' face and realized he was thinking the same thing.

Turning away from his mocking gaze, she closed her eyes and took a steadying breath. *Please be careful, Jase. Please don't make me watch you die.*

Jase was in the middle of stomping his feet into his boots when a knock sounded on the door of his cabin. A second later, the latch turned and Talia stuck her head through the crack to smile at him. She moved the rest of the way in and sat next to him on the bed. He had asked her to wake him when they were within sight of Illiarensei, but it hadn't been necessary. Even asleep he'd felt the surge of corrupted Earthpower; it had jerked him from his slumber as surely as if he'd been slapped.

He could feel it even now, five, maybe ten miles ahead.

"I thought I heard you bumping around in here," she said, reaching up to run her fingers through his hair. It was getting long, he realized. Longer than it had been in years. He wasn't sure if he liked it, but he did like the feel of Talia's fingers as they tickled his scalp. "I was about to come wake you. Illiarensei is just ahead."

"What time is it?" he asked. The gold watch he'd brought with him from Trian was somewhere in his pack, and he didn't feel like looking for it.

"Late afternoon," she answered, lowering her hand from her tickling. "How did you sleep?"

He stood and offered her his hand. "Better than usual, I suppose. I'm still tired, but I'll be all right as soon as I get some blood moving." He guided her toward the door. "Where is Seth? I need to talk to him."

They went topside and stopped to look at the coast of Arkania looming off the starboard side, less than a mile distant. The green wall of vegetation stretched as far as he could see in both directions and looked to come right to the water's edge. It would make mooring a ship difficult.

To the northeast, a thin line of reef stretched for a mile or two, a strip of jagged brown rimmed on both sides by frothy white. Gulls and other sea birds filled the sky, some floating stiff-winged on the higher currents, others diving to scoop fish from below the water's surface. He saw a spray of mist as a school of dolphins broke the surface not more than fifty yards off the port bow. He and Talia watched them swim next to the ship for a moment, then he took her hand and they went to find Seth.

They found him near the helm studying the coastline with a spyglass that was nearly as long as his leg. He lowered it as they neared and turned to face them. "It's going to be difficult to find anything in all that muck," he said, sounding disgusted. "It's so dense you could walk within two feet of someone and not know they were there."

"Don't worry," Jase told him. "I know right where they are. Two of the Agla'Con are holding the Power." He closed one eye and pointed dramatically. "Right there."

"I still say this is a bad idea," the captain growled. "I don't care how powerful Gideon says you are. Going in there," he shoved a finger at the coastline, "after ten Agla'Con is nothing short of suicide."

"Precisely why I'm going alone," Jase said.

Seth's eyes narrowed menacingly. "Like hell you are!" he snapped, and Talia was only a heartbeat behind with a protest of her own. Seth turned to regard her with eyes as hard as stone.

"You aren't going anywhere, young lady," he told her. "If I have to tie you to the mast myself, I will. It's bad enough that Jase wants to get himself killed. But you..." he shook his head. "I thought I lost you once. I will not let it happen again."

"But you're letting *him* go," Talia stated angrily, and Jase realized that part of her anger was for him as well as for Seth.

Seth's silver head swivelled toward him. "I don't seem to have a choice," he said, his voice cold. "He's as pig-headed as Gideon Dymas in matters such as this."

Jase started to smile, but Seth wiped it away with what he said next. "But I'll be damned if you are going alone," he said, his voice harsh. "Even Gideon isn't so foolish as to think he doesn't need someone to watch his back."

"Fine," Jase answered, raising a finger toward the captain's chest. "But you will do as I say this time. If not, I will tie you to the mast with the Power and leave you here with Talia."

Surprisingly, Seth smiled. "It will be as you say, Dymas," he said, dipping his head in a bow. He stepped close, his face serious once more. "It's good to see you've learned something from Gideon," he said quietly. "I hope it will be enough to keep us alive."

I hope so, too, Jase thought, then turned to study the coastline once more.

"There," a Shizu said, and Borilius turned to follow his gaze to where a half dozen Riaki warriors were waving to them from the bank of a sheltered cove. The ship swung right, and Borilius eased off on the amount of Air he was directing into the sails. Stretching into the river with his Awareness, he found that the water was deep enough to bring the ship right next to the bank.

The masts clipped overhanging branches, sending a shower of leaves fluttering to the deck, and there was a gentle bump as the ship settled against the bank. The loud splash of anchors was followed by the rattling of chains as they disappeared into the murky waters. Ropes were thrown to Shizu on the bank, and the ship was secured to some of the larger trees.

Borilius waited for the plank to be lowered to the grassy bank, then moved down to Arkanian soil. Gwuler and the rest of the Agla'Con joined him. Nathal, one of those he'd recruited from Tetrica, ushered Brysia Fairimor down as well. She held her usual scowl of contempt, but her eyes were worried. She'd been trying to hide it, but he had sensed her despair days ago. It was an emotion he liked to feel in other people. It enhanced his ability to manipulate them.

He glanced up at the ship's captain standing at the rail and nodded. "You have your orders," he said. "Fulfill them and your place in Maeon's kingdom will be assured." *Sooner than you think,* he added silently. The man was a loyal member of the Brotherhood, twelve years sworn to the cause. It was a shame that he and his crew would never make it back to Tetrica. With the chapter house destroyed by the Fairimor lad and half the membership likely to perish here in Arkania, it would take months to rebuild the Tetrica Brotherhood.

But such was the life of a Con'Kumen, and these had served their purpose. He smiled. And they would serve one final purpose by waiting here for Jase Fairimor to arrive. The boy was certain to strike them with the Power, and the Con'Kumen — expendable as they were — would perform their final act of service as a signal flare.

He turned to Gwuler. "It may be several days before the boy arrives," he said. "Have your Shizu bring enough supplies to set up at least some semblance of a camp." He glanced at the buzzing insects and frowned. Most looked as if they would bite. "I don't even want to think what this place is like at night," he continued. "Have them search the ship for tents. If there aren't any, I suppose the sails will do. I get the feeling it rains a lot here."

Gwuler's look was challenging. "You aren't getting soft are you?"

Borilius scowled at him. "I've never been fond of suffering unnecessarily. You and your Shizu might enjoy sleeping out in this..." he shot a quick glance at the jungle, "...mess, but I don't intend to." He started down the narrow trail the Shizu had cleared with their swords. "And make sure they hurry," he added. "Show me some of that Shizu quickness you're always bragging about." He didn't have to look back to know that Gwuler was frowning at him.

Well, let him, he thought. When it came right down to it, Gwuler and his Shizu were as expendable as the Con'Kumen. And the rest of the Agla'Con as well. The only one who needed to be standing at the end of the battle with Jase Fairimor was Borilius Constas. He was the only one who mattered. The rest of them could go to Con'Jithar for all he cared.

If I plan the ambush right, he thought with a very satisfied smile, *they just might.*

And then he would return to a place of glory in the Brotherhood. Alone.

Brysia watched as Borilius disappeared into the jungle foliage then turned to study Gwuler as he issued orders to his Shizu. She had sensed all along that the two Agla'Con didn't like each other; the last few days had shown that the animosity between them ran deeper than she had first thought. She had seen the murderous look in the Riaki's eyes just now, and she suspected the only thing that kept him from striking the Zekan down with *Ta'shaen* was his Shizu self-control. That, and the fact that Borilius seemed to be the stronger of the two in the Power.

Nathal, the Agla'Con who had her shielded, moved up beside her and motioned to the trail. "After you, my lady," he said with mock sincerity.

She narrowed her eyes at him, but he only smiled. Hiking up her skirts, she started down the trail.

The ground was soft. In many places her shoes stuck in the mud and were nearly pulled from her feet, and she had to concentrate to keep from losing them. Insects buzzed her ears and face, and she swatted at them with her free hand. There were already circular welts on her arms from where some had bitten her, and the deeper into the jungle they went, the worse the bugs became. She saw several the size of birds and had to suppress a shudder at the thought of being bitten by one so large.

Even worse was the humidity. Less than a hundred paces inland, all traces of the ocean breeze vanished. The air turned hot and suffocating. In spite of the deep shade of the jungle canopy, sweat beaded on her face, and she had to wipe it away with the back of her hand or risk having it run into her eyes. She had always wondered what Arkania was like. Now that she knew, she didn't like it one bit.

Glancing at the dense undergrowth, she wondered if the oppressive climate was part of the reason the Arkanian people were so irritable. They didn't have any kind of stable government. The truces that were sometimes formed between warring tribes were as close as they ever came to any kind of peace. Even then it was isolated. And temporary. It was said that the only time Arkanians stopped fighting amongst themselves was when they went to war against Riak or Zeka. It had happened on numerous occasions but had never produced much more than a lot of dead Arkanians.

In truth, none of the other nations knew much about their neighbors to the south. Except for an adventurous, or perhaps dissatisfied, few, Arkanians as a whole kept to themselves. It was strange to ponder how the other eight nations had flourished in all areas of growth and commerce while Arkania seemed content to live in primitive obscurity. Its way of life hadn't changed much in almost two thousand years. It was frightening to think that such a barbaric society could still exist in a mostly civilized world.

Then again, she had been here less than an hour and couldn't stand the place. No wonder most of the world preferred to leave Arkania alone. If not for the abundance of herbs and other useful plants that grew in these horrific jungles, she doubted anyone would have reason to come here at all. Anyone, that is, except Borilius.

She still wasn't sure what a Veilgate was, but it must be pretty important for a man like him to come all this way. Gwuler was right in his assumption that the Zekan was soft. If he didn't have ability in the Power, she could probably kill him with her bare hands. If the chance presented itself, she might try to anyway.

Something large and scaley bolted up the trunk of a tree to her right, and she flinched at the sudden movement, startled by the flash of reptilian color. Nathal saw it too, and the shield he held on her momentarily faltered. She had to resist the urge to embrace *Ta'shaen* and kill him.

He glanced at her with anger in his eyes, and the shield sprang back into place. She met his gaze briefly before turning her attention back to the jungle, suddenly worried that the bugs weren't the only things that might bite. Whatever they'd just seen shooting up the tree had been the size of a man.

The path opened into a massive circular clearing, and Brysia squinted against the sudden increase in sunlight. The sky, visible through an opening in the canopy, was only partially blocked by the limbs of some of the largest trees she had ever seen. She counted seven in all, evenly spaced around the clearing, each nearly the size of a Yucanter. At first she thought they were Yucanters, but the leaves were deep green and fern-shaped as opposed to the crimson broadleaf of the Yucanters.

She was surprised that an area this large would be absent of the dense vegetation typical of the jungle thus far. A closer look showed that beneath a thin layer of rotten leaves and soil was an expanse of solid rock. She scraped away some of the grime with her shoe and found paving stones. The only joint she found was so tightly fitted that it was almost indistinguishable from the natural texture of the rock. Neither water nor seed could penetrate stones so tightly fit, and so the area had remained free of the encroaching jungle. The stone must also be incredibly thick to have resisted being lifted by the roots of the massive trees growing around the edges.

Borilius and the others moved to the center of the clearing, near what she assumed was the Veilgate. It rose on two thick pillars and was spanned at the top by dual beams. The entire structure was the color of blood and stood out sharply against the surrounding greens of the jungle.

Nathal motioned her forward, and she complied, eager to get a closer look. She had seen its likeness in a sketch in one of the Elvan histories, though at the time she hadn't known what it was or what it was for. The sketch had contained no explanation or description.

As she neared, she saw that it wasn't made of wood as she had first thought. And the red wasn't paint. Not caring if Borilius would object, she moved forward and touched the smooth surface. It wasn't stone, she decided, and it wasn't metal. If anything it looked like —

"It's a type of *chorazin*," Borilius said from behind her, and she pulled her hand away self-consciously. "It is from the Old World and differs from the *chorazin* you know in that it is immoveable. A hurricane could scour this area clean and this gate would remain." He laughed, and from the corner of her eye, she saw him move to stand in front of the gate. "It is believed that these gates were created to facilitate The Gathering." He paused, and she glanced over to find him smiling. "Appropriate since the Agla'Con are once again using them to bring about the destruction of the world."

"You filthy scum will never succeed," she hissed.

He turned to regard her, his eyes filled with a frenzied light. "Oh, but we already have," he said, and the fierceness in his gaze caused her to look away. Hiking up her skirts, she moved off.

Behind her, Borilius' chuckle grew into a cackle of evil glee.

"There is a ship ahead," Seth said, lowering the spyglass. "Helm to starboard. Take us in as close to the bank as you can. I don't want them to see us until we are right on top of them." He turned to Captain Panos. "Ready the archers and the boarding team," he ordered. "Instruct them to kill anyone who isn't female. I don't want them hitting the Sister Queen by mistake. Hopefully, Jase can shield us long enough to rescue her."

"She's not on the ship," Jase said, and Seth turned to find the boy's eyes closed and his face lined with concentration. "And neither are the Agla'Con."

"Are you sure?" he asked.

Jase opened his eyes. "Yes."

Seth reached up to pull at his mustache as he studied the wall of green slipping past the ship. He hadn't expected them to go into the jungle. He couldn't imagine any reason for them to leave the safety of the ship. Then again, he had no idea why they had come to Arkania in the first place. With the Riaki strike team being from Clan Vakala, he had expected them to go there. With as long as it had taken to sail here, they could have been in Vakala already if they had wanted to. It didn't make sense.

"Can you tell where they are?" he asked, and Jase shook his head.

"I didn't dare. If any of them have their Awareness extended very far at all, they would feel my probing. Just searching the ship was dangerous. We are close enough now that if they wanted to they could hit us with the Power."

"We're still five miles away," Seth said, failing to keep the disbelief from his voice.

"But they have the Talisman of Elsa," Jase replied. "Smashing us would be nothing for them now."

Seth nodded grimly. It was true, of course. He had seen firsthand the kind of power a Talisman of Elsa contained when he had watched Gideon use the first one to strengthen the Veil and send Shadan back into the world of the dead. It was a blow that had shaken Mount Tabor to its core and left Gideon so weak afterwards that Aethon and his Darkling hordes had captured him easily.

He closed his mind against the images which threatened to overwhelm him every time he thought of that horrific day. Even now he couldn't fathom how he had gotten out of Amnidia alive. Especially considering the load he'd had to bear. He pushed the thought away and turned his attention back to Panos.

"Those on the other ship are Con'Kumen," he told them. "Unless they surrender, you have my permission to kill them all. Don't let any of them leave that ship. It's possible the Agla'Con don't know we are here. I'd like to keep it that way." He glanced back to Jase. "Don't embrace the Power unless you have to."

Jase raised an eyebrow. "I thought I was giving the orders."

"You are," Seth said. "But you can still listen to reason." He ignored the boy's frown and continued. "If they don't know we are here, we might be able to sneak close enough for you to strike first. You know bloody well you'll need every advantage you can get."

"I know what I'm doing," Jase insisted.

Sometimes I wonder, Seth told him silently. *Sometimes I really wonder.*

Hunkering behind the wall of the forward deck, Talia watched as the last of the trees slid away and the Con'Kumen ship came into view. The helmsman angled *Mist's Fury* in sharply and they were alongside the other ship before the first cry of alarm was raised. Grappling hooks struck the deck of the enemy vessel and ropes were pulled tight, slowing the *Fury* and pulling her in close. The two hulls came together with a thundering scrape and everything jarred to a stop. Bowstrings twanged, and the hiss of arrows filled the air.

Talia cast a glance to where Jase stood with the archers and found him loosing arrow after arrow of his own at any Con'Kumen foolish enough to show his head.

"There," Jase shouted. "Don't let them off the ship!" Three more arrows left his bow in a matter of seconds, but when he tossed the bow down and drew the sword Seth had given him, she knew he had missed. "Blast," he hissed, leaping across to the other ship with the rest of those assigned to board. "Get those three!"

Seth leapt across as well and shoved Jase out of the way. "You stay there," he ordered, then turned and cut down two Con'Kumen who stood to bar his way. He reached the ramp on the other side of the ship and disappeared into the jungle beyond.

Captain Panos' crew quickly overwhelmed the remaining Con'Kumen, and those who weren't killed were taken prisoner. When they were secure, Jase moved to the head of the ramp and stared down at the spot where Seth had entered the jungle.

An eery silence fell across the ship, and Talia rose from behind the wall to cast about in awe. The victory was complete, she realized. Not a member of Panos' crew appeared to be injured. The Con'Kumen may be skilled when it came to murder and deception, but they hadn't stood a chance against the skill of trained naval soldiers.

Ignoring Seth's orders to stay out of the way, she hiked up her skirt and jumped across to the other ship, moving to stand near Jase. A muffled clash of steel sounded below deck, then faded into silence. She let her eyes wander the ship and felt a wash of pity for those who had been wounded. She couldn't risk healing them until Jase dealt with the Agla'Con, and so she steeled herself against their pain as best she could.

Jase followed her gaze to the dead and wounded and pursed his lips grimly. "There was a time when the thought of killing another man made me want to empty my stomach," he told her. "It was something I thought I would never have to do. Something I thought I could never do. It sickens me how I have changed." He glanced back to the forest and frowned. "Yet, here I stand, hoping with every fiber of my being that Seth kills those who fled before they can alert the Agla'Con. All so I can strike them at my leisure."

He looked down at the sword in his hand. "I quit training with one of these a long time ago," he said, leaning the sword against the rail. "It disgusts me that they are so singular in purpose. Bows can be used for hunting. So can spears. An axe is meant for splitting wood. But swords... swords are for the killing of men. That is the *only* thing they are good for." He chuckled softly, a low sound without humor. "And now look at me. I *am* a sword. I have become the very thing I have always hated. I am nothing more than a tool of death."

Talia put a hand on his arm, and he turned to look at her. What she saw in his eyes frightened her. His anger was obvious, but there was more — an element of self-loathing at what he perceived about himself. "Wrong!" she told him firmly. "You are a servant of the Earthsoul. What you do is *Her* will. The power you wield is Hers." He looked away momentarily, but she waited until he met her gaze again before continuing. "*Ta'shaen* is the power of creation, Jase. It is the essence of life itself."

"For you, maybe," he said. "But for me it reeks of death."

She reached up and touched his cheek gently. "Any weapon, sword or otherwise, can be good or evil depending on the purpose for which it is used. The Agla'Con and all those who serve Maeon are enemies to God. I do not doubt that destroying them is His will. Someone has to stand against this tide of darkness, Jase. God has chosen you. Remember that."

He forced his lips into a semblance of a smile and pulled her close, hugging her tightly. "Thanks," he said, kissing her on the head. "I hope you are right." He took a deep breath before continuing in a whisper. "It still worries me that I *want* the Agla'Con to die. It scares me that I want to be the one to kill them."

Before she could respond, Seth's voice sounded from the bottom of the ramp. "Can't I leave you two alone for a minute without you getting all smoochy with each other?"

Jase released her and stepped back. "Did you get them?"

Seth moved up the ramp. "And two Shizu as well. Most likely they were part of a perimeter guard." He paused and his face darkened. "If we hope to keep the advantage of surprise, we will need to act before they are missed. From the look of the trail, they are only an hour or two ahead of us." He handed them each a wad of crushed leaves. "Rub that on your skin," he told them. "It will keep the bugs from biting you."

When Talia finished, she braced herself for the argument she knew was coming. "Do you think we can still surprise them?" she asked.

Seth turned his blue eyes on her, and she knew she had been right in her assumptions. "*You* aren't going anywhere," he told her, raising a hand to silence her protest. "And I don't have time to argue with you about it," he growled. "I meant what I said about tying you to the mast, Talia, so don't fight me on this."

He took a step closer and lowered his voice. "I know of your vision," he whispered.

She stiffened in surprise and glanced around worriedly. No one else seemed to have heard. The look on Jase's face showed he didn't like being left out of what was being said, but he didn't step any closer.

"Gideon told me," Seth continued. "I know how you feel about this, but you must be reasonable. Any injury we sustain won't be something you can heal. And you would only be a distraction for us both. I will *not* risk your life in a battle with Agla'Con." He hesitated once more and reached up push a tendril of hair behind her ear. "Please, daughter of my heart, stay here where it is safe. I cannot protect you from them."

Though she was still angry, the urge to argue with him vanished when she saw what was in his eyes. Seth Lydon, her warder since birth, was terrified of what her coming with them might mean. He didn't admit weakness to anyone. If he said he couldn't protect her then he couldn't. She didn't like the idea of being left behind, especially in light of her vision, but Seth was right. They would be too worried about her to concentrate on the enemy. Going with them would put their lives at even greater risk.

She looked from Seth to Jase, then back to Seth. She had to force herself to do it, but she nodded. The tension left his face, and he relaxed. Jase, too, looked more at ease, and she knew she had done the right thing.

"Captain Panos," Seth called, "take both ships down river and wait for us there. If Jase and I aren't back by tomorrow, then we probably aren't coming.

You know what to do from there."

"Yes, Captain Lydon," the other replied, then began giving orders to his crew.

"And you, young lady," Seth said, taking her hand in his and raising it to his lips to kiss it gently. "Warding you has been a privilege and an honor. I mean it when I say you are the daughter I never had." She threw her arms around his neck and hugged him fiercely. She was pleased when he hugged her back.

"You be careful," she told him, and he laughed.

"I was about to say the same thing to you," he replied, stepping back to glance at Jase. "Give her a kiss so we can get this over with," he said, his usual gruffness returning. He slung a bow and quiver of arrows over his shoulder and started down the ramp. He stopped at the entrance to the trail and waited with his back turned to the ship.

Jase took her hand and stood staring at his feet for a moment before speaking. When he looked up, his eyes glimmered with intensity. "In case I don't come back," he told her, "I want you to know that I love you. I know I said it in the letter, but I want you to hear it from my lips. I love you."

She smiled in spite of the tears forming at the corners of her eyes and threw her arms around his neck, hugging him tightly. "I love you, too," she said, tilting her head back so she could look into his face. He kissed her gently on the mouth, then stepped back and started down the ramp.

Watching him disappear into the forest was the most difficult thing she'd ever done.

"You don't think we can do this," Jase said to Seth as they moved away from the ship.

The silver-haired captain turned to regard him for a moment before shrugging. "Gideon and I have faced worse," he said, then handed him the bow and arrows. He drew both his swords, holding the left one so the blade ran along his forearm. The other he held before him as if to point the way.

"But I'm not Gideon," Jase muttered, slinging the quiver over his shoulder.

Seth turned to grin at him. "So I've noticed." Reaching into his pocket, he withdrew the eagle's claw and handed it over. "You might be needing this now," he said.

Jase fingered the red-gold Orb of Elsa for a moment, then hung it around his neck. He and Seth started forward once more.

A short distance further on, they came across the bodies of the Con'Kumen who had fled the ship. Beyond them lay the bodies of two Shizu. Seth glanced down at the Shizu as he stepped over them. "Clan Vakala," he said softly, "was responsible for the death of Caedikas Tynda, the Riaki Highseat who taught me the ways of the Shizu."

Jase nodded. Gideon had spoken of Highseat Tynda the night they had camped in Yucanter Forest. Tynda had believed Seth to be a figure of prophecy and had taken him in and trained him because of that belief. During their time together, the Riaki Lord and his apprentice had become very close friends. He didn't imagine Seth had taken the Highseat's murder lightly. He cast a sideways glance at his friend and found him frowning.

"I can assume, then, that Clan Vakala knows you?"

"Oh, they know me," Seth said, sounding extremely satisfied. "They definitely know me."

Jase knew not to inquire further.

They had gone about a mile when Seth stopped and motioned for Jase to get down. He did as he was told, slipping into the jungle foliage and kneeling to notch an arrow. Peeking out at the trail, he waited to see what had spooked Seth. The captain had disappeared into the jungle across from him and was nowhere to be seen. Jase took a slow, deep breath and waited, trying to ignore his pounding heart.

It was only a moment before two Shizu appeared on the trail, coming from the direction he and Seth had been going. They moved along the trail purposefully, but they appeared to be relaxed. *At least as relaxed as Shizu can ever look,* he amended silently. Still, he didn't think they suspected anything.

They were just about to him when Seth stepped out of the forest behind them. Whirling, the Shizu drew their swords and... stopped. Jase couldn't believe his eyes.

Seth stood before them, his arms folded across his chest, his swords sheathed. There was a murderous light in his eyes.

"I'm glad you recognize me," he told them softly. "The other two did."

The two Shizu lunged, and Jase rose from his cover, taking aim at a Shizu back. Quick as he was, though, Seth was quicker. His swords appeared in his hands, and he was little more than a blur as he spun between the two black-clad assassins, killing them easily.

Jase eased his draw on the bow and watched Seth flick the blood from his swords. When he finished, he motioned down the trail. "Quietly now," the captain whispered. "I get the feeling we are close."

He was right. A hundred paces further on they heard voices coming from somewhere in front of them. Seth motioned for him to stay put and went on alone. He returned a few moments later, and Jase could tell by the look in his eyes that he had found the Agla'Con.

"Is my mother with them?" Jase whispered.

Seth nodded. "Follow me," he mouthed silently, then slipped into the jungle.

Jase followed, and it took every bit of skill he possessed to move as quietly as Seth. Fifty paces later, Seth sheathed his swords and slowed his pace to a crawl. For the last ten paces they really did crawl, and Jase found himself peering out from under a mass of ferns at a large clearing a hundred yards in diameter.

And clustered in the center of the clearing was the enemy. They were setting up camp near a large, squarish gate, and he could hear some of them arguing about who would be sleeping in the few tents they had. He turned to Seth and smiled. *They have no idea we're here*, he thought with satisfaction. The first strike would be his. He returned to his study of the camp.

He found his mother standing near the gate, and a wave of apprehension flowed through him. He was relieved to find her well, but the thought of what was coming in the next few minutes terrified him. If anything happened to her...

He couldn't finish the thought. He would just have to make sure nothing did.

Only a handful of Shizu were busy setting up tents, so he decided the rest were somewhere in the jungle. He wondered if they would come running when they heard the attack or if they would decide to sit things out once they realized there was little they could do in a battle being fought with the Power. He hoped they would stay away; he didn't want to have to worry about taking a bladestar or an arrow in the back.

In addition to the small number of Shizu, he counted ten men, mostly Zekan, and smiled in satisfaction. *At least all the Agla'Con are where I can see them.*

If he planned this right, he could kill two or three before the others had time to retaliate. But which ones? He could feel one of the men — Kelsan by the look of him — restraining Brysia with the Power; but he was standing too near her to make a good target.

He turned his attention to the loud-mouthed Zekan shouting insults at the Shizu. It was obvious the man was the leader of the group, or thought he was, but Jase needed only one look at the leather bag clutched protectively in the man's hand to know he couldn't strike him either. Even without the vision the other night, he would have known the tremors coming from the bag were caused by a Blood Orb of Elsa. If he opened his Awareness, he could see it shining like a beacon in his mind's eye. He wouldn't risk destroying the Talisman any more than he would risk his mother. That meant he had to select a different target.

The three arguing over the tents would have to do, he decided. They were so engrossed in their argument they would never know what hit them. Now for the distraction. He pointed to the one-armed Agla'Con standing apart from the others.

"Do you think you can put an arrow in that Riaki?" Jase whispered.

Seth nodded.

"Good," Jase said. "When he cries out, I'll kill the three who are arguing. If you get a chance, shoot the Kelsan closest to my mother as well."

"Then what?" Seth asked, taking the bow and notching an arrow.

"I don't know," Jase told him truthfully. "That's as far as I've gotten with my plan."

"Not much of a plan," Seth grumbled as he moved to where he had an angle on the Riaki Agla'Con. "Tell me when," he said. He didn't sound pleased.

"You'll know when," Jase said, rising to his feet.

"Where are you going?"

Jase fastened his eyes on the group in the clearing. "To get my mother back."

CHAPTER 39

First Strike

"We are close now," Ammorin said softly, and Gideon turned to acknowledge the Dainin with a nod. It had been fifty miles back when he had first sensed the tremors the Talisman of Elsa caused in *Ta'shaen*. With each passing mile the presence of so much Power had grown until he could pinpoint the location without even opening his Awareness. It called to him; a white hot point of light glowing like the sun in his mind's eye. And now it was less than two miles away.

The *Nar'shein Yahl* could feel the Talisman's Power as he could, more keenly than he could probably. But it was their ability to hear the whisperings of the Earthsoul that had truly guided them here. Without their aid, he would never have found the Blood Orb so quickly — if at all. Because of them, he was close to getting it back. Closer than he could ever have hoped to have gotten on his own. It was an admission he didn't mind making. He had learned an important lesson at the temple. One he wouldn't soon forget. Never again would he go it alone.

He glanced up at the sails and hissed in frustration. Earlier in the day, they'd had to quit using the Power to push the ship to keep from alerting the Agla'Con to their presence, and it had cost them valuable time. As it was, only the very top of the mast still caught the rays of the sun. The rest of the ship was cloaked in shadow. Far out on the river, the setting sun painted the muddy waters a deep red. It would be dark soon, and darkness favored the Agla'Con.

"There are two ships ahead," Sharrukin said, and Gideon and Ammorin turned to look where he pointed. "They are coming down river."

Captain Eridel lowered his spyglass. "No use trying to hide," he said. "They've seen us. Both ships are Kelsan." Around them, Eridel's crew scrambled into action, grabbing bows and other weapons and taking up positions along the starboard side. Elliott was among them.

Gideon closed his eyes and stretched forward with his Awareness, careful not to touch the minds of any on the ship. He could feel Ammorin doing the same. The lead ship had only a partial crew and a large number of men bound with ropes. Several bodies lay to one side, the arrow wounds still leaking blood. The second ship also had a partial crew, but the decks were empty of dead or wounded. A slender figure with long hair stood near the helm, and he pressed his Awareness closer, wanting a better look before he got his hopes up. The young woman's face came into view: generous lips, dimples, emerald green eyes — he could scarcely believe what he saw. It was Talia Chellum.

"For the love of creation," he said, pulling in his Awareness and opening his eyes. "Signal that we wish to speak with them," he told Eridel. "Then bring us alongside the second ship." He glanced at the crew. "Have your men put their weapons away. They won't be needed."

As Eridel began barking out orders, Gideon turned to Ammorin and found that Elliott was on his way toward them, bow still in hand.

"What is it?" the Prince asked, glancing at the blue and white flag being raised by two of Eridel's men.

"Your sister is on the second ship," he said and watched Elliott's eyes widen in surprise. "Seth and Jase are not with them," he added, looking in the direction of the tremors. "It's my guess they went after the Blood Orb." He shook his head. He knew both men were brave, but he hadn't thought they might be so foolish.

"Ammorin," he said, turning back to the Dainin, "have your men help the crew with the intercept, then gather your things. It's time to finish your Cleansing Hunt." *I just hope we aren't too late to help,* he thought, moving to the starboard rail to watch the ships draw near.

Elliott joined him, and for once the young man was at a loss for words.

The winds coming off the sea were blowing upstream, so both of the approaching ships had their sails furled, allowing Illiarensei's current to pull them along instead. When they saw the Flag of Negotiation being raised, though, they unfurled the sails and swung the ships around. By the time they were pointed up river once more, Gideon was close enough to read the name *Mist's Fury* painted on the stern of Talia's ship. Talia was holding a spyglass in one hand and waving to them with the other.

Eridel's men lessened the sails of *Sea Blade* to compensate for its quicker speed and Gideon watched as they guided her so close to the other ship he thought the hulls would scrape together. It was a dangerous maneuver, especially in light of the currents, but Eridel's crew handled it with the Zekan expertise he had come to expect.

"Elliott!" Talia shouted. Then, before anyone could tell her to stay where she was, she leapt across the gap and landed in front of them. Elliott had to catch her to keep her from falling, but it was just as well. She threw her arms around him and squeezed so tightly Elliott grunted in pain. "By the Light, I'm glad to see you two," she said, stepping back to look at Gideon. Her eyes were frantic as she continued. "You have to hurry," she insisted. "Jase has gone to get his mother and the Talisman back from the Agla'Con. Ten of them. I know he is powerful, but ten is too many. I told him it was, but he wouldn't listen."

Gideon put a reassuring hand on her shoulder and turned to Eridel. "Inform the Kelsan crews to keep up as best they can," he said. "And take us up river. Quickly, now. There isn't much time."

As Eridel moved to the rail to speak with the captain of *Mist's Fury*, Gideon turned back to Talia. "Tell me all that you know," he said softly, then listened as she told of Jase's vision and how it had led them here. The relative ease with which they had captured the Con'Kumen vessel didn't surprise him, nor did the fact that he had been right in his assumption that Brysia's abductors were the same group who had stolen the Talisman of Elsa. What did surprise him, though, was how Seth had allowed Jase to walk into such an obvious trap.

When he told Talia what he was thinking, she firmly defended the captain's actions. "There was no stopping Jase," she said. "His mind was made up. For Seth, it was either go with him and offer what help he could, or be bound with the Power and watch him go after the Agla'Con alone."

"I'm surprised you didn't try to go with them," Elliott said.

Talia's mouth thinned as she leveled a stare at him. "I did," she said flatly and left it at that.

Gideon was about to inquire further when he felt a massive surge in *Ta'shaen*. It was followed almost immediately by several jolts of corrupted Earthpower, and thunder rolled across the jungle canopy in angry peals, scattering birds into the air in fright. Ammorin and the rest of the Dainin raced to the rail and stood looking in the direction of the disturbance. Each held several nets in one hand and a long spear in the other.

Gideon felt Ammorin reach out with his Awareness and moved to stand beside him while the Dainin searched the area ahead. He was tempted to reach out as well but decided against it. One Awareness was risky enough; two would most certainly alert the Agla'Con to their presence. Even in battle, some of them might be sensitive enough to feel the probing.

Elliott and Talia joined him, and Gideon glanced at the Chellum Princess to find her staring at Ammorin in awe.

Ammorin finished his search and turned to Gideon, his brown eyes glittering with intensity. "We must hurry," he said. "My men and I will be in position when you arrive. Just don't take too long to get there or we may be forced to attack them without you." He turned to his men. "Come, *Nar'shein*," he bellowed and dove over the side of the ship. The others followed and the five giant men reached the bank in a dozen quick strokes.

As they climbed from the water and disappeared into the jungle, Gideon turned to Captain Eridel. "Find a place to land," he ordered, "and arm your men."

Elliott chuckled. "Not going it alone this time, I see."

Gideon nodded. "I never make the same mistake twice," he said, then gestured to the weapons crates. "Fill your quiver. It's time to hunt."

With *Ta'shaen* a hair's width away from his Awareness, Jase left the shelter of the trees and walked across the clearing toward the Agla'Con camp. He was pleased at how calm he was. He was even more pleased by how close he got before anyone noticed him. One of the Shizu spotted him first and stopped what he was doing to watch as if he wasn't exactly sure what he was seeing. To his left, two Agla'Con let their conversation die and blinked in surprise at seeing someone coming out of the jungle.

He ignored them, keeping his attention on the three he intended to strike. *Ta'shaen* was a glowing ocean in his mind's eye, and he pressed his Awareness outward, letting it settle over the entire area like a blanket. What he found made him smile. None of the Agla'Con had their Awareness extended. Except for the one shielding his mother, none had yet seized the Power. *They don't know who I am*, he thought. *I've taken them completely by surprise.*

One by one, conversations ceased and heads turned his way. Each time the reaction was the same: no one seemed quite sure what to make of the lone man coming out of the jungle. The shocked silence that fell over the camp caused Brysia to look up from her contemplation. Her eyes went wide as she beheld her son, and her gasp broke the silence, reaching to the far edges of the clearing and bringing the Agla'Con out of their trance.

"I've come for my mother," he told them and watched the light of recognition fill their eyes.

The *hiss-thunk* of an arrow sounded to his right, and the one-armed Riaki howled in pain, clutching at the fletchings sticking from his chest and sagging to his knees.

Jase felt the rest of the Agla'Con reach for *Ta'shaen* but struck before any of them could fully seize it. He hit his three targets with the combination of Air, Flesh, and Spirit he had used on the Darklings in the Dome, and the three men exploded into sprays of blood and tattered robes. There were less gruesome ways to kill these vermin, of course, but he wanted them to fear him. He wanted them to dread what he would do next.

Before the rest could retaliate, he struck again, smashing one Agla'Con's feeble attempt at a shield with a column of Fire that turned the man into a flailing, shrieking mass of flames. The burning figure staggered a few paces to the left before falling into a clump of ferns, a smoldering form no longer recognizable as human.

Jase's satisfaction at the fourth kill was interrupted by lightning streaking toward him from a dozen directions. Instinctively he threw a protective dome of Spirit skyward, deflecting the deadly bolts out into the forest where they shattered trees and sent birds scattering for safety. The Agla'Con attacked again, but this time he held the shield in place, absorbing the white hot stabs instead of knocking them away. He didn't want to hit his mother or Seth by mistake.

Thunder rattled his teeth as it boomed above him, and he had to cover his ears with his hands to keep from going deaf. With each sizzling burst, the hair on his head and arms stood on end and his skin prickled. The air inside the dome quickly grew warm.

Now what? he wondered, directing a strengthening flow into the shield. Striking any more of the Agla'Con was out of the question now; it was all he could do just to maintain the barrier between him and the killing stabs lancing toward him. *Some plan,* he thought darkly, wondering if this had been such a good idea after all.

Kneeling, he closed his eyes against the flashes of lightning and let himself sink deeper into his own Awareness. The sound of corrupted Earthpower hammering at his shield diminished and he found himself gazing at the area around him through the eyes of *Ta'shaen.* He could see the flows of the Agla'Con as they attacked; the blues and whites of pure *Ta'shaen* were tainted red with malice as the vermin corrupted the Power, twisting it to their purposes.

He was surprised to find that only four were striking at him: the one who held a shield on his mother and three others. The Zekan who held the Talisman of Elsa had seized enough Power to collapse Fairimor Palace, but he wasn't attacking. Jase pressed his Awareness closer and heard the man shouting to the others. "Don't kill him you fools! We need him alive!" Oblivious to his commands, they continued their attack.

Jase spotted his mother hiding behind one of the columns of the gate. She was squinting against the flashes of lightning pounding at him, and he didn't need to sharpen his Awareness to see that she was terrified. Knowing her, though, she was probably more worried for him than for herself. If he could get to her and bring her inside his protective dome of Spirit, they could try to flee together.

Jase focused his attention on the Agla'Con nearest Brysia, ready to burn him to ash. He reconsidered when he realized he couldn't attack without losing hold of his shield. The battle had become a stalemate. The Agla'Con weren't strong enough to break through, and he wasn't skilled enough to launch another attack while locked beneath his defense.

He clenched his fists in anger. All they had to do now was wait him out. With five of them still standing, it would be an easy thing to do. He searched the area where he'd left Seth but couldn't find the captain anywhere. He spotted Shizu slipping through the jungle and realized they were searching for the one who had put an arrow into their leader. He knew they wouldn't find Seth unless he wanted to be found, but he doubted the Chellum captain would hide for long.

He was right, and the Agla'Con shielding Brysia staggered forward with a choking gasp as an arrow plunged through his neck. Blood sprayed from his mouth, and he collapsed face down in the thin layer of soil. The shield between Brysia and the Power vanished.

Her reaction was immediate as she dropped to her knees and shoved her fingers into the thin layer of dirt, drawing in as much of *Ta'shaen* as some of the Agla'Con. With a surge of Earthpower he could see in his mind's eye, she struck, exploding the ground beneath the Agla'Con leader in a spray of dirt that sent him spinning through the air. He landed a dozen paces away, and the Talisman slipped from his grasp. Before he could rise, the ground erupted a second time, and he was tossed like a rag doll once more.

Startled by this new attack, the remaining Agla'Con broke off their assault on Jase and turned toward his mother. He felt a surge of corrupted Earthpower surround them as they prepared to unleash their anger on her. Howling with rage, he released his shield and pounded the area around them with a barrage of lightning. Dirt and rock exploded. Ferns and creepers flared into ash. One of the Agla'Con screamed as his legs vanished in a flash of silvery-blue. A second Agla'Con blew apart in a spray of charred flesh.

Jase opened his eyes and stood, throwing everything he had at the remaining Agla'Con. Fire. Lightning. Gouts of Earth. Fists of Air. More Fire. He felt the man's shield weaken and knew it would be only seconds before it collapsed completely. When it did, he grinned in triumph and turned the man into a shrieking column of fire.

That left only the Zekan.

Brysia still lashed at him with Earth, but he had recovered from the initial attack and was wrapped in a protective sphere of Spirit. He had retrieved the Talisman and was moving slowly toward her, laughing as the maelstrom of Earth and debris she was hurling at him glanced harmlessly off his shield. The man actually looked amused by Brysia's efforts.

Smile at this, Jase snarled silently, taking hold of the eagle's claw and sending a white-hot bar of *Sei'shiin* lancing from his fist. It punched through the Zekan's shield as if it were paper, narrowly missing his head. It struck a Shizu racing along the edge of the trees, and the black-clad figure vanished in a flare of white.

Jase saw the Zekan's surprise turn to fear and found himself warding off an attack unlike any he had faced so far. Lightning hammered at him from all sides, and fire erupted along the bottom edges of his shield. It seemed *Sei'shiin* had changed the man's mind about trying to take him alive.

Brysia remained behind one of the gate's pillars and turned her attack on the Shizu visible along the edges of the clearing. Vines and creepers lashed out, snaring the assassins in coils of green death. Swords flashed as the Shizu hacked at the writhing mass, but Brysia's Gift was too much for them. Those who weren't strangled were torn limb from limb.

Jase kept his attention fastened on the Agla'Con. If he could keep him occupied long enough, his mother might very well eliminate enough of the Shizu that she would be able to escape through the jungle. Seth was sure to see her. If anyone could get her safely to the ship it was him.

The thought gave him hope, and he poured every fragment of strength he could muster into his shield. Deflecting the surges that hammered at him, he moved closer to his enemy, trying to turn his attention away from Brysia.

From the corner of his eye he saw the one-armed Riaki struggling to push himself to his knees. The arrow had broken where he'd fallen on it, and blood slicked the front of his *komouri*. Jase felt him seize the Power and braced himself for the added strength the Agla'Con would lend to the attack.

He realized his mistake too late, and the surge of corrupted Earthpower streaked past to strike the ground at his mother's feet. The area around her exploded upward in a spray of brown that sent her flying backward through the air. She struck the ground and rolled several times, stopping in a heap some distance away.

"No!" Jase howled.

His hold on the Power slipped, allowing a stab of lightning to partially penetrate his shield. Heat burned his face, leaving spots of white in his vision. The boom of thunder that echoed inside the protective dome was so loud he thought his head would explode. He clutched at his ears and staggered to the side, trying to shore up the breach, but feeling like he'd been hit in the chest with a sledgehammer.

A second bolt nearly broke through as well. Then a third. The silver stabs kept coming, and he felt his hold on the Power slip further.

And then something dark slid between his Awareness and the shimmering ocean that was *Ta'shaen*, severing his hold on the Power. Everything vanished from his mind's eye. The Power left him in such a rush that he felt as if the marrow had been sucked from his bones. Gasping, he collapsed to his knees in shock.

Shielded!

The thought was as shocking as it was terrifying. As much as he despised what he sometimes did, having his connection to *Ta'shaen* severed was akin to having his lungs ripped out. He had become as used to it as the air he breathed. Now it was gone, and he felt as if he were being strangled.

He pounded at the dark wall with his Awareness but knew he may as well have been pounding on steel with his bare hands for all the good it was doing. *Ta'shaen* was out of reach.

He looked up to see the Agla'Con moving toward him. His earlier smugness was back in place. "I must say you presented more of a challenge than I thought you would," he said, looking pointedly at the remains of the other Agla'Con. "But in the end it seems experience outweighs overall strength." He stopped a short distance away and inclined his head. "I am Borilius. And as you can see, I am not someone to be trifled with."

Jase narrowed his eyes in anger and glanced around the clearing. It was silent save for the distant clash of steel as Seth battled the surviving Shizu. The only movement came in the form of smoke rising from the scorched bodies of the dead Agla'Con. He spotted his mother lying motionless on the ground, and a knot tightened over his heart. If she had been killed...

Snarling with rage, he launched himself at Borilius, ready to break his neck with his bare hands — and was stopped by an unseen fist of Air. Light flashed inside his head as he was thrown backward into the dirt.

Borilius made a *tisking* sound. "We won't have any of that," he growled, and Jase felt a grip of Air close around his throat. It yanked him roughly to his feet and dragged him forward until he was face to face with the man who held him. With one last thrust, Borilius drove him to his knees. "Get used to the view," he mewed. "Because once I turn you over to Aethon, my place in the Brotherhood will be exalted. If you behave yourself, I might let you lick the dust from my boots."

Jase was about to spit a reply when the Riaki Agla'Con staggered over. Borilius turned to regard him with contempt. "I suppose I have to heal you now," he said condescendingly, then motioned for the Riaki to turn around so he could remove the arrow with a far from gentle yank of Air.

The Riaki hissed in pain but remained on his feet as Borilius placed his hand on his shoulder and healed him. For one brief instant Jase felt the shield between his Awareness and *Ta'shaen* weaken, and he reached for it with ever fiber of his being.

The dark wall sagged outward as he pressed against it, and he felt the tingling of Earthpower right on the edge of his grasp. A hair's width more and he would have it.

Exquisite pain lanced through his body, and he found himself flat on his back, convulsing violently as wave after wave of corrupted energy racked him, an invisible fire he was sure had seared him to the bone.

The pain vanished as suddenly as it had come, and he looked up to find Borilius shaking his head with mock sadness. "Things will be easier for you if you'll stop resisting," the Agla'Con said, and the grip of Air closed around Jase's throat once more. It yanked him to his feet, and he felt the bones in his neck and back pop. "Aethon may want you alive," Borilius continued, "but he said nothing about your physical condition. Try seizing the Power again and I will remove parts of your body. An arm perhaps. Or a leg. Do you understand me?" The grip relaxed so he could answer.

Jase ignored him, turning instead to the Riaki. "If you harmed my mother," he growled, "I'll cut your filthy heart out and send it to your clan in a sack."

"You aren't in a position to do anything," Borilius hissed, punching him in the mouth so hard his knees buckled. If not for the fist of Air holding him up, he might have fallen. He tasted blood but kept his hands at his side, refusing to give Borilius the satisfaction of seeing him reach up to rub his jaw. He turned his head slightly and spit the blood onto a clump of creepers, then turned a defiant stare back on Borilius.

The Zekan looked like he might punch him again but didn't. Instead, he gestured to the gate. "Let's call your uncle."

When the clearing fell silent, Seth risked a quick look over his shoulder. His heart sank when he found Jase kneeling in front of the Zekan Agla'Con. It was a distraction that very nearly cost him his life.

His Shizu opponents swept in, and one slashed him across the shoulder before he could turn the blade away and kill the man. As it was, the other blades still almost got him, passing so close to his head he felt the brush of air.

He whirled away, slashing at the Shizu with his left hand and chopping through a tangle of vines with his right. Diving through the hole, he rolled and came to one knee, his swords held before him as he waited for the Shizu to follow. They did, and Seth threw himself at them with a vengeance. Steel rang loudly on steel, and blood spattered the green of the foliage as two black forms tumbled among the creepers.

Another quick glance through the trees showed that Jase had risen to his feet. His posture was defiant, but he was obviously shielded from using the Power. The boy had killed more of the Agla'Con than he had thought he would, so maybe there was still a chance. He started back to where he'd been when the first of the Shizu had attacked. If he could find his bow, he might be able to put an arrow in one or both of the Agla'Con and free Jase. *If I can find the bow.*

He was nearing the area where he'd lost the bow when four Shizu appeared in the forest around him. When they reached for the bladestars tucked inside their *komouri* instead of coming at him with their swords, he knew he was in trouble. He deflected the first two bladestars with his swords, but the third one struck him in the hip. A fourth grazed his cheek and several more whistled past his head. He managed to deflect three more, but there were too many coming at him to get them all. One hit him in the shoulder and another clipped the side of his head.

The pain he could ignore; the warm flow of red on his face was different. If blood clouded his vision, he was a dead man. He might be anyway if he didn't do something soon. Evidently the Shizu thought so as well, because they stayed out of reach of his swords and continued to hurl bladestars at him as fast as they could. With one out of every three or four finding its mark, the pain was quickly becoming difficult to ignore.

The thought that his last act in life had been the failure he'd always dreaded was punctuated by a crackling hiss that sounded from the clearing. He frowned. *Sorry, Jase,* he thought, rushing the closest of the Shizu. He would kill at least one of them before he died. To not even try would be a disgrace.

He'd only managed a few steps when a massive shape burst from the trees in a flash of greens and browns. Steel flashed in a sweeping arch, and *komouri*-clad bodies flew in all directions as blood spattered the foliage like rain.

It was the first time in his life that Seth Lydon had ever truly frozen in surprise.

CHAPTER 40

Through the Veil

Standing in a secluded courtyard in Sagaris' Imperial Palace, Aethon Fairimor studied the men gathered before him and tried to gage their reaction to his gift. The Emperor and the members of the Imperial Clave were the easiest to read; their lust for power was a ravenous light in their eyes. The twenty-five Agla'Con gathered behind them looked just as hungry. The ten Deathsquads standing guard around the courtyard, however... those may as well have been carved from stone for all the emotion they showed. Aethon admired them for their ability to remain calm. It wasn't an easy thing to do in light of the Shadowhounds patrolling the walls above them.

He watched the Shizu a moment longer, then turned his attention back to the artificial T'rii Gate he had constructed for Riak. It was similar to the one in the Meleki camp, but lacked the talismans linking it to the *chorazin* gates he and Falius had discovered scattered across the world. This was to be a direct link to Shadan's armies and nothing more. He knew they would try to use it for purposes other than those he intended, but without the links they would find it very difficult to do. When it came to manipulating the Veil, simply being strong in the Power wasn't enough, there was a large amount of finesse required as well.

"Riak and Melek are now linked in more than just purpose," he told them. "Our Agla'Con, our troops, and our shadowspawn will now be able to move between our armies at will. With such a joining of resources, our war against Kelsa will be that much easier to wage. Even as we speak, Shadan's armies are ready to move through Zedik Pass. They begin their march tomorrow. I will expect the Imperial Army of Riak to join them shortly. Kelsa has strengthened its southern border against a Riaki invasion and will not be expecting you to come from the east. With our combined strength, we will crush any resistance and take the city of Fulrath within the month."

The Emperor, Nisibis Samal, inclined his head. "Forgive me, exalted one," he began, and Aethon could tell that showing obeisance in front of the others angered him, "but some of the northern clans led by Clan Gahara have organized themselves into an alliance against the Brotherhood. There are rumors that they are planning to come to war against Sagaris."

Aethon frowned. "Why have I not heard of this sooner?"

"We only recently learned of it ourselves," Emperor Samal replied. "These rebels have acted quickly." He paused and looked at the members of the Imperial Clave. "We dare not send too great a force to Melek until this new threat can be dealt with."

"Are you afraid of a handful of lesser clans?" Aethon growled. "You are the Imperial Clave. Any act of war against you will be seen as treason against Riak."

"But Clan Gahara leads them," one of the clave members said urgently.

Aethon turned to regard him coldly. "So it is a single clan that frightens you," he said derisively. "Perhaps my confidence in your abilities has been misplaced."

Emperor Samal bristled at the comment. "Gahara is legendary for its role in the Battle of Sekigaroga," he said. "We do not take anything they do lightly. They single-handedly — "

"Silence!" Aethon shouted. "You are the rulers of Riak. A clan has risen up in rebellion against you. Strike them down as is your right. Use an army of Agla'Con if you must. But do it quickly. I want Riak ready to march with the Shadan Cult as soon as they move through Zedik Pass. Is that clear?"

The line of men scowled at his rebuke, but one by one they nodded.

"One other thing," he said, lowering his voice to a menacing hiss. "You are the rulers of Riak as I have said. But remember who put you there. Fulfill your obligations to Maeon or you will be replaced. Understand?"

Again they nodded.

He was ready to add one more threat when he felt a stirring in the Power and the gate came to life behind him. A thin line of red rent the Veil within the metal frame, and his brother Kameron appeared in the opening. In the darkness beyond, several dozen talismans glowed brightly as the Agla'Con who had rent the Veil held it open. Kameron seemed agitated.

"Someone is trying to access the gate," he said, his eyes straying to the members of the Imperial Clave. He hesitated for a moment, unsure if he should continue. "The link indicates the *chorazin* gate in Arkania."

"I'll check it out," Aethon said, then motioned for Kameron to sever the contact.

The rent snapped shut with an angry crackle, and Aethon turned to the assembly of Agla'Con. "You," he said taking in the first two rows with a sweep of his hand, "come with me." He motioned for several contingents of Shizu as well, then touched the minds of half a dozen Shadowhounds with a commanding tendril of *Ta'shaen*. Obediently they walked down the walls to fall in behind the Shizu.

When they were ready, he glanced at Emperor Samal. "Remember what I've said," he told him pointedly. "Fulfill your promises or I will kill you myself." With one last look at those who were to accompany him, he rent the Veil and stepped into the jungle of Arkania.

光

"He comes," Borilius said, and Jase looked up to see a thin line of red split the area inside the *chorazin* vertically down the center. The air parted with an angry hiss, and a tall man with dark brown hair and blue eyes stepped through from a courtyard beyond.

Aethon, Jase realized. The man had the look of a Fairimor.

A dozen Riaki Agla'Con, fire blazing in their fists, followed Aethon into the clearing, and a swarm of Shizu came next, fanning out across the clearing with swords bared. They were followed by a wall of spike-backed Shadowhounds. When the last hound cleared the gate, the rent snapped closed behind it.

Aethon stared at Borilius in surprise. "What are you doing in Arkania?" he asked suspiciously. Then his eyes went to the leather bag in Borilius' hand, and Jase knew by the hungry look washing over Aethon's face that he had felt the presence of the Elsa Talisman.

Borilius bowed deferentially. "My lord," he said, the tremor of fear audible in his voice. "We have accomplished the task you gave us. Gideon Dymas is dead. And here is the Fairimor boy, alive and well, as you requested. His mother is here also, unconscious but alive. And this," he paused, holding up the bag, "is a Blood Orb of Elsa."

Aethon started forward, and the hungry look in his eyes turned ravenous as he stared at the bag. "Where did you find it?" he asked, oblivious to everything but the Talisman.

Borilius watched him warily. "In a temple near Thesston," he answered. "Is my lord pleased?"

"Pleased?" Aethon asked with a smile. "Borilius, my friend, with that I can finish bringing down the Veil. There is no need to fight a prolonged war." He laughed, and the sound made the hair on Jase's neck stand on end. "I can open the world to Con'Jithar right here and now."

Fear and revulsion flooded through Jase, and he struggled against the grip of Air holding him. Desperate now, he shoved his Awareness against the shield Borilius held between him and *Ta'shaen* and nearly punched his way through to the Power beyond. If he could reach it, he would turn the entire area into a mass of flames so great all of Arkania would feel the heat. He would rather die himself than let Aethon attack the Veil.

Borilius felt his attempt to break free and sent a series of sharp pains lancing through him. Jase clenched his teeth to keep from howling and waited until they subsided. When his vision cleared, he found that Aethon had reached Borilius and was holding out his hand for the bag. Obediently, Borilius gave it to him.

"Aethon!"

The shout echoed across the clearing like a thunderclap, and all eyes turned to find Gideon striding out of the jungle. Streamers of green fire arched from his fingertips, and the clearing erupted into chaos as Agla'Con threw up shields and Shizu dove for cover. Lightning stabbed earthward, scattering black-clad bodies, and balls of fire erupted in the midst of the Shadowhounds, incinerating many of the bristly shapes in flashes of red.

Obviously panicked, Borilius let the grip of Air holding Jase vanish and turned to strike at Gideon. By the time he realized his error, it was too late. Jase stepped forward and shattered the man's jaw with a punch that sent him tumbling backward to the ground. As Borilius fell unconscious, the shield between Jase and the Power vanished. He opened his Awareness, and *Ta'shaen* flowed into him in a wave.

Reaching out with a fist of Air, he yanked the leather bag from Aethon's grip, then turned the area around the traitorous Fairimor to fire...

...and found himself diving away as that same fire came streaking right back at him. He hit the ground and rolled to the side as the killing heat flashed over him, singeing his hair and clothes. Before the flames even vanished, he was forced to throw a barrier of Spirit between himself and the lightning bolts sizzling toward him. Obviously Aethon was the most powerful adversary he'd faced yet. And judging from what he'd just seen of the man's abilities, the most skilled as well. With thunder rumbling against his shield, he stretched out with his Awareness and began searching for the man trying to kill him.

He spotted Gideon hunkered beneath a dome of Spirit, and it looked as if the Dymas was taking the brunt of the Agla'Con attack. But Jase quickly discovered that Gideon hadn't come to Arkania alone. Five massive figures spun through the maelstrom of fire, wielding shields of Spirit as deftly as the long spears they used to kill anything that came within their reach. Shizu, Shadowhound, it didn't matter; the steel tips cleared away the enemy like stubble hewn from a field. Arrows streaked from the cover of the jungle foliage, and more Shizu, as well as a few of the Agla'Con, fell clutching at their chests. Everywhere he looked there was death.

But he couldn't find Aethon. The traitorous Fairimor had vanished.

Jase rose and began making his way toward his mother. She still lay where she had fallen, covered with a thin layer of dirt and at the mercy of anyone who might think about sticking a sword in her. A Shadowhound spotted her and was less than five paces away when Jase hit the vile creature with a fist of Air, smashing it into an unrecognizable pulp.

Jase continued slowly forward, and as he moved, his shield moved with him, an invisible wall that pushed the attacking Shizu aside like so many insects. They slashed at the unseen barrier with their swords, but the blades glanced off as if hitting steel. Jase didn't even bother to kill them. His attention was focused on his mother. Bringing her inside his shield was the only thing that mattered.

He didn't feel any kind of disturbance in the Power until a thin line of fire appeared in the air directly in front of him. When it split apart, opening a hole in the spirit fabric of the Veil, his Awareness shrieked in agony.

Aethon stepped through from somewhere beyond, and the bag in Jase's hand flared into ash. The Talisman of Elsa fell away, and Aethon seized it in a grip of Air, pulling it toward his open palm before the flash of the incinerated bag had even faded. Though momentarily blinded, Jase felt what was happening and reacted by punching Aethon in the throat with a fist of Air, sending him staggering backward through the rent with a choking gasp. The Talisman flew wide of the fiery hole and struck the dome of Spirit Jase held above them, shattering it like glass. The concussion of the exploding shield reached the far edges of the clearing, and men were tossed like dolls. Even one of the Dainin was knocked off his feet.

Whirling, Jase thrust out his hand and called the Talisman to him with a grip of Air. It struck his open palm with a loud *thwack*, and he closed his fist around it protectively. His breath caught in his throat, and he stared at his hand in wonder. Like a beating heart, the Orb was warm and alive, a pulsating radiance that made the silhouette of bones stand out sharply against the pinkish glow of his flesh. The bars of light streaming from between his fingers reached the far edges of the clearing. The reservoir of Earthpower waiting to be accessed through the Blood Orb was so immense he thought it might be enough to crack the world like an egg. With so much Earthpower, Aethon really could bring down the Veil, as easily, perhaps, as Gideon had strengthened it years earlier.

And it called to him, a roaring voice of fire that demanded use. He felt himself reaching for it, eager to embrace its vastness, eager to be made invincible. With this much of the Power, he could challenge Maeon.

The light dimmed as Aethon's fist closed over his, and Jase came back to himself in a rush. The tantalizing call of so much raw power vanished like the last vestiges of a bad dream. What had he been thinking? Challenging Maeon? He really was losing his mind.

He glanced down at his hand and found Aethon trying to wrest the Talisman from his grasp. The older man's Awareness pressed in upon his and their eyes met. Aethon grinned.

Now you see why I want it, Aethon's mind whispered to his. *Neither of us could hope to wield so much on our own. Let me have it, and I'll share it with you.*

"Never," Jase hissed, clamping his other hand over Aethon's. "I'll die first."

"You will anyway," Aethon growled, lunging into him.

They fell backward and rolled several times across the ground, Aethon trying to pry his fingers loose while he held on with everything he had. The Power flared white-hot along the edge of his Awareness, and he reached for it, ready to rid the world of Aethon Fairimor once and for all.

A tiny voice of warning whispered somewhere in the far reaches of his mind, and he knew with a certainty that if he tried to call upon the reservoir of *Ta'shaen* without full possession of the Talisman, the entire continent would feel the resulting cataclysm.

Maybe you're not as dumb as I thought, Aethon hissed, and Jase knew for certain that the man could hear his thoughts. Aethon lunged to his feet as if he were trying to jerk Jase's arms from their sockets, and Jase let himself be hauled up without resisting.

I was starting to think Gideon hadn't taught you anything, Aethon continued. *The Talisman binds itself to the wielder. The blood of Elsa will react to Power channeled toward the one who wields the Talisman as if that person were Elsa herself. I hold half the Power. Strike at me and you strike at Elsa. Neither of us would survive. It is the reason I haven't simply sliced your head off with a thread of fire instead of doing this the hard way.*

"It's only the hard way because you're old and weak," Jase growled, spinning Aethon around in a wide arch and slamming him against one of the gate posts.

Aethon grunted but didn't relax his grip. *But it doesn't mean I can't strike at places away from you,* he said, and Jase felt a surge of corrupted Earthpower streak toward Brysia in the form of a lightning bolt.

Frantically he threw a shield over her, and the stab of white exploded short of its mark.

But Aethon wasn't finished. *What of your friends hiding in the jungle?* he taunted, and the foliage at the edge of the clearing blew apart in a spray of greens and browns. Bodies flew through the air, and Jase saw that Elliott was among them.

You bloody — he howled, spinning Aethon around once more. Instead of slamming him into the pillar, however, he took advantage of the Communal link and pulled the knowledge of how to rend the Veil from Aethon's mind.

Grinning like a madman, he directed a massive flow of Spirit into the gate. The air split apart in a hiss of silvery-blue, and he and Aethon tumbled through to the darkness beyond.

This latest Shizu was better than the last three Elliott had faced, and he found himself defending more than attacking. The white of the man's eyes shone in the slit of his *koro* mask and made Elliott think of the rabid wolf he and Seth had killed while hunting together in the Glacier Mountains. The Shizu was attacking with the same disregard for his own life as the wolf had.

An errant stab of lightning split a tree a short distance away, and the Shizu flinched, momentarily losing his concentration. Elliott took advantage of the distraction and sliced the man's sword arm with a quick twist of his wrists, then spun to remove his head. Even as the headless corpse fell, another Shizu rushed in and the macabre dance continued.

It seemed like hours before he could finally lower his sword, though in reality it had been only moments. His hands stung, and his arms felt like lead, but no more Shizu appeared out of the jungle to challenge him. Retrieving his bow from where he'd dropped it, he moved to the edge of the clearing.

What he found turned his blood cold. It wasn't the number of bodies littering the ground so much as the number of bodies unrecognizable as such because of the way they had been torn apart with the Power. He saw a stab of lightning take an Agla'Con in the back and hurriedly looked away as the man's remains began raining earthward, charred shreds of cloth and flesh trailing smoky tendrils. It made killing with a sword seem civilized by comparison.

He set his sword on the ground before him so he could take it up again quickly if needed and notched an arrow. Sighting down the narrow shaft, he took aim at an unsuspecting Shizu and let it fly. The arrow was halfway to its mark when the ground to his right exploded in a flash of white and the world around him went black.

The prickle of energy on her skin pulled Brysia Fairimor back to consciousness, and she lifted her head as a thunderous explosion rocked the air above her. She flinched, covering her head with her hands, and looked up to see the last tendrils of white-hot energy crackling down the surface of what could only be a shield of Spirit. To her right she spotted Jase locked hand to hand with a man who bore a strong resemblance to her father.

Aethon, she realized. It had to be. The man was definitely a Fairimor.

She saw the light pouring from their fists, and her heart froze when she realized what they were fighting over. *Dear God*, she breathed silently, *help my son. Help us all.* If Aethon gained possession of the Talisman of Elsa, life would be over. For everything.

Jase spun Aethon toward the gate, and Brysia's breath caught in her throat when she saw the air open behind them. The black of night filled the square, and a scattering of fires and lamps burned beyond. Jase shoved Aethon through and was dragged in as well. The hiss of the closing gate drowned out her anguished scream. When the shield above her vanished, she knew her son was gone.

Grief and shock threatened to overwhelm her, but she squashed them, focusing instead on her rage. Rising to one knee, she looked around the clearing, eager to enter the fray, hungry for vengeance against those who had taken her son.

Bodies lay scattered everywhere. All across the clearing men were racing for cover. Most wore the black *komouri* uniforms of Shizu, but there were a large number of Agla'Con as well. She saw the remains of Shadowhounds scattered among the dead, and a chill ran up her spine. *Where did those come from?*

Then she noticed other figures — giant figures clothed in greens and browns — spinning through the melee with spears and nets of green fire. Dainin, she realized, smiling. If anyone could defeat the Agla'Con, it was the *Nar'shein Yahl*. She heard the anguished scream of an Agla'Con and looked to see him tumble to the ground. The net which had engulfed him flashed green fire. She saw another Agla'Con fall in two directions as a Dainin spear sliced him from head to crotch. Gruesome, but justified.

From the corner of her eye she saw something move and turned to see Borilius trying to push himself from the ground a dozen paces away. Blood slicked his lips, and he seemed dazed.

She knew that striking him with the Power would draw the attention of other Agla'Con, so she crept out of Borilius' line of sight and retrieved a sword from a slain Shizu. Gripping the long hilt with both hands, she slipped quietly toward him.

Balls of fire continued to explode across the clearing, and the air crackled with blue-white flashes of lightning. The ground shook from every blast, and dust and smoke hung heavy in the air. The clash of steel sounded in the distance. The screams of dying men were all around her. Pursing her lips determinedly, she ignored it all and kept her eyes firmly fastened on the man responsible for this chaos, the man who deserved death more than any other killed here today.

And now it was just seconds away.

She stepped up behind him and raised the sword over her head. Daris had taught her how to use a sword; what she did next was for him.

"Say hello to Maeon," she snarled and brought the blade down with a *shump*.

As Borilius' headless corpse slumped forward, Brysia sensed movement behind her and whirled, bringing the sword up in front of her for protection. The Shizu who had sneaked up behind her slashed with his sword, and her hands stung from the blow she somehow managed to block. He lunged again, and she lashed at him with *Ta'shaen*, exploding the ground beneath his feet and sending him sprawling.

Two more Shizu came at her from the side, and she abandoned the sword completely, striking them with fountains of Earth instead. One managed to hurl a bladestar, and Brysia's shoulder screamed in agony. Yanking the four-pronged star free, she tossed it aside and looked up to find the Shizu already back on their feet and racing toward her, swords and bladestars in hand. She stretched her Awareness into the earth, readying another strike, but green fire streaked in from somewhere behind her before she could attack. The killing surges took each of the assassins in the chest, and they vanished in flashes of incandescent white.

Brysia turned to find Gideon Dymas moving through the smoke toward her. With a shout of joy, she threw herself into his arms and hugged him fiercely, overwhelmed with emotion by what his return might mean.

As his arms encircled her, so did a shield of Spirit, and the sounds of battle faded to a dull rumble. "I told you I'd come back," Gideon said, kissing her gently on the head. "And I always keep my promises." The warmth of *Ta'shaen* filled her as Gideon healed the wound in her shoulder.

Brysia looked into his weathered face, and her eyes filled with tears. "And Benak?" she asked.

Gideon shook his head. "Not yet," he replied sadly. "But we're getting closer to freeing him."

Brysia nodded. She had expected as much. But with Gideon free, Benak's return was indeed closer. Assuming that they could heal the Earthsoul. "Then do me a favor," she told him, taking a step back and smoothing her skirts as if they weren't standing in the middle of a battle. "Get my son back."

Gideon pressed his fist to his chest. "It will be as you command, Sister

Queen."

Ammorin threw back the wall of flames hurled at him by a one-armed Riaki, then smashed the man's feeble attempt at a shield with a thrust of Spirit. With a flick of his wrist, he sent the last of his nets spinning, and the Agla'Con shrieked as the Power-filled weave of *arinseil* bore him to the ground with the weight of ten men, severing his connection to *Ta'shaen* and shocking him for good measure.

Ammorin turned away, his eyes and Awareness once again drawn to the Talisman of Elsa shining like the sun in the center of the clearing. Its light was dimmed by the men's fists, but the light of its power glowed brightly in his mind. Each man held half of that immense ocean. Whoever claimed it all would determine the fate of the world.

He threw off another surge of corrupted Power, then skewered the Agla'Con who'd launched it with a thrust of his spear. Snapping the spear around, he threw the lifeless corpse away like a rag doll. He needed to reach the Fairimor boy before all was lost.

Hefting his spear, he held a shield of Spirit around him and advanced through the maelstrom of fire, throwing back strike after strike of the rapidly tiring Agla'Con. He didn't even bother to engage any of them — his sights were set on their leader. There would be no trial for Aethon Fairimor, he decided, just a swift and long overdue death.

He was nearly there when he felt the Veilgate come alive once more. It parted with an angry hiss, but it wasn't the corruption of the Agla'Con that caused it. It was the pure, undefiled Power wielded by Jase.

Jase swung Aethon around, and Ammorin hissed in surprise when he realized what the boy intended to do. Stretching with a grip of Air, he tried to catch the two men before they crossed through to the darkness beyond. The attempt was turned aside by an Agla'Con who stood between him and the gate, and the Veil snapped shut in a flash of blue. The presence of the Talisman vanished from his Awareness like a snuffed candle. Not even a whispering of Elsa's blood remained.

Ammorin turned his gaze on the Agla'Con who'd prevented him from saving Jase and watched the blood drain from the man's face. *And rightfully so,* Ammorin thought, blowing the man's shield apart with a thrust of Spirit. A moment later the Agla'Con was a shrieking, writhing mass beneath Pattalla's net.

The battle raged for several more minutes, and then a sudden silence fell across the clearing. Ammorin looked around. All the Agla'Con were either dead or captured. None but Aethon had escaped. He spotted Gideon standing with the Sister Queen and felt a quieting in *Ta'shaen* as the Dymas released his hold on it. Pattalla and Sharrukin released the Power as well. Only the residual corruption of the Agla'Con remained to tickle his Awareness.

He strode across the carnage to Gideon. As he neared, he glanced at the headless corpse of Borilius Constas sprawled in the loam. "It seems my Cleansing Hunt is over," he said, indicating the dead Agla'Con. "I offer my thanks to you, Sister Queen, for removing his head. That stroke freed me and my men from having to return him to Dainin."

"What will you do now?" Gideon asked.

Ammorin started to reply but cut off when he felt a disturbance in *Ta'shaen*. The look on Gideon's face showed he had felt it as well.

The Talisman of Elsa was being used.

"Can you tell where it is?" Gideon asked.

Ammorin shook his head. "The distance is too great, but I would say north and east of here."

"That is what I think as well," Gideon said, then hesitated a moment before continuing. "It's probably safe to assume it wasn't Aethon who used it. Otherwise we would be choking to death in a sea of darkness."

"Perhaps," Ammorin replied. "But I do not think Aethon would act so quickly in bringing down the Veil. Shadan would be angry with him. I'm not even sure it can be done."

"Oh, it can be done," Gideon said emphatically. "Trust me."

"What are you two talking about?" Brysia asked, looking back and forth between them, frustrated at being left out of the conversation.

Ammorin dropped to one knee so she wouldn't have to keep looking up at him. "The Power of the Talisman is being accessed," he told her, then hesitated a moment before continuing, "but we do not know who the wielder is."

"So going back to Gideon's question," she said, "what will you do now?"

"The *Nar'shein Yahl* will assist Gideon in finding your son." Ammorin told her softly. "If we fail in that, I will personally deliver you Aethon Fairimor's head."

When the last of the Agla'Con went down in the fiery green tangle of a Dainin net, Talia rose from her hiding place and started across the clearing. Smoke and dust hung heavy in the air, but it was the silence that she found most oppressive. It had fallen over the area like a suffocating blanket, muting the sounds of the wounded and stifling the breath of the living. It was the silence of death.

She picked her way carefully toward the gate, mindful of the bodies littering the ground. She averted her eyes from the awful sight as best she could. Thankfully, it would be dark soon; most of what she saw made her want to empty her stomach.

Like ghosts, the crew of *Sea Blade* slipped from the trees as well, bows and swords still clutched tightly in their hands as they cast about warily, unsure if the battle was truly over. Talia watched them come, and a wave of sadness washed through her when she realized how few in number they were.

She spotted Seth and made her way toward him. As usual, he was completely covered with blood. This time, however, much of it appeared to be his. He saw her as she neared, and the look that flashed across his face showed he was both irritated and relieved to see her.

"Your brother was injured," he told her when she reached him, "but he will be all right." Before he could say anything more, she took his head with both hands and sent a flow of healing through him. He inhaled sharply, then relaxed as the Power left him.

"You are growing in skill," he said with genuine admiration. "There are others who are wounded if you would like to help."

"What of Jase?" she asked, trying to keep the fear from her voice.

Seth shrugged, but she could see in his eyes that he was worried. "I haven't seen him," he answered. "Do what you can for the wounded, and then we'll go ask Gideon."

It took longer than she'd anticipated to heal those who had been hurt because she had to spend a great deal of time just looking for the living among the dead. By the time all were located, it was dark. Several lamps had been placed around the Veilgate, and a makeshift camp had been set up by the crew of *Sea Blade*. She had the last of the wounded brought to her there.

With Pattalla acting as her mentor, she healed what she could and tried to learn from him when something was beyond her ability. She was good with surface wounds such as those Seth had received, but anything internal still made her nervous. Pattalla, on the other hand, was a master Healer and had a way of explaining things that made learning easier. She wished Gideon were able to listen; Pattalla could probably teach the aging Dymas a thing or two.

When the last of the living were accounted for, the grim task of numbering the dead began in full. Of the crew from *Sea Blade*, nearly half had been killed. She hadn't known any of them, but her heart still ached at their loss. All had been good men, ready to fight for a cause they knew nothing about. Many had died without even knowing what it was that had killed them.

The loss of Shaalbin and Bettashin was even harder for her to accept. She had seen them fight and had marveled at their ferocity. Learning of their aversion to using *Ta'shaen* as a weapon made what they accomplished in battle that much more amazing. But it angered and confused her as well. Their refusal to use the Power as a weapon had very likely cost them their lives.

She watched Pattalla and Sharrukin work their magic on the most serious of the injured and felt as if her heart would burst. They may fight like dragons when pressed, but deep inside the Dainin were gentle. Like the crew of *Sea Blade*, the *Nar'shein Yahl* had been caught up in something larger than they had anticipated.

Welcome to the club, she told them sadly, then moved to check on Gideon's progress.

He still stood with Ammorin in front of the Veilgate, and both were probing it with their Awareness, desperate to figure out how it worked. Neither had moved in almost an hour, and she was starting to worry that they never would. She crossed to where Brysia was sitting on a cloak and sat down beside her.

The Sister Queen smiled and reached over to take her hand. "I've been watching you with the wounded," she said softly. "You have quite a Gift. You are not the same girl I remember from those years when you were making my son's life miserable."

"Ah... thank you," Talia said, not sure how to respond. If that last part was a compliment, it was an odd one.

Brysia smiled. "I should be thanking you," she said. "Seth told me what you have done for Jase. He owes you his life on several occasions, it seems. For that, I am eternally grateful." She raised Talia's hand to her lips and kissed it. With a bow of her head, she spoke in the Old Tongue, *"Brelafei 'oin kala susumei en kojyo."* She added the translation, "Welcome to the family, daughter of my heart."

For a moment, Talia was speechless. *Daughter of my heart.* She knew the weight the phrase carried. Only Seth and her father had ever spoken those words to her, and never in the Old Tongue. For Brysia to speak it here was no small thing.

She bowed her head in acceptance of the honor and smiled. "Thank you," she said, wishing she knew the proper Old Tongue response. Brysia kept hold of her hand, and they sat in silence as Gideon and Ammorin continued to probe the Veilgate.

Talia glanced at Seth standing a few paces away and found him pulling thoughtfully at his mustache as he watched her and Brysia. When he realized he'd been caught, he dropped his hand away from his mustache but kept smiling as if he knew some great secret.

"What else did Seth tell you about me?" she asked, doing her best to keep the suspicion out of her voice.

"Only that you love my son very deeply," Brysia said, then laughed. "But I won't repeat the words he used. They weren't very complimentary."

"I can imagine," Talia muttered, raising an eyebrow at Seth. He shrugged, then busied himself inspecting his swords, something he'd surely already done a hundred times in the last hour. Talia smiled and turned back to Brysia. "It's true. I do love him. More than anything else in the world."

As she spoke, her throat tightened and tears formed at the corners of her eyes. She reached up to wipe them away, but it was too late — those few words had caused the dam she'd built against her grief to crumble. She had been so busy healing the wounded that she'd had no time to dwell on the fact that he was gone. Really and truly gone. And no one seemed to know where. What if she never saw him again? What if he was... dead? She pinched her eyes shut and fought to regain control.

Brysia put her arm around her and held her close, smoothing her hair and whispering that everything would be all right.

As the night wore on, though, and neither Gideon nor Ammorin spoke or moved, Talia wondered how Brysia could be so strong in the face of such hopelessness.

Seth watched as Brysia let Talia cry herself out, then brought blankets so the young woman could lie down. The Sister Queen cradled Talia's head in her lap and gently stroked her long, dark hair until the girl fell asleep. Seth marveled at Brysia's strength. And her compassion. He watched for a while longer, then settled in himself, sitting in silence as Gideon and Ammorin continued to study the gate. Around him, the rest of those in the makeshift camp bedded down as well.

Four hours later, Gideon's shout shattered the silence, and the camp erupted into a flurry of movement. Swords and other weapons flashed as everyone cast about for some sign of the enemy. But the shout had been one of celebration, not warning.

Gideon turned to regard the group, his eyes bright with excitement. "I know how it is done," he told them, "though I am not strong enough to do it alone. With Ammorin's help I think I can open the gate."

Seth slammed his swords back into their sheaths and stepped forward. "Where to?" he asked.

Gideon glanced at the Riaki Agla'Con wrapped in the Dainin nets, and his eyes narrowed to slits of blue fire. "Riak," he said decisively. "It's time to resurrect Dunkin's Ghost."

CHAPTER 41

An Act of God

As the Veil snapped shut behind him, Jase took one look at his new surroundings and realized he'd made a mistake. Tents ringed a clearing almost as large as the one back in Arkania, and bonfires blazed in a dozen locations. A hundred or more crimson and black-robed men sat around the fires, every one of them staring in surprise at the two men who had just stumbled through the artificial Veilgate. It took only a moment for them to realize what was happening, and then shouts filled the air as the entire area erupted into movement.

One by one, fists flared red as hundreds upon hundreds of Agla'Con poured from the tents and rushed to watch the two men grappling for possession of the Talisman. Within seconds the night had been thrown back by a hellish red glow.

Oops, Aethon said sarcastically. *It looks like someone was a little hasty in rending the Veil. No matter. This is where I would have brought you anyway. Welcome to Melek, Jase. This is my army. The one I will use to ravage Kelsa in a manner mankind hasn't seen since the destruction of the Old World. Do you like what you see? If so, join with me, and your place in the afterlife will be exalted.*

For his answer, Jase let go of Aethon's wrist long enough to punch him in the mouth. The First staggered backward, but his grip didn't slacken. Neither did his hold on the half of the reservoir of *Ta'shaen* he controlled with his Awareness.

With a growl, Aethon swept Jase's legs out from under him, and the two went down in a tangle, kicking up a cloud of dust as they continued to try to pry each other loose from the glowing Orb.

The Agla'Con formed a ring around them, jeering and shouting as they watched their leader do battle. It reminded Jase of the time he'd fought Heril

Kinsten before school when they were little. A crowd of children had gathered almost at once, each child in the circle shouting encouragement or advice while Tana went to fetch the teacher. It was an odd thought, he knew, and similar to his plight here in outward appearance only. Here, no one shouted encouragement for him, and there was no teacher to break it up. To lose this fight was to die.

Yes, Aethon said, *and you will lose. The question is how quickly. Bringing down the Veil won't snuff this miserable world's life all at once. It will happen slowly, like a cancer. A very painful, ugly cancer. You will long for death before the end, Jase, and I will make you beg.*

You don't have possession yet, Jase snapped, but he could feel Aethon's hold on the reservoir growing. He focused his mind toward it and was alarmed to find that his perception of it had started to diminish. Aethon's Awareness was pressing in on his, a dark wall of malice that was slowly and methodically forcing him away. The more Aethon pressed, the less of the reservoir he could feel. Aethon already held more than half, and his command of the radiant sphere was increasing by the moment. At this rate, he would have complete control over the Talisman of Elsa in a few short minutes.

In desperation, Jase twisted to the side and lurched to his feet, dragging Aethon up with him and kneeing him hard in the stomach. The First groaned, but his grip tightened determinedly. Jase kneed him again and again, but still Aethon held on, his grip like an iron band, unbreakable and secure.

One of the Agla'Con, fearful that Jase was getting the upper hand, sent a tendril of Fire streaking toward him. Jase wove a shield of Sprit to ward it off, but Aethon beat him to it, deflecting the killing fire back into the Agla'Con with a deftness Jase hadn't thought possible. The man crumpled into a heap.

"Don't attack him, you fools," Aethon shouted. "We are linked. If you strike him, you strike me. Release the Power. Now! All of you."

The Agla'Con did as they were told, and the area plunged into sudden darkness — a wall of dark shapes, faceless save for the glimmer of light reflected in their eyes as they stared at the Talisman clutched tightly in his and Aethon's fists.

Suddenly the light changed to a reddish hue, and Jase found himself staring at Aethon's Agla'Con talisman. It had slipped from beneath Aethon's shirt during the struggle, and dangled on the end of a thin gold chain around his neck. The small, oddly formed dagger swung back and forth violently as they fought, the crystal in the hilt an angry sphere of red that burned in his vision like the fires of hell.

Panic forced its way into his Awareness, and he fought to remain calm as the white-hot sphere in his mind's eye slipped that much more into the grip of his enemy.

He knew he was stronger in the Power than Aethon; he had felt it the moment they had seized the Talisman. But what Aethon lacked in strength, he made up for with knowledge and experience. It was enough to tip the balance, and tip it quickly.

He quit trying to regain that part of the reservoir he'd lost and concentrated instead on holding the part that was still his. Aethon's progress slowed, but he was still gaining ground; a minute at most and the Talisman would be his.

It was apparent by Aethon's smile that he thought so as well.

Jase looked at the artificial T'rii Gate rising a step or two behind Aethon, and he momentarily considered trying to reopen it back to Arkania. Perhaps Gideon could help.

I'll open it for you'd if you like, Aethon told him. *It makes little difference to me where I gain control of the Talisman. Perhaps we should go to Gideon. I'd like to see the look on his face when I bring down the Veil.*

Jase set his jaw angrily, sick of Aethon being able to hear his thoughts. It was risky, but he reined in his Awareness until it was a pinprick of what it had been. The communal link between his and Aethon's minds broke, and Jase slipped back inside the protective ward Gideon had helped him create. The raging ocean of Earthpower glowing in his fist faded to a pinprick as well, and Aethon howled in triumph at his perceived victory.

I'm not done yet, you traitor! Jase told him, the thought safe within the sheltering mindward.

Feigning weakness, he released Aethon's wrist and sagged forward, bumping the older man a step closer to the gate. Aethon seemed not to notice. His eyes, glowing with a feverish light, stayed fastened on the Talisman of Elsa and the Power that was now only seconds away.

Jase pretended to stagger once more, and again Aethon was bumped closer to the gate, so intent on the reservoir of *Ta'shaen* that he was oblivious to the metal framework rising only a step behind him. It was then that Jase grabbed Aethon's talisman and ripped it from his neck. The slender chain snapped like string, and Aethon came back to himself in a rush. The First's hold on the Power wavered slightly, but that was all.

Aethon still held nearly all of the reservoir, but what was worse, he was still gaining ground. Jase looked at the dark crystal of Aethon's talisman and frowned in surprise. Gideon had told him Agla'Con couldn't wield without aid. How was this possible?

"Thought I would lose my hold on the Power without my talisman, did you?"

Aethon mewed. "Normally I might have, but the Talisman of Elsa was enough for me to keep the link. I am a Fairimor, after all. The blood of Elsa is bound to me as much as it is to you." He showed his teeth in a grin. "Sorry to disappoint you, Jase," he continued. "But it's time to die."

"For you," Jase snarled, plunging Aethon's dagger-talisman deep into the Agla'Con's side.

Aethon gasped and clutched blindly at the dagger with one hand even as he maintained his grip on the Talisman with the other. His hold on the Power faltered, and Jase opened his Awareness once more. *Ta'shaen* flowed into him in such a rush that points of light formed inside his head and a great roaring filled his ears. With a howl, he jerked the dagger free and punched Aethon in the face with the hilt. He staggered and nearly went down, and Jase channeled Spirit into the gate, opening a hole in the Veil.

Icy cold air poured through from the darkness beyond, and pellets of snow swept in to sting his hands and face. With one last shove, he pushed Aethon into knee-deep snow, then severed his hold on the Power. The Veil snapped shut with an angry hiss.

Jase glanced at Aethon's hand, severed just above the wrist, and smiled as he shook it loose from his fist. Tucking the dagger-talisman in his belt, he opened himself more fully to the Power and turned to face the Agla'Con.

The Talisman of Elsa flared white as he unleashed a torrent of fire.

"Captain Gaufin."

The voice stabbed into his dreams like a knife, and Elam came awake with a start, throwing back the blanket with one hand and seeking the hilt of his sword with the other. He rolled from the cot and brought the sword up in front of him, casting about the tent in alarm. The silhouettes of two men stretched across the canvas door flap, framed in a halo of lamplight.

Elam lowered his sword, embarrassed by his reaction at being awakened, but even more embarrassed that he had fallen asleep at all. When he'd come to his tent earlier in the evening to review Taggert's plan for retaking the pass, sleep had been the farthest thing from his mind. Especially considering the nature of his dreams lately. The one just now had been most terrifying. With considerable effort, he forced the dark images away and pulled open the flap to find Taggert and Idoman. Both men were bare-chested, but Taggert held his sword and his aging face was lined with concern. Idoman's, however, was bright with excitement.

Squinting against the sudden brightness of the lamp, Elam stepped out to meet them. "What is it?" he asked.

"There is a — " Taggert started to say, but Idoman spoke right over the top of him.

"Something is happening in *Ta'shaen*," he blurted, drawing a scowl from Taggert. "Something big. I have never felt anything so powerful in my life." He turned and pointed to the northeast. "It is coming from Melek."

Before Elam could reply, Joselyn Rai ran up to them out of the dark. Her nightgown was hiked to her knees, and her feet were bare. Her blue eyes were wide in astonishment. "Do you feel that?" she asked Idoman.

The young man nodded. "Yes. It's as pure a tremor as any I've ever felt."

"Tremor?" Joselyn scoffed. "Boy, you need to hone your skills. That is no mere tremor; it's a tidal wave. The entire fabric of *Ta'shaen* is alive with its vibration. Why, any Dymas on this side of the world can probably feel it."

"And probably some on the other side as well," Lord Nid said, moving into the lamplight. His dark face was serene, but his eyes glittered with excitement.

Elam stepped in between them. "Excuse me," he snapped, "but would someone mind telling me what this is all about?"

Joselyn turned to regard him, her eyes so bright with wonder that even the Meleki King deferred to her. "An act of God, that's what. It has to be. A thousand Dymas couldn't wield as much *Ta'shaen* as what's being unleashed in Melek right now. Ten thousand probably couldn't."

"And it is pure," Idoman repeated. "Pure and undefiled. Joselyn Dymas is right. God has taken a hand in the battle with Shadan's army."

The thundering of hooves sounded from the dark, and Elam and the others looked up as a young sentry galloped into camp. He came right at them, reining in sharply as he neared and leaping from the horse. "Captain Gaufin," he said, his eyes wide and his voice filled with panic, "Zedik Pass is filled with fire. The invasion has begun."

Elam took the reins of the young man's horse and climbed into the saddle. Before he could ride off, Joselyn moved beside him, her hand extended.

"I'm going with you," she said, her tone leaving no room for argument.

Elam took hold of her wrist and pulled her up behind him. He inclined his head to the others. "There are horses on the other side of those wagons," he told them, then he and Joselyn raced off through the darkness. It took only moments to reach the edge of the forest, and when they did, Joselyn gasped in awe at the sight before them. Elam was equally stunned.

The tops of the Death's Chain Mountains were outlined in a glow of white so bright it looked as if a dozen moons were about to rise behind them. The interior of Zedik Pass glowed with the brightness of the sun, and the light streaming into the Allister Plains had turned the area before them into day. Flashes of red were visible within the brightness, but they were nothing more than brief, insignificant flickers compared to the pure glow of *Ta'shaen*. Like the hint of distant thunder, a muffled rumbling teased their ears.

Elam glanced over as Idoman, Taggert, and Lord Nid slipped out of the forest, and together they watched in silence as light danced across the top of the mountains and filled the narrow slit of Zedik Pass with myriad flashes of color. A short time later, there was one final flash so bright it made Elam and the others shield their eyes against it.

When Elam looked back up, the lights had vanished. The mountains and pass were once more cloaked in darkness. Before his eyes could readjust to the darkness, the sound of a single large *boom* reached his ears.

"Praise be to the Creator," Joselyn whispered. "For truly we have witnessed His hand."

乇

"If we are able to retake and hold the Narrows," Croneam said, pointing to the map of Zedik Pass, "then we can position Dymas here and here. They should be able to hold Shadan's armies back for days or even weeks."

"Assuming we have them in the numbers you are hoping for," Erebius countered gently. "Right now we don't have nearly enough to carry out this plan."

"They will come," Croneam assured. "Trust in the prophecies." He pointed to another spot on the map. "I also want to place Dymas here, on the mountaintop along the cliff face. I don't want any winged surprises coming over the Death's Chain like the last time we fought Shadan's scum."

Erebius studied the map silently for a moment. "Then may I also suggest that we — " he cut off, his eyes widening in surprise. Rising, he hurried to the window and threw back the curtains, flooding the room with light as brilliant and white as the noonday sun.

"By all that's holy," Erebius breathed. "Come look at this!"

Croneam joined him at the window, and a chill of excitement raced up his spine when he found the eastern horizon rimmed in white. He turned to Erebius. "What do you feel, my friend?" he asked.

Erebius closed his eyes. "A powerful Awareness... of a man.... No. A woman." His face pinched with concentration, and he tilted his head as if listening. "No... it is both. And it is wielding the Power of a thousand Dymas.

Fire. White, hot, cleansing Fire." He opened his eyes and turned to regard Croneam with eyes that sparkled with awe. "God has taken a hand in the battle."

Croneam returned his gaze to the east. "This is it," he whispered. "The Night of Fire has come. The ranks of Dymas will soon be filled."

乇

Sitting at the bedside of Lady Korishal, Elison Brey watched Randle Fairimor pace back and forth across the room. The King's face was creased with emotion as he contemplated the magnitude of today's battle and tried to come to terms with how much had been lost. He hadn't spoken in almost an hour. It had been two hours since he'd started pacing the room.

Elison tried to find words of comfort, but there were none. Yes, the Con'Kumen ambush had been suppressed, but it had cost some of the best blood in Kelsa to do it. Twenty-eight *Bero'thai* had been killed. A dozen more had been wounded. Of the City and Palace Guard, one hundred and seventeen would not be returning to their families. And then there was Breiter.

The image of his friend's body, pierced with multiple arrows, flashed through his mind, and he pinched his eyes shut in order to hold back the tears that threatened each time that horrific memory returned. Forcing his grief away, he turned his gaze on Ladies Korishal and Hadershi. Now was the time to tend to the living. He would deal with Breiter's death later.

Both Dymas' faces were ashen, their breathing shallow and uneven. The arrows had been removed from their bodies, and their wounds had been bandaged, but no Healer had been found to treat them properly. Both had lost so much blood that Elison wondered how they still lived.

He looked at Randle. "You're going to wear a hole in the rug," he said softly, forcing a smile. "Come. Sit. It won't be long before the *Bero'thai* return with a Healer."

"A lot of good it will do Breiter," the King mumbled, then looked mortified when he realized he'd spoken aloud. "I'm sorry," he said, moving to a chair to flop down wearily. "I didn't mean for that to sound so... so..." he trailed off, unable to finish.

"It's not your fault," Elison told him.

"Isn't it?" Randle asked. "I'm the one who sent all the Gifted to Fulrath."

"And I sat as a member of the council who okayed it," Elison reminded him. "We did what we thought was best." He sighed. "Considering Elder Nesthius' prophecy, I'm not convinced the outcome would have been any different even had we kept more Gifted here."

"Bloody prophecies," Randle growled, lurching to his feet to begin pacing once more. "I've had about all I can take of fate's meddling hand." He ran his fingers through his hair and continued to mutter under his breath.

Elison watched him without speaking.

Suddenly Lady Korishal's eyes snapped open, and she inhaled sharply. "It's him," she exclaimed, sitting up to cast about the room in wonder. "The Night of Fire has come. Do you feel it? Do you feel? The earth trembles beneath his power. The earth... Spirit and Fire... do you... feel?" Her eyes fluttered, and she slumped back to the pillow.

Alarmed, Elison checked her pulse. It was as faint as ever, but still there. Exhaling in relief, he moved to Lady Hadershi's bed and took her hand. She had begun to thrash as well, but was having difficulty waking up. Her eyelids flickered as she tried to open them, and a soft, unintelligible murmur escaped her lips. As quickly as it had come, the thrashing stopped, and Beraline drifted back to sleep.

Elison looked questioningly at Randle, but before either of them could speak, the door to the room burst open and Cassia rushed in. She moved straight to the window.

"Look," she said excitedly. "The northeastern horizon is bright with light."

He and Randle joined her at the window and found the northern arm of the Kelsan Mountains outlined with a halo of white.

"Please tell me that is something good for a change," Randle whispered.

Elison wanted to answer but couldn't. Awestruck, he stared at the glow in silence.

火

A tickling along his Awareness interrupted Railen Nogeru's study of the map of the Imperial Palace, and he glanced at Kalear who sat opposite him on the floor. The Sarui was gazing intently toward the north, his brow wrinkled in thought.

"You feel it too?" Railen asked, though he already knew the answer.

Kalear nodded. "Yes," he said, his voice filled with awe. "And to be felt over such a distance means the amount of *Ta'shaen* being wielded is tremendous. Never in my life could I hope to wield so much."

Railen frowned. "It feels like nothing more than a tickle to me," he admitted. "Are you sure it's as large as you say?"

Kalear turned to regard him quietly for a moment, his dark eyes shining. "The entire world rings with its vibration," the Sarui said. "Open your Awareness more fully and you will feel it as I do. Something big is happening to the north.

In Melek perhaps. Something that may very well change the course of the future."

Shavis stuck his head in from the other room. "But it won't change anything before morning," he told them. "So finish making your plans. Sagaris awaits. For us, that is where the future will be changed."

"Yes, Dai'shozen," Kalear replied, returning to his study of the strategy he'd devised for *tres'dia's* part in the attack on Sagaris.

Railen returned to his perusal of the map, but his mind was on the tremor in *Ta'shaen*. With a quick look at the door to make sure Shavis wasn't watching, he closed his eyes and opened his Awareness. Clearing his mind, he began tracing the tremors back toward the source of the disturbance.

Darkness vanished in a flare of silvery-white, and Jase closed his eyes against the brightness as he directed *Ta'shaen* into the closest of the Agla'Con. The pure flame of Elsa struck, and their hastily woven shields burst apart in sprays of corrupted Earthpower. The Agla'Con hiding beneath them flashed from existence.

In his mind's eye he could see the spots of black left behind by their spirits, stains of evil against an otherwise vibrant landscape of light. Like wraiths, the dark shapes stood and looked around in confusion while the glowing fabric of the Veil became visible around them. It rippled slightly, and the dead men were pulled through to the world beyond, vanishing from his Awareness as if they had never been.

Even as he marveled at seeing spirits pass from this life to the next, Jase turned the Power of the Talisman on a second group, crushing their defenses and incinerating them, their weapons, and the nearest cluster of tents in one massive flow of white-hot fire.

Darkness fled further, and the Plains of Criet grew bright as day. To the north, Cresdraline Forest glowed greenish-white. To the west, the face of the Death's Chain flashed like giant teeth against the black that was night in Kelsa. The stars and moon faded from view, washed away by a glow that seemed to fill all of Melek.

Everywhere he looked, men were running for cover or holding up shields of Spirit, trying desperately to ward off his attack. Darklings, Shadowhounds, and numerous creatures he'd never seen before swarmed from the tents. Driven by the power of their dark masters, they plunged into the mayhem, only to fall writhing to the ground in pain as the heat of his fires blistered their skin and turned their eyes to smoldering jelly. All across the inner camp, tents and flags, robes and other clothing — anything not made of stone or metal — began to smoke. It was only a matter of seconds before anything not shielded by the corrupted power of the Agla'Con burst into flames.

The torrent of *Ta'shaen* flowing through him was so vast, so utterly immense, that he was momentarily fearful it would consume him as well. Those fears vanished when he realized that he felt none of the heat which was so readily destroying his enemies. The Talisman of Elsa was merely warm to the touch, pulsing like something alive. It matched his heart beat for beat as it channeled the immensity of *Ta'shaen* away from him, sheltering him with a glowing sphere of Spirit he hadn't even realized was there.

He became aware also of a gentle, almost imperceptible voice speaking directly into his mind, whispering words of guidance and warning as the Blood Orb of Elsa seemed to take on a life of its own, lashing out at Agla'Con one moment, deflecting attacks the next.

It knows the enemy, Gideon had said. *It is alive with the spirit of Elsa.*

A whisper of warning tickled his thoughts, and he whirled to face a large group of Agla'Con who had combined their strength in order to strike at him with a literal storm of Fire. He sliced through it with a sweep of Spirit, then followed the defensive flows with a dozen stabs of lightning. The ground exploded beneath their feet in a spray of superheated dirt and rocks, and men were hurled through the air like so many leaves.

No, he corrected. *They aren't men. They're Agla'Con. They are vermin who have given up their humanity by joining their souls to Maeon.* The thought made his cutting them down by the dozens easier to stomach. They deserved to die. They and all those like them. This wasn't killing. It was cleansing.

He focused his Awareness on the flow of Earthpower sweeping through him and traced it back to a reservoir of energy so vast he knew even Maeon would cower in fear before it. *Give me the chance,* he thought, a wave of exhilaration sweeping through him, *and I'll bring the Lord of Darkness to his knees. Give me the chance, and I'll rid the Earthsoul of his evil once and for all.*

The screams of the dying fell to a muted whisper. The booming thunder of his lightning bolts was but a faint echo in his mind. Even the rippling of the Veil as the dark stains of Agla'Con spirits were drawn through to Con'Jithar barely registered in his Awareness. Ridding the world of the filth swarming around him was first in his thoughts. Only the Talisman of Elsa mattered. Only the Power.

He sent a series of lightning strikes into the outer camp and watched through the eyes of *Ta'shaen* as chaos erupted in the cultist army. Already terrified by the battle raging within the inner camp, they threw down their weapons and fled in panic. Horses tore free from their tethers and soldiers were trampled beneath the ensuing stampede. Tents toppled and wagons overturned as the entire Meleki army tried to flee the maelstrom of Light and Fire spilling into their midst.

The barrier of Spirit protecting him flashed red as a corrupted tendril of *Sei'shiin* burned a hole through both sides, narrowly missing his head. He felt the heat on his cheek and smelled the stench of burnt hair. In his mind's eye, the trail left by the corrupted flow looked like dried blood.

Tracing the attack back to its origin, he called on the ancient blood of Elsa, and a thick bar of silvery-blue burst from his fist. The Agla'Con and all those near him vanished in a flash of white.

The ancient blood of his murdered ancestor whispered of retribution, and Jase listened, sweeping the bar of *Sei'shiin* in a wide arch and watching as it incinerated everything it touched. In some areas, the air itself started to burn. A few minutes of this, he realized, and he would destroy the entire Meleki army.

A sudden powerful tremor ripped through *Ta'shaen,* and Jase turned to see numerous Agla'Con pouring through a massive rent in the Veil. Five times larger than any Veilgate, the edges of the Power-wrought hole crackled with angry sparks. Deathmen came through the hole with scepters raised, jeweled tips blazing red. They unleashed a wall of fire that absorbed his attack of *Sei'shiin,* swallowing it in a vortex of fire and shadow.

With the brunt of his attack vanquished, Jase found himself open to the reinforcing ranks of Agla'Con. For the first time since he'd embraced the Power, he went on the defensive, holding off a barrage of fire and lightning that would have shattered the walls of Trian into powder. He felt an odd flow of corrupted Power pouring from the place beyond the rent and pressed his Awareness through to investigate. This new flow had harnessed the efforts of the Agla'Con and was guiding them, focusing them toward him with tremendous skill and power.

As he neared the source of the flow, he felt the brush of a powerful Awareness, and it assaulted him with a vileness unlike any he'd ever known. Cringing, he pulled his mind back through the rent so violently that several Agla'Con screamed and fell writhing to the earth, their minds sliced in two by the razor-sharp edge of his Awareness. He barely noticed, too stunned by what he'd felt on the other side of the fiery opening.

The malice of this new Awareness was as palpable as if he'd been struck by an axe. It was filled with hatred and rage. It screamed of death. His death. And the death of the Earthsoul. His blood chilled when he realized that Shadan himself had joined the battle.

His control over the reservoir faltered slightly, and he found himself retreating toward the Veilgate as Fire and stabs of lightning began to penetrate his shield. In desperation, he harnessed the flows of Spirit necessary and directed them into the gate. The interior of the metal frame flashed blue as the Veil parted before him and he raced through to the darkness beyond. The battle raging around him vanished save for a few corrupted flows that pursued him through the opening.

He turned to face the Agla'Con through the blue-rimmed square and threw back their attack with a surge of Fire so intense the metal framework of the gate turned red from the heat. Sprays of lightning shot from his fingertips, lancing through the opening and blowing apart all those foolish enough to give pursuit.

It looked so odd, that hole in the air, like the door of a dark room looking out to the light. He still didn't understand how it was possible, but he knew what he had to do. The gentle whisper in his mind showed him how.

With a surge of strength, he struck the edges of the metal framework with a tightly woven bar of *Sei'shiin*. The cleansing fire pierced the dark metal, and the entire framework vanished in a flash of white. The opening in the Veil collapsed inward, but he seized it with finger-like tendrils of Spirit and held it open long enough for one final strike.

With the whispering of Elsa to guide him, he drew on the remainder of the reservoir and formed a sphere of Spirit, Fire, and Light. Compressing it as tightly as he could with a fist of Air, he thrust it through the opening and released his hold on the Power.

The Veil snapped shut as the ball of energy detonated with the power of a thousand lightning strikes, and he was blown backward by that portion of the blast that slipped through the last sliver of the closing gateway.

The night plunged into darkness once more, and Jase braced himself for impact as he sailed head-over-heels through the night. The Meleki camp was gone from his Awareness, but he felt the detonation of Earthpower he'd caused in Melek rippling through the fabric of *Ta'shaen*. *Far to the south*, he thought. *Very far to the south.*

Light filled the inside of his head as he slammed into the ground, and he tightened his hold on the spent Talisman to keep from losing it. Slag and bits of shattered rock tore at him as he tumbled several yards down a steep slope. When he finally jarred to a stop among an expanse of boulders, he lay still and let the wave of dizziness sweeping through him subside.

His use of *Ta'shaen* in the Meleki camp had left him too weak to rise, so he remained where he was and closed his eyes. He didn't need to see himself to know his clothes were tattered and seared. And he could feel the blisters on his face from the burst of corrupted *Sei'shiin* that had nearly removed his head. *But*

I am alive, he thought. *By the grace of God and the power of Elsa's blood, I am alive.*

Relieved, he let out the breath he'd been holding and inhaled deeply — only to choke raggedly as the air burned his lungs. It was several moments before he could stop coughing, and even then, it was difficult to breathe. The stench of sulfur and other toxic fumes filled the air. Bits of soot and ash floated on a breeze much too warm for this time of the year. Holding part of his shirt over his nose and mouth, he forced himself to his knees and opened his eyes.

He was on a slope overlooking a shattered wasteland of rock and debris — a desolate landscape that stretched as far as he could see. Steam hissed from fissures in the ground. Here and there the skeletal remains of trees stabbed skyward, misshapen daggers with bark scarred and pitted as if burned by acid.

He closed his eyes in denial, but it didn't matter. He knew where he was. The horror stretching all around him had been burned into his memory by his nightmares.

A rumbling sounded behind him, and he turned to gaze up at the solitary wedge of Mount Tabor rising above him. The symbol of victory for Death's First March, its rim was alight with surging fountains of molten rock. Columns of soot and ash the color of blood boiled upward to form a swirling mass of clouds that rained debris down the back side of the mountain in a storm of death. The near side of the mountain glowed red with snaking rivers of magma. Like tendrils of Agla'Con corruption, they stretched away into the darkness and vapor shrouding the ruined Valley of Amnidia.

Flickers of movement in the lowlands below caught his attention, and he glanced down to see hundreds of dark shapes ghosting through the ruined landscape toward him. Staying in the ravines and fissures, they were never visible for more than an instant, but the fires of Mount Tabor glinted brightly on bared steel.

A wave of terror washed through him, and he opened himself to the Power. It shimmered at the edge of his Awareness, but slipped away each time he tried to embrace it. In desperation, he tightened his grip on the Blood Orb and willed it to help. Nothing happened. He was simply too exhausted to wield *Ta'shaen.*

A moment later the first of the Shadan'Ko stepped from the shadows to face him.

EPILOGUE

The Mith'elre Chon

The Elvan Dymas Elrien was looking down at a ragged band of Shadan'Ko throwing themselves at the Great Wall of Aridan when the disturbance he'd been expecting rippled through *Ta'shaen*. He didn't need to extend his Awareness to know from whence it came. The prophecies had told him that many years ago. The Night of Fire was upon Melek.

Turning from his study of the futile attack by the Twisted Ones, he made his way along the wall's battlements until the sounds of the Shadan'Ko faded from his hearing. His pupils, ten young Elvan men and women between the ages of eighteen and twenty, followed at his heels. When he reached the seclusion of a tower courtyard, he gathered his pupils closely about him.

"What do you feel?" he asked.

One of the young ladies, a grey-eyed beauty from the Midion Valley, raised her hand and spoke. "A tremor, large to be felt over such a distance, coming from somewhere to the east. Primarily Fire, unless I miss my guess."

"That is correct," Elrien congratulated her, then asked, "Can anyone tell me what it means?"

The ten fledgling Dymas were silent.

"It is the fulfilling of prophecy," he told them, then hesitated as *Ta'shaen* rippled again, this time to the north. He turned and pointed to the glowing rim of Mount Tabor just visible in the distance. "Behold," he said, a tingle of excitement running up his spine, "the *Mith'elre Chon* has come. The Third Cleansing is at hand."

How great are the feet of him who comes to the holy mountain; how great the power of his blood as he awakens the light of truth!

Stand fast and await his coming, ye Children of the Gift, for he shall come as a Son of Thunder with Fire and Light as his weapons.

Behold, he shall come like dawn to the east and pierce the Heart of Darkness with his fiery sword, scattering death's army to the wind; and lo, the earth shall resonate with the sound of his coming.

Gird up your loins, oh Gifted, and strap on the armor of God, for the One Who Comes Before has called you. Come forth and join the battle lest all be smitten and die.

~ The *Cynthian* Chapter 183, Verses 11-14 as recorded by the Prophet Heian Tajima.

GLOSSARY

Time: is measured based on two important dates in history. The first, the Farewell of Elderon (A.F.1), marks years in the Old World and was approximately 3000 years in length, though no one can be sure, since it's unclear just how long the people gathered before they went to battle. The length of the Great Destruction is even more vague. Estimates based an fragmented records indicate it may have lasted as long as sixty years. The New World is marked with the letters A.S. (After Solemnizing) and continues to the present, the year A.S. 2300.

Calendar: The Ha'lel Calendar has ten months of thirty-six days each. It was given to the Old World race of man by Elderon during the Age of Instruction. Every twentieth year, five days are added to Bashan and the Feast of Ha'lel is held. The names of the months are: Fayu, Hyr, Morshe, Elul, Corshem, Iathec, Bashan, Jad, Sewil, Corlil.

Distance: is measured in leagues and miles with 1 league being the equivalent of 3 miles.

Languages: Because of Kelsa's location as the heart of the Nine Lands, the Kelsan language became pivotal in trading and economic development. In the year A.S. 486 the Unification Act was signed, and the countries of Elva, Zeka, and Melek adopted the Kelsan language as an official 'second language'. A century later, the Chunin nation signed as well and the Kelsan tongue became officially known as the Common Tongue. The nations of Riak and Dainin became bilingual a half century later. Kunin and Arkania refused to take part in the Unification Act and both countries have suffered financially because of it.

Aarin'sil: Legendary forge in Dainin.

Adgawa River: A river in Gahara.

Adirhah, Raimen: Member of Deathsquad Alpha.

Aebis, Jukstin: One of Jase's friends in Kindel's Grove.

Aebis, Mathin: Jukstin's younger brother.

Age of Instruction: The span of years immediately following the Creation where Elderon walked among those whom He had created, instructing them as to how they should live and teaching them about the world they were to inherit. The precise duration of the Age of Instruction is unknown, but most scholars agree that it was around two hundred years due to the multiple generations of children mentioned in some of the records.

Agisthas, Athar: King of the city of Agisthas.

Agla'Con: Wielders of *Ta'shaen* who have given themselves over to Maeon for an increase in their abilities with *Ta'shaen*. Their true Gifts are forfeited and they must now take *Ta'shaen* by force via talismans created for this purpose. While an Agla'Con talisman helps channel the stolen Earthpower, its main purpose is to protect the Agla'Con from *Ta'shaen* which would otherwise destroy the wielder. In the Old Tongue the term Agla'Con means "Heart of Darkness."

Allisen: Mistress of the kitchen in Fairimor Palace.

Ammorin: A Dainin.

Andlexces: Capital city of Elva.

Aridan: Elvan city fronting the Great Wall. *See also* Great Wall of Aridan.

arinseil: Power-wrought metal of the nets used by the *Nar'shein Yahl.*

Arkania: Southernmost nation in the Nine Lands, the people of this jungle region live in primitive obscurity.

Arrow of the Sea: A ship in Lord Tetrica's fleet.

Asahi, Leif: A leif of Clan Samochi.

Aulious, Maira: Brysia's friend in Seston.

Avalam, Clan: A clan in northern Riak.

Awareness: The term used by Power-wielders to describe the mindlink a Dymas or *Dalae* must have if they are to successfully control the Power. *See Ta'shaen.*

Balasei, Keder: Dai'shozen of Clan Derga.

Battle of Amnidia: Also known as the Second Cleansing, this battle was fought in the year A.S. 1407 between an army of Dymas led by Siamon Fairimor and the legions of Agla'Con led by Throy Shadan. During this battle, so much Earthpower was used that the valley was left in ruin. At his death, Shadan unleashed one final onslaught so horrible it tainted every fiber of the valley, leaving it uninhabitable. The Elvan nation, recognizing this curse, relinquished their claim on the valley. *See also* Great Wall of Aridan; Shadan'Ko.

Battle of Capena: Fought in A.S. 2162 when a Riaki army led by sixty Agla'Con attacked and destroyed much of the city before marching north toward Chellum. They were intercepted in the Shellum Plains by Gideon and a small army of Dymas and were destroyed.

Battle of Greendom: Fought in A.S. 2280 on a hill overlooking the village of Greendom, it is known by many as *The Final Stand.* During this battle, the combined armies of Kelsa, Elva, and Chunin stood against the refleshed Dreadlord Throy Shadan and his Agla'Con.

Battle of Sekigaroga: Legendary civil war battle in Riak between the northern and southern clans. It was headed by Sagaris in the south and Gahara in the north. Sagaris was beaten so decisively, Gahara became the premier clan of the north.

Bero'thai: "Honor Guard" in the Elvan tongue, they are an elite group of warders assigned to protect the ruling families of Elva and House Fairimor.

Betsunin: The name given to the final three races created by Elderon. They consist of the Dainin, the Chunin, and the Kunin.

Bettashin: A Dainin.

Beumestra, Kalear: A Sarui of Leif Tsuto, Clan Gahara. He is a Dymas and was witness to the Agla'Con killing of Highseat Tobdana.

Blood Orb of Elsa: Another name for a Talisman of Elsa.

Blue Flame, the: The symbol of Kelsa and of House Fairimor.

Book of Halek: Old World book of prophecies written by Gamaleil Halek. It is one of the earliest known writings from that time, and though an exact date is still a point of debate for scholars, most agree it was written within the first fifty to one hundred years after Elsa was slain by Maeon.

Brandameir, Cheslie: The woman Seth rescued at the Con'Kumen chapter house in Trian.

Brey, Elison: Captain of the Fairimor Home Guard and warder-advisor to Randle Fairimor.

Brotherhood, the: Another name for the Con'Kumen.

bu'to: Ceremonial helmet worn by the Sarui.

Byoten, Leif: A leif of Clan Samochi.

Callisar Mountains: Mountains south of Thesston in central Zeka.

Callison, Brant: Second in command of Seston's Waypost.

Capena: Large city on the Kelsan-Riaki border and home to nearly a third of Kelsa's military.

Chael'trom: The Elvan name for refleshed. It means "deadman walking." *See* K'rrosha.

Chellum: A city in Kelsa.

Chellum, Decker: King of the city of Chellum and father to Elliott and Talia.

Chellum, Elliott: Crown Prince of Chellum and friend of Jase Fairimor. Born only three days after Jase, his life is closely intertwined with Jase's. His name, spelled *El'Liott* in the Ancient Language, means the "Sword of God."

Chellum Home Guard: The elite special forces who protect the city of Chellum.

Chellum, Talia: The Princess of Chellum. She is in love with Jase and has been since they were kids. Talia is a *Dalae* Gifted with **Sha** - Flesh - and is on her way to becoming a powerful Healer.

chorazin: An indestructible, Power-wrought substance.

Chunin: Land to the west of Kelsa. It is inhabited by a race of people who bear its name and is divided into three kingdoms: Northern, Middle, and Southern.

Church Day: The name given to the days of the month when those in the Church of Elderon hold worship services.

clan: A Riaki "city state" comprised of two or more leifs. Though most clans are associated with a single large city, there are many made up of several small towns and villages. Though largely self-governing, clans are subject to the Emperor and the Imperial Clave. *See* leif.

clave: The Riaki word for council, claves are the ruling body for each clan and are made up of delegates from each leif society. The head of each clave is called the Highseat, a Leiflord elected to the position by popular vote.

Cleansing Hunt: What the *Nar'shein Yahl* call their hunt for an Agla'Con.

Cobblestone Inn, The: An inn in Kindel's Grove.

Colgra, Kradan: The Agla'Con who led the attack against Fairimor Dome.

Common Tongue: The language given to Kelsa at the time of the Second Creation. Because of Kelsa's location at the heart of the Nine Lands, the Kelsan language became pivotal in trading and economic development. In A.S. 486 the Unification Act was signed and the countries of Elva, Zeka, and Melek adopted the Kelsan language as their own. A century later, the Chunin nation signed as well and the Kelsan tongue became officially known as the Common Tongue. The other nations of Dainin, Kunin, Riak, and Arkania retained their own languages but became bilingual nations by adopting the Common Tongue as an official second language.

Communicator Stones: Spheres of crystal that can be used to communicate over long distances if activated by one who can wield *Ta'shaen*.

Constas, Borilius: An Agla'Con.

Con'droth: A demon from the realm of Con'Jithar. One of Maeon's creations, these flesh and blood creatures are worshiped by the Arkanian people. Though no one outside of Arkania can say for sure, it is believed that these demons can be summoned into the world of the living through evil rites performed by village priests.

Con'Jithar: The realm of darkness where Maeon dwells. Sometimes referred to as hell by the different religions.

Con'Kumen: "Hand of the Dark" in the Ancient Language, it is an organization sworn to Maeon.

Core, the: The twelve members of the Kelsan High Tribunal who take over in times of war.

Cresdraline Forest: A large forest in northwestern Melek.

Crompton, Thaddis: Chief General of Capena. Second only to Croneam Eries in rank.

Cynthia: The first of Elva's great cities, it was built in A.S. 12 in the Valley of Amnidia. Nestled at the foot of Mount Tabor, it was a glorious city and served as Elva's capital until its destruction by Throy Shadan in A.S. 1407.

Cynthian: A history of the Elvan city Cynthia. Though most of what it chronicles deals with the secular and political elements of the city's history, it also contains many prophecies concerning the destruction of the Valley of Amnidia, the rise of Shadan as the first of the *chael'trom*, the death and rejuvenation of the Earthsoul, and the coming of the *Mith'elre Chon.*

Dainin: The largest of the races of men, these ten-foot-tall giants inhabit the northwestern-most part of the Nine Lands. See also *Nar'shein Yahl.*

Dai'shozen: Riaki word for First General. A *Dai'shozen* is the head of a clan's military force.

Dakshar, Shavis: A Shizu of Leif Iga.

Dalae: Ancient word meaning "Gifted." It is the name given to anyone who has any one of the Seven Gifts of *Ta'shaen.* Except for Healers, most tend to keep their Gifts hidden because of the mistrust people have of those able to wield *Ta'shaen.*

Darklings: Human-like shadowspawned soldiers of the Agla'Con. They are created by combining the characteristics of Shadan'Ko with those of animals and are the most common of all shadowspawn.

Death's Chain Mountains: The rugged mountain range that separates Kelsa from Melek.

Death's Third March: So-named in the prophecies, it is believed this series of battles will open the way for the return of the *Mith'elre Chon* and lead to the final cleansing of the Agla'Con or the destruction of mankind.

Deathmen: *See* K'rrosha.

Deathrider: The name given to mounted K'rrosha. *See also* Shadowlancer.

Deathsquad: Shizu strike teams. Sometimes used as assassins, they carry out various missions for their Leiflords and act as a military force for leif and clan. Deadly efficient, they are the most feared assassins in any of the Nine Lands. Each leif has one to six Deathsquads. A Deathsquad is comprised of six, six-member strike teams.

Deathstrike: Assassination attempts carried out by Shizu.

Deathsquad Alpha: One of Leif Iga's six Deathsquads.

Deathsquad Amai: One of Leif Iga's six Deathsquads.

Deathsquad Boli: One of Leif Iga's six Deathsquads.

Deathsquad Valhei: A Deathsquad from Clan Vakala.

Derga, Clan: A clan in northern Riak.

Destroyer, the: *See* Maeon.

Destruction, The: The worldwide battle between rival Agla'Con that resulted in the end of the Old World and ushered in the Second Creation.

Diam, Captain: Captain of the *Arrow of the Sea.*

Dome, the: Part of Fairimor Palace, this massive dome is part library, part music hall, and part relaxation area for Trian's most elite citizens. It is also where the Kelsan High Tribunal meets.

Domei, Agaro: Leiflord of Asahi, Clan Samochi.

Dragonblade: Unbreakable, Power-wrought swords, some of which date back to the Old World. They get their name because of the Dragons etched into the blades and hilt. Even though the Dainin are able to craft these weapons in modern times, those dating from the Old World are prized by swordmasters since the hilts are constructed of *chorazin*. Legend says the Old World blades were forged in the fires of dragons.

Drastin, Prometh: Governor of Tradeston.

Dromensai, Tereus: Highseat of Clan Gahara.

Drusi: A city in Kelsa.

Dunkin's Ghost: *See* Fairimor, Dunkin.

Dymas: "Chosen" in the Old Tongue, these men and women use *Ta'shaen* for the benefit of the Earthsoul and the people of the Nine Lands. Though believed by many to be extinct, there is evidence to support the notion that many Dymas are in hiding due to the fear and mistrust people have toward them. What sets a Dymas apart from the lesser *Dalae* is the Gift of Spirit, which allows a Dymas to utilize all Seven Gifts of *Ta'shaen*.

Dy'illium, The: An Old World book of prophecies.

Earthpower: A common term for *Ta'shaen*.

Earthsoul: As is the case with all the creations of Elderon, the Earth itself is a living entity. Her spirit, known as the Earthsoul, sustains the life of all creatures and is the very essence of *Ta'shaen*. It separates the spirit realms of Con'Jithar and Eliara from the world of the living. The point of contact between the three spiritual realms is known as the Veil. Like all living things, however, the Earthsoul will eventually weaken and die unless rejuvenated through the Blood of Elsa. If the Earthsoul does indeed fail, the realm of Con'Jithar will swallow the earth and all Her inhabitants in a blanket of death and Maeon will reign supreme. *See also* Con'Jithar; Eliara; Veil, the.

Earthsoul, Rejuvenation of: In order to keep Elderon's creations from becoming a part of Con'Jithar, and therefore subject to Maeon, it is prophesied that a firstborn son of Elsa will need to take up one of the Talismans of Elsa and use the reservoir of Earthpower it contains to instill new life into the Earthsoul. Although none of the records say exactly how this is to be done, they do say where it must take place: the Soul Chamber deep inside Mount Tabor in the Valley of Amnidia.

Eimei: A serving girl at *The Rose of the Forest* in Seston.

Elderon: Name of the Creator.

Elderon, The Church of: The predominate religion of Kelsa, Elva, Zeka, Dainin, and Chunin. There are several canons of scripture, including the *Cynthian* and the *Book of Halek*; and members meet weekly in churches to read them and to praise Elderon's name.

Eliara: The place of peace where Elderon dwells.

El'kali: Old World term meaning "Soldier of God."

Elrien: An Elvan Prophet and *Dymas*. He has spent most of his life at the Great Wall of Aridan where he helps guard against the Shadan'Ko while waiting for the *Mith'elre Chon* to return.

Elsa: A righteous woman from the Age of Instruction who was slain by Maeon.

Elsa, Blood of: When she was slain by the hand of Maeon, Elsa's blood mingled with the dust of the earth and sprang forth in diverse places as Talismans of great Power. A link was created between her spirit and the Earthsoul which is the sustaining force behind *Ta'shaen*. The Talismans formed from her blood became the access keys to vast reservoirs of the Power. The Blood of Elsa is also a reference to those of her descendants who are prophesied to one day take up one of the Talismans to rejuvenate the Earthsoul. *See also* Earthsoul; Earthsoul, Rejuvenation of.

Elsa, Talisman of: A smooth orb of reddish gold approximately the size of an egg that is the access key to a vast reservoir of *Ta'shaen*.

Elva: In the Old Tongue, "The People of God." Unlike the other nations created during the Second Creation, the first of the Elvan people are believed to have been brought from another world by Elderon.

Enue, Taggert: First General of Chellum's main forces.

Eridel, Captain: Captain of the Zekan ship *Sea Blade*.

Eries, Cam: Grandson of Croneam Eries.

Eries, Croneam: First General of Fulrath.

Eries, Hena: Granddaughter of Croneam Eries.

Eries, Joneam: Son of Croneam Eries and current general of Fulrath.

Eries, Tey: Croneam Eries' five-year-old granddaughter.

Eries, Tress: Croneam Eries' wife who was murdered by Shizu.

Esielliar: An ancient Elvan Prophet.

Eved'terium: An Old World book of prophecies.

Fairimor, Ackster: A former King of Kelsa.

Fairimor, Aethon: Eldest of triplet sons born to Farsenil Fairimor. Tried unsuccessfully to overthrow the Kelsan government and assume the throne with his father and two brothers. Leader of the Agla'Con, he is first among the living in the eyes of Maeon, and second only to Shadan in command. He is called "The First" by those who serve him.

Fairimor, Andil: Randle Fairimor's second-born son.

Fairimor, Areth: Randle Fairimor's elder brother who gave over his throne to Randle in order to go with Gideon Dymas to the Soul Chamber to try to rejuvenate the Earthsoul.

Fairimor, Benak: Husband of Brysia Fairimor, he never returned from the mission to heal the Earthsoul and is believed to be held as a prisoner by Shadan.

Fairimor, Brysia: The Sister Queen of Kelsa and mother of Jase Fairimor.

Fairimor, Cassia: Wife of Randle Fairimor and High Queen of Kelsa.

Fairimor, Dathan: Aethon's younger brother and second of the triplets.

Fairimor, Dunkin: King of Kelsa from A.S. 2001 to A.S. 2008. After his wife and son were murdered, it is said that he died of grief and that his ghost went on a rampage in Riak exacting vengeance against those responsible for his family's death.

Fairimor, Endil: The Crown Prince of Kelsa and son of Randle Fairimor.

Fairimor, Farsenil: A former King of Kelsa.

Fairimor, Jase: A young man from Kindel's Grove.

Fairimor, Jimsalon: A former King of Kelsa.

Fairimor, Kameron: Aethon's youngest brother and third of the triplets.

Fairimor, Randle: High King of Kelsa.

Fairimor, Siamon: A former King of Kelsa.

Farewell of Elderon: A.F. 1. At the end of the Age of Instruction, Elderon gathered the people to Him one last time to bless them and to say farewell. He anointed priests and appointed Kings to guide and rule the people. Time in the Old World was measured from this moment.

Fenian, Captain: Former commander of the Seston Waypost who was killed by the Con'Kumen.

First Cleansing: A.F. 2015. The Agla'Con were hunted down and destroyed by Dymas.

Flag of Transgression: In accordance with Riaki custom, this flag is raised by a majority vote of the leifs of a clan to signify that a leif or leifs is being punished for crimes against the clan. The leif is officially disbanded during this time and the people belonging to it are no longer considered part of the clan. The transgression period is usually for one year, but can be made permanent if further transgressions occur during the time of punishment. At the end of the year, members of the transgressing leif are reinstated or absorbed into other leifs depending on the final judgment of the clan.

Free Zone: The mile-wide section of land surrounding the city of Fulrath.

Frestrem, Galam: A young man of Kindel's Grove.

Fulrath: A military city in Kelsa. Sitting in the highlands of the Talin Plateau, it is the first line of defense against any invading army coming from Melek. The city itself consists almost entirely of the Rove Riders and other soldiers who patrol and guard Kelsa's eastern border.

Gahara, Clan: A very powerful Riaki clan whose seat of power is in the Gaharan Mountains in northwestern Riak.

Galasei, Ino: Former Shozen for Leif Iga's six Deathsquads.

Galatea, Javan: Leader of the Riaki Deathsquad sent to kill Jase Fairimor the night of the Festival of the Dragon.

Gathering, The: In the year A.F. 3000, the people of the Old World, led by two rival groups of Agla'Con, divided into two great armies and went to war against each other. Though the actual duration of The Gathering is unknown, it is speculated that it may have taken as long as ten years. The war resulted in the destruction of the Old World and the near decimation of the First Race of Man.

Gathyrsi, Benak: Jase Fairimor's father.

Gaufin, Elam: Acting Captain of the Chellum Home Guard.

Gavin: A *Bero'thai* stationed in Fairimor Palace.

Gefion, Pel: A general of Fulrath.

Geshiann, Stalix: The Judgment Seat of Trian.

Gideon: A Dymas for more than 300 years, he is known as the Guardian of Kelsa and has served as warder-advisor to the Fairimor Kings for the past three centuries.

Gift of Discernment: The rarest of all the manifestations of *Ta'shaen*, Discernment comes only to those who are faithful servants of the Earthsoul, and then it comes only when She wishes and lasts only as long as serves Her purpose. It is tied to the Gift of Spirit.

Great Destruction, the: Worldwide battle between rival Agla'Con that resulted in the end of the Old World and ushered in the Second Creation.

Great Wall of Aridan: Construction on the wall began the same day Elva relinquished its claim on the Valley of Amnidia in A.S. 1408 and took fifty years to complete. Built at the urging of the Prophet Urias, it was truly an inspired structure. Within weeks of completion, it came under attack by the first of the Shadan'Ko. *See also* Shadan'Ko.

Green Dolphin Pier: A pier in Tetrica Harbor.

Greendom: A city near the Allister River.

Greig: A young warder-in-training apprenticed to Daris Stodd.

Greyling: *See* K'rrosha.

Groben, Resaline: A Healer in Fulrath.

Gyllas: A city in Zeka.

Hadershi, Beraline: A Dymas and veteran of the Battle of Greendom.

harrolia tea: A healing herb of the Dainin.

Hasho, Clan: A clan in northern Riak.

Hasi, Simaru: Tizin Leiflord, Clan Gahara.

Hattoku, Amathus: Shozen of Leif Iso, Clan Ieous.

Hattori Prefecture: Northernmost prefecture in Riak.

Heeda, Moratsu: Former Dai'shozen of Clan Gahara.

Hend: One of Brysia Fairimor's warders.

Herisham, Sereth: A young Dymas and soldier in the Chellum army.

Highseat: The title given to the leader of a Riaki clan. The Highseat is a Leiflord selected by popular vote of the clave to represent the clan.

Highwaymen: Mounted soldiers whose job it is to patrol Kelsa's highways and maintain peace along the roads and in the villages scattered along the way. They also have the responsibility to clear the highways of debris such as downed trees, boulders, etc.

Holdensar Prophecies: A book of Riaki prophecies given by the Prophet Holdensar.

Hom, Gwuler: Former Shozen of Clan Vakala turned Agla'Con.

Hresdom, Gilium: A young man of Kindel's Grove.

Hurd, Calis: A colonel of Fulrath.

Ieous, Clan: A clan in northern Riak.

Iga: A leif of Clan Gahara.

Iga'rala Mountains: Mountain range in northern Riak.

Illiarensei: A massive river in Arkania. Its name means "The mother of all waters."

Imor: A descendant of Elsa and father of the Fairimor bloodline.

Imperial Clave: The governing council of Riak. Members of the Imperial Clave are selected by the Emperor from among the Highseats of the most powerful clans.

Iso, Leif: A leif of Clan Ieous.

Jenin: A village in Omer Forest.

Jersil's Hollow: A village in Omer Forest.

Jiu: Shizu method of meditation through which they achieve a oneness with the world around them both in body and spirit. It heightens their abilities as warriors and enlightens their minds as disciplined thinkers. Though no ability with the Power is required to be able to utilize *Jiu*, it is very similar to a Gifted person's use of their Awareness in relation to *Ta'shaen*. It is simply a matter of strength through a disciplined mind.

Jizo, Benin: Zekan ambassador to Kelsa.

Jyoai College: A prestigious university in Trian.

Kamishi, Bosor: Dai'Shozen of Clan Avalam.

Kamoth: Capital City of Melek.

Kaitan, Emish: Elvan ambassador to Kelsa.

kamui: Old World Dragonblades, these twin short-swords are the rarest of all Dragonblades.

Kashi: A leif of Clan Samochi.

Kelsan High Tribunal: Kelsa's thirty-six-member ruling council.

Kelsan Rangers: Similar to the Roves of Fulrath, these mounted squads patrol the border between Kelsa and Riak to guard against Riaki raids on civilian targets. *See* Rove.

Keries: Member of Deathsquad Alpha.

Kindel's Grove: A small village in the Omer Forest.

Kinsten, Heril: A young man of Kindel's Grove.

Kireinin: Name of the races of men known as Riaki, Meleki, Zekan, Arkanian; and on the Jyndar continent, the races Glendan, Rosdan, and Tamban.

kitara: Traditional robe of the Riaki.

kiisho: A Riaki board game similar to chess.

komouri: Black, tight-fitting uniform of the Shizu. Other elements of Shizu clothing include the *koro* hood-mask and the *kotsu* soft-soled boot.

Korishal, Marithen: A veteran Dymas and former member of the Kelsan High Tribunal.

koro: The black hood-mask wore by Shizu.

K'rresh: A type of winged shadowspawn.

K'rrosha: In the Old Tongue, "Refleshed." K'rrosha are the souls of Agla'Con refleshed into bodies of dead people. Also known as Deathmen, Greylings, and Nightwalkers. Those that travel by horseback are known as Shadowlancers and Deathriders. The Elvan name for them is *Chael'trom* which means "Deadman walking." Shadan excluded, something about the refleshing limits a K'rrosha's ability with *Ta'shaen*, allowing them to wield only Fire. Some of the Refleshed believe the limitation is put upon them by Shadan as a means of maintaining his own supremacy.

K'tyr: A unique and very dangerous kind of shadowspawn. They are the rarest of all because their creation kills the Agla'Con who helped spawn it. They are similar to Satyrs in that they have four arms and carry curved short-swords, but they also have wings and can fly. They have the ability to create voids in *Ta'shaen*, making it impossible for a Dymas to embrace the Power.

Kunin: One of the races of Betsunin, the Kunin are similar in size to the Chunin, but are as dark and loathsome as the Shadan'Ko — the result of a curse that fell upon the nation when they tore down the Temple of Elderon in order to build a shrine to a dark god they call *Uri*.

K'zzaum Pit: The desert valley where Shadan's fortress is located.

Laceda, Erebius: A Dymas.

Laceda, Junteri: A Dymas and daughter of Erebius.

Lailies: A tavern in Thesston.

Lazy Gentleman, The: A tavern in Kindel's Grove.

Leda, Idoman: A fledgling Dymas and member of the Chellum Home Guard.

leif: A society or district within a Riaki clan. Most clans have five or six leifs, but there may be as few as two or as many as twelve. Leifs are formed mainly by the unification of prominent families either through marriage or commerce. The members of these "family" societies are very loyal to one another and sometimes put the welfare of the leif over the rest of the clan.

Leiflord: Each leif has a Leiflord who is appointed by the voice of the people. This lord represents the leif as a member of the Highclave, the clan's ruling body.

Leir, Endaman: The youngest of Deathsquad Alpha's six captains.

Lemorin, Pachus: Clave representative from Leif Shochu, Clan Gahara.

Leva, Nemean: A general in the Chellum army.

Lourin: A *Bero'thai* assigned to Fairimor Palace.

Lyacon, Breiter: A captain in the Trian Home Guard.

Lyacon, Zea: Breiter's wife.

Lydon, Seth: Childhood name: Kellam Goewin. He is known in Riak as *shent ze'deyar*, which means "A Clan of One." As the only non-Riaki to ever become Shizu, he is known as the Kelsan Shizu, and is greatly feared and respected by the Riaki clans. Now serving as Captain of the Chellum Home Guard and warder to Talia Chellum.

Maeon: The name of the demon god who opposes Elderon and rules in the realm of Con'Jithar. Always striving to take souls, he is the enemy of mankind. Other names include: the Great Deceiver, the Dark One,

Soulbiter, Soultaker, the Destroyer, and Soulcrusher.

Mae'chodan: A rank within the hierarchy of the Con'Kumen.

Mae'rillium: A rank within the hierarchy of the Con'Kumen.

Maridan, Clan: A clan in Riak.

Marik, Chavin: King of the city of Marik.

Marriage Feast, The: A song.

Matail: One of Brysia Fairimor's warders in Seston.

Mendel Pass: The pass leading from Trian Plateau northward through the Kelsan Mountains.

Merishal, Pass of: A pass through the Riak's Iga'rala Mountains.

Mertom, Helem: A young man of Kindel's Grove.

Mist's Fury: A ship in Tetrica's fleet.

Mith'elre Chon: In the Old Tongue, "The One Who Comes Before." Prophecies in the *Cynthian* tell of the *Mith'elre Chon* going to battle against Shadan during Death's Third March.

Moirai, Prad: King of Chunin's Northern Kingdom.

Mount Augg: A lone mountain-island in the center of Mirror Lake.

Mount Tabor: The volcanic mountain located in the Valley of Amnidia. Inside the mountain is the Soul Chamber where the Altar of Elsa is located, and where it is said a firstborn son of Fairimor must go to rejuvenate the Earthsoul. In A.S. 1407, Throy Shadan went to Tabor in an attempt to turn the power of the Earthsoul to his own use. The Battle of Amnidia was fought and Mount Tabor was left in the heart of a vast wasteland. It is guarded by a horde of Once-men known as the Shadan'Ko.

Muli, Lughat: Tsuto Leiflord, Clan Gahara.

Murra, Tana: A young woman of Kindel's Grove and friend to Jase Fairimor.

Myrscraw: Giant birds from the Island of Myrdin that are used as transportation by the Shizu.

Nagaro, Aimi: Tohquin's daughter.

Nagaro, Kailei: Tohquin's wife.

Nagaro, Tohquin: A Shizu of Leif Iga.

Nagusa, Orito: Tihou Leiflord, Clan Gahara.

Nanda, Tohan: King of Chunin's Southern Kingdom.

Nar'shein Yahl: A Dainin phrase that means "Keepers of the Earth." The *Nar'shein Yahl* are Dainin warriors called by the voice of the Earthsoul to carry out Cleansing Hunts.

Nesthius, Elder: A Prophet, he is the High Priest and leader of the Church of Elderon.

Nian, Captain: A highwayman of the North Omer Waypost and friend to Jase Fairimor.

Nid, Hulanekaefil: High King of Melek.

Nine Lands, the: A more commonly used title for the Temijyn Continent, which consists of the nations of Kelsa, Elva, Dainin, Chunin, Kunin, Melek,

Riak, Zeka, and Arkania.

Nogeru, Railen: A Shizu of Leif Iga.

Old Tongue: The language spoken by the First Race of Man. After the destruction of the Old World, it was abandoned when the other races were created by Elderon and each was given its own tongue. Though no records document His reasoning behind the addition of so many new languages, scholars believe it was to ensure that no one nation would ever become so powerful as to dominate the world. The Old Tongue is still spoken by an elite few, usually scholars or students of Old World history.

Ole'ar, Teig: Elvan Master of Spies for Croneam Eries.

Olwen, Luas: King of Chunin's Middle Kingdom.

Omasil, Eli: First Captain of the Tetrica Palace Guard.

Once-men: *See* Shadan'Ko.

Oronei, Derian: A Shizu of Leif Iga.

O'sei, Taka: First Captain of the Fairimor Palace Guard.

Osoren, Fendomeir: An Agla'Con.

Overlook: Part of Fairimor Palace, the Overlook is a monolithic structure constructed by the hand of Elderon for the child Fairimor in A.S. 1. It is a seamless block of *chorazin* complete with rooms, windows, doors, stairs, heating ducts, and so on. The top of the Overlook fronts the Dome of Fairimor Palace and holds a lush garden.

Padershi, Halian: Former Emperor of Riak.

Panos, Captain: Captain of *Mist's Fury*.

Pattalla: A Dainin.

Pelias, Crismon: Commander of the Waypost in Greendom.

Pemaru, Dalarus: Captain of Deathsquad Amai of Leif Iga.

Pendir, Bornis: A young blacksmith of Kindel's Grove.

Phipps, Corom: A young man of Kindel's Grove.

Phipps, Tersin: Young boy of Kindel's Grove.

Pit, the: *See* K'zzaum Pit.

Plains of Criet: Located in western Melek below Zedik Pass.

Premala, Clan: A clan in Riak.

Prenum, Lenea: Civilian Governor of Fulrath.

Previnser, Elder: Priest of the Church of Elderon in Kindel's Grove.

Problain, Anosar: Clave representative from Leif Tsuto, Clan Gahara.

Proud Flame, The: An inn in Trian.

Pryderi, Salamus: King of Zeka.

Quatha: A type of reptilian shadowspawn.

Rai, Joselyn: Elderly Dymas who resides in Greendom.

Ras, Shalan: The Agla'Con killed by Thorac Shurr in Yucanter Forest.

Refleshed, the: *See* K'rrosha.

Reiekel, Orais: King of Elva.

Reisten, Leif: A leif of Clan Samochi.

Rejuvenation, the: The act where a firstborn son of Fairimor must take up a Talisman of Elsa and revitalize the Earthsoul.

Rhead, Silas: Mayor of Kindel's Grove.

Robil: One of Brysia Fairimor's warders.

Roe, Glavin: Owner of *The Rose of the Forest* Inn in Seston.

Roliar, Tamind: Leiflord of Kashi, Clan Samochi.

Romari, Tokasu: Leiflord of Iga, Clan Gahara.

Rose of the Forest, The: An inn in Seston.

Ross: One of Brysia Fairimor's warders.

Rove: A squad of mounted soldiers from Fulrath whose primary objective is to patrol the open grasslands of Talin Plateau and the Allister Plains in order to combat the raiding parties of the Shadan Cult and other Meleki groups hostile to Kelsa.

Sagaris: The capital of Riak.

Samal, Nisibis: Emperor of Riak.

Samochi, Clan: One of Riak's largest clans.

Sarui: "Immovable" in the Riaki tongue, Sarui are the Home Guard of the Riaki people. They act as a police force for their leif and guards for their Leiflord and other clave members. Sarui wear lavishly ornate armor of steel and leather and heavy steel helmets called *bu'to*. They carry swords similar to their Shizu counterparts, but their primary weapons are spears and halberds.

Satyr: A type of shadowspawn.

Scloa: A village in Omer Forest.

Sea Blade: The Zekan ship loaned to Gideon.

Second Cleansing: *See* Battle of Amnidia

Second Creation, the: After the destruction of the Old World, Elderon returned to the Earth and created ten additional races of men. These new races included: Riaki, Meleki, Dainin, Chunin, Kunin, Zekan, Arkanian; and on the Jyndar Continent, the races Rosdan, Glendan, and Tamban. The Elvan people are believed to have been brought by the hand of Elderon from one of the many worlds He has created.

Second Rise of the Agla'Con: Took place in A.F. 2515. Much more wary this time, the Agla'Con kept their numbers secret until A.F. 2790 when they systematically destroyed all known Dymas. Eventually the Agla'Con separated into two rival factions that brought about the destruction of the Old World.

Sei'shiin: In the Old Tongue, "Spirit Lightning."

Seston: A large town in the Omer Forest and crossroads of the three highways leading to the cities of Tetrica, Marik, and Capena.

Seven Gifts of *Ta'shaen*: The Seven Gifts of *Ta'shaen* are Light, Earth, Fire, Water, Air, Flesh, and Spirit. Their names in the Ancient Language are **Shiin, Ta, Suzu, Nami, Tei, Sha,** and **Sei**, respectively. *See also* Earthpower; *Ta'shaen.*

Shaalbin: A Dainin.

Shadan Cult: A group of religious fanatics who worship Throy Shadan.

Shadan'Ko: "Curse of Shadan" in the Old Tongue. Several years after the Battle of Amnidia, thousands of Kelsans moved into the valley to try to reclaim the land. Over the next three decades they turned into the Shadan'Ko, a Darkling-like people who lost all traces of their humanity. The Elvan nation built the Great Wall to keep the Shadan'Ko locked away. Many Shadan'Ko have the ability to shape-change and are known as Changelings. Other names for the Shadan'Ko include: Twisted Ones, Ruined Ones, and Once-men. *See also* Great Wall of Aridan; Valley of Amnidia; Shadan, Throy.

Shadan, Throy: Once a powerful Kelsan politician and Dymas, he waged war against the Kelsan heartland in an attempt to take the throne. After his defeat, he went into hiding for several years where he raised an army of Agla'Con. In A.S. 1407 he led his army to the Valley of Amnidia and attacked the Elvan city Cynthia. His reasons for attacking Cynthia can only be speculated, but it is believed he hoped to destroy the Soul Chamber of Elsa in an attempt to bring down the Veil. Shadan and his followers were killed, but the war destroyed the entire region, leaving the pristine valley uninhabitable. Shadan returned in the year A.S. 2273 as the first of the K'rrosha and led an army of cultist followers against the land of Kelsa in A.S. 2280. He vanished during the Battle of Greendom, and his armies were once again defeated.

Shadowhounds: Dog-like creatures that scout ahead of K'rrosha. They have the ability to walk vertically up stone walls and across stone ceilings, and are sometimes used as assassins because of their ability to penetrate even the most well-guarded fortress. To combat this threat, many rulers have installed wooden panels called Houndsbane around access points to prevent the hounds from entering. Other names include: Sniffers and Hellhounds.

Shadowlancer: A name given to mounted K'rrosha. *See* Deathrider.

shadowspawn: Flesh and blood creatures created by the Agla'Con. Shadow-spawn come in hundreds of nightmarish varieties ranging from the very animalistic to the almost human. *See also* Darklings.

Shaloth: The head of the Con'Kumen chapter house in Tetrica.

Sharrukin: A Dainin.

Shizu: "Silence" in the Riaki tongue. These warriors are known among the other nations as Deathsquads. Although they are occasionally used as assassins, their primary duty is the protection of their individual leifs.

shoari: A type of prison cell used in Riak.

Shochu: A leif of Clan Gahara.

Shozen: Riaki word for General. A Shozen is the head of a leif's contingent of Shizu and Sarui.

Shurr, Thorac: Chunin Ambassador General and cousin to Luas Olwen, King of Chunin's Middle Kingdom.

Sigura, Tauro: Waga Leiflord, Clan Gahara.

Silliam, Iveera: Wife of Seston's Mayor.

Silliam, Sigyn: Mayor of Seston.

Solemnizing, the: At the close of the Second Creation (A.S. 1), the Creator solemnized the marriage of Imor, a descendant of Elsa, and the Elvan Princess Temifair. He named their child Fairimor and placed him upon the throne of Kelsa.

Soulbiter: *See* Maeon.

Soulchamber: The sacred chamber of Elsa located inside Mount Tabor where the Rejuvenation of the Earthsoul can be enacted.

Soulcrusher: *See* Maeon.

Soultaker: *See* Maeon.

Sourish, Heppil: A young Dymas and soldier in the Chellum army.

Stodd, Daris: Warder to Brysia Fairimor.

Strembler, Droe: A member of the Con'Kumen captured by Daris Stodd. He was freed by someone in their brotherhood and sent to Trian with a message to Zeniff.

Stromsprey, Galadorian: Ancient Kelsan hero said to have returned to battle after he was killed. He is famous for the saying: "Death dulls not my sword."

Tale of Glendair: A song.

Tate's Mercantile: A shop in Seston.

Ta'shaen: "Earthpower" in the Old Tongue. *Ta'shaen* is the power of God — the power by which all things were created — and is the life force of the Earthsoul. It is bestowed as a gift by the Earthsoul that it might be used to serve and help others. Like all things, however, it can be misused and corrupted. *See also* Seven Gifts of *Ta'shaen*; Agla'Con; Dymas.

Temifair: The Elvan Princess who became the mother of the Fairimor Bloodline.

Tendomi Shrine: More ruins now than shrine, Tendomi Shrine was constructed in A.S. 841 by those who first settled Gahara's mountain valley. It is located within Iga's territory.

Tetrica: A seaport city of Kelsa.

Tetrica, Baikal: King of the city of Tetrica, and youngest of Kelsa's monarchs.

Thesston: Capital of Zeka.

Thought Intrusion: Forbidden by the Creator, Thought Intrusion is similar to the Gift of Discernment in appearance but is in actuality an evil corruption of Spirit *Ta'shaen*. Agla'Con foolish enough to use it often find themselves the target of a Cleansing Hunt.

Tierim, Falius: An Agla'Con.

Tihou: A leif of Clan Gahara.

Tizin: A leif of Clan Gahara.

Tobdana, Gariel: The Highseat of Clan Gahara after the removal of Tereus Dromensai.

Togaru Temple: Clan Gahara's main religious structure.

Tokasa, Madrel: A Shizu of Leif Iga.

Tomlin: A young warder-in-training apprenticed to Daris Stodd.

Tradeston: A city on the shores of Mirror Lake in Kelsa.

Trepenskar, Kallenia: Ancient Riaki Prophet.

tres'dia: "Fire Sword" in the Riaki tongue.

Trian: Capital of Kelsa.

T'rii Gates: Also know as Veilgates, these reddish gates are constructed of *chorazin* and can be used to travel to other gates throughout the world. When using a T'rii Gate, the Veil is parted between two linked points in the spiritual fabric of the Earthsoul. Though some fragmented records mention T'rii Gates being used by Elderon to bring the Elvan people from their homeworld, there is no real evidence to support it. Another legend suggests the gates were used to facilitate The Gathering which preceded the destruction of the Old World. *See* Veilgate.

Troas, Muriell: Daughter of Ren and lover to Elder Zanandrei.

Troas, Ren: Owner of *The Proud Flame* in Trian.

Tsuto: A leif of Clan Gahara.

Tunnel, the: Secret passage leading through Talin Plateau from Fulrath to the Bottomlands.

Twisted Ones: *See* Shadan'Ko.

Tynda, Akota: Senior member of Leif Iga's Shizu and son of Caedikas Tynda.

Tynda, Caedikas: Former Highseat of Clan Gahara and the man who raised Seth Lydon.

Vakala, Clan: A powerful clan in Riak.

Valley of Amnidia: Once a lush and fertile land, it was destroyed during the final battle with the living Shadan. Relinquished by the Elvan people, Amnidia became the home of the Shadan'Ko, former Kelsans corrupted by the taint left behind by Throy Shadan. It is now a wasteland of volcanic rock, ash, and soot. Only shadowspawn and a few of the boldest Agla'Con dare venture into the valley as the Twisted Ones have developed a taste for human flesh. *See* Great Wall of Aridan.

Vantoru, Leif: A leif of Clan Samochi.

Veil, the: The spirit barrier that separates the world of the living from the realms of Con'Jithar and Eliara. It is, in a very literal sense, the Earthsoul — the spiritual sphere within which all life is sustained. As the Earthsoul weakens, however, the realm of Con'Jithar presses ever closer to the world of the living and will eventually swallow it unless the Veil can be strengthened or the Earthsoul rejuvenated.

Veilgate: Veilgates are mentioned in Volume I of the *Elvan Histories* but seem to refer more to the actual 'spiritual' gateway than the physical structure of the *chorazin* T'rii Gate. *See* T'rii Gates.

Viewing: A channeling of Earthpower whereby a Dymas can show images from the past.

Villicks, Reapandry: A member of the Village Council in Kindel's Grove.

Vomanei, Gerish: A young Dymas and soldier in the Chellum army.

Waga: A leif of Clan Gahara.

Waypost: Small military outposts for Kelsa's Highwaymen. They dot the highways at thirty-mile intervals. *See also* Highwaymen.

Winseral, Elder: Head of The Church of Elderon during the attempted coup by Farsenil Fairimor.

Wohlvin: A type of shadowspawn.

Wyndor, Relaiya: Brysia's alias when she travels.

Zabrisk: Zekan seaport.

Zanandrei, Jendus Elder: Assistant High Priest to Elder Nesthius.

Zedik Pass: The narrow, nearly impassible slit through the Death's Chain Mountains. One of only three passes connecting Kelsa to Melek.

Zeesrom, Bresdin: A Chief Judge of Trian.

Zeniff: The Agla'Con who resides in Fairimor Palace.

Zeph, Sallen: Member of the Con'Kumen who led the Riaki strike team to the Eries home.

About the Author

Greg Park was born in 1967 in Provo, Utah, and spent much of his youth fishing the Provo River and hiking and hunting in the Wasatch Mountains with his father and brothers. In 1986, he served a two-year mission in Osaka, Japan, then attended Brigham Young University where he received a Bachelor of Arts in English. He recently returned to BYU to work on a Master's degree in media education.

He currently teaches English and Japanese, and courses in creative writing and science fiction literature at Timpanogos High School, in Orem, Utah. Still an avid outdoorsman, he spends much of his time fishing, hunting, and camping with his wife and children in Utah's backcountry. *Cleansing Hunt* is his second novel.